THE CAPTAIN RANDOM

ADVENTURES

VOLUME TWO

HAYDEN GRIBBLE

The CAPTAIN RANDOM Adventures Volume Two

CAPTAIN RANDOM
AND THE
STRATOS CONUNDRUM
HAYDEN GRIBBLE

CAPTAIN RANDOM

AND THE STRATOS

CONUNDRUM

HAYDEN GRIBBLE

1

AFTERMATH

Unearthly sounds filled the decimated hangar. A wind raged through the vast metal walls, and the small fires that had erupted, scattered like tiny beacons of destruction, whirled their orange flames in unison as the strong breeze blew through them.

The debris of the gantry that had once been held firmly suspended forty feet above the ground began to fall. Screams from stranded beings, terrified and trapped in their surroundings, cowered with arms held high, protecting their heads as the heavy metal smashed on top of them. The screams died and were replaced by the clatter and contact of metal on metal. Explosions began to ripple and tear holes in the walls and floor.

It had become a hall of devastation.

A silver ship, about a hundred feet in height and sit-uated right in the middle of the hangar was fading out of existence as the noise of the wind grew stronger.

Further screams of despair rang out as a few of the survivors had clambered over the falling rubble towards the magic ship but it was too late.

They were confined to their death.

Balls of fire burst the seams of the floorboards and the survivors began to scatter.

Its sporadic nature suggested a series of bombs but to those trapped they would have considered that impossible for a ship that had such tight security.

None of this was in the minds of the terrified people who were still aboard. It was now a fight to get off the ship before it was too late.

Escape pods were the only option left to them before the once grand ship fell out of the sky and disintegrated in the Earth's atmosphere.

In all the ruins, the strewn mounds of rubble lay the aggressor. A man, corrupt by power, believing his own god complex, who promised those in his employ that the invasion would be successful, that they were doing the right thing, lay broken.

Immobile yet still alive, he began to open his eyes.

Groaning in agony, a thought kept ringing in his head.

How had it all gone so wrong?

The heat of the flames licked against the side of the man's face as he lay facing the ceiling in a room of destruction and death. All the prostrate man could feel around him was the violent waves of doom as he came to.

Shaking his head, the man groaned like somebody who had been beaten against a brick wall for over an hour. He didn't know how long he had been unconscious and in a way he didn't care.

He had failed.

And now the fallen was stirring and knew that he was finished.

The sound of the ruined metal timber falling to-wards him made his skin go cold. With his eyes blinking open and shut, he struggled to free himself from his temporary prison.

Staring into the burning abyss of his once oh so magnificent ship, he was pinned by the falling debris to the floor.

Although aware of his perilous position, he struggled to remember what had precisely happened.

He remembered his plan. Oh, how he had worked on it.

He had spent years plotting the attack and after using the millions of Stellerpounds he had at his disposal – not so much earned but stolen through his many business schemes, and the

---

money he had conned out of fellow competitors in the financial market, he was able to do what nobody from his home planet of Draxo had done in over four centuries – reclaim the Earth.

Draxo was one of the first Earth colonies to settle out of the solar system. It was uninhabited and after years of research it was chosen for colonisation to help move the population of the Earth – which was stretching to overcrowding in the big urban areas – to all corners of the galaxy.

And so, with the numbers in the population at breaking point, great ships, built to hold thousands of humans in suspended sleep set off on their long jour-ney, with a crew who took it in turns to pilot them within these suspension cycles and made sure the passengers got to their new world safely.

Many were jealous at those who had been selected for the voyage to Draxo. It was a beautiful planet, rich with emerald green skies and mauve fields. The first human inhabitants were not used to this strange colour scheme but they grew to love it.

It was like no other planet in its system and as far as they knew it had never been inhabited before.

However, it wasn't long until their new paradise suc- cumbed to the same problems that the colonists had experienced on Earth.

The colonists were placed in suspended animation for the decade long journey, as was an abundant supply of food and water, not to mention a self-servicing plantation chamber that would enable crops and vegetation to flourish while they slept.

It was to be a new golden age.

Upon landing, the scientists who had joined the colonists on the journey had taken samples of the soil and rainfall as soon as they awoke from their slumber.

The probes they had sent from Earth had been ac- curate, the soil was able to sustain the crops and the atmosphere was not poisonous. If anything, it was healthier than the over populated and polluted mother planet.

There was a high bombardment of positive neutrons in the air and the new settlers were in a better frame of mind once there.

The planet was tranquil, peaceful and the need for work was more of a hobby as greed was not a common trait.

Unfortunately, Draxo did also have its drawbacks.

There was a nutrient in the soil that meant it was rancid after a week.

They could combat this by managing the supplies appropriately, but as generations came and went and the surplus population grew, famine came and took the lives of some of the colonists. The designated leaders, whose predecessors had been designated on the first voyage and whose roles were inherited, pleaded for aid from the mother planet but it never came. Draxo, for reasons they did not understand, had been cut off and left alone.

And so the planet lay dying, weak and helpless, until the ruler Draxo, an ambitious and some would say reckless King, decided that they should make the Earth pay for what they had done.

Ordering repairs to be made to the ship that had carried them to Draxo centuries earlier, and enlisting the help of those who had come to the planet over the years of his rule, the plans for war began.

The money he had acquired and stolen, along with the technology that was culled from other races during his reign, made him strong and determined to bring the Earth to its knees.

Many of his subjects disagreed with his vision of war and violence.

Some were convinced that the power had gone to his head and as punishment, the King outlawed many and accused them of treason.

The once happy, peaceful humans of Draxo were now ruled with an iron fist and forced into a war with their own people.

The King gave himself a name that struck fear into his subjects and those who were loyal to him. Together they equated to an army that ensured that the King's life was kept safe from the rebels who tried to kill him before Draxo was beyond redemption.

That name was Stratos.

Stratos abandoned Draxo, leaving behind the weak, feeble and those who opposed him, to die. Ordering his troops aboard the ship that brought them to what had been their Eden, Stratos and his army placed themselves in suspended animation and set the coordinates to auto-pilot back to Earth.

The Army was a strong force of twenty thousand, with advanced weaponry that had been stolen from the aliens whom visited Draxo and lived to regret it, and now they were more than a match for the planet.

Whatever the conditions and no matter how sur- prised the peoples of the Earth would be, a ship that was once built to bring peace and new beginnings was now an armoured battle craft set on a course to destroy those who had stranded them.

The plans that had been made were meticulous to the last detail.

A sensor was set to alarm the forces if they were under attack or if an obstacle dangerous enough to cause danger to the mission meant that evasive action would be needed. At that point, they would simply wake up and destroy it.

For the first few years however they were mostly undisturbed, safe in momentary sleep, waiting for the moment they had been preparing for.

It soon became clear though, that even though com- munication had been lost decades earlier, Earth knew that they were coming.

As soon as the ship, now called the Commodore after the engineer that originally made her, scraped the fringes of the Solar System, a fleet of galactic fighters, small and slick in design like an ancient World War II spitfire plane, hung in the sky like a spiders web, waiting for the unwitting fly to fall into the trap.

Fifty in number, the fleet were ready, and that meant the peoples of the Earth were too.

When Stratos awoke to the sound of gun fire on his vessel, he was taken aback by the trap, but in no way unprepared.

Back on Draxo, he heard rumours that the rebels had got word to those lucky aliens who had escaped the bleak prisoners of war camps that stained the planet like blood on a flower.

The word must have got out about what he was planning. Earth knows what we are going to do, he thought to himself, but they will be no match for us.

Ships fell hard like hailstones as the Commodore showed the fleet the full might of its destructive power. The battle raged for two hours. Although slightly damaged, the shields that had been stolen by more advanced races kept most of the fire at bay.

The firepower at Stratos' disposal was devastating. One by one the little fighters were destroyed, the pilots inside trapped in the burning craft and fated to a fiery end.

Then the moment of retreat came when the ships were forced to flee, their mission failed. Licking their wounds, the armies of Earth were defeated. With minimal casualties and a regained sense of willpower and determination, Stratos had won.

Now they had penetrated the Solar System, the Commodore continued its journey of death. Following their excursion past Pluto, the armies of the solar system banded together, in a way that they hadn't done in centuries.

All the political disagreements and differences in opinion that separated the planet were forgotten for the time being.

The only planet that decided not to help the Earth was Mars, whose lifeforms elected to remain hidden from their neighbours, knowing full well what destruction the human race would bring to the red planet if they were detected and known about by the wider population. An outbreak of a contagious disease had also confined them below ground for centuries.

Living in fear and trapped on a diseased world, they watched as the ships from Earth and Mercury took off to hold the Warship away, knowing the effort was in vain.

No matter how big in number the defensive parties were, or potentially successful the campaigns were, nothing could stop the gigantic offense from lumber-ing on through the System. Now only a matter of weeks away from their final destination, Stratos relished the fight he faced.

He kept his best soldiers awake, depriving them of the sweet comfort of sleep and ordered that they stay at their posts, taking it in turns to look out and attack.

One by one the command posts that led to the world of mankind were ceased, purged and eradicated. Slaves were taken, many were slaughtered and it fed Stratos' lust for revenge.

It was as though he absorbed the attacks and let them fester in his mind, further polluting his thoughts and filling his imagination with perverse images of destruction and power. The Commodore was like a cancer wiping through the stars and obliterating all in its path. It seemed as though nothing could stop it.

Until one day, the day that Stratos let his guard down.

Repairs were required as the Commodore began to feel the brunt of the storms of battle it had faced. Shield capacity was strong, but not as strong as it could have been. The loyal followers of the man who would be King, fearful of their own lives, worked endlessly to repair the ship.

Some even succumbed to their weakness and kept awake, whilst some starved to the point of death and began to slip away.

Stratos was as relentless and unfeeling as stone through a plain glass window. He killed those who were too weak to fight or work, knowing that there were still many in suspended animation he could call on.

Work conditions were appalling and his armies were making mistakes thanks to it.

Following a devastating fight on the rings of Jupiter, the Commodore was badly damaged. It was the first time since the ship had started its invasion that it had been defeated. Loathing the decision he had to make, Stratos ordered his subjects to retreat and they fled.

It was just at this moment, unbeknownst to him, that a mysterious ship seemingly materialised out of nowhere on board. Out stepped a purple skinned, spiky haired male, who held himself high and strode into this world of hate like he owned the stage, accompanied by his three friends.

A tall, strong looking female with her black coloured hair dangling in a thick plait, a kind and yet dangerous robot who was in the shape of a skateboard and a young blonde haired scruffy male who looked roughly the same age as the woman with dark hair. The purple one carried an unearthly feel and a yearning to wreak havoc about him. They were wanderers, rebels, chaos bringers.

It was as if they had not been home in a very, very long time.

They brought with them a sense of experience beyond the stars and soon they went about destroying Stratos' world from the inside, like a virus in a computer mainframe.

Stratos, lying in the rubble, winced as he tried to move.

He opened his dry, blood stained lips and uttered the only thing that was in his mind.

'Random,' he spluttered as he struggled to move, dry spit barking from lungs.

'RANDOM!'

Another explosion gave birth to a glow of fire that growled at Stratos like an animal. Every sinew of his being was broken, beaten. His body told him to stay where he was, accept his fate and embrace the inevitable.

His mind spoke another language to him, one of sur- vival, vengeance and hate. The pain worsened now his eyes were open. The ambition, like the fire now raging throughout the Commodore, burned brightly.

He had to get out - and nothing was going to stop him.

At first his small movements ached, and then the pain really set in. Hot, searing pain that shot through his veins and boiled within every sinew in his body. Stratos knew it was futile to try and guess how and where the breaks had occurred. It felt as though nearly every bone in his body was broken.

By all rights, he should already be dead; he knew that, especially after falling seventy feet from a disintegrating gantry onto the stone cold floor below.

From every angle, the man who called himself Random had beaten him.

How an intruder like him aligned himself with rebels who were hiding in the store rooms and saved both himself and his allies and left the others to die was incredible. To have compassion and show no remorse in equal measure was a personality trait that puzzled Stratos and led him to believe that this man was not like any other he had encountered.

To him, Random's behaviour was like that of an old campaigner, whose eyes only reveal his true intentions and his full ruthlessness to his enemies and hides them from those who trust him.

Every inch began to feel like a mile but Stratos was undeterred. Crawling away from the rubble and watching the panic unfold around him, the pain he felt illuminated from his blood shot eyes and pathed the way out of danger.

Desperately, Stratos searched the room, which glowed a brilliant orange. The screams of his men, sup- posedly the best of the best, the ones he personally picked and oversaw the training of, ran around like headless chickens.

The feeling of depression and imminent doom hung like a fog amongst the smoke.

The Commodore was breaking up around him, his beloved ship, the one that was meant to bring to Stratos his dream of revenge, was going down faster than the Titanic in Earth stories of old.

The ship slipped even further out of space towards the planet it was supposed to conquer, pulling away at its metallic seams in the atmosphere.

Many will have already perished, sucked into the vacuum of space or fated to a fiery grave but Stratos was not thinking about them at all. Although he was the King, he wasn't going to go down with the ship.

Still crawling, Stratos' eyes were firmly on the prize. His salvation and only means of escape lay mere metres away.

Through the fire and smoke and his own blurred vision, he spotted an escape pod on the opposite side of the hanger to where he had laid.

In all the confusion, and although some had es- caped and were bound to be picked up by the Space Seals, only one remained empty. Its red, vacant light lit the way.

He was nearly there.

The pain was put to the back of his mind for the time being, he could worry about it later.

Safety was so close for him now. VWOOOSSSHHH!

An explosion, so ferocious in its manner, rocked the hangar.

Stratos stopped his hellish trek and lay prostrate on the floor.

Looking up, he started to feel his broken body being dragged back towards the rubble pit he had awoken in.

Struggling to fit his fingers in a metal grill on the floor, Stratos blinked into the void behind him. The hanger was silent now. No more screams or desperate struggles to get off the doomed craft.

Stratos was now alone in the hanger; the only company he had now was the vast hole that had replaced the hull.

He watched as his faithful soldiers, the ones who had shared his dreams and those who he despised were floating lifelessly in the black, unforgiving silence of space.

A wind that sent a chill along his spine was still tempting the fallen leader to a silent death.

Holding on with the last remaining effort of his being, Stratos, who knew that the only strength he had left in his body was now in his arms, edged his way along the grill the last few feet to the escape pod door.

Grimacing and screaming until his lungs began to burn, Stratos reached out for the release button. His fingertips reached out like a child seeking the attention of its mother.

Just a little further.

More fire and sparks licked his face with vicious intent and the icy touch of deep space dragging him towards death.

His screams inaudible over the vacuum that wanted to embrace him, Stratos' last ounce of strength hurled him onto the button.

In a split second the escape pod door, which was about six feet in height, whipped open. Feeling along the wall inside the pod, Stratos found a hold and swung himself inside, snapping the door shut.

He had made it.

Now, the fun really started.

Sliding to the floor once more, Stratos panted as he rocked about in the little pod. The turbulence created an unstable yet safe environment for the Warlord to tend to his wounds.

He knew, however, that to elude his enemies from Earth and escaping too early, he would have to release the pod at just the right moment.

He felt that it was coming soon.

Around the pod, more and more chunks of the Commodore collapsed, splitting through the stress of the fractures that had been created by the internal damage of the explosions.

The hole that had been torn in the hull was now replicating all over the ancient ship. The loss of life was insurmountable and disturbing.

Not all of the rebels had been lucky enough to escape, something Random had promised they would succeed in doing.

The majority of them were among the first to be picked up by the salvage ship, warning that those who followed were Stratos' personal army, fleeing like flies from a carcass.

The rebels watched from a safe distance as the Commodore, a ship that set sail on a mission of peace and prosperity that had become one of war and death, in a blaze of fury, perished for good.

Stratos flicked the jettison switch as soon as he felt the force of the first shock wave. The sound was like that of an atom bomb and it deafened the lone survivor. He had found no time to secure himself in one of the grey seats that sat to the side of the pod. The pod was roughly the size of a cupboard and would have only fitted two people but with the extra room available, Stratos' tormented frame was thrown to the far side of the pod, screaming as the gravity created by the shock waves crushed him.

Before long, Stratos closed his eyes, giving in to the bliss of unconsciousness.

His body was broken and he now had no feeling below his waist. Only willpower had brought him out of his destiny of fire.

He had cheated death. It was up to the pod now to carry his nearly lifeless form to safety.

Whilst his eyes were closed, a mirage of thoughts flowed through his mind. There was no point answering the questions he had now, he should just let them go, give in to the embrace of sleep and worry about it later.

The pod tore away along with the rest of the debris that once formed the magnificent form of the Commodore. Since its rockets were no longer firing, it could be easily mistaken as a spare part, a piece of a puzzle that was torn away from its body and now littered the black, empty space above Earth. The final explosion had been impressive with the look of a huge firework.

Earth was safe yet again, thanks to the strange purple man and his friends.

The alien with the mysterious silver ship had come and gone and brought with him a world of destruction. His name had betrayed his actions. He wasn't a saviour; he was a bringer of death.

Debris began to shower the Earth, falling over the isolating desolation of Antarctica. Only a few colonies were brave enough to set up home on such an uninhabitable plain. It was here that the pod carrying Stratos was slowly heading for. The rest of the debris would break up in the atmosphere.

The capsule however, temporarily home to one of the worst War criminals in the history of the universe, was on its final journey.

Only the course Stratos thought he was taking, he would never actually complete. Something strange was happening outside in the mists of space, something that would alter the course of the universe. An anomaly was about to occur and Stratos wasn't actually heading towards the planet he once had desires upon conquering. No, he was to arrive in a place far stranger than the third rock from the sun.

With no more shock waves to hold him against the wall, Stratos' unconscious body crumpled on the floor.

It fell like a rag doll and it was hard to believe that this bloody, sickening mess was once that of a strong, evil megalomaniac. His ego would never allow anybody to see him in this weakened, defeated shape.

He was alone, wounded almost beyond recognition but he was not finished. No matter how badly injured he was, he would rebuild, grow stronger than he was before and live to serve his one purpose, his only calling in life.

To kill Random.

2

A QUIET PLACE

Far away in a distant solar system, the light of a thousand stars and suns reflected off the sleek, metallic hull of the ship known as the Venus II.

As it sailed majestically through the blackness of space, it lit up like a beacon of style and sophistication. It was truly one of the most appealing space ships this side of Orion's Belt. But inside, the crew of the Venus II were feeling far from regal. In fact, after their latest ordeal, they were highly willing to never bump into another King or Queen or ruler of any kind ever again!

Jake sat on the side of his bed, running a towel through his shaggy blonde hair with all the tenderness and care of a butcher with a new-born calf.

He was so rough; it was as though he didn't want any of it there in the first place. He hadn't washed it, it was something he had started doing to release his fury and felt healthier than punching a wall.

'Exiled!' he muttered loud enough for the person in the bedroom opposite his own to hear. 'I ask you!'

Anji hadn't asked. In fact, she had been very quiet.

Ever since Spectronia. Ever since the Zedron Flux.

Ever since Random had collapsed and changed colour.

They had bundled their unconscious friend back on board the ship but before they left, with their heads hanging shamefully for what he had done, Random's normally vibrant purple skin complexion, unique to his planet of Rodas, had changed. Now, his pigmentation was split down the middle. His left hand side was as blue as sapphires swimming in a sunlit ocean. On his right, crimson blood red like the aftermath of a battlefield.

Their robotic friend, fondly named Skateboard for his resemblance to a little board with four wheels some people in the universe like to ride upon. As soon as the ship was up in the big black, he had shared his feelings with his companions.

'I've been concerned for some time,' he had said to them.

'Well then, why didn't you tell us?' said Anji, her tone bordering on anger.

'Miss, I was not at liberty to disclose such informa- tion. I was keeping an eye on the situation, seeing if it improved. Random and I have been discussing the matter and until now I didn't have the slightest incli- nation to break his confidentiality. The Captain has a right to his privacy.'

'Nice to know that he didn't feel like he could talk to us!' scoffed Jake.

'Actually, when we were trapped in the cave earlier, he started telling me something. I could tell that he was struggling. He seemed to have more on his mind than he was letting on,' Anji said awkwardly.

Jake looked indignantly at his two friends.

'Oh, right, well I see I'm not included in this heart-to- heart club!'

'Don't be so childish, Jake,' snapped Anji. 'Our friend could be in terrible danger.'

Jake sighed.

'I'm sorry Anj, Skateboard. I just...well, if you'll allow me back in the club, I'm a little scared.'

'Me too,' Anji smiled, putting a reassuring arm around her friend.

'We all are, Sir,' said Skateboard. He left the mid- section and retreated down a corridor, past the living quarters and into the medi-bay. The sound of his wheels clanked against the metal floor as he whirred into the doorway. The medi-bay was a brilliant wash of sterile white, with two beds lying side-by-side. It was the first time in quite a while that anyone had occupied those beds and for the second time it was the same patient who lay still within the silk sheets.

Skateboard thrust himself onto his hind wheels and his body rose up to get a better look at the occupant.

Anji and Jake followed in after him and joined Skateboard at Random's bedside.

The Rodasian was flat on his back, still, no sign of life. He had a tube sticking out of his mouth that was linked to a futuristic bank of machinery.

His skin was wet and clammy and apart from the slightest twinge of activity in the corners of his eyes, there was no sign that he would be getting up anytime soon.

Anji's mind flittered back to the vision of Random on that cliff top, the Zedron Flux held aloft in his hands, using it as a threat to repel an invasion force of what resembled Egyptian gods called the Osirans who in their pyramid ships had desires to hold the Flux in their grasp and rule the entire universe.

That's how powerful the Zedron Flux was. Whoever attained it was gifted sheer omnipotent power, enough to bring life or death to the farthest corners of the cosmos.

And there he had stood, Random, with the power of the gods.

Then just when all hope was lost, as a weapon of supreme power was about to split the entire planet of Spectronia and wipe out the peaceful race of Spectronians, Random was forced to do the unthinkable.

He had opened the Flux and absorbed its power.

From their vantage point far away, Anji, Jake and Skateboard had watched in horror as their friend was consumed by its godly green glow and as he levitated, the force of the Flux burning like fire through his body, he used its awesome might against the Osirans and one-by-one, their invasion fleet fizzled out of existence.

He had saved a planet, a whole race of life, but in doing so had wiped out another.

Random had committed genocide to try to avert genocide.

As the Flux returned to its safe compartment and was relinquished to a man who had risked everything to get it to safety, Random had slumped to the ground.

And now here they were, unaware of the effects such an devastating incident could have had on his body.

Whatever it had done, the Flux had had a devastating effect on the boy.

He lay there, still and silent. Apart from a smudge of dirt on his face, there was no sign that Random had seen any physical injury. But as the most impossible person Anji and Jake had ever met lay motionless, the situation was worrying for them all.

'This is terrible,' Jake stated the obvious.

'What are his life signs saying Skateboard?' Anji squinted at the virtual readouts on the monitor on the wall above his head.

'He is stable, for now, that's what we need to worry about, but we must get him somewhere where he can be treated properly.'

'Treated for what?' asked Jake. 'Do you think the Flux did this to
him?'

'It's highly possible.'

'We've seen him do some highly impossible things before, but
that Flux was something else,' said Anji. She parked herself on the
spare bed. 'I saw it. Close up. And I could understand why Lon
wanted it so bad. All of that energy. All of that power.'

'It ran right through him, polluted every cell in his body. We can
only imagine the damage it might have caused,' said Skateboard.

'So you're saying that he might never recover?' Jake's eyes
looked panicked.

'I'm not a doctor, sir, so I don't want to panic either of you. The
best thing we can do now is to try and find somewhere that can
help him.'

His circuits whirred loudly. 'Goodness me! Just look at you
two!'

Anji and Jake glanced down at their clothes. They were torn and
smeared with the rainbow coloured dirt of Spectronia.

'Get out of here at once! This is a sterile unit, now out, out, out!'

He shooed them out of the room, with little protest from either
of them. As soon as they were clear the medi-bay door slid shut
behind them.

'He's right,' said Anji. 'We'd better take a shower.' 'Together?!'
asked Jake with a mixture of hope and curiosity.

Skateboard heard the slap from inside the medi-bay and tutted
before producing a small vacuum cleaner from a utility cupboard
and proceeded to tidy up their mess.

*

Anji stepped from the shower feeling like a new person. She
covered herself with a towel dressing down and spun her thick
wet hair into another before flinging it back over her shoulders.

Sliding into her slippers, she joined Jake in his room. 'So that's the real reason why you are feeling sore, because you never got to say goodbye to, what was her name?

Bow?'

'Row,' Jake corrected, chucking his towel to the floor and flopping his head into his hands, his cheeks resting on his palms making him look like a furry apple on two plates.

'Don't worry, I'm sure there will be plenty of other exotic, beautiful women out there in this wide old cosmos to not be attracted to you.'

Jake looked at his friend and let out a short laugh. 'Just because you haven't met Prince Charming yet.' 'Jake I'm 13!' she laughed. 'I'm not old enough to have met anyone yet, let alone Prince Charming. Anyway, don't you think we have more important things to think about right now?'

He nodded.

'Yeah, I suppose you're right.'

'We girls normally are,' she smiled. Jake saw that naughty twinkle in her eye.

'God, I'm so glad that it's you I ran away from the Earth with. For someone who is on a spaceship a zillion miles away from home, you know how to keep me grounded!'

'I do my best...I just wish there was something I could do to help Random.'

'Anj, what did he say to you, in that cave?' 'Nothing. He was acting peculiarly. When he was unconscious, it was like he was fighting someone invis- ible.'

'Oh great, that's all we need. First the Sandman, now the invisible man!'

'It might have been a bad dream, for all I could see, but he was...off...the whole time we were together on that planet. Something was not quite right.'

'It definitely isn't now,' scoffed Jake. 'Look, he'll be alright. He will get better. I'm sure of it.'

'Let's hope so,' said Anji, her head rested on Jake's shoulder. 'Why red and blue?'

'Didn't he say that was the colour of his people?'

'Yes, but I didn't think he meant that they were both of them. What if the Flux has done something to his DNA?'

'Okay Doctor Gummadi, like what?'

'I don't know, just...' she gave up. 'Anyway, I'd better get dressed. I'll see you in a bit.'

'Okay,' said Jake as he picked the towel up and started to ruffle his hair like he was using sandpaper on a piece of wood.

'You want to be careful you don't go bald doing it like that,' Anji chuckled as she left the room.

Jake paused and then laughed nervously to himself. He opened the towel and stared at the strands of hair that lay entangled in the soft wool. Slowly, he returned the towel to his head and patted his hair softly.

*

He lay in the dirt barely able to breathe. The liberty of air was indescribably painful. But he didn't want the pain to end. He wanted to harness it. Keep him alive. Maintain his mission objective.

The sun glared down through the broken ruins of the pod. It poured into Stratos' little world like volcanic fire. He tried not to look up directly into it, but when he looked down he wished he hadn't.

There was a hydraulic pipe where his thigh should have been. He ground his teeth as he realised that the pain in his leg was now greater than the pain in his back. Or what was left of his leg.

He snarled like a rabid dog, foaming at the mouth, trying to grit the spaces where his teeth used to be. A horrible throbbing sensation emitted from his fresh new wound. He was losing a lot of blood. If he didn't find help soon, murderous determination or not, he wouldn't make it.

Stratos dare not look at any other part of his body. But then he could not look anywhere else in his crumpled up prison. Wherever he looked there was a reminder of what he used to be, mainly because there was a part of him that had glooped to the inner walls of the pod.

And yet something didn't seem right. This wasn't Earth.

Although the sun shone down upon him, the air temperature inside the capsule was perishingly cold. Where had he landed? Was this some kind of ice moon! He had been so perturbed by his new injuries that he had failed to notice the snowflakes cascading down into the pod where he lay. In fact, not only was the snow falling inside the capsule, it was starting to flood it.

With great effort, and agony, Stratos tried to move his right arm a few inches towards a bank of buttons. With this effort came even more pain. After all that he had been through, it was a miracle that he was still alive let alone able to move a few inches to the right!

The snow continued to flow heavily into the pod. Around where his ankles used to be, pools of snow began to form, stained red in places where bits of Stratos should have been.

With one final effort, on the verge of unconsciousness again, he threw everything he had at the button and pressed it firmly. A little red light blinked on and off in its place and with that, Stratos blacked out.

Outside the pod, an even bigger light began to blink in and out of existence. And not far away, someone had noticed…

*

'Sir, miss, I think you should come and take a look at this.'

Jake and Anji, the latter still changing into a fresh set of jeans and a jumper, pounded out of their living quarters and towards the cockpit at the front of the Venus II.

There they found Skateboard at the controls of the ship in the space that was normally occupied by Random as the main pilot.

'Look on the screens,' he instructed.

On the scanner was an outline of what looked like an asteroid, only with a large complex built into it.

'The Valetudinarium,' Jake read aloud. 'What's that when it's at home then?'

'It's a hospital. The most comprehensive hospital this arm of the galaxy'.

'By comprehensive, do you mean best?' asked Anji. 'For what Random needs, yes,' said Skateboard. 'Let's go there then!' cried Anji. 'Step on the pedal, Skateboard.'

'It's a long way away, miss, and we haven't got the reserves to get us there.'

'So what, we need fuel?' asked Jake. 'Precisely,' said Skateboard.

They both looked out of the cockpit's windows. 'Where?' asked Anji. There was not a moon, no

planet, not even a nebula anywhere near them. No sign of life in sight.

'Roughly 70 clicks away. We have enough to get there, but one of us will have to go outside and...er...fill her up, as it were.'

'A space petrol station?' laughed Anji. 'Don't we need money?'

'Not if we have a wounded person in our party, no,' replied Skateboard.

Anji rushed out of the cockpit. 'Where are you going?' asked Jake. 'To get my spacesuit.'

'What's the rush, we've got 70 clicks to go.' 'I know but I want to be prepared.'

'Can we hyper drive there, Skateboard?' asked Jake. 'That is with hyper speed taken into account, sir,' chirped Skateboard. 'If you fill up the ship to the brim, miss, we won't need to refuel again for another year.' 'Right gotcha,' she replied from within her quarters. 'Oh, and Anj?' said Jake.

Anji popped her head around the mid-section door, spacesuit half on. 'Yes?'

'You couldn't get me some Haribo while you're at it, could you?'

The space-walk was precarious for a girl from Earth who had never spacewalked before. Anji had taken a deep breath, consuming the last amount of air from the ship's oxygen systems before her helmet started pumping through what she needed for her journey and closed her eyes. As the airlock door hissed open, she felt gravity ebb away from right under her feet. Slowly, she began to drift outside.

'Just breathe normally, miss,' came Skateboard's voice over the intercom, pumping communication into a speaker either side of her ears.

'Okay, I can do this...I can do this,' she chanted to herself. With one small push off the edge of the airlock doors, Anji took a giant leap and became the first hu-man being to venture into space to fill up for petrol.

The sensation of floating aimlessly in the dark void was like nothing she had ever experienced before. It was indescribable.

'What's it like?' Jake asked.

'It's amazing!' Anji marveled as she turned around and saw the airlock door shut. 'I feel...light!'

Skateboard took over the comm. 'Okay, Anji, just re- member what I told you. You will find the fuel valve under the port side wing. Can you see it?'

Anji turned to her left. 'Yes, I think I can see it.' 'Good,' said Skateboard. 'Now key in the co-ordinates zero-two-three-mark-five-nine-A into your wrist pad. The suit shall do the rest.'

Anji did just that. Suddenly her body shifted and little hydraulic tubes shot some kind of gas out of the spacesuit and propelled Anji at a gentle pace towards the valve.

Within moments, she was there. 'I'm here! Ooh, this is fun!'

Jake tutted ruefully. I wish I'd had a go now, he thought to himself. Although he was braver than he looked, Anji's appetite for adventure was always greater, even if it had waned slightly after her ordeal back on Genocia with the Mutts in the wastelands. There was no doubting it, although things hadn't quite gone to plan on their last adventure, at least the old Anji was returning back to him.

She proceeded to unscrew the valve and then, using coordinates again commanded over the intercom from Skateboard, propelled herself across the forecourt.

As intergalactic petrol stations go, this one wasn't the glitz and glamour she had expected to find. In fact, it was just as dingy and basic as some of those that adorned the side of motorways back on Earth. Only this one was in space and instead of old Ford Fiestas well past their best, ready for the scrap heap and being driven by teenagers who thought they owned the road but in reality had only just passed their tests, this one has spaceships.

Anji maneuvered to the pump and noticed that there were three options of fuel.

'Er, Skateboard which one do I go for?' 'Five Star.'

Anji tutted. 'Bleeding obvious when you think about it.' She lifted the pump and again, using coor- dinates from Skateboard, began heading back towards the Venus II.

All of a sudden, Anji came to a grinding halt. Something was stopping her from moving towards the ship.

It was almost like she was being anchored back to the pump.

'Anj, what's the matter?' cried Jake.

'Er, sorry guys, you're not going to like this,' she said, 'but you're going to have to move the ship closer. We've parked too far away from the pump!'

A slight adjustment later and Anji was away. She watched as the clock display on the pump spun to full capacity.

'There we are, Skateboard,' she said, making sure the drip at the end of the hose fell within the fuel chamber, 'All done!'

There was no reply. 'Skateboard?'

Still nothing.

Anji looked up at the cockpit, where Jake was mouthing to her that they could not hear her. He pointed to the sign on the wall of the petrol station. It read:

DO NOT USE COMMUNICATION LINKS WHILE FUELING.

'Oh,' Anji gave her friends a thumbs up, replaced the fuel nozzle, screwed the cap on the Venus II and went over to the kiosk.

She floated up to the kiosk operator, who looked as cheerful as a funeral in winter and pressed a button on her chest. Her external speaker system cracked into life.

'Only 16,000 gallons of fuel to declare.'

The creature on the other side of the glass didn't change its expression.

'And?' it replied.

'Well, we've got a sick person on board who needs urgent medical help, so my friend told me we had to declare how much we'd-'

'I can see how much you have used on my system thank you very much,' it said grumpily.

Anji frowned. The creature looked like someone had shaved an otter and had dressed in a company shirt and hat.

The kiosk runner looked down at its screen and then up again.

'Actually, my monitor is playing up, so could I have that amount again please?'

Anji rolled her eyes. '16,000 gallons.'

'And you're exempt because you are carrying a wounded being on your craft?'

'Well, we are, aren't we?'

'Do you have proof that you have said being in your travelling party?'

'What? No?'

'Well how can I believe you then?'

'He's hardly going to come out, blow a kiss and dance a jig now is he?' she said in an exasperated tone. 'He's in a coma.'

The creature gave out a long and hard sigh. Slowly, it flipped a switch.

'Would the craft in bay 5 please confirm its status?' Anji waited and waited and waited for a response until a blip came from the dashboard in the kiosk.

'Oh,' said the attendant, 'He does look ill.' 'They sent you a photo?!'

'Yes, that proves it. Hold on I'll write you a receipt.' 'Quickly, if you please?'

'Hold on, I'll get a pen.'

Anji was beginning to get exasperated. 'You're enjoying this, aren't you?'

'I'm a petrol station attendant. Of course I am enjoying it.'

Anji shot the creature a look of disgust.

'So you're happy to leave someone dying just to alleviate your boredom!?'

'No, actually it's just nice to have someone to talk to.' 'Well hurry up and get a different bloody job!' The attendant sighed again. Anji got the impression he did that a lot.

'I'm a Tamorian. We Tamorians are born and bred for one thing in life. That's to be petrol station kiosk attendants. Now ask yourself, who is the lucky one? Him, or me?'

The attendant scribbled on a piece of paper, ripped it off and handed it to Anji who accepted it gladly.

'Thanks,' she spat. She grasped the paper in one hand and punched the coordinates back to the ship with the other. As she drifted back towards the airlock of the Venus II, she glanced down at the incomprehensible scribbling of the galaxy's worst petrol station attendant and made out four words of the appalling handwriting.

HAVE A NICE DAY.

3

REBORN

He blinked his eyes open. Although his new sur- roundings were as dark and dingy as the deepest well in the universe, his eyes still strained. He forced them shut again and moaned; anticipating that now he was conscious that wave upon wave of agony was to follow.

But it didn't.

The pain was gone.

So was almost every sensation. He couldn't feel a thing! What had happened to him?

Stratos lay on the cold slab confused and alone, unable to move. He grunted, trying to force his limbs into life, but they just would not move.

He tried again but not one part of his body flinched an inch. Stratos was paralysed.

He breathed heavily and tried to look at his sur- roundings, only managing to turn his head left and right. He was unable to move his chin closer to his chest to take a gaze at his body, not that he especially wanted to in this instance. The image of how it looked in the escape pod was enough to haunt him for the rest of his life.

'I thought I heard you wake up,' said a voice. 'Who are you? Where are you? Where am I?' he de- manded.

'I could ask you the same question.'

'If I told you, you wouldn't believe me.'

'Same,' she retorted. She got up and lent over her patient.

'What makes you say that?' said the stranger. 'Are you a celebrity of some sort?'

'You could say that,' said Stratos, 'Why can't I move?'

The stranger pulled up a stool from her work bench and sat beside her patient.

'I am Professor Garben. You're on an unnamed moon and you are unable to move because...well, I'm not sure how to break this to you-'

'Tell me!' demanded Stratos. There followed a brief silence. 'Please,' he continued.

Garben shot him a concerned look.

'I'm so sorry but...your body was badly damaged by the crash. When I intercepted your distress signal, it took me an hour to dig you out and when I found you...' she stopped herself, remembering the horror of what she had found, '...Well, there wasn't much of you left. I stabilised you, the ice had done well to preserve what it could in such a short space of time, but it wasn't enough. It kept you alive until you got back here to my workshop but from then on I'm afraid I had to do anything I could to keep you alive.'

Stratos was starting to fear the worst.

He took short, shallow breaths mustering the effort to ask his next question.

'So...what have you done to me then?'

'You must remember that what I have done was purely a measure to prolong your existence.'

Garben couldn't get the words out. She fumbled around for a mirror in her pocket. In a twisted way, maybe showing him would be easier to comprehend than her telling him.

She produced the small mirror and thrust it in the face of her patient.

Stratos' eyes widened in horror. His body was gone.

There was nothing left of him from the neck down. 'I'm sorry. Your body was broken, diseased. It

couldn't sustain your life any longer. I had to dispose of it. I did the best I could, but there is a solution.'

Stratos was lost for words. All gone, his entire body had been thrown away, probably burnt. Nothing left except his head.

'H-h-how...' he struggled to speak.

Garben got up off the stool and walked over to a bank of complex, important looking instruments.

'These computers are the only thing that's keeping you alive right now. Although your brain is intact, undamaged, these are doing the rest for you. Even though you may think that you are breathing, there is a tube running from here into your brain to keep it pumping with oxygen.

Your motor neuron senses are still working, hence why you are awake. But you will feel no pain currently.

I have turned down your pain receptors. So al- though you have nothing to feel pain, the brain is such a vital component in the body that it can play all sorts of tricks on you.'

Stratos' mouth was dry. He was still reeling from the shock. Who wouldn't be in the circumstances? But there was more he needed to know.

'Why did you keep me alive?'

'Because it is against my code, my nature to leave someone like that. I might be exiled but I am still a doctor. If there is a chance of life, any chance, I have to take it.'

'Look, I don't want your life story. Please, tell me, what are you going to do to me?'

Garben moved back onto her stool.

'It's entirely up to you. I'm a doctor of medicine first but I am also a Professor of electronics and augmented reality. So I am fully qualified to reconstruct your body, although being a long way away from my usual tools I can still build you something that might be crude but enough to prolong your life, if that's what you want?'

'Of course!'

'Forgive me, I know I sound curt but this is a big choice that you must make. I've worked with implants throughout my career, replaced bits of bodies with exact replicas of what people had before, improved them even! But for someone to be given a completely new body, something which isn't their own, well, it can cause all kinds of trauma.'

'Listen-'

'Garben.'

'Listen, Garben, I am just a head. This is a living nightmare. I don't want to be a floating brain in a jar. I want to be able to move again, to be free of pain. Your proposal is a godsend. I'd appreciate it greatly if you could construct me a new body.'

'But you're not listening. I am trying to tell you that what I can do for you is make you a crude bio metric mode of transport. It won't look anything like your old one. I don't have my full capacity here in this workshop and we are planets away from anyone who can help with supplies.'

'So what you're saying is that I will look more robot than man?'

'Precisely.'

Stratos mulled the proposition over. He could be capable of almighty power, impervious to pain and damage. What wasn't there to like about that idea? It was a great upgrade on the fallible flesh he had been born with.

He had made up his mind. 'Good.'

*

As Garben set about her work, far away on the edge of the remote, barren galaxy that the moon that Stratos had been marooned upon, a nondescript, insignificant little scavenger craft had just entered the long forgotten backwater of space known as the Falovarian system.

The Falovarian system is renowned by astronomers the galaxy over as being unique among many star systems in the universe for one simple reason.

There are no planets, only moons.

But their research was never broadcast amongst the population of surrounding systems because for one reason. The dark section of space was used to banish those who had broken laws in the local sectors of the galaxy and whose punishment wasn't to be as harsh as death, although some would have wished it upon themselves rather than a lifetime of isolation on desolate plains.

There were small crumbs of comfort for the exiles, however. Although some decreed that this was a futile method of punishment, others found it truly inspiring. Depending on the length of sentence, after the exile had served their sentence, they and all their belongings were simply beamed back to where they lived. The prisoners, as it were, were given food replicators, that if broken could be fixed remotely by hard light holograms transported across the stars from the safety of their offices, so that they would not come to any harm. The moons all had breathable atmospheres too and although some ecosystems were...unpredictable...to say the least, they were ultimately livable. That was down to the lack of surrounding planets, the scientists who were integral to the exile programme had explained.

It was entirely possible for the weather to be both sunny and cold at the same time. So it could snow whilst also feeling like a warm Spring day or the sun could be blazing down but it could feel colder than the metal that was currently being sculpted around what remained of Stratos' windpipe. It had a maddening effect on the exiles unfortunate enough to live out their sentences in solitude.

However, they were afforded small luxuries. For some, that meant books, a life supply of hard drives stuffed full of their favourite entertainment or in Garben's case, a small workshop to continue on her experiments. Although she was a Cybernetic surgeon, her exile was completely unrelated to her work and so, she was afforded her wish that her workshop and all that was in it, was transported to the nameless moon that had been her home for the past two months.

And in that time, despite her long treks across the boring, tedious looking rock that Garben had been left upon, she had never come across another living soul.

But she was not alone.

And now, someone was coming to be rescued. Samlore Charbok
had said nothing to anybody for four years. In that time, he had
barely left his chair. He had sat patiently waiting, passing the time
recounting his former glories. The cultures he had pulped. The pirates left ravaged by his hand. He had been captured and tried
following a sting operation led by the Sirus Police Corps and his
punishment instead of death, for nothing else than Judge and Jury
had wanted him to suffer a lifetime of solitude, instructed that he
be imprisoned on the moon for life.

He chuckled as the sentence was carried out. He knew it would
only be a matter of time before they found him. Any moment
now, his crew would be here. It had taken them a long time, but
he knew. He just knew.

He pressed his hands into his long, untamed beard. Even for a
Samlore - a race of scavengers affectionately dubbed the vermin of
the universe by those who they pillaged - his patience had been
commendable. Samlores were not well renowned for their
patience. If they got bored, they'd strip the scalp from the heads of
those who opposed them with their long, nail like talons and flew
off into the unknown for another race to steal from.

They were space pirates of the worst kind.

They would always leave a gruesome reminder of who they
were when they had fled the scene of a conquest.

Which left a distinguishable trail for the Space Corps to follow
and eventually they were caught.

However over a few years they had rebuilt their rabble piece by
piece and now they were coming back to claim their Captain.

Aboard the ship, a group of repulsive Salmores were gurgling
out their victory cry like a band of rowdy football fans after
winning a cup final. Only with more head butting. The Salmores
were an abhorrent race of creatures.

Their skin was a putrid green, with the slimy texture of a frog, although anyone who had got close enough to one of them to discover this hadn't lived long. Their eyes were small and narrow and were close to their pig-like snouts, which drooled with unmen-tionable regularity and two huge tusks protruded upwards from their bottom gums.

On top of their skulls bore long swathes of fatty skin that seemed to dribble over their heads like long hair and their stomachs wobbled over their armoured trousers, with their legs bent and long like a horse born backwards.

Two things were well established in the galaxy when it came to Samlores.

One - they were not to be messed with.

Two - they were never going to win any Best Looking competitions.

Luckily for the Samlores, they only really cared about one of these things...and pretended not to be hurt about the other.

'Commander,' hollered a Samlore above the ruckus. The Commander, who was only distinguishable from his crew by his sash of sharp weapons he wore over his shoulder, pushed through the crowd. One of the crew was forced flat against the cramped craft's internal wall and hit his head on a large pipe. He shook his concussion and ignored the gash in the back of his head and went back to celebrating violently with the rest of his comrades.

'Have you located the Captain?' the Commander growled. Samlores gurgled as they spoke, making it sound like they were perpetually trying to gargle salt water.

'We have,' snarled the pilot.

'Excellent...' cried the Commander. He turned to his crew and reached for his laser sword that was fastened to his belt. With careless forethought of where he was jabbing it, he slashed it into

the ceiling and the explosion of sparks garnered the attention of
the noisy ramble.

'We've done the impossible,' he grinned. 'We've es- caped the
harshest prisons in the galaxy, we've found the Falovarian system,
it's taken a long time but we've done what many have only ever
dreamed of doing. And when we go down there and rescue our
Captain, we shall be unstoppable again!'

The crew cheered in unison. 'Right, take us into land!'

*

'Are you ready?'

Garben had worked hard and fast on Stratos' new body. He had
been quite impressed by her skills. In reality, she had been sitting
on a prototype robot for quite some time. It had been transported
with her from her home but she had never got round to finishing
off the head, which was odd, considering the head was something
so complicated, so fiddly, that many cybernetic experts started on
that part first. But she'd always found the actual body to be a
good starting post. As she continued to weld Stratos' organic flesh
to the frame, she did wonder whether he would be happy with
what she had done. The robot that had formed the basis for this
new body was constructed for strength and intimidation. She had
planned to use it to rampage intergalactic bank vaults for her.
After all, how was she going to continue to finance her cybernetic
experiments?

However, on her last raid, which had unfortunately resulted in
two workers being killed in the process, her exile had put her
work on the robot on hold.

She had to live with the guilt of her actions, and had been doing
so well in her isolation. How was she to know how much Nitro 7
to use in that large bank?

And more fool the workers for finding it and being to choose when the explosion went off. That's how she'd come to terms with the guilt.

She'd blamed it on others.

As the final nerve endings were connected to the bio skeleton, she marveled at the work that she had done. Even the work on his eyes, which Stratos had complained were not functioning properly. Upon gouging them out, a practice so much easier when the pain receptors of the patient had been switched off, she'd realised that Stratos' optical ends were severely damaged and he would be blind within months.

She'd also been surprised at how unnerved her patient had been during the whole procedure.

Especially when he had refused to be put to sleep.

It was slightly unnerving that Stratos had wanted to be awake the whole time, especially when his eyes were pulled out.

She decided that upon reactivation of his new body, his strength ability would have to be turned to a minimum. She was still unsure who this man really was and it was only by the good nature of her heart, the bits she had left anyway after the accident that caused those deaths, that she hadn't left him for dead. Anyone in her shoes would do the same, wouldn't they? To save a life. Who knows, saving one might mean that she might be able to sleep at night again. Maybe her conscience would let her off.

But only if this man wasn't as dangerous as she was starting to believe.

Who in their right mind would want to stay awake during such an ordeal?

Come to think of it, what kind of man would survive the injuries he was suffering from in the first place?

No, the strength dial must be kept to a minimum. Especially if she was to spend the rest of her sentence with this man.

Not man...machine.

With a final few tweaks, Garben was finished with her work and stepped back, returned the soldering gun to the workstation and stared at what she had done.

'My eyes...I cannot see.'

The voice was electronic and organic in equal mea- sure.

Garben moved over to the instrument bank. 'Switching optical on...now.'

A flash of light burst into Stratos' view.

'Switching over to independent life support too.' A row of complex hydraulics inside Stratos' new

chest heaved up and down, pumping oil and other es- sential liquids around his new body, lubricating his innards and making sure that vital components would function correctly.

'Switching independent movement to you, now.'

Another switch was flipped and Stratos' new fingers began to move freely.

Stratos grinned. He could feel again. And not just the sensations he could before, they were heightened. He could tell the density of the slab he had been lying upon just by sheer touch.

He was without pain flooding through his body. The feeling of sheer agony and torture had gone. It was re- placed with a feeling of strength, robustness, impervi-ous to pain and suffering.

Wait until the universe got a load of him.

Pleased with her work, Garben was starting to feel slightly alarmed by what she had created.

'I must stress, please, it's all I have to work with right now.'

Stratos detected a level of anxiety in her voice.

'The mirror. Give me the mirror.'

Hesitantly, Garben picked up her mirror. She noticed that her hands were shaking. As her trembling fingers passed the mirror into Stratos' huge mechanical hand she retracted quickly and clenching her fists tight, dug her fingers into her palms. She was clammy with fright.

Stratos, with his new eyes in sharp focus, gazed into the little mirror and was alarmed by what he saw.

'How much of me survived the accident?' Garben gulped. 'About 12% of your body mass.'

'Well, Garben,' he sat up, his new body clanging against the metal slab and swinging his new legs over onto the floor. His feet clapping the ground as he hurled his body weight upright now for the first time, towered over his helper.

His full height must have been nearly nine feet tall. His new eyes, cold and unblinking glared down at her.

'I'd say that this is a 100% improvement,' he smiled through sharp, metallic teeth. Garben, unable to take her gaze off the incredible feat that she had achieved, began to slip to the floor, quivering in fear.

'Don't be afraid,' he cooed. 'I will not harm you. You have given me life again. Thanks to you, I am reborn.'

The sound of metal echoed around the workshop as he moved about, getting a sense of how this new body worked.

'What can this new thing do?'

Garben picked herself up, reassured at Stratos' word, but still terrified and fascinated in equal measure at her creation and propped herself up on the stool.

'Erm,' she recomposed herself. 'The body that you now have has the capacity to be ten times stronger and ten times faster than the average humanoid life form.'

Stratos, his back to Garben, grinned maniacally. 'Perfect. Just what I needed.'

Picking his hand up, he looked at it and made a fist. 'I don't suppose you mind me taking it for a try out?'

'W-where?'

'Oh, I don't know, outside perhaps?'

He crouched down to fit through the door and tried to open it. Gently, his fingers enveloped the handle and he pulled down to open it.

Nothing happened. Stratos tried again. Still nothing.

'What is happening?' he said through gritted teeth. 'Am I malfunctioning?'

'No,' Garben stuttered.

Stratos turned to face her. He stood in shadow, out of the lighting that bled from the ceiling over the slab that Garben had worked on.

The image was the stuff of nightmares. 'Then what have you done?' he hissed. 'I just wanted to be safer than sorry...'

Before Garben had a chance to explain further, the sound of rockets pierced the still air. The noise grew louder and louder.

Garben rushed to the window and looked outside.

There in the snow, was a small ship coming in to land. 'That's impossible,' gasped Garben.

'What is?' asked Stratos.

'This is an exile moon. No-one should be able to find it.'

'And yet, someone has,' said Stratos. He went over to the same window and crouched down to see for himself. The ship had landed roughly one hundred feet away, but with his telescopic vision, Stratos could make out a side door sliding open.

Suddenly, he recoiled as to his horror, a pack of Samlores began to spill out of it and laser swords primed, proceeded to charge towards the workshop.

'Garben, you must turn off my strength inhibitor.' 'Why?'

'Don't argue, just do it!' he yelled.

Garben jumped to it, clambering to the instrument bank. She flicked a couple of switches and instantly, Stratos began to feel the strength grow within his new body.

Without warning, a blaster bolt shot through the window, sending Garben scrambling to the ground. The shot embedded itself in the instruments on the wall, blowing any chances of the inhibitors from limiting Stratos now. There was another bolt at the other end of the workshop. Bits of broken glass lay strewn across the slab. Stratos was unmoved.

Suddenly, the Samlores burst in through the door. They immediately stopped as soon as they clapped eyes on the terrifying machine that stood, unafraid, in front of them.

'Hold your fire!' came a cry from the front. Stratos glared down with murderous intent at the dozen or so Samlores who stood quaking before him. 'You only needed to knock,' he said calmly.

'Samlores like to make an entrance,' said the lead Samlore.

'Who am I addressing?' asked Stratos.

'Samlore Charbok, Captain of the Dangoza.' Stratos looked over their shoulders, which was easy for him given his new head for heights, and looked upon their little ship with utter contempt.'

'What? That little thing?'

'That hunk of junk is not mine, never has been, we shall liberate the Dangoza from the Space Corps.'

'So why are you bothering us then?'

'Well, before I escape this hole of a moon once and for all, we Samlores thought we should do what we do best...scavenge.'

'Well there's nothing here for you to scavenge,' said Stratos.

'Oh yeah? Says-'

Charbok was halted by something cold and powerful gripping his throat. Soon he seemed to be levitating in mid-air. The Samlores remained unmoved, petrified to the spot.

Stratos had picked up the Captain of the Samlores like he was a rag doll. He held him up close to his face. Charbok tried kicking and hitting with all his might, but he had dropped his weapon when he was grabbed. Stratos began to squeeze.

'Says me...'said Stratos. With a terrible blood cur- dling squelch, Charbok was no more and Stratos hurled his body clean out of the door, passed the stunned Samlores and off into the distance.

The Samlores instantly laid down their weapons and dropped to the floor, begging to be spared.

Stratos laughed.

'You pitiful beings need a new Captain...I accept the position.'

The Samlores agreed in unison, still pleading not to be hurt.

'Silence!'

They all stopped instantly.

'Let's go...you are in my command now and anyone who disagrees can rest uneasily that they will not be breathing for long.'

The Samlores began to file out of the workshop. Before he left, he looked over at Garben, who had propped herself underneath the slab.

'I owe you my life, Garben. In return I spare yours.' Garben, tears running down her face, brought up the courage to speak.

'Who are you?' Stratos smiled.

'I am Stratos. Destroyer of Worlds.' And with that, Stratos left.

Garben, still shaking severely, slowly left the con- fines of her shelter and crawled across the broken glass to the door.

By the time she had reached it, the craft doors were shutting and the tiny scavenger ship was ready to leave.

'Oh god,' said Garben as she watched the ship take off. 'What have I done?'

4

THE VALETUDINARIUM

Random awoke from a fever dream in a very strange place indeed. At least, he thought it was a fever dream. Or maybe it was his recollection of events, strange as they were, that led him to feel so...weak? He took a sharp intake of breath and listened to the noises around him. The intermittent beeping and the coughing, the sound of professionals tending to others. Then there was the sickening smell of a sterilised atmosphere. From that alone he deduced that he was in some kind of hospital, but where?

Why and almost as equally as important, how?' He felt cold...and yet hot at the same time. His body hurt and ached like nothing he had ever felt before.

Random wondered why.

He started to dig deep back into his mind to work out what had happened to him.

It all seemed to happen so...quickly.

At first, things had gone swimmingly, then less so. He remembered Spectronia and that immense power of the Zedron Flux. He recollected the ultimatum he had to give to the Osirons to stop them from blowing up the planet.

And then...did he? His blood ran cold. He had, hadn't he?

He'd activated the Flux to destroy an entire race. Genocide.

'Skateboard, he's stirring!' came a cry from a familiar voice.

It was Anji. He could feel her holding his hand. Or was that the other one? Jake? No, it wasn't Jake. The person who was holding onto him smelt too nice to be Jake.

With extreme caution, Random began to open his eyes and instantly regretted his decision.

The blinding white lights of his hospital cubicle made them water.

'Random, buddy, you're back!' came another voice.

Random shut his eyes again and decided to use another of his senses to conclude who this new voice belonged to.

He sniffed the air. The sterile was joined by an over- whelming level of anti-perspirant.

It was Jake alright.

'Please, don't crowd him,' came another, less familiar tone.

'He's going to be okay, right?' Jake spoke again.

Random wanted to assure him he would be fine, he really did, but when he tried to speak his throat was so dry it felt like someone had poured an entire desert into it.

'He needs to rest,' came the stranger's voice again. And with that, Random fell back to sleep.

He awoke again sometime later. This time, he felt stronger, less weak.

Daring to open his eyes again, he felt a great sense of relief when, to his great surprise, the overwhelming lights that blinded him before were gone. With caution, he gently levered himself upright but feeling a sudden dizziness, slumped back onto the bed.

He huffed, his breath rapid as though he were ex- hausted after a long run.

'Sir?'

Random's eyes opened again. He certainly knew that mechanical voice.

'Skateboard,' he croaked. His lips were like sandpaper. Licking them and clearing his throat, he said the name of his faithful friend again.

'It's good to have you back with us,' Skateboard sounded relieved, even for a computer. 'For a while we thought there might be no way back.'

So many questions and yet, Random wasn't sure if he wanted to know the answers to any of them.

'Why? Where have I been?' he joked. 'How much do you remember, sir?' Random sighed. 'Everything.'

'You remember the Flux?'

'How can I forget. I remember what I did. What I had to do. I take it that it nearly killed me?'

'Well, to be precise, sir, the aftershock of the energy the Flux generated has polluted the cells in your body to such an extent that they have been incapable of regenerating, as they would if you broke your leg, for example, to give you sufficient time to heal. So your body was starting to shut down.'

'You could have just said, "yes", Skateboard,' sighed Random.

He fell back in his bed and gazed upward at the ceil-ing. It was very tall, with large chandeliers of lights dangling from metallic beams metres above him.

'What is this place?' asked Random.

'You are in the Valetudinarium,' replied Skateboard. 'Where's that then?'

'Sector 4A of the Hollister System. The biggest hospital in the known galaxy. We are on the largest asteroid on a belt surrounding the planet Fro.'

'Hospital...good,' Random said to himself. 'Anji and Jake, they are here, yes?'

Skateboard looked to the side of the bed. Anji was fast asleep in the visitor's chair situated next to Random's sick bed. Her coat had slipped off her sleeping frame and fallen to the floor, so Skateboard produced his inner claws to tenderly put it over her again so as not to wake her.

'They've barely left your side,' said the AI robot.

'I think I can tell,' said Random, suddenly feeling a heavy weight lying across his ankles. It was Jake. He was snoring softly curled up at the foot of the bed.

Random allowed himself a chuckle.

'I've done a terrible thing, old friend. I don't deserve to have survived this.'

Skateboard got up onto his two hind wheels and lined his vision interface level with Random. He was looking upward, his mind in a very distant place.

'You made a decision. A terrible decision that saved the lives of millions.'

'I know but-'

'The Osirans,' Skateboard interrupted, 'Would have ripped the whole planet apart with the Armageddon beam.

Destroying all life, including ours in the shock wave. They would then have taken the Flux for their own and destroyed countless lives, countless worlds if you had not done what you did. There's a blessing and a curse being the saviour of Rodas. Sometimes you must take action that others simply cannot. On this occasion, it was a blessing that you were there to do the right thing.'

Random smiled, tears collecting in the corners of his red/blue eyes. He reached out his hand, which he noticed was quivering as the various tubes and drips jangled out of them and patted Skateboard affectionately.

'Sometimes I do wonder where I would be without you, Skateboard.'

'Only sometimes?' the robot joked.

Random smiled. He would live with his decision. Just like he lived with the guilt of blowing up Anji and Jake's school and condemning the Sandman to the fire. Like he had done when liberating Genocia.

Like he did, day after day, to not go back to Rodas and meet his destiny.

'If sir does not mind my saying so, I think you should get some rest. Your test results come back tomorrow.'

'Of course not.' Random returned his hand to his side, kicked his ankles that were quickly going dead from underneath the sleeping Jake and very quickly fell back into a deep, dreamless sleep.

*

Meanwhile in another part of space altogether, the little scavenger ship sailed away from the prison system Stratos had found himself in with a new Captain at the helm. Stratos had to admit to himself, as he stooped inside the tin can of a vessel, it had been incredibly easy for him to take charge.

But what he was unaware of was that the Samlore race was, despite their devious, violent nature, quite cowardly and pitiful. They are also loyal until they are conquered, at which point they will turn their loyalty to those who have conquered them.

Stratos smiled. They were perfect for his plans. 'O' Great One,' said the Commander to Stratos as he returned from the cockpit.

'No,' said Stratos, 'Supreme Leader is what you will call me.'

The Commander's heart started beating that little bit faster.

'Excuse me,' he saluted. Stratos grinned. He liked that. 'What do we do now?'

'We need to find a ship. A battle cruiser with the capacity of immense weaponry.'

The Commander moved back into the cockpit and barked the order at his navigator.

'Got one,' said the navigator, who due to his poor sight was wearing what appeared to Stratos as someone else's glasses. Someone he had killed, perhaps.

'Supreme Leader,' said the Commander, gesturing at the scanner screen.

Stratos squeezed into the confined space, jamming not only the Commander and navigator in with him, but also the pilot and another Samlore who seemed to carry out no other function but to serve drinks. As he realised that he was now trapped in the cockpit with everyone else, he awkwardly perched on the end of a chair.

Stratos gazed at the scanner and witnessed a large blob blip in and out of existence on the top left hand corner of the screen.

'The only ship within range with weaponry is the Orbital, 12 clicks away.'

'Then set a course, it's ours.'

The Commander's jaw slackened and the tea boy dropped the foul smelling liquid in the goblet to the floor.

'Supreme Leader...'whispered the Commander, 'The Orbital is one of the mother ships of the Space Seal Corps. It's the most heavily guarded space carrier in the sector. There's no way we can take it-'

'We can and we shall,' Stratos interrupted. 'But...why?' the Commander dared to ask. 'To send a message,' said Stratos coldly.

*

'Welcome back to the land of the living!' Anji enthused.

It was the following morning and Random was still finding his strength but was at least now able to sit up in bed, no matter how many tubes and drips were anchoring him to the spot.

'Morning to you too,' he quipped.

'How are you feeling, buddy?' yawned Jake.

'I'd be lying if I said I was back to my normal self,' he replied.

Jake fished about the end of the bed for something. 'Well if you fancy some breakfast...here you go!' he said, producing a brown bag and handing it to his friend.

Now he came to mention it, Random was famished. It felt like a lifetime ago since he had eaten. Had food even passed his lips when he was on Spectronia?

He dived into the bag and pulled out a bunch of half-eaten, browning grapes.

Random bulked. 'On second thoughts, I'll skip breakfast.'

'Well, I suppose I did buy them a week ago...and I got hungry on the way back from the shop.'

Random's ears pricked up. 'A week ago?! I've been in here a week?!'

'You've been asleep for a couple of days on top of that,' said Anji.

Random struggled to make this new information process in his fuzzy brain.

'So, what happened?' he asked.

Anji shrugged. 'Don't know. You'd seen off the Osirons and by the time we got to the top of the cliff you'd already started to collapse. Random?' she drew herself closer, 'It couldn't be anything to do with what you were trying to tell me in the cave, could it?'

Random frowned. He had forgotten about the voices in his mind, the incessant consciences that plagued him, told him to go home and fulfill his destiny. He hadn't wanted to saddle Anji and Jake with his worries that they were becoming more frequent because at the end of the day they were only human. They'd never understand. Moreover, he didn't want them to worry. But clearly now the cat was out of the bag.

'No. And don't worry you two, your pilot hasn't started to take leave of his senses.'

'We're not worried about our pilot, mate,' said Jake, who in this time had liberated the bag of week-old grapes back off Random and was quietly scoffing them. 'We're worried about our friend.'

'Well,' said a smiling Random, 'You've no need to worry, I'm getting back to where I need to be. Slowly, but surely.'

'Let's hope you go purple again too, eh?' said Anji absentmindedly.

'Sorry, say that again?' asked Random. 'Oh,' said Anji.

Random began to look around for something, any- thing, that would show his reflection. Jake did the same and as Anji struggled to find her mirror inside her bag, Jake found a metallic pan under the bed and handed it to Random.

Random's eyes grew larger than a planet as he saw for the first time, inside the warped image of his bed pan, that his skin had gone red and blue.

'What the-'

The rude word Random said next was drowned out completely by an announcement over the speaker system.

'WOULD DOCTOR KILDER, DOCTOR MADONEY AND DOCTOR SELBY PLEASE MAKE THEIR WAY URGENTLY TO MATERNITY ROOM 39? FOR EVERYONE ELSE, PLEASE RETURN TO YOUR BEDS. THERE IS NO CAUSE FOR PANIC OR ALARM.'

The intercom clicked off and a few seconds later clicked back on again.

'JUST A MESSAGE TO ALL INPATIENTS AND MEMBERS OF STAFF IF YOU DO HAPPEN TO FIND A SELOPTAN BABY IN ONE OF YOUR WARDS, PLEASE STAY AWAY FROM ITS TENTACLES, ESPECIALLY THE SHARP ONES, UNTIL THE MIDWIVES CATCH UP WITH IT, THANK YOU.'

Of course Random heard none of this. He just stared, lost for words, at his reflection.

Red and blue.

How?

Skateboard made his way into Random's ward, doing his best to stay out of the way of the mixture of patients, doctors and nurses en route back from the Venus II. It was a fairly long walk - the ship had been parked on the western wing of the asteroid since they had landed and Random was on the opposite side of the Valetudinarium, which was not ideal but manageable for Skateboard's daily treks back to Random's bedside.

After all, the asteroid was five miles long and two and a half miles across, meaning that although it could be a tiresome trek for Anji and Jake, at least they were all keeping fit.

For the first couple of nights, Skateboard had al- lowed the pair to sleep by his master's bedside but when the hospital management had begun to take a disliking to this, for space reasons, which was ironic considering how big the hospital was, he had insisted that they begin to go back to the Venus to sleep and eat. He certainly needed to recharge his batteries - a lesson he had learnt the hard way on Spectronia - but then he began to realise that they were sneaking back in the middle of the night.

Originally, he put this behaviour down to their age, acting out and being rebellious against authority perhaps. After all, the Valetudinarium wasn't just a hospital. It was a whole new place to explore. But that didn't stop Skateboard worrying about what kind of infectious diseases or terrible things they might encounter here alone without him.

Yet he needn't have worried. The first morning they had done this, when he had panicked and was just seconds away from alerting the hospital security that his friends were missing, he had returned to Random's bedside and found that they were asleep next to their ill friend.

And so the tradition had continued. Every morning, that's where he would find them. He didn't say any- thing, why would he? He just chirped to himself how lucky Random was that he had two loyal friends.

And how lucky he himself was to have all three of them.

As Skateboard neared Random's ward, dodging a sticky, squelchy looking infant Seloptan baby and the nets that a gaggle of harangued midwives were throwing at it, he whirred over in his mind why his friend had changed colour in his stricken state?

Whatever damage the Flux had done to him, they'd know soon enough, but in the meantime, he would have to break the news to his friend gently.

The ward was a hive of activity. Roughly 30 beds, adorning a multitude of aliens with a range of differing ailments, lined the back wall. The ward was a long tube of clinical equipment and white light. It had struck Anji and Jake when Random was first wheeled into his bay, how much it resembled a hospital back on Earth, barring the futuristic equipment, of course and the incredibly tall ceiling. Skateboard had pointed out to them that wherever the hospital may be, it still needed to serve the same purpose and hence why they all looked so similar.

A Doctor nearly swished his reptilian tail right in the path of Skateboard as he made his way to Random's bed and had it not been for a beep from Skateboard's speaker system to let him know he was there, he'd have been swiped right into the wall.

'Do excuse me,' said the posh Doctor.

'Not a problem, sir,' said Skateboard as he merrily made his way to his master's side.

He whirred to himself, he would have smiled if he had a face, when he saw that Anji and Jake were by his side as always.

'Good morning to you all,' he said in his usual posh manner.

Anji and Jake sat pensively in their places. Random didn't move. Barely blinked.

'Oh my, are you all frozen in time?' he quipped. Then he noticed that Random was looking at his reflection.

'Oh,' he said.

'Skateboard...' Random uttered. 'What? How?'

'We should soon know, your test results arrive back this morning,' he cooed. 'Now please put that down sir, you know where that has been, and try to relax.'

'You're getting your results this morning, Random, I'm sure it isn't permanent,' said Anji, trying her best to allay his worries.

'Unless you prefer it?' Jake said, shrugging his shoul- ders. 'And who knows? Next planet we go to, red and blue might be in with the season?'

Anji frowned. 'Oh yeah, because you're all about fashion statements Captain Shabby.'

'That's harsh!' said Jake in defence. Although after looking down at his clothes, which hadn't been changed in a few days, maybe she had a point.

Random dropped the bed pan, which made a horrible clunking noise as it fell to the ground and threw himself back onto his pillow.

'Whatever they say, let's hope it's good news.'

'It's bad news, I'm afraid,' said the Doctor, who de-spite the absence of a mouth - or indeed eyes or nose - on her face, somehow managed to convey the test re-sults to Random and his friends audibly.

Jake wondered where the mouth indeed was on the Doctor's body, before quickly thinking it probably wasn't something he should be imagining.

Random shuffled uncomfortably in his bed. 'Okay, hit me.'

'The radiation from the power you were exposed to has damaged your central nervous system, your musculoskeletal system, your metabolism and your skin pigmentation has been compromised. It's fair to say that it is a miracle that you are still alive.'

'So what does this all mean? Is he going to die?' Anji asked, fearing the worst.

'Everyone dies,' remarked the Doctor, in a tone a local butcher would have been proud of. 'But if you get plenty of rest and some drugs from our chemist, your metabolism should begin to repair your body, but I'm afraid it's going to be a slow process. Truly, we have never seen a body as remarkable as yourself. To which species do you belong again? Rodasian, you said?'

'Yes, but for the sake of my patient confidentiality, please do not tell anyone,' Random replied in hushed tones.

'Of course, if you wish,' said the Doctor.

'How long until he can be discharged?' asked Jake. 'Not for a while yet. Although your body is repairing it will take a while, like I said, until you are back to normal, if indeed you get there. If you do not rest then your recuperation will be compromised. Even for such a unique individual as yourself, remember you have been in a coma for over a week, time will be the teller. Until then, rest up and relax. I have to complete my rounds now but if there is anything else I can do, let me know. I'll get onto the pharmacy and see if there is anything we can do to help boost your metabolism.'

'Before you go, Doctor, does this...radiation mean that I've endangered those who I've been in close prox- imity to since then?'

The Doctor smiled.

'No, your exposure was internal, there is no way that your family have been put at risk. We'll get you started on medication this afternoon. Until then, good day.'

The Doctor slithered away, medical tablet readout in hand.

Random turned back to his friends. 'Family?'

'We had to tell them we were your next of kin,' said Anji.

'So who are you then? My sister?' 'Your wife,' she corrected.

'My Wife?!' said Random before turning to Jake 'And you my Brother?'

'Er...husband actually?'

'What?! Does that make Skateboard my husband too then?'

'Certainly not, sir!' lied Skateboard. 'We had to pretend we were next of kin otherwise they would not have cared for you. So after a little research, we decided that we would say that we were of the faith of the Church of Many and left it there. In that religion you can have up to twelve husbands or wives of your choosing.'

'I bet the divorce rate is insurmountable!' Random remarked.

A short time later, Jake found Anji on the observation deck of the East wing of the Valetudinarium. After Random had returned to sleep, the three of them had gone their separate ways and after a change of clothes, Jake joined Anji's side as she gazed at the planet below.

'Beautiful, isn't it?' she admired.

The planet shone gloriously in the darkness of space. The asteroid belt the Valetudinarium belonged to hung around it like a necklace.

'It sure is,' said Jake, who noticed that Anji's arms were held tightly around herself. 'Hey, don't worry Anj. You heard what they said. He'll be fine.'

'No, they said that he might be. He needs a lot of time to get over this - who's to say that he will be the same when he finally gets over it? Or what long lasting damage that bloody Flux thing has done to him?'

Jake shrugged. 'I suppose we just have to see. What was it the Doctor said? "Time will be the teller?"'

'Very profound,' replied Anji.

'Look, as long as he is here in this hospital resting up then nothing can go wrong can it?'

Almost at the instant that Jake had finished speaking a huge ship blasted past the view screen, making

Anji, Jake and the other dozen or so aliens in the area fall to the floor as it trembled beneath their feet.

'You had to say it!' said Anji as she helped her friend back up to his feet.

'What the hell was that?' asked Jake to nobody in particular.

The pair watched as the ship, a huge battle freighter honed away from the hospital and flew out further into space.

A murmur of discontent surrounded them as fellow patients, nurses and next of kin gathered around the glass to get a better look.

The freighter's engines came to an abrupt halt high above the planet below. A loud crackle abruptly pierced through the speaker system all around the hospital.

On the East wing wards, the patients that were asleep, including Random, awoke with a startle. Random pulled himself upright in bed, a hum of something in the atmosphere sparking his attention.

Suddenly, a voice boomed into life.

'Peoples of this system please attend carefully.' The voice was metallic yet organic and malicious. 'I come looking for the one who has dared to put a stop to my galactic conquest. The one who is known to the universe as the bringer of darkness. Random.'

Anji and Jake looked at each other confused and alarmed in equal measure. Elsewhere on the asteroid,

Random and Skateboard, who had returned to his master's bed, did exactly the same.

'Ever heard of him?' came the voice once more. Those who had gathered by the window begin to chatter among themselves.

'Anj, we've got to get him out of here,' said Jake ner- vously.

'No?' came the voice once more. 'Well, let me leave him a message...'

The tremor became more and more violent as a red light began to shine from underneath the belly of the freighter. It looked hotter and brighter second by second until suddenly with a terrifying finality, a beam of thunder seemed to explode from the huge freighter down upon the planet below.

What happened next was the stuff of nightmares. As the incumbents of the viewing deck were thrown to the floor and the patients on the wards were thrown from their beds, the planet began to split and with sickening finality exploded in a fireball that sent a shock wave of earthquake proportions bursting through the asteroid belt.

Someone on the Valetudinarium must have turned a self-defense shield on the asteroid as debris started to fly towards the hospital and then deflect off an invisible force keeping it out of harm's way.

As the inhabitants of the Valetudinarium, shocked and stunned by what they had just seen, gathered themselves the best they could, a panic began to shriek around the halls of the place. Anji and Jake lay there on the floor, stunned by what they had just witnessed, lost for words.

'I think he got the message,' said the horrible voice once again. 'If he wants to put a stop to all of this...then the purple one will have to find me...'

And with that, in a blinding flash the Freighter went to warp and disappeared, leaving nothing else but a silent, hollow space where the planet, where upon billions of lives had just been lost, was no more.

Anji and Jake, among the chaos surrounding them, turned to each other. Jake looked terrified and managed to break their silence.

'We've gotta get out of here!'

5

SIEGE

The metal monster sat brooding in a tiny corner of the Samlores stolen ship. Waiting. Impatiently.

Revenge for him was best served instantly. Al- though to him it had only been a few hours since the Commodore had fallen to Random's efforts, with this new body, he wanted to move as swiftly as time would allow him - but time was also an enemy to him right now.

Aligning himself with the Samlores, a pathetic race of snivelling vermin not worthy to lace the space boots of his most trusty loyal soldiers, was nothing short of embarrassing to a man of his great stature.

But they would never have to know - those who had survived of course.

As soon as the Freighter was theirs, which it would be no matter what the Space Seals threw at them, Stratos would make sure of that and wreak havoc... just as soon as his message to Random had been delivered.

With the knowledge he had within his head, and the might of his new body, as soon as the arsenal of devas- tation was at his mercy, nothing could stop him.

Not even Random.

He looked down at the two grossly over proportioned fists that sat clenched in his lap. They made a jangling sound as he rested them on his thighs. Well, they were his thighs now. The arms were huge, heavy, dangerous. It was like having two submarines for limbs. But he liked them.

His body had been augmented, improved, and it was going to serve its purpose.

The trauma of losing his own body was so minute it didn't bother him. How was he to obtain supremacy with a broken vessel that was no longer worthy of containing his ambitions. This new one served it just so.

The hydraulics that replaced his innards were pumping toxins everywhere, poisonous to anyone else who came into contact with them and keeping Stratos' poisoned mind on the job in hand.

He was starting to get cross. Why weren't they there yet?

He was yearning to give this new body a test drive. To sample it's destructive force.

Stratos growled loudly, thrust himself upright and marched towards the cockpit, knocking unwitted Samlores aside as he cleared his path.

'Report!' he barked.

The pilot looked nervously over his shoulder. 'We are nearly there, Supreme Leader.' 'Nearly is not now, is it?'

The pilot paused, throwing the question over in his incredibly dense mind.

'Er...no,' he coughed.

Stratos bent down and leered at him.

The pilot stared into his deep, soulless eyes. 'So...how much longer?' Stratos spat, a spray of clear fluid dispersing on the pilot's face.

The pilot gulped. The scavenger ship stuttered to a halt. Stratos glanced up away from the terrified Samlore and took a look through the view screen.

In front of them, a huge vessel swelled over the little craft, blocking out the blackness of space.

'Good,' grinned Stratos. 'I like an efficient pilot. For a moment there I thought I was going to have to kill you,' he said casually, patting the pilot roughly on his shoulder, make the cold sweat pour just that little quicker for the shocked occupant.

'Supreme Leader.'

It was the Commander's weasley voice that broke the silence.

'What are your orders?'

Stratos turned around to face his subjects.

'We get ourselves arrested. And then, as soon as we are aboard, we strike. Who knows? if you're lucky I might let you have some of the fun too. I want the ship, I don't care what you do to the crew, just make sure that they are disposed of. Feel free to get creative.'

The Samlores gurgled in horrible appreciation. 'Crew?' asked Stratos.

'247, Supreme Leader. We are but 12 in number,' said the pilot.

A sickening clash of metal on bone propelled the pilot out of his chair and into a bank of important looking dials and switches on the adjacent wall. The pilot was dead before he hit the ground and as his lifeless form fell to the floor, Stratos retracted his fist.

'I will not stand negativity. It spreads like a disease, infecting unless cured straight away. This freighter may be the size of a small moon, but don't let it intimidate any of you. These ships have a small crew despite their size...we can quell them. You just have to do what I say. Is that clear?'

The Samlores nodded their heads in agreement.

'This is the Orbital. Please state your business in this quadrant.'

The voice came from the ship's communication systems.

'What shall we say?' asked the Commander. 'Nothing,' replied Stratos.

'This is the Orbital. Please respond.'

*

The rookie at the desk clicked the comms button off again. Fresh out of the academy, it was only her second week on board the Orbital. A fortnight out in the real world. It was nothing that she thought it would be.

It was boring.

Her commanding officer, a steal faced, rigid woman twice her age, stood pensive over her shoulder.

'Nothing, Ma'am.'

The commanding officer turned on her heels and paced, hands behind her back.

'How many lifeforms on board?'

'12. Just running a security scan on the ship right now,' said the desk operator.

She surveyed the bridge whilst awaiting the results, large, cavernous, far too big for the crew that she was in charge of. But if they were to maintain the security of the sector, and protect the cargo they had on board, they had to be sure that nothing was compromised.

She turned to the other officers sitting along the long, vast command bank of complex computers and sighed. This was supposed to be her day off. Why did she get the impression it wasn't going to be a quiet one?

'I should have called in sick,' she muttered to no- body in particular.

The scavenger ship was plastered across every single monitor on the bridge. The huge area was a hive of activity, a buzz of electrical instruments hummed in the background as the newbie had finished completing their scans.

'It's stolen, Ma'am.' she confirmed.

The commanding officer leaned back over the desk and peered at the monitor.

'Send a patrol down to Bay 3. Get a tractor beam fixed on that ship. Bring them in.'

The scavenger ship put up no fight as it was dragged into the belly of the Orbital. As it rested on the floor of Bay 3 and as the security patrol surrounded it and cocked their laser guns, the ship itself was silent.

'Hold your positions,' said a voice from under one of the helmets.

The bay was still, like the calm before the storm. 'This is the Orbital. Come out with your hands up,' came another.

Still there was no sign of life.

The patrol seemed unmoved. They had been trained

for situations such as this and seen them many times over.
They were happy to wait. However long it took.

After a few minutes, a creaking sound started to emit from the ship. Within moments, carnage was released.

Without warning, something ripped through the door of the scavenger ship, tearing it's hull away like paper. It leaped out of the hole and with a devastating swipe of its arm wiped a couple of soldiers clean off their feet and across the bay. A volley of laser fire exploded and reverberated around the four walls, as the Samlores began their side of the slaughter.

*

Up on the bridge, an alarm went off instantly. The rookie alerted the commanding officer, who sprung out of her command chair and leapt to her side and watched in horror on the surveillance screen as the carnage unfolded. Her eyes swam in horror as she witnessed a huge cybernetic man rip one of her soldiers to shreds. In all her years of service, she had never seen anything so destructive in one single life form before.

'Seal the bulkhead,' she croaked.

The rookie sprung into action, flicking a number of switches as the bridge crew, snapped out of their shock and back into action.

The Commander made for a cabinet in the wall behind her chair. Pressing a few buttons, the door hissed open, revealing a laser proof vest and a long, shiny laser gun. Fastening the vest over her uniform, she took up arms, closed the cabinet and turned back to the rookie.

'Never call in sick, cadet,' she said.

Stratos had enjoyed the slaughter to such an extent that he had failed to pick up the alarm siren shrieking over the sound of death. As the final corpse slid away from his iron grasp, he surveyed the wreckage. Two Samlores lay slain with their enemy.

'Weak,' said Stratos to his troops. 'We have to get to the bridge. Cut off the snake's head and crush the resistance. Shut off this damn alarm. Follow me.' The Samlores did as they were instructed.

Stratos led them to what should have been the exit out of the bay but a bulk door had slid down to trap them out.

A small hiss of activity could just be heard by Stratos under the sound of the alarm. Soon the Samlores also heard it and started to look around the bay as though they were looking for a swarm of bees buzzing above them.

Stratos turned to see that the bay door that had sealed them inside was starting to slowly open. He growled. They were going to suck them out into space...unless...

Stratos clasped his powerful hands together and started to smash down on the bulkhead. Every blow made a dent and a bone jangling sound as slowly but surely, it was starting to give.

Meanwhile back on the bridge, the commanding officer watched on in terror as she witnessed the monster doing what should have been impossible.

'How long until the bay doors are open?' The rookie checked her read out.

'Eight seconds.'

She grit her teeth. 'It's not quick enough.'

She was right. The rookie shot a look of panic at her superior. 'Ma'am! He's through!'

As soon as the fists shot through the bulk, a dozen or so troops began firing at them, sending beams of energy ricocheting off Stratos' protected armour.

As the troops began to beg for back up, Stratos' mighty hands tore the bulkhead in two. His army of rogues returned their fire and took out a couple of the Orbital's struggling soldiers. Slowly they forced them back as Stratos ran like a bull into them and allowed his fury to inflict appalling violence against all who stood in their way.

Before long, the corridor they were now standing in fell silent. One of the Samlores was sick as Stratos turned back to his men.

'You!' he pointed at the Commander. 'Find the bridge. Now! We do not split up until the bridge is ours!'

As the Commander made for an info port on the wall another volley of lasers exploded towards them.

Stratos laughed at them as every single shot bounced off him, not even leaving a scorch mark upon him. Even a bolt of fire that was aimed squarely at his head deflected harmlessly away. A force field defence system built into his metallic body was doing it's job.

With lightning pace, Stratos pounced like a jaguar at his prey and the rage surged once more inside of him.

Even though the Commander had found their route to the bridge, they could have just followed the soldier who lay waiting for them like lambs to the slaughter, lining their way to the prize. Stratos pitied them. They never stood a chance.

The commanding officer was at a loss as to what to do next. They were so close now and yet so many of her soldiers, her comrades and more importantly her friends had been sent to their deaths in a futile effort to stop the rampage.

'Ma'am, surely we must abandon!' cried the rookie, who was white with fright.

'No.'

'But Ma'am!' the girl was grappling at the arm of her superior, who stood rigid facing the entrance to the bridge, gun in hand, ready to take on the force of nature that was sure to tear his way inside any moment now.

'Send a distress call to all Space Corps ships in this sector...we can't let them take control, not with what we have on board.'

The rookie tightened her grip on her arm.

'Now!' screamed the commanding officer as she threw the girl to the floor. The girl scrambled to her bank and started to send out the SOS signal.

Behind her, the bridge doors buckled and twisted and before she had a chance to complete the message, she was shot in the back by a bolt from one of the Samlores' guns.

The commanding officer watched as her new of-ficer, fresh with promise and too young to die, fell silently and lifelessly away.

She turned back to face her victor and despite the cold sweat that trickled down her face, kept a lid on the terror she was facing.

Stratos leered over her. 'You are the Captain, yes?'

'I am Admiral Quint of the SSC Orbital and you have committed an act of atrocity that in direct opposition of-'

'Save it!' he demanded. 'Admiral Quint, I hereby relieve you of your services. Order your men to stand down.'

He grabbed her laser gun from her grasp and twisted the barrel until it snapped like a twig. Quint did as she was told and ordered her troops to stand down.

'The Orbital is lost,' she said as she signed off her message.

'Just under new management,' replied Stratos. 'Now Admiral. Run.'

The Admiral looked vaguely at him. 'RUN!' he shrieked.

Again, Quint did as she was told and ran as fast as her legs would carry her out of what used to be the bridge door.

Stratos looked up and saw the multitude of officers who were still on the bridge too.

'You too! Get out! Run away like the cowards that you all are!'

'You heard him, move, move!' barked the Commander as he and the Samlores raised their guns threateningly.

They sprang away from the bridge, knowing that any show of resistance was an instant sentence of death. They'd all seen what had happened in the bay and in the corridors leading up to the bridge.

Resistance was well and truly futile.

As the last Space Seal retreated he was needlessly tripped by the Samlore standing nearest the door. Stratos surveyed all that he had conquered.

'Magnificent...just magnificent...Commander, seal the blast doors.'

The Commander made for the command desk and without hesitation carried out the order. A shutter slid down over the wreckage of the bridge entrance and sealed them in.

'Cut the oxygen to all other levels of the ship.' Coldly, the Commander carried out Stratos' want and in doing so, assured that any resistance stupid enough to try and stop them on the Orbital was soon to be no more. As images of the crew suffocating swam on every monitor within the bridge, the Samlores watched on in dread.

'First they fight like cowards, then they run like cowards and now they die like cowards. How pre- dictable,' quipped Stratos. He moved over towards a bank of instruments further down the line of the Com- mander. 'Let this be a reminder to you all not to defy me,' he said as he punched in some information into the computer.

'Supreme Leader,' said the Commander who edged closer to him, 'What are you looking for?'

Stratos gave a truly sinister smile.

'This is more than I could have dreamed of,' he cried. 'This freighter has enough weaponry in their cargo, as well as their defence systems to destroy an entire planet.'

The Samlores grinned to one another and gave knowing nods back to Stratos.

'And that's just what we are going to do!' he leered. On a monitor behind him, the image of Admiral Quint gasping for breath stained the monitor before she too succumbed to the inevitable.

'Let's target a neutral world first. Somewhere that'll really make the universe shake. And Random take no- tice...'

Stratos keyed in the navigation codes and a planet came up on the screen.

'There,' he pointed his bloodied hands at the screen. The Samlores looked upon their doomed target.

'Fro.'

Jake and Anji, running against the tide of frightened patients and staff, made their way back to Random's bed to find their friend already trying to put his clothes on.

'Random!' said Anji breathlessly. 'I heard,' he replied.

'Sir, please you must reconsider!' pleaded Skate- board, 'You are not well enough to leave the Valetudi- narium, let alone take on a genocidal maniac!'

'He's just destroyed an innocent planet, Skateboard. Billions of lives have just been lost,' said Random as he struggled with his shoe laces. 'Not only that but he said my name specifically. The people here will know who I am and will probably arrest me.'

'That won't happen,' said Jake. 'But what are we go-ing to do?'

'We have to follow him, whoever he is, and make sure he doesn't do it again.'

'Random, it's got to be a trap,' said Anji.

'Definitely, which is why as soon as we are back at the Venus II I'm dropping you all off on the first peaceful planet we pass.'

'No!' cried Anji.

'Definitely not!' exclaimed Jake.

'Sir, you have got to reconsider. We should work with the authorities to put a stop to this, I'm sure they will protect you...protect us!'

'But Skateboard, we have no idea why he even wants me. I have
to know. Now, I want you to plug yourself into the mainframe
and download my medical records. The nurse delivered my
tablets before this all started, so as long as you know how to treat
me, I can rest while we try to find this monster and think up a
plan to stop him. Now do we have a deal?'

Skateboard sighed. What Random said about his anonymity
being compromised rang true. They did need to get away, but he
knew how ill his friend still was, and how long he needed to
recuperate.

They also needed more information on this lu- natic...and
considering the weight of the genocide of the Osirons on the
conscience of Random, now a whole planet had been blown away,
somehow, in his name.

'Sir's right, Jake, Anji, we have to get him to the Venus II.'

'Right... I have an idea,' said Jake.

The Doctor was rightly shaken by the events of an hour ago.
They all were. The tragedy of Fro's destruction had led to two
different methods of instant reaction. One was of utter shock, grief
and barely being able to comprehend what had just happened and
the other was mad hysteria. The Doctor had wanted to do both
simultaneously but instead, she shut down and sat in silence,
totally shocked.

She had connections with Fro, very personal ones. Her parents
had retired there. After a combined century of dedication to
medicine, they were her heroes and now they were gone. She
never even had a chance to tell them how much she loved them.
Like so, so many.

So many arguments unhealed. So many unsaid goodbyes.

She had wiped the tears from her eyes and was in

the middle of a sympathetic embrace from one of her duty nurses when she remembered the name that the terrorist gave was also the same name of her patient.

Random.

It was him, wasn't it? The boy whose body didn't make sense. The boy who should have been torn apart by the radiation he had consumed.

The boy who was lying in the East wing right now. She had to get to him.

She had to raise the alarm...but first, there were some questions she wanted to ask...

*

Racing to his bedside, she bolted down the endless corridors of the Valetudinarium, knocking still panicked beings out of the way as she screamed for space.

By the time she made it to the east wing, she knew that she was too late.

There was a mass underneath the badly made bed sheets but the patients belongings were nowhere to be seen. Neither were the bag of half gone off grapes that were plonked on the bedside cabinet.

Desperately, she whipped the bed clothes away, ex- posing nothing more than two pillows in the space that Random should have been occupying. Panting in anger, she tore away to the alarm button on the wall and plunged her slimy tentacle against it.

'Security alert, security alert, we have a sick patient missing from east wing bed 148!'

*

79

Somewhere else in the Valetudinarium, Random, who was hiding under a shroud on a gurney being pushed by Anji and Jake, stopped pretending he was dead and popped his head up from under the sheet.

'Bed 148. That's me!'

Jake, who had raided the utility cupboard after Skateboard had located it whilst downloading Ran- dom's data from the mainframe and taken two over- grown worker's overalls for himself and Anji, rolled up the sleeves of his arms that were far too big for him and gripped the gurney even tighter.

'Leg it!' he screamed.

6

ESCAPE AND RESCUE

By the time they arrived back at the Venus II, the hospital security team was waiting for them.

A line of six heavily armed officers, in baby blue uniforms that made them look like they were dressed in an armoured version of the scrubs the medical team were wearing, saw Anji and Jake wheel the gurney carrying the stricken Random and Skateboard into the hangar. As they cleared the entrance door, several other similarly dressed officers emerged from behind them and readied their standard issue batons.

'Random...' said Anji cautiously.

The Rodasian peeped his head from underneath his shroud and witnessed their predicament.

'Ah, right,' he muttered, unhelpfully.

'What are we going to do now?' hissed Jake. 'Skateboard! Use your knockout gas!' he cried. Nothing happened.

'Skateboard? Do it now!'

The AI robot poked his frame outside of the under- neath of the gurney.

'I'm sorry, sir. I'm afraid I do not have a knockout gas stock built into my mainframe.'

Random rolled his eyes. 'Anything else?'

'You're coming with us,' said one of the security officers.

'No, we can't, you don't understand!' protested Anji. 'Listen to me, all of you!' cried Random, who was

now sitting up and holding court as well as he could in his state. 'We know that this looks bad, but we had nothing to do with this.'

'Then why are you running?' said the officer. 'Because if we don't stop this lunatic then the entire universe could be in great danger!'

'But he asked for you, why would he do that?' 'We've travelled all over this universe, with the peo-

ple we've saved we are bound to pick up an enemy somewhere along the line and look what's happened!' Anji interjected, 'He's got the power to destroy planets! He must be stopped!'

'That's something for the Space Seals to deal with, in the meantime we must place you under close surveillance,' said the officer, who started to move in with the rest of his men and women.

Anji and Jake began to back away towards the gurney. 'Seriously, us being here will mean nothing but danger,

not just for you but for your patients! This psycho will clearly stoop to any level to find us. Please. You've got to let us go.'

'You are not going anywhere and that's final!' screamed the officer.

'Fine!' cried Random.

In that instant a piercing screech exploded from the tannoy system, rendering everyone incapacitated except Skateboard. He looked up at his friends, who just like the officers were crying out in agony as they held their hands over their ears. Gently, he pushed Anji onto

Random's gurney, then Jake, and proceeded to fire up his rockets to hurtle them all out of the ambush and towards the Venus II.

Silently to everyone else but the little robot, the ship blipped like a car alarm as it's runway descended from its belly. In no time at all, Skateboard pushed them all up the runway and into the ship and using his wireless capabilities, instructed the ship to withdraw the runway and fire up the engines. As the officers tried to pick themselves back up and fight the horrendous noise away from their focus, the Venus II lifted up on its haunches and soared above them towards the security door that would see the travellers to freedom.

'No!' protested the officer, who try as he might, was so incapacitated by the noise that he was unable to radio into control to keep the doors closed. The Venus II sailed away towards its escape and as if by magic, the doors opened accordingly and before the officers could act, it was gone.

As soon as the Venus II disappeared from view, the high pitched noise died away. The security officers rolled around on the floor, wounded by their ordeal.

The officer who had confronted Random and his friends finally managed to use his radio.

Shaking, he whispered the words, 'Inform the Space Seals.' before finally losing consciousness.

Onboard the Venus II, Anji and Jake sat shaken on the sofas in the mid-section as Skateboard began to skuttle towards the cockpit.

'Jesus Christ! What the hell was that?' said Jake as he shook his head, the sound refusing to budge from his eardrums.

'I'm so sorry about that,' said Skateboard from the cockpit. 'I managed to hack the Valetudinarium's comm systems and incapacitate their security detail to give us time to escape.'

'You could have warned us!' bit Random, who was lying back on the gurney again, digging his fingers into

his ear canals. Finally he had something else to add to the list of physical ailments he was currently experiencing.

'And give away my escape plan? Apologies, sir, but it was a spur of the moment thing.'

Anji shook her head. 'At least we got away. Now what?'

'Miss Anji, please take Random to the medi-bay,' asked Skateboard.

'No, Skateboard, we need to talk about what we are going to do next.'

'We will do so in the medi-bay, now hurry please.' Anji gave Random a sympathetic look and reluctantly, the red and blue boy allowed himself to be helped by his friend off the gurney. As his feet touched the ground they gave away a little. He was still pretty weak...in no state to rush head first into a war with a man with a vendetta against him.

As Skateboard initiated the Venus II's cloaking de- vice, which hadn't been used in a while but thankfully still worked, the ship sailed silently, noticeably in the blackness of space once again, voyaging close towards the debris of what used to be the planet Fro, leaving the Valetudinarian far behind.

Stratos sat brooding in the Admiral's chair on the bridge of the Orbital. He had ordered his subjects to clear the freighter of the corpses of the dead, demanding that not one was missed and giving them an option to be creative in their disposal methods.

He'd done it. Besieged a battleship the likes the Space Seals couldn't afford to lose into enemy hands and destroyed a planet. It felt good. All of it. The destruction was like oxygen to his demented mind. And yet he was puzzled.

The distant hum of the Orbital's engines was disturbed by a knock on the bulkhead door.

Stratos grunted.

The bulkhead opened and the Commander swaggered in through the door and approached his Supreme Leader. He gave a bow.

'Commander.'

'Supreme Leader. We've finished disposing of the bodies.'

'Good.'

'It's not a pretty sight, you may want to use the wipers on the bridge view screens when we pass through them.'

Stratos ignored this visceral information.

'Tell me, Commander,' he croaked. 'Why that prison moon? Why not Earth?'

The Commander gave a nervous glance away from his brooding ruler.

'I don't understand, Supreme Leader.'

'When I was viciously apprehended by Captain Random I was about to destroy Earth. So tell me,' he pushed the chair's personal view screen towards his subject, 'How I happened to end up thirty million miles away?'

The Commander surveyed the digital readout on the monitor.

'Er...'

'Yes, that's what I thought. It isn't possible, is it? An escape pod has no warp capabilities. So how did I move? Why did I not end up on Earth?'

'Supreme Leader...' the Commander stuttered. 'I'm afraid that I am not the most learned when it comes to star mapping.'

'Did you not attend school?' asked Stratos.

'I'm a Samlore, Supreme Leader...I burnt it down on my first day.'

'A pity...you could have been so much more,' he spat. 'But this...is disturbing me.'

'Supreme Leader, we have successfully obtained the one of the most powerful battleships in the known cosmos. With your adjustments we can make whole systems bow to your might. Perhaps this puzzle can be completed after your universal conquest?'

'You're right, Commander,' Stratos said, pushing the monitor away. 'It's time we continued our breadcrumb trail.'

The Commander smiled a sinister grin.' What shall we destroy next?'

Stratos got up from his chair and made his way over to the long console bank.

He trailed his finger down an image of planets and rested his finger upon one.

'That one,' he smiled.

The Commander licked his lips.

'I'll tell the men to fire up the weapons.'

Stratos took his finger away and looked down on the next planet to face the horrific firepower of his fury.

'No,' he said. 'I have a better idea.'

From the relative comfort of his sickbed, Random sat cross legged as he sat and listened to his friends chatter.

'Could it be someone from Genocia? I mean, there's no way that the Government was ever going to be having us on their Christmas card list after what we did there,' said Jake.

'That's true. And there's no way that its Lon or the others. As we know the Flux went away with Strakonis, he wouldn't do a thing like that, would he?' asked Anji.

'Now there's a word I wish I'd heard the last of,' groaned Random. 'No, it's no-one we have met before, that's for certain,' he scratched his head, 'Could be a hit man, someone acting revenge?'

Another jolt sent them sprawling as another chunk of debris hit the Venus II's shields and set the occupants of the ship at unease.

'Skateboard, we really have got to get away from here. Every jolt is a reminder,' complained Random.

'Of what?' asked Skateboard.

'Of the billions of lives that have been lost in my name!' he snapped. Random threw himself back on the bed. 'This is a nightmare. Like I'm being punished for what I did to the Osirans. I try to prevent genocide and yet I end up causing it two times over. I won't let any of you tell me otherwise so don't even try.'

Jake bit his lip. Skateboard whirred towards his friend.

'Sir, just give it a little while longer. While we are silent, the Space Seals won't detect us. If we hide just a little longer in the rubble then we'll have the information we need and we can go.'

'What are you doing?' asked Anji.

'I'm using the Venus II's long range sensors to scan for the battle freighter's vapour trail. When the scanners detect it, we will be able to follow in its jet stream and catch up with whoever is in control of it.'

'Great! Face-to-face with a madman we know nothing about!' said Jake.

'And someone who knows a lot about us, or him to be more specific,' said Anji pointing to Random.

Random tugged at the irritating drips that were pumping medicine into his bloodstream.

'I need to be stronger,' he said to himself.

'Can we ask for the help of the Space Seals?' asked Jake.

'Negative, sir. The Orbital has been stolen from under their noses. She's one of theirs and what's more Random has been named an accessory to Fro's destruction and they are looking for us. There's no way that they will help us, especially when we know so little about what is going on.'

'Talk about being in the dark,' huffed Anji. She sat beside Random and put her hand on his arm. 'Random, we're not going to let you blame yourself for all of this. What's important is that we stop this guy from doing it again.'

Random sighed. 'You're right. We need to find light in the dark. Somehow. But it's going to be difficult with an ill Captain and a crew who are fugitives from the law. Then again, if anyone can do it, it's us,' he forced a smile across his face. 'Jake, what are my levels at?'

Jake got up and looked at the digital readouts that adorned the wall behind Random's sickbed.

'Hmmm...' he said thoughtfully, 'I'm fooling no-one, I ain't got a clue what any of this says!'

'Fine, Skateboard?' asked Random.

'One of your kidneys is still failing to function properly.'

'Which one?'

'Your fourth one.'

Anji and Jake were wide eyed with shock. 'Say what now?' asked Anji.

'And what about the rest of me?'

'The lumber puncture you had in your spine has cleared up the mess in your back but your ninth ventricle in your heart is a little erratic. Am diagnosing for a cause now.'

'Nine!?' spluttered Jake. 'Aren't you only supposed to have two?'

'The Captain's body has been artificially augmented beyond even the most conventional of Rodasian bio- logical make-up,' said Skateboard. 'For sir to function the way he does he is required to have a more complicated set-up than most lifeforms in the galaxy'.

Anji eyed Random.

'Has he got more of everything?'

'Down girl!' said Random cheekily, making Anji blush.

'No wonder you're so fast with a heart that big,' said Jake.

'No wonder you feel so much loss,' said Anji. Ran- dom didn't acknowledge the remark. It wasn't just loss he felt, it was responsibility. To all in his care and to those who had perished on Fro.

'So, I'm still a bit of a mess, yes?' he asked. 'Statistically speaking, sir, you're running at 68% capacity.'

'That's not bad, just over half!'' said Jake.

'It's not good enough. How long until I am back to my old self, Skateboard?'

'There's no telling, sir. I hate to tell you this but there's no evidence to suggest that you will ever be back to normal. Your strength is way below what it was before the incident and although the drugs that the doctor prescribed will help you heal quicker, there's no telling what that radiation did to you in the long run.'

'Hang on, Skateboard, you're not telling me what I think you are telling me, are you?'

Skateboard's diodes sighed.

'Sir, we have to proceed with extreme caution. If you front up to this menace before you are well enough to do so, there's a very high chance that your body will descend further into radiation sickness. Overexertion could lead to cellular degeneration that would lead to irreparable damage.'

Anji and Jake felt tense and nervous.

'You mean he could die?' asked Anji.

'It's sadly possible, yes,' confirmed Skateboard. His circuitry
was not built to cope with the emotion he was feeling in his
artificial reality chip. He wasn't built to give bad news to people.
He was built to move things and do odd jobs for masters.
Skateboard was never meant to feel remorse or stress and worry.
But now his fears were out in the open, he thought it would help
him feel a little better. After seeing the faces of his humanoid
friends, he realised just how wrong he was.

'But I hasten to add that this is an extreme worst case scenario. If
you stay in bed and let your metabolism heal you then there's a
chance that you shall continue to lead a life.'
'Just not the same as I had before, no?' 'No.'
'Skateboard, I can't do it, man,' Random said, his voice soft and
understated. 'If I don't do anything there's a chance that more
people will die. I can't let that happen. I was made to prevent
things like this from happening and that is what I will do.'
Skateboard sighed and bowed a little. 'I understand, sir.'
'We're right behind you as always,' said Anji. Random smiled at
her. 'You would be even if I asked
you to keep out of danger, wouldn't you?'
'Anything for a friend!' said Jake, who gave Random a big bear
hug. The Rodasian groaned a little, leading a sheepish apology
from Jake.
A little alarm went off, breaking the moment for the travelers.
'What's that?' asked Anji.
'Security warning system,' replied Skateboard. 'The Space Seals
have caught up with us.'
Outside in the vacuum of space, four by-jets scoured the vicinity
for any activity. Light, slim and nimble, these one manned crafts
were able to negoti-ate the huge boulders of rock that were
travelling in their own dead slipstream, parts of what used to be

---

the planet Fro flowed like rocks down a gentle woodland stream. Space was as silent as always. It was the calm well and truly after the storm.

Because of their actions in escaping the Valetudi-narium, Random and the others were now fugitives in the sector and local traffic control had failed to notice a vessel of the Venus II's description leaving the general area. The local space was now awash with activity as the Space Seals not only began their investigation into the abduction of the Orbital but the destruction of Fro and the whereabouts of the Venus II.

Anji was perplexed as to how, with a cloaking device, the had been found.

'How?' she cried.

'They must have picked up on our own vapour trail,' said Skateboard. 'I'd better remember that in future situations.'

One of the by-jets barrell rolled past a massive rock and in doing so, missed the invisible Venus II's hull by a matter of centimetres. And yet, it failed to detect the ship even with such close proximity to it.

'Phew,' Jake blew out his cheeks. 'I don't think we can stay here much longer.'

The travellers, barring Random, had convened in the cockpit and witnessed the close shave. As the by-jet continued to spiral away, the alarm died down.

'Yeah! Have you picked up the vapour trail yet Skateboard?'

Skateboard ran a command through the systems. 'It's going to be difficult with all of this local interference to obtain it so quickly, I'm afraid.'

All of a sudden, there was ding from the cockpit command station.

'Oh,' said Skateboard surprised. 'I spoke too soon.' He observed the read out internally. 'Got it!'

'You know, we could just hand this information to the Space Seals and let them deal with it?' said Jake. 'Then they can arrest us! We can't do that!' cried Anji.

'But Random...what if...' said Jake.

'Don't say it,' she urged. 'Then it might not happen,' she smiled at her friend kindly. 'Remember what Random said, "the light in the dark." Let's find it together eh?'

'Sure thing, I'm all for positivity in a universe of chaos. Right Skateboard, let's do it!'

'Actually, sir, why don't you type in the co-ordinates. This can be a part of your training to pilot the Venus II in the absence of myself or Captain Random.'

Jake looked hesitant. 'Well, if you're sure.' He slid himself into the pilot's seat and with guidance from Skateboard, punched in the co-ordinates that would take them towards the danger that lay ahead.

'Remember to link the coordinates to the vapour trail too, sir,' said Skateboard. 'Let us follow them at a distance at first. It'll be good to give our Captain enough time to rest as possible.'

'Good shout, robot,' cried Jake. He punched in a few more commands and gripped the steering column tightly.

'Ready?' he said to his friends.

Anji gripped tightly onto the headrest of Jake's chair.

'Do it.'

And with that, Jake smiled a stupidly smug grin as for the first time he sent the Venus II into warp and in a blinding flash, they disappeared from the wreckage, far away from the Space Seals, far away from the devastation of Fro and into the danger that awaited them.

It took a couple of hours for them to follow the vapour trail through the warp tunnel that formed like a kaleidoscope of colour around them.

The gang always marveled when they were travelling faster than light. The shapes and colours that enveloped them were enough to put them in a trance and forget about their dangerous mission.

During the journey, in the medi-bay, Random began to stir in his sleep. He had thought it impossible for him to fall into a deep slumber with all that was rushing through his thoughts but with his body still as broken as it was, a two hour nap could be the difference between having enough energy to stop the monster who had destroyed a planet and losing his life to the tyrant.

But unsurprisingly, the sleep was not as restful as Random may have wished. It was when he slept that he occasionally could see the mysterious figures of the ghosts of long ago who had whispered into his mind so often since his birth.

And for the first time since the incident, there they were again.

In the dark recesses of his psyche, Random stood in the mist and saw the familiar outlines of the impossibly tall blue man and the short and red skinned lady. He opened his mouth to speak, but they beat him to it.

'You know what will happen if you confront this menace, don't you?' said the female.

Random took his time to respond. 'I know what's likely to happen, yeah.'

'Then your conscience is clear,' said the man. 'You know your role in the universe. The sacrifices you are yet to make?'

'I have a rough idea of what will happen there too,' he replied.

'Random, there is a force of terrible evil swarming through the cosmos, wiping out entire civilisations like a virus. You were created to bring hope and balance to Rodas. Now, the universe needs you more than even those who you are destined to save back home. But take heed, he thinks he knows you, but he doesn't. Not really. Not the person that you are now, anyway.'

'What?' Random said back to the female. 'How would you know that? Come to think of it, I still don't know how you can contact me from the past!'

'We are not,' the blue man interjected. 'You will learn someday.'

And with that, Random awoke, only slightly less confused than he had been when he fell asleep. But his mind was jolted somewhat by a knock at the door.

'Hey,' said Anji tentatively. 'Sorry to wake you up.' 'I'm not so sure that you did,' he replied and sat up in his bed. 'Are we there?'

Anji nodded. 'We are, yeah.'

Random exhaled deeply. 'Right then, let's-' 'Random,' Anji sat next to her stricken friend and spoke softly, 'Listen, we've...I don't know how to tell you this.'

Random looked blankly into Anji's eyes and saw the sadness inside of them.

'It's happened again.'

Jake and Skateboard looked out of the viewing screen of the cockpit, silent, unable to utter a single word. To their surprise, Random, his bed sheet hugging his shoulders, joined them, closely followed by Anji, to see with his own eyes what she had told him back in the medi-bay.

When he saw what his friends had all seen, he wished it had all been a bad dream.

Finally it was Skateboard who broke the silence. 'The Magari system. Seven planets...three moons.' 'All gone,' said Random in horror.

Stratos hadn't just had his way with one planet. He ended up destroying all of them.

'Scan for survivors,' demanded Random. 'Sir, the chances of anyone-'

'Just do it, Skateboard!' shouted Random. He imme- diately followed it up with a softer, 'Please.'

Skateboard made the command through his wireless connection with the ship.

'Horrible,' whispered Anji. 'All those planets. How can somebody do something like this!?'

'This isn't just revenge for this guy,' said Random. 'This is sport.'

Jake shuddered as he witnessed the stillness of space. 'It must have been over so quickly. Bits of Fro was still floating about. There's barely anything left this time.'

'Completely vapourised,' said Random.

A tiny light began to blip in and out of existence on the dashboard.

'Sir,' said Skateboard. Random leaned over Jake in the pilot's chair and he took a look at the read out dis- played on the monitor.

'One survivor,' exclaimed Random. He bolted out of the cockpit.

'Hold up, where do you think you're going?' 'Well I'm going to rescue them of course!' 'Random, you need to rest!' stressed Anji.

'Anj, we have the chance to save a life, I have to take that chance!'

'No, you don't, but I can,' said Jake. 'I can't allow it,' said Random.

'Oh, so Anji can fill up at a petrol station in space but when there's a chance to be a hero-'

'It's not about being a hero, Jake, it's dangerous, you'll be floating in an atmosphere littered with debris.'

'I don't care, I want to do it!' Random sighed.

'Skateboard, get as close as you can to the survivor. Scan their life signs, give Jake as much time as he can take to get her back here safely.'

Random shot a look at Anji.

'You'd better stand by in case he needs help too.' As Anji and

Jake prepared themselves, Random made for the cockpit and sat down in his pilot's chair.

'This is worse than anything we've ever faced, my friend,' he said to Skateboard, 'Now I can't even stop them from risking their lives again for me.'

'Like you said earlier, sir, there's no telling them,' said Skateboard.

Random sighed. 'Just promise me one thing. If they do get in trouble, don't you dare try and stop me in getting them back in here.'

Skateboard's circuits whirred and he went back to his business of steering the Venus II right into the heart of the rubble of the dead planet.

7

ALL DEAD, ALL DEAD

That brilliant explosion.

The blinding flash that had torn the planet Alfrajetti apart It had ripped open the very core of their world, split it into a million pieces, shredding countless countries to smithereens.

Obliterating a planet that had hung in space like a jewel in a crown.

And for Io, the last Alfrajetti in the universe, it had slaughtered her people.

She couldn't move for the shock, the lightning that burst through the very crust of their world, separating her from her family forever.

Oh god - my family.

An inner voice calmed her. If she had survived, there was every chance they might have done too, right?

The ray of hope shone in her mind as another quake shook all around. It had been doing that ever since she had regained consciousness, but when was that again, she wondered to herself? How long had she been floating about in space on a piece of rubble that used to be her home?

How much time left before her oxygen supply finally diminished and sacrificed her to the coldness of space.

No, she knew she was the only one now. Another voice began pouring thoughts in her head.

All the others were dead.

Her Mother, whose look of terror burned into her as the crash of the explosion happened all around them.

Her Father, who was in the house at the time, readying the meal of which she and her Mother were preparing for outside in their garden.

Her friends, she didn't have a chance to say sorry to after she'd cheated her classmates out of a chance for winning the Interstellar Trigonometry Competition.

Or to her parents for the message they received back at home of her actions and how they led to the school being disqualified.

There would never be a chance for forgiveness, for redemption.

All dead, all gone.

She sobbed uncontrollably as another quake shook her about the rocky plane. She'd lost them.

And no matter what she could do, they would never come back to her. Never would she be able to speak to them, tell them how much she loved them all.

Never would she even be able to hug them.

Then she remembered that light, that flash that interrupted her last, helpless look at her Mother and now here she was. Adrift. Alone.

It was slowly becoming harder to breathe.

Not long now, she thought to herself, not long before her lungs were on fire, gasping for air.

Not long until she would be with them again.

As she closed her eyes, she thought that she could see a ship close by. And a figure, who appeared to be tethered to it, edging closer and closer but still oh so far away. As yet another quake rumbled, and a portion of the ground near her disintegrated into nothingness, she wouldn't dare allow herself to hope that rescue was possible.

For her, it wasn't something that would redeem her for what she had done...

*

'I'm almost there!' cried Jake, who was starting to wonder whether he should have left the space walking to Anji in the first place. Trust him to want to play action man too. No, concentrate, Jake, he told himself, concentrate on the survivor.

It had been Random's idea to tether his friend to the Venus II, in the case of an emergency they could just wind him back into the ship. Skateboard was relieved that his Captain had made that decision as it meant that he could focus solely on piloting the Venus II around the huge rocks that were hurtling menacingly towards them. Even an expert would have had problems multi-tasking at a time like this and one such as he was having trouble keeping Jake away from the rubble also.

'You're doing brilliantly, Jake, just keep doing what you're doing,' said Random into the microphone on the dashboard. 'How's he looking to you, Anj?'

Anji was monitoring her friend's life signals on an- other instrument inside the cockpit they were sitting in.

'His heart rate is through the roof! Couldn't we have just beamed this person up?'

Random gave Anji a quizzical look. 'Beamed up?'

'Yeah. Surely you can do that with a ship like this.' 'Nobody can beam people up as you say, Anji.' She huffed. 'Well, I know some people who can.' 'Are they real?' asked Random.

'Well, no, but-'

'Well there you are then,' he replied. 'Jake, move

0.72 degrees to your left, do it!'

Jake punched in the commands into his wrist computer and yelled as he spun to the left, dodging a huge jagged piece of what used to be Alfrajetti.

'Woo! Thanks for the heads up! I'm almost there!' 'Jake for zarks sake, be careful! The infrastructure of the debris the survivor is floating on is starting to fall apart!' 'Oh great, any other good news you've got to tell me?' he replied sarcastically.

'Random says that there is no way we can beam you out of there,' said Anji.

'That's not helpful,' said Random.

'Yeah, I kind of gathered that when no-one said anything when I was volunteering for this, Anj, but thanks all the-'

The comm link died. 'Jake?'

Random flicked the communications switch again. 'Jake!'

'His life signs have stopped!' said Anji, her words an- guished and worried.

Random punched in a few commands and an image of Jake flickered onto the scanner.

'The radiation from what is left of the planet Alfrajetti is interrupting our communication with him,' said Skateboard.

Random and Anji looked at one another.

'Nothing we can do for him now,' said Random as the Venus II lurched again missing another massive block of rubble. 'Come on mate, you can do it.'

'Hello? Hello?' Jake muttered but there was nothing but silence in reply.

'Oh no!' he looked back to see if the Venus II was still there and to double check that it hadn't smashed into what was left of a fairly big planet. He breathed a sigh of relief. There it was, dancing around the debris like an ice skater around rocks.

'Right, looks like it's all down to you now, Jakey,' he said to himself. He gulped.

As he moved in closer he could see the immobile form of the sole survivor of the terrible atrocity that Stratos had committed. Surveying their surroundings, Jake began to wonder how on earth they had survived. If they had!

No, Jake, he told himself, don't think like that. If his travels with Random hadn't only opened up his horizons to a universe of impossibilities, it had also taught him that there was always a chance.

So close now, Jake prepared the helmet that Random had dug out for him. It had a seal that locked to the person wearing it, so at least the survivor would be able to breathe, but the ravages of deep space would leave them susceptible to radiation without the whole body suit that Jake was wearing, so he'd have to act fast.

Io watched as the stranger tumbled closer and closer. As she supped what little air she had left, she turned her head and remembered.

No, her last memory wasn't of her Mother...it was that man. That thing. Grinning at her. Taunting her.

Telling her to pass on a message...

'I got you!' said Jake triumphantly. He landed knee first and bent down in preparation to scoop the survivor up in his arms heroically like a knight in shining armour. Suddenly, another tremor erupted all around them and no sooner that Jake had put his arms underneath Io's semi- conscious frame, the ground beneath them completely gave way.

Jake screamed and gripped on to her tightly as he was showered with rubble and debris. He did his best to protect her but the devastation was such that she was already caked in it. He had no time to punch in the coordinates back to the Venus II, nor could he call his friends to wind them back in.

He had to do it.

With no time to do anything else, Jake, holding Io close to his chest, pressed the button on his side that activated the system to haul them back in.

With a horrendous jolt, both of them started to hurtle backwards towards the Venus II, slaloming around the flotsam and nasty looking rocks which were ping-ing around them like a pinball in an asteroid field. Jake held onto Io as tightly as he possibly could, knowing that a slip of his hand would undoubtedly send her hurtling off into space and all of this would have been for nothing. He cried out in terror, unable to see their path back, half not wanting to see it for fear that he would probably black out anyway.

The cord snaked around and around the asteroids reeling them both in like a fishing rod. Jake's eyes began to cry tears from how tightly he had screwed them shut.

And then suddenly, it was all over.

With a sharp crash on solid ground, Jake and Io skidded onto the metal floor of the Venus II.

'Anj, close the door, there's a draft!' shouted Random.

With a hiss, the ramp slammed shut. Jake, panting and disorientated, struggled to get to his feet.

'There's no time to waste, get her in the medi-bay now,' cried Skateboard. Jake bent down, picked her up and proceeded to rush as fast as his wobbling legs would carry both of them.

Io took a sharp gasp for air and her eyes exploded open.

'It's okay, I've got you,' said Jake.

'You,' her voice was hoarse, it hurt her to talk. 'You should have left me out there.'

And with that, Io lost consciousness completely.

The crew of the Venus II spent the next couple of hours waiting patiently for Skateboard to run the de- contamination process in the medi-bay and making sure that it was safe for the others to enter.

Anji handed Jake and Random a cup of tea, the for-mer still in his spacesuit with his helmet propped on the sofa next to him. Random sat cross legged on the chair opposite and blew on his drink thoughtfully.

'I can't understand why she wouldn't want to be res- cued,' Jake said as he took the cup in his grasp.

'Nor can I, at the end of the day you'd have thought that she would be nothing else than grateful,' said Anji as she popped herself down next to him.

'Survivors guilt,' said Random. 'She's the last of her kind. Nobody in the universe would want a title like that.'

'She's seen her whole world burn,' said Jake, 'And for what?'

'Nothing,' said Anji, sipping her tea.

'Don't you wait for it to cool down first?' asked Jake. 'All that she has just seen. All that she has just lived through. No-one would ever get over that. No-one should have ever survived that,' Random stopped staring into the middle distance and focused his attention back onto his friends. 'Anji, Jake, I think we should be extremely cautious with how we proceed. There's an awful lot that isn't making sense here.'

'Like a man going about the galaxy destroying planets just to lure you into a trap?' said Anji.

'And not knowing anything about said bloke and why he is doing what he is doing?' continued Jake.

'And how a planet explodes and yet a life form is able to survive, not only that but live in the vacuum of space for a period of time,' concluded Random.

At that moment Skateboard rounded the corner and entered the mid-section.

'How is she?' asked Jake.

'She's stable. The contamination process has concluded its cycle so there is no risk of radiation exposure. I've given her an oxygen mask. She was out there for quite a while.'

'Do you know how long?' asked Random.

'It's hard to give a precise time but I estimate she was without oxygen for roughly thirty earth minutes.'

'Half an hour!' exclaimed Anji. 'That can't be right.' 'Like I said, miss, it was an estimation.'

'Has she come round?' asked Random.

'She has sir yes, but please, try not to distress her.

She's been through a lot.'

'Skateboard, is it possible for her kind to be able to live in space for as long as that?' Random knelt down by his robot friend's side.

'It's difficult to say. The Alfrajetti's lung capacity is stronger than many humanoids, but to the best of my knowledge nothing could survive out there for as long as she did.'

Random sighed. 'Right then. We've been on the back foot since the start. We've had nothing but questions about this whole thing. Now it's time to get some answers.'

Io lay motionless, gazing up at the medi-bay ceiling, her oxygen mask planted protectively over her nose and mouth.

Cotton sheets tucked her into place on a bed that sat next to one that looked like it had recently been used. Suddenly she heard footsteps approaching her. She shot a glance to the door and saw the half red/half blue figure of Random standing before her.

'You should have left me there,' she groaned.

'That's funny, normally someone would say, "thank you" if you'd just rescued them from death.'

'I've died already today.'

Random sat himself on the bed next to Io. 'What's your name?'

'Io Radousen.'

'Nice to meet you, Io Radousen. I'm Random.' Io stared blankly at him.

'You're nothing like I imagined you to be.' 'So you've heard of me then?'

'Briefly,' she shifted uneasily. 'Recently.'

'How come?'

Io closed her eyes. A single tear fell onto her cheek. Feeling her pain, Random changed tact.

'You know I've not been well myself. I might never be well again. The last thing I should be doing right now is taking part in a wild goose chase around the galaxy. The worst part of what I am being led into isn't what is at the end of the journey, oh no, that part that really boils my blood is seeing nothing but total and utter devastation. All those lives that have been lost. All in my name. All in a madman's dream. Apparently this is all my fault. So I can forgive you for not wanting to talk to me right now, Io. I don't think I will ever find the words to express how truly sorry I am for all of this but I cannot put a stop to what is going on unless I know more of what, and who I am dealing with. So please, Io Radousen, help me.'

Io stayed silent, trying to sum up the words.

'You're right. I do hate you. I hate that the very mention of your name has brought me so much pain and anger. I hate that there are billions of souls out there lost thanks to what he has done, but I don't hate you as much as I hate him.'

Random moved closer to her. 'Who is he?'

Io broke down in tears. Random got up and picked up a box of tissues left on the side and handed them to her.

'Please,' he cooed, 'Take your time.'

Io didn't raise the tissues to her face. She held them tightly in her fist as she remembered what had happened to her.

'I don't know why I was chosen. I don't know why he picked on me. Believe me, I wish that he hadn't. But for some reason I was the one he wanted to use.

'My family and I were getting ready for a meal I had planned. I wanted to say sorry to them for the way I had been acting recently. My school,' she snorted, 'Not that it matters but I've not had the best of times there lately. So I wanted to make it up to them. To say sorry. I'd even gone to the trouble of paying for the food myself. It was just us. It's always been just us. That's why I felt like I needed to make a great effort to make things right with them. They don't...didn't have another child to fall back on when I got things wrong.

'Whilst we were readying out in the garden, I heard something strange, like a humming coming from the sky. As my Mother and I looked up, we saw this huge...ship, just hanging there in the sky.

'Before we could call for Father, what good that would have done, there was this strange light, like an explosion that burst from it and crashed down upon us. The last thing I saw of my world was my Mother. She was terrified. I was terrified.

'Then...' she broke off for a second, allowing herself to try and sob the memories out of her system. 'Then, all of a sudden we weren't on Alfrajetti at all. I was somewhere else. I was afraid and so I called out for my Mother and then for anyone who may be listening.

'Suddenly I heard heavy footsteps coming my way. The darkened room became light and,' she shuddered, 'I remember seeing him. I was too frightened to scream. I just stood there shaking, like a coward, as this... mon-ster approached me.

'He was...'

Io broke off again. Random put a reassuring hand on her shoulder. 'It's okay, take your time.'

Io choked back the tears and continued.

'He was made of metal. There wasn't much about him that was recognisable as anything I'd call Alfra- jetti. He was so tall, his arms and legs huge, powerful. His head was similar to ours, I suppose. But he spoke in a metallic voice, and his eyes... his eyes... were black.

'He told me that I was lucky, that I had been chosen, like it was some kind of competition. I said to him, "chosen for what?"

'He said, "chosen to watch."

'The next thing I know a couple of his hideous henchmen took my arms and pinned me up against the glass. I could see it all. My home, the moons of Alfrajetti, the entire system. And then I could feel a buzzing sensation underneath my feet. I tried to keep upright but his thugs did that for me. And then...' Io began to cry uncontrollably. 'I saw it happen. At first they hit my world and I saw everything I have ever known burn up before my eyes. He killed them. He killed them all. And then he told me he enjoyed it so much that he'd do it to them all. They threw me to the floor, I pleaded with him but no matter how much I begged he chose not to hear me. And so it happened. One by one all of the planets burned.'

Random himself was moved to tears. He sat there in silence, listening to the horror of what had happened.

'They then picked me up, held me clean off the floor and held me close to his horrible face. I can still feel his cold grasp squeezing my cheeks as he told me to pass on a message. He said, "Tell Random to meet me at the Eye of Avalon. Tell him that I shall be waiting for him there and the killing does not stop until he is here, on this ship, ready to face his destiny." And then he told me that there was one other survivor. My Mother. He'd also taken my Mother.

'And he said that he wasn't going to release her until you were facing him and I had passed on the message.

'I begged him, I begged him to leave her alone but he threw me away, tossed me away like garbage, laughing at me as he did so. He said he'd do with my Mother whatever he liked. I begged him but it was like I was no longer there. I was just an insect to him. Something to be ignored, swatted away. The next thing I know his vile helpers held me up again and one of them forced something into my throat. I choked as I felt his slimy fingers push whatever it was deeper and told me to swallow it. And then... he told me his name, he told me he would be waiting for you and that you shouldn't keep him waiting too long or else more star systems would burn. He then said I wouldn't have long either and with that, I was torn away just as quickly as I was pulled from my home planet.

'Then something happened. I woke up and I was on a piece of harsh ground. I didn't recognise it but when I looked up I could see the starry night sky.

'The earth around me shook and buckled like an earthquake. I then realised where I was. He had aban- doned me on the wreckage of my home. But I didn't scream. Although he wasn't there I could feel him watching me, laughing at my pathetic existence. I promised myself that I wouldn't scream again and that I should die where I was. I didn't want to continue liv-ing. Not even with my Mother safe. I wanted to believe that he had spared her too but I knew he hadn't done so out of kindness.

It was there that I left my life and embraced the thought of death. I still do.'

Random struggled to take it all in.

'Who is he? What's his name?' whispered Random. Io looked at Random square in the eye.

'Stratos.'

Random left the medi-bay and allowed Io to fall to sleep. Despite knowing how restless she was going to find it, she preferred it to not being awake.

His mind was racing.

Stratos. He had never heard that name before. How could it be that someone hated him so much and would destroy so many other lives just to get through to him, to display such utter barbarity on a scale that was inconceivable and that this person was not known to him?

Silently, he strolled down the corridor leading to the mid-section and finally the cockpit, haunted by Io's account of events. Haunted by what had happened.

Haunted by what he was going to have to do next. Anji, Jake and Skateboard had listened to every word. They had been monitoring the conversation from the cockpit on the surveillance system in the medi-bay, in place in case of a medical emergency. As Random walked slowly into the cockpit, he saw their sad faces. Anji and Jake both leaned in to give him a hug. He accepted it gratefully and buried his head on their shoulders. As they collected themselves, it was he who broke the silence.

'Skateboard, run a background check on Stratos. See if we have had any contact with him, no matter how directly or indirectly, we have got to find out how he knows about us.'

'Yes, sir,' said Skateboard.

'What are we going to do?' asked Anji. 'This Stratos guy, he's destroying whole galaxies. Just to get through to you.'

'I know,' Random slumped in the pilot's chair. 'He hates my guts and he is blowing planets apart just to make sure that I am listening.'

'What kind of a monster would do such a thing?' asked Jake to no one in particular.

'Possibly the greatest threat the universe has ever known,' said Random solemnly.

'Sir,' said Skateboard, 'I've concluded my back- ground check on Stratos and there is nothing in the universal databanks regarding his existence.'

Random got up out of the chair to check the readouts himself.

'That's impossible.' 'I'm afraid it isn't, sir.' 'Check again.'

'I have done, sir, there is nothing on file concerning anyone of that name.'

'Maybe it's a code name?' said Jake.

'Maybe he's hacked in and destroyed his files?' asked Anji.

'I'm not so sure, it would take a genius to do that,' said Skateboard.

'We are talking about someone who can harness weapons together to kill off a planet, it isn't out of the question,' said Random.

'Perhaps not, but we have to accept all possibilities at the moment,' said Skateboard.

'Such as?' asked Random.

'Such, as, sir, that yes, there is a slight chance that Stratos could be a code name, or that he has hacked into the universal databanks, or that my theory is correct...'

'Would you like to share it with the class?' asked Random.

'That Stratos doesn't exist in this universe at all.'

8

FOR WHOM THE BELL TOLLS

Stratos had already inflicted more rage upon the universe than anyone had ever dared to comprehend. The ripples were being felt across the cosmos, news of the horrific atrocities he had carried out were becoming nightmares that haunted neighbouring star systems as they prepared their defences. Yet almost all the rulers of the planets who nervously anticipated the Orbital's arrival on their doorstep knew that there was nothing they could do to stop his wrath without considerable help from the intergalactic military, and Stratos knew that they would be pursuing him even as he smashed his fist repeatedly into the confines of the Admiral's quarters.

His rage had been peaked by something that had disturbed him greatly. Something that had plagued his mind ever since he regained his strength, his life, his overriding ambition to eliminate Random once and for all.

The truth.

It had stared him in the face ever since his ascension from near death to immortal.

There was nothing here in this cosmos he recog- nised. Sure, the star systems looked the same when he looked them up on the computer but there was so much that was different.

Worlds he had vanquished in the past still existed. People he had murdered still lived.

Places he had known were missing.

His fingers had trembled when he requested infor- mation on his own home world of Draxo. It had been so long since he'd left, he'd given up so much for su- premacy but it still felt like home to him.

And there were people who were so dear to him, torn away by his ambitions of power that as far as he knew, were still living on that pile of rubble that had promised so much but now stood on the brink of ex- tinction.

He found the truth in his search...and it shredded what little compassion he still had in his cold metal heart.

Draxo didn't exist.

Draxo had never existed.

They were all gone...or had never been born at all, never colonised from the Earth.

Wherever he was...this wasn't home. He was marooned.

He had let out a cry of pain and fury so loud the whole battle freighter had heard him.

But how? And then as he delved into the reason why he had ended up in a different part of space and a completely different universe to the one he knew and conquered, he discovered it.

The Eye of Avalon. That was what had brought him here. And when he'd marooned the girl he sought to manipulate to lure Random into his trap, he'd returned to his work and the answer to the question he so desperately needed to see was finally sitting there waiting for him.

All those calculations had led to this.

When he saw the answer, the formulae staring out at him from the computer screen, it pushed him past his limits.

The Commander stood outside the room quaking in his boots. He recoiled with every blow he heard, the savagery sound of metal being torn apart, ripped from the walls made his sweat cold.

He was welcome for the distraction of one of the Samlore foot soldiers approaching him.

'Commander, we have received confirmation on the long range scanners that a ship is approaching us.'

'The Space Seals?' 'No, Commander.'

He sighed. 'That is good news.'

Another bellow of fury exploded from within the quarters.

'You should tell him yourself.'

The foot soldier gave a whine of discomfort. 'Commander?'

'Well, go on, then.'

The foot soldier gulped hard and head butted his commanding officer hard in agreement, which did little to settle his nerves as he knocked tentatively on the door.

The banging stopped immediately.

'What!' barked the barely humanoid voice from within.

The foot soldier cleared his throat. 'Supreme Leader, we-'

The foot soldier never finished his sentence. In a split second a huge metal fist smashed through the door and splattered the him across the opposite wall.

As the Commander witnessed his bloody remains drip to the ground, he thanked his luck that it wasn't him who had interrupted the Supreme Leader's wrath.

Tentatively, he peeped through the hole that Stratos' fist had made and saw his Supreme Leader almost slumped against the view screen that gazed out onto the harsh blackness of space. The room was dark, save for the sparks and the small fires that had sprouted all around. All the furniture was splintered, the walls gutted, jagged tortured pieces of metal dangling down from the ceiling like daggers. A pipe had also been torn apart, flooding steam down upon Stratos' hulking frame.

'This better be good news Commander...' said Stratos, his voice chillingly calm.

The Commander rediscovered his composure. 'Supreme Leader...they are on their way.'

Stratos, his back to his loyal subject, grinned maniacally, his reflection staring back at the Commander through the hole in the door.

'At last.'

'So, what are you saying, Skateboard? And make it easy enough for Jake to understand,' said Anji in a vain effort to cut the tension within the mid-section.

'Hey!' said Jake before thinking to himself so hard that Anji could almost hear the cogs whirring within his brain. 'Actually, yeah, you'd better make it easy enough for me to understand.'

'I think I get what he's trying to say,' said Random, who placed a tray of drinking chocolate tenderly on the table that the gang surrounded in conference. They all took a cup except for Skateboard, leaving one for their guest who had insisted she would be well enough to discuss their next move with them. 'It's a parallel world, theory, right?'

'Indeed, sir,' said Skateboard to Random.

'Oh come on, that's way too sci-fi to even be a real thing!' said Jake.

'Really? After all we've seen and NOW you com- plain that things have gotten a little "sci-fi?"' said Anji, agog at her friend's reluctance to accept the idea.

'It is a pretty conclusive theory among many renowned scientists. In fact, it's a universal theory. That every decision you make sets you on another path,' said Skateboard, who although his diodes were not compatible with drinking chocolate, was doing his best not to be affronted by Random not even asking what he could get for him. 'For example, if we had decided not to return the engine part to the Osirans, Random would never have changed colour, creating an alternate timeline where the consequences of that inaction would have set a completely different future for us all.'

'Thanks for reminding me,' said Random, who re- turned to blowing on his drink to cool it down.

'Yeah, we might never have left that relaxation planet in the first place!' said Jake.

'Ugh, what I would give to be there now,' said Anji, who had been decidedly against the decision to give up their holiday in the first place.

'So somewhere out there, are an infinite number of us running around or sitting by a pool doing nothing?' said Random.

'Precisely,' continued Skateboard. 'And my theory is that Stratos is from a different universe to ours altogether. In his reality, you two are the worst of enemies but here a decision or action resulted in either Stratos not existing or something happened to him that stopped him from becoming a murdering scumbag.'

The gang looked in surprise at their little robot friend.

'I'm sorry,' he said sheepishly, 'Just trying to dust off areas of my language chip I barely use.'

'No, you're right, Skateboard, this man has de-stroyed billions of lives. He has the blood of a whole star system on his hands now...and he must be stopped,' said Random.

'Machine.'

A new voice joined them. it was Io, who was looking much better.

'Hey, how are you feeling?' asked Anji.

'I just saw my home planet explode before my eyes, my Mother could be being tortured by the machine who did it as we speak and I'm leading a group of strangers to their deaths.'

'You could have just said better,' replied Anji sharply.

'Io, pull up a pew and have some hot chocolate,' im-plored Random.

'I'd rather stand,' she replied.

'Well, I'd rather you didn't. You're still recuperating. You did nearly die of asphyxiation you know and if I've learned anything today it's to rest up,' Random pointed out.

Io tentatively took up a place beside Anji, who still couldn't put her finger on why she had taken such a dislike to the new arrival.

After all she had been through, she thought she may be a little more forgiving. Yet despite her recent tragedy, Anji felt a sense of distrust within her.

'I will do as you ask but my people are quick healers. Well...physically speaking.'

'You said machine?' probed Jake.

'I did, and I see that as an accurate description,' she took up the lonely cup and blew on the hot liquid.

'So not a man then?' said Random.

'He must have been once. Now he is more metal than flesh.'

'Great, a psychotic cyborg then!' said Random. 'Yes. Are we going to confront him?'

'That's the plan,' said Anji. 'Just us four?'

'Actually, Skateboard's a pretty mean bad ass when he wants to be,' glowed Jake, patting the AI robot on his back.

'You do a great service in saying so, sir,' he clucked. 'Don't mention it. Maybe just don't go back to sounding like a space butler after I've said it, it dampens down the effect!'

Io ignored Jake. 'But I haven't told you where to find him. All he gave me was a message.'

Random leaned in towards her. 'Now sounds like a good time to hear it again.'

Io nodded. 'Stratos is waiting for you at the Eye of Avalon.'

'The Eye of Avalon?' asked Anji. 'Yes...erm...'

'Anji.'

'That's the rendezvous he gave me.' Io confirmed. She took a sip of her hot drink and replaced it on the table.

'Where's that when it's at home?' asked Jake.

'It's not somewhere that I am familiar with, I'm afraid, sir,' said Skateboard. 'But I'll consult the navigation system immediately.'

'Then as soon as we've found it, that's where we'll be going,' said Random determined.

'But it's a trap! It's so clearly a ploy to reel you in,' said Anji.

'My Mother is on that ship...if there is any chance that she may still be alive, I will do anything to get her back.'

'Oh, and that means setting us up?' said Anji.

'Anji!' replied Random. 'Io has been put in an impos- sible position. And we must do what we can to save her Mother and to save the universe from Stratos.'

'Can't we call for help?' asked Jake.

'I'm not sure the Space Seals will take our word that we are innocent in all of this,' said Anji. She shot a look of distrust at Io. Despite her tragic tale, Anji was concerned at how accepting Random was of her story. Yes, she had pointed out the obvious, but how could the five of them stop a man with the ability to destroy whole planets?

'Strength in numbers would be advisable,' said Skateboard.

Random placed his fore fingers on his lips in thought.

'Who else can we call upon? If we give away Stratos' location, supposed we drum up as many ships as we can, it could be full scale war. I'm not willing to do that. There should be as little opposition as possible.'

'So we're just going to go ourselves?' asked Jake. 'Yes.'

'With no back up plan?' asked Anji.

'I didn't say that, did I?' Random got up from his seat and paced around the mid-section. 'There's a chance that the Space Seals could already be on Stratos' trail. If that's the case, then we just have to make sure that we get there before they do. We would have to convince them we had nothing to do with events so far, however, and that would be a massive task in itself.'

'Sir,' came a voice from the cockpit.

Random, Anji, Jake and Io all got up and followed the voice.

'I have located the Eye of Avalon.' 'Where is it?' asked Anji. 'What is it?'

'I think this backs up my theory somewhat. The Eye

of Avalon is a recent phenomena that was classified by astronomers on the edge of a prison star system known as the Flavorian system. It was identified as a reality fissure according to the universal data banks, which healed itself up and returned to its intended destination almost as soon as it appeared.'

'So it's a blip in space then?' asked Random.

'Yes, sir, it quickly healed itself and then returned to the actual place that Stratos had fallen through from his universe to ours. Call it an auto correction, as it were.'

'But what created it?' asked Anji.

'It's difficult to say without analysing it further.

Best guess is that it's a sort of wormhole. It could have been pre-planned, perhaps your counterpart in the other universe intended to imprison him, sir,' said Skateboard to Random.

'I'd like to think another version of me wouldn't have so little disregard for others,' he said.

'Perhaps he intends to go back? Maybe he's figured it all out for himself. Maybe we don't have to go and follow him at all!' chirped Jake.

'You forget that Stratos has already callously wiped out entire civilisations to catch my attention. Would you really think he'd just pack up and go home now after going to all of that trouble? No, there must be another reason. We need to go now. Skateboard, where is the Eye of Avalon?' asked Random.

'On the cusp of SOL 3.'

'You're not narrowing this down for us, Skateboard,' replied Anji.

Random leaned over to inspect the read out. 'Oh,'

'Oh?' said Jake.

'SOL is your solar system and the 3 is...Earth.' Anji and Jake turned in horror to one another.

'Earth? Stratos is going to destroy Earth!' Anji cried. 'Not if we can help it! Skateboard, how long until we

---

reach the solar system?' asked Random. 'Approximately 92 clicks,' came the reply. 'What are we waiting for?' said Anji. 'Let's go!'

Random hurled himself into the pilot's chair, pushed some buttons and forced a lever down and with that, the Venus II tore away and was thrown into lightspeed, leaving nothing in its wake as it shot off towards Earth.

As the brilliant colours of the lights peed tunnel whirled all around them Anji took Random by the arm.

'We can't let Earth be destroyed...' tears began to flow from her eyes, '...we just can't!'

'We won't' said Random, who got up and put a re- assuring arm around her and Jake. 'No more chaos. No more death. This ends with us.'

Io allowed herself to be swallowed by the shadows. She was sending these brave strangers to their deaths...

*

Stratos marched onto the bridge of the Orbital, its banks of instruments manned unconvincingly by a group of Samlores who had heard the powerful hy- draulics of their Supreme Leader's legs long before his brutal frame stood before them. All of a sudden they all decided, almost telepathically, to look busy.

'Report!'

'The ship is nearly here, Supreme Leader,' said one of the Samlores.

'Shall I power up the weapons?' asked the Commander. 'You would deprive me the pleasure of killing him with my own hands?' spat Stratos. 'Don't you dare sug-gest such a thing again.'

'Coming up on the viewer screen now, Supreme Leader,' said the Samlore sitting at the scanner bank.

'On screen!'

The huge image of space shot up above them and nothing else. For a few minutes, they all looked for signs of a ship approaching until naturally it was Stratos with his bionic vision who spotted it first.

'There!' he pointed. 'Increase magnification in quadrant zeta four!'

The Samlore did as he was instructed. A slightly larger spec of silver came into view.

'Magnify 200 percent,' Stratos instructed. The image zoomed even closer.

'There she is!' exclaimed Stratos. 'There she is!' 'It's not a vessel that I recognise,' said the Commander.

'You wouldn't,' said Stratos, his eyes transfixed on it. 'It looks in better condition than the last time I saw it.'

The sleek, streamline spacecraft shone and twinkled on the viewing screen.

'The Venus II,' said Stratos in almost a whisper. 'It's heavily armed...and has a cloaking device which is currently active!' exclaimed a Samlore.

'Then how are we seeing it?' asked the Commander. 'This is the Space Seals most powerful battle freighter. It wouldn't let something as cowardly as a cloaking device deceive it. How far away are they now?'

'14 clicks, Supreme Leader.'

'And it cannot see us just yet, no?'

'No, Supreme Leader. Due to our location we are obscured from both they and the planet below this moon.'

Stratos grinned. 'Good.'

He walked closer towards the screen. A alarm bell rang, alerting the Samlores to action stations.

'Oh Captain Random...for whom the bell tolls...'

*

118

The Venus II left light speed several hundred miles away from Mars to give its crew adequate cover if needed.

'Mars!' exclaimed Jake. He and Anji breathed a col- lective sigh of relief.

'So they haven't destroyed anything?'

'Negative, miss,' said Skateboard, 'The solar system is just as you left it.'

'It feels good to be back!' sighed Jake.

'We've got a lot to do to make sure it stays this way,' said Random. 'Skateboard, see if you can locate Stratos' ship.'

'Shouldn't be an issue, sir.'

'Won't it be difficult to locate with all the local traffic?' asked Io.

'What local traffic?' said Anji. 'There won't be any other spaceships around here. Well...a few satellites...'

Io tutted. 'What a primitive place you come from.' 'Oi!' said Jake, 'It may be primitive but at least it's still here.'

Io scowled at him.

'I'm sorry, that was quite mean, wasn't it?' 'Jake...remind me when I'm having a personal crisis

again to not go to you about it,' said Random.

Jake felt his cheeks flood with hot shame. 'Sorry again, Io.'

'Stratos should be here...why isn't he here?' she said, ignoring Jake's apology.

'Don't be afraid, Io, you're safe here,' Skateboard re- assured her.

'If you had met the monster like I have...you'd never feel safe.'

'Any updates, Skateboard?'

'No, sir. There is no sign of Stratos' ship anywhere.' 'I don't like this,' said Anji.

'Could he be cloaked like us?' asked Jake.

'It's a possibility,' said Random. 'He's here somewhere...'

'Sir!' exclaimed Skateboard. 'Incoming!'

Random looked up and from the cockpit window saw a bolt of energy fizzing towards them through the whirls of space.

'Evasive maneuvers!' said Random, as he picked up the Venus II's port wing. The spaceship shuddered as the volley of fire burnt right underneath it and continued to hurtle past them.

'No damage,' reported Random.

'A warning shot,' confirmed Skateboard.

'Can you get a fix on where it came from?' asked Anji.

The crew's breathing became collectively a little heavier.

'Already confirmed, miss,' said Skateboard. Random read the read out and pointed into the far distance.

'What? The moon fired at us?' said Jake.

'It came from behind the moon,' confirmed Skate-board.

'The dark side of the moon,' said Anji.

'There appears to be quite a build-up of background radiation obscuring it from our instruments.'

'Do we go and meet them head on?' asked Anji. 'No, we need to hang back, we can't be tempted any

further,' said Random, 'for now at least.'

All of a sudden, the communications system cracked into life and a sinister, malicious voice bled over the airwaves.

'Do I have your attention...Captain Random?...'

9

THE ORDEAL

'Stratos,' Random said with utter contempt.

The malevolent, almost robotic tones shook the cockpit of the Venus II. Anji squeezed Jake's arm. He gave her a look of utter dread.

'Your voice is different and yet...it remains as arro- gant and foolish as it always was to me.'

Random's frown fixed itself on his brow.

'How come you know so much about me? Because I've never even heard of you!'

'I have many an advantage on you, Captain. The odds are overwhelmingly stacked in my favour. You may think that you are safe, cowering like rats in your little tin ship, hiding from my sight. But I've always been able to get through to you someway, somehow.'

'You unspeakable abomination!' shouted Random, whose anger was rich for all to see. 'And you think destroying whole star systems is a justifiable way of trying to get through to me!?'

'Well...' said Stratos calmly, 'it worked, didn't it?' Random's blue/red eyes began to burn intensely. 'And now I have you where I want you...well, almost...' the voice continued.

Suddenly a bright green light began to shine around the cockpit.

'What's happening?' cried Anji. She let go of Jake and moved away from the light which had begun to envelop Random.

'Stay away!' ordered Random but it was too late.

The beam reached out like a claw and trapped Io too and due to his close proximity, Jake had also been caught up in its grasp. As the brilliant light shone brighter still, the figures of Random, Io and Jake disappeared altogether. Anji had fallen against the dashboard, shielding her eyes from the light and as it ebbed away, she put her arm by her side and gazed in horror at the empty cockpit.

'Skateboard?' she muttered.

The robot had also been left behind. He checked the computer. 'They have been taken...'

The next thing they knew, Random, Jake and Io were no longer in the relative safety of the Venus II. The green light dissipated and the trio were left alone in a strange place.

'Where are we?' asked Jake.

'Oh no!' cried Io, who began to back up with extreme caution.

'We're on the Orbital...' said Random, '...he must have found a way to get past our shields.'

'How?' asked Jake.

Random took a look around and observed his sur- roundings. It looked as though they had materialised in a cargo bay, its grey decor yawning off the walls around them.

'The man can destroy planets, a little abduction clearly isn't past his capabilities either,' said Random, who noticed Io receding in the vast room. 'Io! Don't worry, you're safe,' he tried to reassure her.

'We are far from safe!' she screamed. At that mo- ment the bulkhead door hissed open. A gaggle of Samlores marched into the room, armed with Space Seal issued laser rifles. There was nowhere for Random and his friends to run. Jake was repulsed by the Samlores salivating tusks, the hideous creatures clearly salivating at the prospect of torturing their victims.

The boy lifted his hands above his head. Random re- fused to offer them the gesture of surrender.

'You'll do my friends no harm otherwise you're get-ting nothing from me!'

The Commander leveled his gun squarely at Random's head. 'Come.'

*

Anji was pacing up and down, unable to relax. She'd just seen her best friends abducted by a madman before her eyes. Her mind was playing havoc with her anxiety.

'But they are going to kill them!' shouted Anji.

Skateboard, despite his emotional limitations as a robot, was also feeling anxious at the prospect of what their friends could possibly be enduring right now as they were doing nothing but fretting.

'Please, Anji.'

He dropped the usual "miss" that he usually desig- nated to her, hoping that addressing Anji by her actual name might actually help to calm her down. 'Hypothe- sising about the possibilities will not help them or us.'

'Well, what then?!'

'We need to take action...' 'Can we beam them back?'

'Negative, miss, we do not have that kind of technology on board.'

'You mean to say that we can replicate food and stop the need to go to the toilet but we can't beam about the place?'

'Yes, it's hard to conceive when you put it like that, but even if we could, I doubt that we could penetrate the Orbital's shields like they did ours...'

Skateboard left his sentence hanging in the air as his diodes began to whir, trying to form some kind of a plan in his main frame.

Anji sat on a chair, her left leg jiggling and pro- ceeded to bite her nails, staring into space. She was sure that Random could handle himself. She'd seen it all before with him, even if the Rodasian was still recovering from a massive dose of radiation poisoning that had scrambled his body, but Jake...poor Jake. Why did he have to get taken with them? Why couldn't it have been her. If she could guarantee her friends' safety over hers, she'd sacrifice herself in an instant. And yet now she was stranded without them, again! Just like on Genocia.

Then she had an idea. 'I've got it!'

'Yes, miss?'

'We call the Space Seals!'

Skateboard's diodes moaned. 'Unfortunately my CPU has already calculated 2,793 possible plans of action and enlisting the help of the Space Seals didn't make it past the "bad idea" stage of elimination, miss.'

Anji got off her stall and knelt down beside her AI friend.

'Think about it. They are already looking for Stratos AND for us. If we can tell them we have nothing to do with all of this then we can get them onside!'

'Presuming, miss, that they believe us,' said Skate- board.

'We tell them the truth then, we have nothing to hide...come on! If you continue on your parallel world theory while we fly to them, we'll have even more evi- dence to back us up!'

A beeping alarm went off in the cockpit. The pair rushed into the small room.

'What now?' Anji complained.

On the cockpit view screen a large battleship loomed before them. Then another. And another.

And another.

Huge vast vessels, armed to the teeth with turrets and missiles, engulfed the tiny space that the Venus II was parked in. Anji gasped audibly at the sight of them, five by now. They looked a little like massive aircraft carriers in space, with smaller ships balanced on top of them. The battleship at the front was now so vast, so magnificent, Anji was terrified they were going to crash into them.

'It appears,' said Skateboard to his human friend, 'they've already found us.'

Random allowed himself to be manhandled roughly by the gang of vicious Samlores who clawed at his flesh as he was pulled and pushed towards what he assumed was the bridge.

Between the shoving and the horrific feeling of his captors long nails scratching his skin as they continued their short journey from the detention cells, Random thought of Anji and Skateboard and how he hoped and prayed that they would not be stupid enough to mount an attack on the Orbital.

Not yet, at least.

With Jake and Io imprisoned behind a translucent shield, and both he and his friends manacled to make any chance of escape even less likely, he thought of all the chaos he could wreak given the chance.

He could easily tear the manacles apart, radiation poisoning or no radiation poisoning, he was sure that he still possessed the strength to decorate the blank corridors of the battle freighter with whatever made the Samlores the slimy weaklings he was sure they really were.

But for what?

No advantage. Nowhere to run. And so he was left with the inevitable.

Random had to face his enemy.

They came to a bulkhead door that hissed upward into the ceiling upon approach.

Random stared into the bridge of the ship. It's huge, multi leveled structure until recently was a hive of activity of people protecting the lives of countless species across the cosmos. Now, the monstrosity who stood imperiously before him dominated even the biggest of control rooms. For the first time, Random clapped eyes on a man who hated him more than anyone in the entire universe.

'Leave us,' growled the metallic voice. The Samlores obeyed their order and untidily filed out of the bridge back through the bulkhead door, which slammed shut behind them. Random didn't turn once from his enemy, not one second was lost.

He was never going to let him see fear...because there was none to feel.

The only emotion Random felt was rage.

'You look very different to how I last saw you,' whispered Stratos, looking out of the bridge into the vast blanket of space.

'Oh yeah, when was that then?' said Random snarkily.

'You were older. Much older. And purple. If my suspicions hadn't been aroused before our meeting then they would all be confirmed to me now.'

'Older? How? Who are you?'

'I am Stratos. And you are Captain Random.' 'I know who I am, thanks all the same!'

'A boy who was too scared to face the responsibility of saving his own planet that he ran across the stars, searching for a distraction, anything that would help him sleep at night...even if it meant the destruction of others.' 'Hypocrite!' cried Random, trying his best not to rise to the bait. 'You've destroyed countless lives just to get my attention and here you are claiming that I am a killer when you have the blood of star systems on your hands!'

'One day,' continued Stratos, 'that little boy realised the power he possessed and what he could do with it and it was on that day that the universe fell into darkness. You see, Captain, that the Random I know and despise had been boiling away entire galaxies long before I encountered him. And that Random is very much a part of you too.'

'Lies!' Random spat.

'No,' Stratos moved in the shadows and proceeded to punch some instructions into a computer. A hologram of a star map, showing what Random presumed was the universe projected out of an unseen lens and swamped the space that divided them.

'Your universe...' said Stratos before punching in more instructions. Suddenly, several of the nebulas and star systems flickered and disappeared from view.

'Mine.'

Random gazed at the map, his breathing began to fall deeper. There were now gaping holes where twinkling stars used to be.

Stratos stayed in the background, circling his captive like a lion stalks his prey, ready to pounce, but he wanted to make this poor imitation of his best enemy squirm. Make him truly suffer for his other selves crimes against the universe. For whatever atrocities

Stratos had committed in this universe, they paled in comparison to those of the Random he knew and de- spised.

'Oh you saw to it that they all went. Tatmaria. The Dools of Mareen. Even the Kibarium cluster. All gone, destroyed, turned to nothing but dust. Even Spectronia.'

Random's eyes widened. 'Say that again?'

'That was where the power overwhelmed you, where you became the destroyer of worlds. Until then your lust for destruction was simply palatable to a rival like me but after that, you were simply unstoppable, you and your human friends. And when I realised that their home world was also the same that had left my people to die, it didn't take a split second to make me want to burn the Earth too.'

'The Flux,' Random said under his breath. His skin crawled. Sweat began to pour from his brow and his hands became clammy with terror.

So he had done it. Somewhere out there, there was a version of him who had used the Zedron Flux, just like he did, and allowed its power to consume and distort him. The thought that there had been a version of him in another universe who had made the same de-cision as he, to use the Flux to stop the Osirans, but then proceeded to committing incredible acts of genocide afterwards, sickened every fiber of his being.

'Little did I know that you were going to be there. You ambushed my armada before I had a chance to destroy the Earth and obliterated my plans. but putting an end to my revenge wasn't enough for you. You showed no mercy. Not even a little. As my men lost their lives all around me and my ship disintegrated under the might of your war weapon, I watched as you laughed at my pleads of mercy.

'And in that moment, you killed what little good may have ever been alive in me.'

'Stratos, this is insane,' said Random as he paced to- wards his enemy with intent. 'You're taking a horrific vengeance with me that does not exist in this universe, on the lives of innocents on a scale that is terrifying. The revenge that you are wreaking is not in this universe, I am not the Random you think I am.'

'No, but I know what you could become. Besides, you are forgetting. Although I realised that I had fallen sideways in space to another dimension, I still deci- mated this universe. My desire for revenge is dwarfed by my hatred for you.

'I cannot go home. I can never get back to my uni- verse. The rift in space time will not allow it. So why shouldn't I transfer my power of destruction to this universe instead? I'll tell you why,' he pushed his face right into that of Random's. The red/blue boy saw the hideous biomechanical implants protruding through his flesh, his veins blue and puckered, his eyes as black as the heart of death itself.

'Because I can,' he snarled.

'Stratos,' said Random calmly, trying to regain his composure, still meeting the gaze of his enemy hard, 'The killing must stop now. It goes no further than here.'

Stratos emitted a blood curdling laugh, like a rusty chainsaw revving up in an echo chamber.

'Why? Who is there to stop me?' he cackled again, 'You?'

In a split second, Stratos' mighty claws had clamped around Random's arms and the boy was crashing against one of the walls. Random felt the sharp frag- ments of buckled metal dig themselves in his back and before he had any time to react, he was flying across the room before he landed in a heap, his head hitting the control bank hard at the opposite end of the bridge.

He coughed, a tinge of copper washing his taste buds. He tried to pick himself up but he was still too weak.

Not ready, not ready at all, he thought to himself as he began to black out, the final image he saw as he fought back unconsciousness was that of Stratos hurtling towards him, the floor shaking as he landed just inches from Random's stricken frame.

Random's tormentor knelt down in front of his prisoner and laughed.

'Evidently not.'

And with that, Random's eyes closed and everything went black.

Skateboard hated being lectured. An AI robot with the intelligence he possessed, talked down to at a rate of condescension that was off the scale? It was so embarrassing. Especially when the woman in authority who was talking to him and Anji was telling him nothing he didn't know already.

They had been forced out of the Venus II at gun- point and escorted to the bridge of the massive battle freighter and forced to endure a dressing down of epic proportions by the Admiral of the ship.

Admiral Bagari was an impatient, no-nonsense woman at the best of times. This was not one of them.

'What's more,' she continued, as Skateboard no- ticed she seemed to have more stripes pinned to her tunic than there are on the American flag, 'Without full jurisdiction from the Space Seals you are nothing more than space vigilantes. I should have you both locked up for running away!'

Skateboard acknowledged the rank displayed on her tunic and thought it was best he stop her there, exactly eleven minutes forty-nine seconds after she started speaking. From the very moment they had strolled into the bridge of the battle freighter after the Venus II was brought on board, as a matter of fact.

'Admiral,' he said politely.

'Don't interrupt me, I haven't finished!' she barked. 'We have the Orbital in visual range, Ma'am,' said one of the exotic looking soldiers that sat, working away at their post. When Anji's mind started to wander, roughly three minutes into the Admiral's tirade about how they should both be arrested for harbouring a suspect, she'd been taking in her surroundings and admiring the vast array of alien beings who were working together. The officer who alerted the Admiral reminded Anji of a cross between a parrot and an octopus, an image she had never concocted before and probably never would again.

The Admiral strode away from Skateboard and Anji, who both made to follow her but were forced to stay exactly where they were by the dozen or so Space Seals who were leveling their rifles right at them.

'Magnify,' ordered the Admiral.

The Parropus did as he was told. A vision of the Orbital flooded the huge viewing screen.

'How far away are we?' she asked. 'Three hours, Ma'am.'

'Can't we just beam there?' Anji interjected.

'No we cannot just "beam" there. Their shield will be at maximum. Plus we don't want to startle the threat before we know precisely what they want to do.'

'That, Admiral, is what I've been trying to tell you,' said Skateboard. 'Now, please, listen to me. The Orbital has been hijacked by a criminal from another universe, who seems hell bent on revenge against our friend for a rivalry they possess in his reality. Stratos was destroying those planets to lead us here for one reason alone, the total destruction of Random.'

'Listen, robot, your story would sound more believable if you dropped this whole charade. If there had ever been a being as powerful as you say he is we would have known about him long ago, let alone this whole parallel universe delusion you seem to think magically explains this whole thing.' A prominent vein began to pulsate near Bagari's temple.

'But that's exactly the point, Admiral,' Anji inter- rupted, 'You don't know about him because he doesn't exist in this universe, that's what Skateboard is trying to tell you!'

'Then explain this to me,' she said through gritted teeth, patience busting at the seams, 'Where did this "Stratos" of yours pop up from? Huh? People don't just come into existence like that!'

'Err...Ma'am,' said another officer, this one looking more like a jellyfish in a uniform.

'What!'

'We've picked something else up on the long range scan.'

'Well go on then, what is it?'

'I...don't know,' stuttered the officer.

The Admiral marched over to the bank, her legs pumping with anger.

'We've got to convince her of our story!' said Anji quietly.

'I have a feeling she won't need much more convinc- ing,' said Skateboard smugly.

He was right.

On the other side of the solar system to them, sitting between the Earth and Venus was something that no one in the history of the galaxy had ever seen before. The stuff of legend, the kind of thing little boys and girls write about when they want to grow up and become science fiction writers.

'What on Sevestia...' exclaimed the Admiral. There, for all to see on the long rang scan, was a large swirling fissure in space.

Random awoke from his nightmare with a horrendous splitting headache. Upon braving the harsh white light that shone in his face, he soon wished that he hadn't woken up at all.

He felt his arms and legs being pulled apart, heavy iron bonds lashed around his ankles and wrists, hoisted up in the air like meat in a butchers shop.

'How kind of you to join us again, Captain,' beamed Stratos. 'I thought I'd invite your friends to join us. I wouldn't have been much of a host if I left them in their cell now would I?'

Random did his best to break free of his bonds, but it was no use.

'Don't you dare hurt them!' cried Random. 'Random!'

It was the familiar voice of Jake. Random's heart sank. He sounded terrified.

'Jake! Don't worry, it's going to be alright! Where are you? This light...I can't see anything!'

'He's not in a very comfortable position, Random,' chuckled Stratos. 'You wouldn't be either if you were pinned to something as uncomfortable as he is.'

'Random, please,' came another voice. It was Io. 'Oh, yes, she's still here too, my bait,' Stratos hissed.

Jake and Io were fixed with magnetic bonds to two identical slabs. Their heads were encased in what looked like hard hats to Jake. He tried his best to act calm but considering the Samlores that circled them and the horrific sight of Random being hung high in the air with a blazing light shone in his face, he feared the worst.

He knew that before the incident with the Zedron Flux, Random would bust them out of this no problems. He would break out of his bonds like they were paper and send Stratos' big metal bottom back into his own universe with one swift drop kick.

But Random was weak, injured. Defenceless.

And now for all the hope in the universe Jake was starting to lose faith that they would ever get out of this alive.

'Do you know what these are, Captain? No of course not, you can't see them, can you. Well let's just say that the Space Seals have a rather unethical way of dealing with prisoners from time to time. From what I can make out from the instruments, these helmets send pulses into the brain to make the poor tortured souls wearing them submit the truth. Well, I doubt there is any information these two can give me that would be handy so why don't we play a little party game?'

Random tried his best to keep pulling at his manacles, but every time he did he was zapped by an electrical bolt that seemed to come from nowhere.

'Oh, don't think I wasn't going to include you in this game,' said Stratos. 'Every time you yelp for mercy, or cry out in pain, another bolt surges through your bodies. Every time you bargain for your lives, the voltage will go up. Within minutes you'll all be too weak to put up any form of resistance but don't worry about that because the effects aren't long lasting...so we get to do it again. And again. And again! Are you ready? Let's play!'

It was the surge of lightning and the screams of Jake and Io that Random heard first before his own body was riddled with an indescribable searing heat.

'Stratos!'

'No, no, Random, you know the rules, don't go breaking them already now!'

'Please!' cried out Io.

'Oh dear, it looks as though the urchin from Alfragetti is the first to lose a point,' he turned to the Samlore who controlled the voltage on the torture instrument. 'You know what to do!'

The screams echoed around the chamber, as did the crackling energy of the electrodes that were boiling their way into Random and his friends.

'I think I have a name for my new game!' Stratos cried as he did little to hide in vain the pure enjoyment he was getting from seeing his enemies writhe in agony.

'No mercy...'

10

FOR ALL THE STARS IN OUR GALAXIES

Admiral Bagari was cross.

She paced up and down her bridge, arms behind her back, scowling at the two intruders who had so skillfully talked their way out of a prison sentence for accessory in galactic genocide. Not only were their powers of reason so on point and their words rang so true, but they'd also somehow managed to coax her last name out of her, so not only would she have to put up with them showing her up in front of her crew, who had spent the last three years hiding behind corners from her whenever she was on deck patrol, but now they saw her as an agreeable person.

She groaned.

Loudly.

'I thought you said you knew all about spatial anomalies?' she growled at Skateboard, who had posi- tioned himself precariously balanced upon one of the command chairs.

'I do, Admiral, but not about this one.' 'So you tricked me?'

'Not tricked, Admiral,' cried Anji, 'He'll know soon.' 'Thank you Miss Gummadi,' he said in his usual polite manner. 'This is indeed fascinating. It appears that this anomaly is indeed a gateway into another dimension. Call it the Beta universe to our Alpha.'

'Why?' asked Admiral Bagari.

'Well, because we knew about ours first,' he said smugly.

'Alright, Skateboard, what are you getting at?' asked Anji.

'According to my calculations, the anomaly is a one way gateway into our universe. Caused by a cataclysmic explosion that had the ability to rip a hole through space/time. This is how Stratos managed to end up in our universe.'

'Then we are lucky he didn't blow up the Earth when he arrived!' said Anji.

'Negative, miss. The anomaly originally materialised in the opposite end of the galaxy, before snapping back here. Hence, why Stratos was able to snatch the Orbital.'

'Killing all of our people in the process,' Admiral Bagari interrupted. 'We got there first. No ship, no Stratos. Just hundreds of bodies, scattered around the quadrant, suffocated. Some of them we knew, we grad- uated with. Gone now. One day I might be able to cope with the responsibility of telling their loved ones.'

'That's horrible!' said Anji, her mind flicking straight back to what kind of hell Jake and Random must be facing as they spoke.

'That was nothing compared to what we saw next. As we followed the vapour trail we came across more and more death. Too late every single time. Continuously playing catch up. Too slow to save them.

The universe will mourn the worlds that have perished. Just as soon as our armada has put an end to him once and for all.'

'Not without rescuing our friends first,' said Anji stoically.

Bagari sighed. 'We've a job to do. To protect the lives of billions of people. If I have the opportunity to blast the Orbital out of the sky before Stratos kills again then I will take it.'

'Then let us go and save them before you do!' 'Anji, no.'

'Why not Skateboard!?'

'You're leaning on the navigation port.'

Anji looked down and noticed that she had knocked the coordinates out of alignment when she forced her hands down on the control unit.

'We'll discuss that in a moment,' said Skateboard. 'First of all, we need to work out a plan to stop Stratos.'

Anji bit her lip.

'I'll have to call a conference meeting with the Admirals of our fleet. There's too much that could go wrong here and I alone am not able to make a definitive decision on what we do next, no matter what I say.'

'Fine,' she murmured. 'I bet NASA are having a field day.'

Admiral Bagari, Skateboard and a smattering of officers looked blankly in her direction.

'Y-know? The space people from Earth! With that massive portal hanging right over them they'll probably be running around like headless chickens...bit hard denying the existence of aliens after all of this!'

'Oh please, this is the Earth we are talking about. They couldn't detect a sandwich in a fridge with the crude science they have down there!'

'How are they NOT going to notice that?! A big wib- bly-wobbly swirly thing in space?'

'By doing what they always do.' said Admiral Bagari. 'Ignoring the facts staring them in their face! They'll probably even blame it on fake news or something equally as dismissive.'

'Fake what?' said Anji befuddled.

'We have intelligence on your home world, Miss Gummadi,' the Admiral smirked. 'Can't let the human race go unsupervised now, can we? Although you will have to tell me how you come to be this far out in space.'

'Another time,' said Anji defiantly. 'First, we've got to get Random back.'

Random awoke on the floor of his prison cell. Aching, tired, broken.

What he had just been through was like nothing he had ever experienced before. It was all a game to Stratos. He didn't even interrogate them.

Random had no concept of how long he had been lying there but judging by the pool of dribble that lay underneath his mouth, it must have been a little while.

The boy groaned as he pressed his palms down and used them to elevate himself off the floor.

Swinging himself around to sit up, he noticed his friends lying in a similarly undignified fashion, like rag dolls strewn across a play area. He dragged himself to be beside them. Even though they only lay roughly three feet away, the effort Random used to get to them drove him to the edge of exhaustion.

He checked Io first. Her skin was still warm and she appeared to be breathing. Then Jake.

Oh no, what had Stratos done to his best friend?

Random had sworn when he lay recuperating in the hospital bed in the Valetudinarium that he would not put them in danger again.

And once more, he'd failed them. 'Jake, come on, wake up buddy!'

He shook his friend's shoulder vigorously until Jake let out a faint moan.

'Not now Mum, five more minutes please,' he mur- mured.

Random laughed. 'Oh Jake, even in the darkest times you shine a light on things.'

Jake's eyes opened. His skin was pale and yet dirtied, scorched even, from his ordeal at the hands of Stratos' torture devices.

'How are you feeling mate?' asked Random.

'Like I never want to lick a battery ever again. I haven't been this shocked since a certain someone crashed in a pond on our school trip,' he joked.

'That's two jokes in as many sentences,' remarked Random. 'You must be feeling bad.'

'I've felt better,' Jake agreed as he allowed himself to be pulled upright by his red/blue friend. The pair sat crossed legged, leaning against one another, allowing their life force to slowly flow back through their bodies. With every intake of breath, they felt better.

'Stratos was right,' said Random as he rubbed the back of his neck. 'No long term side effects.'

'Yeah, considering I've been electrocuted for god knows how long, I don't actually feel so bad now I'm awake.'

'We can be thankful of that,' said Random. 'Come on, help me wake Io up.'

'Random, why hasn't he fired on Earth yet? With the other planets he didn't seem to hesitate.'

'Now he's got us he must want us for something.' 'Come on though, if someone hated you that much you'd think they'd kill you straight away. The bloke's only gone and blown up half the galaxy just to get your attention. I mean, why go to all that bother if all he's going to do when he's captured us is give us a little torture with no lingering side effects.'

'I don't know,' mused Random. 'Perhaps he needs me to get home?'

'No,' said a third voice.

It was Io. Unbeknownst to the boys she had already been stirring throughout their conversation. She dragged herself to the opposite side of the cell of her two fellow prisoners.

'He wants to make you watch.' 'Watch? Watch what?'

'The end of the planet you all love so much.' 'The Earth! It's alright I suppose,' said Random.

'There's no suppose about it! We've got to stop him!' cried Jake.

'Calm down, Jake. With any luck Anji and Skate- board will have found help. I mean for all we know they might be constructing a rescue mission right now. Plus if Io's right, he won't blow up the Earth while we are in this cell. He'd want our eyes right on the action...'

Jake shuddered. 'Well, let's do something now before he gets a chance to do it!'

'Not before we find my Mother,' said Io.

Random and Jake looked at one another, both thinking the same thing but daring not to say anything to the girl who had led them into this terrible situation in the first place.

'Io,' said Random tentatively. 'You've got a better view than I have from here. What do you see?'

Io craned her head. Past the wavering wall of energy that fizzed and crackled, holding the three of them in the cramped prison cell, was a corridor leading out of the detention block. She thought to herself how little Stratos must think of their chances with so few guards leering over them!

Just in eyesight, was the shoulder of a Samlore with his back to them, the angle of his arm suggesting he was armed, ready to pounce on the slightest inkling of danger.

'One guard...that's all I can see from here,' she con- firmed.

'I want to test something, so I apologise Io,' said Random.

'Apologise for what?'

'Oh don't give me that! You're the one who led us into this trap. If anything it's your fault, not ours you yellow bellied charlatan!' Random shouted, making Jake jump and Io's mouth flop open in disbelief.

'I'm sorry,' stammered Io.

'Oh don't give the sob story, sweetheart! You're a filthy turncoat!'

Io ignored the ebbing pains of her electrocution, stomped to her feet and glared down upon Random, her eyes fierce with anger. 'Who are you calling filthy you schbarp!'

Jake gasped.

'I'm presuming that's really rude isn't it?' he said. 'You can shut up too you spotty, smelly adolescent.

With a face as punchable as yours no wonder it looks so ugly!'

'Hey!' cried Jake. 'Who are you calling ugly, zit face!' 'Only the girl who has led us to our deaths!' screamed Random. 'You don't deserve to get out of this alive!'

The guard posted at the end of the detention block sighed. It had been a long day. He'd been standing to attention, worried for his life that if he put a clammy paw out of place that his Supreme Leader would crush his skull like an egg for even so much as itching his nose.

He hadn't even been allowed a coffee break.

Now this, a skirmish between the prisoners. But what if…

No, this couldn't be a ploy to escape now, could it? 'Hey! What's going on back there?' he hollered down the corridor.

'Stay out of this!' came the breaking voice of a teenage boy. 'This is personal!'

'Don't make me come back there…' the guard warned but the commotion was on going. Reluctantly, the guard sighed and allowed himself to be drawn into the argument.

As he made his way towards the chaos, he could hear bits of the cell being thrown about the place.

'Hey! If you break anything in there I'll make you pay for it!' he said as his walk broke into a trot.

As he made it to the cell opening, he could make out that the boy and the girl were tearing chunks out of one another.

'Stop that!' he demanded but it was no use, as Io began to choke Jake in a headlock so hard that his lips were beginning to go blue.

'Right!' cried the Samlore who had no choice but to intervene.

Dropping his weapon to his side, he found the access key in his pocket and swiped it in a slot in the wall. Instantly, the energy wall holding the prisoners in captivity disappeared and the Samlore stepped into the cell.

Then suddenly, that itch he had wanted to scratch went in an instant as a perfect right hook from Random sent his nose flying off his face altogether.

The Samlore was sent hurtling back against the wall, smashing the back of his skull at high-speed impact before leaving a nasty stain trailing down the wall, like a fly having been swatted against a pristine wall, as he slumped unconscious on the ground.

Jake and Io stopped fighting instantly and looked in astonishment at Random, who in turn was staring at his still clenched fist.

'Wow...' said Random. 'Jake...I think my powers are coming back!'

'Never mind that,' said Jake, kicking out at Io as he got up out of the head lock. 'Did you hear what she called me!'

'Oh, like you're faultless in all of this!' said Io, rubbing her shin.

'Well, that's what I am, faultless,' said Jake smugly. 'Tell that to your acne,' she retorted.

'There you go again getting all personal with me!' 'That's so below the belt you're practically kicking me in the-'

'Shut up you two,' implored Random. 'Don't you see? Being electrocuted must have somehow helped me recover a bit of my former strength...do you know what this means?'

'It means you're in with a chance of winning the next series of the Universe's Strongest Man?' said Jake sarcastically, still hurt by the jibes Io had made about his skin.

'It means,' said Random ignoring Jake's last com- ment, 'that I can take Stratos on! We can beat him!'

'And save my Mother?' asked Io.

'We can do that and more, Io. If my powers are re- turning then we can stop Stratos and save the entire universe!'

'Great!' said Jake, 'How?'

Random put his arms around their shoulders and drew them closer.

'Here's the plan.'

'What's taking them so long?' Anji's arms were hugged against her stomach, impatiently jostling with Skateboard as the pair waited nervously for an update. They were looking on with invested interest at the con- versation Admiral Bagari was having with her fellow Commanders in the Space Seals fleet. They sur- rounded her, looming large in hologramatic form, with Bagari in the centre, discussing their next move.

'The anomaly has thrown them,' said Skateboard confidently. 'They were expecting to find a battle waiting here for them but instead they've encountered a problem and don't know how to deal with it.'

'So?'

'So, they're soldiers. Killing is easy. Thinking outside the box isn't.'

'But Stratos is sitting there doing nothing!' 'As far as we know, miss.'

'All this time we could be trying to mount a rescue mission.'

'I know,' said Skateboard ruefully. With his ultra-sensitive hearing, he was not only paying full attention to Anji but also the meeting itself.

'What makes it worse is I don't agree at all with what they are proposing to do.'

'What's that then?' asked Anji.

'The council agrees that the presence of a time and space anomaly is unprecedented and this does indeed call for drastic measures,' said one elderly looking officer.

'Add to our current predicament the possibility of other potentially deadly forces that may have escaped from the Beta dimension into ours, this has indeed made things worse,' said another.

'Might I interrupt if I may be so bold?' asked Skateboard.

'You most certainly cannot! snapped Admiral Bagari.

'Is this the prisoner you spoke about, Bagari?' asked a kinder looking lady.

'I'm afraid so,' said Bagari under her breath.

'Then he is the one who discovered the anomaly too?'

'Correct,' said Bagari through gritted teeth. She hated conference calls and hated it even more so when a prisoner she should have thrown in the brig by now was snatching centre stage and undermining her command of the situation.

'Let him speak, er?'

'Skateboard, Admiral,' replied Skateboard.

'Mr Skateboard, what can you tell us about this anomaly. Is it possible that other life has leaked into our universe through it?'

'No, Admiral. From my calculations the structure of the anomaly is not stable enough even for a return visit, let alone repeated passage.'

'How so?' asked the older officer.

'The anomaly was created by a huge explosion on their side of the dimensional rift. And like a paper cut, before long the space around begins to heal itself. The anomaly itself is almost closed but not fully. It needs something a little stronger to repair it.'

'Why not get it a plaster?' said Anji sarcastically.

Unsurprisingly, her comment was completely ignored. 'Is it possible that it can be opened again?' asked the kind looking female officer.

'Negative. As soon as the anomaly is shut that is that.'

Bagari smiled. 'So there you have it, my fellow mem- bers of the Admiralty. So all we have to do today is seal a tear in the fabric of time and space reality and stop a madman with modified technology powerful enough to destroy planets from doing it again.'

'Admiral, might I make a suggestion?' asked Skateboard confidently.

Admiral Bagari rolled her eyes. 'Go on.'

'Members of the Admiralty, the anomaly is currently 47,000 clicks above the Earth. The Orbital is currently hiding behind the dark side of the moon, but itself is only 8,000 clicks away. If we can attack it and somehow lure it towards the anomaly, then Stratos will perish when the anomaly begins to seal itself. Taking into account the firepower he has at his possession, the explosion would be enough to turn the anomaly into a black hole, sucking the Orbital in and the resulting implosion from that would fold the anomaly in on itself.'

'But doing so will also drag the Orbital out of its hiding place and towards the Earth itself, exposing its presence to the peoples of the Earth to the truth that there is life on other planets,' said the elderly officer. 'Despite there being oblivious to certain expeditions in the past, for them to witness a strategy such as we are planning it could blow the secret out of the water.'

'Sorry, Admiral but it's highly likely they've already spotted it,' said Anji.

'It's risky, very risky,' said another new voice, this time coming from a tall, squid-like looking being. 'It risks dragging the Earth into the fight. They could suffer collateral damage. We must protect them, not put them further at risk.'

'There is also the question of us causing permanent damage to our prize vessel,' said the elderly officer. 'The Orbital is our newest, strongest and most ad-vanced ship in the fleet. If it perishes we face the pos-sibility of weakening the Space Seals resolve.'

'Unfortunately it doesn't look like we have much of a choice,' said the kindly looking Admiral.

Skateboard responded. 'Sir, this Stratos threat is like none we have never faced before. He almost single handedly took the Orbital and killed all of your people on board. I know it's hard but we cannot simply afford any lives to be put at risk by going back there.'

'We could go!' chirped Anji. 'No!' snapped Bagari.

'We are not a part of the Space Seals, and our friends are on board!'

'So you keep saying. But I cannot allow you two to be put at risk. You're civilians.'

'I thought we were prisoners?' questioned Skateboard. 'At least allow us to return to our ship and take part in the attack.'

'What part of, "I won't put your lives at risk" do you not understand?' said Admiral Bagari.

'But we've fought before! And if there's a chance to save our friends we must take it! We can't abandon them to die while you're busy blowing up the ship they are on!' Anji wouldn't relent.

'We have to be careful of the Samlores who are working with Stratos,' said Bagari.

The elderly Admiral groaned. 'Samlores...I should have known they'd be so easily corroborated into working for Stratos. Parasites that they are...'

Anji's frustration was fast reaching breaking point. Random and Jake were alive, she was sure of it, but they wouldn't be for long if they didn't get a move on.

'Do you have experience of combat?' asked one of the hologrammatic Admirals.

'Yes!' cried Anji. 'Without us the people of Genocia would still be slaves. Without us an alien made of sand would have taken over the Earth. And just before we got into this mess we had helped save the people of Spectronia from a race of Egyptian gods!'

'I have to admit,' said the elderly Admiral, 'that is quite a CV. Okay, as long as you are with us then I think you should be allowed to go ahead.'

Despite being granted permission to rush headlong into a deadly situation, Anji couldn't contain her delight.

'Oh thank you, Admiral!'

'Admiral, are you sure?' said Bagari.

'I'd have thought you couldn't wait to get rid of us?' said Anji.

'I'm not a fan of civilians getting caught in the crossfire.'

'Pardon me, Admiral but our friends are trapped over there. This is as much our fight as yours,' said Skateboard.

'Plus we will need to use smaller ships to take on the hornets,' said the squid-like Admiral.

'Hornets?' asked Anji.

'One man fighter ships. They are difficult to lock on to from our guns on board our freighters.'

'We can back you up with some of our own,' said Bagari.

'I can also try to hack into the Orbital's mainframe. I presume that Stratos has changed the codes since he stole it, yes?' asked Skateboard.

'Sadly, yes,' said Bagari.

'Not a problem, I can make a start on hacking in and setting the navigation systems on a trajectory towards the anomaly,' said Skateboard.

'You can do that?' asked Anji. 'Yes, but I need to get closer.' 'Then you could also beam Random and Jake out of there!'

'Oh please, what is your obsession with "beaming up?" Is it an Earth thing?' sniped Bagari.

'You could say that,' said Anji.

'We'd have to get very close to the Orbital to make it even conceivable, miss. I shall work on it simultaneously to hacking the navigation systems and see what I can do.'

'Nice one, Skateboard!' said Anji, the adrenaline was flowing through her body now. Her heart wouldn't stop pumping. 'Well, what are we waiting for, let's go and get them!'

'We'll send the battle freighters in. Top priority is to stop Stratos and protect the Earth. Further written instructions will be sent imminently,' said the elder Admiral. 'This is a message to all Space Seal personnel. Commence battle stations.'

The bright lights on the bridge switched to a dull red and sirens began to wail.

'Get a move on you two!' snapped Bagari. Anji jumped onto Skateboard's back and the pair zoomed out of the bridge.

'We won't just be protecting our universe but making sure that not only is it safer by us doing our duty but that this anomaly, this threat, never happens again,' the elderly Admiral's voice echoed over the alarms.

'So to that end, may we succeed...for all the stars in our galaxies.'

11

THE BEST LAID PLANS...

Back on the Orbital, Random, Jake and Io had met with minimal resistance as they escaped their prison, which struck Random as odd, considering how much Stratos seemed to enjoy tormenting them. Surely, he would have more than just one guard on them at all times? He tried to shake the idea from his head as the trio made for their first destination.

Before they had left the detention centre, Io had insisted that they look for her Mother.

'There's no time!' Random said.

'I'm not going any further until I find her!' Io replied adamantly. Nothing, not even her fear of Stratos and his gang of vile Samlores would shirk her from finding the dearest person to her in the whole universe. 'I'll stay here, you two go on and do what you've got to do.'

'Io, we must stay together if we can. If we don't sab- otage Stratos' weapons then the Earth will surely be next. We can't let anyone else perish. Please, do it for Alfragetti. Do it for your Mother.'

Io had given Random and Jake a pleading look. 'Please, just let me check the database for further prisoners. The terminal is just over there.'

Random sighed and nodded. 'You'd better cover her, Jake,' he said without looking at either of his companions.

Io ran across the detention centre floor to a computer bank that jutted out of the wall.

'What if she isn't here?' asked Jake.

'She could be anywhere,' said Random. 'If she is though we can't let another person slow us down so you might have to stay here with them, now go on, cover her.'

Jake saluted and instantly dropped the gun, making a loud metal clunking noise in the process.

'Careful!' Random hissed.

Jake sheepishly picked the gun up, which he had confiscated from the guard they had left without a nose in the prison cell, and shuffled over to Io's side.

He took a glance at the look on her face and thought about asking the obvious.

'Any luck?'

Io's face had fallen. 'No.'

'Chin up. She could be anywhere on this huge ship.' 'She's a prisoner, she should be here!'

'Stratos might be playing mind games with you. He could be playing with all of us,' said Random. 'I'm sorry Io but if she's here we will find her. Please, the Earth is in danger. Help us stop the murder of seven billion people. Come with us.'

Io nodded slowly. 'Yes, alright.'

'Thank you,' Random smiled in appreciation. 'Now then, we need to know how to get to the weapons chamber and a way out of here.'

Random took Io's position in front of the computer bank and started scrolling with his finger on the screen for information.

'So the plan is to sabotage the weapons then get the hell off this ship?'

'That's about the long and the short of it, Jake. If we can carry out as much damage as possible we may be able to disable the Orbital completely.'

'But Stratos would still be alive,' said Io.

'Leave him to me,' replied Random. 'A-ha! Got it!' he cried.

'The armoury is stationed directly 43 decks below us.'

'Great, how do we get down there?' asked Jake. 'Simple,' said Random. 'We take the lift.'

'Oh, that's alright then,' said Jake with relief. 'I thought that you were going to suggest taking the stairs!'

'We have to act fast,' said Random. 'Stratos will know we've gone as soon as that guard comes around.'

'If he ever does,' said Io. 'I have never seen anyone hit with that much power before. Especially from a boy like you.'

'I'm not just any boy,' said Random. 'I'm Random.' 'He certainly is,' said Jake.

'Right come on, let's move out, be aware of any Sam- lores on the way and try to avoid the security cameras whenever you see one! We will be laying a trail but if we work quickly we can keep clear of any conflict.'

The trio left the detention centre and made for the nearest lift, but Jake, who was already heaving the heavy gun around, was already starting to flag a little. Not that he'd ever mention it to the others, of course...he'd already been teased enough for one after- noon!

They made their way down a nondescript grey cor- ridor, which led to another, then another.

'Which way now?' asked Jake as they turned into yet another identical corridor.

'Next left,' said Random. 'Hey, Random?' said jake. 'Yes, mate?'
'Did you mean to hit the Samlores' nose clean off his face?'
'Nope. Just a sign that my powers are coming back.
Also that I've had a really bad day.'

They arrived at the lift section and pressed the buzzer. All the time Io could not stop thinking about where her Mother could be. Then she promised herself, if she had the chance, the first sniff of an opportunity, she'd find out for herself, alone if she had to.

And if Stratos had done anything to harm her...then somehow she'd see to the end of Stratos herself...

It wasn't long before they arrived in the weapons chamber, which was bigger than the bridge on the Orbital itself.

'Wow!' Jake had marvelled as he looked up at the sheer vastness of his surroundings.

'Jake!' barked Random. 'Sorry!'

'Zarks. What has he done?' muttered Random as he stood surveying the machinery in front of him.

Towering over them, an array of electrical equipment was bolted together, linked by a complex menagerie of engineering.

'So that's how he's done it!' said Random. 'Stratos has managed to combine all the heavy weaponry on board to make them into one.'

'So that's how he destroyed my home,' said Io.

'Yes, this battle freighter wouldn't have had the capacity to have this form of firepower before he got to it. He's created a doomsday weapon - from scratch!'

'Okay, so he's a genius and a megalomaniac, now come on, let's destroy it!'

'Jake, I don't think you understand. If we blow up this room then the whole ship could go up.'

'So?'

'So will the moon. The devastation it would make would split it into pieces, causing the debris to smash into the Earth.'

Jake's mouth fell open. 'Oh my god, the human race would be extinct! Just like the dinosaurs!'

'The resultant asteroid shower would kill them all,' replied Random.

Jake gulped. 'What do we do?'

'Find the off switch instead. Power the planet destroyer down. Now where is it...' he looked all around the room before lastly taking a look upward into the deep recesses of the huge machine. 'Oh, there it is, right up there.'

Io frowned. 'You can see it from here?'

Elsewhere, the relief guard was idly strolling along the corridor leading to the detention centre to start his shift. He wasn't sure why it was needed, especially after he had witnessed how much they had suffered at the hands of the "lie" detector Stratos had cannibalised into a torture device. But who was he to argue with his Supreme Leader? He'd seen the chaos disobeying his master would bring.

Yet still, he'd taken his sweet time to start his shift. He knew it probably would result in a fight.

Good, he purred. He loved fights.

As he rounded the corner into the block that held Random and the others, the Samlore was startled.

There was no guard in sight.

The Salmore grinned. He could be useful and report it. He hadn't been useful in a long time.

If ever!

Then he noticed the blood stain on the wall. His eyes followed the trickle of green liquid to the floor, where there appeared to be the end of a Samlores nose. He recoiled. What could have caused such a terrible thing to happen to his comrade? Then he laughed. Somewhere one of his fellow troops was walking around without a nose. Samlores took great pleasure in the hardship of others but they took even greater delight when something terrible happened to one of them!

Being a part of such a twisted race, the Samlore bent down and picked the nose up and raised it to his own. Mockingly, he fastened it to his and then had the terrible image of a Samlore with a heavy cold and two noses and promptly dropped it to the floor again.

As he moved to take his post, he saw something move within the cell.

Of course, the prisoners!

He took a closer look at the shape that was starting to move behind the energy barrier keeping the prisoners inside.

There was only one blur inside. A blur without a nose.

Without a moment's hesitation, he scrambled back to the command bank and sounded the alarm.

Deep inside the dark recesses of his decimated quarters, Stratos heard the alarm in the split second it began to sound.

His eyes opened and he bolted straight to the door, tearing his recharge socket out of his shoulder and the wall simultaneously. His metallic teeth gnashed together and bit down hard. The anger and rage began to boil within his bionic body.

Stratos knew what the alarm meant.

He also knew the first place they would go...

Down in the weapons chamber, Random, Jake and Io jumped as the sound of the alarm blared over the ebb and flow of the sounds made by the pulsing weaponry.

Random turned on his toes. 'Right, you two! Head to the spacecraft hangar and get yourselves out of here.'

'We can't leave you!' cried Jake.

'We can't leave my Mother!' replied Io.

'Listen to me, both of you. I can't reach the off switch in time. I need to work out how to sabotage this thing just enough so it doesn't cause another disaster.'

'Fine!' said Jake, 'but when we do find a ship, I'll keep the engine ticking over until you get there.'

'No you won't, I must stay here to make sure Stratos does not escape. Go now!'

'But...'

'Come on!' said Io as she took Jake's arm and began to drag him away from his friend.

Random watched as his friends left the chamber and disappeared out of the room. He took a sharp in-take of breath and looked up at the colossal magnitude of the weaponry system.

'How to break it but not blow us sky high...'

'Red group leader, standing by!' 'Blue group leader, standing by!' 'Gold group leader, standing by!' 'Venus II, standing by!'

Now that the call signs were out of the way, Anji and Skateboard were ready for take-off.

'Right, Skateboard, what would you like me to do?' asked Anji as she fastened the seat belt in her co-pilot's chair.

'Nothing that I can think of, miss. I believe I have complete control of the ship and the means as to which enable us to engage in combat.'

'Well, I'm not sitting here doing nothing, come on, there's got to be something I can do to help?'

Skateboard's diodes whirred.

'I don't suppose you've ever had any experience prior to our meeting of firing a weapon?'

'Yeah,' Anji's eyes lit up. 'Plenty!'

'Good, then let me show you how to work our weapons systems.'

He paused.

'I was not aware that children on Earth were allowed to use firearms?'

'Yeah, course we were, I used to shoot things all the time back home.'

Skateboard's curiosity was well and truly stirred. 'Really? Where was that then? On a shooting range?' 'Nah. PlayStation.'

'ALL UNITS PREPARE TO DISEMBARK.'

A voice piped over the speaker system into the huge spacecraft hangar.

The room was a hive of activity. Swathes of Space Seals had rushed into their crafts while others in over-alls worked as quickly as possible to finish fuelling and arming them, who were now running full pelt to clear the runways and leave the area. The Space Seals called their fighter crafts "Hornets" after the Earth insect of the same name, which had led Anji to question just how they had so much information on her home world.

The ships themselves were only big enough for the pilot, small in shape and slight in design with a huge sting protruding out of the front of it, just below the view screen.

Two tiny wings either side hummed loudly making the hangar echo with the sound of a swarm.

The Hornets were black in colour, all except for the pattern at the front, distinguishing which group leader it and its fighter pilot had been assigned to. Like hornets themselves it was waspish, quick in the air and if provoked, deadly.

'That's the order, get ready, Skateboard, hold on to your wheels!'

'FIVE.'

'I feel as though you're getting quite a thrill from all of this, miss.'

'FOUR.'

'Really?' she winked. 'THREE.'

'I wonder what gave that away?' 'TWO.'

'I just want my friends back, Skateboard.' 'So do I, Anji,' he chirped. 'So do I.'

ONE

'Well then shall we?'

The hangar door burst open and with a collective explosion of noise and fire, the Venus II, followed by the sound of dozens of engines roared into life tore off the tarmac and shot out into space, closely followed by the swarm of Hornets.

The blackness of space became a wash of red, blue and gold colour as the swarm burst out the battle freighter like a nest.

As they did, more swarms pierced into space and joined up with those that erupted first.

Then another exploded from a third battle freighter and the Hornets settled into triangular formation, with the Venus II at the point and behind them four of the battle freighters also formed a solid wall of defense.

Back on Admiral Bagari's bridge, the officers on board paced up and down noisily setting about their preparation for attack.

'Ma'am, the battle force confirms it is in formation,' said the Parropus.

Admiral Bagari, sat imperially in her command chair, clicked a switch on the arm control panel.

'Bagari to the Swarm...take us in.'

On the command, the Venus II and the Hornets shot off from their present location, closely followed by the battle freighters towards the Orbital...

Meanwhile, Jake and Io had reached the spaceship hangar.

As they entered the area, Io stopped on her heels. 'Io,' Jake huffed. 'What are you doing?'

'My Mother, I can't leave her here!'

'Io, they know we are here, we've got to go!' 'Not without her!' Jake turned back and ran towards her.

'Listen to me. Random is smarter and stronger than he looks. He will save her, I'm sure of it. Now let's get out of here.'

Io paused and watched as Jake tore off towards one of the multitude of Hornets that sat with their cockpit hatches open. She spotted the hangar door. It was shut.

'He's not as clever as you make him out to be,' she sighed. 'Someone has to open that to let you out.'

Jake turned and just heard her over the alarm siren. 'Io, I know we might have got off on the wrong foot, but'

'Just get out of here, you silly little boy. Don't worry about it, honestly. I got you into this mess. By getting you out of it, we can call it quits.'

Jake sighed. He hadn't the time to argue with her. 'Are you sure you know how to do it?'

'No more than you probably do flying that thing!'

She had a point. Jake took a peep inside the hatch. He saw a steering wheel, two big buttons and a pull lever.

'Seems easy enough,' he shouted back. 'You'll need this!' he sprinted back to her and gave her his gun. He stood silently, panting for breath, trying to wish her luck.

'You too,' she said. Io gave Jake a tiny peck on his cheek. 'And I'm sorry, now go!'

Jake did just that. He pelted back to the Hornet as Io ran to the control box directly in the middle of the hangar. She familiarised herself with the controls and noticing a huge lever, surmised that that must be for the hangar doors.

She watched as Jake pulled himself inside the Hornet. When inside, he pulled the lever and the hatch snapped shut.

'Right, I passed that test then,' he said to himself as he heard the sound of the huge metallic hangar door start to snap itself open. He looked down on the two big buttons. Now in theory, he thought to himself, one of these is the start-up button and the other is the one that fires the lasers. He hovered over the button to the left and then decided to press the right one. A barrage of laser fire exploded out of the sting at the front of his craft and promptly blew the Hornet in front of him into pieces.

'Ah,' he cried and gave a nervous grin to Io in the command box, who herself was covering her face in terror.

Jake pressed the other button with all his might and the engine burst into life. Using the logic he had recently acquired on his flying lesson in the Venus II, he pulled the steering column up and the Hornet noisily rose into the air. He smiled a big dopey grin.

'I'm a space pilot!'

With one final shot, and a fairly cheesy salute to Io, Jake pulled the steering column forward and the Hornet shot out into space and away from danger.

Io pushed the lever back down again and raced back into the corridor. She ran as fast as her legs would carry her, gun in hand, looking for an information port. Luckily she found one quickly, the sound of the alarms throbbing inside her skull. Desperately, she did what she could to blot it out of her mind as her focus fixed solely back to her Mother.

She searched for lifeforms on board. There were not many.

There were nearly a dozen Samlores. One metal machine.

Two organic creatures. Then her heart sank.

Only one of them was an Alfrajetti. Herself.

Io's eyes began to flood with tears. She blinked hard and they trickled down her face. A great pool of emotions engulfed her. Grief, Anger.

Stratos had lied to her.

He hadn't saved her Mother. Io swore knew the truth now.

As she collapsed to the ground, allowing the tidal wave of loss wash over her, she hugged herself as she cried out loud.

She was all that was left of the Alfrajetti. Stratos had killed her too.

How could she have been so stupid? Io had been used.

It was the sound of the weaponry chamber door blowing open that Random heard first. He swore to himself. Unable to sabotage without causing a massive explosion, he'd decided to try and climb up to switch the weapons off. He was only three quarters of the way up the huge scape of the doomsday weapon and nowhere near the shutdown switch and he'd already been discovered.

A gaggle of Samlores burst into the room and took a look around.

'There!' cried the Commander who spotted Random doing his best Spider-Man impression far up above them.

With one word, he gave the command for his sol- diers to fire. They assumed their positions, raised their weapons and sent a volley of laser fire crashing all around Random. He did his best to avoid them but with his back to the attack, he was stuck.

The hulking frame of Stratos crashed through what was left of the entrance to the chamber and glared upwards.

'Stop! You'll kill us all!' he commanded, swiping a Samlore clean off his feet in the process. The Samlores ceased fire.

He glared at the far-off image of Random continuing his ascent. 'He's mine...'

With a mighty spring from his powerful legs, Stratos propelled himself high into the air.

Random looked behind him and his eyes grew wide in terror as his nemesis hurtled towards him.

Before he had time to act, Stratos landed a mighty punch square on Random's jaw, forcing the boy's head to brutally smash into the metal housing that he was climbing up. Involuntarily, Random lost his grip and started to fall, only to be caught by Stratos instantly.

Before long Stratos, with Random being held by his t- shirt dangling at his side, landed firmly back on the ground. The Samlores felt the force of the landing and the vibration sent those nearest to the impact centre falling to the floor.

'Fire up the device,' yelled Stratos to the Commander as he strode out of the chamber. Random, too groggy to put up a fight, dangled within his grasp, trying to collect his thoughts. As they left the room, Stratos smashed the alarm button with his free hand.

As the Samlores filed out of the chamber, the alarm was silenced and the weaponry chamber fell back into its usual hum of energy.

But where the laser fire had burrowed into the doomsday weapon, the metal, unnoticed by all in the room, was starting to buckle ever so slightly...

Jake screamed out loud as the Hornet wobbled and jutted. Although he had felt fairly confident about flying a spacecraft, he quickly realised that his inner bravado was ever so slightly misplaced. For a start, in the recent past he'd had Skateboard sitting beside him, guiding him with every misjudged acceleration of late breaking, but there was no AI robot with him now. He couldn't even see the break!

As he wrestled with the controls something strange struck him. The Orbital wasn't firing on him. Either Random had succeeded in his sabotage of the doomsday weapon or maybe, just maybe, Stratos and his cronies hadn't noticed that he had slipped out.

Come to think of it, he hadn't seen many of those horrible looking Samlores when he had been held captive. On a ship of that size, he'd have thought it would have taken a whole army to abduct a battleship. But no. It was only Stratos who had done it.

He didn't want to let on but his encounter with the terrorist had really unsettled him. His callousness, the unfeeling way in which the cyborg had tortured them. Jake had never been tortured before. He'd never come up against a man of such brutish capabilities.

It had hurt him. Deeply.

He tried to shake the thoughts from his mind as he continued to pilot the little Hornet the best he could. He dare not look behind him so putting the pedal to the metal Jake shot the Hornet away from the Orbital as fast as it would go.

As the cockpit juddered and shook, Jake looked out of the view screen and tried to get a fix on where he was going. He could see a huge greyish moon to his right that swamped his sight so he concentrated on the little bit of starry space that was just past it.

And as he did, he thought that he saw something. No, not something, several things.

More than that, lots of somethings!

As they got closer, Jake recognised what was he was flying towards.

It was a full on armada in space.

Dozens of Hornets, just like the one he had com- mandeered, were growing larger before him. Following them was what looked like large slabs of grey but it was the ship that was way out in front, with its sleek silver finish that brought the biggest smile to Jake's lips.

It was the Venus II. His home!

'This is Admiral Bagari of the Space Seals Corp. Please state your name and intent.'

Jake began to scream. 'It's me! Anj, Skateboard!'

'I shall ask again. Please state your name and in- tent.'

Jake took a look around. They could not hear him. 'Uh...'

'If you do not co-operate we will be forced to take offensive action.'

'Woah, alright alright!' he started waving. 'I don't mean any harm!'

Suddenly a more familiar, friendly voice broke over the speakers.

'Random?'

'I don't think they can hear us, miss,' said another familiar, more robotic voice. 'I'll patch into the comm system.'

A blaring distortion exploded over the airwaves, making Jake put his hands over his ears and lose control of the Hornet. It began to barrel roll towards the fleet.

'He's attacking us!' cried Bagari.

'No!' screamed Anji.

Jake grappled with the steering wheel and eventually brought the Hornet back under what little control he had.

'Bloody hell,' cursed Jake.

'Jake!' Anji sounded absolutely relieved as she heard the voice of her friend. 'Admiral, it's Jake, don't shoot!'

'Then why is he in attack mode?' came the unim- pressed Bagari.

'Uh, sir, ease off on the accelerator if you would be so kind?' asked Skateboard.

Jake did as he was told and instantly the Hornet became more controllable.

'I take it that's why you have the stabilisers on when you let him fly the Venus?' said Anji on the sly.

'You leave the stabilisers on?' said a rather indigent Jake.

'Never mind about that, get out of the way!' cried Bagari. 'You're directly in the path of our battle fleet!' 'Guys,' said Jake ignoring the Admiral's order. 'Ran- dom and Io are still on board. He's got this weapon...he's going to use it on Earth! Random's trying to sabotage it right now...that's if he didn't get him.' 'Stratos?' said Anji.

'Anj, he's evil. Like, really evil. We've got to stop him.'

'We will if you get out of the way!' Bagari was start- ing to get a little exasperated. First the talking robot had shown her up in front of her peers, now some teenage boy was stalling possibly her greatest moment in the field.

'I'm going to help.'

'Then stay where you are and we'll come and get you,' said Skateboard.

'Nope. I want to fight in this thing.'

'Seriously?' said Anji, Skateboard and Bagari all at the same time.

'Yeah, I feel like I've got the hang of it.' 'You'll be much safer here, sir.'

'No, I want to do my bit to stop him.'

Back on board the Orbital, Random was strung up in the restraints once more as the Samlores prepared him for torture. Slumped and barely with it, Random tried to prepare himself for more of the anguish he had been forced to endure.

If his theory was correct, it was going to be the only thing that would ensure that he would defeat Stratos once and for all.

'Supreme Leader, we are ready to move the Orbital towards the target.'

'Good.'

The Orbital began to sway as his huge engines began to slowly pull the gigantic battle freighter out of its hiding place.

Stratos paced up and down the bridge. His anger was barely brimming underneath the surface. He had Random back in the torture device, barely conscious.

'Captain, you didn't have to go to all of this trouble. If you liked my therapy you only needed to ask for more.'

He grabbed Random by the hair and forced him to look his nemesis in the eyes.

'We won't want you missing the fireworks either now, will we?'

Random coughed. 'Why...the-'

'The Earth? Well it's always been your favourite planet. No matter which dimension this may be, the third rock from the sun has always been a jewel in the eye of the butcher of the cosmos. That's why you protected it so viciously. I've never seen you care so much for anything more than you do that miserable little planet.'

'But...you don't know me, Stratos.'

'But I do! And although my plans have altered some- what since I came here I thought it would be rude not to complete what I was destined to do and then go home.'

'Bet you can't...'

Stratos paused. 'What did you say?'

Random smiled.

'You heard.'

Stratos strode up to his captive and smashed his face with a swipe of his back hand.

'Explain what you mean by that.'

Random reeled. That hurt. That hurt big time. But he was well past the pain threshold to stop now.

'Either/or.'

Stratos looked at Random furiously. 'How did you know?'

'Know what?'

'That I can't go back.'

'I didn't,' said Random. 'You just told me.'

Stratos pulled his backhand down on Random yet again, the savage blow nearly knocking him out of his restraints.

'It will be good to get you from underneath my skin,' spat Stratos. 'Yes, I located the anomaly that brought me here. And when I saw that it had appeared above Earth, I thought it good to destroy that vacuous rock and its stupid lifeforms before going home and doing exactly the same on the other side. Two universes. No human race.'

'Lemme guess,' Random spluttered. 'A one-way ticket?'

'If anything tries to enter it from this side it will be torn apart and the anomaly will close.'

'And poor old Stratos can never go home. Face it, you're stranded.'

Stratos thumped his fist through a control terminal.

'You've always talked too much,' he raced over to the torture device, pushed the Samlore operating it clean out of the way and set it to full.

A shock of lightning cascaded out of the impulses digging into Random's brain and the brilliant flash of blue flooded the bridge as the boy began to writhe and scream in agony.

'Not for much longer. You'll be kept in a state of perpetual torment for as long as I see fit. And when your precious Earth is nothing but dust, you'll be no more.'

Stratos roared maniacally as Random did his best to stay awake and absorb the pain.

If he could, if his strength would allow, harness it.

Stratos turned to look outside and he gazed upon the blue/green planet that had begun to hone into view.

High above it, and not far away from the Orbital at all, was the swirling image of the anomaly.

It should have been his gateway home. Now it hung there in space, teasing him. Playing with what was left of his heart. A reminder of what once was.

But now he could make this universe his. Nothing was going to stop him.

'Sir!' came a cry from the Commander. 'There's a fleet of ships coming in hot.'

Stratos tore himself away from the screen.

'How many?'

'Four battle freighters, thirty Hornets and a ship I don't recognise, Supreme Leader.'

Stratos peered into the monitor. 'I do,' he spat. All too well.

It was the Venus II.

'Commander, I want all of you to go out there and stall them.'

The Commander gulped. 'But Supreme Leader, they outnumber us.'

'I don't care, go!'

The Commander didn't budge. Not out of insubor- dination, but out of fear.

'NOW!'

He jumped to it and began to rally the small group of Samlores on the bridge together.

'You heard our Supreme Leader, every Samlore to the hangar, now!'

Random just about heard the commotion. And al- though his screams had died down as he was becoming too weak to even cry out in agony, Stratos was provoked further by his prisoner as Random emitted a little smile.

Disbelieving at how she had been manipulated, Io wiped the tears across her face with her sleeve as she walked slowly back towards the weaponry chamber. Suddenly, she heard footsteps growing nearer. She instantly ducked inside a crescent and hid from view as she witnessed what must have been every Samlore on board tearing down the corridor back the way she came. When the commotion had passed, she took a cautious look from her hiding spot and when she thought it was safe, continued on her journey.

Far below, a little girl was practising her shots with her basketball, whilst waiting for her friend from the next block over to where she lived with her Mum in Brooklyn to meet with her. Despite being only eight, she had convinced her only parent that she was big enough to play outside by herself, but had settled on the compromise that it was fine as long as she agreed a time and a place to meet and did not come home any later than the curfew time.

Happily, the girl grabbed her basketball, which was still slightly too big for her and tore off across the busy street to the local park.

The weather wasn't exactly the best on this particular day in New York but the windy weather didn't bother her. The sun was still shining and for once, the court was empty.

She hadn't been exactly straight with her Mum and had gone out to play ten minutes earlier than her friend to practice shooting hoops. Who knows, one day she may even throw the ball high enough to get it through the hoop!

Of course she would. Everyone in the NBA had started out somewhere.

As she dribbled with severe concentration, she picked the ball up and threw it without looking where she was chucking it.

She did it.

She made the hoop.

The ball trickled tantalisingly around the rim and actually dropped through the net.

The little girl should have been ecstatic but she didn't see it.

The spaceship in the sky had distracted her.

Dexter Mackay was having a bad day. Not only was the office a state, but his dreams of getting his recycling plan off the ground lay in tatters, much like the rubbish that had been accumulating in Hyde Park over the last few months.

His idea was foolproof. It had gone through the planning stages no problem. It was cheap, clean and easy to put in place.

Plus it had a snazzy slogan.

DON'T BE A LITTER BUG. PICK IT UP.

Or so he thought.

Maybe that's where he had lost the interest of his fellow MPs in the cabinet meeting. They'd been all about slogans of late.

But now that the Prime Minister had flatly denied him his chance, he was in a funk. Although it was late at night, he couldn't sleep. His office chair was too lumpy and there was no chance his wife would let him in the house at this hour. Especially if it meant waking her up as he'd left his keys at home again.

Rubbing his eyes, Dexter picked up the cold take-away and walked over to the window. He expected to see nothing but the busy streets of London. In particular, the bright lights and the throngs of people going about their Friday nights along the River Thames. But everyone was standing still. Looking upward.

Up until then, to Dexter there was nothing happening out of the ordinary.

Nothing except for the huge spaceship that ap-peared to now be hanging in the sky.

As the people of Earth should have been waking up or going to bed or going about their business, events occurring hundreds of miles above them were about to take place...and the fate of them all was hanging by a thread...

12

THE BATTLE FOR THE SOLAR SYSTEM

The Samlores were like lambs sent to the slaughter. The Commander knew it. But whatever they did now, they were dead. If they disobeyed their Supreme Leader's order, he'd have annihilated all of them before they had a chance to mount an attack. No matter how futile.

As he led his small band of troops towards the on-coming storm that was the Space Seals battle fleet, some how he felt content with his fate.

There was nothing he could do. If they ever so much as attempted a runner, the Space Seals would catch up with them in an instant. If they went back, they'd have the wrath of Stratos to contend with.

They were his decoy.

He only needed them to buy him a little time. So that was what they were going to give him. Not for Stratos.

But for them.

What little honour they had.

Back on Admiral Bagari's battle freighter, the Parro- pus officer had spotted the enemy Hornets approaching the fleet.

'Targets are in sight,' he said.

'Shields up. Hornets...on my mark,' said Bagari. Just a little closer.

And then something happened that startled her. She left it too long.

One of the enemy Hornets fired, taking out one of the Space Seals own, right next to the Venus II.

*

Anji cried out in shock.

'Skateboard, that wasn't Jake's was it?'

'I'm still here, Anj,' came a voice over the speakers. The Samlores had blinked first.

Bagari took her microphone in her grasp. 'Fire!'

And with that, the battle for the solar system began. The Samlores had little to no battle tactics. They flew all over the place, no formation and opened fire wherever they liked.

The Venus II looped the loop and attempted to chase one of the enemy Hornets down but the craft was elusive, fast.

Jake flew his own craft to be close to his friends and in doing so narrowly missed being blown sky high by a volley of fire from the nose of a Samlore that had clearly had its eyes on him. But the Space Seals pilots were impeccable in their co-ordination and one of their own immediately blasted the Samlore out of the sky.

'Let them get on with it!' cried Bagari, who spotted that the Orbital was now within firing range of the Earth. 'All freighters, all freighters, engage the Orbital.'

The battle freighters moved on, letting the Hornets clear up the mess that their fight with the Samlores was creating.

'Skateboard, please tell me that you have hacked into their navigation computer already?' there was an element of nervousness in Bagari's voice.

*

Back on the Venus II, not only was Skateboard doing his best to tail the Hornet which had provoked him, but he was also still trying to hack the mainframe on the Orbital.

'Almost there, Admiral,' he said, lying slightly.

Of the possible 96,489 combinations that he had calculated, he'd only attempted 13,592 so far but at least one of his objectives was almost complete. Within moments, he was done.

'The Orbital's shields are powering down,' he de- clared before turning to his co-pilot.

'Miss, ready when you are,' he said, buying enough time to attempt another couple of thousand.

Without replying, Anji fired the laser cannons and obliterated the Hornet.

'Good shooting, girl!' said Jake, who in watching his friends in battle had completely failed to notice a Samlore on his port side, half on fire, but still capable of taking him out.

Anji had noticed his predicament but it was too late. To his surprise, Jake's Hornet was sent spiraling out of control as the Samlore rammed him, embedding the gun sting at the front into his cockpit, sending both ships cartwheeling off into space.

*

The first thing that Io saw was the huge doomsday weapon. The instrument that destroyed her home planet. She readied her gun and leveled it up at the vast housing that held it in place and saw the stress and strain of the buckled metal.

'Looks like Random's left the rest to me,' she said to herself.

She thought of Alfrajetti. She thought of her family. She thought of her Mother.

'This one's for you, Mum.'

Random blinked his eyes open, his jaw throbbing red hot. Stratos must have brought him around with another savage blow. But he didn't mind. The pain would not be permanent. Any moment now, the tables would be turning.

'I thought it would be a pity if you missed this,' said Stratos, who loomed over the command port, cold metal fingers poised over the red button.

Smiling sinisterly he relished the moment. This was going to be a moment to savour. But something didn't feel right.

'No final pleas for me to stop, Captain?'

'You've gotta do what you've gotta do,' Random rasped, his throat dry as sawdust.

'I want to see the look in your eyes as the Earth burns...'

Stratos pressed the button.

*

171

Far below on Earth, the human race collected to- gether, watching the strange and slightly scary vision of a spaceship hover high in the sky.

But no-one ran and nobody panicked.

Instead they stood there and watched the fate of their world play out...mainly through their camera phones...

*

Nothing happened.

Stratos pressed the button again. The same outcome.

Something very wrong had occurred.

Instead of the sound of a magnificent explosion and

the brilliant light of destruction flooding his field of vision, Stratos could only hear the hum of the ship's engines. Then came a sound that made him even angrier than he had ever been before.

The sound of a boy laughing.

'What have you done?' he demanded.

Random's laugh was becoming more vigorous by the second.

Stratos' black eyes looked Random square in the face.

Random stared back at his enemy and tried suc- cessfully to stop.

'It's nothing I've done, your lab rats fired on the weapon system, not me!'

'No,' said Stratos. 'It can't be! It can't be!'

'Oh, I'm afraid it is. This is what happens when you enlist the help of mercenaries. They were never your soldiers, Stratos. They were just idiots with guns.'

Stratos hollered out in sheer frustration. He went over to the security terminal and punched his fist clean through the image on the screen.

'The girl...' he spat.

Random stopped laughing instantly. 'No...' Suddenly the ship jolted. Random pulled at his manacles. Io must have stayed on board, he thought to himself. He had to stop her. She'd caused the doomsday weapon to fail. He had to stop her as much as Stratos did. One false shot would blow them all sky high.

What's more, he had to save her... 'Stratos, we have you surrounded.' A new voice bled into the bridge.

'This is Admiral Bagari of the Space Seals Corp. You have taken our vessel and committed genocide. We will give you ten seconds to surrender. Lower your shields and turn yourself over.'

'NO!' screamed Stratos. He spotted Random trying to break free and thrust himself into the torture device's instruments and threw it into maximum. Random immediately stopped what he was doing and began to writhe in pain again.

Bagari's voice boomed once more. 'Stratos, we have hacked into your mainframe. Your shields are down and your weapons are offline. You have five seconds...'

But Stratos wasn't listening. He had to get the doomsday weapon functioning again.

'Four...'

Stratos had left the bridge. It was only Random, screaming in agony left. Despite the torment, he was straining at his bonds...

'Three...'

As the bolts of lightning continued to riddle his body, Random grimaced as the manacle holding his right arm in place snapped...

'Two...'

There went the one holding his left leg down... 'One...'

With one herculean effort, Random exploded out of

his bonds, tore the helmet off his head and threw it to the floor. As he jumped through the air, the first volley of fire from the battle freighters smashed into the side of the Orbital, sending sparks and jets of smoke cascading out everywhere.

Random didn't allow it to distract him. He had his strength
back.

The torture had the opposite effect - it had made him better
again.

Without a moment to lose, Random sped his way af-ter Stratos
towards the weaponry chamber.

There was one more life to save today…

*

The sound of Jake screaming bounced around the walls of the
cockpit as Anji and Skateboard chased his ship. There was not
much left of the battle. The Space Seals had obliterated the
Samlores, but one ship was proving elusive and had set off in hot
pursuit of the Venus II.

Bloodied and wounded, the Commander sneered as he set his
sights on the silver pearl in the black of space.

'Er…Skateboard…'

'Sorry, miss, I'm a little busy with this final code…' said
Skateboard, who was just one thousand combinations from
sending the Orbital hurtling into the anomaly. Despite his
capability to do any number of things at one time, he was
adamant he needed to dedicate as much of his concentration on
this final task as possible.

The Commander raised his sighter and prepared to fire. 'Anji…'
said Skateboard, with just five combinations left. 'Six o'clock…'

Anji looked perplexed. Then she remembered her job. Instantly,
she swung her laser gun towards the blip on their scanner and
fired.

The Commander, who had his finger on the button, had no time
to press it as his Hornet exploded into a million pieces.

'Excellent shot, miss,' said Skateboard. The final combination had been cracked.

He switched off the audio of Jake, who by now sounded like he was throwing up, and made contact with the battle fleet.

'Admiral Bagari, I'm in.'

Bagari grinned. 'Send him to hell...'

*

Back on board the Orbital, Stratos' bionic legs had powered him way ahead of Random and he sprinted back into the weaponry chamber.

It was a complete mess.

Shards of blasted metal and plastic lay strewn all over the place. The ship jolted again as the battle fleet continued its relentless attack, causing more explosions all over the ship.

'What have you done!?' he cried...the room appar- ently empty of other life.

Suddenly a blast shot Stratos in his back. It did little but to singe him where other men it would have burrowed clean through.

Stratos turned and spotted Io, shivering in the shadows.

As he advanced, she shot again. Once more, the bolt deflected off him. The same thing happened again and again, until Stratos snatched the gun from her grasp, snapped it in two and picked her up by the throat.

Io's face turned blue as her eyes began to pop out of their sockets.

'To think I nearly saved your Mother...you just weren't quick enough...'

Stratos squeezed his grip.

And with that Io's eyes flickered shut.

Random bolted down the corridor and could see the silhouette of Stratos holding Io's lifeless body up against the flames.

'No!' he cried as he tore straight into Stratos' midriff, sending Io's body tumbling to the ground and Stratos himself flying like a bullet into the wall, where he almost tore a hole through it.

Random scrambled to Io's body but he was just too late.

His eyes began to well up. Not another life...

The roar of Stratos hurtling towards him took his glaze away from Io's pale face. The force of him tearing him away and throwing him down the corridor sent him reeling. He regrouped quickly and threw as good as he got back at the metal monster. He landed a punch full on Stratos' jaw and sent him sprawling.

Stratos looked down. Blood was pouring from his mouth. Black, tar-like blood.

'Finally...some guts...' he jibed as he sent a devas- tating blow right back at Random, who ducked and sped around the back of Stratos, punching with all his might, denting Stratos' monstrous body.

He had to keep going. Punching and kicking. Ignoring the fire around him as the Orbital continued to buckle under the strength of the battle fleet's assault. He had to stop Stratos here and now.

Even if it meant the death of him, too.

*

Jake's eyes stopped spinning. Retching again, he had no more to give. Falling back to the floor, his stomach ached. Looking around, he was dismayed at what he had done to the decor of the cramped vessel.

'Jake, are you alright?'

'Anj...I'm fine. Just give me a few minutes to regroup and possibly hose myself down and I'll be right with you.'

'I've got the ship's laser triggered on the Hornet. You might want to hold onto something...'

'Oh no!' cried Jake. 'Please, not again!'

Meanwhile, on board the Hornet that had embedded itself inside Jake's cockpit, the Samlore, now the last surviving Samlore in the whole solar system, had similarly stopped himself from vomiting at the sheer velocity of the spinning Hornets and looked up to see nothing but the side of his enemies craft. He noticed the gun was embedded in the cockpit. So, all it would take was one shot and his enemy would be blasted out of the sky and he would be free.

Unfortunately for him, Anji was just too quick. With a squeeze of her trigger, the Samlore was no more and once again, Jake's craft was sent spinning into space.

'We'd better go and pick him up...when he's stopped of course,' said Skateboard.

'How's the rest of it going?'

Anji looked up as the Venus II's scanner showed her the current events.

The Orbital was sailing closer and closer to the anomaly and a barrage of fire was exploding from the four battle freighters and blowing chunks out of it.

'I suppose you're going to say that we can't fly in and help Random, aren't you?' Anji said.

'If we fly into the carnage we risk being hit our- selves. If we get too close to the anomaly we also risk being pulled in by its gravitational field. I'm sorry, but we've done what we can, miss,' said Skateboard. 'It's up to Random now.'

A light bulb went off in Anji's head.

'We've still got to save him...and you know what, Skateboard? I know exactly how we can do it...'

More and more debris began to tear away from both the interior and exterior of the massive battle freighter. At Admiral Bagari's command the Space Seals threw more aggression at a ship that was once theirs, but now they were willing to sacrifice it to destroy the threat that it carried. As it lurched closer and closer to the anomaly, two enemies fought it out on board.

*

Random's super speed was back and although Stratos was able to land blow after blow upon his frame, he had been able to counter attack. Punch after punch and kick after kick sent them sprawling into their surroundings, further damaging the internal structure of the Orbital. Random and Stratos had torn whole chunks out of it and each other.

As the fight moved onto a high rise of pathways and corridors that dangled high above nothingness, Stratos fell back over a precipice and crunched through the floor of a walkway below. In doing so, he tore a massive part of his chest plate off.

Random leapt down to join him but spotted from a distance the exposed wiring and broken circuitry of a cyborg who was surely now on the edge of complete failure.

Random landed a clean right hook squarely in the eye socket of the creature who had claimed so many lives just to spite an enemy who in this universe he didn't even possess.

Stratos cried out as the punch knocked him free of his grasp on the walkway and he fell further below.

But Random wasn't finished yet. He dived after him immediately, caught him by the exposed chest unit and began to punch and tear at anything he could. They seemed to plunge towards doom for ages before the back of Stratos finally broke their fall against the very bottom of the ship.

The force of the crash sent an echo that even the silence of space would have heard. Random tumbled to the ground, panting, bleeding all over. He craned his neck to see Stratos, his circuitry wheezing, all that was human still groaning and crying out in agony. He was broken, again, at the hands of his worst enemy.

'It's shocks me to hear that you still feel,' said Random as he rolled onto his front. Both adversaries were moving gingerly, defying the injuries and damage they had both sustained.

'You think that you are better than me?' growled Stratos, his voice sounding broken. 'That compassion and valor set us apart. You're wrong Captain. I've seen what you are capable of. I KNOW what you can do. In defeating you I had to become like you. But I've seen what happens to Captain Random when he succumbs to temptation. To evil. Believe me, in killing you I'd be saving your pitiful universe!'

'You're wrong, Stratos. I've seen temptation. I've looked right into its green envy and I rejected it. Right there and then. I allowed it to consume me and it very nearly destroyed me. But I'm never making that mistake again.'

Random grabbed Stratos by the throat. Stratos choked and then began to laugh.

'But I have won,' he coughed. 'Because I've brought you down to my level...you're willing to kill to pro- tect...don't you think that's what I had to do?'

'I really don't care what you had to do,' said Random, tightening his grip. 'This isn't your universe. You have no say over what it does. Because of your mon- strous terrorism billions of lives have been lost. The universe won't ever forgive you and it sure as hell will never forget.'

Stratos grinned a sickening smile. 'Then I really have won...and the best part of it all? You die in the fire with me.'

Random frowned.

'This ship is falling into the anomaly...in a few minutes we will be nothing but a memory...an indelible one, stained across the cosmos. What a victory...' Stratos croaked, black blood oozing out of his mouth.

Random looked around him. He'd been so wrapped up in his wrath that he had failed to notice that the ship was indeed falling apart and had felt like it was being pulled against its will. He thought it had been the gunfire from the Space Seals, but he was wrong.

'Someone must have hacked your navigation sys- tem,' he mused. Then he smiled, 'Skateboard!'

Random leaned in so that his face was right up against his foe. One of Stratos' eyes had burst and the other was still as black as its owner's heart.

'Sorry, Stratos, but this ride has room for one person only...'

He let go of his enemy, letting him tumble back and walked towards some hanging debris. If it could support his weight for just a couple of seconds, he could hop his way back up to the top of the ship and then leg it back to the bridge. But the walls had begun warping all around him, buckling as the dimensional strain of the anomaly was beginning to suck the Orbital into its void.

Stable for a moment on the remains of a gantry, Random yearned to have the final say in this horrible fight. 'You know what your biggest failure was, Stratos? Your ego. You tried to do it all yourself and look where it got you. Your weapons sabotaged, the ship defenseless, your minions useless and wiped out in an instant and now you're plunging into oblivion. I have my friends and I know that they will always, ALWAYS have my back.'

The Orbital began to warp out of shape, buckling and screaming as it twisted and snapped.

'You got distracted and it cost you. The chaos you create means nothing to the chaos that has been your downfall. Normally I'd have some shred of compassion for my enemies but you, you've deserved everything you get. Goodbye Stratos...it hasn't been pleasant.'

Stratos shrieked an inhuman chorus of agony. Ran- dom's face wore that of defiance and finality as he turned and sped away out of the hole.

As he pelted upwards, his speed and agility sending him flying up the shaft and using the momentum of the falling debris and buckled walkways, he could still hear Stratos' scream as he was pulled towards a fitting but very nasty death.

Stratos got to his feet gingerly and tried to follow after him but the damage to his circuits had spread to his legs and he crashed to the floor, his world burning all around where he lay.

Stratos tried all he could to free himself but the drag factor of the gravitational pull of the anomaly was starting to warp his metal body. Stratos watched as parts of him began to pull away and break. Little explosions where his circuitry was failing burst out all over him.

His optical sensors shut down.

He was blind but continued to hear the horrific screeching of chaos all around him.

He prayed for mercy that his bionic body would ter- minate itself, shut down to spare him the terrifying reality of what lay in store for him but it kept going right up until his final seconds.

It was happening again. His body was destroyed but he could still feel the icy grip of death engulf him once more.

Only this time, there was no way to cheat it.

*

Random dodged and weaved his way around the falling beams and fires that littered his journey back onto the bridge. He made his way over to the intercom and flicked a couple of switches, not really knowing what he was doing but hoping that he could make contact with anyone who could help him.

But he needn't have.

Within seconds, the same energy that had enveloped him on the Venus II shone its glowing light upon him again.

And as he faded away, Random smiled.

*

From the safety of her battle bridge, Admiral Bagari watched as the Orbital plunged deep into the anomaly. A colourful display of cosmic brilliance exploded across the view screen and a final blinding light and tremendous roar rippled across the entire battle fleet.

Some of her officers took cover as the amazing light bled all around them.

And yet within minutes, the light was gone.

The roar had faded to nothingness and the anomaly, the Orbital and Stratos were all gone...

Back on Earth, the gatherers on London Bridge whooped and cheered as they watched the incredible fire display. A burst of applause and hundreds of people whooping and cheering reverberated all around the world.

Dexter turned back to the newsflash he had got up on his work computer and stared in disbelief at what so- called experts were already surmising as a highly advanced light display.

He watched in astonishment as the newsreader said that there appeared to be no cause for alarm.

Instantly, he texted his wife, who had not seen his messages telling her that he loved her and that he was sorry for being forgetful all the time and reassured her that it was just a false alarm and that the world was not ending.

Yet.

Immediately, he picked up his office phone and punched some numbers into the keypad.

'Yes, get me the PM,' he said. He took his glasses off, rested them upon his desk top and rubbed his eyes. 'I know he's busy, but this is an emergency! I know everyone else is saying that but...look, I'm happy to hold, okay?'

The minutes drifted by until finally, the terminable hold music ended abruptly.

'Prime Minister? Did you just...well, yes I'm sure it was just a fireworks display, but don't you think it looked too...real to be...no, no I suppose you're right...yes, we do have much more important things to get on with than just ano...sorry, what do you mean by another alien invasion!?'

Meanwhile in Brooklyn, the little girl gave out a cry as she saw the weird spaceship looking thing in the sky disappear.

As soon as it went, she wondered if what she had just seen had indeed been real. Her Mum was always telling her what an overexcited imagination she had.

Sighing, she picked up her basketball and steadied herself.

This time she was definitely going to shoot through the hoop.

As she took her shot, the ball travelled through the air...and as the ball sailed through the net she suddenly had two reasons to smile today.

*

Random re-materialised in the familiar mess that was the Venus II's mid-section. He heard the smash of crockery under his foot and immediately realised that he had reappeared on top of Anji's favourite mug.

He'd beamed back on top of the table!

Anji, Jake and Skateboard appeared in the cockpit doorway and tore towards their friend. Random jumped down and gave them all a warm embrace..

'I'm so happy that you are safe!' said Anji, tears trickling down her cheeks. 'And I told you Skate- board...didn't I say all along that we could beam him up!'

'That you did, miss, it seems that we did it just in time!'

'How?' asked Random.

'Skateboard found the command code when he hacked the Orbital's mainframe. So with its shields down he could throw the transporter into reverse and give you a return trip.' replied Anji, squeezing Random tightly.

Random blew his cheeks out. 'For a while there I really thought that was a one-way ticket...'

'So Stratos is gone?' asked Jake. 'There's no way he can ever return?'

'You saw the Orbital plug up the anomaly...it's all gone now,' Skateboard reassured him.

Random's head fell.

'Io gave her life to stop him. She succeeded. So many have suffered thanks to what that man has done...'

The group huddled together again, collected in their grief and relief.

Stratos was gone.

13

REFLECTION

Some time had passed since the day in which the universe was saved and the time felt right for the peoples of the galaxies to mourn the loss of so many.

Stratos' words had echoed back through Random's head every day between then and now.

His mark was indeed stained across the whole cosmos.

Planets and entire solar systems that had grown and supported many unique species over millennia had been blown away in just a few seconds.

All those cultures, all those races. All those people, gone in an instant.

And so, after Admiral Bagari and Admiralty of the Space Seals had officially pardoned Random and his friends of any association with the intergalactic terrorist known as Stratos, they were decorated for their part in the victory, which had now been dubbed "The Battle of the Solar System."

Bagari herself was awarded the Premiership of the Space Seals Corp and under her leadership one of the first things she wanted to do was reward those who had saved so many.

Random, Anji, Jake and Skateboard had all humbly accepted the Medal of Honour, which they were awarded during a ceremony on the Space Seals HQ planet of Xarephas. But before the ceremony, Bagari had one request that she wanted them to fulfill.

That evening, the universe turned off the lights. At a coordinated time, everywhere went black. And then, little white lights began to fade into existence on Xarephas. The entire planet began to twinkle as its residents all lit a candle and held it in their hands.

Its neighbouring planet, Dorva, did exactly the same. Then its neighbours. Then the next planet along, and another.

Before long, every planet still in existence shone back into light as everyone held a candle high for those who had perished and for those planets that were no longer there.

For the stars that were no longer in the sky. Random and his friends looked up and around them as they and millions upon millions of others showed solidarity and remembrance.

When Bagari had asked them to take part, there was nothing else they felt they should do.

It was an honour for them all and a reminder to them that even in the darkest situation there can always be light...

As the travellers said their goodbyes, Random shook hands with Bagari, who had offered to see them off.

'Captain,' she said dryly. 'Admiral,' he said back.

'Once again, on behalf of the Space Seals Corp I thank you all for what you have done.'

'Ah,' Random snorted. 'All in a day's work for us.' 'I take it that if we need your co-operation again then you will give it?'

'Of course,' he smiled. 'You know where to find us.' Bagari frowned. 'Actually, we don't.'

Random began to follow his friends up the platform into the Venus II.

'Ah, that's okay, if there is trouble, you can be sure it will find us first. Until next time, Bagari.'

'Let's hope there isn't one,' she said as the platform raised fully and the Venus II, cleared for take-off by the Space Seals air traffic control, rose high in the air and flew majestically back out into space and far away from Bagari and Xarephas.

A while later, the crew of the Venus II were gathered in the cockpit as Random stood behind Jake, who was occupying the pilot's seat, watching with bated breath.

'Okay, Skateboard, stabilisers off!'

Random and Anji held onto the nearest solid fixtures for dear life as Skateboard silently clamped himself magnetically to the floor. But the Venus II didn't jolt, didn't stutter to a halt or stall completely.

'I've done it!' exclaimed Jake. 'I can fly this thing! I mean, I knew I could but still, big moment for me, this.'

'Yes, Jake,' said Random looking at Anji in disbelief. 'Seems that you can.'

'My turn next!' cried Anji. 'About time too,' smiled Random.

'So, Bagari's going to become the leader of the Space Seals then?' said Jake.

'She deserves it,' Anji replied.

'Yeah, and so did we!' said Jake, taking his hand off the steering wheel to kiss the medal that he still had draped around his neck. The Venus II buffeted a bit as he did so.

'Eyes on the road, Jake!' said Anji. 'Sorry, you lot,' he said shame faced.

'I'll put it on auto-pilot,' said Skateboard. 'Cool, so where to next?' asked Random.

'Well, first of all maybe we should get you looked at again,' said Anji.

'Why?'

'Have you not noticed? You're still red and blue!'

Random took a look at his reflection in the view screen.

'Yeah...well, the rest of me seems fine again. Run a scan over me if you don't believe me, I feel like I'm back to my former self!'

'Yeah, but you don't look it!' said Jake.

'Maybe it's time I showed my true colours…' Random said to no one in particular. He looked up at his friends and grinned and made his way out into the mid-section.

'As for where we go next, I'm easy, but somewhere quiet would be good. After all we've been through. You'll never hear me grumbling about having to go on holiday again!' he said.

Anji laughed as she too made her way after him before Jake's hand pulled on her sleeve.

'Er…Anj, can I have a minute?'

The pair walked back to the living quarters and sat on Jake's bed.

'Listen, I don't want to panic you or anything but…some quite nasty stuff happened to me when I was on board the Orbital. I don't want to talk about it now, but I will, I have promised that to myself. When I am ready.'

Anji looked concerned at her friend and placed her hand on his.

'But when I can, I want you to be the person that I talk to. Is that okay?'

Anji gave Jake a kind smile and leaned over to kiss his cheek. 'Of course.'

Jake smiled back, but Anji could sense that he wasn't quite right. The bravado had slipped. She wasn't going to tease him. They'd all seen some nasty stuff over the last few weeks.

'You just say the word and I'll be there.'

Jake pulled her in and gave Anji the biggest hug he could. He began to well up.

'You always are.'

Back inside the cockpit, Random was sitting on the floor with Skateboard helping his AI robot carry out his tasks of routine maintenance all the while filling his friend in on what had happened on the Orbital.

'So this torture technique...it restored your powers?' asked Skateboard.

'Yes. Not sure how.'

'I think I can explain it,' he said whilst shocking some new wiring into place under the dashboard. 'Your synaptic reflexes were rejuvenated by the electrical impulses. So, all the time Stratos thought he was making you weaker, he was in fact making you stronger.'

'Wow. I need to talk to Jake...he put up with so much. And Io...' Random broke off. 'I know you'll say I couldn't have given anymore but I'll always feel guilty I couldn't save her. And the rage...the anger I had for that man, that machine. If that other Random was just like me then no wonder he let the Flux overtake him.'

'But you didn't. And for that you are nothing like your alternate self.'

Random sighed. 'Yeah, I suppose you're right.' 'I often am,' said Skateboard.

Random moved forward to install another new set of wiring. Clumsily, he spilled his hot chocolate, making Skateboard jump who in turn accidentally shocked Random with one of the cables. A bolt of energy cracked loudly like a whip.

The robot watched in horror as the red/blue coloured boy tumbled backwards.

'Sir! Are you okay?'

Random groaned and Skateboard's diodes sighed. 'Really Skateboard,' he said as he picked himself up,

'You're so jumpy!'

Skateboard recoiled in surprise. 'What's up?'

'Sir, I think you should take a look for yourself...'

Random got to his feet and checked his reflection in the dashboard. He check it again. His skin seemed to be shifting, changing.

Anji and Jake raced into the cockpit.

'What's going on?' asked Anji. 'We thought we heard lightning!'

Random turned to face them, his face beaming with the biggest grin he'd had in a long time.

'Guys,' he said, utterly delighted. 'I'm purple again!'

JOURNEYS IN THE RANDOMVERSE
HAYDEN GRIBBLE

JOURNEYS IN THE RANDOMVERSE

A collection of Captain Random short stories

HAYDEN GRIBBLE

To the memory of Terrance Dicks

Contents

INTRODUCTION

'It was only a matter of time before the worlds of Captain Random were further explored in the form of an anthology. I had always intended to find new ways of telling the adventures of Random and his friends and here it is; the book that you hold in your hands is a truly fantastic collection of the good Captain's travels, even if I say so myself!

But Hayden,' I hear you saying…probably, 'why tweak the formula? Surely after four novels, you had a good thing going. Why tamper with it?'

Well, faithful reader, I'll tell you.

Captain Random has existed in my imagination since 2014. That's yonks ago, isn't it? Since then, I've had many an idea about the kind of scrapes that he and his best friends Anji, Jake and Skateboard (everyone's favourite, it seems when I speak to people about the books!) get into. Some of them are grand and long such as those that preceded this anthology, like *The Sandman, The Eater of Souls, The Rainbow Chasers* and *The Stratos Conundrum*, and some are like little golden nuggets. Treasured short trips like the ones you are about to read and hopefully enjoy.

I've always been of the thinking that the story was king and that word count doesn't matter.

It would be silly of me to stretch out ideas that couldn't be lengthened just to make a novel out of it. The story would suffer too much and the reader would have a very thin tale to delve into. So instead, I decided it was better and more exciting to have them in one bumper volume.

This also gave me greater scope for a varied range of ways to tell these adventures. In this book, stories are told from the perspective of the characters, some old and some new, and new horizons are chartered in doing so, both for the Randomverse and for me as the writer of this incredible character's worlds.

Onto the Randomverse in the book title. Yes, I know that as you read this, the whole multi-verse theory has probably been done to death. From the popular *Marvel* films to *Rick and Morty, Family Guy* and *Community*, many TV shows and movies have explored the concept with aplomb in recent years, and I was initially keen to avoid it.

However, after the events of *The Stratos Conundrum*, it was a possibility too good to resist and I have opted for a different angle to the others I have named previously, at least I hope so, and I'll let you be the judge at the end of the day.

Plus, the book title is true in that it explores Random's universe, it's a rather apt title if nothing else, right?

Another change I have made to Random and his friends in these pages is their age. I've always envisaged the characters aging as their adventures continue, and this seemed to be the best way to show how they are becoming adults and how their experiences are changing them as people. There's another reason why I have chosen to do this. Prepare yourself for the next line, Random fans...

The next book will be the last...

..now please don't cry!

It's been a fun ride, it really has, but all good things must come to an end and *Captain Random* is no exception. That's one of the reasons why this anthology carries the bulk of stories this special character will have.

I've poured my heart and soul into these books and I want it to end on a high, leaving you wanting more and me still loving to write them. True, the series could continue for twenty books or so, but where's the fun in that? Isn't it more special when there isn't a lot of something? Don't you love them even more for it? I know I do!

So to give these golden nuggets a chance to breathe in their own right, collecting them into an anthology of short stories, to show where Random and his friends have been and where they are going in a way that celebrates them for who they are seemed a fitting way to start drawing the curtain down on them.

But not yet. You've got so much ahead of you, dear reader, fifteen short stories, all stuffed with the humour, adventure and fun that I have endeavoured to give the *Captain Random* adventures before the big one at the end.

I'll stop myself from saying any more as that's another story for another day...

From brief encounters to space heists, diary entries from the crew of the Venus II to a holiday for Skateboard and a trip into another reality altogether, these fifteen adventures are the very best of *Captain Random* and I should know, I've written them all!

To space zombies and oracles of fate via a trip to the very birth of the universe, *Journeys In The Randomverse* is brimming with excitement and it all culminates in a beckon across the stars that will lead Random to his final adventure, it's all here.

I really hope you enjoy it.

Happy reading!

Hayden Gribble

March 2022

OUTSIDERS

Trelorma is one of the most boring places to grow up in the entire universe. You can trust me on that, I've lived here since I was a baby. Baby Flav, that was me, indistinguishable from any other baby, bored as soon as I hatched. Once in school, we learned about the moons of a neigbouring solar system that did nothing.

Not one thing. They just hung there in the starry sky, ruining the starscape like bits of rubbish floating in a lake. No means of supporting life, nothing to do on their rocky desolate surfaces.

Not even any signs that anyone has ever been to one of them, well, except a few dusty footprints and some flag waving to no one in the bleak vacuum of its surroundings.

I mean, it's true we have a jungle on Trelorma, well, most of the planet is a jungle, as a matter of fact, but when you've spent almost all your days surrounded by nothing but leaves and insect life, you'd find it boring too.

Sure, if you saw it for the first time you'd probably fall over at the silver and golden orange skies but to me, I yawn in boredom.

It's like...try eating ice cream every day of your life. That sounds like a good idea, doesn't it?

Oh sure, you'd have a wide range of flavours to gorge yourself with day in/day out, but by the time you turned sixteen you'd be crying out for something else to live off, wouldn't you?

Well, that was me, and this is where my head was at when my story begins. It was an ice cream sundae of a day!

With nothing to do and no one to meet up with since all my friends were at school and, uh...what should I say in case my Mum ever reads this...forget school, let's say church! As I said, it was an ice cream sundae after all! (Ooh, I should keep this bit in, very pun-ny, Flav!)

So, with nothing to do but go on the same walk I have tread every day of my upwardly mobile life, I decided to be a bit adventurous…

My house is slap bang in the middle of a very busy street of roughly 30 houses on either side of a brown mud road. If you saw where I live, you'd think you'd had a bang on the head and were seeing multiple versions of it because they all look the same.

Every single one of them was carved into thick trees.

Everyone a two up, two down, with a working toilet at the rear. And it was the same country-wide. PLANET wide, even!

Over 60 billion Trelormans living in blissful ignorance of adventure, doing what they were told, not questioning anything ever. Why? The answer has terrified me all my life.

Everyone is happy.

So why question the norm when there is little to complain about. I'll tell you why...BECAUSE I AM NOT LIKE ANYONE ELSE!

I get in trouble at school for challenging my teachers. I get lectured at home for challenging my parents.

I get all manner of unpleasantness kicked out of me for challenging my classmates.

All because I ask questions about why we do this? Why do we do what we do?

Leave our houses at the same time every day, come home at the same time, eat the same meals, read the same books, listen to the same music, go to bed AND get up at the same time, without fail? We all even wear the same clothes.

It's not like we'd have any distinguishable features to any outsiders because, yes, you've guessed it, we all look the same!

After sixteen years of following the same path as everyone else and not getting anything new out of my life, I decided to forge my own, and honestly, I had arrived at a point where if there was something so scary and dangerous that it could end my life, it would almost be worth it.

Who knows, maybe I'd die of the shock of finding something new!

So, I stopped in my tracks, at the end of my road, which turned onto another one identical to mine, which in turn led to yet another road identical to mine and thought against the usual routine.

I looked out of the corner of my eye and spotted what I would like to think was a Flav-sized hole in a hedgerow.

Looking around to make sure that nobody spotted me, and who cares if they did, it wasn't like anybody would follow me, I dived through it.

Landing in a crumpled heap on the other side, my clothes dirtied and torn from getting caught on the branches on the way through, I chuckled to myself.

I had done it. The circle had been broken.

I had escaped!

So, what now?

Why is this all so important I hear you thinking, dear reader?

Well, I'm getting to it, but that little decision changed my life forever and led me to the greatest thing that has ever happened to me.

To the greatest person I have ever met.

A person who even now when I think of him, my hearts will skip a beat and then proceed to beat a conga at different times.

It was the day I met a strange outsider called Random...

But there I am again, getting ahead of myself. Oh, and I'm blushing again!

Excuse me, I'd better get back on track with my tale.

Picking myself up, I suddenly realised what amazing wonders might lay ahead of me.

The circle of monotony had been broken and now the predictability of my life lay in ruins, much to my merriment.

I hopped and whooped as I danced through the outback, instantly stepping in something that neither looked nor smelt pleasant.

Doing my best to wipe the foul mound of horribleness off my left sandal, I proceeded with my other two feet to step over the offending hurdle, trying to not let this small hiccup ruin my mood.

Very soon it felt like I had been walking a long time.

The jungle was thicker than I had ever seen on this planet, and the wildlife, the animals that we as a race have never been allowed to see, were so...beautiful.

I had no names for them because the powers that be on this planet never told us anything about the planet we lived on, so I had nothing to call them.

But as I continued my walk through my dense yet colourful surroundings, I started giving nicknames to what I saw.

The multi-eyed small hairy things that dangled in the trees, squeaking, and playfully whipping each other with their long tails I decided to call Dinkys.

The five-legged long-snouted mammals that used their vine-like tongues to strip that bark from the trees on either side of me I dubbed Nonkey-Noos.

Well, I never said I was a genius with names now, did I?

The flies and insects that I had grown accustomed to my Mother shooing from our kitchen that liked to also eat the insides of our house, seemed to buzz freely in this haven, and although she would be ashamed to read it (again, put this story down now if you have read on, Mum!) seemed to love buzzing around me.

As I raised my hands towards them, allowing the glorious Trelorman sun to shine down upon me, they seemed to have a great time weaving in and out of my fingertips, their noisy wings fluttering soothingly as they sang around me.

All seemed right with my world.

Until it no longer was.

I should have noticed the light grow darker as I stared at the insects.

I should have had a suspicion all was not right when they scrammed faster than hunted prey.

I should have felt the ground beneath my feet start to shake as the thud of deadly hooves began to shatter the peace and serenity.

And when I turned to see what was now looming over me, I really should have done something more heroic than scream!

The sight of the intruder still makes me shudder. It stood what must have been twenty feet tall, much more than my five-foot frame.

Its huge wet nose globbed a mass of unpleasant gloopiness down upon me like a horrible gunge of snotty soup. Its eyes were both black and blood red at the same time and its teeth, which seemed to make up most of its long, hideous face, would be too many to count before being torn to pieces by them.

Terrified, I couldn't move. My brain thought of nothing else but to curse me and my infernal need to challenge the norm.

So, this was why Trelormans stuck to the roads, did what they were told and never questioned. Because there were things, so close to our doorsteps, that if we went looking for them, could send us to our deaths!

Suddenly, an ungodly roar burst through its jagged teeth and I was splattered by its bad breath and saliva, both of which make me want to gag just remembering what that was like.

My paralysis of fear was broken, and I started to run like I had never run before.

I ran as far as my legs would carry me, trying to keep my balance as the thunderous legs of this mighty creature tore after me.

I wasn't much of a sport for this beast, which I am ashamed to say I still haven't given a name to because let's be honest, no name is as awesome as Nonkey-Noos or Dinkys now, is it?

Before long, it had caught me, its massive claws pushing me to the floor.

I fell front first onto the leafy ground, winded by the surprise of it all.

I suddenly realised whatever it was had probably only galloped a few strides to catch me.

I whimpered and thought of my Mum as it growled high above me. Its claws raised, ready to strip my body inside out.

I held my arms up in vain and cried out, pleading for it to leave me alone.

Suddenly a blaze of light shone diagonally down upon my attacker and a crackling sound of energy reverberated around the jungle.

I tried to peer at the light but within moments it was gone, and my attacker with it.

In its place stood someone completely different.

'Oh!' cried the being. 'Sorry about that! I hope I wasn't interrupting anything!'

I lowered my arms and gazed at the stranger. He was like no one I had ever met before.

He looked odd with only two arms and two legs and his head burdened with a shock of spikey brown hair, not like the bald palate we Trelormans are used to having.

His clothes seemed to be made up of a strange black-and-white arrangement, almost identical to the suits I had seen people wear in alien films.

And his skin, and this was the weirdest part, was a vibrant purple.

'Sorry for the abrupt arrival but we were unable to dock so my co-pilot thought it would be best if he beamed...' suddenly, this alien seemed to be aware of his surroundings.

His face dropped.

'This isn't the Oceanic World Ball...' he muttered.

I gulped and plucked up the courage to speak.

'Who are you?'

The alien looked directly above and did a complete 360-degree spin on the spot. 'This isn't the High Priest's Chamber, tell me, have they put me down in his greenhouse? Does the High Priest even have a greenhouse?'

I picked myself up. 'Look, I don't know what you are talking about!'

'Argh, I'm going to kill Skateboard. If I get mud on this suit, I will lose my deposit!'

I screwed my face up, unable to make sense of his words.

'Oh well, maybe you can help me, I need to get to the Chamber as quickly as possible, please. I am receiving an award,' a look of unbridled joy beamed across his proud young face. 'My friends should already be there, that's if they haven't been matter transferred into the bathroom or worse the swimming pool, that reminds me, I should have brought my trunks for after-'

'Please, be silent!' I spat.

The alien looked hurt. 'Oi! I'm the guest of honour, you can't talk to me like that, where's your master, I'd like a word,' he pushed past me. I pulled him back.

'Listen to me, I honestly have no idea what you are talking about. There is no High Priest, no Chamber, no swimming pool!'

The alien looked me deep in the eyes. They were a bizarre blue/red pigmentation.

Despite my frustration with this weird newcomer, I could have swum in them for days.

'So, what you are telling me,' he said in a quieter tone, 'is that I am going to be late for my award ceremony?'

I sighed. 'It looks that way.'

The alien pulled away from me and let out a frustrated cry.

'Zarg it, I should have told Skateboard a matter transfer won't work every time. I knew we should have just parked up instead. Oh well,' he sighed,

'serves me right for wanting to make an entrance I guess.'

I couldn't take my eyes off him.

'So where am I then?'

'Trelorma,' I replied.

He frowned. 'Where's that when it's at home?'

'It's a planet in the ninth-star system.'

He looked me up and down. I blushed a little.

'Oh, I am a long, long way off,' his face seemed to age slightly as he grew serious. 'That really shouldn't have happened. What's your name?'

I drew myself to my full height. Finally, he was asking the right questions.

'Flav.'

The corners of his mouth gave a little smile. 'Nice to meet you, Flav, I'm Random. Nice get-up.'

I blushed again as he teased me. I looked down at the mess of my clothes, hoping he couldn't smell the remnants of what lay on my sandal, I jumped towards him for protection suddenly remembering the creature that had wanted me for dinner.

He allowed me to huddle near him.

'I was being chased by this…thing!'

'Really? Where is it now?'

'I have no idea. You appeared right where it was and now…well, it couldn't have got away without us knowing.'

Random turned and stared at me.

'This thing that was chasing you, did it look vicious? Like it was about to eat you?'

'Very much so,' I nodded.

'Ah,' he replied.

'What's the problem?' I inquired.

'I think your creature may have just turned up at the Oceanic World Ball,' he gave a strange smile to such an odd statement. 'Oh well, I'm sure security can handle it. They are notoriously hot on things like that on that world, that's why we couldn't land. They didn't recognise our number plate!'

Every sentence Random uttered implored me to delve further. 'You keep making references to others. Who are they?'

Random had started inspecting his surroundings, allowing the same insects who had swarmed around me minutes earlier to envelop him. 'Friends of mine. I travel with them. Righting wrongs, saving planets and getting awards and free days out at theme park worlds in return, it's not a bad life,' he chuckled as the insects appeared to tickle his fingertips. 'These aren't poisonous, are they?'

'No,' I replied. 'We call them Bark strippers. They love to eat our homes.'

'I've never seen a fly eat a house before, sounds incredible.' I went over to his side and watched as he seemed in awe of the insects and marveled at everything about him.

How can someone who had literally just burst into my life be so calm? I know for a fact if I had been in his shoes, I would have panicked as much as I did when the horrible creature dribbled its snot

on me!

Whoever this Random was, he seemed easily distracted, absorbed by something new that allowed him to forget another more important or uncomfortable thought.

'How will you get home?' I asked.

Random's face fell a little and his eyes diverted off into the horizon.

'I don't know. I'm sure Skateboard will sort it out for me. Although let us hope for your sakes he won't bring your friend back at the same time!'

I panicked again. 'He wouldn't, would he?'

'Nah, I doubt it.' Random snapped his fingers and the insects flew off. He made his way over to a fallen tree and sat down. 'He will figure something out.

Could take time, but I know he will. Could be seconds. Could be days. But he'll get me out of this mess...he normally does.'

He gestured for me to take a seat next to him, but I was hesitant.

'I would like to but...' I gestured at the mess I was in.

'Don't worry about all of that,' he waved, 'You were being chased, it must have been scary.'

'But the smell...'

'Don't worry about that either, I've been worse when I've been in a scrape.' he smiled. I did not know what he meant but his smile reassured me.

Hesitantly, I sat beside him.

'So, tell me more about yourself, Flav.'

'There is nothing much to say,' I responded.

'Really?' he gasped. 'In all my travelling I have never met someone who had nothing to say for themselves. Except for the Silent Nuns of Ancordica. Zargs what a rough social gathering that was,' his mind was wandering again, I could tell.

'There really is very little I can say, nothing interesting ever happens here.'

'You see Flav, that's where you're wrong. That entire sentence has got me gripped. Somewhere where nothing happens. That sounds interesting to me!'

'We Trelormans live a life of routine, of monotony.'

'Many worlds do, you should see Earth,' he scoffed.

'I have,' I replied.

'Huh, funny how so many people have. But this planet Trelorma, I can hear you find it boring given your tone!'

'It is! We never explore, we never question, we never challenge the daily routine.'

'Well, you have,' Random interrupted.

I looked at him. Those eyes...God how I wanted to be closer to him.

'I mean,' he continued, 'You seem to be off the beaten track here, Flav. A planet of slaves wouldn't have the freedom to go against the norm and yet you have.'

'We are not slaves,' I bit back before smiling.

'Sorry, everyone here is happy. There is no hunger or war. We get all that we want. Nobody challenges what we do every single day.'

'Well, that's not true,' Random nudged me in the side. 'You do.'

'I want more. Normal isn't enough for me.'

'Normal never is for me either,' he replied. I gazed into his eyes again. My hormones were going into overdrive. Although I had only known him for a couple of minutes, I wanted nothing more than to be with this alien who was appropriately named Random.

'So, you travel the stars?' I said, edging slightly closer to him. He must have noticed me but didn't seem to resist.

'Yes.'

'Not alone, though?'

'No, never alone. Well until now.' he tutted, looking upwardly as though he was willing his spaceship into existence.

I took my chance and put my hand on his arm.

'You've got me.'

'Yes, for now at least,' he patted my hand before straightening up and leaving his sitting place. 'But I could be gone in a flash so I wouldn't get too

close.'

I got up too. 'Or as you said, it could be days. You would need somewhere to stay. You could stay with me?'

He grinned. 'I doubt so if the insects keep trying to eat your house!'

I snorted back, much to my embarrassment. Then I plucked up the courage to ask him a very big question indeed.

'Can I come with you?'

He looked stunned. 'What?'

'Random, you can travel the stars. On this planet we do nothing, but work, eat and sleep. I want the freedom you have to roam the galaxy.'

'But you must have family here, surely?' My face fell a little. How could I forget about them?

Although my Mum does my head in sometimes (I mean it Mum, stop reading!!) of course I would miss her. I would miss all of them.

'I do, yes.'

Random stood facing me and took both my hands in his.

'You see, the people I travel with, we do not have anyone else but ourselves. It would be unfair to your family if I was to rip you from this world. Without a guarantee that I could ever get you home safely again.'

I tried hard not to let Random see the tears that were forming in the corner of my eyes. He smiled.

'Hey, hey, it's okay, you're alright Flav.'

I sniffed back the frustration that I had allowed to fester within me ever since I was young.

The feeling of being an outcast, standing outside of what everyone else thought was right.

Of course, they had a right to be happy but didn't I also?

Now, this boy has dropped out of the sky and was refusing to take me with him, the frustration was starting to overflow again, although I knew deep down he was right.

I couldn't leave my family.

'Can I not bring them with me?' I joked. I wanted to break the mood a little before I fell apart.

Random scrunched his face up and laughed softly. 'I'm sure you couldn't guarantee they would do their fair share of tidying up. Besides, if any more people started to join me, I would probably have to start charging rent! You'll find your place in the galaxy one day, Flav, I am certain of it. If you can diverge from the path your people have forged before you then who knows? Maybe you can make another path for them to follow...starting with this place!' he said kicking some leaves from beneath his feet. 'Although I wouldn't tear the jungle down of course...no...better to leave it like it is.'

Random put his hands in his trouser pockets.

'Besides, it all looks really pretty to me.'

I wiped my eyes. Nobody had ever spoken to me as frankly as Random had just done.

My actions in the past had always been scorned, not because they were bad but because they were misunderstood.

'Maybe you are right. Maybe one day I can effect change. If all that fails then I can always stow away on one of the crewless ships that bring us our supplies!'

'That's the spirit,' he grinned. 'Although running away isn't everything…'

Suddenly, a quizzical look passed over Random's expression. 'Hold on, crewless..so your people have never left this planet?'

'No,' I answered.

'Has anyone ever been here?'

'Not to my knowledge.'

He raised his eyebrows. 'Huh, so this is what First Contact feels like!'

Random spun on his toes and held his arm out for me to take. 'Right then, Flav, I'm all yours.'

'But as I said, this planet is boring.'

'Well if you insist. You're clearly off looking for your new path. Let's find it together.'

And so, we did. We walked on for a few hours. I told him about my life, about school, about my Mum and what people really did on our planet and he took it all in with wide-eyed fascination.

As did I when he told me about all his adventures.

And yet at times, a sadness passed in his eyes (which I refused to leave every time I gazed into them) that he dare not let me in on. I did not feel the need to press him on certain details.

There was no key in the lock to those stories.

What made our time together even more special, as I discovered more wonders in the untouched jungles of my planet with this handsome stranger, was that I knew it could end at any second.

Within the blink of an eye, he could be gone forever.

So, I made it my goal to not let a precious second be wasted. He must have thought that I talked for my whole planet.

In a way, I did! But when he spoke, I drank in the knowledge and the experience of a boy who in the space of an afternoon I had allowed myself to fall totally in love with.

And yet, I knew he wouldn't allow himself to do the same.

He showed me nothing but kindness alongside his window into such a different world to mine but he was stoic in not allowing the same thoughts to flood into his heart.

How could he?

He was so…different. I truly disbelieve even to this day that there is anyone else in the universe the same as him.

But all good things must come to an end and as darkness fell, just as we had ventured back along my new path near the place where we first met, in a blinding flash, he was gone.

The monster that attacked me did not materialise in his place and once again I was alone in this world.

I wept silently knowing that the inevitable had come.

After a while, I left that jungle and stepped through the Flav-sized hole in the bush that I had dived through in a moment of rebellion that seemed like forever ago.

I went home, made my excuses to my mother about how I looked (I know if you've found this you are still reading, Mum so yes, that's why I was a mess that day!) and went upstairs and sat with my arms wrapped around my legs and hugged them as I stared out into the night sky, hoping that one-day Random would come and visit me, that one day I could be with him again, even if it was just for one more afternoon.

Thinking about that day again has led me to a moment of realisation.

That's the thing with important people in your life. Some you can know for years and still not leave as big an impression as those you only catch in a fleeting glimpse.

That's why I am writing this story now. That's why I am sending it out into the stars. I hope it is found. I hope that he finds me again.

I really do.

NIGHT TERRORS

Jake opened his eyes and immediately realised this had been a bad move.

For every time he stirred, the pain began to burn within him. Next time, he would do himself the biggest of favours by staying unconscious for as long as humanly possible. Maybe that way he could avoid the waves of torture he was being subjected to. He stopped, remembering he had tried that before, mere minutes earlier, and then he reminded himself of how that went.

A disembodied laugh echoed all around him. It was a laugh that he knew all too well. A laugh that curdled within his mind and seemed to solidify there, sticking to his memories and haunting his every moment.

Jake shivered. His body may have felt like it was on fire but he was saturated in water.

He sobbed involuntarily which made his evil tormentor laugh even harder. Jake tried to free himself from his bonds for what seemed like the millionth time, hoping to break away at last.

But he never could.

'Stop whimpering, pitiful child!' growled his captor.

Jake screamed even louder for help, which never came no matter how loud he yelled.

The captor laughed again, almost choking on his spit.

'You know what they say,' he whispered, brandishing the electric rod in his hand and raising it to Jake's helpless form.

'In space...no one can hear your dreams...'

As his senses became awash with the blue bolts of lightning, Jake's eyes sprung open.

With a start, he squealed and fell out of bed, landing on the metal floor of his quarters with a dull thud.

'Do they say that?' he panted.

He scrambled against the door and out into the corridor, panting heavily.

As his eyes began to adjust to the darkness, his breathing became more controlled and the calm of the night soothed him back into reality.

Jake took in deep gulps of air, he allowed his eyes to close again. It was just a dream. It was always just a dream.

Suddenly he became aware of how wet his bedclothes were.

He felt his t-shirt and sighed as he discovered it was sopping, clinging to his chest like a second skin.

He picked himself up slowly, moaning to himself and felt out in the dark for his bed, narrowly avoiding the litter of sharp objects that seemed to lie beneath his frame like mines in a minefield.

Crouching down, he felt his duvet and the top sheet of his bed. Feeling the marshy dampness beneath his fingertips, his face contorted in annoyance.

All was quiet aboard the Venus II at this time of night.

Although it was always dark outside the ship as it sailed through the timeless blackness of space, the ship's onboard robot, affectionately named Skateboard by its juvenile crew, had set up a timed environment to help the human members of the ship to find a routine pattern that mirrored the one they were used to back on Earth.

Even the Venus II's pilot had grown used to the sleeping patterns his friends had adopted and was also at this moment fast asleep.

With a hiss, the door to Jake's quarters slid open. The boy's head poked out into the corridor, looking for any signs of life in the area.

After checking that the coast was clear to his left and right, Jake looked through the door leading to the room next to his that belonged to his friend Anji. Relieved that he hadn't woken her up, he proceeded to smuggle his bed sheets up in his arms and rush out into the corridor.

Occasionally tripping up over a corner of loose bedding, he barely made a sound louder than the gentle hum of the ship's engines.

After turning a couple of corners, he finally made it to the mid-section of the Venus II, which consisted of a communal living area, before leading into the cockpit. Upon entering, Jake peered tentatively to check for any signs of life. He was mere metres from his destination – the washing machine.

Hurriedly, he dived for the appliance but somehow managed to knock Random's favourite mug over on the table with his sheets.

Jake froze on the spot as though standing still would somehow make him indistinguishable to the eyes or ears of his sleeping friends. After a few agonising seconds, he continued to the washing machine.

And then, just as he opened the washing machine door, he was discovered.

'What are you doing, sir?'

Jake jumped as the metallic voice seemed to come out of nowhere.

'Skateboard! You frightened the life out of me!' he squealed.

'I can assure you sir that it is beyond my abilities to commit such an atrocity,' the little AI robot said scanning the contents of linen in Jake's arms.

Jake tried to distract his gaze. 'Don't you ever sleep?'

'I do not need sleep, sir,' Skateboard replied.

'Then what do you do to unwind?' he asked, trying to pass the bed sheets behind him and hide them from view.

'There's always a cache to clean out, memories to wipe. There is only so often I can learn all of the lyrics to *ABBA*'s back catalogue. Miss Anji's karaoke nights can be a little repetitive so I like to forget and then relearn the words to give myself something to do. But I'm afraid sir, I have to ask, isn't it a little late to be doing housework?'

'Ah, well,' Jake stuttered trying to find a believable story in his head, 'I missed the last load.'

'And you didn't feel like this could wait until morning?' said Skateboard. Jake looked at him at a loss.

'Fine,' he exploded, throwing his sweaty sheets onto the floor. 'My bed sheets are all wet. I can't sleep in wet sheets, so I thought I'd save myself the embarrassment of waiting until morning when everyone's awake and wash and tumble dry them now before everyone wakes up and takes the mickey out of me!'

'Oh, I see,' said Skateboard. 'But sir, I do not understand, you seem to need your sheets washed on an almost daily basis. I should know. I seem to do the majority of housework on this ship. Is it normal for a teenage boy such as you to need his bed sheets cleaned so frequently?'

'No!' Jake blushed.

'Forgive the rather personal question but have you yet to master our in-built synaptic toilet system?'

'For god's sake, Skateboard I'm thirteen, not three! I am fully capable of going when I need to, not when I don't expect to! Honestly, I am fine.' Jake looked indignantly at his robot friend.

Skateboard fell silent, allowing the teenager time to tell the truth.

Jake sighed in defeat. 'Okay, you've got me. I'm not okay.'

Time passed for both of them. At Skateboard's behest, Jake had made himself a drink and took up a place at the meeting table. Using his hind wheels, the AI robot lifted himself to Jake's level and listened patiently to Jake as they waited for his bed sheets to wash and dry, taking in the horrors that his young friend was currently experiencing. As Jake nursed his cup of hot chocolate, he poured over the details, again and again, not being afraid to let Skateboard see him cry.

'And this is happening every night, you say?' Skateboard asked.

'Yup,' said Jake. 'Without fail. Always the same dream.'

Skateboard's diodes whirred, making a very similar noise to the rattle the washing machine was making in the background.

'I am fairly confident that I know what you appear to be suffering from.'

Jake leaned forward. 'Go on Skateboard.'

'I believe that you are experiencing a severe case of recurring nightmares.'

'Well, that's clear and obvious, but the question is why?' said Jake.

'From what you have described to me, and from your vivid description of the dreams, it sounds like you are still disturbed by what happened aboard the Orbital a few months ago.'

Jake stared off into the middle distance. Of course. That voice. The torture. He had told Anji, not long after they had saved their planet from destruction at his bloody hands, that one day he would want to talk to her about his treatment at the hands of the evil Stratos, but he hadn't been ready. Now his memories were triggering in his mind as he slept...not that he had slept very well since the experience.

'Do you think about it when you are awake?' asked Skateboard.

'What with all the things we get up to daily?' Jake scoffed. 'I barely have the time to scratch my ar...nose...most days.'

'So your trauma is becoming present when you are unwinding then.'

'Wait, do you think I have developed some kind of a disorder?'

'Of the post-traumatic stress kind, yes, sir, but I believe we can help you.'

Jake jumped and put his hand on Skateboard's top. 'No, Skateboard. Please, don't tell the others. Not yet.

I don't want them to think anything bad of me.'

'I'm sure they wouldn't think that. If you were, to be honest with them, sir, I think that you may find them very understanding.'

Jake puffed his cheeks out. 'Soon. Maybe.'

Skateboard found his friend's stubbornness slightly hard to comprehend.

'When Captain Random hid his feelings from you both it nearly destroyed him. I implored him to talk and look what that led to.'

Jake looked away. He knew the events that Skateboard was referring to. It was months ago now but it seemed to all of them like it was yesterday.

He could remember staring up as his friend used a power that wiped out a race of gods and running to be by his friend's side when the energy was ripped out of him.

Unable to cope, his body started to break down as every cell began to die.

It was as he recovered that Random had finally confided in his friend's the inner turmoil he had been suffering.

The voices telling him to go home and face his destiny.

Then came Stratos and his arsenal that wiped out whole planets. Even after he had been vanquished, Jake suspected that Random's conscience was still ripping him in two.

Relenting, Jake sighed. 'Okay, I'll talk.'

Skateboard's diodes whirred. 'In the meantime, let's see if we can do something to help you.'

The washing machine continued to rumble on behind them.

'Like what?' asked Jake.

Moments later, Jake and Skateboard were in the medi-bay. As Skateboard busied himself with the complex computers in the darkened room, Jake lay flat on his back with sticky pads on his temples and his chest. He clenched his fists anxiously.

'Now then, sir.' said Skateboard, 'this should monitor your heart rate and brain activity. Shortly I shall give you a hypodermic dose to a state of deep sleep. When you are under, I shall start the electro-hypnotic process that should allow you to speak to me while you are in your dream. I shall connect myself to the medi-bay computer remotely and when I am integrated with its matrix I should be able to monitor you closely and be able to bring you out of the dream should it all get too much for you. Before we start, do you have any questions?'

'Yeah,' Jake gulped nervously. 'This isn't going to hurt, is it?'

'Not at all,' Skateboard cooed. 'You'll be in a state of deep hypnosis. Just relax.'

'No, I meant the syringe!'

Skateboard looked down at the large needle jutting out of his claw. 'Oh...just a scratch. Are you ready?'

'Um.'

Jake tore his eyes away from the pointy implement and let his head rest back on the bed. 'As I'll ever be.'

Skateboard proceeded to administer the hypodermic. As the drugs entered Jake's bloodstream he sucked his teeth in discomfort.

'Skateboard you liar! That stung like a-'

Before Jake could finish he was under.

Skateboard placed the syringe in a kidney dish on the table next to Jake's bed. His circuitry whizzed and spun.

'Let us begin.'

Jake awoke in a swirl of mist. Feeling the cold dusty floor below him, he sat up, observing the blue haze all around.

'Master Jake,' said an echo that seemed to whisper in the air. 'Can you hear me?'

The teenager was mystified. 'Skateboard?'

'That is correct, it is me.'

Jake waved his hands. 'Where are you?'

'Where you left me. Back on the ship. You are now under my hypnosis. Tell me, where are you?'

Jake pulled himself up and brushing the dust off the palms of his hands, he looked all around him.

'Kinda hard to say.'

'Please try, sir. Concentrate.'

'Uh..I dunno. It's dark. Well, not completely dark. I can see myself and all. Hey!' he patted himself down. 'I'm not wearing my night clothes!'

'That must be a little embarrassing,' said Skateboard.

'I'm wearing clothes you plum, just not what I am wearing in real life!'

'That must be of some relief to you. So what else do you see?'

Jake squinted into the gloom. 'Just a blue mist. Like fog. I can't see past it.'

'Are you moving or are you on the spot?' asked Skateboard.

'Er...' Jake placed a tentative foot in front of the other. 'I can move around. Should I?'

'Yes please.'

Jake twirled around. 'Which way?'

'Whatever way you prefer.'

Slowly, Jake began to walk forward, before turning on his heels and heading in the opposite direction.

'Skateboard?'

Skateboard detected a quiver in his voice. He checked the computer.

'Your heart rate has increased to 120 beats per minute. Are you running?'

'No, I'm just scared. This blue mist seems to be following me. I can't see past it!'

'Try to calm yourself a little, sir.'

Jake began to breathe heavier. 'You're still with me, Skateboard?'

Skateboard observed his friend's life signs.

'Every step of the way, sir. Is there anything else you can sense? Can you hear anything except my voice?'

Jake held his arms outstretched like he was feeling in the dark. 'No.'

'No smells either?'

Jake sniffed the air. 'Yes, I can smell...it's not very strong but it smells like burning.'

In the distance, Jake could make out the shape of a man. He squinted for a better glance.

The man was tall and slender, with what appeared to be a travel bag in one hand and a cigarette in the other, the glow of the tip not enough to expose the man's face from the silhouette.

'Hey!' Jake cried. 'Who are you?'

The mystery man seemed to hear him.

He pulled the cigarette out of his mouth, trod on it when it fell to the floor and threw the travel bag over to Jake before turning his back and disappearing into the shadows.

'Wait! Come back!' Jake rushed towards him but he was gone. He looked at the bag and knew who that mysterious man was instantly.

Suddenly a brilliant flash of light exploded above Jake.

The floor began to shake and Jake cried out as a shockwave knocked him back into the dust.

Skateboard saw his vital readouts climb higher and Jake's body seemed to jerk on the bed.

Back inside his dream, Jake tried to shield himself from the light.

'Jake? Are you okay?'

'Y-yes! It's like...'

Skateboard didn't like the pause.

'...Oh my god!'

As the light began to fade, Jake could make out what he had just witnessed.

Out of the misty gloom, he had just witnessed a planet blow up.

He relayed the information to Skateboard.

'It's terrible. There's nothing but rocks floating all around me now. No sound, nothing.'

Another explosion sent Jake flat on the floor again.

He pressed his face into the dust, crying out in terror as the tasteless particles stuck to his tear-stricken cheeks.

'It's him, isn't it, Skateboard? It's him!'

'Breathe deeply, sir. Take your time.'

'I can see it this time! It's Stratos blowing up those planets. All of those worlds...all of those people...' he sobbed loudly as another distant bang tore through the mist.

Desperately, Jake tried to hide his face from what he was seeing.

One of the small mercies of their battle with Stratos, who had arrived from an alternate dimension with a cybernetic body and a plan to wreak havoc on the cosmos in revenge to

another version of Random was that the crew of the Venus II only saw one planet perish at his hands.

But it was enough to have left a scar on Jake's mind.

One that felt like it was opening up.

All of a sudden, Jake felt the ground beneath him give way.

He seemed to be plummeting deeper and deeper inside his nightmare.

He screamed before the soft sand seemingly broke his fall.

He jolted upward instantly. All was dark around him now except a rectangular beacon of light directly above.

The light still seemed to be blue all around.

'I seem to be in some kind of hole now!' Jake said out loud.

'A hole?' asked Skateboard, who was doing his best to keep up.

Suddenly, a strange outline loomed high above him.

'Oi! Who are you? Let me out of here!' Jake called out. 'Wait...I know you...'

The figure, which looked female in outline with her tentacle-like hair cascading down into the hole, produced a flat-looking implement with a handle.

'It's not a hole, Skateboard...it's a grave!' Jake screamed. He was back on Spectronia, on the night that a twisted archaeologist had buried the terrified boy alive.

'Jake, it's not real, remember, none of this exists. It's all in your mind, sir, you must fight it!' implored Skateboard.

He peered at his friend, who was moving about so much on his bed that the robot began to worry he may do himself physical damage by falling.

Reluctantly, Skateboard activated the restraints, which snaked out of the bed and held down Jake's limbs and head, the strap swiping over his forehead and sealing him in.

Back in the nightmare, Jake felt restricted all of sudden, like he could not move.

Paralysed with fear, he watched helplessly as his tormentor proceeded to tip a hideous amount of sand over him.

Jake cowered against the wall of his tomb and let out a horrible cry but seconds later, the sand that tumbled towards him like a skyscraper about to crush him, began to transform.

Within moments, the sand took the form of a man, a man who continued to fall towards him and whose face Jake knew instantly.

It was the Sandman, a mutated soldier from Random's home planet Rodas who had followed Random and Skateboard to Earth after they had stolen the Venus II from him.

'The Sandman!' Jake shouted, enough to make even Skateboard shudder.

The AI robot had been compromised when flecks of the deranged soldier's sand infiltrated his motherboard and corrupted his systems and he too remembered the horrific atrocities he had been forced to do against his will.

'Fight him Jake!' the robot demanded but it was too late. Jake scrambled again to the foot of his grave and curled into a ball, just as the Sandman's jaw dislocated like a python and seemed to stretch impossibly wide. Skateboard's words began to echo all around him.

With great effort, Jake pulled himself upright and stared at the creature head-on. 'Come on then, think you can hurt me? Think again sandy pants!'

A piercing scream of sheer lunacy screeched from above Jake as the sand crashed down all around him.

'No, you can't get me!' he protested, brushing imaginary sand off himself. Jake's eyes snapped open.

He was alone again. The Sandman had gone. His grave was no more and the debris from the planets in the sky above him had disappeared. Standing once more in the blue mist, his world was silent again.

'What happened?' he asked out loud.

Skateboard was relieved to notice that his vital signs were climbing down once more.

'You fought back, sir. You stood up to your fear.'

Jake placed his hand on his heart. It was still thumping madly in his chest.

'I'm still alive!' he cheered, wiping his eyes as he went.

'Of course you are, sir, remember, none of this is real,' came Skateboard's voice.

Jake fist-punched the air. 'Yeah, like the Sandman thought he could get me. We showed him, didn't we?'

'We did indeed,' replied Skateboard.

'So is that me cured then? Now I've stood up to my nightmares? Can I come out now?'

Silence.

'Skateboard?'

The shapeless voice of his friend had seemingly abandoned Jake.

Back in the land of the living, something had gone wrong with Skateboard's connection to the sleeping boy.

The lights of the medical computer seemed to blink off in unison, plunging the medi-bay into total darkness.

Skateboard also felt the ship's engine grind to a halt under his wheels.

Without hesitation, he searched the ship's mainframe, to which he was wirelessly connected, for an error report.

'Oh my...' he said to himself, before tearing through the doors of the medi-bay, leaving the sleeping, sweat-saturated Jake alone in the dark...

'Skateboard! Come on man!' Jake's throat was beginning to go hoarse but no matter how loudly
he shouted, Skateboard seemed to have disappeared.
Shortly after, he gave up.
Jake stood in the blue mist. He was alone, really alone.
Suddenly it dawned upon him, as the blue mist swirled all around his body, that he was very much still in his nightmare.
Taking a very deep breath, he walked forward, puffing his chest out, he summoned all the bravery he had.
He knew he would face another terror, soon.
But this time, he thought he would be ready for it.
Unfortunately, he wasn't.
With alarming speed, Jake felt like he was pushed by something invisible.
His limbs seemed to be forced outwards. Jake grunted as he was now strung out in a starfish shape on a metal slab.
The boy tried to force his bonds open, wriggling with all his might, but the straps across his wrists and ankles welded him in place.
In the distance, he could make out a streak of what appeared to be lightning.
Mustering his spirit, he confronted his new tormentor. 'If you've got something nasty planned, I've got news for you,' he said, 'because no matter what you've got for me it's nothing I haven't seen before. Nothing I haven't already survived. You on the other hand. You're nothing but dust. Ashes, even. A bad memory. You can't hurt me now.'
A hiss of metal crunched toward him. A hulking form loomed over Jake, who could do nothing but look directly into the face of his enemy.
It was him again. It was his worst memory. Of course, it was. Now he remembered why he was surprised at his clothes when he entered the nightmare. Why a detail so trite was so important. They were the clothes he wore on his worst day.

Terrified, Jake knew where he was. He was back where he always was.

'Stay away from me!' but it was no use. The sadistic, terrifying form of Stratos rose in the mist, a rod of pure electricity brandished in his vice-like fist.

'You can never run from me,' he spat, a fleck of oil falling on Jake's sweaty face.

Jake gulped hard. 'Whose running? Not me. So why don't you just do it, eh? Come on, you seemed to relish torturing me that day, why don't you finish the job this time huh? Put me out of my misery?'

Jake's nightmare version of Stratos appeared to waver a little. His expression changed slightly.

'The hard act doesn't suit you, Jake...hollow words from a hollow creature. I'll change your tune.' He held the torture device up to Jake's face, which was awash with the electric blue fizz of energy threatening from within it.

'Only one person is changing my tune and that's me.' The adrenaline flooded Jake's body as he lent into Stratos' face until he was mere centimetres away.

Suddenly his bonds didn't feel as tight. The terror he had felt before was gone. Jake pushed his forehead against Stratos.

'I'm not afraid of you now, big boy.'

Stratos screamed pure rage in his face.

'YOU HEAR ME?' Jake hollered back. 'READ MY LIPS YOU BIG RUST BUCKET...' he smiled madly

'...I. AM. NOT. AFRAID!!'

Instantly, Stratos and all of the terror lurking in his head sunk away as Jake was pulled back into the real world and he awoke with a startle.

Jake sat up. He looked around. The medi-bay seemed lighter now.

The silence of the nightmare realm he had inhabited was replaced with the gentle hum of the Venus II's engines. Straps that had held him to the bed now lay limply over the bed edges. He breathed deeply. His mind seemed clearer.

'I did it!' he cried in delight. 'Skateboard! Skateboard?'

There came no reply.

He was back in the real world but Jake was still as alone as he had been during the final confrontation in his nightmare.

Sodden with sweat, Jake pulled his lanky sleeves up and started to peel the sticky pads off his body.

He had to find his friends.

Meanwhile, in the mid-section, Skateboard was looking rather sheepishly at Anji as the girl was furiously throwing a mop around her.

Jake entered the room and was relieved to see his friends.

'Anj!' he said delightfully before spotting the lake of water that was sloshing about the mid-section's floor. 'What the hell happened in here?'

Anji threw the mop down in a huff. 'Nice to see that someone got a good night's sleep!'

'It's my fault, miss,' Skateboard said, perched up on the worktop to stay out of the wet. 'The load that was in the washing machine got jammed in the drum and caused a leak which in turn hit a socket in here and tripped the ship's power.'

Jake nodded his head. So that explained why Skateboard had left his dream so suddenly.

'I only got up early to make a cuppa to take back to bed with me, wish I'd stayed in bed now,' she turned to Skateboard. 'I was having a lovely dream as well Skateboard, I mean what were you doing?'

'Actually, Anj, I can explain,' interrupted Jake. 'It worked Skateboard,' he smiled.

Skateboard's diodes whirred. 'I am so glad, sir. So no more wet sheets? Well...' he gestured at the broken washing machine.

'What?' asked Anji.

'Nothing like that!' Jake hastily interjected. 'But...maybe it's time I did talk to you.'

'About what?' she enquired.

'What I said I would one day talk to you about,' Jake replied.

Anji's mind went back to her friend's enigmatic plea for help not long after they had defeated Stratos. 'Oh, sure, can you take it from here for a bit, Skateboard?'

The robot gazed blankly at the swimming pool currently sloshing where the mid-section floor used to be.

'Err..I'm not sure I am fully waterproof, miss,' he lied.

Anji took Jake's arm and led him back to the sleeping quarters.

'Then wake Random up..and tell him we need a new washing machine!'

Sat on Anji's bed, Jake opened up about everything. How he had felt about the horrors of the universe that they had faced together.

How those he had faced alone had plagued his thoughts and stopped him from sleeping at night.

He felt a vulnerability he had never felt before..because he had been so honest about his feelings in the past.

Although he would never want to admit it, it felt good.

Anji held his hand throughout and sat in silence, listening, until he had finished.

She took his head in her hands and kissed him softly on the forehead.

'Jake,' she sighed. 'You really must talk if something is bothering you. You wouldn't have needed to suffer in silence.'

'I know,' he said. 'It's just, you and Random, you seem so strong. Like nothing can hurt you.'

'Don't be silly. I'm terrified most of the time. I mean look at us. Look at what we have been through. If I wasn't affected by the things that had happened to me I wouldn't be human and neither would you. Jake, this is a mad, bad universe. It's brilliant but it's also dangerous. We knew it would be, Random said so, but nothing can ever prepare us for how amazing yet scary it is.

But we can always help each other throughout. No matter what we face, we never have to do it alone.'

Jake smiled at her. He hugged her tightly. Then he said something he meant to think but said out loud.

'I love you,' he whispered into her shoulder.

'Say what?' she cried back.

'Nothing!' he replied sharply, pulling out of the hug like he was about to embrace a venus flytrap.

Anji looked her flushed friend in the face and ruffled his tangled mane of blonde hair playfully.

'It's alright, I heard you, I love you too.'

They both giggled like the school kids that they were. They both meant it.

'I'm lucky to have a best friend like you,' Jake said.

'Me too,' Anji beamed back. 'Just promise me that in the future you will talk and not bottle it all up again.'

'I promise.'

Anji swung her legs off the bed and looked out at the porthole in her room into space. A swirling nebula passed by, interrupting the usual view she saw of the twinkling stars and the blackness of space.

'I mean if it ever gets too much for us, we can always go home?' she said, resting her head on his shoulder.

'Nah, we are home.'

Anji erupted into laughter. 'Oh my god, that was corny.'

'Corny. Me. Never!' he shouted back.

Anji shushed as she tried to hide her giggling. 'Not too loud, Random's still asleep.'

'He can't hear down the corridor.'

'You don't know that. He's got super speed and strength, he's probably got super hearing too!'

Jake went white. 'I hope not. That'd be properly terrifying!'

They both laughed some more before allowing time to be lost in their thoughts again.

'Jake?'

'Hmm.'

'I do have one question.'

'What's that Anj?'

'The man you said you saw…in your dream…who was he?'

Jake's face fell a little. 'I don't know.'

Anji left it at that. There were some things that she understood should stay private. She had an idea who he was, but there was no need to go further. Jake's reluctance to answer confirmed his identity to her anyway and she knew it was right to say no more.

Jake put his arm around his best friend.

Anji snuggled up to him, not minding that he was still a little sweaty. She'd let that slide on this occasion.

'No more nightmares,' Jake said defiantly. 'No more night terrors.'

UNUSUAL SUSPECTS

SPACE POLICE INTERNAL MAINFRAME

..PERSONAL LOG INITIALISING...

..PLEASE ENTER YOUR LOG-IN NAME...

..SUPERINTENDENT DAYLISH RAWKSBEE...

..REGISTRATION CODE ADDITIONAL 576314B...

..PLEASE ENTER YOUR PASSWORD...

...

..PA55W0RD...

..LOG IN SUCCESSFUL...

INCIDENT FILE RECORDS

THE SOLON FACTOR

..LOG UPDATE...

On the forty-ninth day of the month, Thoros of Zen, at approximately thirty-nine past the trib, I was called to an incident that had taken place in the bowels of the central Diamos bank.

Myself and my colleague, Officer Amstaff, proceeded on foot as we were by the location in question and upon entering the main doors of the bank we found to our utter astonishment that all living creatures within had been rendered unconscious with some kind of gas.

It would appear that a worker had pressed a security alarm before succumbing to the plumes of purple smoke that had filled the room.

Luckily, Amstaff and I were prepared and after fixing our masks and whilst she checked up on the dozens of sleeping bankers, I went in search of the main safe and, I hoped, the perpetrators.

After a few minutes of struggling to see through the smoke, I felt my way along a long and narrow corridor, where the smoke, which I could now make out was cascading out of the air vents, was not as dense as it had been in the main reception.

As I made my way closer to the main safe, I started to hear voices. Readying my gun, I strained to listen to what they might be arguing about.

Although I was confused by what I could make out were incoherent rantings, it was quickly apparent that there were four of them.

Before long I was practically on top of them, standing in the doorway of what should have been a heavily guarded entrance to the main vault.

But all of the security checks, every heavily bolted door, guarded checkpoints, had an unconscious guard slumped in a heap on the floor.

I checked the pulse of one and was relieved that they were still alive, and although the reasoning as to why the bank had been attacked was unknown, who carried out the attack was very apparent indeed.

I backed against the wall and cocked my gun, setting it to stun. I widened the bandwidth of the weapon, knowing now for certain that with or without Amstaff I would be outnumbered.

And then, without warning, I jumped through the door and ordered them to drop their weapons and put their hands up. You see, I didn't want to fire upon them straight away.

What if they had something of value on their person and it got damaged?

They were found in the main vault after all...and considering the valuables stored in that vault, I used my initiative to work out just what they were doing in there.

In my experience, the kind of people who break into the planet's biggest bank this side of Diamos are organised, ruthless, violent individuals. Dangerous crooks, hell-bent on obtaining the biggest collection of weapons of mass destruction in the cosmos, and who will do anything, and kill anyone, to get them within their clutches. So, imagine my surprise when there, through the smoke, stood three very surprised-looking children and a flat metal robot. I was almost as surprised as they were! But then I noticed what the purple-skinned one had in his arms. It was a golden, glowing box that illuminated through the dispersing smoke.

It was the Solon Factor.

They were trying to steal the Solon Factor!

I demanded that he placed it on the ground in front of him.

The boy, who was the ringleader, did so hesitantly, all the time telling me that they could explain and that the Solon Factor was dangerous.

I mean, every idiot on Diamos knows that!

With the motley crew now unarmed, I delayed no further.

As they protested, I blasted them with my pistol, the blast knocking all of them unconscious.

Even the robot seemed to stop moving, his circuits having been affected by the blast.

At that moment, Amstaff caught up with me and alerted me to the fact that backup was now on its way. I checked that the Solon Factor hadn't come to any harm.

Luckily, it wasn't active. I breathed a huge sigh of relief. We proceeded to approach the assailants to cuff them and as the smoke began to clear, people began gingerly waking up and proceeded to take them in.

Upon placing the assailants into custody, we began to carry out background checks on them individually whilst we waited for them to regain consciousness. However, upon logging into the mainframe, and as the eyewitness accounts began to trickle in, it soon became clear that they were not native to Diamos...

What follows are the transcripts of the audio files given to me by Amstaff, who alongside me conducted the interviews.

The young girl, the only female in their gang, was the first to come around and so, faced our interrogation first. Disorientated and confused, I hoped to use her current state against her to obtain my answers.

INTERVIEW#1

ME: Name?

SUSPECT 1: Anji, Anji Gummadi.

ME: Miss Gummadi, you have been arrested on suspicion of attempted armed robbery, assault and use of a weapon of mass destruction. You do not have to say anything...but we would love it if you told us why?

SUSPECT 1: Hold on, I'm arrested! *THE SUSPECT TRIES TO FORCE OPEN THE CUFFS BONDING HER TO THE DESK* I thought these were for my safety. God, I must have been drugged, I feel so...hold on, you've got to let me out, you are making a terrible mistake!

ME: I'm sorry, little lady, no can do.

SUSPECT 1: Listen, pal, I'm not little and if I could get out of these cuffs I'll show you I'm not much of a lady either!

ME: I wouldn't recommend threatening a police officer, not on top of your current record.

SUSPECT 1: But you don't understand, you've got to let me go!

ME: You're not going anywhere until you've answered my questions. Now, why were you and your friends trying to steal the Solon Factor?

SUSPECT 1: We weren't trying to steal it!

ME: Oh, what were you planning to do then exactly? Borrow it?

THE SUSPECT FELL SILENT BEFORE RESUMING

SUSPECT 1: Look, officer, I know it looks bad, but believe me, I'm trying to do you all a favour!

ME: If that is so, then why did you assault and apprehend all those people inside the bank?

SUSPECT 1: I didn't.

ME: Was it one of your accomplices who did that then?

SUSPECT 1: Probably. I didn't know they were also going to be there.

I PRODUCED A FILE

SUSPECT 1: What's that?

Me: You'll see.

I OPEN THE FILE

ME: For the record, I am showing the suspect CCTV images of her and her colleagues breaking into the bank. As you can see here, your friends appear to be working the front as it were, while

in this one, you sneak in through the air ducts and are seen to
abseil down inside the vault.

SUSPECT 1: I had no idea they had been recruited too.

ME: So, you were all recruited.

THERE IS A LONG PAUSE

SUSPECT 1: It's not all there, in my memory. Please, just let me
go. You don't know what danger you are in!

ME: Officer Amstaff, take her back to her cell. Let's see if one of
her friends has woken up. Interview terminated at 41:92.

INTERVIEW TERMINATED.

INTERVIEW #2

ME: Interview conducted with Superintendent Rawksbee,
speaking and Officer Amstaff in attendance. Name?

SUSPECT 2: Skateboard, sir.

ME: That's a funny name for a robot.

SUSPECT 2: Would Clive suit better, sir?

ME: Don't get smart with me, robot. Now I want some answers
and I want them now. Why were you trying to steal the Solon
Factor?

SUSPECT 2: I wasn't, sir.

ME: Really, that's a coincidence. Neither was your friend and like her, you were found to be breaking an entry and assaulting members of the public in the process.

SUSPECT 2: That isn't what happened. I thought I was alone.

ME: We have CCTV footage of you entering the bank through the maintenance doors and proceeding to tamper with one of the air ducts.
What were you doing?

SUSPECT 2: I was installing an infusion that was to temporarily render the inhabitants of the bank unconscious.

ME: So that you and your friends could break in and take the Solon Factor!

SUSPECT 2: No.

ME: You are a robot, no doubt with hacking capabilities. Is that how you broke into the bank and if so, why didn't you turn off the security cameras?

SUSPECT 2: I thought I had. I admit I have a bit of a blind spot when it comes to Diamos technology.

ME: And you could have gassed your friends in the vault.

SUSPECT 2: As I said, sir, I had no idea she was there. We must have been recruited separately.

ME: By who? Who wants the Solon Factor?

SUSPECT 2: I wish I knew, sir. It would get us out of this terrible mix-up.

ME: Stop speaking in riddles robot and answer my questions!

SUSPECT 2: Sir, shouting will do you no good.

ME: If you fail to cooperate, we have another way of finding out the truth...

SUSPECT 2: Sir, if you mean to threaten me with torture then might I evoke the universal rights of...

ME: You may not because we would never be as callous to use torture...despite how tempted I am! Amstaff, take Mr..Skateboard to have his memory files checked. If anyone will tell us why the Solon Factor was almost stolen, it'll be him.

INTERVIEW TERMINATED.

At this point, I was asked away from the interview room to join forensics who had just come back from the bank with an interesting new development.

I was astonished to learn that there had been a fifth person caught on camera lurking outside the building roughly ten minutes before the assailants turned up.

Cloaked, with their features cleverly hidden, they had entered the building to use the depositing system and left fingerprints on the digital keyboard before proceeding to wait outside once again for a while and upon the arrival of the purple-skinned suspect, had abruptly left.

When my team was asked to check the keyboard, which hadn't the time to be used since the attack, it was found that a residue was left on the keys.

I asked the team to analyse it to try and work out the keys that had been punched in by our mystery figure. Meanwhile, I decided to pass the time by interviewing a third member of my most unusual suspects. Surely this next one would be easier to get something out of...

INTERVIEW #3

ME: Interview conducted by Superintendent Rawksbee on the…

SUSPECT 3: What are you talking to?

ME: Excuse me?

SUSPECT 3: You just seem to be chatting to nothing. It looks a bit weird.
ME: Please will you refrain from interrupting my…

SUSPECT 3: Or what? You'll arrest me.

ME: Fine! Have it your way. Let's get on with it. Name, please.

SUSPECT 3: Jake.

ME: Last name?

SUSPECT 3: No, first actually.

ME: I didn't mean it like…ugh…fine. Tell me, Jake, what were you and your friends doing trying to steal the Solon Factor from the Diamos Bank?

SUSPECT 3: We weren't trying to steal it. To tell you the truth, I had no idea my mates were involved. We landed yesterday and thought we'd check the planet out. Next thing I know, this weird alien thing, if you pardon the expression, comes up to me in a bar and tells me that he needs my help. Well, you could say my friends and I are in the business of helping when asked, so I wondered what he wanted. The next thing I know…I am in that bank you're talking about, knowing I need to obtain this Solon Factor thing of yours. Armed with a gun!
ME: And you don't remember anything in between?

SUSPECT 3: Nope.

ME: Were you being controlled?

SUSPECT 3: Must have been. I haven't broken into a bank before. To tell you the truth I don't know why I was after this...Solon Factor...thing of yours, all I knew was that there was a good reason I was there.

ME: So you admit to breaking into the bank and threatening the staff with a firearm?

SUSPECT 3: Oh no, I didn't have time! All of a sudden there was this gas-like stuff that engulfed everyone and they all fell to the floor. Not me, though. Must have a strong constitution!

ME: Or because you are an alien, it didn't affect you...

SUSPECT 3: ...No, I prefer my version.

INTERVIEW DOOR OPENS

ME: Interview paused.

At this point, I was led out of the room by an officer from forensics who implored me into the lab. They had made a breakthrough in the case.

He proceeded to explain to me that the residue on the keypad in the bank was Vervovan slime. In context to any officers reading this who are unaware as to what Vervovan slime is, I shall explain. It is a substance that is secreted through touch that can infiltrate the nervous system and influence the actions of others through psychic thought.

Suddenly, the dots were starting to join up. The reason why all three suspects had given me conflicting and confusing accounts so far was that they had clearly been influenced, even the robot, whose files must have been corrupted to be manipulated so easily.

But Vervovan slime is a potent compound. Used by one and one only.

The Voss.

The most dangerous terrorist on Diamos. My blood ran cold. If The Voss was loose and after the Solon Factor then we were all in danger!

I had to know more. I instructed Officer Amstaff to send a SWAT team to the bank and alerted all units to track down The Voss. The Solon Factor had to be protected at all costs.

And while all my team went to battle stations, there was one more person I needed to speak to...

INTERVIEW #4

ME: Interview commencing at 52:89, Superintendent Rawksbee in attendance. Name, please.

SUSPECT 4: ...

ME: That's the part where you answer my question.

SUSPECT 4: Not until you listen to me...

ME: You're not in any position to demand anything from me, but I would love to hear what you've got to say.

SUSPECT 4: Then you will not be getting any answers from me. Believe me, I wouldn't be that stubborn if I were you. You have little time to listen to me as it is.

ME: Is that a threat? Your friends are all in custody for the attempted theft of a very dangerous weapon kept safe in a secure bank...but we are not so sure that they acted knowingly.

SUSPECT 4: That's putting it mildly.

ME: Then how would you put it?

SUSPECT 4: Superintendent, I had no recollection of why I was in that bank vault. None whatsoever. But while you've been wasting my friend's time with your questioning, my memory has been repairing. I remember the reason why the Solon Factor was so needed, and the clock is ticking.

ME: Then why don't you tell me?

SUSPECT 4: Because you have my innocent friends banged up like criminals and the longer you waste time interrogating me, the more danger we are all in.

ME: So, were you acting knowingly? Did you drug them?

SUSPECT 4: What? No!

ME: Are you in league with The Voss?
SUSPECT 4: If by The Voss you mean the creep who we met yesterday, then no, I wasn't.

ME: Good...your stories are starting to melt together. Okay, Mr-

SUSPECT 4: -Captain. Captain Random to you.

ME: Fine, Captain Random, tell me everything you remember.

SUSPECT 4: Fine, I'll play it your way... I'll be quick so keep up. I remember going into the bank when the smoke was billowing, not knowing why or how I got there but knowing I had to get inside the vault. So, I proceeded to the vault, finding all the

guards slumped on the floor and the security gates open. And
then when I got to the vault, I knew exactly what to find, which I
suppose can be explained by this Voss person. I could feel a
whisper in my head, telling me what to find and what it did.
Somehow, I was drawn to this golden box-like object and upon
picking it up, was surprised to find my friend dangling from the
ceiling like an unprofessional cat burglar, my robot friend
wheeling into the room and finally my other friend brandishing a
gun at my head!

So, we started to row, not knowing why we were all there and I
could feel the spell starting to break with all four of us in the
room.

Then in all the confusion, you turned up and shot us just before
I could warn you.

ME: Warn me, about what?

SUSPECT 4: Why we were taking the Solon Factor.

ME: Well, go on then, Captain Random, enlighten me.

SUSPECT 4: The Solon Factor had been tampered with. I don't
know how, but with a touch of a Diamosian it is rigged to start a
countdown-

INTERVIEW PAUSED.

Now, at this point, I must confess to you reading this that I was
terrified by what this strange alien had told me.

The Voss, a known terrorist on this planet, had somehow come
into contact with the Solon Factor in the past and rigged it to
explode.

Possibly as a bargaining chip, we thought after the event, for his
freedom and a promise of anonymity.

Although The Voss has proved hard to catch, what with his known repertoire of mind control through the strange substance he secretes, our guys and gals at the lab have been getting better at finding him and the net was closing in.

But on this occasion, this was not so.

Before it was a genuine mistake made by The Voss when we discovered later, that he had controlled the Head of Weaponry in the Diamosian Army and left a biometric print on the bomb when it was installed in the vault just days before this incident.

So, it turned out that he needed to repeat the whole trick and this time on four alien visitors to the planet, who could easily be blamed and mistaken as the people who stole it.

After all, they would be caught red-handed, what with The Voss leaving the CCTV running and instructing the robot named Skateboard to not turn it off.

But in using the deposit machine himself, and forensic confirming that he had used the keypad to check that it hadn't been touched with the Head of Weaponry's code, he had given himself away.

But now, time was not on our side...

INTERVIEW TAPE RESUMED

SUSPECT 4: Superintendent, I don't have the time! None of us do. You need to stop with this red tape and listen to me! If one of your officers touches the Solon Factor it'll explode!

INTERVIEW TERMINATED

Okay, so that's a bit of a cliffhanger, I'll admit, but at this point, the audio ceased as I made headway to inform my SWAT team not to touch the Solon Factor under any circumstance. Random begged me to release him, squawking about his super speed or something, but I told him it was no use.

You see, I had just remembered. I had checked to see if the Solon Factor was damaged after I had stunned Random and his friends.

I had set the bomb off.

No matter what we did, it was going to blow.

He pleaded with me, telling me that he had a ship nearby. He could take it on board and eject it into space but we had to let him go.

What could I do? I knew no matter what there was little chance of saving the planet now. The Solon Factor was activated and Diamos was on a

countdown to destruction.

So, I relented. I freed him of his bonds and in a flash of purple light, Captain Random vacated the room.

I was soon to learn that he had vacated the police station altogether, just like that!

I ran to the office, ordered my SWAT team to evacuate the area, warned them of hostility towards the suspect and allowed Random into the bank once more.

The worst thing about the whole incident was that I did not know how long we had. No-one did. At any second the planet could be torn apart.

I watched on the surveillance monitors alone in the office, my team in the thick of it, as the same flash of purple I saw vacate the interview room burst into the bank and then like a shot burst out again.

And then there was nothing. Every precious second felt like a stay of execution.

Suddenly, the silence of my office was broken by an incredible explosion overhead which blew all the windows and glass into little pieces. I shielded myself from the blast until the sound of the blast was replaced by distant alarms and people screaming.

Then I hurried to the space where my office wall had once been.

Peering high above me, I saw the tremendous aftermath of a horrendous explosion that seemed to have happened miles above our world.

He had done it. Random had saved us.

But what about the strange purple boy himself? Had he made it?

I am happy to report that moments later, a ship landed in the police car park and from a platform that descended from its belly came the form of Random.

I rushed out to greet him, just as another officer, who was oblivious as to what was going on, was trying to give him a parking ticket.

Although he was soaked with sweat and heaving from exertion, he proceeded to pat me on the shoulder and asked if he could have his friends back now.

Whilst the cleaning robots were understandably miffed about the amount of work they now had to do in the place, and the papers blew around the office where the glass windows and walls had once been, our forensics team confirmed with samples taken from the suspects, Random included who gladly agreed to the samples as they all did in exchange for their freedom, that there were indeed traces of Vervovan slime in their system.

The robot ran a diagnostic on himself and confirmed it also. His memory files checked out too.

The effects of which had started to wear off, clearly not so much when I interviewed the girl, but sufficiently with the others and they were all

clear to go, they were lucky that being aliens from another world the slime wasn't deadly or longer lasting!

And so, it was proven that the four aliens were innocent. Their part in the heist was over. And with that, the blonde-haired boy told us he would give Diamos a one-star review on Planet Advisor, something I must confess I have never heard of, and they entered their ship and sailed off into the sky.

Sadly, I was unable to obtain any more information about them, something I regret to this day.

Leaving me to explain the incident to the authorities and news stations that were demanding answers for a terrifying world, I straightened myself up and told them that the Solon Factor had been activated but that the threat had been dealt with.

If only that were completely true.

You see, The Voss evaded us and is still out there...

INCIDENT FILE RECORDS CLOSED.

THE HOSTS

The icy chill and snow bit at Anji's neck as she pulled her bobble hat further down in a vain attempt to keep out the cold.

The wind continued to swirl around her, blowing tiny shards of snow into her eyes and nose, she coughed as she picked her laser gun up from her side and trudged on after her friends, who were unaware that she was lagging behind. The sound of the wind snapped and whipped all around them as they struggled towards their destination.

Jake turned back and called out for Anji to catch them up, although he thought it was unlikely that she could hear him. The wind and snow were appalling, like the worst snowstorm Britain had to offer but ten times over.

'What a place to break down!' he muttered to no one in particular.

Random heard it alright but chose to ignore it.

'Never mind that, why did we park so far away?' cried Anji, who could just about hear her friends after all.

'Because you don't park when you break down,' replied Random. 'Besides, we shouldn't be here long... I hope.' He whispered the final part of that sentence to himself.

It had all been going so smoothly. Since Anji was now as efficient at piloting the Venus II as the others, it had taken quite a lot of pressure off Random to be manning the wheel as often as he had been.

Although Skateboard was completely able to pilot the ship at all times, the crew had made a collective decision to be as qualified as each other in the case of one of them getting lost or kidnapped.

Considering how frequently the inhabitants of the Venus II found themselves in trouble, it wasn't a bad contingency plan to have in place!

Nonetheless, when Random climbed into the pilot's seat, little did he realise that within a few minutes he and the rest of the

---

Venus II would be plummeting nose-first towards an ice moon. Nor did he bank upon the rather fortuitous crash site being within walking distance of another ship that had also appeared to have suffered more than just a bumpy landing. He did click his tongue in frustration, however, when due to the damage report machine ironically becoming damaged and the weather conditions interfering with the Venus II's long-range scanners – and Skateboards – that they were left with no alternative but to go outside.

And so, armed with the laser guns the crew had acquired from a previous adventure in the mines of Genocia, they ventured out into the cold.

Using Skateboard's short-range scans as a compass, Random, Anji and Jake stumbled their way across the tundra.

'Any sight of it yet?' called Anji to Random, who was several metres ahead of her.

'Nothing,' spat Random as a volley of snow blew into his mouth.

'I can't see a thing!' cried Jake.

The landscape was nothing but a brilliant white. All of them, even Skateboard with his electronic circuitry were struggling to see.

'How far now, Skateboard?' Anji shouted, not knowing if her question had even reached her friend as the horrid wind carried her words right back at her.

'About twenty metres, miss,' came the response.

'We need to be careful that we don't lose the Venus II,' said Random.

'Don't worry about that, sir. As I am linked to our ship I can home in on it.'

'Well, let's hope you really are waterproof then and don't short circuit!' Anji tutted.

The travellers soldiered bravely on. Twenty metres in such harsh conditions might as well have been twenty miles for what they were concerned but eventually, the black outline of a huge octopus-shaped vessel honed into view.

'Blimey! I wonder what could have brought that thing down?' asked Jake.

'I'm sure we'll find out soon enough,' replied Random. 'Skateboard, can you locate a way in?'

The little robot's diodes whirred. 'Yes, sir. There's an airlock roughly forty paces to the left.' He whizzed off, somehow managing to stop himself from skidding on the ice as the others followed.

Anji groaned. 'Well let's hurry up before my legs freeze!'

'You should have worn something more appropriate,' chuckled Jake.

'Actually, you won't be able to notice in all this snow, but since I didn't have much in the winter department of my wardrobe I decided to borrow your combat trousers. Besides, it's better than what you've got on.' Anji thrust the laser gun over her shoulder and pointed to his attire.

Jake held his arms out wide. 'What's wrong with them?'

Anji smiled. 'They're mine!'

Jake's face fell.

'I must have mixed up the wash last night,' he sulked as they neared the entrance.

'They look rather good on you. I'm surprised you're not cold yourself,' said Anji.

'Not now I am burning with embarrassment,' he replied.

The travellers came to a sudden stop. The exterior of the vessel was caked in ice.

Random went to work scrapping the ice and snow off what to him looked like an entrance panel.

'It's no use. The ice must be inches thick!' said he.

'Come on mate, I've seen you punch through walls. Surely a bit of ice isn't going to defeat you?' said Jake.

'For all we know, Jake, this ship isn't hostile. I don't want to go punching a hole through their wall and then asking them for spare parts now do I? What kind of guests would that make us? Skateboard, can you override the entrance code?'

The little robot scanned the panel. 'Negative, sir. It doesn't seem to be operational.'

Random drew himself up. 'It's a good thing we brought the lasers then. Anj, you take one side of the door and I'll take the other. We'll cut our way in.'

'But what about that "bad guest" malarkey?' asked Jake.

'Well, it's that or freeze to death,' said Random curtly.

Random and Anji stood on either side of the door frame and on Random's mark, fired up the laser guns. The heat from the laser beam was enough to melt the build-up of ice forming on Skateboard's body and before long, the metal seams that held the airlock door firmly in place melted and buckled.

They turned the laser guns off and turned to their friends.

'Ladies first,' Anji gestured with a mischievous grin on her lips.

Jake's eyes narrowed. 'Funny, I don't remember ever putting those trousers in the wash...'

Suddenly, Anji looked alarmed as Jake's smug little face pushed past her and inside the airlock.

'Make sure you wipe your feet, Anj,' he called back.

As the friends entered the ship one by one, Anji looked down at herself and started to walk like a crab and followed them.

Having blasted through the other airlock door just metres away from the outside one, the travellers were standing at the bottom of a dark and hollow gantry.

'Skateboard, see if you can get the electrics working,' said Random looking up into the murky black. 'We'd better step away from here, it's a bit drafty...'

The robot switched on his local sensors and made off into the dark. He turned on his night vision and shone a torch, which was built into the front of his bodywork, to help the others see.

They walked a little further inside the spaceship not wanting to take their woolly hats and gloves off.

Anji rubbed her arms. 'It feels colder in here than it does out there somehow!'

'What is this place?' asked Jake. 'Where is everyone?'

'No idea. But you saw how thick the ice was outside on the airlock door. I think this thing has been here for a very, very long time...' Random said, an echo reverberating around the room.

'Either that or the snow out there is worse than we imagined!' Anji said with dread.

'Worse?' asked Jake.

Random shone a light from a tiny torch in his coat pocket. Following the light, he observed his surroundings. Rows of tables lay broken, overturned in the dirt, and shining his torch upward, he could make out an abundance of flecks of dust hanging in the air. Then he noticed the bars, rows upon rows of cages yawning down the corridor before him.

Just as it began to dawn on him what this ship might be, he heard a scream.

In a heartbeat, Random pelted towards the cry, a shrieking, high-pitched noise that he had not heard before.

He stopped when he saw Anji and Jake holding one another.

'What's the matter?' he said to Anji.

'Him not me!' she cried back. Jake's eyes were unable to look away, entranced by the terror of what lay in front of them.

There, lying backward over a broken chair, was the body of a man. A petrified, rotting corpse, his flesh looking like it had been eaten away in patches.

'Step away, both of you!' Random demanded and Anji did her best to pull Jake out of the way. He crouched down and used the butt of his laser gun to prod the corpse.

'Yep, he's dead alright,' he declared.

'We know that, what killed him?' replied Anji.

'No idea. Look at his skin...'

'I'd rather not,' said Jake retching. 'I think I'm going to be sick!'

Jake peeled himself away from Anji and went to sit down on one of the benches as Anji crouched beside Random.

'Could he have been bitten by something?'

'I don't know. We'd better keep our distance though.'

Anji got up and looked around. She produced a similar torch to Random's from her pocket and shone it along the walls.

'There's more,' she declared, starting to feel a little sick herself. It was as though the putrid smell of rotting flesh had only hit their nostrils upon discovering the bodies; the stench had been hiding in the dark.

'Oh god!' said Jake, before puking loudly.

'They are all wearing the same uniform,' Anji said, holding her sleeve up to cover her nose.

Random made for a communicator that dangled on a lanyard around his neck.

'Skateboard are you picking up my frequency?'

The communicator popped and Skateboard's reassuring tones bled through.

'Loud and clear, sir. I've found the bridge, just currently working on getting the power switched back on.'

'Skateboard we've found dead bodies in here,' he counted with his torch as he spoke, 'roughly two dozen. It looks like they all went the same way. They are missing chunks of flesh... are we in danger here?'

'Not now, I don't think sir. But you'd better join me up here. I'll direct you from your current location. Just switching the lights back on now.'

With that, a shock of life buzzed around the walls for the first time in what could have been years and suddenly, Random, Anji and Jake knew where they were.

'Oh great...' said Jake, wiping his mouth with his arm, 'we're on a prison ship!'

Soon after, the travellers were all together again on the bridge of the abandoned vessel. For such a large ship, the bridge was tight and pokey and the banks of computers and instruments looked either
burnt out or lay in pieces on the floor.

There were more bodies in there too, much to Anji and Jake's displeasure.

'Are you sure we can't stand somewhere else?' said Anji, her words muffled through her sleeve.

'The whole ship appears to be like it,' said Random. 'Can you get the black box working Skateboard?'

'The entire ship has been in the ice for decades in my estimation, sir. It's going to take a while to boot the whole system back up again.'

'What do you think could have done something like this?' asked Anji.

'Cannibals!' replied Jake. 'Mutant space cannibals. You saw the skin on those guys. They had more holes in them than a tennis racket!'

'At least if what you say is true, Skateboard, and what you are guessing Jake is true, then whatever caused it should be dead now,' said Random calmly.

'How do we know that though, we could have an alien on our hands who lives in the ice and eats people!' said Anji.

'But how could it have got in?' asked Random. 'You saw the struggle we had. Whatever caused the crew and inmates to die must have resulted in the crash.'

'That's a sound prediction, sir,' said Skateboard.

'I prefer mine,' said Jake, 'now seriously, can we at least cover the bodies or something? This little meeting is giving me the creeps!'

'I'm with you on that,' said Random. 'Right, Skateboard, what are we looking for here exactly?'

'The Venus II crashed due to a break in the stablilisers that keep the ship afloat when in flight. From a quick examination of the internal computer system, I've managed to conclude that the prison ship does indeed have the component we would require to take off and stay stable. However, I am not sure where the component might be. Due to the expansive nature of the prison ship, there are two drive rooms and the stabiliser circuit we need will be in one of them.'

'So, what you're saying is that we need to split up and find this circuit?' asked Anji.

'Precisely. I'll demonstrate what we are looking for imminently. We will need to cut our way into the drive plate, which I shall also highlight to you all.'

'But we don't know what we are dealing with here!' said Jake.

'Maybe not, but if we all know where we are going then we can be out of here before we need to find out,' replied Random.

'Fine... I'll just try and ignore the scores of dead bodies lying around the place, shall I? Or maybe walk around with my eyes closed and let someone shout left and right so I don't trip over a dead man!?'

'Yes, if it helps,' said Random who smiled as the sarcasm in Jake's voice was completely lost on him.

Anji took his arm. 'Come on, mate. We can get through this. In ten minutes, we'll be back on board the Venus II sipping hot chocolate and...'

'...Booking in next month's therapy sessions?' Jake interrupted. Random patted his friend on the back. 'That's the spirit!'

Jake fired a withering look in Anji's direction.

'He doesn't get me, does he?'

Anji silently agreed and they all huddled around Skateboard as he began his demonstration. Little did they know that behind them, as the ship's computer systems slowly booted back up again, the temperature dial on the thermostat started to flicker...

A little while later, Anji and Jake were alone, the latter carrying a crudely drawn map of their destination that seemed to jangle in a non-existent breeze.

Anji had noticed her friend's pensive look. 'Are you that cold?'

'It's not the cold, it's this place, it's the corpses. It gives me the creeps!'

'You and me both, how much longer to the drive room?'

Jake inspected the map. Now that the lights were back on it had made their journey much easier, but he dare not look at anything but Anji and the piece of paper in his hands.

If anything, the lighting had made this place much, much worse.

'A few corridors left to go... any chance we can swap?' he asked, gesturing to Anji's laser gun.

'Not a chance,' she retorted. Jake gulped.

The duo continued their descent, unaware that one of the bodies that they had passed twitched slightly. As they walked on, another body close by seemed to twitch a little too. Slowly, their eyes blinked open.

Meanwhile, on the other side of the ship, Random and Skateboard were also making their way gingerly toward the opposite drive room.

'To think I thought I could have a quiet afternoon...' Random cursed, laser gun ready and primed.

'I can assure you, sir, that there is no need for that,' Skateboard reassured him calmly.

'Well, it makes me feel a little safer.' He adjusted his scarf. His skin was starting to feel clammy. 'Is it getting hotter in here?'

'Yes sir. Now that I have powered up the generators the ship is starting to wake up. Any minute now the main computer should be back online.'

'If the main computer is booting back up then why do we need to cut the stabilizers out of their housing?'

'This ship has been here for many years, sir. We are dealing with antiquated technology that has been lying forgotten on an ice moon. I doubt even if the main computer comes back online that the instruments on board will work.'

'Fair point... wait!'

Random cocked the laser gun. Something up ahead had caught his gaze.

'What's the matter, sir?'

'I saw something, up ahead!'

'It's your mind playing tricks. We are quite alone.'

'It was a shadow!'

'I can assure you, sir, it's your mind playing tricks.'

Random relaxed a little. 'Come on, let's get this component and get out of this morgue.'

Skateboard's diodes made a humming noise. 'Wait a moment sir. My sensors indicate that the main computer is online.' The little robot whirred off back in the direction they came from.

'Hold up buddy!' cried Random. 'You're going the wrong way!'

Random followed him to an office nearby. Skateboard was already working on the information port. He scrunched his face up. Yet another room with bodies inside it.

'Skateboard what are you doing, let's get going!'

'Do you not want to know what happened here?'

'Yes, of course, but can't we do that after we've got what we needed?'

'This won't take long, sir. I'll punch it through the loudspeaker.'

'Punch what through?'

'The last black box entry.'

Random looked at the monitor on the wall and watched it blink into life. The picture and sound quality were awful.

The snowstorm outside was nothing compared to the fuzzy reception on the old video. Random squinted and made out a bald middle-aged man peering desperately back at him from the past, carnage all around him.

'This is Chief Russell Parkley, relaying a distress call on behalf of Captain Tardelli of the SS Argonian...'

Random quickly made for his communicator. 'Anj, Jake you're going to want to hear this...'

The video continued. 'We contracted something on our last pick-up that seems to have spread to both prisoners and staff on board. Our vessel has been badly damaged as we fought to contain the spread and our engines are failing...'

A loud explosion and screams washed out the screen and audio for a few seconds.

'...I am relaying the mayday. We are going down! But the bridge has been overrun and there's no way to the escape pods without running into the

infected. Our situation is now critical. Do not come and find us. I repeat do not come and f-'

The screen went blank.

'Er...guys...did you get that?' Random stared at the monitor.

'Every word,' came the reply from Jake.

'How long ago was that message recorded, Skateboard?' asked Random.

'Nearly 24 years ago,' came the response from Skateboard.

'Surely anything that infected this ship back then is gone now?' asked Anji.

'Oh, you think?!' came a panic-stricken Jake.

Anji turned to face him and screamed.

'Anj!' Random frowned. 'Come on Skateboard!'

As Random and Skateboard tore away from the office they ran headfirst into a corridor of utter terror.

The corpses of the dead were alive... and heading straight for them!

PART TWO

Anji and Jake ran as fast as their legs could go. Neither dared look back even though they could hear what sounded like a swarm of hornets tearing after them. Both were trying to breathe through their screams. As the dead gathered apace it was hard to keep ahead of the wave of death that followed the two teenagers. Suddenly, Anji spotted a little alcove and dived for it, pulling Jake along with her. They managed to find a tiny room and slammed the door shut before sinking to the floor. Both of them gasped for air.

Jake wiped his face and dared to peer through the grill at the bottom of the door. His sweaty face turned white.

The dead bodies of the prison inmates and uniformed officers, which were rotting and diseased, were scratching against the walls and doors in the corridor, each one emitting a horrible blood-curdling noise that chilled the travellers to their core.

Anji reached for her communicator. 'Random, do you read me?'

Jake swiped it out of her hand. 'Hey! They'll hear you!'

Anji sighed and continued to drink in the air.

'Wait a minute. The video said there was an infection. Do you reckon it could be airborne?'

Jake panicked. 'Oh my god, could we be infected already?'

Anji pulled her scarf up over her nose and mouth. 'Well, I'm not taking any chances!'

Jake followed suit and then looked around at his surroundings. There were no exits... and the room seemed a little colder than the corridor had been. It was still a pig sty, piles of rubbish lay everywhere. Then, he noticed the blood stain that smeared down the wall.

Jake nudged Anji in the ribs and nodded over toward it.

Slowly, the pile of paper and debris directly below it started to writhe. Jake clambered up to Anji, who was desperately fiddling with the laser gun.

'Is it just me... ' Anji gulped. '... Or has it got hotter in there?'

The paper dispersed and made them both jump and shriek. Underneath was the mutilated remains of a woman, whose skin, grey and torn apart like the other corpses they had seen, was looking up at them and struggling to her feet. Her eyes were hollow and glowing a radioactive yellow. She glared fiercely and growled a horrendous scream.

Suddenly, her shrieking was ended by a blast from Anji's laser gun, which exploded in her chest and sent her reeling.

Jake was astonished and looked in a mixture of disgust and surprise at Anji.

The woman fell to the floor as the laser burrowed through her sending a volley of unpleasantness against the stained wall.

'I can't believe you just did that!' said Jake.

Anji didn't feel any remorse. 'You can't kill the dead, Jake. Whatever this virus is, it took her long ago.'

'Well, you just did!' he gingerly went over to the corpse, as did Anji.

'At least we know we can fight them,' she said before she picked up her communicator. 'Random, come in. We're trapped but we think we know how we can fight these things... Random?'

She waited for a reply but there was none. All the pair of them could hear on the other end was a wave of chaos...

Random and Skateboard had been backed into the office by the hosts of the virus, and no matter how many volleys of laser fire Random threw at them, more kept coming. Furiously, Skateboard kept working at the main frame, averting corrupt files and zig-zagging his way past pathways that kept leading to dead-ended encryptions; from functions
on board the prison ship to instruments that through time had rotted and no longer worked. Finally, he found a file path that did.

'Step back sir!' he instructed and as Random stopped firing and got out of the way of the door, a slab of metal swiped from left to right and sealed them in.

'Right, now that's bought us some time,' he reached for his communicator and noticed he had left it on. 'Sorry about that Anji, you all good your end?'

'No, we're trapped. We had company but we managed to deal with them but there are so many corpses out there.'

'Hosts,' said Skateboard.

'What did he say?' asked Jake into the communicator.

'They are hosts for a deadly infection. I'm reading into the crew logs as we speak and it seems that this ship transported prisoners from a wide variety of planets. Their destination was a penal planet in the Pentagonian galaxy, not far from your Earth, as a matter of fact.'

'Keep to what we need to know, Skateboard please,' said Random irritably.

'It seems as though the infection was passed from prisoner to prisoner initially, taking anyone who came into contact. Before long, almost all the prisoners were carrying the disease and had started to overpower their guards, which led to a bigger outbreak. It also says that despite repeated pleas for help, it never came and the ship eventually crashed on this ice moon, killing all those who had

not been infected yet on impact.'

'That's terrible,' said Anji. 'So that explains why not all the bodies came back to life then.'

'They are not "back to life," miss. The virus is just looking for new hosts. Without any, it will just die so it's using the motory sensors of the brain to send signals to other parts of the body to make it move.'

'Like space zombies...' Jake frowned.

'No. The hosts are faster than zombies and the virus knows what it is doing. Plus these hosts are very much real,' Skateboard continued.

'So why now?' asked Random. 'After so long. Wouldn't the virus have died as soon as the ship crashed if all the remaining crew perished?'

'I'm afraid not, sir. Judging by the medical records on the computer, this virus was put on ice, as it were, in the event of the crash.'

'What made it wake up?' asked Jake.

The penny dropped with Random. 'We did.'

'Captain Random is correct, sir,' confirmed Skateboard. 'When we boarded, one of the first actions we took was to turn the power back on.'

'Including the heating!' Anji interjected.

'Precisely,' said Skateboard.

'Can't we just turn the power off again? Will that stop the hosts from attacking?' asked Random.

'I'm afraid not, sir. It would take days, possibly weeks for the temperature to freeze the virus to such a degree it will become dormant again,' Skateboard confirmed.

'This virus, does it have a name?' asked Jake.

'More importantly, does it have any other weakness?' asked Random.

'According to my data banks, the virus was named CoMin2v4 and was discovered on the planet Quadros not long after the prison ship had left it. It was discovered in an animal that lived on that planet and sadly passed to all other humanoid life. Within days the planet was quarantined but a cure was never found. Quadros died out and has been blacklisted by the Federation of Planets as a no-go-zone ever since.'

'Brilliant! So we can't stop it,' said Random, throwing his arms up.

'Not so. Just as the ice stored the virus and the warmth revived it, extreme heat can stop it in its tracks. And as long as there are no new hosts to infect, it will die in the fire.'

'So, we can turn the temperature up?' asked Random.

'No, it needs to be immense heat to stop it,' Skateboard replied.

'So, we blow the ship up!' said Anji.

'But what's stopping us from getting infected?' asked Jake.

'Not much, sir, I'm afraid. The virus is airborne but much more prevalent in areas close to the hosts. I think it would be best if you haven't already to cover your mouths and noses and keep away as best as you can from the hosts. You too, sir.' He looked over at Random who was already lifting his scarf over his face.

'What's the plan now, Captain?' asked Anji.

'Simples. You two find a way to get out of the ship and wait for us at the Venus II. Skateboard and I will salvage the stabilisers and blow this place sky high.'

'No, sir. I must insist that you too leave with Anji and Jake,' said Skateboard. 'My organic make-up is far less than any of you three so I insist that I be left on board and you three leave immediately. We will have to deep clean and quarantine when we get back so I insist you all keep your distance from one another until I have the chance to bio-check you all.'

'You got that, you two?' Random spoke into his communicator.

'Gotcha, we'll blast our way out and meet you back at the ship,' Anji replied.

'Good luck,' Random clicked the receiver off. 'It's a full-proof plan Skateboard but you still need protection from the hosts.'

'I have my defensive stun gun, sir, that should be enough to hold them off.'

'I insist. I know there is a chance I might catch this thing but if we don't get the stabilisers then everyone is doomed. I'm staying with you... and that's an order.'

Skateboard hummed. 'Sir, if you don't go you could be putting the others in serious danger.'

'And if I do you might die and they will forever be stuck on this moon. It's not up for argument, Skateboard, I'll take the risk. Plus, you need my speed to find the stabiliser.'

'It's an awfully big risk... maybe your Rodasian immune system will give you a little more protection...'

'Good, it's settled then. I'll take the drive room Anji and Jake were heading for, you take the other. Keep in radio contact at all times. The first one to the stabiliser gets out as fast as they can. The other blows up the drive room and runs for life. Got it?'

'Yes, sir.'

Random cocked his laser gun.

'Get ready to run, sir...'

Random could hear the drumming of the hosts on the other side of the door. He hadn't picked up on it before, but it made his brow sweat nervously.

'Go, sir!'

With the door snapping open Random fired on the hosts, the red searing heat of the lasers shooting all around as he sped off back into the corridor, barely able to escape their grasp as he felt rotten fingers pull at his clothes.

Skateboard covered him with stun fire, the little pistol shooting tiny beams of blue energy into host after host rendering them inactive once more and creating less of a horrible visceral mess than his friend.

Meanwhile, Anji readied her weapon as she stood in front of the only way out for her and Jake.

'Are you ready for this?' asked Jake as he prepared to open up.

'Yup,' said Anji, her finger wrapped around the trigger. 'Get behind me and stay low as soon as you open the door.'

'But Anj, these were people once, don't you feel a bit weird about that?'

'I can't right now, Jake. The hosts have taken them and stand between us and getting out of here alive. We can think about the ethics another time. Ready?'

Jake nodded. She was right, but these weren't robots they were killing, it was flesh and blood. Reanimated or not, this wasn't something he thought either of them was at liberty to do. Then again, it was their only shot at survival.

'Now!' cried Anji. Jake yanked the door handle down and the door swung open. He scampered behind Anji who squeezed the trigger and a ray of red exploded from her gun into a waiting crowd of screaming hosts.

Jake closed his eyes throughout it all, not bearing to watch.

Within moments the swarm of diseased corpses now playing host to a horrific alien virus were no more blasted to pieces at the hands of a teenage girl.

Anji lowered the laser gun and wiped her eyes, silent tears started to flow down her cheeks. Jake heard the empty silence and opened his eyes again.

'The coast is clear,' she sniffed. 'Come on.'

Random had fought his way through corridors and corridors of infected Hosts, all grappling and trying to tear him to pieces and no matter how hard he fought them, there always seemed to be more on the way. His eyes were beginning to feel heavy. His vision was washing in and out like waves on an ocean shoreline. He had no time to check his person for bites or scratches; he had to reach the drive room…

Skateboard, being made up of robotic components, had gone largely ignored by the Hosts as he made his journey to the other drive room, only relying on his stun gun to repel the odd threat of attack. Considering how he was not pursued, he deduced that the virus may be able to overrun the nervous system of a humanoid host but that's as far as the brain matter went.

It didn't know what he and Random were planning to do. If only Random hadn't insisted on staying, Skateboard thought to himself.

He was well aware of Random's powers but he was more than aware of his fallacies too. In the future, he would have to insist strongly because if Random never made it out alive, Skateboard would never forgive himself.

'I've made it,' said Random over the communicator system. Skateboard noticed how exhausted he sounded.

'Sir, are you okay?'

'Yes… the drive room is deserted. I think I've managed to lose them.'

'Good, I am almost at the other drive room. Can you see the compartment I told you about?'

Random was on his haunches. His vision was doubling up. He shook his head and tried hard to refocus. Searching for the compartment that Skateboard showed him, he began to worry that the hosts had passed their virus onto him.

'No, I don't think it is in here,' he sighed.

'Okay, sir, no problem, that means that my side has the stabiliser that we need. Even if it is not entirely compatible with the Venus II, I can fashion something out of them that we can use.'

Random panted and sat down. He went to pick up his communicator but missed it entirely. He tried again and was successful on the second attempt.

He noticed droplets of sweat dripping down his brow and wiped them away as his temperature began to soar...

Anji finished off another group of hosts and brought down her weapon as her communicator started to blink into life.
'Random, we're nearly there.'

Random huffed and puffed as he gasped for breath. 'Anj...'

'Random, are you okay mate?' asked Jake into the communicator.

'Fine, just out of... breath. Make sure that when you open the airlock door... that you contain... contain... keep the hosts inside.'

'Okay, gotcha,' Anji looked at Jake with concern.

'Lay down some covering fire when Skateboard gets out...then run...back to the...Venus...'

'Random?' Anji and Jake spoke at the same time.

The radio went dead.

'Skateboard?'

'Do what he says, miss. He's right, we need to keep the hosts inside. I'll contact you as I leave and so will Random.'

Skateboard rolled into the drive room and immediately spotted the compartment that housed the stabiliser parts that would guarantee he and his friends escape from this nightmare. Immediately he went to work, a little torch burst out of his metal body and started to cut the housing free. All the time, not knowing that Hosts were coming into the room...

Whilst Anji kept watch, Jake forced the buckled airlock door open and the teenagers ran back into the snowstorm that greeted them when they crash-landed.

Blinded by the whiteness and the flurry of snow that blew fiercely into their faces, Jake managed to force the inner airlock door firmly shut, falling to the floor as the horrors within were trapped.

He scrambled up and ran towards his friend, who had her weapon trained on the door.

'We're out! The hosts have been contained, you'll have a bit of a fight to get out of there now though.'

'Not to worry, miss. I have the component,' said Skateboard as he slipped it onto his back and fastened it magnetically.

'We'll deal with any problems we find. See you in a bit. Over.'

Skateboard turned and was shocked to see several Hosts were now circling him. 'Oh my. Greetings to you all. Sorry I can't stay to chat.'

Suddenly, Skateboard's stun gun fired rounds into each and every one of the hosts, who shrieked and fell instantly. A pity, he thought as he rolled over one of them, the coolest thing he may ever say and nobody was there to hear him. Now, to check on Random.

'Sir, come in, sir.'

Random pulled himself over to the engines and readied his gun. He was losing it. He could feel the virus starting to overtake him. All that made him who he was, his memories, all of him was losing the fight. But all he had to do was wait until his friends were clear.

'Skateboard,' he grunted. 'Are you clear?'

'Almost there, sir. Are you at the entrance?' replied Skateboard as his little wheels burned rubber hurtling past the attacking hosts.

'Just let me know when you are clear.'

Random slid to the floor. If only he could keep control for just a little longer. He could hear a swarm of hosts hurtling towards him from outside.

'I'm coming through,' declared Skateboard. He had reached the airlock. Seeing the Hosts grappling and scratching at the airlock door, he stunned the lot before they had a chance to see him.

'Open the door,' he asked politely.

Jake and Anji heard him and pulled at the buckled door and as soon as a slither of space appeared, Skateboard flew through.

'We're out, where are you Random?' Anji barked.

Back inside, staring his future right in the face, Random smiled.
'Get clear!'

He continued to smile as the hosts raced toward him.

'Not today, thank you.'

At that moment, Random dialled the laser gun up to full, jammed the trigger down, threw it behind his shoulder and then rolled for cover.

The gun hit the engine fuel tanks and ignited.

'Run, run, run!' screamed Anji as she, Jake and Skateboard struggled in the snow to make a quick getaway.

Suddenly an explosion erupted a short distance away, followed by another even closer by.

The trio threw themselves into the snowdrift, the bangs became louder and they were hit by a wave of heat as the entire prison ship went up in flames.

Jake pressed his face into the cold snow and waited for the chaos to end.

Before long the prison stopped exploding and the
travellers picked themselves up and looked back in horror.

The prison ship was nothing but a mountain of twisted metal and roaring fireballs of destruction.

'Oh my god...' cried Jake.

'Random. Come in Random,' Anji spoke into her communicator.
The radio was dead.

'No!' Anji dropped her gun and ran towards the disaster area.

Jake did his best to pull her back. 'Anj, no!'

'Let go of me,' she struggled to push him off her.

'Miss, please stop!' cried Skateboard. Another explosion rocked the landscape.

Anji fell to the floor and sobbed. Jake knelt beside her and held her.

Not a word was spoken.

Skateboard slid up beside them. He'd failed to save one of the crew. One of his friends.

His diodes made a slow humming sound like a robotic sigh.

As the trio mourned, a little crackle from their communicators started to fizz over the airwaves.

Anji and Jake looked astonished at each other and grappled for them, snot and tears frozen on their faces.

'Random! Random! Are you okay?'

'Ugh... I'll live.'

The travellers whooped and cheered, hugging and sobbing tears of happiness.

Skateboard, who had been fighting the temptation to shut himself down in guilt, took charge of the situation.

'Sir, what happened?'

'Remember on Genocia, when we used the laser gun to blow up the mine?'

'You did that?' cried Jake.

Random sounded proud. 'Yep. The hosts were killed in the fire and so was the virus.'

'So that's the hosts gone then?' asked Anji.

'Yes. The virus would never have been strong enough to sustain itself in that heat. To be perfectly honest, I'm surprised Captain Random could,' concluded Skateboard.

The gang waited for their friend to make his way to them. When they did, with all the terror they had faced, they could do nothing else but burst into laughter. Random staggered from the wreckage looking scorched and black like he had been caught in a comedy explosion.

'How can you laugh after all of that?' he limped a little as he reached them.

The trio stepped away from him.

'Hey! I just saved our lives and all you can do is laugh!?' he continued.

'Well, we could hug you but-'

Skateboard interrupted Jake. 'You seemed to be suffering earlier sir like you were succumbing to the virus.'

'I was. I managed to crawl to cover and the heat of the explosion did the rest.'

'Hold up! You might still have some traces left on you!' said Jake.

'Jake is correct, sir. I'm afraid I shall have to ask you to remove your clothes,' said Skateboard.

'What? Out here?' said Random.

'Yes,' replied Skateboard.

Random looked offended. 'I'm not taking my clothes off in front of you!'

'Fine, we'll turn around,' suggested Anji.

'But it's freezing out here!'

'If you can live through an explosion, you can survive the cold.'

The trio did just that as Random stood flabbergasted.

'We can't let you on board before you do, sir.'

Random stood indignantly. Reluctantly, he started removing his coat. 'Fine!'

Before long he stood before them in nothing but his pants and socks, his knees knocking in the chill.

Anji and Jake laughed uncontrollably.

'Oh, this is brilliant!' said Jake as he fell to the floor holding his ribs and struggling for air.

'I don't know why you two are smiling. All your clothes might be contaminated too.'

That stopped the laughing.

'But...' said Anji and Jake simultaneously.

'No buts, miss, sir, we all need to decontaminate and quarantine on board.'

'How long for?' asked Jake.

'A week. You'll all have to stay in your rooms all of that time.'

All three of them began to protest.

'No ifs or buts, sirs and miss.'

They began to undress.

'You'll see plenty of butts in a minute!' said Anji cheekily.

As they reluctantly stripped down. Skateboard decided to rub it in a little more.

'Don't worry. It's only a couple of miles back to the Venus II.'

Jake, Anji and Random protested further but did what they were told.

Soon after, as the embers of the prison ship rose in the snowstorm, the travellers made their way back to the Venus II, somewhat less well-dressed than before they left it.

That'll teach them, thought Skateboard to himself, especially Random for nearly dying again!

As the Venus II, half covered in a snow drift, honed into view, Skateboard lowered the gangway remotely.

'Can we at least have a warm bath first?' asked Jake hopefully through chattered teeth.

'No,' said Skateboard sternly.

As they all went up the gangway, under strict instructions to go straight to their quarters and freezing to death, Skateboard wondered if he was

being too cruel.

After all, he'd bio-scanned them when they left the prison ship and even Random was clear of the virus now.

But then he thought against it.

After all, he could do with a week to himself.

MAROONED

'Mayday, mayday. This is Captain Random of the Venus II. I have been ejected into space and have approximately 20 minutes before my air supply runs out. Do you read me, calling on all frequencies, do you read me?

Nothing. Typical. Just typical. To pick the only spacesuit with a diminished oxygen supply. It's so...so...Jake! Suppose it was my time to have bad luck. Oh well, I guess I had better wait here until there is help. I wonder if this radio pad on my wrist can send out a long-range frequency message...yes. Maybe it will be broadcast to everyone in the area. I can be rescued!

Right, let's take a look at this. Huh, as if I can pick up the radio on here! It must mean I am not too far away from someone if I can pick up a signal. Almost have it and...there!

Hello. This is an urgent SOS call to anyone and everyone. My name is Random, Captain Random. My ship, the Venus II, intercepted a distress signal from a vessel called the Maxim at coordinates...ah, what were they again? I think it was 0745 by 902 binary.

If that doesn't help, it was near this greeny/blue planetoid. Hopefully, that will narrow it down.

My crew, consisting of two teenage humans and a robotic AI accepted the Maxim's distress call and upon landing, we discovered what can only be described as utter pandemonium.

It turned out that the reactor had been compromised and was about to explode, causing a monumental explosion that would not have only vapourised everyone on board but also would have been deadly enough to create airspace pollution that would have seen the area un-passable for months.

Well, that's what our AI robot said, anyway. I let him deal with the science bit whilst myself and my two friends boarded the ship and started to help evacuate the area.

As the Maxim's systems began to overload from the impending explosion, I set about organising the evacuation, but as the life support systems were starting to fail, as was the gravity that slowed things down, it became apparent that everybody needed to don spacesuits to ensure that they wouldn't die of oxygen starvation.

I didn't want to tell them they could also be sucked into space with the airlocks opening intermittently and without warning.

Well, they had enough on their plates!

So with help and coordination from the Captain of the Maxim, the rescue began!

It turned out that the crew of the Maxim was roughly 200 in number.

The ship itself is a scientific research vessel that monitors the atmospheric conditions above the greeny/blue planet... zarks, what was it called again?

I'll keep thinking while I tell my story. I know I might be using up precious oxygen supply but it'll be worth it if you rescue me.

Plus, I couldn't stay quiet for my final precious minutes alive. If there's one thing worse than dying, it's being bored while it happens!

Imagine dying of boredom! Besides, if I drifted aimlessly in space alone for too long... ah... okay, I'll admit it, I'm afraid. So I'd rather yak on and on about what happened to stave off the terror of certain death if no one comes.

But, before I bore YOU to death about how dire the situation is for me, I'd better get on with the story...

... It turned out, following a symmetric rundown of the ship's capacity, that the designer of the Maxim hadn't allowed room for the full quota of staff on the escape pods, I mean, who does that?

So luckily my ship, the Venus II, was able to lend a hand, even though we could only take on board a few dozen at every turn.

And so, my robotic friend suggested that my friend Anji should pilot the Venus II to the nearest planet and start dropping off the evacuees before returning for the rest. Since the escape pods on board could only fit 70, we had no time to lose.

In the meantime, Skateboard, that's my robot friend's name, by the way, remained on board the Maxim and attempted to safely shut down the reactor. Since he was the only lifeform on board who didn't require oxygen and could magnetise himself to the ship, it made sense that he was the one who would stay behind. Plus he's a bit of a genius!

So, whilst I and my other human friend, Jake directed the crew towards the escape pods and the Venus II, I noticed that one of the crew members was unaccounted for.

Considering the Captain had requested that this missing person were allocated one of the escape pods on offer and ordered them to wait in line, which was fun when the gravity kept failing, I can tell you, I did a head count of those waiting for rescue from my ship.

I contacted the Captain immediately over the internal communications in my space suit and he confirmed that the Head Scientist, a creature called Yovak, could not be found.

I asked Skateboard to locate him and he confirmed to me that, although he was rather busy trying to avert a major catastrophe, he could see a life form in the engine bay.

Did I mention that Skateboard can connect to computers and talk to them?

Honestly, he's amazing. So whilst I left the evacuation in the capable hands of the Maxim captain and Jake, I made my way towards the engine bay.

The Maxim isn't the biggest ship I've seen, it has to be said, but it was still a bit of a distance to get to the engine bay. Naturally, I was hoping that Yovak was still there.

With all the explosions and gravity failures I experienced on the way, it's amazing that I ever got there, even with my speed advantage. I'm pretty fast if I'm being modest. Eventually, I made it and found her.

To say that Yovak wasn't a looker is... well... I shouldn't be mean, I'm not like that.

Hey, if you're into ten-foot-high slugs who salivate pools of acid, then who knows, maybe you'd buy her a drink!

I have no idea whether her dating profile would include the words GOOD AT SABOTAGING SCIENCE VESSELS WITH MY SPIT but from what I saw, it should be there above enjoying walks and listening to music if it wasn't!

It took just a split second to clock onto what was happening here. Yovak's acid was eating away at the equipment running the ship, corroding everything as quickly as sugar dissolves in a cup of tea.

Man, I could do with a cuppa now. My mouth is so dry... NINE MINUTES!?... okay, I'll crack on with the story before my lungs burst then.

I notified Skateboard. The overheating reactor and life support failure wasn't an accident. All this time, in my head, I was questioning the Captain's skill at recruitment campaigns.

Surely employing a being whose species can corrode metal by gobbing at it shouldn't make it onto the shortlist! A blacklist, more like. Anyway, Yovak was deliberately sabotaging the Maxim!

Before I had time to listen to her response, a volley of acid shot my way. I ducked instantly, which was a sensible thing to do considering the horrible liquid melted a hole in the wall where I had been standing.

As I continued to weave and swerve my way around the bay, I enquired as to why Yovak wanted to kill all on board.

Amongst the chaos, I have to admit I didn't catch every word so the excuse was a little sketchy to my ears.

I heard something about illegal experiments, endangering her kind, something like that. My response was pretty measured I thought.

I replied that two wrongs don't make a right and people can be brought to account for their crimes, but this must have been lost in the moment because in that instant Yovak proceeded to fail in attempting to melt my legs.

The next few moments are a little patchy. I think I managed to notify the crew, but I cannot be sure.

But the main takeaway was that although

Yovak hadn't managed to slime me to death; she had succeeded in melting a nearby bulkhead.

Unfortunately, I was slightly taken by surprise when the room seemed to buckle all around me.

The next thing I knew I was holding on for dear life as the floor was worn from under my feet.

The rush of everything within the engine bay began to fly past me.

Before I knew it, I had the full force of a translucent ten-foot-high slug smacking into me, forcing my grip away from the only thing that was keeping me inside the spaceship and then, as the back of my head smacked against something hard, my helmet, I guess, I was rendered unconscious, falling towards the stars…

… and then… God, it's getting hard to breathe… here I am.

Drifting aimlessly. Marooned in space.

The Maxim was nowhere to be seen.

Yovak herself, or what I presume is all that's left of her, completely vanished.

I awoke with a startle and a headache, unable to recognise any of the star systems in my vicinity.

And then I made a horrific realisation. I wasn't just floating in space. I was hurtling.

The force of the explosion must have thrown me into the vacuum and anyone with a grasp of science knows that when force has been used but gravity is missing, there is nothing to stop an object from moving in space. Judging by my speed, there didn't seem to be much slowing down either.

I attempted radio communication immediately. I was well out of range of the Maxim, the Venus II and the people I was supposed to be saving. I was alone. I mean, I AM alone.

This really could be it.

After all the things that could have killed me in my time. That should have killed me. I didn't have any money on a giant space slug's bum knocking me out into space as the winner!

Oh well, at least I gave my life-saving others. Just as it should have been.

As you can tell I've given up hope now. It's okay, whoever is listening… if anyone is listening. It was a good run, you know.

I saved so many lives in my time. It was so worth it. All of it.
Even the bad moments.

Not the failures, of course, there was always more I could do.
Like for Io, like the Osirans...

..and Rodas...

I never went home. I never did what I was born to do there.

Even with my good work elsewhere... I will die knowing I
never went back. I never saved my own people.

I always meant to... when I was ready, but that time never
came.

And for that... I deserve this end...'

'Oh, please, cry us a river!'

'Anji?'

'The one and only!'

'But... how... where?'

'I discovered what had happened, sir, not long after I shut the
reactor down and upon Anji's

return we all came along and tried to find you.'

'Skateboard too! I knew someone would be listening... I should
have known it would have been you!'

'Hey, Skateboard, it was me who thought about checking for
distress calls. Okay, well, not quite. I forgot to turn it off when we
landed on the Maxim. But hey, at least we got to listen to why you
were out here in the first place! We managed to track you thanks
to your space suit.

That Captain bloke told us that every space suit is fitted with a
device that can be detected and followed. Apparently, the Maxim
crew are always going missing on expeditions.'

'Where's Jake, Anji?'

'Back on the Maxim, Random, helping to clear up the mess. As
soon as we pull you in we will go back and pick him up.'

'That glow... the tractor beam!'

'That's right, sir, the Venus II managed to stop you travelling
thanks to my precise calculations.'

'Stop showing off, Skateboard, let's get him in!'

'Thanks, guys. Just in the nick of time. Hold up, you said that
Jake was still on board the Maxim!'

'It's okay, Random, I managed to find out what was going on and alerted the authorities on Trapaxia when I dropped off the first load of evacuees. They liked to talk about what they were up to... a lot. So I made sure that on my return

journey when Skateboard told me he'd saved the ship, I was not alone when I came back!'

'Nice one, Anji! Now get me in, please. It's cold out here!'

'Commencing matter transfer now, sir.'

'You guys... where would I be without you? With... wow... two minutes of oxygen left! Thank zarks for that! Quick, get me in! That's it. I'll be with you in a minute. Now then, how do I turn this radio thing off?'

CAUTION
NO
ENTRY

HOME

From the smoking husk of what was once a school, a pristine set of unfamiliar apartments now stood in front of her. It hadn't seemed that long ago since she had played a part in the building's downfall, but the site she had been staring at for a good time now confirmed that she had not been back home in a long, long time.

The girl continued to stare aghast. She hadn't expected a mountain of twisted metal and rubble to greet her. Now the whole area had gone to dust, seemingly now only a memory for her former schoolmates and those who had lived in the local area spoke volumes for how she had dealt with the fallout of that night.

It had been a strange few days when it happened. A spaceship had fallen from the sky and she, along with her best friend, had helped the injured alien to fit in with them in a futile attempt to pass him off as human. Yet, what had their actions resulted in? A night of devastation.

First, the home that they shared with orphaned children such as they, had been attacked and destroyed by a vengeful monster who was hell-bent on killing their strange new friend.

Luckily, no one was hurt, but the fight had then moved to their school, which was also pulverised to oblivion in a contest between the two impossible beings from another world.

Then, before the dust had truly settled, the girl and her friend had run off with the victor, sailing the stars and writing the wrongs of the universe all in the name of adventure.

However, they were all running away from something and no matter the good that they had done for the cosmos, and the countless lives that they had saved, they left a trail of damage in their wake.

Just recently, the responsibility had begun to weigh heavily upon her shoulders.

And so, one day on the other side of the galaxy, Anji Gummadi decided that she had been running long enough. It was time to go back.

Now she was home, Anji began to wonder to herself if she had left it too long.

Maybe it was best to let the past be the past? No children had died, indeed, nobody lost their lives that night except for the Sandman, so now she was here, was there really anything to have lingering guilt about? Maybe the school was gone but the kids who had attended it were having much better lives now. She wasn't the only person who had thought the place was a dump, she knew that for a fact! The less said about some of the teachers too, the better.

Now she was here, she didn't need to see anymore. Anji breathed deeply and turned on her heels.

It had been a waste of time to drag her friends back here again but now she had seen it, she could move on. Just about.

This ghost could be laid to rest.

Yet at that moment, another rose from the grave.

'Shut. The. Front. Door.'

Anji's heart started thumping hard. She recognised that voice... and had hoped that she would never hear it again.

'Er... hi,' she responded timidly.

At the corner of the street, gauping in amazement was Jemima Wright.

In all her adventures Anji had faced down power-mad tyrants, soul-sucking aliens from the dawn of time and even Gods themselves.

But none of them evoked a sense of dread in quite the same way that Jemima did.

Jemima dropped her bag, her eyes wide in amazement. 'Oh my god, we all thought you were dead!'

'Surprise...' Anji cringed.

Suddenly the girl began to hunt in her handbag, a collection of bracelets jangling like prison cell keys against the opening.

'What are you doing?' Anji asked needlessly. She knew exactly what Jemima was looking for.

As she produced a mobile phone from the handbag, Anji threw herself at Jemima and slapped it to the floor.

'Hey, you headcase!' Jemima drew her fist and aimed a punch at Anji's face.

But this dance had been had before by the pair and Anji, remembering every bruised cheek, every split lip, every insult she had endured at the hands of the bully, decided enough was enough.

With cat-like reflexes, Anji ducked and grabbed hold of Jemima's arm and threw her to the ground. Not knowing what had hit her, Jemima lay crumpled on the floor, a glob of unwanted chewing gum having splatted against her school blazer, making a nasty mess for her to discover later. Anji breathed heavily and leered over her.

Jemima coughed and looked up at the victim of so many of her cruel words and actions. The sun was blotted out by the outline of a girl that she recognised but wasn't the one that she had once known.

'Fighting back now, are we?'

Anji knelt down. There was no need to take this any further.

Much to Jemima's surprise, a hand was offered to her.

'Always, but I'd never stoop to your level, Jemima.'

Hoping that no on-lookers had witnessed her one and only defeat, Jemima swore and accepted the help.

When she was back on her feet, she straightened herself and looked down at her dirty blazer.

It had been raining earlier that day and the grime of the suburban street had coated itself upon her.

'You're going to pay for that!' she cursed before looking up and realising that Anji was already walking away from her. 'Oi! Come back!'

Anji did not turn around. 'I'm not fighting with you, Jemima.'

Anji continued to walk calmly down the quiet street.

'Just wait for a second, please!'

An outstretched hand clawed around Anji's arm.

'Leave me alone!' snapped Anji.

Jemima withdrew her hands and held them aloft in surrender.

'Look, I don't want to hurt you anymore, it was a long time ago now, Anji.'

'Yeah, well, what you did still hurt.'

'I know, I'm sorry.'

Anji started to walk away again.

'Anji please, just wait a second.'

Anji turned and pressed her head against Jemima's.

At that moment, Jemima saw the reflection of the rumours she had started, the fights she had picked, the venom she had spewed in the direction of her

rival stream uncontrollably from the tear-stricken eyes.

'You made my life a living hell. Because of you, I lost friends. Because of you, I was never able to tell someone how I felt. The things you called me, hurt more than any punch you could ever throw at me. So why would I ever give you anything?'

Jemima gulped and couldn't bear to look her in the face.

'That was a long time ago.'

Anji blinked her tears back. 'It doesn't mean that they never happened.'

She tore off again.

'Everybody thinks you did it.'

Anji stopped again.

'What?'

'Everyone thinks you burnt the school down.'

She walked back towards Jemima, who now stood looking quite sheepish.

'Well, I didn't, okay? End of.'

'Then why did you run away?'

'That's my business,' screamed Anji.

'Even when everyone thinks that you are dead?' Jemima screamed back.

Anji was stunned.

'You are wrong Anji. People cared about you more than you knew.' Jemima had to be careful how much she said.

'Dead?'

Jemima nodded.

Anji wiped her tears away and walked back to face her. She took her gently by the arm.

'Come with me.'

Jemima felt like she had been given detention. She had been pushed and pulled by the still furious Anji towards a local greasy spoon called Syd's Café.

This had been a frequent haunt for Anji way back when.

She would hide from the bullies who threatened to ambush her on the way home from school when she didn't have the relative security of Jake to hand.

Inside, the décor was just as rancid as ever. Streaks of grease that had stained the walls for many a year was now contesting for space with patches of rot and mold.

And yet, as she forced Jemima to buy her a coffee, much to the bemusement of the café owner, and made her way over to her usual table, she looked

around the run-down, deserted old place and finally began to feel like she was finally home.

Enough nostalgia, she told herself, she wanted to hear what Jemima had to say and as the girl made her way over to Anji with two steaming cups of coffee in dirtied old mugs, it was time for the old scores to be settled.

'You're lucky you came back today. This place is being torn down next Monday,' said Jemima as she plonked herself opposite her old rival.

Anji was still smarting. The heat inside the café, in contrast to the cold miserable day outside, made it look like steam was rising off her black plaited head inside the hood she had kept up for sake of anonymity.

'Alright Jemima, talk.'

Jemima scoffed. 'You've changed. All this attitude. I think I prefer the old you.'

'The one you used to bully?'

'Oh, come on, you were asking for it most of the time!'

'It's never an excuse. You made me feel like nothing. Daily! Why would you do that?'

Jemima huffed. 'Only one of us could be popular. As I said, it was ages ago now. Water under the bridge.'

'For one of us...' spat Anji.

'If you want me to talk, you had better keep me sweet.'

Anji lunged over the table and grabbed Jemima by her school tie, spilling the coffee all over the place.

'Oi! None of that in here!' came the voice of the old and grizzled café owner.

Anji simmered and released her. Jemima, alarmed by such aggression, started to collect her things.

'Where are you going?' Anji demanded.

'I'm not staying here if this is what you're going to be like.'

'Then why did you come, eh? Where is the old Jemima Wright? You loved a fight. You loved to hurt me. Why would you even let me drag you here? I'm not the only one making sense, Jemima. You want answers from me as much as I want answers from you.'

'I've left her well in the past, what about you Anji? Because this isn't you, it never was. I'm not staying here just for the goss so if you'll excuse me.'

Anji got up. She noticed the way the café owner was looking at her, as he dried a coffee mug with the grimmest tea towel you could imagine. She sighed. 'No, look, please. I'm sorry.'

Jemima looked her in the eyes. So much had changed in the girl that she used to know. She had no right to keep her there but then there was so much that she wanted to find out. So much had been concealed between them. Could she let her out of her sight without letting her know?

'Okay,' said Jemima as she placed herself back down at the table. She looked dismissively at her spilled drink.

'But before we go any further, you're getting me another one... and clearing that up!'

A few minutes of relative tranquility passed.

Having cleared up the coffee mess, Anji returned with a fresh mug as Jemima tried to create space among the mound of sodden paper napkins.

'We could always just move tables?' she suggested.

'I've always liked this one,' said Anji stubbornly. 'So, you said that everyone thinks I am dead?'

Jemima picked up her fresh mug of coffee. 'Well, you did go missing after the school burnt down. Mica and I thought you'd done it yourself.'

'Why would I do that?' she asked and then realised why two and two could be put together. When she felt frustrated and isolated, Anji had a habit of smuggling lighters into school property and then setting fire to the student's clothes in the changing rooms when they were out for PE.

'When your blazer has a habit of catching fire four times a term, you kind of join the dots,' said Jemima, raising the mug to her lips and blowing on it gently.

'It wasn't me,' said Anji quietly.

'The news said differently. Then as you and your boyfriend had disappeared, along with that new kid, it all made sense. Especially when your home burnt down too. It was everywhere, Anj. The TV, the web. The story of the purple alien and his human friends who went mad and started blowing things up. Luckily no one was hurt, well, except you three who were never found.'

'Didn't the kids home say anything?'

'They did! They had to list you as missing, presumed dead. The guy who ran your home lost his job. They blamed him for the fire and for you going off the rails.'

Anji gasped in horror. James was the only adult in the world who she respected and trusted. She had let him down terribly.

'Oh my god. Is he okay?'

'Yeah, he didn't go to prison. No evidence. Works somewhere else now. He moved in with Miss Carter, do you remember her? She fell in a cow pat when that alien ship crashed. Happy days. Anyways, I think they rebuilt your home. All the kids got re-homed too. Well, after the counselling.'

Anji began to feel awful. Running away from that night had left horrific consequences for others, caught up in the collateral damage like refugees in a war.

'But they were all okay in the end?'

Jemima slurped her coffee. 'Would you be? Anyway, enough about this, what's your side of the story.'

'Why should I tell you?'

'Because I've sat here telling you what you want to know. Now it's your turn.'

Anji sighed. 'Not much to say,' she lied. How could she tell her all about the wonders of the universe, all the amazing places she had seen? The
fantastic adventures she had experienced. The terrifying monsters she had fought.

If there was one person in the world who didn't deserve the exclusive story, it was Jemima Wright.

And so, hiding behind her coffee mug, Anji began.

'I ran away. Seemed like the burning down of the school and my home was the perfect excuse to start afresh.'

'But you were there, Anj. All three of you were. They had you on CCTV. You and the aliens!'

'I'm not denying that we weren't. We were trying to stop it all. After the attack on our home... we had to do something. But we couldn't stop the school from burning and knowing we'd be arrested we ran. We kept on running.'

'Until now,' Jemima interrupted. 'So, why did you come back?'

Anji gulped coffee. 'Sometimes to move forward you've got to go back.'

Jemima laughed. 'You're a poet too now, are you?'

'It's the truth. I had to come back. Something about that night and this place... I just wanted to see it again... for the last time.'

Jemima looked down. Her heart was pounding loudly in her chest.

'If this is to be the last time, then maybe I should say what I need to say.'

Anji looked up.

'All that time I spent making your life hell. It was wrong. I had some stuff going on. Big stuff,' she scoffed. 'You weren't the only one who was angry.

When my Mum left... it sounds like a bad excuse but... I had always been Daddy's golden girl. It's
hard to deal with your parents breaking up when you are all alone. He wasn't for long. No, he was soon shacked up with some strumpet he found in a pub. When she came along... well... my Dad was never around anymore. Then you joined our class.

Suddenly I wasn't the best-looking one anymore and you were better than me at so much. I needed a release.'

'You needed a punching bag,' said Anji.

'I did. It was wrong. I've done a lot of thinking since then, and a lot of growing up. And truth be told...' her eyes began to well up.

Anji looked concerned, surprising herself. Jemima was being sincere.

'...Um...' Jemima ran her fingers along the bottom of her eyelids, catching the tears. 'It's hard for me to say but...there was another reason why I picked on you. There was a lot I wanted to tell you... but couldn't...'

'You can now, Jemima,' said Anji, her natural understanding washing over her anger.

'...Let's just say it wasn't just the boys who liked you...'

Anji frowned for a second and then understood completely.

'Oh.'

Jemima's eyes were streaming. Years of bottled-up feelings were flooding out now.

'And I knew I couldn't tell you because of the way I had been to you... and you always had that Jake kid with you. I was so jealous. Just when I had no one, even when I made you unpopular with those stories, I knew you had won. You were never going to be as lonely as I felt because you had him.'

Anji shook her head. 'Jemima, we weren't going out. We never have done.'

'But you were so close. It was so obvious you loved him and he loved you.'

'Love can mean a lot of things.'

'Not to me.' sniffed Jemima.

Anji sighed again. She leaned over the table and placed her hands in Jemima's. 'Look, Jemima, this doesn't change anything. I appreciate your apologising, I do. It's what I have always needed to hear. And I'm sorry for how I retaliated. All those times I could never understand and now I do. It helps, it does. But I could never feel the same. Besides, I'm a missing person. I can't stay here, there would be too many questions asked. Questions I could never answer.'

'Then answer this one. If the school hadn't burnt down... if you hadn't run away and I had changed... do you ever think-'

'I can never say... it's not something I have ever thought about. To tell you the truth, I never have the time to stop and think.'

'Then do so now. Please.' Jemima poured at her palms, imploring the shared feeling.

'I can't. I'm sorry.'

Jemima scrunched her eyes up. All that time, they had both been lost souls. Both in pain and needing something to hold on to. If only she hadn't hurt her, again and again.

If only it had all been different.

A beeping sound broke the mood.

'Excuse me,' said Anji, as she checked her phone. 'I need to go.'

'It's okay... I understand,' said Jemima. She wiped her face with her sleeve.

Anji slowly got up. She noticed the gentle patter of rain against the window. It was a fairly long walk back to the others. She could stay a little longer, and let them know she wasn't ready yet. But now her heart was calm again, the scars of yesteryear beginning to heal, her mission was complete. She had come home to look for a reason to leave this all behind in the past. Now she had closure, she could.

'Wait,' asked Jemima. 'I know it sounds forward of me but... just once... just so I know how it would have felt... please?'

Anji looked at her tear-stricken face for an answer to what she was asking and found it quickly.

'I don't think that would be a good-'

'Please. See it as an apology and... what could have been... if I wasn't such a cow!' she chuckled through the tears.

Anji felt very awkward.

'Okay... close your eyes...'

Jemima, quite aware of the mess of makeup that was streaked across her face, did just that. As she closed her eyes, she waited, imploring Anji closer.

But nothing ever happened.

The ring of the bell above the door of the café jingled loudly and Jemima opened her eyes.

Anji was gone.

Jemima sat alone, the two half-finished coffee mugs swimming in a sea of stained napkins in the deserted café, the rain cascading against the window outside.

Silently, Jemima's face fell and as the rain poured, so did her regret.

WARM IN WINTER

She didn't know how close they were; only that she had to keep running. It was becoming a regular occurrence for her, this daily race for her life between her and the big bad people wanting her dead. At the end of the day, all that she was doing was trying to help. Was that such a crime?

Sadly, on Rodas, even compassion for others seemed to be a reason for death.

She had never known the planet to be any better. Ever since she could remember, red and blue factions of soldiers seemed to be battling an embittered war amongst themselves. Even as a child, she knew it wasn't they who were suffering. No, it was the innocent civilians who were caught in the crossfire.

It was the same passive natives who had gotten her in trouble this time. Well, of course, it wasn't their fault. They didn't ask to be rescued, not until the armed thugs in their crimson coloured uniforms had readied their guns at them.

The poor innocents had done nothing wrong at all. She would have known, she'd been staking the area out for the past couple of weeks. A family, trying their best to survive, like everyone else on the war-torn world of Rodas, had been selling and buying basic foods to give back to the people of the district.

The family themselves were nine in number, made up of a Mother and Father team helped out by their seven children, ranging from adult to very young, to get the supplies out.

But as the girl knew, whilst ducking around a dusty back street corner as she evaded more laser fire from her pursuers, such activity had become illegal. Especially since the Crimson Empire had captured the district from their enemies, the Sapphire Regime. Now, like so many before them, the family was being persecuted for the colour of their skin.

It was a race war that had started the bitter conflict on Rodas, centuries upon centuries ago.

An argument over colour had split the planet straight down the middle.

The row spiraled out of hand so quickly and was exploited by those who had always had a negative opinion of the other half of the planet's incumbents. So the fires were stoked, the rage roared and before long a never-ending battle ensued.

Sadly, for people like the family who were just there to help, no matter what colour the needy were, this act was punishable by death.

So the girl took it upon herself to help in the only way she knew how and to travel the planet putting the fire out where she could.

When she had been younger, she had sought to keep her head down, much as her Father had implored her to, but then something happened one night that would change her life forever.

As the heli-fighters clashed and their burning twisted remains rained down upon her house, the girl got lost during an evacuation of the area.

Whilst she screamed as loud as she could to be heard above the mayhem, calling for her parents to save her and take her with them, scores of Rodasians continued to barge past her in the narrow hallways of their city.

She had seen attacks before but none with such ferociousness as this. Glass and noise shattered all around her and then, after being pushed out onto the streets by the scrambling refugees, she spotted something in the sky.

In the eye of the storm, she stopped dead in her tracks and watched the most curious of events.

High above, but below the security net that had been built around Rodas to contain the planet and trap it in its endless fight, she saw two battle freighters directly opposing each other.

She recognised them instantly. One belonged to Kalor Maloso, the evil dictator of the Crimson Empire and the other belonged to his bitter rivals, the Sapphire Regime.

Not much was known about their leader, mainly because they were in retreat and did not broadcast their desires of conquest as much as Maloso did, but the girl knew she was on their side due to her blue skin.

Peering through her tears, she saw a tiny spec situated between them. Curiously, the spec began to travel upwards towards the barrier. Any idiot could see that it was a suicidal move. The barrier pulsated waves of energy, making it impossible to escape. And yet, this tiny spec in the sky did. It disappeared into space and the battle freighters had instantaneously fired on it.

Then, something even more miraculous happened.

When the laser fire combined it created a shockwave on the ground level, knocking everyone to the floor. Soon both battle freighters were gone, blanketed by a glorious sight of such awesome majesty it even stopped the conflict for a time as both the Crimson Empire and the Sapphire Regime tried to work out what had happened.

The girl's world was frozen in time. She looked up and smiled, her tears now falling silently into the dust.

The red and blue lasers had combined and exploded like a giant firework and washed the sky of Rodas with the most beautiful deep shade of purple.

The colour that had started the war.

The colour that could end the war.

She knew what she had to do now.

She knew how she could put a stop to it all.

The girl, even at her tender young age had seen enough and learned enough to survive on her own. Tearing herself away from the chaos, she instantly made for the ruined citadel. That astonishing colour she witnessed for the first time, was purple. She knew how to make it. She'd seen it happen right in front of her eyes.

All she had to do was mix red and blue. It was as easy as that.

With a goal in her mind, she spent the next couple of years living hand to mouth, roaming the ravaged plains of Rodas, fighting the aggressors from both sides with a simple combination of purple paint and purple coloured weapons. It worked, for a while. Even the hardest most embattled soldiers ran away like cowards when she splattered them with her traps.

But before long, they realised that this new combination wasn't harmful and so, her campaign rumbled, and the girl had to resort to her instincts to stay alive.

She never found her parents again but she knew that they were safe, deep down in her stomach. One day she would find them again. One day, when Rodas was free.

Right now, however, as she narrowly avoided her head being blasted to pieces by a shot from a laser rifle, she had other things on her mind.

As the street lights descended into darkness she took her chance. Spotting an opportunity for cover, she took it without a moment's hesitation. The girl skidded into a pile of rubbish that sat in the corner of the narrow pathway and buried herself within its putrid remnants. As what smelt like a ton of rotten fish heads had slopped over her frame, she held her nose and pushed her head down. The noise of the soldiers bundling their way past her disgusting hiding place began to subside.

Before long, the girl decided to risk it and popped her head up from behind the bins and peered with nervous eyes at the street. All was quiet again. Some people, used to the fraught nature of life on Rodas and who seemingly ignored the commotion as though it were just another day on a fighting planet, continued about their business.

The girl straightened herself up and felt the sickening gloop of the rotting food plop down her slight frame and onto the sandy ground. She wretched, succumbing to the aroma now clinging to her clothes like black-death and took in her surroundings. She knew this place.

Having spent the last few years on the streets she had grown accustomed to every back alley and darkened street on this side of Rodas.

Further ahead she knew of a crossroads splitting the path and taking her back toward the outskirts of the citadel border.

That way she could reach safety... and with the river nearby there was a place to wash away the stink of dead fish!

As she made her way cautiously, she stopped now and then to give a weak smile to any poor soul who came within a few feet of her.

As the path was quite narrow, it was quite a slow journey. Every face she glanced at looked the same. The eyes were sunken and void of hope. The mouth's pencil thin. Their faces were drawn and lined. Even the children seemed to look aged beyond their years, their youth, much like hers and countless generations before, taken away as the full horror of war was stained throughout their lives.

On the two-mile walk to the river, she continued to keep a cautious eye out for any soldiers of the Crimson Empire who were still looking for her. From previous experience, mercifully after several minutes they always seemed to give up. So many times in the past had she avoided them, sometimes only by the skin of her teeth, but never did she think they would catch her.

As the stars began to twinkle high above the pulsating barrier shield in the sky, she picked up her speed. If there was one place she didn't want to be, it was out in the open at night time.

Days were bad enough on Rodas. What happened in the evenings was almost inconceivable. Before long she found herself alone, the streets far behind her and now the open, desolate plains embraced
her. Conscious that scouts could be picking her up on their long-range scanners, she couldn't break into a full sprint as she knew that such an act could draw the wrong kind of attention. As long as she could reach the river, she knew she would be safe.

Over the dunes she went, trickles of the abrasive material beginning to rub her feet through the holes in her battered shoes, her breathing becoming heavier and heavier. Before long she could make out the river and all around it appeared to be shacks that lined its banks as far as the eye could see. The dwellers lived there. She was known to them and they frequently helped her out as much as they could. The dwellers were the homeless refugees of Rodas who had escaped the horror of the citadel and tried as hard as they could to shelter from the chaos. In comparison, they had a much quieter life and the girl was proud to be one of them. As she skidded on her backside towards the river bank the sand grew softer and she tried her best to avoid the darker parts that looked to her like quicksand. A few souls had been lost to them in the past and she wasn't going to be one of them.

317

She jumped over the final few feet of the dune and arrived on the muddier banks, the black sludge covering some of the putrid smell of the rubbish she had been forced to hide in.

As she cursed the mud, she picked herself out of the sticky slime and trudged towards an open-roofed shack.

'Thalo!' she cried as she passed an old woman, washing her clothes in the river.

'Up to no good again I see, Nkite,' the old woman said back hoarsely.

'Never me, Thalo, always them,' she replied.

She passed more faces, those happier to see her. A group of small children surrounded her. They were always so relieved that she was safe after her adventures. It always brought a little hope to their lives when she came back. A loud man's voice boomed above their giggles and the children scattered back to their homes.

The girl was a hero around these parts but a dangerous one no less. Many times the dwellers had vouched for her whereabouts and every time she went on a mission to help others, she brought members of the Crimson Empire to the river bank. And yet, every time they hid her. The dozens of families who lived there had become the family she had lost and she felt compelled to save them.

She knew she could never do it alone.

The girl, known to the dwellers as Nkite, walked fully clothed into the river, discarding her paint gun and binoculars at the bank's edge.

The water was warm and shallow at the lip of the bank but she was aware of just how deep it became very suddenly. With a huge splash, she allowed herself to slip under the water, the stench and filth floating off her, cleansing her once more.

After every mission to the citadel, she allowed the water to welcome her back.

She burst above the surface again, she breathed freely and pulled her long blue hair behind her neck.

As she emerged and went back to the river bank, she thought about why she does it.

Sodden to the bone, she made her way to a space near a gathering of sleeping dwellers.

She grabbed a piece of metal and laid it over a pool of liquid she thought it best not to inspect, she took her wet coat off and lay down, slipping the coat back over her.

It was a cold night on Rodas, it always was in winter, even on a topsy-turvy planet like this.

Yet the hope that one day soon, when the stars burn brightly and the purple sky high above Rodas brightens the planet once more, all will be well with Rodas one day, kept her smiling.

She'd be there, she would make sure. Even if it took a thousand years, she'd hold back the chimes of time to make sure she could be there for Rodas' salvation.

In her mind, amidst the horror this planet had seen, she knew it could be a peaceful place once more.

For all the lost souls caught in the crossfire of a pointless struggle between two violent armies, there were still many good people here.

She's seen them, repeatedly. Every time she did her little pranks with purple paint or the countless times she'd fired her paint gun at a Crimson or Sapphire soldier, she had been protecting the good and the kind. With every little contribution, her purpose in this world seemed more intertwined with the saviour that she knew was coming soon.

As she closed her eyes, the flames of hope within her heart were enough to keep her warm in winter.

HEADSCRATCHERS

When the Venus II began its twelfth involuntary barrel roll, Anji started to wonder whether she had, as Jake accused her of doing, flicked the wrong switch. The occupants of the cockpit, well three of them as Skateboard was able to use his magnetic capabilities to stick himself to the floor and stay relatively safe, continued to fly from one wall to another, all unable to find something to hold onto. As Random's brain lurched violently around in his skull, he searched high and low for a solution to their current predicament. It was too hard, even for him, and so his mind told him this wasn't the time to problem-solve and that blacking out was the only sane option left to him.

Amongst the screeching of the ship's engines tearing themselves apart the screams of the crew were like a drop in a very noisy ocean. However, as the Venus II lurched closer and closer towards oblivion, Skateboard's audible circuits thankfully broke in the hullabaloo, meaning he was finally able to fully concentrate on getting them out of this mess.

First thing first, he thought, stop the rolling. He connected to the control circuits of the Venus II and tried every trick in the book, but to no avail. They were still hurtling uncontrollably in space.

Okay, he pondered, let's change tact. What's causing the problem? He scanned the ship and ran diagnostics that probed every single connection within the Venus II.

Millions upon millions of potential faults were located and sorted in an instant and still the ship and its inhabitants were being thrown mercilessly about the place.

Right, so that didn't work, he mulled over, what about outside influences? Atmosphere, traffic, it must be something outside…

He switched his visual sensors to full stabilisation mode so that he could make out a clear vision and it was at this moment that the cause of their problem became known to him.

Ah, he cried, so that's what's causing it.

Outside the viewscreen was a sight so magnificent it could live in the memory of the stars for centuries.

Swamping the Venus II was a legend, a myth that circled the cosmos and yet no living being had ever seen.

The Quantum Narcosel.

Skateboard searched his memory banks for all he knew about it.

At this point, he would normally have shown off all his knowledge on the matter to his friends but as they were all currently unconscious and being tossed to all four corners of the cockpit, it was better to digest it all, considering he had only heard of it as a fable before himself.

The Quantum Narcosel was a fissure in space/time that acts as a wormhole to another part of the galaxy, like a motorway shortcut to a far-flung place, only there were no intersections, no place to hop off the ride.

If the Quantum Narcosel had you in its gravitational pull, you were going where it wanted you to go whether you liked it or not.

And so, with the amazing, huge multi-coloured fissure pulling them helplessly down the kaleidoscope plug hole, Skateboard embraced the inevitable and began to look at the positives.

They were not going to die, they were off on another adventure and it wasn't like the crew of the Venus II had anything particularly planned today anyway.

As the Venus II shook more violently than before, the little ship was swallowed whole and Skateboard, entranced by the whole experience of it, witnessed the entire terrifying, brilliant thing.

The journey was surprisingly short. Within seconds the Venus II was spat out in a completely new part of the galaxy. Mercilessly, at the same time that the ship escaped the Quantum Narcosel's clutches, the Venus II's operating systems returned to normal, the buffeting ceased and the barrel rolls had subsided to nothing more than a light lull.

The alert sirens were replaced by the hum of the engines, which were no longer fighting against the elements.

All of this was of great relief to Skateboard, until he realised that the Quantum Narcosel had spat them out directly onto the face of a planet and they were slipping softly through giant, dense brown tree trunks.

Skateboard checked the systems and couldn't believe his diodes. The Venus II seemed to be smoothly crash landing and before long, with a light plop on the planet's surface, they were down.

Immediately his attention turned to his friends. The cockpit was a complete mess with bits of paper and debris from discarded sandwiches that had escaped the lidless bin and ended up at the side of the pilot's chair. It looked like the inside of Jake's room! Skateboard detached his magnetic couplings and plonked himself off the roof and onto the cockpit floor. He ran a medical scan across all three of his friends and was worried for a second by a large red blob that had appeared on Anji's forehead. Thinking it to be a gash, Skateboard wheeled over to her. On closer inspection, he was relieved to discover that it was no more than a tomato slice. His investigations were interrupted by a groaning noise coming from underneath the dashboard. Slowly, the crumpled, battered figure of Random began to crawl from underneath it.

'Zarking hell, what happened?' he said, rubbing his forehead softly. 'I feel like a scrambled egg!' he noticed Anji and Jake, the latter of which was bent

double over the co-pilot's seat in a pose that he wouldn't have ever described as comfortable.

'Please tell me they are okay?'

Skateboard concluded his scans. 'Aside from some bumps and bruises... and vegetation, they are well.'

'Ugh,' groaned Anji, who hissed through her teeth as she lent on her palms. 'Before any of you start, I didn't do anything wrong.'

'Correct, miss,' said Skateboard. 'I'll go and get the painkillers from the medi-bay.'

Random picked himself up and groaned loudly as he made his way gingerly over to Anji and helped her up.

'Did something hit us?' she asked.

'Not sure,' said Random, who then noticed the strange forest they appeared to now be in. 'Hey... where are we?'

'Don't mind me, I'm fine,' said a muffled Jake.

'All right then, we won't!' Anji joked back. She helped her shaggy-haired friend back onto his feet and noticed a small cut on his cheek. 'Hey, we'd better get that checked out.'

'Leave it,' said Jake proudly. 'With any luck, it'll heal into a scar and make me look hard!'

'Guys, come and have a look at this,' Random said beckoning them to the viewscreen. The three friends looked out at the lush, thick brown trunks they seemed to have nested at the base of.

'Look at the way they sway,' said Jake.

'It's so thick and dense!' said Anji.

'We'd better get outside and take a look,' said Random. At this point, Skateboard arrived back in the cockpit carrying a tray of medical supplies.

'I'd advise that we check that the Quantum Narcosel is still operational before we go anywhere,' he replied.

Random, Anji and Jake looked quizically at him. The little AI robot knew that this might take some time. As his diodes sighed a little, Skateboard proceeded to patch them up whilst telling them all he had discovered about the mysterious powers of the Quantum Narcosel. As he finished attaching the bandage around Random's forehead, the penny finally dropped for Jake.

'Oh! It's a wormhole in space!'

Skateboard whirred. 'Similar principles to a wormhole, yes, sir, but with one element that is more familiar to the principles of black hole phenomena.'

'That it's supermassive?' asked Anji.

'No, miss. It's vast in size, yes, but it can be known to condense the object at the other side of the fissure.'

'Meaning?' asked Jake, hopping down off the dashboard.

'It means that we could be compressed to about the size of a can of baked beans if we're not too careful,' said Random.

Jake sighed. 'Great, I hate beans.'

'So there's no guarantee that we can get home?' asked Anji. 'Or back to our area of space at all? Actually, just how far away did the Quantum Narco-wotsit throw us?'

Random checked the instruments. 'Roughly sixty-four thousand lightyears away from our galaxy.'

'Might take a bit of time to go the long way round then!' said Jake sarcastically.

'To answer your question, miss, we can go back the way we came, but it may take some time. The Quantum Narcosel picks up on the genetic signature of all that is pulled through it and allows it safe passage back, but we have to wait for our window of opportunity.'

'Why?' asked Random.

'Well, the fissure is sucking all kinds of stuff in with its gravitational pull. Ships, debris, satellites. It can't all go in at once,' replied Skateboard.

'But you said this thing was supermassive?' asked Anji.

'In principle, yes, although I believe that was your terminology, miss,' said Skateboard. 'But if too much goes in at once at any end it will just compact whatever tries to enter it. We have to wait for the time it gives us to go back.'

'Which is?' asked Jake.

Random pressed a few buttons on the dashboard again. 'Three hours and twelve minutes.'

Anji mulled the time over. 'Why don't we check out where we are then?'

'But it could be dangerous!' cried Jake.

The cockpit fell silent and then after a few seconds, all four of its inhabitants broke into unanimous laughter.

'Ah,' said Jake, eventually wiping away a tear. 'Imagine if we ever said that seriously, eh?'

'All the same,' said Random, his pulse racing at the thought of another adventure. 'We'd better check the scanner. See what the locals are like if there are any.'

Random carried out the commands. 'Oh, wow.'

'What's up?' said Anji who moved closer to look at the read-out on the computer.

'There's quite a settlement here,' replied Random.

'How many lifeforms are we talking about?' asked Jake.

'Nine billion, five hundred and eighty-three... no hang on... six hundred and twenty-one... wait, it's going up again!'

'Whatever they are, they can reproduce at an alarming rate.' said Skateboard.

'Sounds like your dream planet, Jake!' said Anji, who upon nudging Jake in his ribs made her friend wince in pain.

'All joking aside,' said Random in a more serious tone. 'We'd better be careful. We don't know where we are, if the atmosphere is breathable or if the
natives are friendly. Other than that, we should be fine. Better grab the oxygen packs just in case. Right... just over three hours until home time. Who wants to explore?'

*

A short time later, the crew of the Venus II made their way down the gangway of the ship and onto the surface of this strange new world. The odd branches and trees had bent around their location almost like they had crashed down on a log cabin.

Wearing breathing equipment over their nose and mouths, Random, Anji and Jake led the way closely followed by Skateboard.

Random looked wearily around. 'Stay close to the ship. We don't want to get lost or go too far away to miss our chance back.'

'Or run out of oxygen,' said Anji. She walked off the gangway onto the pale, springy surface below. 'Hey! It's squidgy.'

'Yeah! A bit like being on a bouncy castle!' said Jake, who began to spring up and down
enthusiastically.

'You can take off the oxygen masks,' said Skateboard. 'The air is quite breathable.' The trio did so and the little AI robot took the apparatus back into the ship before returning to finish his scan of the local area.

Random made straight for the trees. There was something about the way that they swayed all in the same direction that entranced him. He held his hand out to touch the thick trunk of one of them.

'Amazing,' he said to himself. 'It's so soft!'

Skateboard felt his wheels dig a little into the ground. He scanned it instantly and cursed a delay in his findings. His diagnostic relay must have been damaged a little in the crash. Impatiently, he waited.

'I concur, miss, the ground almost feels like flesh,' he said.

'These trees are so close together, there are only a few feet between them. How comes we didn't get torn apart when we crashed?' asked Anji.

'Feel this!' implored Random. Anji made her way over to her friend and also felt the tree trunk.

'Do you see?' Random continued. 'It's so soft here. That and the buoyancy of the ground made for a nice landing!'

Oblivious to his friend's findings, Jake spotted something at the base of one of the trees. 'Hey, guys! Check this out,' he called over, but they were too deep in conversation to notice him. 'Fine!' he muttered as he approached his discovery.

There, at the foot of the tree, was a large oval-shaped white ball. It was about half the length of Jake's body and when he pressed his hand upon it, it felt soft and delicate to the touch.

'What the hell is this?' he said, feeling rather nervous.

Suddenly, as if reacting to his touch, the ball cracked a little at the top. Jake gulped.

'Guys, I really think you should get over here,' he called out as more cracks began to appear.

As Random and Anji finally heard him and made for Jake's location, only just able to make him out in the dense wood, Skateboard's diagnostic finally finished.

Adjusting his read-out, he began to panic.

'We have to get back to the ship!' he cried out, but his friends were all gone.

Suddenly, a cry of terror blew through the stiff breeze.

Skateboard hot-wheeled it in the scream's direction, only to be stopped in his tracks by the sight of Jake tearing past him, crying in horror.

'Jake, wait!' came another voice. This time it was Anji, who along with Random, was running after him.

Pretty soon they all caught up with him just as the teenager hurled himself to the floor, his face buried in the fleshy ground. Random and Anji knelt at his side immediately and pulled him onto his back.

In doing so, they saw the terrible thing that was happening to him.

There, clamped to Jake's face, was a hideous transparent creature.

'Hold still, buddy!' cried Random as he tried to wrestle it off him, which was hard to do given all the kicking and muffled screaming coming from their friend.

'What the hell is it?' cried Anji, who could barely watch. 'Hurry, it's strangling him!'

Eventually, Random found a narrow gap between the creature's belly and Jake's cheeks and as it dug its multiple legs further into the boy's flesh, Random yanked it with all his might. The creature flew through the air and hit a tree trunk.

Jake coughed excessively and clung to Anji's arm.

'Are you okay?' asked Random, putting a reassuring hand on his friend's arm.

'Would you be!' came the reply.

'Sounds like it,' said Random.

Skateboard made his way over to the creature and surveyed it carefully. It lay on the ground, motionless now.

'Jake, you've got two marks on your neck!' cried Anji. She wiped her hand over what looked like two puncture wounds. A smear of blood oozed from both.

'The little bloodsucker!' said Jake, still panting and now panicking again.

'Take it easy, mate, I'm sure you're fine, but we'll get you back to the Venus II to check you out, okay?' said Random.

He got up and walked over tentatively to join Skateboard at the creature's prone body.

The monstrosity was huge. It had sat on Jake's face but its full-length had been almost down to his knees. Random got down next to it. It looked insect-like.

Its transparent body was hard like a shell and its multiple mandibles and bug-like eyes and antennae reminded Random of something he had read about back on Earth.

'Dead?' he asked Skateboard.

'Yes,' the robot replied. 'The shock of your action was enough to stop its heartbeat before it hit the ground.'

'What is it?' asked Random.

'I'll answer your questions when we are safely back aboard the Venus II, sir, but for now, we must get back there before anything else happens.' He rolled his way over to Anji, who had produced a handkerchief and was using it to stem the flow of blood from Jake's neck wound. At the same time, Random noticed that there was an unusual swishing pattern beginning to emerge in the trees ahead of them.

Skateboard scanned the injured boy. 'You'll be fine, sir, you've lost a little blood but luckily there is no infection and your breathing apparatus is intact.'

'What was that horrible thing?' asked Jake.

'I'll tell you soon, sir, but for now, I recommend that you sit on my motherboard and I'll transport you back to the ship. Come along, all of you,' he commanded.

'Guys!' cried Random. Suddenly they all noticed that the forest was swishing oddly around them.

The sound of many, many feet was upon them.

'Quick, run!' he said, grabbing hold of Anji's hand to pull her and the others away but it was too late. The travellers yelped in shock.

Bursting out of the trees was a whole army of the same type of creature that had attacked Jake. Only these were four times its size and closing in on them.

Random for once, was quite scared. He tried to protect his friends by performing a one-man barrier but to no avail. As the terrifying monsters loomed over them, their mouths salivating with unspeakable slobber, he cleared his throat.

'Look, we don't mean any trouble. We crashed here. I'm Random and these are my friends, one of them is hurt. Will you help us?'

'You have killed one of our own,' came the reply, in all its hoarse deep menace.

'It attacked me!' cried out Jake.

'Please, there has been some misunderstanding. Can we talk this over? What shall I call you?' asked Random.

The leader peered down at him, making the Rodasian feel smaller than an ant.

'We are the Larvae and you will pay...'

It was after the long trek back to the Larvae's base, through the vast, identical fields, that it had

occurred to Anji exactly where they were.

And now they were alone, kept locked in what looked like a hut made from the same trees they had seen all over this planet, she felt compelled to share her theory.

'We're on someone's head, aren't we?'

Jake winced as he continued to paw over his wounds. 'What gave you that idea?'

'Think about it, you lot! Did you not see the fields we were marched through? All those trees, sure they were shorter, but what was at the base of them?'

'Eggs,' said Random, who was observing their prison with great interest.

'Exactly!' cried Anji. 'Or should I say, "Eggs-actly!"'

'Get to the point, Gummadi,' warned Jake, who was in no mood for jokes following his ordeal.

'It all adds up. First the ground, you said it was fleshy, right Skateboard?'

Skateboard, already knowing the reality of their situation, agreed, deciding to give someone else the chance to be the clever one for a change.

Anji continued. 'Then there's the monster that attacked Jake, it's not a monster at all. It's a nit! Jake broke its egg and so it acted in self-defense!'

'Hey! It wasn't the only one!' said Jake.

'Then, there are the trees, they are not trees at all. How can they be? They are too soft! It's-'

'Hair... each tree trunk is a strand of hair,' Random butted in.

Anji looked indignant. 'I was just coming to that,' she said as she slumped against the hairy wall.

'Only this hair is roughly two feet in width,' Random tested its texture by pressing his palm against it, 'and incredibly strong.'

'So we've been miniaturised?' asked Jake.

'No,' said Skateboard. 'We are on a planet alright, only it's a living organism.'

'How?' asked Random.

'I am not sure,' said Skateboard.

'Are we currently sitting on the scalp of a mahoosive alien that has nits then? One that can breathe in space?' asked Anji.

'It's hard to say but it is an interesting premise though,' said Skateboard.

'One we don't have time to investigate further,' said Random. 'Skateboard, how much time do we have left to get back through the fissure?'

'We have just under two hours. It took us an hour and a half to be brought here.'

Random frowned. 'That means we only have roughly half an hour to argue our case for freedom.'

'But you're super fast and super strong Random. Why can't you just blast through the walls, punch a few of these big nits out and race us back to the Venus II?' said Jake.

'We don't know if the Larvae are hostile or not. I will not harm a species without reason too.'

'Way to stick up for a friend,' said Jake.

Random got down on his haunches and looked him square in the eye.

'Violence is only ever a last resort. You should know that by now.'

'But I was attacked!' whined Jake.

'By a baby,' said Anji.

'Which I then killed...' said Random. Anji and Jake fell silent. The realisation set in that their friend had indeed carried out that appalling deed.

'Sir...' said Skateboard.

'I know what you are going to say Skateboard, but please save it, I should have known better. I only hope the Larvae will accept my apology.'

At that moment, three giant Larvae scuttled into the hut, their maniples making a swishing sound as they moved across the soft ground.

They each appeared to be carrying some form of weapon and to Random it seemed to resemble a whip made from the hair on this planet.

'Come,' said one of the Larvae. 'You are required.'

***

Once more the travellers trudged through the strangest of planets they had ever encountered. On the short trip to the throne room, they witnessed a kingdom built from strands of hair.

There was a small town, of which all the houses were modest in size and a population of Larvae was happily going about their daily business, some of them stopping in their tracks to gaze upon the weird three humanoid aliens and their robot friend.

All the time Jake thought about Random's words. It was true that while their lives could quickly descend into violence, they never started it themselves.

Except for today.

Today had been a blot on their copybook and made all the worse that the creature that attacked him had sadly not lived past the commotion Jake had caused.

If only I hadn't put my face near that egg, he thought to himself.

If only Random hadn't had to step in for me once again, he reflected.

He wasn't the only prisoner to feel the burn of shame. All four of the travellers felt guilty for what had happened but none more so than Random.

In the past few years he had saved countless civilisations but with every life saved, somewhere his actions had caused the loss of another.

It was his burden to bear and the feeling it left him never felt better, no matter what good he had done for the universe.

This time, he would face the consequences of his actions and he would allow himself full responsibility, for whatever came his way.

As Random, Anji, Jake and Skateboard were marched up a mountain of stairs that led to an incredibly impressive palace, the

334

eyes of the inhabitants burnt on their necks and when they got to
the top and the huge, hair-bound doors to the throne room
enveloped upon them, they gulped hard.

Inside the long throne room, a hundred Larvae stood in line on
either side of a runway, leading to a distant yet large throne upon
which Random could make out a Larvae much vaster in scale than
his subjects.

Random's face fell even more serious. 'Leave the talking to me,'
he ordered.

With a prod in their backs, the foursome was
forced inside the throne room and as the inhabitants far below
began to go about their daily business again, the heavy doors
slammed firmly shut.

Inside, they were introduced, after a long, rough walk, to the
huge creature on the throne. Its shell-like skin was darker than the
others, and it wore a crown woven from hair.

Random moved forward from his friends and dropped to one
knee before the mighty ruler of the incredible world the travellers
had fallen upon. 'Am I addressing the King of the Larvae?'

The creature rubbed its mandibles in annoyance. 'In your
culture, the male might be King, but here, it is those who lay eggs
who rule.'

'My apologies, your Majesty. Not just for the confusion but our
conduct here on this planet.'

'Silence!' the Queen clicked. 'Magister read them their rights.'

An inferior Larvae scuttled forward and partially unravelled a
scroll.

'Strangers of the daughter planet, you have been found near the
body of a member of our tribe. The charges that have been
brought against you include trespassing upon our egg farm, the
actual harm to one of our young and finally the murder of one of
our number. How do you plead?'

Random bowed his head in shame. 'Your Majesty. I cannot deny
the accusations you have brought against us but we are strangers
here. We were under attack from the infant Larvae and in fairness,
my friend here would have died if I hadn't stepped in. I never
meant to kill. I was only

---

thinking of saving the life of another. It was a mistake that I greatly regret, I can assure you. If you would like proof of the attack, take a look yourselves!'

Random pulled Jake by the arm in front of him.

The Queen lent forward, as did a number of the congregation as Jake pulled his collar down and took an improvised bandage away to reveal the two sucker spots in his neck. Members of the congregation murmured as the evidence was produced. Jake looked around him nervously.

'Chief,' said the Queen, 'Is it possible that this wound was self-inflicted?'

The Chief wore a stern expression. 'No, your Majesty. This attack was unprovoked, I can assure you of that.'

'Oh yeah. how?' Anji butted in. 'Were you there to see it happen?'

'I did not need to be! Our younglings are not dangerous. It is obvious that these... foreigners... came here and felt threatened by our differences and began a cowardly attack on our kind.'

'Of course, we felt threatened, it attacked me!' cried Jake.

'Don't agree with him Jake,' warned Random.

'What's your problem with us?' asked Anji.

'Please!' said Random sharply. 'Chief, I know that our appearance here has come a little out of the blue, and I can see that you are not used to

strangers on your world but we came here by accident. If you look outside right now, high above us, you will see a fissure in space. You may not believe us but we fell through that. Others will follow if you do not let us go and pass back through and try to stop something like this from ever happening again.'

'"Others will follow",' the Chief huffed. He addressed the congregation. 'Did you hear that? Your Majesty, Lords and Ladies, this murderer intends to threaten us with more aliens upon our land. How will they treat us? With the same disdain as these abominations! The only future that lies for them is the same as those who dare come to our world in the future. Death.'

Random's fists clenched. It was clear that the Chief didn't like strangers on this planet and now he was trying to stoke the flames of a crowd who were scared and bewildered.

'There's only one dangerous person in this room and it isn't me!' screamed Random.

'There is only one murderer in this room and it is you!' The Chief loomed into Random's space, slobbering maliciously down on him.

'Chief, that is enough!'

The Chief purred. The Queen looked alarmed.

'My apologies, your Majesty, but you can see how their mere presence has terrified the room.'

'The only terror going on here is the words of a man who is oblivious to his prejudice,' said the Queen.

'Nice one, Queenie!' Anji whispered to Jake. She squeezed his hand in excitement, as though she knew they were in the clear.

'Stranger, might I ask what your name is?' she implored Random forward again.

'I am Random, your Majesty, and this is Anji, Jake and our robot Skateboard.'

'And you fell through this... fissure, you say?'

'Yes,' Random replied. 'It's called the Quantum Narcosel. If we don't get back to our ship soon we will miss our window back to our universe. If we do not fix it, many other beings will also fall through. Some will be peaceful, others might not be.'

The Queen sat back on her throne. 'Strangers, as you can see we are not used to alien life visiting our world. Indeed, it seems that there are those in my council who are not ready at all for this to become a regular occurrence. It is for this reason, and for the story that you have indeed given us, that I believe that it would only be right if all charges against you were dropped.'

The travellers breathed a collective sigh of relief. Even Skateboard, with his eyes nervously checking the time they had left to escape this universe, allowed his hydraulics to relax.

The Chief was seething. 'But your Majesty, they murdered in cold blood!'

'They did not,' chimed in a new Larvae member. Random surveyed him curiously. He approached Jake and stared in fascination at his wound. 'Just as I thought. The puncture wounds are comparable to the diameter of the mouthpart of a newborn Larvae.'

Jake, relieved that the truth was believed, pointed his finger at the Chief. 'Ah! Take that then!'

The Chief was incredulous.

'Have you anything left to say?' the Queen asked him.

The Chief was silent. His rage began to bubble underneath. This wasn't fair. It was his wife's egg farm that had been compromised, the Queen knew that, he had told her before the trial had started. If she wasn't going to make these unwelcome foreigners pay, then he would.

'Random, Anji, Jake and Skateboard, I hereby declare that you have been found not guilty of the accusations brought against you,' said the Queen loud enough for the whole congregation to hear.

The travellers whooped and cheered, all except Random. 'Thank you, your Majesty, and I will forever regret the event that brought us to you in the first place.'

The Queen nodded. 'You may go.'

The travellers high-fived and bowed respectively, all except Skateboard.

'Sirs, miss. We need to go now!'

'Thanks once again!' said Random as he along with the others raced towards the heavy door outside. The Chief clicked two of his six legs and the guard who had brought them in came to his side. 'Wait until they are outside,' he said in a low tone. 'Time that the Queen was overthrown...'

'How long have we got, Skateboard?' asked Random as he and his friends spilled out onto the grand steps they had minutes earlier been forced up as prisoners.

'I'm not sure telling you would help the situation, sir, but we'll be lucky if we get back in time!'

'Can we use your super-speed?' asked Anji to Random.

'I think we are going to have to,' said Random. 'Right everyone, hop on Skateboard.'

'But sir, my speed isn't as fast as yours,' said Skateboard.

'I know, you're going to have to let me go manually,' replied Random.

Jake was rather quiet and with good reason. He had made the mistake of looking behind them as they were running.

Finally, he found the words to alert his friends.

'Er, guys?'

Random and Anji were busying themselves on Skateboard's motherboard and almost fell over when they saw what Jake was witnessing.

Down the steps, a swarm of Larvae was beginning to tear after them.

'Well, this isn't going to help matters,' said Random with a sigh. 'Skateboard, bond us to your motherboard and direct me back to the Venus II please.'

'Sir,' obeyed Skateboard.

Anji pulled Jake onto Skateboard's back and his shoes instantly bonded to it.

'Right, hold on tight everyone!' cried Random.

'Wait, I'd better tie my shoe-' Jake never had a chance to finish.

In a blinding flash, the four travellers sped away from the scene.

The Chief looked on, his mouth dribbling with unspeakable saliva. 'Cowards... after them!'

The army of Larvae picked up speed leaving the throne room empty, except for the dead bodies of the Queen and her bodyguards.

'Left!' Skateboard instructed.

The travellers swung in unison.

Anji was crouching down, trying to get a better balance which was hard, considering she was also holding onto Jake's arm with all her might.

The blonde-haired teenager was screaming with terror, his sockless feet being beaten by the long strands of hair that they were weaving past.

'Straight on for two miles!' Skateboard said calmly.

'Gives me a chance to build up some momentum!' Random said to himself, his left leg furiously pounding the fleshy floor propelling them toward escape.

Suddenly, the Larvae burst through the hair, narrowly missing them.

'How much further?' asked Anji.

'Just under two miles, we are on the home straight!' said Skateboard.

Random peddled like mad. Soon enough, the Venus II honed into view. Without hesitation, Skateboard remotely lowered the gantry and the travellers tore on board. They stopped abruptly in the mid-section and as Skateboard uncoupled their bonds, all three of his friends were sent sprawling to the floor. Before they had a chance to regroup, Random was already crawling to the cockpit.

'Oh come on, give us a break!' he moaned as he saw on the viewer screen that the Larvae had started to swarm the Venus II.

In the mid-section, Anji screamed as a Larvae had begun dragging her by the ankle out of the ship as the gantry started to recede upwards, trapping the insects out.

'Anj!' Jake leaped to her defense and picking up his shoes, started smacking the Larvae as hard as he could. Skateboard, who was already trying to speed up the retracting gantry and fire up the engines, produced his stun gun and hit the Larvae with a precise shot to its head. A high-pitched scream emitted from it as it slid back outside the craft just as the gantry slammed shut with a heavy thud.

Jake opened his mouth to ask if Anji was okay but a curt, 'no time!' from her, stopped him as she followed Skateboard up to the cockpit.

When inside, they were stunned to see the Larvae had completely obscured the viewscreen.

'There's loads of them!' cried Random, who had gripped the steering column and as the hum of the engine got louder, realised there was only one way to escape and that was to shake them off.

'The drag effect of their weight is too much!' he shouted.

Outside the Venus II, almost every square inch of the craft was covered by the Chief and his army. Hundreds of them were now scuttling all over it.

The ship had become infested.

The Chief hammered on the hull to no effect. He grimaced and thought quickly. 'Tear this ship apart!'

Back inside, Skateboard was doing his best to compensate for the drag effect of the weight of the Larvae.

'Sir, they are trying to damage the ship!'

'How much time do we have Skateboard?'

Skateboard checked. 'Seconds!'

'That settles it,' said Random. He lent over to the dashboard and flicked a few switches.

Suddenly, all the Larvae began to shriek in agony. A blue web of electrical current burst out of the Venus II's hull, causing the Larvae to stiffen and fall one by one off the ship. The Chief's final order had ultimately led his charges to their deaths and as his still body fell onto the soft ground below, slowly the Venus II began to pull away from the surface.

'Punch it now!' exclaimed Anji as Random powered them all away from danger. As the ship tore through the long hairs of the planet of the Larvae and nearer the edge of space, the incredible sight of the Quantum Narcosel replaced the unpleasant one of Larvae trying to get in.

'Skateboard?' asked Random through gritted teeth.

'Now!' came the reply.

With a blinding flash, the Venus II disappeared.

Moments later, on the other side of the universe, the Quantum Narcosel exploded into life and belched out the Venus II. Inside, its occupants stayed motionless in the cockpit.

'Are we home?' asked Jake tentatively.

Random checked the scanner. 'We are!'

They all jumped for joy. Anji threw her arms around her friends as Random fell back in his chair exhausted.

He wiped his brow with the sleeve of his t-shirt. 'How much time did we have left?' he asked, turning to Skateboard.

The AI robot checked. '0.054 seconds.'

Jake burst out laughing. 'I'm making that my lucky number!'

'Look!' said Anji.

As they watched, the Quantum Narcosel suddenly shrank into nothingness.

'What happened?' asked Jake.

Skateboard ran a quick diagnostic on the local area. 'It seems as though our coming back through the fissure has healed it.'

'What?' Random said disbelievingly. 'You mean our passing back through sealed it up?'

'It would seem so. I think I shall carry out further tests if I might be so bold. This experience might just change our methods in the fight against these occurrences of anomalies in space.'

Random swooped his hand in an "after you" gesture and after setting the controls to autopilot, made his way out to the mid-section.

'Hey,' Anji called out after him. 'Don't blame yourself for what happened back there, you hear me?'

'Yeah,' Jake continued. 'You shouldn't be feeling down after saving my life. I mean, where would you lot be without me?'

Random smiled. 'Probably making escapes quicker! You're both right though, thank you.'

He continued out of the mid-section. Of course any life, no matter whether it is good or bad he would feel the burden of it lost if he had a hand in its demise. One day, he'd allow himself time to heal from it all.

But first, he needed a shower. For some reason, since they crashed on the planet of the Larvae, his scalp had been itching like mad!

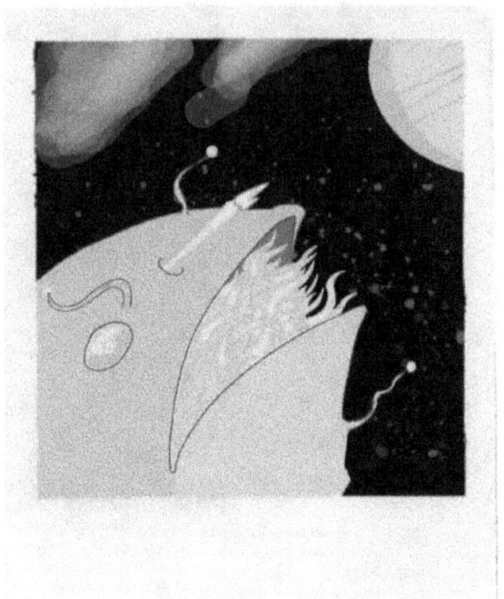

DEAR DIARY

Dear diary...

...by Anji Gummadi...

aged 15 and three-quarters.

Hey!

Is that how you start a diary entry? No idea, that's why this is my thirteenth attempt, but I'll be damned if I have to scrub it out and start again, so we are stuck with it.

Anyway, why have I decided to start a diary now, you might be saying? Especially since I am a bit of a celebrity in some parts of the galaxy. Well, maybe not by name but by association.

You see, today marks the third anniversary since Jake and I left the Earth with an alien with purple skin and his robot skateboard. Three years!

Doesn't time fly when you are saving the universe twice weekly?

So before I pull myself away from my room and dig into the very special cake we picked up from Argolas IV (it's telepathic, seriously! Really!

You can choose the flavour of your slice as long as you say out loud what you would like as you cut it.

That way, everyone gets a fair piece and we don't have to buy four individual cakes!), let me tell you about what has been happening recently.

What about the previous three years, I hear you cry, in my head! Well... I'll get around to them one day, I'm sure.

But seriously, you really must be confused. Why start now? Why not back when we ran away from our mundane lives? I'll get to that.

First, I want to tell you about something that happened last
Thursday.

Thursday... er... whatever month it is this part of the star system
we are in.

It started like any other day. We were being chased out of the
nostril of a space whale the size of the solar system by a band of
space pirates we had been asked to investigate by a local planet.

That's what we do. We go around, minding our own business
and then suddenly someone's asking us to do something that
might lead to certain death.

A typical Thursday, then.

After we had negotiated a wave of what can only be described
as asteroid-sized bogies, we were back out in the darkness of
space just at the point that the bomb we had planted exploded
within the space whale's stomach, blowing both the whale
and the space pirate's ships out of the sky and
into the atmosphere of all twelve planets in the
star system we were protecting. Sounds callous, almost evil,
doesn't it? Well, it's not!

You see, the reason why we had to deal with the space whale in
such a way was that it had drifted into the star system, called the
Narzoski system, from a rogue wormhole. These things have been
opening up all around the place, ever since our terrible encounter
with Stratos a few years back. I say it was terrible because... the
things that he did are almost too awful to mention. Like I said, one
day I'll write about it, I am sure.

Since then, fissures leading to alternate realities have been
opening up like supermarkets on this big old high street we call
the universe. Even though we fell down one recently but we were
lucky to get out of it! They haven't come about that often, I hasten
to add, but these can be dangerous. Leaks from parallel worlds
can lead to instability within the fabric of reality itself, or so
Skateboard put it, and so now and then we are called to look into
it by the Space Seals Corps.

They are a sort of space military operation that we've worked with before, now run by Admiral Bagari. She loves us a lot; she just doesn't like to show it.

When the Space Seals are unable to find a way to stop something from escaping these fissures, we step in like the absolute professionals we are and help where we can.

So why did we kill it? The space whale was a planet eater. We've seen whole worlds burn before and we were not willing to see it happen again. Also, it was an evil space whale.

Sentient, though it was, the huge creature did this for a living in its reality. After Random had tried negotiating with it, we were left with no choice but to take drastic action.

It was only after we had stolen the bomb that we needed from a local gang of space pirates, who themselves had been terrorising one of the moons in the Narzoski star system, that we killed two birds with one bomb, so to speak, and BOOM! One dazzling fireworks display later, the Narzoski system was safe yet again.

As the Space Seals healed the rift in the fissure, we caught our breath, said our piece back to Bagari and left for another adventure.

It was only when I sat down on my bed and drank the experience that I realised what we had become.

We were agents for the Space Seals, employed without pay or reward to do their dirty work.

I mean, I'm not saying that we would accept it. Far from it! All we ever ask in return if it's offered to us is a couple of freebies, I swear!

A spa week here, a holiday there. Maybe some free fuel for the Venus II or in this case a telepathic cake! We are not mercenaries, but I was starting to feel like we were.

*

Not long after, there came a knock at my door. It was Jake. It was always Jake.

You see, me and Jake have this thing. No, not like that! It's unspoken... I don't want to use the word but I suppose you could call it love. Not that we have ever acted on it. I mean, I suppose as time has gone on and Jake has matured (in body only, I hasten to add, not in mind!) I would have never said no to starting anything. We had this long-term agreement when we were at school, if we were both single come the day of the prom we would go together. Prom's technically only a year or two away by my estimation, but I doubt we will ever act on our relationship.

Well, he wouldn't anyway, I know that for a fact! His head is turned more than an owl on a roundabout. But that promise has got us through some very sticky situations in our time travelling the stars... and I sure as hell won't stop using it if one of our lives are in danger again.

I let him in and he takes up his customary spot at the foot of my bed and I have to tell him off for the umpteenth time to keep his shoes off my quilt. Then we start talking. It's like a de-brief/counselling session we always have whilst the other two are carrying out repairs or doing something high-tech and spacey.

He's having problems with it too. Not just that but also with the killing.

Our motto has always been to be kind and friendly until someone tries to kill us, and even then Random prides himself upon giving them a chance! But like myself, Jake worries about it and now that we seem to be unofficial agents for the Space Seals it seems to confirm it. I tell him that we should speak to Random and see what he thinks.

Naturally, he thinks slightly differently. First of all, Random is an addict. So am I to some extent. He likes adventure. More than that, he LOVES it! It's a distraction from what he really should be doing, which is saving his world, although from what he has told me over the years it sounds pretty irredeemable if you ask me! But he insists on keeping in touch with the Space Seals and keeping an eye on these fissures.

Random feels responsible, I get it, I do. If you were a superhero created from all the best of your people with powers beyond our own, you'd feel like that too. What's that old movie saying? "With great power... something-something?" Never mind. Random's link to the fissures is closer than you might think. You see, Stratos killed in his name.

Random seeking out the wormholes and alike is kind of like him erasing the bad that evil cyborg did. He said so himself. And so, for the time being, he is willing to work with the Space Seals.

That led to me going back to my room in a bit of a huff. I didn't show it mind, although I did give Random the silent treatment for the next couple of hours.

As I lay on my bed thinking about what to do next, a thought suddenly occurred to me.

I needed some time away. Not just from travelling but from Random and Skateboard, even Jake!

But what? I mean, the holidays are all well and good but I wanted something more. As I mentioned I am as addicted to adventure as Random is, for reasons I will get into, so what to do? Where could I go?

I hurled myself into the cockpit and typed into the computer an amalgamation of my desires. Adventure, action, new faces.

Then I reeled in shock at what it suggested to me.

It said that I should join the Space Seals...

So the following day... whoops, I should write that bit a little more formally, hang on...

Friday... of whatever the month was again.

... There.

I've done it. I've only gone and bloody done it.

I've enrolled in the Space Seals Corps.

The night before, Jake and Random had pleaded with me in equal measures to change my mind. Skateboard had been his logical self and said that if it was what I wished then I should just go for it.

But I wasn't sure. I mean, it seemed to fill all of the categories of what I needed right now, but to join the thing I was wanting to run away from, was it such a good idea?

I quelled their fears and told them that the course I had looked up was only a short one.

It was an intense two-week training programme that was to take place on one of their space freighters known as the Archangel.

Well, my Dad, what I remember of him, used to say I was his little angel, so it seemed like it was fate that I would sign up.

That morning, the boys reluctantly ran me to meet with the Archangel. Jake was really worried that he might be losing me for good. I told him he was stupid and that I'd see him in a couple of weeks.

As I packed my things, Random asked me again if it was really what I wanted to do. I was truthful and I told him that I wasn't sure but that I needed the challenge.

He then asked if this was me getting back at him for wanting to work for the Space Seals in stopping the fissures from opening.

I said no, I wasn't doing this out of spite and as soon as my bags were packed I gave him a cheery smile and made for the mid-section gantry.

There, Jake and Skateboard awaited me and we all hugged and said our goodbyes and without looking behind me, I stepped onto the gantry and into the cold isolating embrace of the Archangel.

When I was clear of the Venus II, I allowed myself a glimpse of home as it sailed away from me. I gave a smile and a little wave as it flew out of the landing bay and out into space.

I'd be back... wouldn't I?

I was escorted to the barracks that I would be sharing with a dozen other females who had also enrolled in the programme. Tell you what, the Space Seals badly needed a decorator on board the Archangel.

To be frank, both of the freighters I'd been on, were military grey. Like a deep, dingy grey. I've known black holes to have more colour!

But oh well, it was home for two weeks so maybe I shouldn't have grumbled. I then met my fellow inmates, sorry, cadets, and they more than made up for it.

What a colourful bunch! A rainbow of races! But their demeanours, almost to a woman, were very bleak.

Almost as though they didn't want to be here. Maybe they didn't have a choice.

It was also clear from the off that I was the youngest.

On account of my 16th birthday being so close, and because I have a professional acquaintance with Admiral Bagari, I got in, but even now I was beginning to feel out of my depth.

They weren't particularly friendly either. I was shunned to the corner bed, which was nothing more than a camping one with a bluey-grey Space Seal uniform, complete with boots and polishing kit, sat neat and tidy at the foot of it.

I ran my hand along the single-sheeted quilt. It was sharp to the touch, like wool laced with barbed wire.

At that point, a fight broke out between two Regolarians, which are slug-like creatures, only twelve feet tall and fire-breathing!

Sitting on my bed I sighed.

Maybe it was a holiday I wanted after all?

The next day, oh bum, I've done it again!

Saturday

You see, not much else happened that Friday. I put on my new uniform, was told... well... shouted at about how to keep it clean and neat, ate dinner at the food hall and then went back to my bunk and got ready to sleep. It would be needed. The next day we were to be deployed on a training exercise on the desert planet of Kronas.

With live guns.

And live grenades.

Now the day was upon me and we had all been cramped up inside this tiny shuttle.

Not before we were barked at whilst standing to attention by Commander Silas, who to me seemed the kind of man who was probably bullied as a kid, became a football referee and then thought to himself, "Nah I want to make people's lives more of a misery. I think I shall become a Space Seal Academy trainer, that'd show 'em!"

He seemed to enjoy picking on me. Probably because he knew I was the youngest or possibly because I was the only cadet with two arms (everyone else had at least four) so maybe he was trying to toughen me up.

Fool.

I lost my parents as a kid. I lived unwanted in a children's home. I too was bullied mercilessly (although I recently discovered my bully had the hots for me, which might have confused matters). I have taken on aliens from other worlds, cyborgs from other realities altogether and helped save millions of lives.

As he spat blue flecks of spit at me, roaring in my face, I stared unblinkingly and thought to myself.

Oh, hun, you're going to have to try better than that...

A short time later, I was squashed in with the other cadets into this tiny shuttle, a gigantic machine gun thrust against my chest by the attending Captain, about to run out into god knows what!

All we had been told was that there was something out there that needed sorting out... and by the manner of artillery we were taking, it wasn't going to be friendly.

The instant we touched down, the shuttle door peeled down onto a bright, humid plain. It was the heat that hit me first, full-on in the face like someone had opened an oven door.

I wasn't given much time to dwell upon it though. No, like everyone else I was running headlong into danger with no idea what to expect. So no change there then.

Before long, however, we certainly knew why we had been thrown into this pressure cooker.

The sandy ground below our boots shook like an earthquake was about to strike. A sound, as though a load of hornet nests had just been upset, started to grow louder and louder.

I looked to my left and right at my cadets, cocking my machine gun just as they did. I noticed one girl was shaking and then slightly distressingly a trickle of liquid began to seep through her trousers onto the dry sand below. I gulped... feeling nothing else but a need to go and put my arm around her shoulder and comfort her.

I couldn't though. Not because of what the Captain would do or the harsh words of Commander Silas that would await me when I got back to the Archangel. No. The hive army of insects that were flying straight for us confirmed that my words of assurance would have to wait some time yet!

The Captain's cry of charge seemed to switch something on in my mind. Instead of running away from danger, I was tearing toward it! The hum of the enemy burrowed into my skull. I noticed that my fellow cadets were starting to attack, firing their guns with varied precision at the enemy and yet, I noticed that the creatures themselves weren't attacking. I wasn't going to fire on anyone unless they tried to kill me first, that's what we do.

That's what Random would always do. I looked for cover. There was none to be found. Before long the hive was right on top of us; they were about to attack. Something was up here.

Then it hit me, almost as hard as the searing heat that felt like it was melting my face.

This wasn't a training exercise.

This was pest control.

Suddenly, the Captain hollered a halt to proceedings. To every man and woman, every single cadet did what we were told.

It had only been a day for us in the academy - had we been conditioned to obey already?

Not me, clearly as apparently to the Captain's rage, I was the reason for the pause in the exercise.

Then, within moments the entire world began to melt around us.

The hive disappeared into thin air, the sand beneath our feet evaporated into nothing and the unbearable humidity faded into the cool breeze of an air conditioning system.

The desert moon of Kronas was gone. We had never left the Archangel.

It was all a simulation!

As I felt the hot stares of all the cadets on the back of my neck, I heard the piercing scream of Commander Silas aimed in my general direction.

Before I knew it, I was being frog-marched into his office by a couple of his heavies. Good, I thought. I was in the mood for an argument!

Boy, it didn't disappoint!

Silas sat down behind his desk, which looked as immaculate and tidy as any Headmaster's office I had been to (believe me, I've seen quite a few!) and stewed.

He asked the guards to wait outside and as soon as the door shut, he blew a fuse, man!

He blew up so hard I swear that there was steam rising off his shiny bald head.

The small, slight man standing before me grew smaller and smaller the more he shouted at me.

Apparently due to my lack of participation the team had failed our objective. I asked him what it was as nobody told us and he rather curtly shouted back to follow our orders.

I took issue with this. Following orders blindly? We didn't even know if the creatures we were instructed to massacre were dangerous or not. There was no intel given to us about who we were fighting and why. He said that we didn't need to know. I said that it was asking us to commit murder.

He then pointed out that it was a simulation, but I was adamant that the principle remained. When he threw back that I shouldn't dare talk to him in this manner I came right back at him with the opinion that he and the Space Seals needed someone to remind them that we among them aren't murderers.

I can't quite remember what he replied now. Something about me being an "insubordinate delinquent, a disruption, someone who would never amount to anything, I could get others killed, I don't listen to authority," yada yada yada.

To be honest, I wasn't paying much attention.

You see, I've known so many like him.

In the past I was angry. I was a disruption.

I acted out in ways that soothed my pain. The pain of sticking out like a sore thumb. The pain of not allowing myself to feel or care again.

The pain of being alone.

And so, just as he launched into what felt like the final chapter of his novel-worth of put-downs and insults, I decided to shout back.

It was at that point that I realised why I had enlisted with the Space Seals.

I needed a reminder of who I am.

I'm not a number, I'm not a cadet who needs pushing around, breaking then re-molding in someone else's image.

I'm Anji Gummadi.

I lived through my parents passing away. I have a hatred that will last a thousand lifetimes for drunk idiots who drive and have no idea what suffering they cause further down the line for those who have been left behind.

And I have learned to deal with my grief, in ways far better and healthier than setting fire to stuff at school and getting into fights.

I looked Silas square in the eye, so close I could smell the salty sweat pouring from his little round face, and told him why I was so much better than all of this.

"Do you know why I'm none of the things you accuse me of?" I yelled when he had finished his pathetic tirade. "I help people. I have helped to save more lives than you and your toy soldiers will ever do. I have seen my weaknesses and through others, I have learned from them, not by wearing a uniform or following orders blindly to kill, but by using my initiative and having the best team I could ever ask for around me. Because do you know what, Commander? We might not all be perfect, and we might not be neat, but when something doesn't feel right, we don't just reach for our guns and fire at will, we question. You can't break me, no one can! And one last thing about me, by God, do I know how to be there to help when it is needed and don't you dare for one-second lecture me on my manners, or my temperament because it's more than you and your stupid army ever deserve!"

And with that, I slammed my fist on the desk, breaking a little model of a ship that looked like it had been lovingly painted recently.

Commander Silas looked down at the splintered remains and began to shake. His skin was redder than an angry bottle of ketchup and he shook so violently I'd have been worried that his brain might explode out of his skull if I wasn't so angry myself.

"You have one hour to get off my ship," he said quietly.

I smiled at him as I unfastened the cadet nameplate that was fixed to the lapel of my uniform.

I threw it at his face and turned on my heels, not bothering to see his churlish reaction.

"I've already left," I said heroically as I left the room. Silas began to shout and scream like a toddler who had been told to go to bed.

I gave the guards outside his office a withering look.

"I'd sit him on the naughty step until he's calmed down if I were you," I said and with a wink, I walked back to my barracks to collect my things.

Sunday

Okay, so I didn't leave straight away.

There was a lot of paperwork and official stuff to sort out before I was allowed that sweet chance for freedom.

When I returned to my barracks, I was shocked to see that it was full of my fellow cadets.

I had thought they would all be off on some other crazy exercise in which they were asked to shoot at poor creatures (okay, I know it was a simulation but come on, the principal stands in my book!) so when I heard them all talking, some about me, it didn't surprise me how silent it went when I entered the room.

God, it was like being back at school, the daily walk through the dining hall to the seats.

People would stop and stare at me then too, so naturally, I was used to this.

Unlike school, this time I was escaping... and someone stopped to say something to me!

As I sat down on my bed, which even after one night's sleep I felt had given me a rash it was so
uncomfortable, I heard a small voice asking if they could speak to me.

It was the girl who had wet herself during the exercise.

She was rather tomboyish in looks but wore a kind, slightly scared face.

I returned my kindest smile and said sure, even though I didn't feel like talking to anyone.

She said that she just wanted to thank me for making them stop.

She had no idea it wasn't real and felt bad that we
were just being asked to shoot for no apparent reason.

I said it was a rubbish thing for them to ask us to do straight out of the gate and that the Space Seals was no place for people who were capable of independent thought.

She agreed. She said she'd had the chance to join up and please her family, as her Father was a Space Seal, or go off to Space University to study something to do with plants.

I told her to thank God there was a 48-hour cooling-off period and that she was better off doing what she wanted, not what she thought others would like.

After agreeing with me, she patted me on the shoulder, said thanks again and disappeared to the other side of the room.

If only I remembered her name.

Sunday was spent packing my things and doing a few paperwork-y bits and pieces, which meant I had to confront the smug-looking Commander Silas again. It wouldn't have been so bad had he not quipped, "I thought you had left already?" in my general direction. I'll let you have that one, I thought to myself; it was a silly thing to say.

And then, I was left alone, waiting in the massive landing bay of the Archangel for my old friends to show up and take me away from this massive mistake of a venture.

I felt alone, which was fine, I've been alone a lot in my life, but standing in a huge hangar with so many people going about their day around you, oblivious to your existence, it makes the air feel a little bit colder. Especially when you've made a bit of an arse of yourself!

But then, a familiar voice made me turn on my heels, kicking over my rucksacks in the process.

'I contacted your friends especially. They wanted me to inform you that they might be some time; apparently, they have been on a treasure hunt on the other side of the galaxy.'

It was Admiral Bagari. Her usually stoic expression had softened somewhat since the last time I saw her and her uniform carried with it a golden tunic highlighting her promotion to Admiral of the fleet.

I sighed and turned back to the landing bay doors, the final layer between me and freedom.

'I thought you might like some company?'

That made me turn to face her again. 'Haven't you got better things to do than keep a delinquent company?'

Bagari came closer, her hands held behind her back. She chewed her cheek. 'Not when you're the boss; in a way you can have as much or as little time in the world depending on your choices.

I have to say that I was shocked to see your name on the academy register. What made you want to give it a go?'

I explained to her that I needed a change, some form of challenge to myself and ultimately, I
discovered that what I needed was confirmation that I was already on the right path.

She seemed to like that. I'll never forget what she said next.

'You might not believe it, but I admire you, Miss Gummadi. You used your judgement when things didn't seem quite right and acted in a way that anywhere else you would have been commended.

Your determination and willingness to challenge authority is a credit to you and your friends. Believe me, you can do things we never can here at the Space Seals. However, let me give you some advice. It's one thing to question, yet it's another to be hot-headed-
'

I interrupted. I knew instantly what she was referring to. My battle with Commander Silas. I said he was a massive windbag who let his rank be an excuse to make others feel rubbish.

Bagari didn't disagree. She said that there were thousands like Silas in positions of power, not just in the Space Seals, but all over the cosmos.

'But people like you will make them think twice about the way they handle people and situations so use your disdain for authority to your advantage, Miss Gummadi, it won't make you a soldier but it might make you stop someone from going too far one day.'

I was reeling. Here I was, thinking that a woman in her position would strip me down for my conduct and here she was complimenting me!

It was probably the first time someone with power had ever done so.

I knew where the Admiral was coming from. She wanted me to be me. Having a little belief can go a long way, especially when it comes from an elder. In saying what she had said, I had a new-found respect for her and for once in my life, an authority figure had shown belief in me.

She extended an invitation for me to wait in her ready room but I politely declined and thanked her for her kind words. We said our goodbyes, until the next time our paths cross, and she disappeared into the throng of activity, officers pausing to salute as she passed them.

I decided to put my bags in a big pile and plopped myself down against them. I had no idea how long Random and Jake would be, so I began to regret not accepting the invitation for a moment! But then I found solace in my solitude and rummaged through one of my bags.

I wanted to make a start on something I had wanted to do for a few days now, but I had never had what I needed.

Since I'd swiped it from Silas' office, and a pen too, I thought now would be the best time since I had a little peace and quiet.

Plus I didn't seem to be in the officers' way so why not stay put until I was leaving?

Picking up the pen, I took the lid off and instantly lost it down a metal grill on the floor.

Tutting, I went back to the office equipment I had stolen and observed the front cover of the book in my hands.

Pen in hand, I furiously crossed out the name Ulrich Silas and wrote my own over the top and flipping over the front page of this brand new, yet-to-be-written-in exercise book, I wrote the words DEAR DIARY in large obnoxious letters.

Oh yes, I lost my train of thought. I promised you that I would answer your question right at the start of this diary entry. Why start now?

Well, I'll whisper it... in visual form!

Recently our adventures have become more dangerous, and Random especially has been carrying the weight of the universe on his shoulders more than he ever has before.

I can sense that a time is coming, and believe me, I hope that I am very wrong here, but you know the impending sense of doom you get when you are caught outside and a storm is rumbling close by?

I have this funny feeling that we are about to be caught up in the worst storm ever.

Maybe it will pass, but with a life like we have all led for the past three years, it would be criminal if nobody had ever heard of anything we had achieved.

Then again, if we come out of the other end of what we have before us, I'll have to keep writing!

I wonder if any publishers in this big old cosmos would have it?

JOURNEYS IN THE RANDOMVERSE

'First, there was the big bang and then there was everything.

The explosion that occurred created life in the universe, the expansion that gave birth to everything there has ever been and everything there ever will be, forming early stars and galaxies, which is the reason why all life exists.

Without it, there would be nothing.

For billions of years, many a civilisation has tried to unearth the mysteries of what caused it and how the big bang came to be but the spark that ignited the flame has never been pinpointed.

Many theories suggest that every speck of energy of our infant universe was condensed together into one incredibly dense focus at an impossibly small point.

This point exploded in what should have been an almost impossible, unimaginable moment of force and from which, billions of galaxies were born, stretching themselves out across the immeasurably vast gulf of space.

The immense velocity of the big bang surged outwardly like an infinite tidal wave.

The surge of matter stretched so far that the incredible energy created life as we know it in our universe. This has led many of the greatest scientists who have ever lived to theorise that the big bang was so big, its magnificent power didn't just create one universe.

It created multiple universes...'

'What are you doing there, Skateboard?'

The enquiring tone of Anji broke the AI robot's concentration. He sighed.

'I thought I'd take the opportunity of our journey to Sarrus to write my speech.'

Anji wearily pulled her dressing gown around her middle and plonked herself half asleep next to her friend in the pilot's chair.

'Speech?'

Skateboard saved his progress in his memory bank and closed the file. 'Yes, I wanted to explain the alternate realities theory to the Admiralty.'

'I don't think you need to convince them that it exists, every one of them knows by now, after all of this,' she stretched her feet up onto the dashboard, almost pressing the eject core button with her heel in the process.

Skateboard's diodes breathed a sigh of relief as she narrowly missed it and continued his argument.

'Some do not. Admiral Bagari has personally asked me to address the council.'

Anji huffed. 'How can some people not believe it? I mean how long have they been sending us after the wormholes to close them up?'

'People will always deny the facts - even when they are staring them in the face and it doesn't fit the narrative,' said Skateboard.

'Seems pointless to me, and it's more work for us!' Anji swung her legs off the dashboard, again making Skateboard fret for a split second as she nearly turned off the oxygen supply with her foot. His diodes sighed as her feet touched the ground and he thought about putting a sign up banning his friends from putting their feet up in the cockpit. 'Ignorance is bliss, isn't it?'

'We shall see,' replied Skateboard.

'I love your optimism, but it's a waste of time in my book.'

'Possibly, miss, but I intend to give it a try.'

Skateboard accepted her skepticism at face value. He understood that she was frustrated by their involvement with the Space Seals and appreciated that after her short weekend as a cadet with them she'd want to escape their clutches, especially after such a negative experience.

Yet Skateboard knew that they were getting closer to stopping the anomalies from opening up to alternate dimensions. None of them liked working for Admiral Bagari, Random very much included, but they all felt a responsibility to put it to an end.

Chaos followed them, and they not-so-secretly loved it, but it was time to stop danger from other universes from harming their own.

Suddenly, a small yellow light began to flicker on the dashboard.

'Here we go again!' huffed Anji.

Months earlier, following their run-in with the Larvae after falling through reality into another dimension, Random had helped Skateboard rig up an anomaly detector on the Venus II. As the molecular structure of all that exists outside of their known universe was different from any object from theirs, they used remnants of Larvae to break down the genetic code to a point that enabled Skateboard to discover an energy pattern that would enable them to distinguish when another anomaly would open.

All the while they had done so, Jake and Anji had tried their hardest not to be sick as Random had brought the Larvae's appendage inside the spaceship.

Now they were able to spot an oncoming tear in the fabric of reality from as far away as neighbouring galaxies, and since Skateboard had given the Space Seals the ability to use it also, Anji didn't see why they should still be involved. Moral duty or not, she was fed up with all of this.

Still, as she sounded the alarm klaxon, which turned the cockpit a deep blue and the loud noise
emitted to the living quarters, beckoning Random
and Jake to battle stations, she yawned and strolled into the mid-section to make herself a cup of tea.

Skateboard checked the read-outs. 'Strange. This is close... really close.'

Jake entered the mid-section, yawning loudly as he finished doing up his trouser buttons.

'Not another one,' he sighed.

'Yup,' replied Anji, who was busy stirring milk and sugar into her mug. 'One lump or two, Jake?'

Jake, used to her dismissiveness by now, ignored her and made for the cockpit.

Although also slightly jaded by their recent adventures dealing with the multiverse, he retained a small interest.

'How far away is it going to occur?' he asked Skateboard as he slumped into the pilot's chair.

Skateboard's diodes went haywire. He started to panic.

'Right on top of us!' he cried. 'Hold on tight!'

A shockwave sent Jake flying out of his seat as the Venus II was sent spiraling backward. A green ribbon of energy bolted through the ship like a shot of thunder. Anji fell to the ground, somehow managing to stop her tea from spilling in the process.

Then, just as quickly as the ribbon exploded into their world, it was gone again.

The Venus II stopped rocking like a boat on a stormy sea as Skateboard restored the systems to normal.

He instantly carried out a diagnostic.

Jake leaped from the cockpit into the mid-section and helped Anji back to her feet.

'On second thoughts, I will have that coffee!' he quipped.

'Is everyone okay?' asked Skateboard, raising his voice over the blaring klaxon.

'We're alright,' said Anji, 'but no idea about Random!'

'Ugh... I didn't ask for an alarm call,' said a new, unfamiliar voice.

Anji, Jake and Skateboard turned to see where the deep, masculine tones had come from.

In the doorway stood a tall man. His hair was shoulder-length and it dangled floppily like curtains over a window in front of his kind-looking eyes, which shone red and blue in colour even in the relative gloom of battle stations. His muscular yet slim frame towered over them all and the vest in which he wore showed off his taut arms in a vulgar fashion.

As the stranger trained his eyes on the ships' three astonished occupants he shot a similar expression right back at them. The air was thick with confusion.

'Who the hell are you guys?' asked the stranger.

Jake's mouth fell open, trying to find the words. Anji picked up a nearby saucepan and pushed it in front of Jake about to ask the same thing.

Yet, after she had stopped staring at the massive muscles the stranger possessed she noticed something even more prominent about this person.

His skin was purple, just like Randoms.

'What have you done with my friends?' the stranger demanded.

'One moment, sir, I think I can explain everything,' said Skateboard politely.

'Oh really?' asked a panicked Jake, 'who is this guy?'

Skateboard turned to the teenager.

'He is Random.'

'Don't be silly, Skateboard, that's not Random.'

'It is,' he replied.

'What, does puberty happen overnight on Rodas or something?' said Jake sarcastically.

'I'd better put it another way,' said Skateboard, acknowledging that he wasn't exactly helping matters. 'This is Random, just not our Random.'

Anji was still confused. 'Then whose is he then? And where's ours?'

Skateboard turned back to this new version of Random, who looked like he was furious with what was going on.

'I believe I can explain everything. Would you all care to sit down? I'll go and boil the kettle again.'

The older version of Random sat glaring at the three strangers who stared from the other side of the table. His deep resenting eyes met with theirs.

'I don't think you're listening to me,' he barked. 'There is no other Random, only me!'

'Well, that ain't right,' replied Anji. 'Because the Random we know and love isn't a thirty-year-old hunk with bangs to die for.'

Jake gave her a quizzical look. 'Hunk?'

'Well, he must be an imposter. There is no way there can be more of me. It's just impossible.'

'It isn't, you know. You're living proof,' said Skateboard.

'So I'm meant to believe that I have been taken from my own universe and this isn't my ship.'

'Take a look around,' Anji implored. 'Does it look anything like YOUR ship? Do we look like your friends?'

'Well...' Random had to concede that his Venus II was a lot tidier... and cleaner... but he didn't want to say so. 'You guys are normally a couple of decades older, I admit.'

'Really? What do we look like? Am I bald? I'm bald, aren't I?' said Jake whilst pulling at his blonde locks for comfort.

Random decided not to tell him – the truth was a best-kept secret – and he had more pressing questions to ask.

'Okay, so maybe this isn't my ship then. But how did I get here?'

'Captain, I'm sorry to tell you that not only is this not your ship, but it also isn't even your universe,' replied Skateboard.

The adult version of Random looked shocked. 'How?'

'Since you arrived onboard I have been scanning your molecular structure. You don't belong in our universe, I'm afraid, sir.'

The handsome newcomer clenched his jaw in thought, making Anji's heart flutter yet again. Is this really how Random would look when he became a grown-up? She started to consider her long-time prom and marriage promise she had made to Jake!

'What do you remember, sir?' asked Skateboard.

Random huffed. 'I awoke in my bed... what I thought was my bed... and walked into the mid-section, that's it.'

'You don't recall anything funny happening?' Skateboard probed.

'No. How did this happen?'

Jake interrupted. 'Also, how do we get our Random back?'

'I believe we can find solutions to the problem, sirs but once again I must apologise for this unfortunate event,' said Skateboard.

'Why, what did you do?' asked Anji.

'Well, technically it's something we've all done. In your universe, sir, have you been chasing a phenomenon known as the Quantum Narcocel?' Skateboard asked Random.

'We picked up an anomaly on the scanners a few months back but thought nothing of it, why?'

'Did you see the anomaly in question?'

'Yes, but we ignored it.'

'Ignored it, how could you ignore a massive kaleidoscope in the stars?' said Jake, remembering the one that gobbled them up.

'We don't tend to go looking for trouble,' said Random. The travellers were shocked.

'Well, you're certainly not our Random then!' joked Anji. 'What do you do then?'

'Mainly we just travel around, looking for places to hang out for a bit before moving on and pitching up again somewhere else.'

'But you run from danger?' asked Jake rather forthrightly.

'Wouldn't you?'

The travellers huffed. 'We live totally different lives,' said Jake.

'If I might get back to the matter-in-hand,' said Skateboard as he tried to gain their attention back. 'It seems as though Random's quantum signature is entangled within the occurrence of the anomalies.'

'Can we have it in English, please?' asked Anji.

Skateboard did not understand what Anji said and checked his translation chip to see if he was speaking an alien language.

'We all have a quantum signature. Every living thing in the universe binds to the same code. For every alternate reality, this signature is unique. So when our Random brought the Larvae's remains

on board, he came into contact with the quantum signature of something that didn't belong to his universe, meaning that when an anomaly appears, the quantum energy from its appearance ripped our Random from our universe and transferred him somewhere else. And because we and the ship were also in an alternate reality, the anomalies have begun to trace this signature which is why they have been appearing more frequently.'

'And always near us,' Anji interjected.

'Yes, miss. Because the anomalies are chasing us, not to threaten us but because we can heal the rifts between reality.'

'How?' asked Jake. Random just looked at them all open-mouthed, trying his best to take it all in.

'Think about it. The Venus II visited an alternate world, yes? It was dragged into the Quantum Narcosel and managed to fly back again, right?

Well, it wasn't because of the flight path timing we thought could do that but it was because our universe's signature was able to heal the rift by pulling through and out again.'

'Meaning?' asked a slack-jawed Random.

'With our quantum energy, we can heal the anomalies and put a stop to them opening up completely!'

Jake's mind was going a mile a minute and it still wasn't enough to keep up with his robot friend.

'Woah, woah, woah, slow down Skateboard, I'm starting to get a headache.'

'I think I get it,' said Anji.

'Okay then Dr. Gummadi, what's he on about then?' said Jake.

'Think of it this way. The anomalies are tears in space, right? And because we've been through one and back again, and thanks to Skateboard's anomaly detector, we can act like a needle sewing up the wound.'

'All because we survived one of them?' asked Jake.

'Precisely, you two,' said Skateboard.

'So why has Random been torn away from us and how do we get him back?' asked Jake.

'And how do we get Captain Handsome back home?' asked Anji.

'Oh please, just call me handsome,' said Random.

'I think that Random's entanglement was caused by his overexposure to the Larvae's limb. He did help me extract the DNA and the quantum signature and harness it to make my detector,' said Skateboard.

'Then why didn't it take me?' asked Jake. 'After all, I had one of those suckers on my face, remember?'

'So you did, but it was for a brief time compared to how long Captain Random was working on the remains.' Skateboard confirmed.

'You guys are sick!' said the alternate Random.

'And our Random's signature has been blended with those that bear similarities with others, so when an anomaly surfaces, it gets confused because there is a rift between realities and it tries to pair him off with the anomaly that has appeared,' Skateboard continued.

'And the alternate universe spits out their version of Random because they think they've got the wrong one!' cried Anji.

'Which explains why you, sir, are with us right now,' said Skateboard in conclusion.

The alternate version of Random sank back in his chair.

'Heavy,' he said with a sigh. 'How do I get home?'

'And how do we get our Random back?' asked Jake, feeling like his question still hadn't been fully answered.

'We keep flying through the anomalies, sewing up the rift as we go and Random should just appear back with us when we have finished, and you, sir, will automatically go back to your reality when we do,' said Skateboard to the newcomer.

'Awesome!' said Anji before another pertinent question crossed her mind. 'Hold on, how many of these anomalies will we have to pass through?'

'It could be as few as a couple and as many as a thousand,' replied Skateboard. 'It depends on how many similar quantum signatures have become entangled.'

Random, Anji and Jake sighed. 'That could take years!' said Anji, breaking the silence. 'Plus, when can we be sure that one will spring up?'

'Well, there is one outside now isn't there?' said Skateboard, 'and remember we have the detector. If I could ask Captain Random's permission, I can amplify his signature and use both as a signal to bring all the anomalies to us now.'

'Isn't that dangerous?' asked Jake.

'Won't a thousand or more anomalies appearing all at once destroy space or something too?'

'Not if I use the signal to make them pop up one after the other,' said Skateboard. 'If we do this, my friends, we can bring our friend home, send this version of Random back to where he belongs and ensure that the fabric of space reality will be healed for good.'

'So, no more anomalies?' asked Anji.

'No more anomalies,' confirmed Skateboard.

Random beamed. 'Great! So if you need my signature, where do I sign?'

***

Sometime later, the crew was seated in the cockpit along with
the alternate version of their friend, ready for what was going to
prove to be the craziest journey of their lives.

Random felt like an imposter in the chair that should have been
so familiar to him and yet clearly belonged to a stranger. In this
reality, he was an imposter. These weren't his friends. He even
doubted why they would be risking so much for him if it wasn't
for their friend being missing. Who did they think they were?
Their apparent thirst for danger troubled him. Back in his
universe, he and his version of Anji and Jake were deserters. They
had thrown off the shackles of all responsibility that had ever held
them back and run away and they had kept on running, never
looking back. Just like his counterpart, this Random had also been
tasked with bringing an end to the bitter, senseless war on Rodas
and like he, as soon as the Venus II and Skateboard had come into
his life, he had scarpered also. Yet his conscience had been left
unprovoked until today.

Seeing Skateboard again stirred up a mixed feeling of emotions
and regret. He thought as the others prepared themselves for the
anomaly jumps, about how Skateboard had felt bad about
deserting a planet that needed them so much.

And then, he shuddered as he remembered the day that
Skateboard went home...

'I have adjusted the driving stabilizers so our jumps should be
less bumpy than our encounter with the Quantum Narcosel,'
Skateboard said from his co-pilot's position.

'Thank god for that!' replied Jake who immediately discarded
the waste paper bag on the floor. He turned to Anji, who like he
was strapped into the fold-down chairs that jutted out of the back
wall of the cockpit and sighed.

'We'll get him back, Anj. Just you see.'

Anji smiled. 'I know.'

'Right, are we all ready?' asked Skateboard.

'Yes,' said Anji.

'Yup,' replied Jake.

'Go for it...' said Random. His stomach was tying itself in knots. He looked at the fantastic anomaly that hung incongruously in front of them. As soon as they flew into that thing, he would be torn away, back to his own universe. He started to ponder. Would it hurt? Would he even remember what he had experienced? He was about to find out. Before he did, there was something he had to say.

'Skateboard?'

The little AI robot turned to the stranger.

'Yes, sir?'

Random's throat went dry. He had to say it, no matter how difficult it was.

'I'm sorry.'

Skateboard's circuits whirred. 'It wasn't your fault, sir,' he chirped back.

Tears formed in the corners of Random's eyes.

If only this Skateboard had known what had happened.

'In three.' Skateboard fired up the thrusters. The incredible engines inside the Venus II groaned louder and more urgently.

'Two.' The cockpit began to shudder and Jake began to regret throwing the sick bag away.

'One.'

With a jolt, the Venus II tore with ferocious speed through the blackness of space and surged with unswerving purpose toward the fantastic impossibility of the anomaly. Within seconds, the little ship was swallowed by it and in moments the wormhole began to fall in on itself, like a black hole that was late for a very important appointment.

Almost as soon as they had flown into the jaws of the unknown, the anomaly was gone.

Then an incredible explosion ripped through the stars and as quickly as it had gone, the anomaly was back. What looked like a small craft was belched out from the middle of its spectrum and in an event that only took a matter of seconds, the anomaly was gone again, leaving the Venus II alone once more in the emptiness of never-ending space.

Anji dared to open her eyes.' Was that it? Is Random back?'

Jake breathed a sigh of relief. 'Did it work?'

Skateboard looked to his left for confirmation.

'Sort of.'

'Uh?' said Anji.

'What am I doing here? And who the hell are you?'

The travellers froze. That wasn't Random's voice.

It was the voice of a woman.

'Let me out of this seat at once!'

Anji and Jake craned their necks to get a better look but they didn't need to. The pilot's chair swiveled to face them and they were shocked by what they saw.

'Random?' asked Jake timidly.

Sitting before them was a beautiful lady - a woman whose eyes shone like moons, whose hair cascaded over her shoulders like a heavenly waterfall and with legs that made Jake want to drop down on the floor and thank god that he was a man.

'Anj, Jake? What's happened to both of you?'

'Sir, er, miss, let me explain,' said a rather flummoxed Skateboard.

'Since when have you both had sex changes?' demanded the female.

'Skateboard, what's happened?' asked a bemused Anji.

'It seems the quantum signature is still trying to untangle itself,' he explained.

'Does this mean that this will keep happening?' asked Jake.

'Until all of the rifts are healed and our Random is back, yes,' Skateboard confirmed.

'What are you all talking about?' asked the female Random.

'Try again Skateboard, quick! She's doing things to me,' said a rather embarrassed Jake.

Skateboard quickly calibrated the signal he had made and summoned another anomaly before them. As he did, he thought of the consequences of what they had just witnessed.

With every jump, they would be getting closer and closer to their goal, closer to stopping the anomalies from coming back and bringing their Random home but for every jump into another reality, they would encounter a different Random.

Skateboard thought about this and realised that not all of the Random's out there could possibly be as nice and accommodating as their own.

Moments later, a huge anomaly exploded before them, rocking the Venus II violently.

The female Random flicked her hair off her face and stopped struggling to escape her safety belt, which Skateboard had magnetically sealed as a precaution, and gazed at what now stood before them.

'What on Rodas is that?' she shouted before trying to get out of her bonds again this time, with the intent to run to the nearest escape pod she could find and get away from all this madness.

'There's no time to explain, miss, in we go again,' exclaimed Skateboard.

In seconds, they had vanished back into the anomaly, which in turn vanished itself before exploding back into existence again and as before they were vomited back out into space as it evaporated behind them.

Jake heaved a heavy sigh of relief. He looked up at Random's seat and was delighted to find that the intimidating yet attractive version of Random had gone.

He was, however, rather startled and disturbed to see that a huge, slimy octopus-like version of his best friend had replaced her.

The creature lifted its slimy, dripping tentacles in alarm and screamed back at him and Anji, who was unfortunate enough to cop a mouthful of the unspeakable saliva from the alien's suckers right in her face.

Skateboard looked in alarm at the purple-skinned creature that sat next to him now and was then even further alarmed when he noticed that it was trying to reach for the controls on the dashboard.

With no time to lose, he summoned yet another anomaly, which again exploded into reality in front of the Venus II, and with no hesitation, repeated the same procedure he had run twice before.

The next time they left an anomaly, which disappeared as soon as they left it, the cockpit was

---

a state, dripping with the unmentionable slobber that the octopus Random had left behind.

Only on this occasion, there didn't seem to be a different version of Random sitting in the pilot's chair.

'Er, where's Random?' said Anji, who was wiping her face with her sleeve. As distressing as the moment had been, being hit full-on in the face by alien goo was made all the better that it smelt and tasted to her like strawberries, not that she was trying to let any of it into her mouth!

'I am here,' came a semi-familiar voice.

The travellers looked all around them.

'Right here,' it said again.

They looked around them again.

'You just looked at me, Skateboard.'

Skateboard dialed up his optical circuits to full capacity and made out the outline of a transparent being with a familiar outline in Random's chair.

'Sir?' he asked.

'I take it this isn't my reality?' the invisible Random asked.

'How do you know that?' asked Anji.

'Believe me, I'd be boring you if I told you,' he said, his voice sounding posher than that of their friends. 'If you could be so kind as to do... whatever you just did and take me home again, I would be ever so grateful.'

'Of course, sir, my full apologies,' replied Skateboard.

The invisible Random snorted. 'My dear thing you were not to know. Charmed to meet you all.'

And with that, Skateboard summoned another anomaly and plunged the Venus II back in and out again.

This process lasted many hours. Upon every jump, Anji, Jake and Skateboard met another facet of the person they know as Random, including among many; a black and white silent film version, a cartoon, a mouse, a version of Random who looked like he hadn't shaved in decades and had a beard that had slunk out of the cockpit into the mid-section, one that spoke backward, a Random who bore a passing resemblance to a melding of he, Anji and Jake like they had been caught in some form of a transporter

malfunction, one whose actions were backward, one that was half
man/half horse, one that was a half squeezed tube of toothpaste,
one that was a mute, one whose head was seven times bigger than
his body (which Jake had joked to an exasperated Anji, to lighten
the mood, WAS their Random) one that only spoke in song and
one that had multiple limbs that made damn sure that nobody
was going to not have a nightmare that night.

   After the nine hundredth and forty-seventh jump, Anji and Jake
were ready to give in. Skateboard himself was fighting back the
urge to give up.
   Only the thought that they were potentially only thirty-three
jumps or so away from ending this nightmare and rescuing their
friend kept them going.
   So far, Skateboard had been counting their blessings that they
hadn't bumped into any evil versions of Random.
   With the next jump, he wished he hadn't spoken so soon.
   As the Venus II emerged from yet another healed anomaly, the
pilot's chair was again taken by a Random. As soon as Skateboard
clapped eyes on him, the middle-aged man with the bionic right
arm, the battle-torn clothes that barely kept his hairy muscular
body concealed and the false-eyed version of Random, he knew
he had to restrain him immediately.
   Only this time he didn't act quickly enough.
   'Who the hell are you?' barked the metallic tones.
   'Skateboard look out! He's got an axe!' cried Jake.
   He's right, thought Skateboard as he jumped off the seat just in
time for the blue laser outline of the axe to narrowly miss him and
split his chair in half like an old oak tree. Anji and Jake screamed
and released their restraints.
   'This is my ship! I am Random, a destroyer of worlds. Don't you
dare!' he cried as he buried the axe in the dashboard, sending a
sea of sparks and fire up from the gash that now sat within it.
   'Oh my god,' said Anji as she and Jake dived for the midsection.
'It's Stratos' Random!'
   Random spotted her and readied his axe.
   'Good, I like them when they run!'

Before he had a chance to use it, Random stopped in his tracks and his body convulsed in agony. As his body became as still as a statue, he toppled to the floor unconscious, revealing Jake behind him with a laser gun.

'Insert cool line here,' he said knowingly.

Anji got up from the floor.

'You killed him!'

'That's a funny way of saying thank you,' he replied, 'and no, never, he's just stunned.'

Anji hugged her friend and they were both reminded of what had happened in the cockpit.

'Skateboard, are you okay mate?' asked Jake as they both pelted back, smoke pouring out of the cockpit.

Skateboard was busy battling the small army of fires that had erupted from the damaged console.

'My apologies, friends, but after seeing Jake I thought I'd better deal with what I can only describe as an utter disaster.'

The travellers gazed through the smoke at the damage.

It looked bad.

Really bad.

'Can we keep jumping?' asked Anji.

'Negative,' said Skateboard. 'The damage is too severe.'

Anji and Jake went cold. Not now. Not after all they had been through.

Random was lost.

It couldn't be. They were so close. And now they had no chance of getting him back.

'Is there nothing you can do?'

Skateboard's circuits whirred, trying as hard as he could to find and build connections with the ship's mainframe again.

His actions took a couple of minutes, during which the evil version of Random soon began to stir.

'Jake,' said Anji.

'I'm on it,' said Jake, who picked up his laser gun again and leveled it at their enemy.

'Yes,' Skateboard said finally. 'Yes, I can still make a connection.'

Anji was delighted. 'Then do it!'

'The only trouble, miss, is that there is only enough energy in the console to make one more jump. If we don't act quickly and the power shorts out we might ourselves be stuck in another reality.'

Anji's face fell. 'You're kidding.'

'No, either we make this jump, our Random comes back to us and the anomalies all heal or he will remain missing.'

Anji thought quickly. 'But we can just keep flying the anomalies if they keep cropping up, like we have been, surely?'

'No, the quantum signature is repaired sufficiently that they will not find us anymore, especially since the detector and signal I have made have been destroyed. I'm sorry, Anji. We make one more trip and make it count or we spend years

chasing what's left of the anomalies across space.'

Her face fell.

This could be their only chance to see Random again.

She wiped a tear from her eye. 'Do it, Skateboard. Just do it.'

Jake had overheard the conversation, his eyes and trigger finger not leaving the man laying semi-conscious before him who had damaged their chances of succeeding. 'Do it, mate. Do it for Random.'

Skateboard acted instantly. He didn't even wait for his friends to find something to hold onto. He had to act now before the power died altogether on their ship. He summoned up all the power he could to bring the last, final anomaly they could use before them. It shot into existence, engulfing the windscreen of the Venus II.

With all the power the groaning engines could muster, Skateboard wasted no time in sending them back in for one last chance.

Before the evil Random was able to grab Jake's gun and snap his thin, chicken-like legs, the Venus II disappeared from existence, as did the anomaly, potentially the last that this universe would ever see.

There was a silence and stillness that embraced space once more. It stayed that way for longer than any of the previous anomalies and jumps had allowed.

Suddenly, there was a crashing boom that burst from the same anomaly as it exploded back into the universe and from it, a damaged, spluttering little ship spun out from within, allowing it to close in on itself for the last time.

All that was left now was the Venus II.

They had made it.

Anji came to as the smell of burning touched her nostrils. She sat bolt up and raced out of the cockpit and the subsequent fire, which Skateboard was trying desperately to put out again and tripped down the steps into the midsection.

The smoke had seeped all around, making it hard to see if they had been successful in their mission and so she gravitated towards the coughing she could hear.

'Jake!' she cried, pulling her friend up to his feet.

Jake spluttered as he tried to clear his lungs. 'Did it work? Tell me it worked?'

The power was all but out on the ship, making it hard to see even without the smoke.

Skateboard had initiated the emergency backup systems so his friends wouldn't lose the ability to breathe or their gravity.

In doing so, the fans began to work and the smoke began to retreat.

As it did, another person was heard coughing before them.

As the smoke cleared, Anji and Jake cried out and threw themselves toward the spluttering.

'RANDOM!'

Skateboard joined them in the mid-section and his diodes gave a massive sigh of relief as he saw his two human friends playfully wrestling a familiar face on the floor.

'Easy, guys,' Random laughed. 'It's like you haven't seen me in days!'

'It feels like we haven't,' said Anji as she planted a big kiss on Random's cheek.

'Welcome back, sir,' chirped Skateboard as the three teenagers picked themselves up off the floor.

'Good to be back, Skateboard,' he said as he looked around at the damage the Venus II had endured.

'What's been going on here? How did I end up universe hopping?'

'We've closed all the anomalies, sir. We never need to worry about them again,' assured Skateboard, who along with the relief of curing the universe of dangerous anomalies and rescuing his lost friend, was also very happy that he didn't need to deliver his speech later on Syrrus.

'Where did you go?' asked Anji.

'What was it like?' asked Jake.

'Ah, I'll fill you all in with the gossip later,' he said, 'but you'll never believe half the things I've seen!'

'Trust us, we will!' said Anji.

Random smiled. 'It's good to be home... even if... well, home's a bit broken. We'd better get to work on repairs.' He went into the cockpit and saw the damage that the axe of his alternate self had caused. 'Zarks! Who did all of this?'

Anji smirked.

'You did!'

HEAVY IS THE HEAD...

Solenia sat lost in her thoughts.

Tapping her fingers against the plush velvet cushions on the arms of her throne, she breathed slowly and sank deeper into her mind.

It had been a long time since the Battle for Spectronia had taken place. Years had flown by since the biggest test that Solenia had ever faced as Queen of her people and it still haunted her.

Every single decision she had made on that terrible day continued to twist and turn within her. Many of her army of Valkaryies had perished in the line of fire, in the line of duty to the people that she had kept safe under her protection.

Until then, Spectronia had been a peaceful planet, largely ignored by the mightier races in the universe and so Solenia, like her Father before her, had ruled with no blood upon her hands.

Never before had fighting taken place on the planet and never would it again.

To this day, her hands were still clean but her mind was awash with the genocide of others.

She sighed again and looked around her. Her throne room, resplendent in gold and the
magnificent colours of the rainbow collated in the grains of sand that made up her underground palace, was as dark as her mood.

No one, not even her trusted bodyguards, was among her.

She was truly alone.

Why she needed bodyguards in the first place she did not know, but after she remembered her tempestuous outburst at them, and her closest advisers, to leave her alone, she thought better of them for never coming back. She had instructed them all to go and never return.

When Solenia gazed upon the broken orbs that lay scattered on the dusty floor, the ones that had once adorned the sides of her throne and bore ceremonial sentiments, she sighed harder.

Her physician was right.

She had let the guilt get to her.

His original prognosis for her problems had been survivor's guilt, but she had dismissed it out of hand.

Now, as Solenia sat all by herself in a place that once thrived under her rule, she began to think that he had a point.

Random. It had all been Random's fault.

If only he hadn't used the Zedron Flux.

If only he and his friends had never chosen Spectronia as their battleground.

If only he hadn't wiped out the people with the flying pyramids.

He'd promised her when he had been prisoner within the bowels of her palace that he meant no ill-being on Spectronia.

If only she hadn't been gullible enough to believe him at face value then hundreds of her subjects wouldn't have been put through their grief.

The aftermath of the battle had been terrible.

Solenia had taken it upon herself to do her birthright and lead by example. She had fought, though it had been to no avail. The people with the flying pyramids could pick them off like fish in a barrel. The Valkryies' weapons had been useless. Their laser spikes were too far away from the hull of the mysterious ships to do any real damage. Even after they had gone, evaporated in the sheer might of the Zedron Flux, the stench of death had hung like a fog high above the corpses of the fallen.

So many families lost a loved one that day and Solenia had attended every single funeral. She had witnessed enough tears shed to fill their graves and had wept more than her fair share.

It was the stress and strain of putting herself through the repetition of grief and witnessing the sorrow her people felt that she had begun to doubt herself.

What was the point of being a ruler if she couldn't put a stop to suffering? To have the power to hold life and death in her hands and decree that the latter should not befall her people in the crossfire of other people's squabbles.

Then a darker thought would approach Solenia's head.

What if I had possession of the Zedron Flux?

Maybe she could have brought them back to life. What a power to have.

To possess the mysteries of the greatest, most brilliant element in the universe, what good could she have done?

And then she remembered why she banished the Flux.

No living being should have that power.

Not even her.

Solenia cupped her face in her hands and wailed. It echoed off the walls of the throne room and reverberated around her, mocking her for her moment of weakness.

As the scream died away, she slumped off the throne and sank to her knees. Little pools of tears fell into the sand and she began to sob uncontrollably.

All the while, in the shadows, lurked the figure of a man who Solenia trusted more than any other. His colourful brow furrowed and he stepped forward tentatively.

'Your Majesty?' came the soft voice.

Solenia looked up towards it, her eyes were red with tears.

'I beg you for your time.'

'Not now, Proctor,' she croaked. 'As you can see this isn't a very good time.'

Proctor approached his Queen and sat down next to her.

His thinning hair unfurled off the top of his shiny head as he climbed down to sit next to her.

As soon as he sat beside her, Solenia allowed herself to collapse in his lap and continued to weep bitterly.

Proctor tutted and placed his hand on her shoulder and hugged her close. 'Your Majesty, you need to seek help.'

'A lesser man would pay for those words,' cried Solenia. 'But I have always held your council in higher regard than many.'

Proctor smiled. 'I'm flattered. Your Father thought the same.'

'And that is why you are the most trusted and learned man on Spectronia,' she replied. 'How do I rid myself of this feeling? For too long I have felt like I let my people down.'

Proctor thought about how to tell her once more what he had told her so often. How could he make her see sense?

'Your Majesty, you let nobody down. You did what you thought was right in the most impossible of scenarios. You made the decisions that nobody else in this world could make because it is your birthright to do so.'

Solenia pulled herself away from Proctor gently.

'Your words are a strength to me, my dear Proctor, but when I close my eyes at night I am haunted by the death that I saw on that day.'

'A ruler's job is to rule no matter what the consequences. Those that you led into battle followed you willingly, not just because you are their Queen but because they believed in you and they still do. They want to see you. For too long you have kept yourself away from the public eye. The people of Spectronia need to see that their Queen still cares.'

'I care still... too much,' she replied, rising back to her feet. 'Is it not that I do something right by the people who lost their loved ones that day? Is it not right that I punish myself for what happened?'

'No, it is not,' said Proctor. Many times before had he taken part in a conversation like this with his Queen and many times before had the outcome been the same. He needed to break the cycle. 'Your Majesty, our peoples were not prepared for an attack of such magnitude. What the outsiders did was unjust and unfair but the actions of the few saved billions.'

Solenia's eyes narrowed. 'You mean that you think what Random did was right?'

Proctor gulped and then stood firm. 'If you truly trust my judgement you must listen to me. Without the intervention from the purple one, the planet would have been destroyed. None of us would be here. This conversation would be taking place in the next life and believe me, we would bemoan the fact that our entire species were wiped out on that terrible day.'

Solenia pondered on Proctor's words and steadied herself back into her throne.

'For years I have seen the eyes of the bereaved staring back at me. Those dark, tragic eyes were swollen and red with grief and anger. They burn in my mind every time I close my eyes as has my hatred for that man Random and yet... he did save us.'

'He made a terrible decision, Your Majesty,' said Proctor who walked to his Queen's side. 'For all the guilt that you are feeling, his burden must weigh heavy too.'

'You want me to feel pity for a murderer?' she spat.

'I want you to find it in your heart to forgive a hero.'

Solenia snapped. A hero? The boy whose very presence on her planet had cost the lives of her people?

'You watch your tongue,' she sneered, tears still streaming down her face. 'That word does not befit one such as he and never will!'

Proctor was losing the argument. 'But Your Majesty, he saved us! You must see that?'

'Silence!'

Proctor uttered not one more word. His change in tact hadn't worked. The softly-softly approach that he had tried a hundred times before was the only course now.

'I only want you to see another way of thinking to help you through your grief.'

'Grief? I'm not grieving, Proctor. I'm angry. I'm angry that I couldn't do more. I'm angry that we as a planet were not ready but more than anything I am angry that I wasn't ready! I should have done more.'

'You did all you could and you know that,' said Proctor in a soothing tone.

'It wasn't enough!' spat Solenia. 'I didn't save Spectronia, he did! An outsider, who in the process killed another race just so that we live.'

'Survivor's guilt is common after such an event, Your Majesty, trust me, people can help, but this obsession with the past does not alter what you do next. All it does is temper what you are capable of doing now. Spectronia needs its Queen. Spectronia believes in its Queen. It needs... I need... a Queen who believes in herself.'

Solenia's face fell. She had let her guilt and her jealousy impede her ability to rule, it was true. For years she had been pushing people away. Proctor, her ever-faithful adviser had been in her family for generations. He WAS family. How could she push him away after all that he had done for her?

Defeated, she gazed up at her old friend. Proctor sighed.

Looking back at him was the face of the little girl who told him that one day she was going to be Queen. The same little girl who would collect butterflies and name each one after a family member and tend to them lovingly. The same girl

that he had witnessed crowned in front of billions of people on the day that her Father passed away, all too soon. As he had watched the crown descend upon her head he could almost see the responsibility weigh down upon her much as it had upon her Father.

'Your Majesty. No one else can rule but you. We need you now more than ever. Spectronia is still afraid of the outside world. Instead of hiding, maybe it is time to come out from the shadows and show the universe that Spectronia is not afraid.'

'You wish me to extend the hand of friendship?'

'I do.'

'And what if we encounter a threat again?'

'Then the people of Spectronia will be protected by a Queen who has seen battle and knows how to win but above all else will always seek to find a diplomatic path to peace first.'

Solenia smiled, much to Proctor's relief. He hadn't seen her smile in a long time.

'It will take me time but I feel, Proctor, that my time in the shadows is coming to an end and hopefully, one day, so is Spectronia's.'

Proctor bowed and allowed himself to smile.

He'd done it.

'Shall I fetch your court, Your Majesty?'

Solenia shifted uneasily in her chair. 'I dismissed them all... I doubt they will want to come back after all I have been putting them through.'

'They are waiting outside for your word,' he smiled. 'As I said, the people of Spectronia haven't given up on you, even if you had given up on yourself.'

Solenia beamed. 'Thank you, Proctor. Thank you for everything.'

The pair shared a silent smile, which was interrupted by another voice entering the fray.

'This is the Venus II calling Spectronia. Spectronia, do you copy?'

Solenia's face turned to one of shock. 'Random...'

Proctor made his way over to a small console in the far corner of the throne room. 'It's a distress signal, Your Majesty, one that seems to be playing on every single frequency.'

'How?' Solenia asked.

'This is the Venus II. We need your help. Request permission to land.'

Solenia turned to Proctor. 'But I banished them.'

'It sounds as though they are in trouble,' said Proctor.

'If they land here I am sworn to execute them.'

'Then maybe it's time to un-banish them... or at least listen to what they have to say?'

The robotic voice broke through all the speakers in the throne room and interrupted Solenia and Proctor once more.

'I seek a counsel with Queen Solenia. Please, my friends are in terrible danger, I must speak to Queen Solenia immediately.'

Solenia's heart was pounding.

This was all too soon. Moments earlier she had been happy to stay in the darkness and wallow in her pity but now this. Proctor was right. Now was the time for her and Spectronia to emerge from the shadows.

'Proctor. Bring him to me.'

To be continued in the next Captain Random book...

HA
HA
HA
HA
HA
HA
HA
HA

FRAME OF MIND

Four minutes had passed since Random's heart had stopped. Anji continued to press down with as much might as she could muster, not caring how Random would moan at her after hurting him when he awoke – if he awoke, she just wanted him back with her. She broke for a second and wiped away the snot that was cascading from her nose, ignoring the stream of tears that streaked across her face. Taking a huge gulp of air, she descended again, pinched Random's nose and sealed her lips around his, and blew hard.

'Come on, Random, please!' she pleaded.

Anji thumped down on his chest again and again. She didn't know CPR, especially not the correct technique to use on an alien like him, but she did what she could. It still wasn't enough. As she conceded defeat, she fell upon Random's lifeless form and buried herself in his chest and sobbed uncontrollably.

There was nothing more that she could do.

Random was dead.

Anji's body convulsed in grief. How had this all happened? Why had this happened? He had seemed fine that morning. When they had landed on the planet Dolja, they had checked that the air was breathable. Skateboard had double-checked! Maybe he'd made a mistake? The planet was uninhabited. Not one living thing lived on this mysterious yet beautiful world. Not that Anji was thinking of her surroundings right now, or how she was still alive.

Anji's head was full of confusion. It had been so out of the blue.

How was she going to tell Jake and Skateboard?

She didn't care how they would react to her. They could blame her all they wanted if it made them feel better.

She would if she were in their shoes.

She picked herself up and looked upon Random's dead body.

'I'm sorry,' she choked, stroking his arm affectionately.

The beautiful countryside that surrounded her felt like it began to zoom in on her. The gorgeous hilly fields were rolling towards her and the sun felt like it was burning the back of her neck, creeping up on Anji from high above as the sky somehow grew darker.

Suddenly the wide open space felt like it was trying to suffocate her. Anji closed her eyes tight until...

'Hey, Anj, what are you doing down there?'

Anji's eyes sprung open.

'Random!' she exclaimed, hurling herself at him.

'Woah, what's going on?' Random sounded surprised.

Anji pulled herself away from him and looked at him intensely.

'Wait, hold on a second.'

'Anj, I hope you don't mind me saying this but you look a mess, what's happened?'

Anji was dumbstruck. She looked back at the place where Random had fallen. The wheat shoots he had splintered when he fell were still standing tall. His clothes didn't look dusty either. There was no evidence that he had ever fallen to the ground at all.

'But...you died,' she whispered.

'What?'

'Just then you were...' Anji pointed to the floor. 'I tried to save you but I couldn't.'

Random observed Anji's face. She was confused and terrified in equal measure.

'Anji, I wasn't with you. I went on to see if I could find a place for us to stop and eat. Remember?'

Anji frowned. 'No, no I don't. It happened, I saw it happen.'

'But I'm here, Anji.'

'I know, none of this makes sense!'

Random took Anji by the shoulders and brought her in tightly. He hugged her.

'Anji, I'm here now. I don't know what you saw but I'm telling you right now this is me.'

Anji pulled him in even tighter and let herself sob again.

Random was concerned.

Whatever Anji had experienced must have scared her half to death.

He sought to reassure her further and ended their hug, took her hand and placed it on his chest.

'See,' he said soothingly as she felt his heartbeat against her palm.

Anji breathed freely. She tumbled back a little before regaining her balance. 'I must be going nuts!'

Random took her hand and smiled. 'We're alone on a strange, uninhabited world. We have no idea what to expect here. Anything can happen. Anything at all. I won't leave you alone again, I swear. As long as we stick together we're safe. Trust me.'

His eyes seemed to twinkle as he spoke.

Anji raised a wary smile. 'Random I've known you for years. Of course I trust you. Just goes to show how mad I am.'

Random smiled. 'That's better. Now come on. I've found a nice spot on top of the hill. We'll go up there, should give us a nice view of the whole place.'

Anji nodded and wiped her nose with her sleeve. She followed her now well friend again as they
progressed through the crops, although she was haunted by what she had just experienced.

It had unhinged her. It must have been real. Maybe it did happen and then she had been killed too? No, don't be silly, she told herself. But what had caused such a realistic hallucination? She made a note to ask Skateboard when they got back to the Venus II. She felt her forehead to check for a temperature to rule out being ill with some kind of space bug. Then she felt for her pulse as she looked up and saw the hill they were walking towards.

Anji blinked as the sun caught her eyes.

'Random?'

'Uh?'

'Who's that up there?'

Random turned around and followed Anji's pointed finger.

'I can't see anyone.'

Anji tutted. 'There!'

Random looked again.

'Anj, stop it, you're scaring me now.'

Anji snapped. 'I'm scaring YOU?!'

'I can't see anyone up on that hill.'
'Well, I can!'
'Okay, tell me what you see.'
Anji squinted. The two figures were far away but close enough
to distinguish if she concentrated her gaze. She saw a man and a
woman.
The man had thick, parted hair and wore a dark green jumper
and brown trousers.
The woman had similarly dark hair worn in what looked like a
plait down the back of her head and stood slightly shorter than
the mysterious man. She wore a gorgeous bright orange sari that
glistened in the bright sun making her glow. Her glamour was
unmistakable to Anji, whose heart skipped a beat when they
appeared to start waving.
'Oh my god,' said Anji as the full realisation of who they were
hit her. She fell back.
'Anj, are you okay?'
Anji began to cry again. 'How can they be here?'
'Who?'
Anji stuttered, barely able to bring herself to speak.
'It's… no… it can't be…'
'Anj, please. What do you see?'
Anji looked at him, her eyes red and puffy. The colour had
drained from her cheeks. Random thought she had seen a ghost.
Anji finished.
'…it's my parents.'
Random looked back.
'Anji, I don't know what's going on but-'
'How can they be here?' Anji repeated.
'Listen to me, Anji,' said Random softly.
'I've got to speak to them,' said Anji as she made to get up.
Random pulled her back. 'Get off me!'
'Anji, listen please.'
'I've not seen them all these years, I've got to speak to them!'
She began to try and release herself from Random's grip.
'Anj, please!'
'Get off me, why won't you let me go?' she shrieked.
'Because they aren't there!'

'They are. They're just as I remember them!'

'Anj, stop this!' the fabric on her t-shirt started to rip.

'Random, please!'

Random grabbed her and pulled her down to the floor. Anji started to kick him in the shins.

'They aren't real, Anji, I'm so sorry.'

Anji was hysterical. 'But they must be.'

'Anj, something is playing with your mind, you must fight it.'

But Anji didn't want to fight it. She wanted to embrace it. As she broke down again, realising that Random would never let her go, no matter how much she kicked, punched and screamed at him, she relented.

Random's eyes began to well up too. 'There's no one there, Anj. I'm so sorry.'

Anji blinked through the tears and looked up again. Random was right.

The two figures were gone.

She fell back and allowed herself to be consumed by her emotions. She was angry and confused and above all her heart ached.

That's how she had last seen them, waving her off to nursery. That image was etched in her mind for life. She let rational thought bleed in through the fog of confusion.

'There's something in my head.'

Random hugged her again and as he felt ready to let her go, now that the danger of the unknown had gone, for now, he rubbed the feeling back into his shins and steadily got back to his feet. Dusting himself off, he stood next to Anji, who was staring back at the hill.

'It's nothing but a mirage. Something's playing on your thoughts. I think we'd better get back to the ship.'

'I could have sworn it was them, just like I could have sworn I saw you...' Anji didn't want to finish the sentence.

'I think we should forget about this break and get back to the Venus II, quick. I don't want you going through anything else,' said Random. He took Anji's hand and started to lead her away. 'It's a bit of a trek back but the sooner we start making tracks...'

'Oh no,' cried Anji.

'What now?' asked Random.

'Listen...'

'Anj, I can't hear anything, it's all in your head.'

'Please, just let me listen.'

Random fell silent. All he could hear was the soft breeze brushing against the crops. In Anji's head, she was stuck in another nightmare.

'Those voices... I haven't heard them in years. I didn't think they'd affect me now.'

'Come on,' said Random, taking Anji's hand again.

'I know it's in my mind, I'm not listening to you!' she screamed.

Random led Anji back the way they came and started gathering speed, dragging a protesting Anji behind.

The voices were suddenly louder and to Anji's anguish, the faces of many a school bully began to poke through the crops that they were running past.

Every one hurling abuse, everyone calling her something that felt like a cut through her heart.

'Random, I don't think I can put up with much more of this,' she said.

'Block it out, Anj, fight it!' Random was growing more frustrated.

There was nothing he could do but try and take her mind off it. 'Remember the good times. Remember visiting the planet Algaros. Anything positive in your memories, think of them now!'

But the abusive schoolchildren's voices grew louder and louder, as Random and Anji broke into more of a sprint.

Pretty soon, as Anji screamed and shouted behind him, Random took complete control and whisked her off at his own pace.

Anji's mind became a whirlwind of torment. She started to see people, situations she thought she had left far behind in the past and yet here they were, manifested before her eyes, each moment plunging her further into torment.

Mercilessly, the Venus II honed into view.

'Nearly there, Anj, just a little longer-'

Random's sentence was halted by the most devastating explosion.

It lifted both he and Anji off their feet and sent them sprawling back into the crops. Moments later, as the fireball mushroomed high in the sky, Anji looked up and her eyes were ablaze with horror.

'Jake... Skateboard!'

She got up and looked where the ship had been. It was no more.

'Anji,' said Random calmly.

'Oh my god. They're gone!' she was paralysed, her mouth was dry. 'Can't be... Random please tell me that didn't just happen.'

'What didn't happen?'

'Did you just hit your head?! The Venus II just... blew up!'

Random shook his head. 'No, Anji, it didn't. The Venus II isn't there.'

'But you saw it, we were running towards it! You fell with me. How could you possibly say that.'

'Because what you just saw isn't real!' he calmly announced. 'The Venus II is close by but fine, I can see it.'

'Then what stopped us?' Anji asked.

'This thing...' he said pointing in front of them.

Anji couldn't see anything but the charred remains of what had once been their home.

'I can't see anything except...'

'Anj, concentrate. Try and look past the mirage.'

Anji squinted and screwed her tired mind shut as tightly as she could. Like an old washcloth, she tried to drain herself of all her negative thoughts and as she did, slowly a creature began to emerge.

Finally, her vision was clear and she saw what Random had noticed and what had stopped them in their tracks.

There, looming high in the air, was a beautiful white-lighted creature. It looked like a huge jellyfish, its tentacles moving majestically and slowly as it bobbed in the bright blue sky. Random pushed Anji behind him and approached it to speak.

'Hi,' he said in a friendly tone. 'We mean you no harm. Might I ask who you are?'

The creature stayed silent for a moment and then spoke in an ethereal female voice.

'I will speak only with your friend.'

Anji looked bemused. She walked tentatively towards the bright light that shone all around the mysterious creature. 'What are you?'

'I am Dolja,' it responded.

'You're named after the planet?' she asked.

'I am the planet,' came the reply.

Random and Anji shared a quizzical look.

'I am all around you. I am the night and day. I am the earth and the sky. I am the very air that you breathe. You are present upon my skin.'

'Then it's you who's been messing with my head, why?' asked Anji.

'Anj, go easy,' warned Random. 'We're dealing with a sentient planet here.'

'Screw that!' she said angrily, 'I want to know why you have been torturing me!'

'Torture?' it replied.

'Look, I don't know how you did what you did but I want you out of my head now!'

'Please, I did not mean you any malice,' replied Dolja.

Anji's fury grew. She looked around her and picked up a big stick and made for Dolja.

'Woah!' said Random, 'Put that down.'

'It's lying!' spat Anji.

'Anji, you can't hit a planet with a stick!'

'Watch me!'

'This is all so unnecessary,' said Dolja quietly.

'So was torturing me,' said Anji, whose stick was quickly confiscated by Random.

'I am very sorry if my means of communication harmed you in any way.'

'What's wrong with "Hello"?' replied Anji.

'As I am the only habitant of my domain I am un-used to your means of speaking,' Dolja reassured.

'Which is why you tried to communicate through thoughts?' asked Random.

'I am unaccustomed to visitors. There has seldom been many in the millennia that I have existed,' it continued.

'I can see why!' said Anji. 'Did you treat them the same way? How long did they last?'

'I did and sadly they were not with me long.'

Anji gritted her teeth. 'You nearly drove me to despair too!'

'All I did was read what was in the forefront of their minds at the time.'

Anji sighed. 'How do you expect to make friends if all you do is read people's minds and think that bringing their nightmares to life will make them want to be friends with you? People don't want something getting inside their heads without consent! You have no idea what people are dealing with.'

Random looked over at his friend. After today's ordeal, he had a fairly good idea of what was on Anji's mind.

'I see,' said Dolja.

'Dolja, I understand you're lonely, but if you were to appear as you are now from the start then I wouldn't be feeling like I do now,' said Anji.

'Might I ask... how do you feel?' asked Dolja, tentatively.

'Violated, scared, traumatised. You made my dead parents come back before my eyes. You made me see my friends die. You made me face the abuse I used to face every week as a child and for what? The chance to say hello?'

'Anji,' Random interjected. 'Dolja doesn't understand emotions. It can't tell the difference between memory and imagination.'

'I can't believe you are taking sides with the planet!' said a gobsmacked Anji.

'I'm not at all, believe me, Anj, I'll always fight your corner,' replied Random.

'But with your help, I can learn to understand,' said Dolja.

'Why didn't you just appear like this and why did you only haunt me and not Random?' asked Anji.

'I was unable to infiltrate your associate's mind. His brain's genetic structure was more complicated than yours. Upon your arrival here I immediately picked up on both your brainwaves and yours was an open door. I must confess that I find it somewhat difficult to speak as I am with you now.'

'Because you don't know how?' asked Anji.

'And because I don't think that my visitors will want to make acquaintance.'

'Then don't get in their heads! Find the courage to say hello and stay out of what is not yours!'

'But if I were not to sense the visitors who come to my domain then how will I get to know them?'

'By talking like we are now!' replied Anji. She was slightly exasperated but relieved that she seemed to be getting through to the planet.

'I see,' said Dolja. 'I believe that I owe you an apology.'

'You do,' said Anji, whose crossed arms then flopped to her side as she sighed. 'Thank you.'

'I would like to extend my hand of friendship to you both.'

'Only if you stay out of our heads,' said Anji.

'Of course, but there is so much more I would like to learn if you would be willing to teach me how to communicate better than my previous methods?'

Anji paused for a moment. 'How long have you got?'

A few hours passed before Anji and Random, who along with Dolja had found time to sit and talk on the hill that the travellers had been aiming for before Anji's nightmare had started.

After a time, they said their goodbyes and watched as Dolja's physical form vanished into the air. As the sun began to set, the two friends made their way back towards the Venus II, their path lit

by a beautiful auburn night.

Random looked at his friend and broke the silence.

'You didn't have to do that, you know? Not after what it put you through.'

'Yeah well, I didn't want whoever else comes here next to experience that again. Besides, it wasn't dangerous, was it? Just… shy.'

Random smiled. 'I'm proud of you Anji Gummadi.'

Anji smiled back. 'Aren't you always?'

'That's true,' he replied. The pair became silent again as the stars began to twinkle high above them. Random knew what he wanted to say, just not how to say it.

'Anj, I... er...'

'I know,' she sighed. 'I'm a mess.'

'Isn't everyone?' said Random.

'Depends on how we learn to deal with it all, I guess.'

'That's true. I suppose the question is how do you?' asked Random.

'By wearing them on my sleeve.'

Random thought about this for a moment. 'Memories are what make us who we are. And our deepest fears, well, how many of them come true?'

'Hopefully none of them,' said Anji who shivered as she remembered the sight of Random lying dead on the ground before her.

'As long as you're not wishing me dead then we're cool!' Random joked.

'How is that even funny?' replied Anji.

Random put an arm around his friend as the Venus II appeared in the distance.

'I wonder if Jake's got off the AI machine Skateboard made up for him. Imagine if he had come here too! Anj, listen if you ever need to talk-'

'I always do. But I can't change what's shaped me. I don't want to either.'

She looked over her shoulder back at the hill and imagined that her parents were there once more, waving and looking out for her.

She smiled. 'Not all memories are bad.'

MECHANICA

Skateboard's little wheels trundled gingerly down the ramp that had descended from the belly of the Venus II.

'Honestly mate, it'll be fine!' came a cry from within the bowels of the ship that the little AI robot called "home".

'Jake's right. You deserve the rest, we'll be fine!' came another, this time a female voice.

'I still fear you have conspired to get rid of me,' said Skateboard in response.

'Look Skateboard, it's only for a week! Surely you can't pass up an opportunity like this?'

'No Captain.' Skateboard really couldn't pass up a chance like this.

Not so long ago, the crew of the Venus II had wandered into a pocket of the galaxy that was dominated by non-organic beings. Planet after planet, uninhabitable for the likes of Random and his friends with polluted, poisonous air seemingly unfit for any form of life whatsoever.

Every world they encountered was like a large metal sphere in space. Differing in size and mass, it was like a collection of metallic orbs hanging ominously in the sky.

The crew of the Venus II had begun to panic that they had drifted into a very bad part of space indeed.

Populated by rogue androids and simulants ready to drain their bodies of their blood and convert them into one of their own.

And yet, along the belt of stars in the system, many did roam without malice and upon further inspection, the galaxy was home to what seemed like the nicest bunch of occupants they could have wished for!

As the Venus II sailed past all 459 planets and moons in the system, each one was scanned and each one said the same thing.

Bionic life existed. Not just existed, it was booming. 600 billion machines went about their daily lives, unaware of how unique their little pocket of mechanical utopia was to the universe.

Among this unique star belt, the astonished crew discovered that one was a holiday home for resting robots, those who needed a break, like a giant robot spa in space.

After discovering that he had never had a proper holiday amongst his own, Random, Anji and Jake then proceeded to goad him into having one there.

They researched it thoroughly. 24-hour mud baths, oil changes, file and cache recycling hubs. It was a robot's heaven.

On top of all that bliss and more importantly, it was free.

Now here he was.

Mechanica.

A utopia for robots.

There was just one tiny flaw. For all their goading and encouragement, Skateboard harboured a secret from his friends and as he made his way down the gantry, in a vast pure white concourse where other robots like he was being dropped off and parking up, the halls awash with all manner of robotic life.

As he turned and witnessed his ship ascend back into the stars and fly away from view, he wished he had told them.

He hated other robots.

Like really hated them.

He had grown used to his adventures with his humanoid friends and how they worked.

Real-life, non-manufactured seemed so much more natural to Skateboard.

The fact that organic life can evolve and change in ways that robots like he could never do.

Plus, prior conversations with those of his kind had always been awkward and stilted.

Even back when he was a slave robot for the Sapphire Regime on Rodas, he couldn't stand those in his unit.

He told himself he wasn't robotist, especially since he had such a fantastic relationship with the

Venus II's onboard computer.

There were even some food blenders which whom he'd had
better conversations than other robots. And now they had left him
for a week with nothing but them.

Skateboard's diodes sighed. Slowly, he maneuvered through the
hustle and bustle of the concourse, which looked very much like
an airport runway and catered for nothing but androids and alike.

As he trundled to the arrival queue, which was thankfully low
owing to there being dozens of identical kiosks, he wondered how
many robots like him were there.

'64,519,823,' came the answer. Skateboard looked up at the robot
one place ahead of him in the queue.

'I beg your pardon?' he enquired.

The robot, which stood tall and stoically above him, its metal a
slightly rusted rouge and gold, peered down with its hollow eyes
and repeated itself.

Skateboard looked as astonished as a robot with no facial
features could. 'How did you know what I was thinking?'

'I can wirelessly link to low-security levelled intelligence and
read what they are thinking. I can also interpret your data matrix
and anticipate what you are also about to say.'

Skateboard hastily changed his internal security firewall and
silently moved to the end of another
queue.

'Robots,' he muttered to himself.

'I heard that too,' came a distant cry from the robot again.

*

It had taken Skateboard all of 0.329 seconds to stay in the queue
before he thought better and asked the nearest robot for the
direction of the complaints department. The eavesdropper had
freaked him out somewhat.

If there were all manner of robot life here on Mechanica, how
could he be assured that there won't be others who violate his
personal space and thoughts?

Amongst his busy surroundings, Skateboard finally found a
little booth with the letters COMPLAINTS welded expertly onto a
part of a table overlapping a long desk.

Skateboard picked his front wheels up and placed himself at the lip of the desk.

'Is anyone there?' he cried into the empty booth.

A horrible grinding sound split over the background noise of the concourse, to such an extent that Skateboard thought it correct to retune his audio input.

After doing so, the sound remained. He peered into the booth and all he could see, except for the perfect glimmer of shiny metal, fitting uniformly

with the rest of the décor he had seen so far, was a crude printer, swimming around a mountain of ink-stained and torn pieces of paper. He peered closer. It appeared to be the culprit of the bad noise.

The printer had been placed on a little stool in front of the desk that Skateboard was leaning against. Mercifully, the grinding noise stopped and a single piece of A4 paper plopped out onto the desk and rested on the peak of the papery mountain.

Skateboard read the text.

WELCOME TO COMPLAINTS. I AM P. RINTER, HOW MIGHT I ASSIST YOU TODAY?

'Oh no,' Skateboard groaned. He recognised the make now. A printer so unreliable that it had been outlawed in all the known galaxies and now here someone deemed it capable enough to run the complaints department. Weirder still, it appeared to be wearing a tie.

'I would like to lodge a complaint. One of your guests was able to scan my thought patterns.'

The printer started to grind again. A piece of paper began to poke out slowly from below it, before stopping suddenly.

A beeping sound accompanied a red light that flashed on the top of the printer's digital readout screen. Skateboard read the message.

PAPER JAM.

'Oh for... is there anyone else who can help me?'

He looked all around and realised there wasn't. Skateboard sighed and produced a claw from within his body and proceeded to pull the paper out of the printer's feeder.

Upon doing so, he noticed that the paper had printed at a funny angle. Thankfully as he did so, the printer stopped beeping and the red light changed back to a green one. Skateboard looked at the paper. The text was smeared and unfinished, but Skateboard could make out what the printer was asking him.

CERTAINLY, SIR, CAN I HAVE YOUR ROOM NUMBER PLE-

'No, you have mistaken me, I haven't checked in yet. Is there anyone else I can talk to please? The manager, perhaps?'

The printer began to grind and shudder again. Skateboard turned his hearing sensors down to spare him the horrendous noise.

How on earth an inkjet printer had got here from Earth he would never know, but no wonder the people on that planet always seemed to be so cross and in a hurry all the time – it's because their days were being constantly ruined by paper jams!

Once more, the paper got stuck.

Once more, the beeping sound and red light started flashing and beeping simultaneously.

Once more, Skateboard had to help out the struggling piece of machinery. He read the paper that had caused the jam. This time it was all corrugated up like a bad piece of origami and the text seemed more faded than before. Still, he read it.

I AM THE MANAGER

'I see,' he said as the printer corrected itself again. He was starting to use his usual calmness. Machines always seemed to bring out the worst in him. 'Then I guess this is why according to Planet Advisor that Mechanica doesn't receive many complaints. It's because no one can do anything about it. After all, you can't respond as a normal robot would!'

The printer seemed to start shuddering from side to side as if it were in a rage. It began to print more furiously this time and Skateboard wondered how much longer he could put up with this. The printer's printing ribbon moved from left to right furiously before the inevitable happened. The machine stopped once again.

Skateboard let out a cry of sheer frustration and looked at the digital read-out again.

REPLACE THE INK CARTRIDGE.

'Forget it!' he screamed. As he rolled away from the desk in a cloud of stormy frustration, Skateboard cursed his luck and went to rejoin a checking queue, vowing that if he ever had to make a complaint ever again, he'd do it online.

*

The rest of the day had gone surprisingly pleasantly for Skateboard.

He checked in with the service droid, he was allocated one that would tend to his own special needs, although he found it hard to tell it apart from the others as they all seemed to look alike.

At check-in, he was given a password that would make his droid come and help him at his every beck and call. The droid, who had introduced itself as 2PQ4, would beam to his very location whenever he wished and furnish him with whatever he desired.

Upon being shown to his room, Skateboard had told him he desired nothing more than peace and had promptly told him to go away.

Despite his ongoing annoyance with the company he had met so far, he couldn't fault Mechanica on its presentation. It was a beautiful metropolis of the very best of technology.

There were no wires to be seen, except some of the visiting robots who had seen better days and were in dire need of tender loving care.

The metal shone like it was new and despite there being a lack of organic matter like plants to decorate the place, there were reminders of the cornerstones of mechanical society. Indeed, in the short trip to his room he had passed statues of them all.

There was Rod 96, the first robot with an in-built personality chip.

Not forgetting VLE0, who had helped decipher the code that put a stop to the horrific atomic war in the Argonian Cluster.

And then, Skateboard marveled as he saw the granddaddy of them all; the unrivalled *PSOne*.

Skateboard connected himself to the room's wi-fi, which had been given to him on the room key. As the connection was made, he felt a similar connection to the one he had with the Venus II.

A selection of new commands flooded his matrix giving him a warm sensation.

The room was wireless, just like his ship, his home.

'Most sufficient, I must say,' he clucked. Surveying the room, which had a balcony and a hollow step down in the floor, he thought he would try out his newfound connection... and hastily ran a diagnostic on his security systems again, worried that the eavesdropping robot he had crossed in the concourse would probably end up being his new neighbour.

As he ran himself a crude oil bath and gazed thoughtfully into the thick dark sludge slopping into the deep basin in the middle of what would be his home for a week, Skateboard gave into the thought that had nagged him since he arrived.

Something was very wrong here.. .and he had to find out what.

As the steam cascaded upwards towards the ceiling, Skateboard prepared himself for the immense bliss of his first bath in a while when he realised that the rising vapour wasn't going all the way to the top of the ceiling.

It seemed to be collecting over what was looking ever more likely like the body of a creature.

'Curious,' he said to himself as he wheeled towards the bath and turned it off.

Suddenly, Skateboard's stun gun shot out of his motherboard and fired at the mysterious shape.

With a yelp, the figure plummeted from its hiding place straight into the bath and disappeared into a sea of crude oil.

Skateboard recoiled as the boiling liquid splashed all around, caking the pristine floor and walls.

Peering into the bath, Skateboard readied his gun. 'I know you are in there so come out and show yourself!'

Ever so slowly, as the thick gunk dripped all around them, the intruder drew to their full height.

Skateboard observed, ready to shoot once more, as the tall sensual figure of a woman stood before him, all the while slipping and trying to keep her arms aloft.

'Please accept my humblest of apologies,' came a robotic female voice.

Skateboard was taken aback by the soft tone. 'Might I enquire as to why you were hiding in my room... and why you have ruined my bath?'

The robot bowed. 'Of course you can, Skateboard. I had no desire to disturb your peace. This is not how I wanted us to meet I can assure you.'

'Well, there's the apology but I am still waiting for the explanation,' Skateboard replied, stun gun primed.

'And you will get it but before I reveal to you my being here might I make one small request?'

Skateboard felt affronted. Such barefaced cheek considering she was the one breaking an entry and yet... such manners!

'You may,' he found himself saying, somewhat seduced by her aura.

'May I have a towel?'

Skateboard's diodes whirred. 'I had no idea that we robots required them.'

'Unfortunately, the Dialohpy 5000 series were not built to withstand such copious amounts of crude oil in our optical system.'

'They also do not seem very capable of maintaining their camouflage under pressure,' quipped Skateboard.

'On this occasion, it has failed me,' said the intruder, who started to wipe her eyes but only achieved rubbing more oil into them. 'I am unable to see presently.'

'And yet clearly you can still speak so I will ask you again. Why were you spying on me?'

'Because I know who you are... and I think that you can help me.'

Skateboard lowered his gun slightly. 'That doesn't explain why you couldn't just knock.'

'The service droid. You know that every guest on Mechanica is allocated one. They are spies, watching your every move. I had to make sure that I could get you alone, to talk to you. Hence why I was hiding. Please, your stun pistol is not required, I can assure you.'

Skateboard remained more intrigued than angry at the robot standing before him.

'Okay, start from the beginning. Who are you and what are you doing here?'

The intruder climbed out of the bath and wiped her face on a nearby wall, which struck Skateboard as curious until he remembered the towel situation.

When she was ready, she began to speak.

'I am designated Android S319 of the Galactic Cyber Patrol of Beta Nine Sigma.'

Skateboard assimilated the information. 'Galactic Cyber Patrol, so you are a trained spy.'

'Covert operative. I am here on unofficial business from Station Five. Ever since the patrol signed up to the Universal Worker Laws I was granted a fortnight's leave. And so, upon researching the best possible place to make the most of my vacation, I chose Mechanica.'

'I highly doubt that,' Skateboard replied. 'Cyber Patrol agents are the crème-de-la-crème of robotic intelligence. Your team knew what they were doing in sending you here.'

'I came on my own accord. It's hard to switch off, especially when you've never been on leave before. I'm an Android. Like yourself, you must feel I have no use for leave or downtime.'

'So, you decided to carry out a background check on the complex to satisfy your curiosity,' said Skateboard, filling in the blanks.

'Affirmative. And when I discovered what was going on I knew I had to do something.'

'Then please, er, Android, what was it again?'

The Android tilted her head. 'There is no need to ask me, you have full access to your memory banks surely?'

Skateboard whirred. 'Yes, but it's a bit of a mouthful, as my humanoid friends would say.

May I call you Anne for short?'

Anne's circuits warmed slightly inside her.

'If you deem it necessary.'

Tell me, Anne, what is going on? And how did you know about me being here? Also, why have you chosen me to help you?'

'When I managed to infiltrate the records system I noticed that you had just checked in. I recognised who you were straight away. The Cyber Patrol knows all about the Venus II and the good that you and your friends do. In fact, you've prevented our intervention on a couple of occasions. A hero like yourself is pretty hard to ignore.'

'I'm flattered, but it does lead to the question as to what you were doing in the records. Surely that is a breach of confidentiality.'

Anne nodded. 'Which is exactly the reason why I hacked my way in. The service droid knew too much about me. It knew my every desire. My room looked as though it had been tailored exactly to my wishes. A little like yours.'

Skateboard looked around sheepishly at the blank interior of his room. It didn't speak volumes for his personality.

'Well, indeed.'

Anne continued. 'I hadn't given them any indication when I booked as to my requirements. The only thing I had done upon arrival was sign into the wi-fi.'

'And you think that someone on this planet hacked your details?' asked Skateboard.

'Not just mine,' said Anne. 'Everyones.

Everybody who comes here. All their information is laid bare to the mainframe network. After further examination of an abundance of file paths that should have been locked, I realised what was happening here. Someone is harvesting our data.'

Skateboard's circuits buzzed in alarm. 'That means...'

'Affirmative. Mechanica is taking away our very essence.'

'My friends would compare it to someone selling souls,' chirped Skateboard.

'A quaint comparison. You are very much domesticated compared to me. We've got to put a stop to this. Will you help me?'

Skateboard calmed himself and pondered the proposal. He had come here to relax. And yet, he was a robot. Did he need a period of relaxation? If he were honest with himself, no.

Not while there was a mystery to solve.

'I accept your proposal,' he responded. 'Do you have any leads?'

'I believe so. We must get to the mainframe. It's located fifty kilometres from our location.'

Skateboard wheeled himself over to Anne's side. 'But how will we get there?'

'We have to get to the tube shaft. It looks like a routine up-and-down elevator, but it is a complex junction of turbo lifts according to schematics. I can hack into the system and it can take us to our desired location.
There we should find our answers.'

'I can do that if you will allow me access to the codes you have acquired?' asked Skateboard.

'Affirmative. Will you allow me to make contact?'

Skateboard was a little taken aback by the question. 'Your request has been granted.'

Anne held her hand out and pressed her exo-skeletal fingers to Skateboard's motherboard. If he were able to, he'd have been blushing like a teenage schoolgirl at that moment.

Suddenly a flood of information shot through both their circuitry. It was a sensation Skateboard had never experienced before.

The closest he had got was the time he accidentally got his wireless connection tangled with the vacuum cleaner onboard the Venus II.

It was indescribable but they were intertwined, linked forever.

Within seconds, they parted, and Skateboard seemed a little embarrassed. 'Sorry, first time.'

Anne tilted her head to one side. 'Apology accepted. Now, you must hide within my camouflage so that we can get to the tube shaft. You should have the codes to do so with you now.'

Skateboard shook himself, trying to find the codes, let alone the words after such an experience. 'Got them.'

A violent knock made both robots jump.

Then there was another, harder knock, followed by another.

It sounded like someone was trying to bludgeon their way into Skateboard's room.

'Oh dear,' sighed Anne. 'I emitted some important information.'

'What was it?' asked Skateboard, although he didn't need to as he was fairly certain he knew how Anne was going to respond.

'There was another reason why I was hiding in here.'

Another loud bang exploded against Skateboard's door, causing it to buckle inward slightly.

'When I hacked the records I might have tripped the security myself,' Anne continued.

Skateboard had no time to react. With a mighty bang, his door splintered inwards, shards of metal exploding all around the room as a gang of Service Droids burst into the room.

It was empty.

'Search the vicinity,' cried the main Service Droid. From Skateboard's hiding place he could make out that the digital facial expressions of them all were not the smiley blue faces he had seen on the concourse escorting their masters, but they were now red and looking downright murderous.

Skateboard looked over at Anne who stood on the other side of the room to him.

Luckily her camouflage had worked for the both of them as she extended its protective bandwidth but then he witnessed something he was unable to warn her about.

A long thin piece of debris that had once been his door had impaled her in the abdomen and was sticking out just far enough to stop a Service Droid from proceeding forward.

The Service Droid in question stopped in his tracks as he clanged against the sharp metal. Upon observing that it hadn't gone all the way into the wall and seemed to be hovering in mid-air, he held his arm out menacingly.

'Target found!' it screeched as the other Service Droids spun and also presented their arms. Skateboard noticed a laser gun sticking out of their palms.

'Run Anne!' he cried as he tore towards the wall. Anne did just as he demanded and in doing so, pulled the metal shard from her abdomen and proceeded to use it to crack the Service Droids in the face like a baseball bat. A couple of them got their shots on target but she was too quick for them, skidding out of the room just as the fire from the Service Droids exploded behind her.

She regained her composure and joined Skateboard in the hallway. They both tore away from the scene with all the speed they could muster.

'Are you okay?' he asked.

'In perfect working order,' she said.

'Unlike your camouflage. I'd get that checked out after this,' he quipped.

'If we get out of this alive. All the Service Droids will be after us now. There are millions on this planet. Our mission has become much harder to accomplish.'

'Harder, but not impossible,' Skateboard reassured her, knowing full well that as the Service Droids followed them, the camouflage he and Anne had no longer worked and he wasn't fully convinced they would get through this.

To perpetuate his miserable prediction, the crude oil that Anne had plunged into from her hiding spot was having a severe impact on the speed of her escape. As Skateboard watched her slipping and sliding, he asked politely for her to allow him to help her and in doing so, swept underneath her feet, turned on his afterburners and bolted away.

As the crashing of very unfriendly fire fizzed and burnt its way all around them, Skateboard became wary that if Anne was hit they could both go up in flames.

'Hold on, Anne,' he cried.

'To what?' she replied.

'People always say that,' he responded.

'We are not people,' she corrected.

Mercifully they reached the turbo lift, and as Anne pushed the button for the doors to slide open

and allow them both within its relative safety, they saw the magnitude of Service Droids chasing after them.

'Get behind me,' she said as she strode heroically in front of him. Skateboard did as he was told and witnessed her left arm suddenly morph into what to him resembled a rocket launcher.

As the din of laser fire and Service Droids spouting unspeakable ills rang all around, a loud boom, similar to that of a rocket taking off, shattered the noise into a million pieces.

A horrendous bang, loud enough to set off a hundred car alarms all at once, exploded all around and Skateboard and Anne were engulfed in a thick cloud of black smoke.

All became silent.

As the cloud cleared and very little was left of their attackers, the lift door pinged and Skateboard and Anne, her arm having reverted to normal, calmly climbed on board.

Anne examined the endless rows of buttons and pressed the button for the bottom floor.

A few moments passed before Skateboard broke the silence.

'If that was your left arm, I'd hate to see the damage the other one could do!'

'It's one of the perks of the job. My body is made of multi-forming adaptable molecular alloy.'

Skateboard was very impressed. 'Better than having spare parts.'

'Indeed,' Anne agreed. 'Back to our mission. Intel confirms that the mainframe that collects all our
data is held underground. I managed to track the signal that infiltrated my wireless connection to the source and that is where it appears to be.'

Skateboard hummed. 'So, whoever or whatever is doing this certainly isn't wanting to advertise their power, hiding down there.'

'Whatever it is, we'll put a stop to it.'

Suddenly their conversation was halted by a jolt. Seconds later the lift shook again.

'I think you had better reload,' he said dryly.

Outside the lift, a swarm of Service Droids had descended upon it and were in the process of attempting to rip open its roof and scoop out its occupants. Their metal fingers began to tear down on it, shards of debris coming away as they pierced down and started shredding in.

Inside, Skateboard could see murderous fingers ripping through. He was helpless to stop them, knowing that his stun gun would be as useful as a traffic cone stopping an airplane from taking off.

Their only hope was Anne, and she was more than prepared.

'I will need to wait for a clear sight of them, otherwise, I risk blowing us both up if I hit the roof,' she said.

'Well, let us hope they don't try and shoot us before then!' grumbled Skateboard.

He spoke too soon. As soon as the Service Droids had made holes big enough to shoot through, they opened fire again. Skateboard and Anne did their best to evade the fire, but all it was doing was making holes in the floor!

The situation was becoming unbearable, not to mention inescapable. All of a sudden, a sharp sensation broke across all of Skateboard's instruments. A damage report flicked up on his visual display.

'Blast!' he yelled. 'They've hit my back-left wheel!' He looked down at the shard of broken metal and did well to miss another volley of lasers in the same instant.

He felt like blacking out. He'd seen bad injuries before but now it had happened to him he wanted nothing else but to shut off.

Anne sensed his thoughts through the connection they had made. 'Robot up! We're getting through this!'

She looked up. The roof was almost gone. The time was right.

Another rocket exploded out of Anne's arm and into the Service Droids, sending the whole lift into chaos.

As the down blast of the rocket fired into the lift's floor, it managed to sever the cable at the top of the shaft, sending Skateboard and Anne and bits of Service Droids cascading down upon them.

Before long, with a hideous sound of twisting metal, the lift crashed into the floor and as Skateboard and Anne tried to make

---

sure they didn't shut down in the commotion, the lift doors apologetically pinged open, revealing a dark and gloomy corridor waiting for them.

Skateboard picked himself up. He looked at his wheel again. He was unhurt on account of him being a machine but lamented his missing wheel. He produced a claw and helped Anne out of the rubble and lifted her onto her feet.

'Are you damaged?' he asked.

Anne ran a quick diagnostic. 'Minimal abrasions to my outer shell. Otherwise, I am unharmed.'

'Good,' said Skateboard. He looked up at the lift shaft from where they had come. There didn't seem to be any Service Droids coming after them for now.

He looked at the corridor before them. 'This is where we need to be, I presume?'

Anne checked her information banks. 'Yes, the mainframe is precisely fifty-two metres down the corridor.'

'Let's go. But first, maybe next time it would be safer to take the stairs.'

They took off cautiously down the dank and dark corridor.

Skateboard put himself into reverse and kept his audio/visual sensors tuned to the highest
frequency.

The advantage of being in a corridor is that you can only be ambushed either in front or behind; not from all angles. The downside though, was that in a corridor, if you ARE ambushed from both sides, there was nowhere to run and hide.

Before long, they had reached the epicentre of Mechanica. A horrific chorus of what sounded like modems struggling to connect greeted Skateboard and Anne as they stood in awe before the miles upon miles of huge computers. A network of wires and machinery made up the mainframe that snaked around the walls and floor like blood vessels pumping vital life into enormous ventricle-like chambers. The chambers looked to Skateboard like they were throbbing in and out of a computer too big for Skateboard to comprehend.

'Is this what I think it is?' he asked.

'The heart of the planet!' Anne cried in wonderment. But the noise was becoming unbearable to both of them. The chamber seemed to be crying out in pain, every wire and every processor appeared to be screaming in agony.

'What is causing that noise?' Anne asked Skateboard, who was already connecting to a nearby computer bank, searching for information. Instantly, he had the answers to all of their questions.

'The same thing that is causing the data compromise,' he confirmed. He paused as he listened to the mainframe wheeze and groan.

'I believe I have solved the mystery.'

'Would you care to share your findings?' Anne's tone almost evoked an impatient tone not befitting of an android of her design.

'Of course. It seems as though the mainframe's files have become corrupted.'

'By what?'

'A robot who should not have ever been allowed near Mechanica. By the looks of it, an android who works for the Alzonian government arrived here quite some time ago and upon linking up with the wi-fi appeared to allow his corrupt files access too, leading to a knock-on effect when the main frame tried to process his information. It created a two-way link between the guest and the planet which has led to the main frame feeding our information back.

Anne was shocked. 'But that goes against every privacy agreement in the known galaxy. How did he do it? Why did he do it?'

'How - he was a politician, his files were bound to be corrupt. Why? I don't know. The link should have been broken as soon as the wi-fi connection was out of range, so I highly doubt he even knew that he had broken the planet's mainframe.'

Anne struggled to comprehend what she was being told. 'I am curious. My findings told me that our data was being leaked. So where is it going?'

Skateboard searched the mainframe's memory banks. 'It is, but it isn't going anywhere. The main frame itself is living off regurgitated information. So even though there is a leak, it appears to be on a loop.'

'In a way, that's a relief that nobody has our information then,' she said. 'It doesn't explain why the Service Droids want to destroy us.'

'Doesn't it? Think about it. If the main frame is living off the corrupt data files of a powerful politician, where does that power extend?' asked Skateboard.

Anne computed the question. 'Theoretically, it depends on how powerful the android was to start with, and what power he has back on his planet.'

'Precisely, and judging on the welcome we got upon discovering this, the Service Droids appear to be carrying out the orders the corrupt android would on Alzonia.'

'Which is?' asked Anne.

'Kill when normality deviates. The Service Droids see us as abnormalities like we are the corrupt files in a computer that needs purging. Alzonia isn't the most pleasant of planets, after all. There is no attempt to fix or repair, just purge.'

'Remind me never to go there on holiday,' she quipped. 'Sorry, my humour capabilities are not appropriate at this time.'

Skateboard would have smiled if he could. 'I found it rather endearing, personally.'

'So how do we put things back to how they should be?' asked Anne, getting back to the problem at hand.

'It's simple. We run antivirus software. As soon as it is complete, Mechanica will return to normal. I can do it from here with relative ease. I shall also include a command that does not allow robotic life with corrupt personality files from entering or ensures they are fixed before connecting to the planet's wi-fi system. That way, this should never happen again.'

'How long will that take?' asked Anne.

'Roughly two minutes.'

'Good,' she said. 'Because we've got company.'

Skateboard whirred to Anne's side. She was right. The Service Droids had caught up with them. The noise of the main frame had hidden any sight of an ambush and now there were hundreds of them.

'Do it now!' Anne cried as she dived for cover and began shooting rounds of laser fire at them, taking out a few with her first shot, who failed to shoot back.

Anne and Skateboard looked confused. 'Why haven't they fired?' asked Anne as she picked herself up.

'Of course! Because we are in the main frame. Any damage in here would have horrific consequences, not just to all on the planet, but to the whole planet in general!'

The Service Droids' claw-like hands burst open in unison, a terrifyingly sharp sound echoing around the mainframe chamber at the same time.

'Oh,' said Skateboard. 'It doesn't mean they won't attack us directly.'

'Run the programme,' ordered Anne, 'and run!'

Skateboard picked up Anne and they sped away, the murderous Service Droid army in hot pursuit.

'Luckily, my dear, it's already running. T-minus sixty-nine seconds and counting.'

The next minute-and-a-bit was the longest in Skateboard's life as he heroically carried Anne and they passed rows upon rows of machinery. All the while they were being chased by hundreds of Service Droids who were providing such a direct violation of their employment that if this was a humanoid planet they would all be destined for the scrap heap after. If only he could keep ahead of them for eleven seconds longer.

Ten.

A Service Droid reached out for him.

Nine.

'That wheel I lost has slowed me down!' Skateboard cursed to himself.

Eight.
'What?' asked Anne, whose feet were magnetically clamped to him.

Seven.

'Nothing!'

Six.

The Droid was mere centimetres away now.

Five.

'Are you sure?' Anne asked.

Four.

'Positive.'

Three.

The droid stopped them in their tracks and clamped his claw on Skateboard's body. Both he and Anne stopped dead in their tracks.
The Service Droids were all around them now.

Two.

'Oh.' said Skateboard. Death was upon them both.
The Droid's spinning claw began thrusting forward to destroy.

One.

Suddenly, the noise ebbed away. The army of Service Droids all seemed to disappear pretty sharply, not even batting away the curious occurrence of them all being away from their masters and their duties. The Service Droid that had been ready to attack Skateboard put him down and its face, once red with murderous intent were now calm and pleasant again.

'Would you like anything else, sir?' it asked him politely.

Skateboard and Anne looked at each other bemused. 'No, that'll be all,' said Skateboard in reply.

'Very good, sir,' the Service Droid said before it wheeled away in blissful happiness that it was doing its job to the letter.

Anne and Skateboard picked themselves up off the ground.

The noise and the hum of the mainframe had changed to a more melodic, harmonious tone.

'It appeared that the antivirus worked,' said Skateboard.

'Confirmed,' said Anne. 'Thank you. We saved Mechanica.'

'Indeed,' said Skateboard. He looked at Anne's scuffed bodywork and the hole that the debris had left in her side and then scanned his injury.

'Three wheels,' he sighed. 'I feel so inadequate.'

'It suits you,' said Anne. 'Makes you look rugged.'

Skateboard's diodes whirred. 'Anne. Might I be so bold as to ask how much longer you intend to stay here on Mechanica again?'

Anne's processor ground in her head. 'I have seven days left of leave.'

'Would you mind sharing it with me?'

If Anne could have smiled she would have.

'No, that should be sufficient,' she said, those seven words had been the best words she had heard in that sequence in a long time.

Skateboard's claw snaked out of his bodywork and took her hand. 'Great. If I may? I think before we do anything else we both need to book ourselves in for a service.'

After that, both Skateboard and Anne shared the best week of their lives.

They took full advantage of the break that had been afforded to them and indulged in their passions on the hologramatic programmes that the guests of Mechanica were gifted as part of the package.

For Skateboard, he introduced Anne to his interest in 20th-century Earth hardware whilst she
let him in on her interest in interstellar warfare. Although both could not fully see the attraction to one another's hobbies, they enjoyed spending time with one another and now that Mechanica was fixed, they could use the spa facilities and Service Droids without fear of being killed.

But Skateboard knew that like all good things, this was soon to end.

On the day that they were both to be leaving Mechanica, Skateboard had escorted Anne to her ship on the concourse, knowing that she had to go but not wanting the inevitable to happen.

'I must thank you for all the time we have spent together,' Anne said, breaking a silence that had started upon Skateboard escorting her up from her room.

'Indeed, it has been most satisfactory,' he agreed. Hesitantly, he plucked up the courage to ask Anne a really important question.

'Anne, might I be so bold as to ask you to keep your connection open with me? Just so that if we happen to be in the same star system we can reconvene our friendship?'

Anne tilted her head. 'I would love nothing more.

But I am an agent, Skateboard, I would have to do it behind my company's back otherwise someone could hack our connection and we both know what manner of problems that can lead to!'

Skateboard's diodes sighed. 'I understand.'

Anne knelt and placed her hand upon his shell. 'But who knows? Maybe I might. I also might one day tell you my real name.'

Skateboard perked up. 'I would like that. I respect the boundaries you have to work within.'

'Thank you,' she said as she patted him affectionately. 'Remember, we'll always have Mechanica. Until next time.'

Anne straightened herself upwards and turned her back on Skateboard and made her way through the busy concourse towards a transparent tube that led to her allocated docking bay.

Skateboard watched her leave his life and hoped for a wave or even a glance back. But nothing.

He'd spent too much time around humans to expect a more meaningful goodbye.

As he made his way towards his own designated docking bay tube, in turn missing the backward glance from Anne he had so craved, he reflected on his past week and how much it had made him appreciate mechanical life and how Anne had imprinted herself upon him forever.

Quickly he concluded that although they can be sometimes slow, infuriating and cold, machines
weren't all that bad after all.

After a busy queuing system had clogged up his arrival in the docking bay, Skateboard walked out of the tube and into a vast hangar containing many impressive ships, his eyes immediately clamped onto the one he called home.
Halfway down the hangar, there she stood, the good old Venus II.

As he made his way towards the gangway, which descended slowly as he got closer, a familiar voice bellowed down from within the bowels of his oh-so-reliable ship.

'Hurry up Skateboard, non-mechanical life is only afforded twenty minutes of air in this hangar!'

'Coming, sir,' he cried as he made his way home. On board, the owner of the voice, a purple-skinned boy, was waiting for him at the top.

'Welcome home, Skateboard!' he cried as the gangway groaned back into place now that Skateboard was safely onboard.

'Thank you, sir,' said Skateboard. His connection with the Venus II was firmly back online.

'Quickly, we have to get out of here. I only have a couple of minutes of air left,' said Random as he made his way toward the cockpit.

'Oh, by the way, Anji and Jake say hi. They aren't here right now. They wanted to go on holiday too so I left them to it. I thought I'd go and pick them up after a quick trip to Galaxy 4.

I hear there's a concert raising funds for the Feed the Worlds charity and I thought we could catch it. They didn't seem interested but I thought we could catch it if you fancy?'

'Of course, Captain, that sounds lovely.'

Random sat in his pilot chair and operated the controls. 'I'm glad you said that. These tickets cost me a fortune! Which reminds me, I pawned that old washing machine to pay for them on this little second-hand asteroid. Hope you don't mind?'

Skateboard didn't. He thought to himself that the washing machine hadn't been working properly for months but it would probably still do a better job than that printer in the Mechanica complaints department!

With that, Skateboard was right back where he had always been. Soon the Venus II was leaving Mechanica far behind. As Skateboard felt the connection with the planet – and Anne – fall out of range, his diodes sighed sadly.

He made his way next to Random in his regular co-pilot's position.

'So go on then,' piped up Random as he did his best to keep his eyes on the stars. 'What was it like? What did you get up to?'

Skateboard thought quickly about his response
and decided to plump for the easiest.

'Oh, nothing much.'

GODS AND DEMONS

In the history of the cosmos, no other civilization burnt so brightly, and yet so briefly as the benevolent, peaceful Synoians. In the space of a millennium, the race was completely extinct, all but forgotten by those who were no match to the power and sheer might that they had once possessed.

They were but a myth, a whisper amongst some planets that hung high in the far-flung dark waters of the galaxy, a mere fairy tale children were told in hushed tones at school. It was a pity, because the universe, certainly those star systems that they saved, simply would not exist if it hadn't been for the sacrifice that the Synoians made.

It has been argued, by those in the know, that without the Synoians, there simply wouldn't be any life in the galaxy anymore, except for one race.

The Yarvesh.

At the beginning of creation, the first planets that formed and supported life were blessed with unbelievable power. The big bang seemed to have given those who rose out of the dirt first a chance to establish themselves as superpowers amongst the rest, especially those who had been lucky enough to have been created close to where the big bang occurred.

This collection of life, which developed as the universe continued to expand, were to become known as the elders of the old times and though so many of them are now extinct, they were the protectors of all life and maintained peace far and wide.

Among them, were the Synoians.

The Synoians evolved from the primordial slime and after several hundred years had learned to walk with their long spindly arms and legs developing multiple limbs that carried their slender frames elegantly like regal spiders underneath their fantastic sun. As they began to evolve, their numbers continued to grow as millions upon millions bred and lived on the lush and fervent landscape that the planet that would soon be called Syno had been gloriously given.

The gifts just kept on coming. They learned to communicate through the power of their minds and did not need food or water as they bathed in the astonishing red sunshine that could be seen, morning and night, on every part of their vast world.

As their skills and capabilities continued to evolve, so did their power.

Many Synoians believed that these capabilities were given to them through absorbing the power from the sun, which had been one of the first in the galaxy, and since Syno was the closest to it out of the twelve planets that huddled close to it like ducklings to their mother, it became the dominant recipient of the power source.

Syno was not the only planet that was given such fantastic possibilities. Worlds elsewhere in the universe had been born into a similar scenario and so, space travel was established early by the genius possessed by the gods of the cosmos.

When civilizations of such awesome power and might come together, it can result in fear, intimidation and the want for supremacy over all and yet, the Synoians were instrumental in making sure that above all, peace was maintained throughout the cosmos, and this is how the galaxy was for many a century.

But not everybody was happy.

Quietly at first, races began to see the futility of peace.

One, in particular, the Osirans, who had designated themselves the status of gods, abandoned their home world when it crumbled under the sheer might of the sun in their solar system and boiled away into nothingness.

Escaping in a fleet of pyramid-shaped ships, they silently stalked the gulf of space, formulating plans to invade wherever they please and find the supremacy they craved.

One by one, others like the Osirons also began to raise their voices on the treaty of peace that bound the universe.

Among those leading the dissent was a race of beings called the Yarvesh, who, unlike the Synoians who absorbed their life force through natural means, could only stay alive by sucking the life out of other life forms.

They discovered this when their race began to die as they were coming to the end of their natural life span of roughly eight hundred years.

Without the life force of others, and unable to reproduce, the Yarvesh faced the inevitability of extinction.

To stay alive, to survive, they knew they would have to kill.

And so, while the gods of the universe had turned their backs, they began their relentless slaughter.

As planet upon planet was cultivated, the peace holders of the universe did their best to hold the Yarvesh back, but to no avail. Little by little, the vampires of space drained whole life forms to death.

As the natives of Syno watched on passively, one-by-one the stars in the night sky were going out.

Centuries flew by until collectively, they knew they had to do something, and unselfishly, they knew it would probably result in their extinction.

For so long they had resisted involvement in what had become a full-scale war in a relatively new galaxy.

Those who had signed the treaty of peace with them were slowly ebbing away, falling back,
unable to fight to keep the universe safe.

Like the Synoians, they had reluctantly become involved in what was a very dark time for the elders of the old times and the war against the Yarvesh raged like wildfire across the stars and had burnt longer and more devastatingly than anything the cosmos had seen, until Rodas millennia later.

It was when the battle raged in a far-flung part of the galaxy called Andromeda, that it mercifully came to an end.

After decades of travelling through space, seeing the trail of misery and devastation that the Yarvesh had left, the Synoians bore witness to the dead stars that lined their journey like a mass funeral possession.

It didn't take long for them to close their eyes in shame at their ineffectiveness. They could have stopped this before it started.

Through peaceful means they had tried to avoid this ever happening but deep down, they knew it would. The might that the elders of the old times had been gifted would mean conflict at some point.

Now, seeing how the universe had suffered at the hands of one race was appalling.

They hadn't even tried to find a solution to the Yarvesh's real threat of extinction. No other race had cared. Now they were all paying for their negligence.

It was the loss of the Vards that hurt the universe more than any other. With a population of nine billion, they possessed the might to halt the Yarvesh in their tracks. By far the most powerful gods of them all could put them to the sword.

The Vards, with their huge muscular frames and teeth that were sharp enough to tear chunks out of any creature that dare oppose them, were a vicious yet fair race of aliens that maintained peace and order in the universe like a planet full of gangsters looking after their patch in a big city. But the Yarvesh, though outnumbered greatly, drained the life from the first line of defense and grew in power. Wave upon wave of Vards fell like dominos as the Yarvesh decimated them.

And so, another cornerstone of the old times was gone. It was true that the Synoians had kept a watchful eye on the Vards from their position of privilege, aware that they too could one day take aim at any of the elders and do exactly what the Yarvesh were doing.

It was also the last chance for someone to take the responsibility that the Synoians were about to finally have - to rid the threat and put an end to a truly horrific happening.

As they approached Andromeda, those from surrounding worlds had to turn their heads away from the fear and hide as best as they could in their native lands as they knew what was about to
happen.

They were about to be saved or fated to their end.

Either way, not one civilization could bear to watch and when the Syonians arrived on the edge of Andromeda and witnessed the black, dead stars, completely drained of all life, they wept. The entire population had come to fight. The weight of guilt had become too much to bear. For so many, their inactivity meant destruction and death. But after the day of reckoning, the day that was now, no one would ever have to fear the Yarvesh ever again.

It was then that an almighty battle ensued between the Synoians and the Yarvesh.

They battled in the cold dark embrace of space, high above the Yarvesh's home planet. The Yarvesh, like their opponents, had brought their entire force. Knowing that the Synoians were on their way, they had to be ready to meet them head-on, so instead of splitting their race up and harvesting areas of the universe in groups, they regrouped for the battle that defined the older times.

It was the Yarvesh who drew their swords first. An energy wave of amazing power burst from them all, lined up facing their enemies, and immediately the Synoians telepathically countered with an amazing blast of pure energy which created an incredible explosion in space that splintered the dead stars of Andromeda and blew them into millions of pieces, creating huge chunks of meteorites and debris that would spend
thousands of years hurtling through the galaxy.

The Synoians might was brought under tremendous strain from an alien force that was more than a match for them.

As the battle raged on, the Yarvesh sensed blood. Having taken the life force of a few hundred Synoians, even though they were immensely outnumbered, it gave them the power they needed to begin to crush the resistance.

More and more Synoians were falling.

The Synoian leader, although a race like the Yarvesh had no chain of command, had been elected to her post because her telepathic strengths were superior to those around her, and had also succumbed to the sheer force the Yarvesh were exhibiting.

Those that were far below on their homeworlds shielding from the fight would have given up on their hopes for the universe being saved if they'd had seen the numbers of Synoians begin to dwindle.

Like little stars going out in the night sky, one by one, the Synoians were being defeated.

But then, to the Yarvesh's shock, they realized what they had done.

As more and more of them digested the souls of their opponents, they had begun to feel strange.

Some Yarvesh stopped fighting altogether and began to probe this odd sensation they felt within them.

To their horror, they knew exactly what had happened.

The Synoians were telepathic and they had absorbed their life force.

The life force that relied on their remarkably powerful sun, which they ingested themselves, was now burning within the bodies of the hungry Yarvesh.

An incredible terror and dread flooded the Yarvesh race.

They had made a deadly mistake.

Now, they could kill them from the inside.

Slowly, the Yarvesh that had been gorging themselves on their enemy began to boil. Then, their slimy, tough-like rubber skin began to creak and tear.

Terrified screams went unheard in the vacuum of space as the Yarvesh started to explode inside out leaving nothing but a disgusting trail of their remains as they burst out of existence.

The small band of Synoians who had survived ceased their defense as the Yarvesh gave up their attack and began to retreat.

Dodging the millions of exploding bodies, the Synoian survivors chased straight after them, some allowing themselves to be caught by the Yarvesh as they reached them.

Yarvesh were hunters by design, so if a life form was within a certain vicinity to them they could kill them instantly as long as the life form in question
had its eyes open and was gazing straight at their ghastly appearance.

The keys to the soul were in the eyes of the beholder, so the more the Synoians looked upon them as they flew through space after them, the more the natives of Syno were digested and more Yarvesh burnt from the inside out.

This painful extraction of life went on for some time until no more than a few Synoians remained and only one Yarvesh was left.

Immediately, it surrendered and awaited the inevitable.

Two vast races, each possessing abilities unmatched since the universe had been obliterated in the battle for peace.

The Synoians, who had spent too long travelling through space to stop the terrible atrocities the Yarvesh had committed, were too far away from their sun to draw any more power from it and were as good as dead.

The Yarvesh, the only one that now existed, was entombed in the core of a planet that was starting to form in a new part of the galaxy, weakened by the attack and unable to suck the life force from any new being, it would now die a slow and
painful death, living off the life it had drained but forced to go hungry for millennia.
Lost and abandoned in the core of a planet that in hundreds of millions of years would become
known as Genocia, it would fester, kept alive by its greed and left to wilt its energy away. The Synoians took no pity, just as the Yarvesh hadn't shown any in their quest for survival. There was no point in regretting helping them sooner after all they had been through either. For now, the Synoians only mourned those that the universe had lost as they started their final, futile journey.

The few Synoians that had captured it agreed not to tell the other elders of the old times what they had done and instead allowed the Yarvesh name to pass into myth.

The battle was won at an appalling cost. So many races who were there at the start of the universe were gone and now the last Synoians to exist set off on a fruitless journey back home, fully aware that they wouldn't make it in time.

As though it knew, as the final Synoian passed away, the very sun that had once sustained them also faded into darkness and their home planet Syno, crumbled into dust.

THE ORACLE OF FATE

'What did I tell you not to do, Jake?'

Random towered over his young friend, a scowl etched across his face like a parent who was angry at their young child.

'Don't go in the fountain of youth,' said a rather sheepish Jake.

'So why did you do it then?' shouted Random.

Anji stood in the doorway to Jake's room, struggling to contain her squeals of laughter.

'Well, I didn't think it was real, did I?'

Random glared. 'What about now?'

Jake looked down at his body. His clothes were way too big for him. His trouser legs had bunched up around his clown-like shoes and the sleeves on his favourite red jumper drooped over his hands like sad snakes.

'I'll admit there's a possibility it does exist, yes.'

Anji guffawed with laughter.

'But it wasn't a fountain, was it? More of a lake if you ask me,' said Jake defensively.

'Does it matter?' Random burst. 'I mean, look at you! Thank god we got you out before you turned back into a baby!'

Anji roared with laughter again.

'I fail to see what's so funny!' Random snapped.

Anji collected herself. 'Sorry, I'll be good.'

The pair of them looked on at their friend, who despite his sixteen years of age now appeared to have regressed to how he was when Random had first met him.

Gone was the acne, the bad body odour, the rag-tailed hair and the deep yet sometimes squeaky voice. It was the voice that made Anji laugh the most. Jake sounded like something had sped him up!

'Anj, can you take him to see Skateboard in the medi-bay? See if he's found a way to reverse the process.'

Anji moved forward and took Jake by the hand, missing completely and clasping at his baggy jumper sleeve instead.

'Come on, let's see if we can find your Mummy and Daddy, shall we?' she teased as she led him from the room.

'Hey! It's not funny!' Jake replied indignantly. He was so embarrassed by his predicament. Here he was, about to hit his prime and then BAM!

One slip down a slippery embankment and he was five years younger than he should be!

As soon as his body had been polluted by the chemicals in the water, he instantly felt something shift and change. It was a painless transition but instant, as he felt certain parts of him recede and

change, he knew that he'd found the fountain of youth the gang had been searching for.

That'd teach him for not believing them, he thought. Especially as this new turn of events was about to severely hamper his chances of getting a date anytime soon!

As he watched them leave the room, Random shook his head. He wasn't annoyed at Jake, not really. He was annoyed at himself. Yet again his curiosity had gotten the better of him and one of his friends had paid the price.

When Skateboard had told them about the planet Neptania, and the myth that the actual fountain of youth was somewhere on its dusty terrain, Random had bugged them all to go down and look for it.

Two weeks later, after much trekking and, to everyone's dismay, camping, they had finally come across what looked like an oasis in the dunes. Surrounding the crystal-like water was a slick crust of thick oozy sand and mud.

He'd taken care to ask his two friends to stay away from it just to be on the safe side, but Jake hadn't taken heed and proceeded to, what Anji would call, "prat around" on the edge and inevitably tumbled in.

A few minutes later, after throwing a rope at him, Random and Anji pulled Jake out and discovered to their horror that the fountain of youth was indeed real, and had youthed their friend!

Random allowed himself a little chuckle as he made his way alone down the corridor towards the mid-section of the Venus II, the place he had called home for the last five years.

He had to remind himself that Anji and Jake were almost adults. He couldn't be held responsible for the mistakes they made anymore. In a way, it was a relief. He'd carried the blame for many a mishap or scrape in the time he had known them. Not that they would ever blame him, of course, but deep down, the feeling of putting them in danger burnt brightly.

As he made the short trip up the stairs that led up to the cockpit and slumped into his familiar pilot's chair, he gazed out through the windscreen and mused for a while about his life.

A lot had changed since he had been created back on Rodas, and despite having the same physical age as his two Earth friends, well, one of them at least, he felt so much older than his years.

He tutted. Fighting will do that to anyone.

In a way, he thought, the years that Jake had inadvertently regained felt a bit like those that Random had earned himself.

It could have been all so different. He'd kept himself alive. He'd kept them alive.

He shivered.

He'd been privileged.

Long may that privilege continue.

Suddenly, Random was awoken from his thoughts by a blinking green light on the dashboard. It was the distress signal light.

Someone out there needed him.

He pulled himself over to the monitor to his left-hand side and read the message. Random squinted at what looked like coordinates. There were only two words that accompanied them, two words that stoked Random's intrigue and felt ever-so-slightly ominous.

He picked himself off the chair and leaped out of the cockpit, leaving the green light blipping in and out of existence and the mysterious message flashing up on the screen.

FIND ME.

'How do you know it isn't a trap?' asked Jake as he was reaching for the top shelf and failing miserably.

'I don't. It's a cry for help though,' said Random, who reached the shelf with ease, opened the cabinet door and produced Jake's favourite mug from within and handed it to his small friend.

'Sounds to me more like it's a beckon,' said Anji.

'Skateboard, have you got a trace on the coordinates yet?' asked Random.

The AI robot, who was also running a diagnostic on Jake's condition simultaneously, announced that he had.

'It appears to be the planet Javor.'

'Where's that exactly?' asked Jake.

'In the Didactalonia system,' replied Skateboard.

'Of course it is,' said Anji sarcastically.

'Is it hostile, do you know, Skateboard?' Random enquired.

'According to the logs, it doesn't appear to be much of anything. There are a few known inhabitants of the planet, but there is nothing to suggest that we should be expecting hostilities when we get there.'

'Correction,' said Random. 'When I get there.'

Anji, Jake and Skateboard looked at each other.

'You're going alone?' asked Jake.

'It seems the safest bet,' said Random. 'Besides, I need someone to babysit you.'

'Hey!' cried Jake.

'Why don't you want us to come with you?' asked Anji, who was quite surprised by this change of tone from her friend.

'Because if it is a trap, then I won't be getting you all in trouble, will I? Besides, you guys need to find a way of getting Jake back to how he was.'

'But you could be in danger,' replied Anji.

'When am I not?' replied Random with a wink.

He had a point, thought Anji, but she began to worry that Random knew more about this message than he was letting on.

'Skateboard,' said Random. 'How long until we can be there?'

'If we left now we could be on Javor in a few hours,' came the response.

'Let's get a move on then,' said Random as he walked back into the cockpit.

'Random?' Anji called after him but he was lost in his thoughts. She looked down at Skateboard, a concerned expression etched upon her face.

'Something doesn't feel right about this,' she said to the little robot.

'I know,' he agreed. 'We shall stay nearby and keep an eye on him from afar, don't you worry, miss. We won't leave him completely alone.'

Anji felt slightly reassured.' Well, that's alright then. I can't help but think that he's getting himself involved in something he shouldn't be.'

'Doesn't he always?' replied Skateboard, with a withered tone. 'We'll be there to clean up the mess if needed, miss, don't you worry. He knows what he is doing.'

'Don't we always!' she responded, a little smile breaking through the concern.

'Er, guys...' came a squeaky voice. They turned around to notice that Jake had accidentally spilled his drink down his front. 'Can one of you pour me another? I can't reach the sink.'

'Is it me or is he getting younger?' said Anji.

'I'll see if there are any nappies on board, miss, just in case he is,' said Skateboard as he wheeled away from them both.

Meanwhile in the cockpit, Random was swimming in his thoughts.

After punching in the coordinates in the message, he turned the Venus II around and they were soon on their way.

As he gazed out into the wide expanse of space, he could almost hear the two words in his head being spoken by a woman he did not recognize.

The thing that was concerning him most was the noise of two familiar old voices, who had haunted him during his early adventures, who were also back and chanting the same two words over and over.

FIND ME...FIND ME...FIND ME...

As Random trundled down the gangway, the heavy snowfall trickled onto his thick spiky hair.

He peered out at the horizon as the sound of the Venus II's engines roared, leaving him truly alone.

He surveyed his surroundings and saw very little before him.

Nothing but towering icy mountains and fresh snow that crunched underfoot and the solitary whistle of wind filling his cold ears.

Random sighed to himself and bemoaned the fact that he had forgotten to ask Jake if he could borrow his bobble hat.

He sighed again when he realised that the coordinates must have been wrong.

Even through the shower, which wasn't too heavy but thick in volume, there didn't seem to be anything else in sight but snow.

Random didn't know what to expect. A crashed ship, perhaps? 'Hello?' he cried out.

The whistle of the wind was the only sound that replied.

Random tried again.

'Is there anybody out there?'

Still, there was no one to be seen.

He huffed. Then he felt a slight twinge of dread.

Maybe this was a trap after all.

He prepared himself for a scrap.

'Look, I received a message. It led me here.'

The still, snowy silence was deafening.

'I've come to help. I'm Random.'

All of a sudden a brilliant white light shone in the distance, blinding Random and sending him tumbling to the cold ground.

He shielded his eyes with his arms and tried in vain to peer at the silent explosion.

After a few moments, the light began to evaporate and in its place, as Random picked himself up and began to brush the snow from his coated arms, was what appeared to be a small igloo.

Random blinked furiously, trying to shake the mysterious light from his eyes and spotted the oddity in the distance. He swore to himself that he hadn't seen it before when he landed. He looked all around him. The snowfall had not subsided. It must have just appeared.

Random frowned. Whatever had lured him to this desolate world must have greater power than he had expected.

Pulling his collar up to his ears, he glared at the igloo that had materialised what looked like a couple of miles away and made his way tentatively towards it.

Whatever was waiting for him, he'd be ready for it.

As he shielded himself from the cold, Random got closer to the igloo and saw it for what it was; a tiny little icicle in the vastness of the snowy plain.

When he was just metres away, the door, which looked barely tall enough to allow him through, creaked open slowly.

Random observed this strange building with extreme caution.

Then, suddenly, he was disarmed by a voice from within.

'Well, if you're coming in you should hurry up about it, you're letting in a draft.'

The voice sounded like it belonged to an elderly woman.

It rang with authority and experience and Random pushed his frame through the opening, knocking a shower of snowflakes over his head in the process. As soon as he was inside, it slammed shut, making a sound like a heavy iron drawbridge closing on a medieval castle.

The interior of the igloo took Random's breath away. It was enormous. The Rodasian nearly fell over in surprise as he took in the impossibility of it all.

Before him was a large tropical forest.

'If you could take your shoes off that'd be lovely,' said the voice again.

Random did as he was asked, all the time gauping in amazement. The forest was lush and fervent with incredibly tall trees, some of which had all manner of delicious-looking fruit dangling from them.

The temperature inside this impossible igloo was incredibly hot, leading Random to sweat profusely as he tussled with his snow boots. The sweat was beginning to cascade down his back into his trouser legs and his hands were so clammy that he was struggling to take his gloves off.

At that moment, the voice spoke again.

'I'm sorry, I'll turn the temperature down a little for you.'

With that, the soaring heat was replaced with a more bearable temperature instantly and Random, who by now had managed to take his warm clothes off, looked around once more.

'How is this possible?' he called.

'Please, if you could leave your clothes on the peg provided that'd be most kind.'

'But there isn't a-' Random stopped himself immediately when he noticed there was now a whole row of pegs on the side of the door where there had been none before.

He looked back around. The voice seemed to echo around the place.

'Where are you?'

'I'm right here.'

Random peered carefully into the forest.

'Can you make it a bit more obvious please?' he said, defeated.

A section of what looked like mango trees shifted and swayed.

From within them, the body of a small, plump-looking woman emerged, with black corkscrew hair draped elegantly onto her shoulders and her lined face betraying her friendly, youthful eyes. It was the eyes that Random fixated upon as soon as he saw her. There were too many to count.

'Who are you?' he asked.

The woman moved towards him and as she did a black leather sofa rose from within the floor of the forest. She sat down upon it and crossed her legs.

'I'm the Oracle.'

'Whose that when she's at home?' said Random nonchalantly.

'I'm the surveyor of all things. The time that has passed. The time that is now. The time that will come.'

Random nodded. 'And, what do you want from me?'

'Well, for a start your drink order,' said the Oracle. She snapped her fingers and as if by magic a man in the shape of a waiter, buttoned up to the nines like he worked in a fancy restaurant, materialised next to her.

'What would you like, sir?' he purred.

Random shook his head.

'Sorry, how can you do that?'

'I just do,' said the Oracle unhelpfully. 'Go on, it's okay, whatever you have it won't be poisonous although do stay away from the Belgassian wine, never been to my taste.'

Random felt wrong-footed by the entire encounter.

'Er, just a glass of water for me please.'

The waiter nodded in acknowledgment.

The Oracle's eyebrows rose. All of them.

'Well, for someone with such a varied life your drinks choice wouldn't be considered as adventurous,' she quipped. 'I'll have a bottle of your finest Rajestar whisky. Two glasses.'

Random looked at the Oracle curiously.

'Are you trying to get me drunk?' he asked.

'You're going to need it,' she replied. 'Please, sit down.'

Another sofa, identical to the one the Oracle was sitting on, appeared behind Random and tentatively, he sat down opposite her slowly as their drinks appeared on a little oak table between them.

'What is this place?' he asked looking around him.

'It is my sanctum. Well, it's a little more than that. It can be anything I want it to be. All I have to do is... will it into existence.'

'How?'

'With the power of my mind. If I do desire it to be, the sanctum can be as raucous as the wildest party you've ever been to.'

The Oracle snapped her fingers and the tropical forest that Random sat within was instantly turned into a nightclub, its throbbing music, neon lights and throngs of people dancing suddenly popped up around them.

'Or...' the Oracle shouted to be heard over the music.

She snapped her fingers again and all of a sudden, she and Random, along with their sofas and a little table, were floating in the vacuum of space. '...we could talk out here...'

Random started to panic, gasping for air.

'...but I much prefer this environment,' said the Oracle, who upon a snap of the fingers changed their surroundings back into the tropical rainforest

Random had found himself in when he entered this world of madness.

Random stopped panicking, his heart beating a thousand times faster than it had in a long time. 'How can you do that?'

'I have a power that is as old as time itself.'

'Wow, you're looking good for your age,' said Random trying to rediscover his cool.

'I choose this form because it is the closest approximation to how I appeared in my youth. If you saw my true appearance it would take you a thousand nights to sleep again.'

Random smirked. 'Well, I thank you for that. Tell me, why did you bring me here?'

The Oracle's face turned from playful to serious.

'You have been a hard one to track down, Captain Random. For years I have kept a keen eye out for you and your friends but you seem to be continually on the move.'

'Well, Oracle, space is a really big place. That explains the number of eyes you have; there must be quite a lot to keep your eyes on, as it were, in this big old place,' said Random, reaching for his glass and taking a gulp tentatively. He looked at the glass. 'Well, if it is poisoned then it sure is a refreshing way to go.'

'You're safe with me. Safer than you have been on many of your adventures.'

'Ah, so you found me eventually then?'

The Oracle smiled. 'Evidentally. Once I had established what to look out for.'

Random smirked back and crossed his legs, making himself comfortable. 'Oh yeah, and what was it you looked for to find me?'

'Chaos,' said the Oracle. 'You have a knack for finding trouble.'

'And helping out where we can,' added Random.

The Oracle sank back into her sofa, nursing her drink.

'Every time you run into trouble you risk the lives of not only yourselves but the people you seek to aid.'

Random's face wore a serious expression. 'And what's that supposed to mean?'

The Oracle took a measured sip of her whisky.

'I don't need to tell you that now, do I? You may fight those who are violent, but in your means, you sometimes have to take lives in return for liberation.'

Random slammed his drink down. 'Look, Oracle, maybe you have the wrong person here, but my friends and I have only ever intervened to help those who cannot help themselves. If someone had died at my hands I can assure you that there was no other option left for me to take.'

'The Sandman, The Yarvesh, Consula, ruler of the planet of Genocia, the Osirans, Stratos, the Samlores, the Larvae, the Primards, the list is a long and bloody one.'

'What are you implying? That I'm a murderer?'

The Oracle could sense Random's blood pressure rise. 'No Captain. In the grand scheme of things, you have helped the universe become a safer place but innocents always suffer...'

She let the sentence hang in the air.

Random shifted awkwardly in his seat. 'Is this why you called me here? To teach me a lesson in morals? If you have watched me as much as you've claimed then you'll also know how heavy my heart is for every life that has been lost. I carry the souls that I have failed to save in my heart. Every single one of them is a reminder of my failure. So whatever you have to say, you can't hurt me more than I hurt already.'

'The same way that you hurt for Rodas?'

That name hit Random like a train. He went cold.

'So, that's why you brought me here...' he said with dread.

'In all the years you have been running away from your responsibilities, your home planet has fallen further into chaos. Millions upon millions of people who deserve far greater suffer at the hands of oppression that you, Captain, are destined to put to an end.'

Random gulped hard. 'Hasn't my work across the universe made up for my failure to save Rodas?'

'I think that's a question you should ask yourself,' the Oracle replied.

Random knew the answer already.

'I can't...'

'You can't or won't? What stopped you from fulfilling your destiny? Shame? Cowardice?'

Tears began to collect in Random's eyes. 'If you can see and know everything, Oracle, then you don't need me to answer that.'

'I don't, but I think you need to hear yourself confirm it,' she replied.

Random sank and sighed heavily. 'How bad is it?'

The Oracle waved her hand. High above them, a screen appeared depicting the horrors that were occurring on Random's home planet. Random glanced quickly and then turned his head away. He dare not bring himself to look at the devastation that was happening, the devastation he could have stopped a long time ago.

The Oracle watched on impassively. Explosions and the screams of men, women, and children could be heard. Random started to cry.

'Okay, I get it. Please. Turn it off,' he pleaded.

'I don't think you do. As much as the universe is grateful for what you have done, you've failed to protect those that you were meant to save. You've picked fights far smaller than the ones you were meant to face.

It brings me no pleasure, Captain, in telling you that Rodas is on the brink. I have watched the war for centuries and the time is coming when the planet will be beyond salvation.
Its disease will spread across the star systems…the Crimson Empire will rise and the universe will fall.'

Random shot daggers at the Oracle.

'And yet here you are,' he said, his voice breaking with emotion. 'You sit here, with all of this power, all of this knowledge. If you have been watching Rodas for centuries you could have stopped the war long before I was born. How dare you accuse me of turning a blind eye when yours have been trained on it all along!'

'The war on Rodas is not my fight to win, it never has been, the same as any interplanetary war.'

Random moved over to the door. 'I've had enough of this.'

'It was never my fate to fight. That fate is yours.'

Random put his hands against the ice-cold door and sank. 'And yet it's my hands you expect to get dirty.'

'It is your birth right, Captain Random. Not mine.'

Random laughed. 'If I had your power I would end all conflict, all suffering with the snap of my fingers and yet you sit here lecturing me on morals and destiny. It's always the same. Those in power sit on their high ground while the foot soldiers are slaughtered and left to pick the pieces up.'

'I am cursed to fulfil my destiny, just as you are cursed to yours,' she replied, as impassively as before.

'Then who's stopping you?' said Random as he moved over to the Oracle. 'You can put an end to it now!'

The Oracle stared him down. 'I have been blessed with a power beyond the stars. Can you imagine that?'

'Yes!' said Random, remembering his experiences on Spectronia. 'You're not the only one here who has had the power of a god.'

'So you also understand why such a power should never be used.'

Random's eyes fell. He sighed again.

'Yes… you're right I do.'

'So you appreciate my predicament.'

Random scoffed. 'I wouldn't say that.'

He stood with his hands on his hips and breathed hard.

'Rodas, your home planet is almost at the point of no return. If you don't go back now and fulfil the prophecy then there will be more damage, more deaths and more chaos than the universe can stop.

I ask you to go, not as a punishment or because it brings me enjoyment, but because it is the right thing to do and you know that… even if you also know the cost it may bring to you.'

Random let his tears fall.

'Yes. Yes, I do.'

'Then we are done here,' the Oracle moved towards him, carrying a glass of whisky for her

troubled guest. 'Here, if nothing else it will keep you warm whilst you wait for your ship.'

Random took the glass and chucked it back into his throat. It tasted rancid now. Good, he thought.

'I wish you luck, Captain Random,' said the Oracle. 'I have faith that you will do what is right.'

Random didn't move. He just stared at her. He knew what must happen now.

***

As the Venus II's landing clamps lowered, Random watched through the soft snowflakes as his ship, his home, floated slowly to the ground. His eyes stung, tears almost turning to icicles as they dripped down his cheeks. He turned back to face the Oracle, her little igloo-like house a mere blip on the horizon, the grey smoke rising slowly from her chimney, and wished he had never come.

He turned his gaze back towards the ship, his haven, and slumped up the gangway after it dropped from the belly of the Venus II and trudged slowly towards his friends inside.

'Good news!' said Anji as Random walked into the mid-section, her exuberance instantly dampened as soon as she saw the look on her purple friend's face.

'I've managed to determine that Jake's condition is only temporary. You managed to get him out in time,' Skateboard concurred.

'Yeah, a few minutes longer and you'd have been changing my nappies for the next couple of years,' said Jake, who like Anji became very concerned when he saw Random.

Their friend began to unravel his warm clothes and place them softly on the sofa. He was trying his best to hide his face.

Anji went over to him and placed a hand on his shoulder tenderly. 'Random, what's happened?'

Jake shared her concern. 'What's up, dude?'

Skateboard stayed silent. He knew. Somehow, he knew.

Random turned towards them, his face was puffy and pale. His cheeks were wet, not from the snow, but from the tears, he had been crying since he left the Oracle's home.

He tried to clear his throat, yet his voice was still croaky.

This was it.

'It's time...'

CAPTAIN RANDOM
THE
BATTLE FOR RODAS
HAYDEN GRIBBLE

CAPTAIN RANDOM

AND THE BATTLE

OF RODAS

HAYDEN GRIBBLE

In the light of the bright moon stood a figure bathed in darkness. An eerie calmness betrayed the malicious storm in his heart, as the fire of a thousand suns raged through his veins. He had stood upon the precipice of death for centuries and witnessed the destruction of all he once held dear.

His planet was a battleground. It had been for as long as he could remember. Since the old times, many had said to him when he was young, so long ago. As he had sat in the libraries of the citadel, taking in his studies whilst the carnage of war was happening all around him, he had watched as explosions far away had rocked the mighty timbers high above. The tremors and terrible sounds of destruction haunted his every waking moment. Even as he slept, the horror of battle poisoned his mind every second of his life, like a tinnitus that wouldn't go away.

Some days he'd cry. Only to himself, not to those who looked after him. An orphan like him had to be tough on a planet like his. Any sign of weakness, the slightest glimmer of deviation from normality, a slip of keeping his head down and getting on with life as best he could like everyone else, was dealt with harshly.

His people were sick enough to let a war rage throughout time, both sides refusing to concede defeat. Whole families were regularly torn apart. Mothers and Fathers were captured, enslaved, or slaughtered and their children equally so if they were not careful. Just to be alive was supposed to make little boys like him grateful. So how could he openly admit how scared he was?

As time moved on, he noticed that it never rained on his world. As the madness of war bore its way into his soul, he soon began to realise why.

If everyone like he had spent a lifetime holding back the tears, why would a planet so broken weep for itself?

Time marched on like the good little soldier he became. Suddenly, any shred of emotion he had felt; the sorrow he felt for missing his Mum, the not knowing if she was alive or dead, in danger or safe, the hope that one day the killing would end for everyone in his world, drained out of him.

It had all happened in the heat of battle. The years of cowering from laser fire, of dusting himself down when the building he was in had split into pieces and the heat of the flames that had licked at his flesh seared into significance when he had to face the enemy.

All children, no matter how hard they had studied, no matter their brilliance in whatever they did ended up picking up a gun. It was expected of them. After the horror of it all had engulfed him once and for all he finally saw the sense in all the madness.

He had to do it.

He had to kill.

If he didn't, he would be killed himself.

He'd just be another corpse rotting in the street, forgotten.

If he wanted to find his mother again, he'd have to fight.

He'd have to win.

On the day of the Battle of Endos, the continent he had grown up on, the bloodiest war that had stained his planet took place and in the face of it all, in the heart of the storm as all around him perished, he remained.

His life came at a price.

Captured by the enemy he had been brought up to despise, he was tortured mercilessly. For years that felt to him like decades falling away through the hourglass of time, he felt the pain of being a red face.

The pain of his whole life was stretched out before his very eyes. The things they did to him would make any other man die and yet he survived.

For all that the blue faces did to him, the horrors they imposed upon his person mentally and physically one thing kept him alive whilst his fellow prisoners succumbed. He had to see her face again. He had to know she was still alive.

He had to keep fighting.

Before long, his captors, the Sapphire Regime as they were known, began to fall back against the might of their enemies to which he belonged; the Crimson Empire. Every rumour that whispered around his tiny, dank cell, the one he was forced to share will fellow prisoners of war, was that they were winning. No act of recrimination would stop them, the Crimson Empire was a tidal wave of hope that told him to keep going. They would be rescued soon. As long as they kept fighting back, he'd be out soon and then he could find her.

But it wasn't to be. If the Battle of Endos had told him to carry on no matter what, then what happened on the day of its end would crush whatever spark of love and hope he had left in his heart.

One morning an explosion of sheer apocalyptic velocity shook the prisoners around their cage. As they struggled back to their feet, dazed and confused by what had happened, he peered through the bars toward home. He forced his eyes open as the shockwave continued to wash towards them and as he gazed at the awesome destructive horror before him, his eyes filled with tears for the last time.

Endos was gone.

The Sapphire Regime had wiped it out.

She was gone.

If she had even been alive still, any hope of that had burnt like the rest of Endos.

He cried out in horror, gripping the bars and pulling at them so hard that one of them began to creak, no match for the grief that was exploding from within him.

He was restrained but it had taken many guards to do it, far more than it should to contain a man who had spent years at the Sapphire Regime's merciless hands. He had even killed a few of them in the struggle, driven insane by the finality of what he had witnessed, he possessed a strength no one could understand.

Finally, the man was subdued enough to be put to execution for the murder of the guards and yet, the promise of death didn't stop him.

On the day of his trial, which lasted mere minutes before he was brought before the firing squad, he had laughed in the face of his accusers. He had been laughing to himself since he had awoken after he had witnessed the burning of Endos. A deep, low rumbling chuckle that sat in his throat.

As he stood manacled to the post, awaiting the inevitable, he told himself that this was not the end. When the volley of lasers pierced his flesh and sent his body back at such a velocity that the pole snapped in two, his burnt and twisted body hit the dust at such speed that a cloud engulfed him. The laughing had suddenly stopped. They felt no need to check for life signs. No one could have survived such an ordeal.

But this was no ordinary man.

This was a man whose spirit had been possessed by the devil.

A man whose heart had become black with evil.

The very core of his being had become rotten, corrupted by the lunacy of the world in which he lived.

As he blinked his eyes open, his beaten, bloodied body thrown onto a heap of the corpses of his fallen comrades, he felt the strength begin to flow through him again. As he rose off the pile he slipped quietly away before his captors had a chance to burn them and attempt to hide their shame.

He felt his flesh as he walked back to where Endos had once been, finding it odd how quiet the world had become outside of his cage in the prisoner-of-war camp. It was wet, torn to ribbons and sore with infection. He liked it. It made him feel alive.

How he was still alive was a mystery to him. He lived to keep going. This was no second chance. He was still on his first and he was determined to make it work for him.

As he heard footsteps approach him, he was disturbed from his thoughts of the past. The clicking of boots against the floor of his private chamber grew louder and yet he still faced the window, looking out upon the world he called home.

The home he was about to act upon his salvation.

Suddenly, the footsteps stopped and clicked together in a salute.

'Supreme ruler,' came the voice, a strong, feminine tone that echoed around the desolate chamber.

'Are we ready?' came the reply from the man at the window, his hood hiding his features.

'Yes, my Lord,' was the reply.

'Good,' the man's voice was harsh and yet possessed a velvety tone, polite and dripping with malicious intent. 'Prepare your troops, Admiral.'

The Admiral nodded in response and turned to leave.

'Oh, and Admiral?' said the hooded voice.

'My Lord?'

The hooded figure turned to face her, his blood-red eyes shattering the darkness that surrounded them.

'Failure is not an option.'

The Admiral gulped. A bead of sweat formed on her brow.

'Of course not, my Lord.'

He continued to glare at her as she left his presence before returning to the glorious view of battle outside.

His name is Kalor Maloso. His world of chaos is known and shunned by the universe that surrounds it. But the war that has shattered it is soon to come to an end. Its name was a stain on the cosmos.

Rodas.

Book One

DECIMATION

Worlds away from hell was a little ship that transgressed the stars like a butterfly fluttering through the sunrise. Its sleek, curved quicksilver exterior betrayed the chaos that ensued most days within the body of it all. In the years it had sailed the galaxy it had seen much, just like its inhabitants. To those who had seen it, they had instantly fallen in love with the look of such a beauty. For any who had stepped on board, which was few in number, the thought that immediately crossed their minds was that it needed a really good spring clean. Then again, it was to be expected when three teenagers, whose days were like cracks in the pavement, who spent most of the time righting wrongs and eating and sleeping, lived on board.

To them, it was home. To anyone else, it was the Venus II. The only ship in the history of the universe to have escaped the war-torn planet Rodas and on board were the only two life forms who had the pleasure of doing just the same.

But recent events had brought about an abrupt end to the adventures of the occupants of the Venus II. At the orders of the captain of the ship, the AI robot who acted as chief science officer, medical officer, counsellor and reluctant

housekeeper to his teenage friends had set the coordinates to return to their home world.

As the Venus II made its way home, the four travellers inside were all contemplating the horror of what they were doing. And although two of them were going back to the place they had escaped; the other half were wondering just how awful their immediate future was about to become. But none of them, not even the robot who seemed to have an answer for everything when a question was asked, knew just how dangerous their return was to be than Random.

'Knock knock,' came a voice from outside the door.

Random's deep thought was ended abruptly by the interruption.

He licked his lips. His mouth was drier than a desert in raining season.

'I'm not here,' came his response.

'Oh, okay then, can you let Random know when he's back that Anji wants to see how he is?' was the jovial reply.

Random allowed himself a little smile. 'I'm not sure she wants to,' he said as he got up to unlock the door. As it hissed as it slid up into the ceiling the face of Random's friend Anji stared back at him.

Her chirpy question clearly betrayed the concerned expression that was etched on her face. Random had grown used to seeing her worried

over the years they had travelled together. They had seen so much, but this was new territory.

'You've been in here for hours. Skateboard was beginning to wonder if you wanted some food so I said I'd come and ask you.'

Random sat on his bed. His quarters were a state. Anji looked around as she made to sit beside him, dodging the piles of dirty clothing and books. She spotted many trinkets and souvenirs he had picked up from their multitude of adventures. A laser gun from the time they helped liberate the planet Genocia from a creature from the beginning of time sat half slumped down the wall near the foot of his bed. A file of sand, encapsulating the gorgeous multi-coloured memories of Spectronia sat on the window sill that sat above the bed and looked out onto the twinkling majesty of the stars as they blazed past as the ship was currently in hyperspace. Anji took them all in a way she never had before.

'I'm surprised you keep this stuff,' she said as she made herself comfortable and crossed her legs on Random's bed.

'They are a reminder,' he said bluntly.

'Of past glories?' she asked.

'Not quite,' said Random glumly.

Anji placed a hand gently on Random's shoulder. He felt clammy; like his trademark yellow t-shirt was clinging to his skin for dear life. 'Talk to me. Please. What happened on that moon?'

Random sighed. 'I wish I had never insisted we check out that distress signal.'

Merely hours earlier, the travellers had intercepted an SOS
signal that was emitting from a remote ice moon situated in a cold
and forgotten corner of the universe. It had been a welcome
distraction from their current predicament, thought Random, who
had just rescued his other human friend and Venus II incumbent,
Jake, from the fabled fountain of youth and who had de-aged back
to the very beginning of his puberty.

Plus, it was instinct, for Random at least, to help when it was
asked for, or needed.

Only on this occasion, he regretted caring so much.

On the ice moon, he had proceeded alone to explore the signal at
his own insistence. He was fine with risking his own life but he
was not as ready to throw his friends in the line of danger. Indeed,
most of his free time was actually spent rescuing them after they
had either ignored his

pleas or he'd inadvertently misread a situation and placed them
in peril at his own hand. He was sick of the responsibility of it but
too much of a

coward to send them home. They were his friends after all, so
why wouldn't he want them around to share in the good times?
But on this occasion, he had a funny feeling that things would not
be so smooth..and he was right.

What followed when he finally found the origins of the signal,
would change the course of his life forever.

'I met the Oracle,' he said.

Anji furrowed her brow. 'Who?'

'The Oracle. There are corners of the universe where the oracle is
a myth. A creature that can see all of the cosmos, all of what will
happen. All that should be. All that might be if nothing is acted
upon. Others deny her existence completely, as did I until I met
her. How foolish I feel now.'

'What did she do to you?'

'Nothing. It's what she showed me that scares me.'

'Fine, what did she show you then?'

Random stopped staring in front of him and faced his friend.
'Home.'

Anji realised the implications. Random had told her a long time ago, back when they first met that he had run from his home world. She sympathised with him at the time and even more so now as she had fled hers just like him. But then she remembered the little boy she knew

back then, his purple skin unique and alien, those red/blue eyes glowing as he explained to her that was supposed to stop a war that was raging back there.

'How bad is it there?' she enquired.

'Hell,' came the response. 'Rodas is falling. The planet is turning to ash and dust. The flames of battle that have been raging there since anyone can remember are about to burn their last.'

'And you've got to put an end to it falling? Is that what she said?'

'Anj, remember when I told you it was my destiny to put an end to it all?'

'Like it was yesterday,' she replied.

'Well, today is that day. I've got to stop it. No more excuses. No more time finding distractions. This all ends now.'

Anji shivered. The finality in Random's voice was haunting. She took his hand.

'We've fought wars before. We shall do it again. Together.'

Random snatched his hand away. 'Not this time.'

Anji frowned. 'What do you mean by that?'

'I can't allow you and Jake to get involved. This is my mess that I have to clear up, no matter the cost, but you two should never have to bear my brunt with me.'

Anji sighed and smiled a little. 'Random, we'd never leave you to fight alone. You've always done your best to protect Jake and me but we are older now. We're grown-ups. None of us are kids anymore. We can make our own decisions and nothing would make us change our minds. Nothing.'

Random frowned a little. 'Jake's a kid again.'

'Skateboard said he's sorting that out. Random, if this is what you were made to do surely, it's easier to do this with others?'

Random allowed a little smile. He wasn't so sure this time.

It was still early morning and yet Jake wanted nothing else but to go back to bed. Indeed, when he had awoken from a dreamless sleep he had wondered if he was stuck inside his own nightmare. Then, as he had hopped down from his bed and wandered over to the bathroom, with his room and the corridors of the Venus II looking more intimidating than usual, he spotted his reflection and realised he was in a nightmare.

So, it had happened after all. He was young again.

Why was it always him? At least, that's how it felt to Jake. He'd been sure that the fountain of youth was just a legend. He'd assured his friends they were wasting their time wanting to go on a silly quest to find it. Even as he had teetered on the precipice of a pond which Random had categorically said not to teeter off, he was still disbelieving that such a concept existed. Oh sure, he'd seen space whales, been to parallel dimensions and even watched as a whole planet had turned itself inside/out and managed to not blow up in the instance, but the fountain of youth? What a load of rubbish.

Whether that thought was still running through his mind as he was plunging head first into the very thing he did not believe in, he couldn't say.

But just as it's as likely to be driven in a car by a ghost, they'd found the fountain of youth alright. At least he could claim that he was the first being in the entire universe to have discovered it properly. If only it hadn't reset his adolescence by seven years, that's what he was thinking as he sat stirring his spoon absent-mindedly in his bowl of cornflakes.

Skateboard entered the mid-section of the ship via the cockpit and noticed straight away that Jake was away with the fairies, which was a rather common thing to find Jake away with but he made for the brooding teenager anyway.

'Do you mind if I sit down?' he asked inquisitively.

Jake turned his ache-riddled face towards him and moaned. 'I don't see anyone else sitting there.'

Skateboard was caught a little off balance. 'Pardon me, sir, but unless that's a turn of phrase it doesn't really answer my question.'

Jake put his head in his cornflakes and groaned. 'Look mate can't you just leave me alone I'm busy.'

'Doing what?' asked Skateboard.

Jake didn't have time for his friend right now. 'I don't know, something to come along and stop me from being bored.'

'May I help you with that?' asked Skateboard.

'I don't know. May you?'

Skateboard's wheels squeaked out a sigh. 'I'm sorry Jake if I am speaking out of terms but when you were eleven were you this obtuse?'

Jake picked his face out of his bowl and rubbed the cornflakes off his eyes. 'I'm sorry mate. I'm feeling as stroppy as a toddler in a toy shop and my dad's forgotten his wallet.'

'An...interesting analogy, sir. I have taken the liberty of carrying out a biometric scan with my sensors and I have noticed that your GnRH levels are through the roof.'

'In English?' asked Jake.

'It means that your hormonal fluctuations are erratic. This will explain the irritable behaviour that you are currently displaying. I suggest taking it easy whilst the effects of the fountain of youth wears off.'

'How long will that be?' Jake enquired.

'It's hard to say. It could be days or it could be weeks.'

'Uh, what!?' groaned Jake again.

Skateboard moved to reassure his young friend. 'It's all temporary, sir. In time you will look back and laugh at all of this.'

'Oh, like Anji and Random did?' Jake said sarcastically. He huffed. 'Look. I'm sorry Jake. I know this whole thing is sending me haywire and we should be worrying about Random

but...just this once I'm more worried right now about myself.'

Skateboard propped himself up next to Jake.

'I don't know. I feel like if I was me, the normal me, I can help more. I don't feel like I'm going to be able to do anything the way that I currently am. And I can't help thinking the worst. You and

Random have spoken in the past about what a dangerous place Rodas is.'

Skateboard nodded. He hadn't told him half of the story. 'There are many dangerous places in the universe. Many of which we have visited. When you and Miss Anji joined us, you were both the age that you have regressed back to. I don't recall either of you bemoaning the fact that your ages were going to stop you from saving the people that you did or defeating the evil that you have met. Whatever I have told you about Rodas in the past, it will not prepare you for what you will see when you get there because nothing ever prepared you when you went to Genocia, for example. But you've always taken these things head-on with all the bravado and carefree nature that you've always shown, so what is it about Rodas that makes you feel so negatively?'

'Random seems scared of going back. He's never been like that before,' said Jake.

'Unlike our other experiences, this is going to be a very personal one for Random.'

'And you,' nodded Jake.

Skateboard paused for a moment. Jake was right. He hadn't really allowed himself time to think about it much but yes, the prospect of returning to Rodas filled him with as much dread as it did Random. He knew why also, but dare not speak of the subject with either Anji or Jake.

'Indeed, so it's going to be hard. But if we all look out for each other and support where we can, then we can be greater than the sum of our parts.'

Jake scoffed a little. 'Like little toy cars linking up to make one big robot.'

Skateboard had no idea what Jake was talking about. 'If you say so, sir.'

'I get the feeling this won't be as easy as it has been in the past. And if it's the end...'

'Why would you think that?'

Jake paused. 'Anji...and I have a pact. It's something we've said to one another whenever we've faced certain death, you know, day-to-day usual situations like that. Back on Earth, we'd be finishing school around about now. It's a big deal. You do your exams, all go your separate ways, drink legally, start going out with...you know, the fun stuff in life starts to happen. Anyway, we had both agreed, years ago now, that around the time this would be happening back home, we'd have a big leavers party called a prom and Anji and I...had agreed to go with one another.'

Skateboard was still listening but had noticed on his biometric scanners that Jake's hormones were about to explode through the roof. Not wanting to panic him further, plus as it wasn't life-threatening, he thought it was better if he didn't mention it and let the boy continue.

'So, I've...' he continued, 'I know I've fancied other girls in the past but with Anji, it's always been different and that promise we made, well, let's just say that promise has got me through a lot.'

'I understand, sir. As much as a robot with artificial intelligence can. I once felt the same.'

Jake looked surprised. 'You did? Skateboard you dark horse!'

'Well, it wasn't a relationship of sorts but, there was someone I met a little while back who I connected with.'

'Woah-ho, you're not holding back on the details there are you chum!' giggled Jake. 'Go on, what else happened?'

Skateboard was startled by Jake's juvenile take on his story and then reminded himself that his friend was currently experiencing a compressed period of adolescence.

'Maybe I'll save it for another day.'

'Spoilsport,' said Jake, who was genuinely miffed that he hadn't managed to get any gossip out of his metal friend. 'So anyway, now that we are both eighteen, well, I will be again soon, finishing up school and life would be changing for us and we'd be going to prom soon. So, I kind of hoped that Anji would want to still go and...oh, I'm an idiot. This is all so silly.'

'Why?' asked Skateboard.

'There is no prom is there? And look at me. It would be like I'd taken the babysitter if we did go!'

'Jake, I'm confused. Are you telling me that you want to go to a party?'

'No. Well, yes. Let me put it this way. I want us all to survive whatever is coming so that we can go to the prom. But what's the use anyway, we've probably missed it. I mean, what month is it? It's hard to tell in space, isn't it?'

Skateboard tried gesturing to the calendar that was hung unevenly above the worktop in the kitchen but then quickly gave up on that idea too as Jake's self-pitying was starting to break his biometric scan capabilities and he was beginning to feel like he needed a lie-down.

'You two can go to the prom whenever you want. The universe, as they say, is your oyster,' the little AI robot said trying to be helpful.

'Maybe if we get through this,' replied Jake.

'You don't have to come. In a way it would be a relief if you both didn't, to put it bluntly,' said Skateboard.

Jake looked a little surprised. 'Skateboard, are you trying to get rid of us?'

'In a way yes but in many ways no. Random and I know how dangerous Rodas can be, far more than you can ever imagine. I want to protect you all from ever getting hurt and yet Random needs you...we need you.'

Jake put his arm around his friend. 'I guess what we are both saying is we had better not get killed, eh?'

Skateboard's diodes purred. He didn't know how many more chances he and his friends would have to be all together. Moments like this needed to count.

Suddenly, the alarm klaxon began to shriek all across the Venus II. Little red lights replaced the normal lighting and all four crewmembers jumped out of their skins.

'What the bloody hell is that?' cried Jake. Both he and Skateboard ran towards the cockpit and were soon joined by Random and Anji. Skateboard busied himself with the onboard computer whilst Random slid into his pilot's chair and took command instantly.

'Have we hit something coming out of hyperspace?' asked Random.

'Negative, sir, it appears that there is a warning up ahead,' replied Skateboard.

'What kind of a warning?' asked Anji who was gripping the back of Random's seat as the ship's ride had become less stable.

'Sensors are picking up a blockade up ahead, roughly seventy kilometres from the edge of Ursa-17,' said Skateboard.

'How far ahead?' asked Jake. 'Maybe we should slow down a little bit. If there's something blocking our way, we could hit it.'

'Good idea Tiny Tim,' said Random mockingly, which made Jake glare back. 'Dropping out of hyperspace...now.'

All of a sudden, the bright, psychedelic features of hyperspace melted away and the Venus II came to a stop.

The four travellers look out of the cockpit and were stunned.

'Those ships,' said Jake. 'They look familiar.'

'They are,' said Anji with a level of disdain in her tone.

'It looks like we've encountered a space block,' said Skateboard.

Random tutted. He was always surprised by his metal friend's capacity for stating the obvious.

In front of them lay three huge battle freighters lined up in a row and several dozen hornet fighters in attack formation.

'Just when I thought I'd seen the last of them...' said Anji ruefully.

The comms system on the dashboard of the Venus II began to blink into life.

'There's an incoming message coming from one of those freighters,' said Skateboard.

'Put it through,' said Random instantly.

Obeying his Captain's order, Skateboard accepted the message. A hologrammatic display enveloped the viewscreen showing the face of someone that all four travellers knew very well.

'Admiral Bagari,' said Random.

'Captain Random,' replied Bagari in her usual unimpressed manner. 'I had a feeling I'd meet you here.'

III

Nkite moved quickly as the heli-fighter's laser fire continued to explode all around her. Round after round of the deadly blasts threatened to strike her down as she weaved the cavernous ruins of a long-desolated part of her hometown. She breathed heavily, carrying under each arm the two children she had found cowering in a delipidated building. As she struggled against their kicking and screaming, terrified of the danger she was trying to save them from, she stole her sights off the winding, crumbling road and looked high up in the burnt sky at her tormentor. She knew that the heli-fighter's pilot was toying with her. The chopping blades of the craft whipped in the air high above her and seemed more than content to give her the run around than finish her off for good. The sound of the heli-fighter roared alongside that of its open fire from the laser cannons to such an extent that Nkite couldn't hear anything else. The roar of chaos was now deafening. Inside the heli-fighter, the pilot grinned manically as his thumb continued to squeeze the trigger on top of his steering wheel.

'Like fish in a barrel,' he smiled to his co-pilot, who was looking pensive next to him.

'Can't you just finish her off now, sir?' he said through green-tinted cheeks. 'I feel sick.'

The soldier scoffed to himself. A seasoned man like he had resented taking on another co-pilot since he had lost his last colleague, who during a heated battle in the skies above the ruins of Rodas had sadly fallen from his heli-fighter. Granted, his superiors had not known that it was the pilot himself who had pushed him but they were never to know, lots of things happen in battle. What he didn't tell them saved them time on paperwork after all. He had rebuked even more when he discovered that his new partner possessed no experience of aerial combat whatsoever.

Then his horror had been well and truly confirmed when those in charge of his sector revealed to him that his new partner would eventually become his replacement as he was being moved out.

He loved killing. Nothing else in life came close for him in his quest for fulfillment. A desk job in a never-ending war just didn't whet his appetite as much as blowing people up. So, while he was up there in the sky, blowing people up and having enormous fun at the same time was what he was going to do, and no one was going to stop him.

'You know what makes killing these stinking blue skins so satisfying?' he purred. 'No matter how hard they run they can never escape. It's a battle with only one victor – the hunted.'

The co-pilot's stomach lurched as the heli-fighter continued its pursuit of the stubborn girl it has been chasing ever since it had spotted her leaving the ruins. The powers that be had started to task members of the Crimson Empire army with destroying the ruins of the capitol through any means necessary and they didn't care if anyone was caught up in the demolition project. Like rats fleeing the fire, they would soon run and those who did, no matter what side of the war they sat on, was fair game for a murder chase. They had shunned the war effort, so why save them? Recruiting them would only result in people like the pilot's newest recruit being handed a gun and if they were the future of Rodas, to him, he'd rather the gun was turned on them.

'I can't take this anymore,' cried the co-pilot as he hurled his breakfast out of his person and onto the ground far below.

'Your generation, you just don't have the stomach,' quipped the pilot. 'Right, I'm getting bored of this.'

He squeezed the trigger again and through his sighter, set his gaze firmly on the fleeing girl. 'Game's up, blue skin.'

Nkite weaved and ducked some more and then suddenly she stopped.

The heli-fighter that persisted in terrorising her did exactly the same.

For a brief moment, there was an air of calm that came between them and for the first time, Nkite could hear the cries of the children she had under each arm.

She put them down without looking at them, glaring upwards at their pursuers. 'Girls, find somewhere to hide. Now.'

The children did exactly as they were told and made for the relative safety of a nearby collapsed wall.

'You want to play games?' Nkite said out loud. 'Let's play.'

Without any hesitation, Nkite pulled her stick out of her backpack and tore towards the heli-fighter, which although not as high as it had been before, was still hovering at roof level above her. The nose of the craft pointed downwards as the pilot trained his guns. Nkite gritted her teeth. Just what she wanted him to do. As her legs pumped faster and faster, she used a pile of rubble as a ramp and threw herself off the end of it. At that moment, the lasers began to fire again. The pilot smiled sickeningly as Nkite flew through the air. His sights locked on to her frame as it flipped in mid-air.

Suddenly the windscreen of the heli-fighter cracked. Something had penetrated the glass.

The co-pilot, still wiping the sick from his mouth looked over at his sadistic pilot and

gasped.

The pilot's twisted smile was indelibly stained upon his lips and his bulging eyes stayed motionless. Everything else was just as it should be in the cockpit except for one thing. A spear was sticking out of his chest.

The guns had stopped and the heli-fighter was starting to fall from the sky. The co-pilot pulled himself together and reached for the steering wheel but it was too late.

Even if it hadn't been his first day, or if he had been given more than just one practice run in a craft such as this, he was too close to the ground to stop it crashing now.

As the pilot's lifeless body fell forward, so did the heli-fighter and death for the co-pilot became just as inevitable.

Nkite continued her pirouette in the air and landed less than gracefully in a pile of sand and dust, hurting her ribs in the process just in time to see the heli-fighter explode in a ball of flames. As the fire began to die down, she shakily got back up to her feet and wandered over to its burning remains.

'I win,' she muttered. Nkite made for the children's hiding place and winced as she walked. She noticed a deep throbbing in her right ankle and her ribs felt sharp all of a sudden. 'It's okay, kids, you can come out now.'

She waited for a response and yet there was none.

As the sound of the flames that scorched the crashed heli-fighter
grew distant, she refocused her senses.

'Kids?'

Nkite started to panic. The crash had occurred far away enough
for them not to be caught in the blast, and then she remembered
where she was. The capitol was teeming with Crimson Empire
soldiers. No matter if they were in the air or on foot, they teamed
the capitol like lice sucking what was left of the life force dry.
They could have been picked up by foot soldiers whose attention
had been alerted by the hullabaloo she had caused.

Despite her injuries, which had begun to gnaw at her attention,
she hurried her stride towards the wall that the children had
hidden upon and through her wheezing lungs she finally drew a
sigh of relief as she rounded the corner and saw the pair of them,
huddled together, paralysed with fear.

'It's okay, my loves,' she cooed. 'You're safe now.'

'Please, don't touch us!' shouted the bigger of the two girls.

Nkite's outstretching hand recoiled instantly, as though she
were about to have it bitten.

'I mean you no harm. I'm here to help.'

'You're one of them, keep away!'

Nkite gave the girl a puzzled look. 'One of them?'

A searchlight from a nearby heli-fighter illuminated them briefly
and it dawned upon Nkite what the little girl had meant.

The two girls that she had rescued, the two who looked back at
her with pained, judging eyes, were red. crimson red.

Nkite shook her head. 'Look, it doesn't matter what colour I am
or what colour you are.'

'It does to us,' said the smaller girl. Nkite saw the terror in her
young eyes, a terror that no girl her age should ever witness and
yet it was the same horror that had scarred her at her age. The girl
turned to the older of the two and began to cry. 'Where's Daddy?'

The older girl turned back to Nkite. 'Leave us alone. Please.'

Nkite looked at the floor. She had risked her life for the children
and saved their lives from their own race. A race who didn't want
them alive. She couldn't guarantee them safety but she could get
them to a safer place than where they were.

High above them the sky became busy with the sounds of battle once again.

Nkite grabbed the girls. 'Listen to me, if you stay here you will die. These people, YOUR people, are killing everyone who can't fight. You must come with me.' Nkite's eyes began to cry as she pleaded with them to come with her. 'Please.'

The older girl held her sister tighter. 'No.'

A chill shot down Nkite's spine. 'I'll carry you if you don't.' She winced again. Clearly to the girls she was in no fit state to rescue them by force. To them, it wouldn't be a rescue. It would be a kidnapping and blasphemy upon their names if they were to allow themselves to be taken by a blue skin.

'We'll scream in you do,' said the oldest sister defiantly.

With that, a little bit of the hope that kept Nkite fighting went out. She had risked life and limb and now, as the battle continued to rage all around them, as it had done for century upon century on Rodas, she knew she had to go.

The tears began to stream down her face. As she wiped her nose with the back of her hand, she heard more laser fire from heli-fighters like the one she had destroyed descending upon them. The whole area was about to burn and she could do no more than to save her own sorry skin.

Finally, she croaked one single word to the girls, telling them to run, turned her back and limped away, too ashamed to look back. As she crouched in and out of the debris and ruins of a once great city, one that the Crimson Empire was too ashamed to keep alive, like the people who dwelled there, her heart ached inside her chest.

She had held onto the hope of salvation for so long and yet, as she slipped quietly away, hearing the terrifying noise of gunfire emit from where she had just been, that flame started to diminish.

As she slinked and hobbled her way back to the hideout by the river, the dwelling she had been adopted into when she had been no older than the little girl who had just turned her away, she tried not to let any of the hurt stop her.

That girl and her sister, she could have saved them, they could have survived, maybe they still did.

They had scorned her and why? Because she was different from them. A difference that they had been taught was dangerous and evil.

Nkite dragged herself through the desert towards the river, her body burning with pain, she saw the shacks which made up her neighbourhood and collapsed to the floor, sobbing like a little child.

She had waited for salvation. She dreamt of it all her life. But her heart couldn't take it anymore.

A few distant lights burst the darkness of the riverbank as Nkite's fellow dwellers heard her cries.

She punched the sand over and over, the injustice of it all was too much to bear.

Salvation wasn't coming. Rodas was beyond redemption.

IV

'Get out of the way, Admiral.'

Random's anger at the Space Seals sudden appearance on the cusp of Ursa-17 was enough to boil his blood. Anji looked at her friend and could see his fists were clenched by his side.

'I'm sorry, Captain but I can't do that,' came the response.

'I wouldn't advise you to try and stop me,' Random said.

The Admiral sighed one of her trademarks, long and unimpressed sighs. 'Captain, you are a truly remarkable man. You are outnumbered sixty to one. If we liked, we could transport your friends out of there and leave you to try our patience, at which point one single blast from any of our freighters will totally destroy you. Now I know you're healing powers are beyond comprehension but I doubt your metabolism is good enough to withstand the vacuum of space now do you?'

'I wouldn't go making threats,' replied Random.

'And I wouldn't stoop that low,' Bagari responded. 'I was just pointing out that it'd be stupid to disobey my order.'

'I'm not one of your soldiers,' spat Random. 'You can't tell me what to do.'

'I'm the Admiral of this sector among many others and I am in charge of this space. So yes, I can. Look, I understand that this isn't ideal. Come aboard, I'll bring you up to speed on everything. Then we can discuss what the next steps shall be. How does that sound?'

Anji, Jake and Skateboard looked at Random, who stared unblinking at Bagari's image on the monitor.

'Sounds a lot nicer than being blown up,' he replied.

Bagari gave a little sigh of relief. 'We shall send you our coordinates now. Docking Bay 48 is free. I shall meet you there.' Bagari nodded to someone out of the image and disappeared from the screen.

Anji and Jake breathed a sigh of relief. 'Blimey,' said Jake. 'I thought we were going to war with the Space Seals for a minute there.'

'You're not afraid of the Space Seals, are you?' asked Random.

491

'No…but Admiral Bagari gives me the jeebies!' admitted Jake.

Random allowed himself a smile. He registered a new message that had come through the onboard computer. 'Docking bay 48, Skateboard. Take us in slowly.'

The Venus II turned and made for one of the massive battle freighters.

The fleet of hornet fighters that had blocked their route started to part like the red sea in the bible story as the travellers made their procession.

'Just when I thought I had seen the last of Admiral Bagari,' said Anji ruefully. Just over a year ago, she had spent a weekend training to become a Space Seal herself in the Academy. It had shocked her just as much as it had shocked her friends. At the time the crew of the Venus II had found themselves being unofficial freelancers for the Space Seals after it was discovered that from an earlier adventure, that an evil tyrant from another universe called Stratos, had infiltrated their reality from another. This had created a knock-on effect where anomalies had opened up in all corners of the universe and all sorts of weird and dangerous creatures had started to seep into the wrong reality altogether. Since it had been Random and his friends who had caused the first one, in Bagari's eyes, she thought they should tidy up after themselves. They eventually stopped the anomalies but in a break from their battles against parallel universe monsters, Anji decided to take a sabatical and ended up, to her surprise, enrolling in the academy.

Much to Anji's relief, it didn't last long.

Her stubborn streak and issues with those in authority had put pay to that but Bagari had been rather kind just before she had left so although her respect for the Space Seals was non-existent, she had bucket loads of it for Bagari. Where countless teachers, social workers and people in uniform had failed oh so many times before, Anji had finally found a person in authority to look up to and all it took was for someone to show her respect and value. It didn't make going back there any easier though.

When the Venus II flew through the forcefield barrier between the outer hull of the freighter and the docking bay, Anji began to worry a little about bumping into any of her fellow cadets. As they looked out of the viewscreen at the rows of soldiers, standing to attention in banks of ten, she gulped hard.

Random, Anji, Jake and Skateboard descended down the gangway, leaving the relative safety of the Venus II and onto the cold, non-descript floor of the battle freighter, a loud click echoed all around. Someone in the crowd of soldiers bellowed an order and everybody, every man, woman, diaphone and subjakeat alien lifeform snapped into a smart salute.

The travellers didn't know what to do. Jake gave a rather feeble salute back that looked like a wet fish slapping a teenager on the forehead.

'At ease,' came a familiar voice. The soldiers' salutes instantly disappeared as their arms snapped back down to their sides and their heels clicked again as they relaxed.

The voice belonged to Admiral Bagari and she walked to greet her old friends.

'No salute from you I, see?' said Random quizzically.

'You know me, Random, I am hard to please. To get a salute from me you'll really have to earn it.' She said back with a hint of cheekiness in her voice.

Random didn't feel like joking around. 'Might I hazard a guess as to why you've stopped me?'

Bagari nodded. 'If you'll follow me to my ready room, I shall brief you all personally.' She turned on the spot and led the travellers out of the docking bay.

V

'It's worse than you think, Captain. Much worse.'

Bagari unbuttoned the top of her tunic and made for a drink cabinet in the corner of her ready room. Jake took in his surroundings. The room was furnished beautifully. The walls and floor seemed to shimmer a pinkie, purple colour and there were three push sofas arranged neatly in a U-shape around a big desk, which was impeccably tidy and to which itself sat a few feet in front of a big leather chair and a huge wall of monitors and diagrams.

'Blimey, pays well does it, being an Admiral?' said Jake.

Bagari ignored the comment and instead busied herself with pouring drinks.

'Please, do make yourselves at home. I've been meaning to ask. Jake..have you always been so?'

'Annoying?' asked Anji.

'Young?' finished Bagari. 'Or is this a new thing?'

'Second puberty,' said Jake. 'I enjoyed the first one so much I thought I'd like to go through it all over again.'

Bagari frowned and shook her head. 'Anyway, back to more pressing matters.'

She finished pouring a filthy, dark-looking liquid into five tumblers, put them on a tray and proceeded to take them to the travellers, who had arranged themselves untidily on the sofas.

'Forgive me, Admiral, but I cannot drink,' said Skateboard.

'It's Alturian vodka and it's consumable by any humanoid or android in the known universe,' Bagari reassured.

'Vodka!' replied Jake excitedly.

'You're too young to drink,' said Random.

'Believe me, when you've heard what I have to say I think you'll all be asking for the bottle,' said Bagari. 'First, I'd like to ask you Captain why you chose this moment to return home?'

Random took the tumbler offered to him from the tray. 'Is it important?'

Bagari shot him a look whilst offering the others their drinks. 'I wouldn't be asking you if it wasn't.'

Random nodded. 'The Oracle. She sent me a distress signal. I answered it. Never been one to ignore them. She showed me what was happening on Rodas. How the war had developed while I had been away. She convinced me to come back.'

Bagari took to her chair. 'The Oracle...until now I thought they were just a myth.'

'I wish she was,' replied Random who took a brave swig from his tumbler. Jake and Anji gave him a disgusted look as he let the disgusting-looking liquid cascade down his throat. 'It's just like honey, honest!' he said.

Hesitantly, they too took sips and looked pleasantly surprised at each other. Skateboard produced a tiny metal straw from inside his casing and proceeded to take little sips as he listened on.

'Then she must have foreseen what we have been dreading for quite a considerable time,' said Bagari.

'And what's that then?' asked Jake, who even after one sip of the vodka was starting to feel a little merry.

'We've had news from the security border that protects the galaxy from Rodas that the leader of one of the warring factions has started putting together plans to break out.'

'Kalor Maloso,' said Random coldly. He had encountered him once before on the day that he and Skateboard had stolen the Venus II and become the only people in the history of the cosmos to break the security barrier that contained the war on Rodas and fled the chaos. 'We've met. Kind of.'

'In the past few years, the Sapphire Regime has all but crumbled.

With little resistance left the Crimson Empire are now committing genocide against their own people.'

'That's horrible!' cried Anji.

'That's not the half of it,' replied Bagari. 'Since he learned of Random's birth and escape he had been conducting experiments to raise an army of unbelievable force.'

'Has he succeeded?' asked Random.

'We are not sure. Intelligence tells us that he has been conducting similar experiments for decades but now he has acquired the technology he is going further than he ever had before. It'll end Rodas. His plans are to ultimately destroy his own world and then spread his infection of war across the galaxy. It's the universe's biggest fear.'

Random scoffed. 'The universe's biggest shame, more like.'

Bagari scowled. 'How do you mean?'

Random slammed his drink down, his anger raging through his body. 'Rodas has always been scorned. I didn't spend long there but you didn't have to be a genius to see what had happened. The people there. The billions of refugees from both sides of the planet; took me a split second to see how the rest of the universe had turned its back on them. Their faces have haunted my life. If the universe was so concerned about Rodas then why did it never intervene? Think about it.

The countless lives that have been lost and for what? And now I'm forced to go back there to finish off a job that no one else ever dared to do. I mean look at you, sitting all safe and sound in that cosy armchair when you have an armada out there, all just to stop me from doing what I'm so-called "destined" to do. You could put an end to this war. You and all the other Space Seals. But no. You're all just watching. Observing from afar. You're no better than the rest of them Bagari and you know it.'

'That's not true, Captain and you know it,' said Bagari calmly.

'No! No, I don't know it! There are zillions of armies in the cosmos. All it would have taken was a warning from them all. But they all sat back and let it happen,' he continued.

'Captain there are treaties and agreements too many in number that I could bore you with that prove otherwise,' Bagari said springing out of her chair and meeting Random's frustration head-on. 'I don't like having to sit back whilst millions of people die, believe you me. I'm in this job to save lives, just like you are, but there are times when all I can do is protect and serve. Take our current location for example. We are allowed no further, not one inch closer to Rodas than here, and why? Because there are forces on that planet that the people in charge of this big, bad universe fear even themselves.'

Anji and Jake sat pensively, the electricity in the air was cracking.

Random's clenched jaw relaxed a little. He saw the sincerity in Bagari's eyes. He heard it ringing in his ears. It didn't make him feel any better.

'Why? Why is the universe so afraid of Rodas?' asked Anji.

'Because of the war. Because the people were stupid enough to start a conflict over the making of a colour,' said Random, showing that he had acknowledged Bagari's counterargument.

'Making of a colour?' parroted Anji. 'Which one?'

'Does it matter?' asked Random. 'The point is that Maloso and the Crimson Empire have got to where they might just be strong enough to get out...and take Rodas down with them. It's not just the people in charge who are worried about war spreading across the stars. It's the guilt of never putting an end to it. They can't sleep at night and now their dirty little secret might just pollute those they are sworn to blind from the obvious.'

Bagari didn't argue back. It was hard to. 'Even so, we cannot advance further than this point.'

'So that's it? Rodas is contained here if the security barrier goes? Who says that it will? It's impregnable, isn't it?'

'No, sir,' Skateboard interjected, tearing himself away from his delicious drink. 'We got out,

remember? So, us doing it will have given Maloso the drive and hope to do it himself.'

'And according to our people on the ground, he will,' said Bagari.

'And yet you won't let us stop him,' said Anji.

'It's not that,' said Bagari.

'Well, it sounds like you won't even let us try,' slurred Jake, who had finished his drink already.

'I never said I wouldn't let you try.'

Random tried to hide his surprise.

'You mean?' squealed Jake.

'I'm not happy about letting anybody go down there but I'm not allowed to do a thing. My superiors have spoken. No-one is to enter Ursa-17. But having seen the reports about what is going on down there, I cannot stay passive. If you youngsters want to go to Rodas, you can and I give you my word that I shall say nothing. I have to ask. All four of you. Do you really want to go? You haven't seen what is happening down there.'

'We have to,' said Random.

Anji and Jake gave the same confident look. 'We're staying with Random.'

'I'd prefer if you two were to remain here,' replied Bagari.

'As would I, Admiral,' said Skateboard, whose drink was keeping him unusually quiet. 'I've seen Rodas. I'm worried that if you two follow us down there you won't come back to the same people. War changes people.'

'So?' said Jake. 'We are sticking with you. No matter what.'

Random sighed. 'A part of me prefers you to stay. At least then I would know that you were safe, but another part of me wants you by my side.'

'We'll listen to that side then,' quipped Anji. 'But how do we get in? If by what you say the security barrier is still up then how do we get through.'

'I have a contact,' said Bagari. 'They can get you in. I'll send you the coordinates Skateboard.'

'Thank you, Admiral,' Skateboard replied.

'Bagari,' said Random. 'This could be the last time that we see you. If that's the case…thank you, for everything.'

Bagari looked at him. 'A lot can happen if you go down there. You might put an end to it all yourselves or it might be the case that the Space Seals change their stance. Whatever happens, I'll be keeping an eye on developments. Just make sure you all get back safe.'

Random said nothing. 'Right, you lot, finish your drinks. There's no time like the present.'

'Wait,' said Bagari. 'Before you go, we need to speak about the condition of your craft.'

'The Venus II? It's in brilliant condition,' said Anji.

'That's the problem,' said Bagari. 'It's a stolen, very famous ship. The only one that has ever escaped Rodas? It'll be seen.'

'We have cloaking capabilities, Admiral, I'm sure we will be fine,' said Skateboard, who had a horrible feeling that he knew what was about to be suggested.

'And the entire fleet don't want me to send you down there.'

'So, what are you saying?' asked Random.

Bagari raised her eyebrow. 'Let's create a show. You all try to escape, we open fire, the Venus II crash lands and you turn off your sensors so it looks like there are no survivors. No questions asked by anyone else, you get where you want to be and I don't have to write any reports or be dragged towards a disciplinary committee.

'You mean you want to shoot us out of the sky?' cried Jake.

'In a way, yes. We'll only leave surface damage; I'll make sure of that. It's the only way that can get you past the fleet's sensors and to the security barrier. You can switch the cloaking device on before you get there.'

Random pondered on the idea. Skateboard and the others looked on anxiously.

'Alright, fine,' he said finally. 'But please, mind the paintwork.'

'You'd all better run out of here too. Make it look as though you've escaped,' Bagari said.

Skateboard diodes whimpered. He knew it was inevitable that their ship would get scuffed a bit during this mission but now he was starting to worry about how long it would take him to carry out repairs.'

'Okay, Admiral. As I said, go easy. Don't actually blow us up.' Bagari nodded.

'I'll drive,' slurred Jake.

'No, you won't, you've been drinking,' replied Anji.

'Right, come on you lot, let's go,' said Random. He looked at Bagari again and pelted out of the room, closely followed by the others.

Bagari gave them a ten-second head start and then raised the alarm from her desk. She smiled to herself. For all the annoyance they had caused her over the years, she was looking forward to shooting at them. Then she remembered where they were about to go. If this didn't work, her career would go up in smoke. Were they worth it? She grabbed her beret and made for the ready room door.

'Godspeed, Captain Random.'

VI

Meanwhile, as the travellers fought their case away from Rodas, Kalor Maloso put the finishing touches to his master plan. He stood alone, brooding over a strategy map that sizzled a neon red into the darkness that was his domain. The warlord allowed himself a smile, something he was rare to do unless he had taken a life or ordered the death of many. He glared over the map, which showed a three-dimensional live feed of what was happening on the battleground. He watched in delight as the areas that had once been blue were starting to flash a crimson red. The audio of his troops putting to action his orders surrounded him and he closed in eyes in glee as he heard the declarations of liberation and the screams of their enemies being extinguished like flames in the night.

He opened them and proceeded to monitor the bombardment of the ruins that scattered around the capitol. Dozens of little dots buzzed all over the place like ants.

He thought to himself how he was rather like a giant, pouring scalding hot water upon them to wipe them out altogether. He found that good.

Kalor Maloso has grown weary of the weak and infirm.

He had no use for those who couldn't fight or did not wish to fight. All they did was take up valuable food and shelter, resources which in his mind should be the bare minimum his soldiers should be given. After all, no one except he had a home anymore, but why should they all go hungry? Maloso purred as he watched the sheer magnificence of his genius and switched the map off with a wave of his hand, plunging the room into darkness once more.

Without hesitation, he proceeded to stalk slowly across the vast gloomy room and made for the far wall. With a click of his long, bony fingers, a panel spun out of the rock face. Pressing a few buttons, Maloso stepped back as a low-pitched hum began to emanate around him. The ground started to shake as a trapdoor appeared in the floor and out of it a glass chamber began to rise. Maloso grinned, his demonic eyes glowing blood red.

Before long, the long tubular chamber, and a bank of complex instruments came to a halt. Maloso considered the chamber for a moment.

So far, his plan had worked. But there was so much more he had to do. There was little resistance on Rodas that could stop him now, but he knew that at any moment, the threat of the one who could destroy his conquest of Rodas could return. The prophecy had been told and he knew better than anybody that destiny was something that could not be stopped.

Only he didn't know that. He knew that he could hold back death, that his purpose in this cosmos was to rule. It was his right and no coward was going to stop him.

That's what the people of Rodas had started to call their savour. A coward who ran away instead of fighting for them. All hope of salvation had left the planet at the same time that his little ship had somehow broken through the security barrier which contained the madness within Rodas.

Maloso opened the chamber door and stepped inside, laying down inside the empty tube. He thought to himself as he fixed a breathing mask around what was left of his rotting nose and mouth. If he could break through the barrier once then it would happen again. Only there would not be a barrier to pierce this time. If his plan was to work, then the coward would probably return too late and find himself on a dead planet.

As Maloso made to close the chamber door, his communication system fizzed into life.

'I'm sorry to disturb you, sir, but we have some urgent news.'

Maloso stopped in his tracks and bolted upright. 'I told you,' he said in his malevolent calm voice,' that I was not to be disturbed.'

The voice paused for a second and then continued with a significant amount of fear in its tone.

'Supreme Ruler, I can only apologise but we have received intelligence that the chosen one is on the outer edge of Ursa-17.'

Maloso's eyes grew wider. 'I see,' he said, calculating his next move. 'Then we had best be sure that we are prepared in all things, isn't that right, Commander?'

'Yes, Supreme Ruler,' came the reply. 'Shall I proceed with the plans?'

'That would be most satisfactory,' purred Maloso. 'And Commander? Oversee the experiment personally. We don't want to add yet another abomination to the pile now, do we?'

'No, Supreme Ruler.'

'Good. I shall now retire for the evening. If what you say is true and the coward is indeed on his way then I shall need every ounce of strength I can muster. Until then, make sure that your troops keep driving the Sapphire Regime out and kill anyone who gets in your path.'

'As you desire, Supreme Ruler.'

'Oh, and Commander?'

'Yes, Supreme Ruler?'

'If you disturb me one more time, I shall pull apart every inch of bone in your skull inch-by-inch while you are awake, do you hear me?'

The Commander whimpered. 'As you wish, Supreme Ruler.'

'Good,' said Maloso. The comms went dead and he was left alone again.

So Random was coming back sooner than he had thought. No matter, he said to himself. He calculated how long he would need in the chamber to combat this news. Several hours, perhaps? As he laid back leather straps snaked out from under him and fastened his limbs in place. Then another shot out and wrapped itself around his hooded head. Sighing heavily, he grinned. He looked forward to their meeting.

As he closed his eyes the chamber door shut automatically and an orange gas seeped out of invisible holes in the chamber as tiny little operating needles and sharp implements plunged down from the door and proceeded to plunge deeply into Maloso's hideous flesh. It began harvesting what was left of him, taking what valuable DNA it could.

He did not wince, he did not cry out in pain. It was all for the good of the Crimson Empire.

After all, if he didn't spend several hours a day in the chamber, there wouldn't be a Crimson Empire for him to rule.

VII

Two knocks at the door awoke Nkite from her dreamless sleep. She groaned loudly and refused to open her eyes.

'Gron. I know it's you, please not now.'

'How did you know it was me?' asked the gruff, elderly voice from outside Nkite's little shack.

'It's your knock,' she moaned.

'I didn't know I had a knock,' came the rather puzzled response.

'Well, you do and it's woken me up,' groaned Nkite as she turned on her rough straw bed. She waited a minute to make sure that her unwanted visitor had gone and then allowed herself to start falling back to sleep.

'Are you still awake?' came the old voice again.

'No,' said Nkite, she tutted loudly and shuffled off her bed, wiping individual strands of straw off her person as she got up. She reached for the door. 'Alright Gron, you win.' She opened the door. The silhouette of a hunched figure appeared before her, the luminous moon of Rodas shining aggressively behind him.

'I heard,' he said as he took a well-worn leather hat from off his head, revealing thick yet dropped white hair that matched the colour and texture of his beard, 'that you were a bit of a mess when you returned here tonight.'

Nkite stood upright as though a superior officer had ordered her to attention. 'That doesn't sound like me.'

'You're right, it doesn't,' replied Gron. 'May I enter?'

'If you must. I warn you, the place is a bit of a mess,' she said as she walked over to a little table. On top sat a metal kettle which was perched above some glowing vegetation. 'I think that water might still be hot, did you want some tea?'

'No, thank you. I had some earlier.' Gron shuffled his way into the shack. Although he had use of a crude walking stick, he used his other hand, the one with the beaten-up hat in it, to steady himself inside. 'But I'll trouble you for a chair as always if you don't mind?'

Nkite smiled as she made the tea. 'I never would. Please make yourself comfortable.'

Gron's bones ached as he lowered himself into the wicker chair that sat near Nkite's bedside. He watched her finish pouring the contents of the kettle into a metal cup and perched next to him on her bed.

'What happened?' he asked.

'You wouldn't want to know,' she said, not making eye contact with him.

Gron smiled. 'Do you remember when we first met? You came to my shop, the little one on the other side of the river. I caught you trying to steal one of my fish.'

Nkite scoffed. 'You're not wanting me to pay for it now, are you?'

The pair of them laughed. Before long Nkite fell into a serious mood again. 'If I'd had money to pay you Gron, I would have done.'

'That's exactly what you said to me. And I gave it to you, for free, remember?'

'Yes,' said Nkite. She was taken back to that day several years ago. 'I broke down. It was the first time anybody had been kind to me in a long time.'

'You poured your little heart out to me. You told me that you had lost your parents and that you were all alone. I told you, so was I. My family were long gone, I had only my shop and my relative safety to my name. Then you told me about what you had seen in the night sky around that time. We talked about it, remember? How the sorrow in our hearts just melted away when we spoke about that brilliant wash of purple in the sky. You had a look in your eye as bright as the sun. It was hope. It sparkled inside you. And now, my dear, I can see in the moonlight how that sparkle is diminished.'

Nkite's eyes began to well up with tears. 'They wouldn't come with me, Gron.'

'Who?' Gron asked kindly.

'They were just kids and they didn't want to be saved,' Nkite's lip began to quiver.

'Every time I set out on a mission; I swear that I will help someone. It's an offer that has never been refused. But now, the children..even the children don't want to be saved,' she started to sob. Gron began to cry too. He placed a sympathetic palm on her head and lowered his head.

'Oh, my child I am so sorry,' he whispered.

Overcome with grief, Nkite threw herself into his arms and sobbed heavy, heartbroken tears into his shoulder.

'How bad has it got that even children would rather die than go on?' she wailed.

Gron's face fell. Through the tears, he looked out of Nkite's open window and saw past the tranquil sight of their river pockets of sparks igniting in the night sky. He knew that the bombing was getting closer. He knew that it would only be a matter of time before their little corner of Rodas would turn to rubble and dust.

'Some people, no matter their age, just don't want to be saved, my dear. It's a sad fact of life. You don't know what their lives had been like. Maybe they weren't lucky like yourself. You found shelter and strength upon the riverbank. They probably never had the chance to see the light like you did.'

'But to refuse me..because of the colour of my skin?' she sniffed. 'To favour death over being saved by someone like me?'

'This world has long been poisoned. The night of the purple sky invoked a hope that had not been seen on Rodas in my life until then, believe me. Those who believe such ridiculous notions that we are different are wrong. Take you and me for example. Both of Sapphire complexion and yet do we look alike? We are all of the same race. The Sapphire Regime, the Crimson Empire, we are all one and yet we have never been further apart.'

'Try telling the Empire that, I've seen them slaughter so many people.'

'And it's begun to eat away at you. I know. Every day that you venture out I pray to the stars that you'll return safe. We need more people like you Nkite. You carry the flame that will one day take us to peace. But please, do not lose that spark just yet.

The war must end sometime and people like you will make it happen, I am sure of it.

Someone like you, who'd scare off soldiers by firing purple paint at them, do you remember when you used to do that?'

Nkite allowed herself a smile. 'If only that tactic worked now.'

'That takes guts and belief. War can destroy such gifts. Don't let that happen to you.'

Nkite picked herself up and looked into Gron's sweet old eyes. He'd seen so much. He'd been a soldier a long time ago.

But the war had moved on and worse was on its way. She just couldn't make that promise.

'Otherwise, my hope dies a little too,' he said.

'Now, that's just putting pressure on me,' she retorted before giving Gron a smile of appreciation. 'Thank you for coming.'

Gron took her hands in his. She was like a Granddaughter to him. 'Thank you for letting me in. If you ever need me, or find yourself at a loose end and want to listen to my stories, I'm just a hop over the riverbank.'

'Always. Now then Gron, time for me to help you. Let's get you back home.' She got up and offered her hand, to which Gron took it and using the walking stick in his other hand, lifted himself off the chair. He stood and admired her.

'Not all heroes are up in the stars, Nkite. You'll always be mine,' he smiled.

Nkite scoffed. She was about to reply with one of her usual witty retorts when suddenly she could hear something in the distance.

'What's that?' she said, making her way over to the open window.

'Ha, I wouldn't ask me. My hearing went years ago. The Battle on Blon-Fuge it was,' replied Gron.

'Ssshhh.' Nkite put a finger to her lips. It sounded like an army of noisy crickets but it was getting ever louder. 'Oh zark,' she exclaimed.

She ran over to the door, on which her satchel was hanging on a crude hanger that stuck out of it like a nail in a bit of wood.

'What, what is it?' asked Gron, the panic palpable in his voice.

Nkite fetched her binoculars from inside the bag and ran to the window again. Training the sighter, her jaw dropped when her eyes focussed on where the noise was coming from.

'No, please, no,' she muttered. She threw the binoculars onto her straw bed and ripped through her door onto the riverbank outside. Confused, Gron made for the bed and picked them up. His old hands trembling, it didn't take long for him to realise why Nkite had run away.

'Mercy,' he whispered as he lowered the binoculars. Terror began to flood his mind. 'The monsters...'

Nkite ran as fast as her legs would carry, losing her balance in the soft sand under her feet every now and then as she tore towards a large bell that stood incongruously next to the river.

'Wake up everyone, we have to go!' she screamed as loud as her lungs would allow. Some of the people living their lives on the riverbank stopped and saw her and too began to feel panic. 'To the boats, quick! Everyone, get to the boats!'

She reached the bell and using the rope that dangled below it, yanked it with all her might.

The loud ringing was deafening but it alerted the river folk that they had company.

Nkite continued to shout her warning as she watched the dozens of river dwellers leave their little shacks. Men, women and children, some as young as babies in arms enveloped out onto the sand.

'They're here. They're here!' she screamed.

As the river dwellers prepared themselves for evacuation, the terrifying image of hundreds of heli-fighters, their engines roaring like fire grew ever closer.

And Nkite watched as every single one of them was about to destroy them all.

VIII

As Admiral Bagari's ship continued to pummel the Venus II with its heavy artillery, Random was so lost in his thoughts that he barely registered that they were under attack. He sat, unblinking as the ship lurched sickeningly from one side to the other, the outer hull screeching as the searing heat of laser fire scolded its surface.

Anji and Jake, like Random himself, were clasped into their chairs as Skateboard magnetically fastened his frame to the dashboard as more and more sparks and tiny explosions erupted all around them.

'I thought she said she would go easy on us!' shouted Jake as the Venus II rolled to avoid a particularly nasty volley of missiles.

'She is!' said Anji, who was starting to feel pretty sick.

'Just twenty more clicks and we shall shut the engines down and trip their scanners. I've readied the cloaking device too, sir,' said Skateboard to Random but he wasn't listening. Skateboard channelled his optical sensors towards his friend and Captain expecting a response but there was none.

Random just sat there, staring past the viewscreen and beyond the stars.

If Skateboard had an arm to wave, he'd have frantically whirled it in front of his face to bring him back with them but it was no use. Random might have been there physically but not mentally.

'Nearly there,' Skateboard reassured, just as the contents of Jake's stomach emptied into his lap.

'Clean up in aisle...er...everywhere!' quipped Anji, who thought that humour might from deflect from the fact that her dinner was about to vacate her soon too.

'Three...two...one, cutting engines!'

As Skateboard spoke, he shut down all power except life support and, just as was planned, Bagari's battle freighter ceased firing upon them. The Venus II, now chard, a scorched mess of a ship, was drifting aimlessly behind a nebula cloud, out of sight of its attacker.

508

'We should be out of the way of their sensors now. This nebula cloud will help us get to the security mainframe,' said Skateboard. 'Feel free to unfasten your safety belts. The gravity inside the ship should be stable now.'

He looked back and saw the mess that his two human friends had created.

Skateboard's diodes sighed. 'I'll get a mop.'

As he turned off his magnetic feature and left the cockpit, Random stayed motionless, still staring blankly out into the wideness of space.

He couldn't move, he couldn't think about anything other than his mission at hand. Not for his friends, who were now being mopped up by his obedient and ever-faithful robotic friend. Not for the fact that the ship that he had called home most of his life had small fires inside its cabin that sprinklers were currently putting out. As the Venus II lurched through the nebula, on the other side of the cloud a net began to hone into his sight.

'We're here,' he muttered, diverting his friend's attention away from their clean-up job.

The travellers continued to see to themselves as they joined Random at the front of the cockpit. They watched as they drifted closer and closer to what to them looked like a giant net in space. Before long they could see the electric pulse that shook through the net, a blue energy keeping the danger far below it at bay. As they left the relative safety of the nebula, the image of the security mainframe became clear to see and beyond it and the people who worked within the net could be seen moving in their little command post which clung to the net like dew on a web.

Past it, there it lay. The planet that had haunted Random's dreams.

'What is that?' asked Anji.

'It's the security mainframe,' replied Random.

'And that stops anyone from leaving Rodas?' asked Jake. 'Why didn't it stop you two?'

'We knew how to get out,' replied Skateboard.

'Now we need to get back in,' Random added. 'Okay, Skateboard, let's open a channel.'

'We cannot do that, sir. If we do, we will risk making the mainframe aware of our whereabouts.'

'How do we do that?' asked Anji.

'They will contact us, apparently. Leave the comms open, Skateboard, we'll wait for their signal,' Random got up and made his way down to the mid-section of the ship, avoiding the puddles of sick his friends had failed to clear up yet. He ignored the sparks that were spitting at him from broken electrical cables and the singed walls and floor. He even ignored the little puddles of water that now swamped the room. His feet were wet instantly through his shoes but he didn't mind. Ignoring the calls of his friends as he embarked down the corridor back to his room.

More remnants of the attack littered his path and still, he ignored it.

'Everywhere I go I cause destruction,' he cursed himself.

'But you also leave hope.'

Random stopped in his tracks. That voice. He had heard it before but not for years. She had left him alone for so long after plaguing his conscience with pleas to go home.

That had all changed after the time Random used the powerful element the Zedron Flux to wipe out a race of gods known as the Osirans to save the peaceful planet of Spectronia. After the incident, the voices stopped never to haunt him again. Or so he thought.

'I thought you were leaving me alone now,' he spat. Random wondered if their return had anything to do with him being so close to home. As if he didn't have enough to contend with...

'You need our guidance. The Oracle foresaw what is to come. She knew you would need us but we were always here with you. We would never abandon you,' came another voice, this time that of a male.

Random sighed. 'Why now? Why not any other time since I left? The Oracle never told me, she couldn't tell me.'

The two mysterious voices burnt fiercely inside his mind, so powerful that he believed that they had manifested themselves whole right in front of his eyes. He'd never seen their images so clearly before.

The unbelievably tall and gangly blue man and the normal-sized and fierce looking, her crimson red eyes aflame with the same determination that Random possessed. They stood before him, side-by-side, their ghostly vision hazy in the gloomy dark of the Venus II corridor.

'The Oracle can only do and say as much as she is allowed,' said the woman.

'Allowed? I've met gods before and they never seemed to believe much in rules.'

'Look what happened to them,' said the man. 'You have the power to change Rodas for the better. It's what you were destined to do.'

Random sighed. 'I don't feel ready. I've allowed myself to come this far and now...' he hammered his fists down upon the wall, leaving two dented panels looking like they had seen better days.

'We understand, we really do.'

Random scoffed. 'That doesn't help me much.'

'Then let your friends help you more,' said the woman.

'I can't! I've already led them here. How do you think I feel about that? I'm too much of a coward to let them go and I'm too selfish to admit I can't do without them.'

'To have friends is not selfish,' replied the man. 'Random, you must open your heart. You're about to embark on the most dangerous mission you've ever encountered. You're meeting your destiny head-on. You need them now more than ever. Don't leave them in the dark. If there is light, there is hope.'

At that moment, the visions faded away and Anji, Jake and Skateboard appeared in the gloom.

'Who were you talking to?' asked Jake.

'If I told you, you wouldn't believe me,' sighed Random.

Skateboard knew instantly who Random was referring to. 'The voices, sir?'

'Got it in one,' came the response.

'Random, while we were waiting for the signal, we thought you might want to hang out?' Anji asked.

Random smiled at them all. 'No. Sorry.'

Anji and Jake's smiles faded.

Random watched their changed expressions. He could see how hard they were trying to lighten the mood and he was ruining it. He looked down at the ground and allowed himself a little laugh. 'After all, you both stink of sick. I know that my room is a mess but still, at least it smells nice right now.'

The pair of them looked at themselves and laughed. 'Yeah, good point. We'd better get changed,' said Anji.

'Then can we hang?' said Jake. He was eager, just as much as Anji as they knew it might be the last time to have a laugh.

'Depends on how badly you still smell,' said Random cheekily. 'Of course, I wouldn't want anything else.'

As they both made it down the corridor, Skateboard was left alone with Random.

'I know, Skateboard, I know. Is the auto repair on?'

'It's functioning, sir. The question is, are you?'

Random turned to Skateboard. He couldn't answer.

IX

They had barely made it onto the boats before the shelling started. Just as Nkite had helped get the last remaining stragglers on board they set off down the long and dark river, completely exposed to the descending madness of war. Gron, who was sitting on the same boat as his beloved Nkite, had known this was coming. They all had. For too long they had sheltered away from the atrocities unharmed. It was only a matter of time until their abstinence in the long, bitter war would be punished. But in all that time, the river dwellers had been able to set up a contingency; a place to go if their peace was ever disturbed. They had defence mechanisms to help them get there but no way to attack. As the heli-fighter's artillery torched their homes, they had to get away.

Nkite watched as the homes of her neighbours burnt to the ground. The distant crackling or embers drowned out the steady rowing of the people who had manned the oars. Not one river dweller was able to take their eyes off the destruction of the place they had once called home.

Many of them cried. Men, women, children. Gron himself sat solemnly, forcing himself to close his eyes like he was trying to escape a

nightmare. Against his chest, he clutched a tattered leather-bound book with all his might.

Nkite sniffed and picked up an oar to help the rower on her boat. It was one of a dozen that were fleeing the flames and as she began stroking the water, she cursed their luck. The escape plan that they had all learned, like a myth handed down through time to each and every new dweller, allowing for more time to escape than that which reality had allowed. She began to feel suspicious. How come nobody had alerted them of oncoming heli-fighters earlier? Whose turn was it to keep watch tonight? Now they had to negotiate roughly two miles of river before they could slope out of harm's way and through a complex system of underground caves.

Someone had given them away, she felt sure about that.

As she saw her own shack succumbed to the flames Nkite couldn't keep her suspicions to herself any longer.

'Who was keeping watch?' she shouted.

'Nkite, this is no time for blaming anybody,' came an older, female voice. It was that of Bakal, an elder of the river dwellers close to Gron's age, but lacking his calm head and tact. 'We must get to safety first.'

Nkite bit her lip. Bakal may have been an old woman, but she wasn't the kind of person she wanted to get on the wrong side of.

In the old days, she had been a fighter and led a resistance battalion across the jaws of a battleground known as Ellipsis. Despite heavy gunfire from the Sapphire Regime, she survived and was tortured and finally tried as a war criminal. Only she had escaped and Nkite had never found out how, but whenever Bakal spoke about the night she made it across the sand dunes to the river, the old woman's eyes turned to stone. Having been taken in by the other side, she had grown to appreciate acceptance and as the years wore on, she grew to love her quiet retirement out of the claws of her enemies and even grown to admire her blue-skinned neighbours.

Bakal placed a reassuring hand on Nkite's broad shoulder. 'First, we survive, okay?'

Nkite nodded and turned back to the task at hand. She noticed a few of the boats in front of theirs were already falling under cover of darkness as the reeds and overhanging trees afforded some visible camouflage from the heli-fighters whose engines and fire poisoned the night sky. Then she looked back and noticed that maybe, after all these years of luck, it looked like it might finally run out.

'Bakal,' said Nkite. She nodded into the distance and Bakal turned around.

A heli-fighter had spotted them and was soaring through the air.

The dwellers on the boat, which had managed to hold roughly thirty refugees, began to panic.

'Stay calm!' barked Bakal. 'Everybody, stay calm!'

The screams of the river dwellers became just as loud as the heli-fighter's engines.

'Raise shields!' cried out Bakal. Her words were echoed across the boats and one by one, a bubble-like protection formed and shimmered a calm blue over those in the boats. As Nkite remembered helping to fit the boats with this defensive capability, stolen by herself from an experimental craft the Crimson Empire was developing, she allowed herself a moment to feel proud.

Up ahead, she breathed a sigh of relief as the mountain containing their hideaway started to feel closer and closer. But then, she watched in horror as the heli-fighters opened fire on the boats. She bit her lip. If their defences were compromised or failed to work, it would be her fault.

She found the shield mechanism and promised the camp that it would work.

They had only managed to test them out with handguns and what few grenades they could thieve from the soldiers that had up until now left them well alone.

She had been told that the shields would be a match for anything. The plans she too had stolen and reported back to Bakal with said so also. But there was always a chance they wouldn't. Recent events in her life had taught her not to misplace her hope.

Voices cried out into the night sky as the laser fire exploded all around and began pummelling the boats. Nkite's heart beat faster than it had ever beaten before as she witnessed explosions of light all around her and her fellow refugees. The water boiled and hissed as the lasers burrowed deep beneath. As the fire sent the water rushing into the air like an inverted waterfall, the squadron leader of the heli-fighters led a flyover, surveying the magnificent chaos they had created below.

As the waves settled, she was astonished to see that their malicious attack had failed. All of the boats were still going. 'Why have they stopped?' she said as she turned to Bakal. The old woman dared not take her eye off them.

'We've bought time; that's all that matters right now,' she noticed that the boat had stopped. The rest of the refugees continued their journey into the cave.

One in fact had already entered through the narrow entrance and was safe from the barrage.

'Don't stop!' cried Nkite to her fellow passengers, 'keep rowing!'

The rowers snapped out of their trance, frozen with fear and even slight relief that they were no longer being shot at. But the fleet was starting to converge.

Nkite knew what they were doing straight away. 'Come on, come on, go!' She took up an oar herself and began pounding the river with it, imploring, willing her little boat with all her might towards safety. The faster they went, the more the water seemed to lap up and over the side into the cabin. Water was sloshing around the feet of the river dwellers. Nkite's face went pale.

'The shield...' she looked at Bakal, who seemed to have a telepathic understanding as to what Nkite was going to say next. She said nothing but looked at the half dozen heli-fighters that had adopted an attack formation. Nkite looked forward, trying her best to ignore the fact that they were now vulnerable and of all the boats in the river dwellers' fleet, they had now lagged behind so drastically that the other boats were almost all inside the mountain and yet they still seemed so far away.

Without warning, the heli-fighters opened fire on the boat.

'Plan B, now!' screamed Bakal.

Immediately, those among the dwellers who were not holding onto infants or loved ones deliberately rushed the port side of the boat, causing it to capsize instantly.

As the dwellers plunged into the water, the fire raged and spat against the hull of the boat.

Nkite, along with a few others had gone under but was now floating back to the top of the water, gasping for air in the little bubble that the boat had created.

She looked back, choking as the hideous sound of artillery raged against the hull above her.

She looked for Bakal, but could not find her. 'Is everyone okay?' she cried.

There was no reply. So many of her fellow refugees were half drowned, recovering from the shock of the cold water and were trying to hold on as best as they could to what had been their seats but now acted like sturdy beams of salvation above them.

Nkite still looked for Bakal but could not see her. She could not work out whether there were tears or river water dripping down her face.

So many old and young were struggling to hold on, clambering for safety as their eardrums were ripped apart by the fury of the heli-fighters' guns.

'The hull is going to give; we need to swim now! Hold on and swim!' she implored. 'If you can, just do it!' As she barked her order, a shard of the metal hull buckled above her head. 'Now, now!' she hollered.

With all their might, they kicked and kicked until the boat began to move forward. As she gritted her teeth, Nkite realised the horrible possibility that there could now be friends of hers floating helplessly in the water behind. She tried to shake the thought from her head as she and her friends pulled themselves inch by inch, closer to safety.

Nkite took a moment to stop kicking and taking a gulp of air, ducked her head underwater to see their progress. She saw the opening of the cavemouth was closer than she originally thought. Luckily, they were on a straight piece of the river.

'Keep going!' she screamed, hoping that her friends could hear her over the noise of the heli-fighters. 'We're almost there!'

With all the strength left in them, the dwellers kicked and kicked, sometimes hitting each other in their effort to reach the cave but nobody was giving up. Not one of them was giving in.

As more fire ruptured the hull above them and one refugee was sent sprawling by something that had struck him, Nkite swept him up in one arm and grimaced as the current of the river pushed them along.

With one final effort, the boat passed through the cave opening but the heli-fighters continued their assault, sending waves of artillery fire into the cave mouth opening and causing the rock formation that had allowed the boat's safe passage to close in a massive explosion of dust and rubble. Once the sound died down, Nkite knew they had made it. She sighed loudly whilst others among her whooped and cheered and some just sobbed.

'They made it!' came a cry from outside the boat.

'Quick, let's get this thing off them,' came another. Nkite could hear the sound of people jumping into the water. She held on tight to the wounded man whilst she let go of the bench above her head.

'It's okay, we're safe,' she smiled at him as she tried to keep both of them afloat. Her smile then faded as she saw the vacant, unblinking eyes of a man she had not known well but did know had a family elsewhere on this boat.

She tried to shake him back into life gently at first but then rigorously but it was too late. As the boat was lifted off them, and many were picked up and taken to one of the banks on either side of the river, Nkite held onto him tight as she drifted to dry land. A couple of dwellers tried to pick her up when she got there and she asked them to be gentle with the dead man.

Soaking wet, she pulled herself up without the help offered and looked through the gloom in the cave. Although it was dark, there must have been light coming through as she could make out figures and people all around.

They had made it. The river dwellers were saved.

'Are we all here?' she said to nobody in particular, the cold water dripping off her making a wet puddle in the rocks below her.

'We are missing a few from the last boat,' came a familiar voice. Nkite looked up and saw the crooked figure of Gron. 'All the children were saved. You saved them.'

Nkite ignored Gron's final three words. 'And Bakal?'

Gron shook his head.

Nkite's face fell. 'It's my fault. The shielding unit...it's all my fault.'

Gron used what little strength he had left to sit down beside her. He put a reassuring hand on her shoulder.

'Nothing is your fault, don't ever think that for one second Nkite.'

'What do we do now?' asked a woman who was clutching a crying baby to her chest.

Nkite quickly gathered her thoughts and got up, helping Gron do the same.

'We rest for a while. Find your loved ones and rest. We'll be safe in here for now.'

'But what about the heli-fighters?' asked one voice in the dark. 'There's a river running through this mountain, they will know to check the other side, we have to keep moving!'

Nkite frowned. 'There are dozens of rivers running through the mountain, it'll take the Crimson Empire a while to work out which one we are in so we rest and then soon we shall make our way to the base.'

The man paused for a moment and then answered back, frustration naked in his tone. 'I'm not listening to you, Nkite. Your shields we supposed to protect us.'

'And they did,' Gron said leaping to her defence.

'Tell that to my brother,' came the response.

'I am so sorry, but we are all casualties of war. We must stick together,' came another voice.

'Very poetic,' came another dissenting voice.

'People please!' pleaded Gron.

Arguments broke out among some of the dwellers whilst others did their best to shut them down.

'Nkite, please?' asked Gron.

The girl gave a withering look to her old friend and stood up.

'Listen!' she cried, stopping the majority of the heated exchanges immediately. 'You can fight amongst yourselves all you like but it isn't going to help us. If you don't want to listen to me, fine. If you don't want to follow the plan, the one we all voted on if we were ever attacked, also fine. If you want to blame me for anyone's death and it makes you feel better be my guest. But the one thing we cannot do is despair. We are alive and when we reach the heart of the mountain, we can send an SOS to the Sapphire Regime and they will help us. Now if you do not agree, and you think that allying yourself to me for any longer is intolerable then go, find your way. I won't worry about you. You'll be doing me a favour, but for now, we have all just lost our homes and some of us have lost loved ones in the process. We need time to gather and if you don't want to, go find the other end of this river and leave.'

The dwellers were silent. The grieving man who had started the argument was the first to break the awkwardness.

'I don't need you to excuse me, I go on my own accord...anyone else?' a few people walked over to be with him. Nkite could hear their feet shuffle over the rocks.

'Good luck then,' she called out and with that, she heard their footsteps grow further and further away.

Gron sighed. 'Right, does anybody need medical attention?'

A mumble replaced the silence.

Nkite left him to it and walked off to be by herself as she heard her old friend ask for children to be seen first. She retired into a little cave mouth on her own and collapsed on her haunches. Hugging her knees tightly she let her shoulders drop and she descended into an uncontrollable sob. Gron looked back, his heart full of sadness. Now that Bakal was gone, he knew that people would look to Nkite for leadership. Knowing the toll that the war was beginning to have on her, he worried for Nkite and as he set about his work with others who were kind enough to volunteer to help, Nkite just let the pain flow out of her.

X

Now that the Venus II looked like it had been battered and damaged by battle, it sailed closer to the mainframe without raising as much fanfare as it usually would. In the years they had been travelling together the Venus II and its occupants had become infamous across the galaxy. There was notoriety that came with Captain Random and his friends being in the area sometimes to such an extent that whole countries, nay, even planets had been named after them. In fact, one such planet that they had saved from extinction when they helped redirect a flaming meteorite away from it was so grateful it even renamed itself. So now, when the peoples of the universe attend carefully to their A-Z of the Fadrigo cluster in the Margalonian system, they would have to scratch out the planet named Hardrafamagorian and simply replace it with the name, Jake, instead.

Even so, just to be on the safe side, the crew of the Venus II were still cloaked as they sailed closer to the rendezvous point. Inside the cockpit, Random and Skateboard were at their usual pilot and co-pilot seats whilst Anji and Jake stood behind them.

'I've been looking down on that planet for a while now and I keep little flashes,' said Anji. 'What's causing it? Bad weather?'

'Fighting,' came Random's one-worded response.

'It's so bad that you can see the battle from space?' asked Jake.

'It's so bad there is a security mainframe defending the rest of the galaxy from what's going on down there,' replied Random.

Jake gulped. 'Great.' He looked down at himself. His body still had not fought off the effects of the water from the fountain of youth. Inside he was growing more and more worried that he would not recover in time to be of any use to his friends in what lay head. Yet instead of worrying them, he decided to keep it to himself for the time being.

'Incoming transmission, sir,' said Skateboard.

'Punching it through,' replied Random, who leaned forward to flick a switch on the dashboard.

The image of a green-scaled reptile flashed onto the viewscreen. 'Captain Random, I am Commander Serridian of the Rodasian Security Mainframe.'

'Commander, good to meet you, I trust that our mutual acquaintance has been in contact?' replied Random. Anji watched as Random conversed

with such natural flourish and style that she often wondered why he didn't always talk like this.

In moments where he had been required to be diplomatic, or was meeting a new life form for the first time, Random would switch on the charm and really surprise her with his eloquence. Pity he couldn't just be himself, she thought.

'I have, Captain, yes but I'm afraid the plan has changed.'

Random's face sank. 'Well, not with us, schmuck!'

Anji raised her eyebrows. So much for the eloquent tone.

'I'm afraid that there is the possibility that our message was intercepted by someone.'

'What, someone managed to hack you?' asked Jake. 'Considering you're a security mainframe that's pretty rubbish.'

'Skateboard can you verify this?' asked Random.

'I'm afraid that due to confidentiality I am unable to allow your AI robot access to our systems. I'm sorry, Captain.'

Random was dumbfounded. It had taken him a lot of effort to come back to Rodas. It was a place that deep down in his heart he knew he had to save but wanted to be further away from it than anything else in the universe.

He thought back to the Oracle of Fate, the strange being who had set him on the path back to his destiny and cursed her. 'I bet you're having a right laugh, Oracle,' he said below his breath, knowing that he was probably being watched by her at this very moment.

'This does not mean that I cannot assist in your landing on the planet, Captain, I merely cannot meet with you in person, nor can you come here.'

'What can you do then?' asked Anji.

'I can give you a code. Once you have loaded it into your ship's computer, it will mean that your ship will be impervious to the effects of the mainframe,' replied Commander Serridian.

'Meaning?' asked Jake.

'We can come and go as we please, sir,' Skateboard answered. 'But that's potentially very dangerous, isn't it Commander?'

'Yes,' said Serridian, who had suddenly adopted an even more serious tone. 'Once you land on Rodas your ship could be picked up by the Crimson Empire of Sapphire Regime. Even under cloaking you might be captured. For centuries the mainframe has contained the horror of the atrocities on Rodas.

If the Venus II falls into the wrong hands – any hands apart from your own – the code can be replicated and the war will spread throughout the galaxy.

I am risking not only my command but my life in giving you this message...potentially the future and safety of everyone in this star system, Ursa-17, and beyond.'

'So how are you going to give it to us if you say that your messages are being compromised?' asked Random. Skateboard's diodes whirred as he searched for an answer.

'I think I may have the answer, sir. Commander, you can send the information to me. If ship-to-ship communication is being compromised then sending it directly to me should be safe. My firewalls are tighter than a Space Seal freighter hull.'

Commander Serridian nodded. 'That is a wise suggestion but I am currently scrambling this message through my personal computer so I can always tell you the code now.'

'If it's all the same, sir, I trust my method more. Would you care to oblige?'

The Commander nodded then out of shot he began to tap away at something. 'Bagari tells me that you are the ones who can put a stop to all of this once and for all. I don't doubt her, this isn't the first time that I have placed my life and career in her hands. I hope she is right.'

'She is,' replied Anji.

'You should see our track record,' said Jake.

'I know...I come from the planet...Jake,' the Commander hesitated before finding his planet's new name. 'Call me old fashioned but I preferred what it was called before. No offence.'

'Hold on, there's a planet named after me?' chirped Jake.

'Not now, Jake,' said Random. 'Skateboard?'

'I am processing the code now sir,' said the AI robot, who then used his connection with the Venus II to process the code.

'Protect the code with your lives,' warned Commander Serridian.

'We will, thanks Commander,' said Random. 'Give our regards to the Admiral when you see her next. Oh, and tell her that if she suggests staging a planned trashing of my ship again for no good reason it's coming out of her wallet, not mine!'

Serridian smirked. 'Good luck, Captain.'

The viewscreen went blank.

'Right, are we ready?' asked Skateboard.

'Nope,' said Random.

'Nah-ah,' replied Anji.

'A whole planet, named after me!' said the still-startled Jake.

'But that's never stopped us before,' said Random. 'Take us in somewhere quiet Skateboard, please. We don't want to be captured instantly again.'

'Again, sir?'

'We always seem to be captured as soon as we land anywhere, it's the best way to find out what's going on!' said Anji.

'Not this time. We don't know what we might come up against when we get there. It's best to stay undercover for as long as we can on Rodas,' Random looked deadly serious.

'Understood, we'll go and get ready, come on Captain Planet, let's go find those laser cutters we use as guns all the time,' said Anji as she picked Jake up off the floor and led him out of the cockpit.

'I've found a suitable landing site, sir. Not much activity but not far away from any Rodasians' either,' said Skateboard.

'Wait, Skateboard,' Random paused for a moment. 'How do you feel about going home? Honestly?'

'I cannot lie, sir.'

Random smiled. 'I asked as I know I'll get a straight answer from you. I mean we are home and yet...I can't think of anywhere else I'd rather be further from.'

'I feel exactly the same, sir.'

Random bit his lip. 'I can't help but feel like we've made a bad decision coming back.'

'Not a bad decision, sir, only the right one,' said Skateboard.

Random pondered for a second. Skateboard was right. He is always right. There were many innocent people they were about to try and save. 'This whole planet needs salvation. Are we really the ones to deliver it?'

'Aren't we always?' Skateboard hoped that his words would fire his friend up.

Random smiled. 'Okay, but before we go, I think you and I had better have a Plan B...'

Random imparted his plan to his oldest friend. The AI robot poured over every detail, taking in every piece of information that he was given and storing them as tightly as he would the code the Commander had given him. However, it was the first part of the plan that made him wary.

'You're sure about that?' asked Skateboard.

'You and the Venus need to be kept safe and out of the picture, you heard what the Commander said.'

'But, Anji and Jake and you... you'll be alone down there.'

'Not for long, not if you follow the plan.'

Skateboard's diodes sighed. 'It'll take time.'

'Then as soon as we are down on the planet's surface you start with the plan.'

'But I thought it was Plan B, sir?'

Random sighed. 'It was but I realised when Serridian was telling us about the code that this probably would be safer for everyone.'

'Except you three. Are you sure that you want to risk their lives too?' asked Skateboard.

'Absolutely not, but I know they won't take no for an answer, as do you,' replied Random.

'Do we tell them the plan?' asked Skateboard.

'No, keep it private for now. I'll tell them if I need to when we are on Rodas,' said Random. 'Do we have a deal?'

Skateboard sighed. 'Reluctantly, sir.'

'Good, well then, Skateboard. What are we waiting for?'

Random picked up his steering column and the Venus lurched in space, spinning in a graceful spiral before settling on the coordinates set by Skateboard.

'Next stop,' said Random. 'Rodas.'

XI

The dead, cold fingertips of Kalor Maloso passed over the giant viewer map. He was waiting impatiently for news on the bombings that his army was carrying out. He tapped the bony, fleshless digits on the map and then finally thumbed it with all his might, sending a tiny fleck of glass somersaulting through the air.

He strode over to his communication terminal, still as strong as ever but feeling slightly weaker from his latest ordeal. 'Commander, report!'

'The enemy troops are continuing to retreat. We have levelled many pillars of the old capital,' came a trembling voice through the speaker.'

'Are there many survivors?' asked Maloso.

The Commander hesitated. 'I have seen reports that some from a river-dwelling managed to escape inside Mount Dschali. The heli-fighter unit leader told me that they opened fire on refugees and sealed them in.'

'Send troops inside the mountain to flush them out, Commander. There can be no survivors this time.'

'As you wish, my Lord.'

'Oh, and Commander?'

'Yes, my Lord?'

'Have the unit leader and his team killed for their incompetence.'

The Commander was silent for a few moments. 'As you wish.'

The communications link clicked off and Kalor Maloso was alone in the silent darkness again. He walked over to his main view window and basked in the glory of his work below him. The fire that raged kept him alive and perked up his spirit. 'The time is so nearly upon us,' he said to himself.

Suddenly, he noticed the security mainframe shimmer in the distance. Maloso frowned. He picked up a pair of binoculars that sat close by and fixed them in that direction. There was nothing that his old eyes could see other than more fighting and far-off explosions, so nothing other than the norm.

He replaced the binoculars and turned from the window and made for his chair.

He placed his hand on his chin and was lost in a sea of thought.

XII

A barren, desolate wilderness greeted the eyes of the travellers as their spaceship settled down on the sand dunes of the decimated world. The landing gear let out a whine - groaning under the stress and strain of hundreds of tons worth of titanium and seda metal that crunched the legs of the Venus II further into the ground like a mallet hitting a tent peg into place.

Its battle-worn colours and bleak, dense appearance blended in well with its surroundings on this occasion but given any other landscape and it would have attracted all manner of attention had the cloaking device not been firmly switched on.

In fact, given the huge exterior, that's what the Venus II normally did. But on this occasion, there was no fanfare. As the dust snaked and roared around the bottom of the ship, it began to settle on the stabilising pads that the Venus II stood on.

The only sound that could be heard now was the faint vibration of the inner door mechanism whirring away. All of a sudden, there was a mighty hiss from the hydraulics and the door began to slowly drop down from the belly of the ship.

Footsteps could also be heard clattering down the metal gangway.

Well, if there was anybody around to hear it, but the spot they had picked to land upon was indeed as Skateboard had assured, deserted.

The shadows of three bodies illuminated the gangway – exposed by the bright, white lights from inside the spaceship. The first figure, Random's, took a deep breath as he stood at the front of the pack. 'Let's go,' he said and made his way heavily down the bottom of the ramp.

He bent down and touched the sand with his gloved fingers, feeling the coarse grains fall through the gaps between his digits. Sniffing, he shot a look back to his two companions. Jake stood on the ramp scratching his blonde hair, whilst observing the calm that surrounded them all.

Anji played nervously with her bag that swung irritatingly on her right shoulder. After several seconds of awkward silence, she decided to speak.

'So, we made it then?'

The first person looked away, knowing the answer but not wanting to dignify his friend with a response.

'Yes,' he eventually croaked. 'Yes, we made it.'

'It's not what I expected,' cried the blonde-haired boy.

He looked up at the strange fluorescent moon.

Even though the moon was as bright as anything he had ever seen, the horizon still looked as dark as a harsh winter night back on Earth.

'I was expecting huge towers high in the sky and flying cars. What happened here?'

'The war to end all wars,' exclaimed the leader of the party as he straightened his legs and stood up. He could make out a faint outline of the once, great citadel in the far distance. 'Yet, it still rages. For centuries my home planet has been a battlefield. Millions upon millions have died and it was my responsibility to stop the fighting.'

Anji tore forward and put a reassuring hand on the shoulder of her companion.

'None of this is your fault, Random!' she insisted.

Random turned towards her and gave a glimmer of a smile from his dour expression. For all of the adventures both he and these two-earth people had experienced, all the fun and laughs and the ever so slightly dangerous places they had visited in the quest to get back to this world, he knew he had made a terrible decision bringing them here.

'Anji, you will never know what suffering I have caused. It's time I made up for it.'

'How?' Jake asked Random.

'By making sure that this is the final day. I have to put it right, Jake. It is my destiny.'

Jake was worried. He had never seen Random so serious, so morose and so determined before.

Was this really the same boy that had whooped and cheered his way down a thousand-foot rainbow on the planet Spectronia? Or the same spiky-haired, funny costumed-wearing guy who had used a discarded feather to tickle his way out of the prison tombs of Catacombe 62? Gulping hard, he took Anji's hands and followed his friend towards the unfriendly outline of what looked like a city.

Together, these three had been through so much.

It had been their choice to leave their planet behind and join this funny-looking boy who fell from the stars and since they didn't have a home to go back to anyway, it didn't matter to them if they ever made it back.

But at the same time, both Jake and Anji didn't want to get hurt. So far, they had endured many bumps and bruises on the planet hop back to Random's home world, but this time, there was a full-scale war staring them in the face. And why had Random allowed himself to be talked into bringing them into the hornet's nest?

If I had a dad, he'd never have let me come, Jake thought to himself as he trawled along the sand, which had entered a hole in his favourite pair of trainers and was causing more than a little irritation to his left foot.

A pang of guilt about Anji and Jake's accompanying him to Rodas sparked in his chest. He remembered what Skateboard had said to him in the cockpit earlier, about endangering his friend's lives.

'Remember way back when? Back when we first met, I had no intention of letting you come with me,' Random said as he walked, the chilling night air carrying his sentence back into the direction of his two friends. 'I just wanted to forget about my responsibilities, run away and never come back here. But you two, you two showed me how to be a better person and for that I thank you, but after we assess the situation and analyse what our next move should be I am taking you back to the Venus and locking the door. Do you understand?'

Jake and Anji nodded as they clambered through the soft sand.

'And what if you don't come back?' Anji's lips were beginning to feel sore as the wind continued to blow the sand in her face.

'Then Skateboard will pilot the ship to wherever you want and you can live your lives out however and wherever you like.'

'But you are coming back, aren't you?' Jake craned his neck to see if he could make out Random's face in the gloom.

Random felt terrible. Although he had the physiognomy of a boy just a couple of years older than his counterparts, well, when Jake recovered from his accident, he was in fact a far more advanced being than they were.

He was not as susceptible to illness and disease as humans were but right now, he had a throbbing feeling in his chest that he had never felt before. The most human of emotions.

Fear.

The trio jumped as Random's wrist communicator crackled into life. Over the wind, he could just make out a metallic voice.

'Sir, I must warn you that my sensors have picked up hostile life forms in your vicinity. It would be wise to come back to the ship as soon as possible.'

Random strained to be heard as he continued to walk.

'How many of them?'

Fifteen, Sir. They appear to be on land hawkers, roughly 80 clicks away.'

'Okay, no problem. We are getting close to the edge of the citadel now. I will report back to you when we get there. Await my instruction please Skateboard,' Random ordered before clicking a switch on his communicator and returning to the task in hand.

Random sighed for so long it was heard by future generations. 'Come on, we are nearly there.'

The trio got down on their hands and knees as they negotiated the slight curve on the ground that licked up into the sky. 'Stupid bag!' Anji grunted as she swiped it over her shoulder, almost knocking Jake out in the process.

After a few minutes of crawling in the dirt, they heard something they had not heard before.

The wind had died down and all they could hear now was the sound of explosions, screams of pain and terror and the very occasional whizz of hyper jet fighters and laser fire.

Random's heart was thumping so loud that he thought he could hear it over the sound of destruction.

'Right, that's it. Back to the Venus now, both of you!'

'We are not going anywhere,' Anji protested. 'We are staying by your side and that is final.'

'What? Are you mad!' Jake shouted. 'Can you not hear that down there!? Let's go while we still have the chance!'

'I'm staying.'

'Oh yeah? Well, I'm going!'

The boys' protests were interrupted by an explosion so loud it made the ground tremor for almost a minute.

'...On second thoughts, I'd better protect you, Anji!' Jake declared, despite cowering and holding onto the legs of his friend. She shot him an unimpressed glance.

'Stay low now, we have to get to the edge,' Random implored.

The three youngsters crawled their way closer and closer, the pitch-black landscape was giving away to a blood-red horizon, like a doomed sunrise. Slowly, they pulled themselves up to eye level and saw one of the most indescribable scenes of devastation it had ever been their misfortune to witness.

'Anji...Jake,' Random stuttered. 'This is the citadel of the planet of Rodas. My home...'

XIII

The sheer scale of the conflict took Anji's breath away. She looked on as peculiar, waspish vehicles swarmed what must have once been a magnificent city and rained fire down upon it. She had always understood why Random had no desire to come home. There was so little of it left.

'Right,' he said, shaking her thoughts from her mind, 'What's the plan, Random?'

Random was staring blankly towards the citadel. He remembered it well from the only day he had ever spent on this hell hole but its splendour was now just a rotting husk.

'We have to find the Sapphire Regime,' he replied.

'Who are they?' asked Jake.

'About as close as you can get to the good guys on this planet,' said Random. 'The Crimson Empire are the aggressors. The Oracle told me that it was the Empire whose plans would bring about the destruction of Rodas. We need to find out what they have planned.'

Jake pondered for a second. 'So why don't we just go straight to the Crimson Empire then? Do some spying?'

'Let's just say that we wouldn't fit in,' said Random.

'Story of my life,' Anji retorted. 'But seriously, Jake's got a point.'

'The Crimson Empire are the red-skinned inhabitants of Rodas. The Sapphire Regime are blue. See what I mean?'

'I getcha. So where do you fit in?' asked Jake.

'I don't,' replied Random. He scouted the area for a safe passageway down onto the surface. The sounds of war filled the air and the three friends were having to shout to make themselves heard so he pointed in the direction he wanted them to move instead of continuing to holler.

'What?' said Jake unhelpfully.

'Down there!' said Random as he rolled his eyes.

A screech of sound started to loom close to them. Random peered through the smoke and felt alarmed as the land hawkers that Skateboard had warned them about were now almost on top of them.

'Quick!' he cried as he pulled both his friends down into the mud. Anji screamed as a formation of the unimaginably sharp-looking craft was suddenly on top of them in the blink of an eye.

'Get down there you two and hide, I'll see you in a minute now go!' ordered Random. Anji and Jake didn't argue and began to make their way down the steep decline to the ground surface.

Random pulled his hood up over his face and stood before the fifteen land hawkers that had now stopped in front of him. The horrible-looking things had long, rusty daggers on the end of them and the masked men who piloted them revved their engines to intimidate the hooded figure who stood before them. But Random was far from intimidated.

'Are you with the Sapphire Regime?' asked Random. 'I request to speak with your leader.'

The head land hawker sped towards him full pelt.

'So, that's a no then,' Random said to himself. The rest of the land hawker crew also took off in Random's direction.

Random crouched down and prepared himself for the fight. With breathtaking accuracy, he jumped over the daggers at the right moment and leap high over the head of the lead land hawker and landed on the seat behind him. Before his attacker even had time to register where Random had gone, he found himself flying through the air before landing with a sickening thump against the ground and losing consciousness.

His land hawker, now under Random's control, spun around to face the rest of them.

'Come on then fellas, let's get this over with,' cried Random, who squeezed the right handlebar and sped on towards them, relieved that he had luckily found the right one and he hadn't rather embarrassingly squeezed on the brake instead.

Not far away, Skateboard sat watching the fight on his monitor, completely helpless. Long ago, the biomolecular capabilities of the Venus II had scanned all four of its regular inhabitants and Skateboard could keep an eye on them when they left the ship.

It had sounded unethical when he had told them, but in reality, it was to ensure their health wasn't compromised by the alien atmosphere or that they weren't about to succumb to something which would make them poorly. But in the safety of the cockpit, it was the AI robot who felt ill as he noticed that Random was outnumbered while Jake and Anji were left open to danger.

He was powerless, unable to help, and forbidden to get involved. Plus, he had another mission, one that he and Random had agreed on and one that would take him away from Rodas for some time. He had to leave soon otherwise time would really be his enemy, let alone the Crimson Empire. With a heavy heart, he decided he would have to tear himself away from the danger and do what he had been told. Sighing loudly, he set the controls of the Venus II to a new destination, where he wouldn't be able to step in and help his friends or keep them from danger.

The Venus II's landing gear groaned as its engines roared and sent it flying upwards into the air. Still cloaked and invisible, Skateboard knew even if he had wanted to stay that the ship couldn't. If its security mainframe dodging code was ever found out, the consequences could be catastrophic. Instead, he consulted the navigation computer and inputted coordinates. He took one last look out of the viewscreen and saw down below the tiny figure of Random, who appeared to be making light work of the fight that he was currently winning. As the smoke and smog of destruction began to bleed into the dark starry space and the mainframe also honed into view, Skateboard implemented the code again and the Venus II tore away from Rodas and into the vacuum of space once more.

The computer started to bleep and Skateboard, his mind still on the planet far below, was brought sharply back into focus on the mission in hand. He scanned the readings and followed the navigation computer's instructions. With some minor adjustments to the ship's speed output, he sent a wireless command to the computer and threw the Venus II into hyperdrive and in doing so, brought himself closer to his first intended destination.

Spectronia.

XIV

'Don't look back, Jake just, keep moving!' screamed Anji as she slid and stumbled her way down the muddy embankment to the ground. She had spotted Jake lagging behind, clearly more concerned about how Random was getting on. She'd wanted to stay behind to help but she knew better than to become embroiled in a physical fight when Random was more than capable of handling them himself.

'Sorry, Anj, I think he's winning anyway,' said Jake.

'I can't believe what we're seeing here,' said Anji. 'It's awful. How can anyone live like this?' she looked around her as they continued their descent. 'The sky seems to be on fire. I can't tell where it begins and where it ends.'

'Terrible, isn't it?' said Jake. 'By the way, I noticed the calendar on your wall earlier. Do you know what today is back on Earth?'

'Really Jake? While we are in a war zone trying not to fall down a slippery bank you want to discuss my calendar?'

'Yeah, I want to take your mind off it all,' shouted Jake over a nearby explosion which nearly knocked the two teenagers off their balance.

When she had brought it with her on their latest visit back from their home world, it had bemused Jake. Then he began to understand that a link back home, no matter how tenuous, was perfectly understandable, especially after the years they had been out having adventures in the big wide cosmos.

'Go on then, enlighten me,' she gave in. It was sweet of Jake to want to take her mind off their predicament she had thought. It would be rude of her not to humour him.

'July 13th. We'd be graduating from school around now.'

Anji stopped in her tracks, her footing losing a little bit of traction in the process. 'Really?'

'You'd circled the date. Had you been back to our school?'

Anji sighed. 'What was left of it.' She remembered the day that it had burnt to the ground and the part that she and Jake had its demise.

Then she remembered Jemima Wright, the school bully and the surprising reunion she had unexpectedly had with her. She shook the thought of it all from her mind, wanting to forget again. 'We'd have finished our exams now.'

'And had our prom. Remember our promise, Anj?' Jake said nervously.

Back on Earth, just before their lives had

changed forever, the pair had made a promise to one another that they would attend prom together if they were still single when the time arose. It had been a promise that had got them through some tough times over the years, especially on the rainbow planet Spectronia where Jake had been buried alive by a crazed archaeologist and Anji had managed to help him keep it together while he awaited rescue over a communication line.

'I mean, I know I have the body of a child right now but I had never forgotten-' he continued.

'Jake, I don't mean to sound mean or anything but this doesn't feel like the time or the place that we should be talking about this.' Anji interrupted.

Jake sighed. She had a point, especially as all hell was raining down around them. Here they were, surrounded by all manner of death and destruction and he was asking her to remember that they had promised each other a date! He started to shirk. Maybe she had forgotten? Maybe her feelings had changed? Maybe it was because the fountain of youth had robbed him momentarily of his strapping good looks and to her, he looked like a toddler. Either way, he tried not to take it too personally and fell silent again.

'I mean, we can always talk about it lat-'

Jake was unable to finish his sentence because just at that moment his balance gave way and he found himself slip-sliding into the filthy mud. As he cursed and continued to tumble, his momentum also took Anji down with him and the pair began to hurtle towards the harsh-looking ground. Before long they came to a grateful stop at the foot of the embankment in a tangle of limbs and swear words.

'For goodness' sake, Jake! You muppet!' said Anji as she tried to pick herself up.

Her hair and clothes were caked in thick sludgy mud and she could feel her plait being weighed down by the filth she and her clumsy friend had just rolled around in.

'It's not my fault!' spat Jake, clearly annoyed. He hated it when Anji blamed him for things. Granted it had been him who had caused this incident but had she taken the entire weight of him when they fell on the hard floor? Had she grazed the palms on her hands trying to stop her before the slippery mud became hard gravel? Highly unlikely on both accounts since he'd done his best to stop her from coming to any harm by trying to keep his body under hers so that he took the brunt. 'Okay, it is but I didn't mean it.'

'You never do!' said Anji as she picked herself up.

'That bank was slippery. What was I supposed to do, fly down?'

'In a way we did!' said Anji.

'Well at least we're safe,' said Jake, unaware that his words were famous and if they weren't too careful, last.

A bright light shone on their faces. They both strained their eyes through the lights but all they could see were the outlines of a number of what looked like soldiers pointing guns at them.

Anji and Jake involuntarily put their hands up.

'You and your big mouth,' said Anji.

*

High above them, Random has just knocked the fifteenth member of the land hawker gang unconscious.

He hadn't needed to end on such a flourish as to triple somersault in mid-air whilst performing a roundhouse kick into the face of two of his attackers simultaneously but as he glided to the floor with the grace of a ballerina, it had certainly made him feel better.

He looked around him.

All of the dangerously sharp bikes had crashed into the dirt. Some were even on fire and the gang were all lying in a state of unconsciousness.

As Random dusted his hands, admiring his work, he wanted to say something cool as the cherry on the cake. Then, breathing through the dusty foggy air, he noticed out of the corner of his eye that down at the bottom of the precipice, his friends were being held at gunpoint and it would be rather a waste of time if he did. Especially as he didn't have anything particularly cool to say.

At the speed of light, he tore down the embankment, missing the trail of slippery mud that had entrapped his friends and hurled himself in front of a rather startled Anji and Jake.

'Woah. Woah, before you kill my friends there's something vitally important that you should know,' he cried, throwing his hands above his head just like the other two.

Through the legion of soldiers that stood before them, one moved out of the straight line.

'You. Come closer,' they implored, a strong booming voice emitting through. Random did as he was told. Although he was more than capable of taking this lot down much in the same vein as he had the land hawker gang, it wasn't in his – or his best friends – interests for him to do so. For now, he was at the mercy of these mysterious people.

The soldier took their left hand off the barrel of their laser rifle and pressed a button on the side of their helmet. His visor retracted neatly into the roof of his helmet and continued to recede backwards until it was like he hadn't been wearing a helmet at all.

Random peered through the gloom at the soldier's features. The man's hair was thick and dark and slicked back but it was his face that held his more prominent features. His chiselled jaw and long straight nose were all that remained of what had possibly once been a fairly handsome face. Everything else spoke volumes of the ravages of war that this stranger had witnessed. The scars, overlaying and protruding each other made a cobweb of flesh that had grown back in all the wrong places. But crucially, for Random at least, it was the pigmentation of his skin that would prove the difference between friend and foe.

Luckily for them, the stranger's face was blue.

'You're face it's-' the soldier gulped.

'Purple,' replied Random.

'It can't be,' said the soldier in hushed tones.

The soldiers all stood blankly in identical pure black outfits and began to shift uneasily. Their helmets had reminded Anji and Jake of the same one motorcyclists wore back on Earth, only much cooler to look at and just as sleek and dark as the rest of their outfits. Their guns were still trained on the trio but their aim was beginning to waver.

'But you're a fairy tale, a myth,' said the soldier.

'Some fairy tales are true,' said Random.

The soldier shook his head and snapped back at his staff. 'Keep your eyes on them.' He looked back at Random and the other two. All three looked nothing like he had ever seen. A white boy, a dark-skinned girl and a purple boy. None of which looked as though they belonged on Rodas and yet in one case he knew that one did.

'Tell me quickly,' he barked. 'You said that there is something important that we should know.'

'Yes,' said Random. 'We make much better hostages than we do corpses.'

The soldier turned back to his battalion. 'We're taking them with us, I want three soldiers on each of them at all times, do you understand?'

'Where are you taking us?' asked Anji, suddenly able to shake the mild terror she was experiencing from her mind.

'Underground. We can't let you out of our sight,' said the soldier.

'Takten, the mission cannot deviate,' said one anonymous soldier to the scar-faced man.

'I know, that's why we are taking them with us,' he replied.

'They could slow us down. Distract us even from the rescue,' stressed the soldier.

'Sorry, Mr Takten, is it? Did you say rescue?' enquired Random.

'I am not at liberty to discuss our concerns with you. Yes, Djanga. They must come with us,' said Takten, 'Now quick, we must get inside the tunnels.'

The soldier, whose name Random, Anji and Jake now knew was Djanga took one look at them and then hurried over to them. 'You heard him, get moving.'

'Where?' asked Jake. 'And can we take our arms down now?'

'You heard the man now move forward,' said Djanga, who failed to answer the second part, much to the annoyance of the already harangued Jake and Anji.

The soldiers surrounded the three travellers who began to march quickly towards a nearby mountainside roughly two hundred yards away from the mud slip. As the bombs and explosions continued to rain around them, Jake risked the wrath of the soldiers by putting the palms of his hands over his ears to protect himself. Despite years of listening to all kinds of music as loud as technically possible, he was hoping to protect what little he had of his hearing left.

Before long they reached the mountain side and Takten produced what looked like a magic wand, only it was as thick as a broom handle and

pressed a button on it. A door suddenly shimmered into existence in the rocks.

'A secret tunnel, nice!' gasped Anji.

'In here, quick!' cried Takten and before they knew it, Random and his friends had been pushed through the door and suddenly they were in a brightly lit corridor inside the mountain.

Takten counted his soldiers through and then produced the wand again and as the door shimmered away again shutting the harsh realities of war outside, he pushed his way to the front of the pack.

'Djanga, how far to the group's location?'

Djanga peered at a monitor on the back of his wrist. 'We're six hundred metres away.'

'Better get moving then. Come on.'

'Can somebody please tell us what the zark is going on? We might be your prisoners but you could do us the common decency to tell us where we are going?' Random was clearly a little ticked off. Jake on the other hand was just happy to be safe.

'I can't tell you anything,' said Takten. 'Now come on.'

'Takten. I am here of my own free will. All those stories I'm sure that you have heard of me, they are all true. If I had wanted to apprehend you, I would have done by now, believe me. I'm not the enemy of the Sapphire Regime. I want to help you.

I know how the war is going and I don't like the look of the future on Rodas anymore than you do. Now if you let me and my friend's help then we will be more than happy to, but we won't be herded like cattle by you or by anybody.'

Takten took no time to reach for his laser rifle, but Random was one step ahead and had already placed his hand upon it firmly. His soldiers all turned their weapons on Random, who was staring intently into Takten's stoic eyes. Anji's heart jumped up into her mouth whilst Jake let out a rather embarrassing yelp of surprise.

Takten tried to counter Random's strength by pushing against his hand but it was to no avail.

'How dare you make an example of me in front of my men.'

'I'm sorry but I have to know where you are taking us.'

'Why, are you scared?' Takten's words felt like barbed wire to Random.

'Of course not,' he replied.

'Are you sure? You don't know what people think of you here, do you?'

'I can imagine,' said Random.

'No, I don't think you do. But I'm telling you now your reputation will be further tarnished if you don't let us complete our mission.'

'And what's that then?'

'We have people trapped inside this mountain who if we don't reach them soon will be slaughtered by members of the Crimson Empire. We already think of you as a coward so how do you think their families will feel when I tell them that you stopped us from doing our duty in saving them?' despite Random's physical advantage it was Takten who truly held the upper hand.

'That's all I wanted to know,' said Random.

'Come on mate,' said Jake. 'Please, we've only just arrived. Let's not get killed already, eh?'

Random stared into Takten's eyes. 'What better way to prove you wrong than to help?'

Takten laughed. 'You'll have to do more than that to redeem yourself, Random.' He spat Random's name out in a volley of disdain.

Random snapped his hand back and released Takten who with dignity straightened himself up. 'At ease men, save your ammunition for the red faces. We don't want it wasted on him. Now come on!'

They made it down the corridor, leaving Random, Anji and Jake no time to collect their thoughts.

'I take it they want us to help then?' asked Anji.

'I gathered that too,' said Random as they followed hurriedly.

'So, from that frank exchange that you're not too popular on this planet?' said Jake trying to break the tension.

'That's mildly put,' said Random. 'Now come on, we've got people to save.'

XV

Nkite had known that there would be more trouble the moment she heard a communicator buzzing through the crowd of recuperating river dwellers. She had got up from her position sitting on the rock and helping Gron tend to a little girl's head wound and made her way through the crowd of people all huddled in the narrow corridor in the mountain.

'Let me through please,' she demanded, obtaining a few curt looks from the people she barged past before reaching the person with the communicator. It was a young man, whose blue skin was pale and clammy. He shot a look of panic at Nkite, who instantly hurled her frame against him and after pulling the startled man up against the wall, clasped a hand around his throat.

'Spying on us are you!' she spat.

The river dwellers were all regarding Nkite with watching eyes. 'Nkite, let him go,' said one man, who tried to come between them and was rather surprised at the struggle to wrestle Nkite's claw away. 'Nkite leave it, you don't understand,' he said as the man Nkite was attacking was finally detached from her vice-like grip and fell back.

He coughed vigorously, his communicator still buzzing for attention.

Nkite held both he and the man who had stopped her in condemnation. 'He's a spy, he's led them to us!'

'I have not!' coughed the attacked man. 'Bakal...she...'

'She had friends inside the Sapphire Regime,' said the other man, who took over from his friend who was clearly struggling to find his breath again. 'She tasked us with communicators to alert the Regime when we are in trouble and things got worse.'

Nkite's breathing steadied. She bought the story. Bakal was indeed well connected still to the army to so why wouldn't she have agents along the riverfront in the chance that they were ever in danger? 'So why wasn't I informed?' she said.

'You're a loose cannon,' said the man hoarsely, still rubbing his throat. 'Bakal didn't trust you.'

'She trusted me enough to take over if she was killed!' screamed Nkite. 'She trusted me to keep going back into the war. What did you guys do, huh? You ran away like cowards!'

The other man stepped in again and confronted Nkite face-to-face. 'And if we don't start running again soon, we'll all be dead!'

Nkite looked shocked.

'The Crimson Empire. They have found us.'

'How?' demanded Nkite.

'One of our agents was a part of the group that broke off,' said the man who Nkite had attacked. 'He sent a signal before...' he broke off, visibly upset by the reality of what had happened to someone Nkite assumed had been a friend once.

'Look, Nkite, Bakal had her reasons to not tell you, we all have secrets to keep, but now is not the time to debate. We have to move.'

'Where?' asked Nkite, who was feeling her command slipping through her fingers. Bakal had kept her in the dark. She was on the back foot and these guys seemed to know what to do better than her. Some leader she made...

'We have a rendezvous point with Commander Takten, not far from here, but we have to move quickly. He and his battalion are on their way but so are the Crimson-'

A rally of laser fire shot all around them, sending some of the river dwellers falling to the ground, dead on impact. Nkite gazed in horror as she among others ran for what little cover they could find.

'Get back to the opening!' she hollered as more bodies fell around her. As the river dwellers panicked and tried to make their way back to where they had entered the mountain, she felt a sudden burning sensation graze the top of her left shoulder, the pain of which sent her falling to the floor on top of what was now the corpse of a fallen comrade. The fall saved her from certain death and as she remained lying in the dirt with those who had been killed, she witnessed pandemonium all around her.

At the other end of the corridor, there was nothing but a murderous outline of soldiers mercilessly gunning down all who lay in the line of fire.

The Sapphire Regime were too late. The Crimson Empire had already found them...

XVI

Random's ultra-sensitive hearing had picked up on the sound of gunfire long before Takten and his men had.

'They've found them!' he shouted before taking off with immense speed, tearing towards the sound. 'Quickly!' shouted Takten as the battalion shot off behind him. He turned back to Anji and Jake, aware that they were unarmed. 'You two, try and find cover!' Anji and Jake also picked up the pace. They both felt their hearts beating hard against their ribcages, fear beginning to set in with the scenario they found themselves in. In all the years they had fought for good in the universe alongside Random they had never killed. Now they were racing headlong into a bloody gun battle, unarmed, where people were being shot dead where they stood. Anji began to fret.

She couldn't kill. Never. But in the chaos, they found themselves in there was a very real possibility that she and Jake would have to take up arms and fight.

And no matter how much she pushed the thought to the back of her mind, it wouldn't budge. Suddenly, for the very first time, she regretted not listening to Random.

As the cries of people in terror and deafening laser fire filled the corridor, she started to wish they had never come to Rodas at all.

Random burst into the corridor and immediately smashed his fists into the back of two unsuspecting soldier's helmets, cracking the metal-like frames like eggs and sending them sprawling forward into their counterparts, which in turn sent a volley of laser fire into the roof of the rocky corridor. As debris rained down, Random's super speed and all-out aggression sent more crimson soldiers all which ways, and for perhaps the first time in a long time, he was showing them no mercy.

Slowly, the sound of gunfire was replaced by the screams of the Crimson Empire battalion. Nkite, holding her injured shoulder and on the verge of blackout from the pain, opened her eyes and witnessed a figure in the far distance moving with such blistering speed and power, she knew instantly who their saviour was.

Then she began to think she was hallucinating or dead already. As the laser fire ceased, she saw the figure smash the final two standing soldiers together and then witnessed them fall lifelessly to the floor like ragdolls.

As Takten and his men rounded the corner, they saw Random surrounded by dozens of motionless bodies.

The battalion leader pushed his way forward. Random stood there, panting, his face contorted with anger.

'You could let us have some of the fun,' muttered Takten before turning his attention where it was needed most. 'You,' he pointed at his men, 'Search for survivors quick. We've got to get them out of these tunnels fast.'

Anji and Jake rounded the corner. Jake spotted the bodies first and felt instantly nauseous. Anji did her best to blot out the death all around them and they both went over to Random, who was still standing taut, his fists clenched, staring down at what was left of the Crimson Empire soldiers.

'Random? Random, it's okay its-' Anji cautiously put her hand upon Random's arm which seemed to diffuse him immediately.

'Anji,' he whispered. 'I didn't hold back. I couldn't.' He started to look at his battered hands.

Anji gave him a little smile. 'You saved them, that's all that matters.'

'Yeah, and let's face it they deserved it! I'm going to go and help those people down there,' said Jake as he made off towards the river dwellers.

'This is why I ran away. This is why I didn't want you here. Not only for your protection but...I didn't want you to see me like this,' his hands were covered in the debris of battle.

'You're fighting for good. Never forget that,' she said. He gave her a look of immense sadness but before they had time to talk any further, they heard Jake from further down the corridor.

'Hey, this one's still alive!' he shouted. He was horrified by what he had been forced to walk through. This was the first time he had seen so many people dead. They had been lucky on their adventures up until this point.

Most of their do-good actions hadn't involved conflict as bloody as this but now the war was staring him right in the face and he was unable to blink away the nightmare. But amongst the fallen had lay a girl, her shoulder bleeding and she looked in a bad way. Hearing her groan, he knelt down next to her.

'Hey, are you alright?'

Nkite opened her eyes. Through her double vision, she could make out the young, white face and shaggy blonde hair that drooped down over her. She shot Jake a confused look.

'Does it look like it?' she moaned.

'Well now you come to mention it, no, but are you hit anywhere else except your shoulder?'

'That's more like it,' she bluffed, failing to mention the atrocities she had witnessed today had also left her with a broken heart. She struggled to her feet and Jake gingerly helped. 'Woah, easy, take it easy Miss?'

'Nkite. Who are you?'

'I'm Jake.'

As Jake pulled Nkite up to her full height, he noticed Random and Anji standing next to them.

'You're with him,' said Nkite without question.

'Well, yeah.'

'Then I want no part of your help,' she yanked herself away painfully, wincing and stumbling a little as she did so.

'That's no way to say thank you,' said Jake.

It was completely the wrong thing to say. Nkite's eyes welled up. She gritted her teeth and strode right up to Random's face.

'Why would I say thank you to the man who could have put an end to this long ago? You see these bodies all around us?' she gestured to the waste of life at their feet.

'We got here as soon as we could,' said Random in defence, his face burning with shame.

'You should never have left in the first place! Thank you...you should fall down at our feet and beg for our forgiveness never mind ask for thanks!' Pools of tears fell from the corners of Nkite's eyes. All the years of hope had been shattered into a million pieces thanks to the horrors she had endured today.

All of it for nothing. So many of her people were gone and it wasn't the soldiers who has pulled the trigger on them in the corridors or the pilots who had capsized their boat in the river or set fire to their homes that were to blame. They could have been dealt with so many years ago if Random hadn't fled Rodas at the earliest opportunity. Her dreams of peace and prosperity were gone. All that she had now was sorrow.

'My people need me,' she whispered. Saying nothing more she gingerly made her way towards the survivors who were being tended to by Takten's men at the other end of the corridor. For the first time the noise of people crying, screams of pain and the hum of talk filled the bloody air. Anji and Jake stood stunned at Nkite's defiance.

'Well how do you like that?' said an indignant Jake. He began to feel anger bubble to the surface as if Nkite's words had unlocked his perception and the devastation surrounding them had finally gotten to him. 'After all that you just did. I mean honestly. She'd be dead if it wasn't for-'

'Jake, leave it,' interrupted Anji. Random stood there silent, his cheeks wet with remorse.

As the trio walked away towards the throng of river dwellers that were looking shocked and stunned as they recuperated from their ordeal, one of the Crimson Empire soldiers began to stir from amid the pile of his stricken colleagues. His entire body was wracked with a burning agony, not surprising considering minutes earlier it had been hurled at the wall with a force that would break any man over and over. As he slowly regained consciousness, he was also aware that this burning agony was also the fire in which his life was slowly starting to fall away. He had to report back. Although his vision inside the helmet was impaired, he could make out the purple one who had attacked him. He knew exactly who he was. He knew that he had to let his master know that Random was finally back on Rodas.

Suddenly his attention was diverted by the muffled sounds of soldiers talking. Considering how his battalion had been decimated he was fairly certain that the voices were not those of his comrades.

In fact, if any like him were still alive, lying twisted and broken in the pile of corpses with him, he'd wish nothing but death upon them like he was now yearning for himself.

To be captured and tortured would mean no way back to the Crimson Empire, even if they were to recover and escape.

To be incarcerated was a weakness that Kalor Maloso would never tolerate.

But as he listened intently to the words of the Sapphire Regime officers, he was relieved to hear that they had no intention of taking prisoners. No, an instant shot from a blaster rifle to any who were still alive was to be the order.

The injured soldier knew that he had to move quickly and quickly he did. It took all of his energy to reach for the distress signal on his wrist and activate it. That'd let the command know that they had perished and that for the Crimson Empire, their worst enemy was here and ready to annihilate them. With a little smile, he winced as a bolt of laser fire shot right through his head and he died with a smile on his face, the executor failing to realise what he had just done.

*

As Kalor Maloso was preparing himself in the chamber the distress signal reached him. An intermittent beeping rang around his dark room before a voice fizzed over his speaker system.

'My Lord, I-'

'Save your breath, Colonel, I am well aware of the situation,' Maloso butted in. 'In fact, I have the answer to all our problems. Take a battalion to the mountainside and bring Random here.'

The Colonel seemed hesitant. 'He may not come willingly.'

'I believe he will,' said Maloso.

'As you wish, sir,' said the Colonel before the sound of both his voice and the distress signal faded away into the darkness.

Maloso looked down at the chamber he was reclining in, patting it graciously. 'For so long you have sustained me now...it's time to sustain Rodas...'

He heard a raucous thumping from below his chamber.

He smiled.

From time to time, the things he had long trapped down there tended to do that.

Whether they were hungry or just disgruntled at their situation, he tended to give the abominations what they wanted so they would be silent and still for a long time.

For so long he hid the unmentionables in the dark beneath his feet.

Now, they appeared to be stirring, almost like they knew what he was about to do.

Maloso pressed a button on the side of the chamber and the door hissed slowly shut, a hot vapour swirling all around him.

He input the command into the computer and took a deep breath as a multitude of sharp-looking needles and horrific spiky implements snaked menacingly out of the top of the chamber and shot deep within his body.

He tried not to scream but the operation that the machine was carrying out on him was excruciating and beneath the swirling clouds of smoke and steamy vapour a truly horrendous experiment was taking shape.

He could feel the implements pulling and tearing at his body, ripping him piece by piece. As he suffered the torment, he remembered how many times he had done this before and how this time, it would be more worth it than anything else he had ever had to endure. This would be the last time he had promised himself that, but this time the machine had more of him, so much more of him than before.

As the banging from beneath the floor of the room became harder and more urgent, Maloso couldn't hold back his agony anymore and a shriek of terrifying proportions echoed over the sounds of the banging and the machine operating.

Outside the room lay a thick metal door and two guards in ceremonial crimson robes. The stead-fast issue of Maloso's personal guards were notoriously ruthless and hard-nosed but even they were shaking a little in their boots as the piercing shriek of pain penetrated their armoured helmets.

They had never heard Maloso like this before and although they
had been briefed, along with the high command of the Crimson
Empire, on the details of his master plan, to hear it being carried
out meant that there was no going back.

From this moment on, Kalor Maloso, and Rodas, were never
going to be the same again and as the cries of pain reached a
horrible velocity, the entire planet of Rodas was about to shake in
the aftermath of what the terrible man had done...

XVII

'The Crimson Empire has entered a new phase of warfare,' said Takten to his audience. As the soldiers cleared up the mess that their ambush had caused and patched up the survivors, he took the time to explain to Random, Anji, Jake, Nkite, Djanga and Gron the latest on the war effort. He had wanted to get them all out as quickly as possible before a further attack, which he knew was oncoming, but while his troops were working as hard as they could evacuate the mountain, he felt it was time to open up about how badly the Sapphire Regime were fairing – especially after seeing Random's powers first-hand. 'For years now we have been suffering losses. Our battlegrounds have fallen and we have been driven back, forced to live like rats underground.'

'So that explains these tunnels then?' said Anji. 'I had wondered.'

'The tunnels were built by our forefathers as a solution to trench warfare but before long they were abandoned and instead rebels from both sides would use them.'

'Rebels from both sides?' asked Nkite.

'It's true. I was a soldier when they were dug,' said Gron, who was perched with the others on one of the giant boulders that were scattered around the place. 'There were whispers among the ranks so when I deserted, I came down here, long before I found the river.'

'And you lived with people from the other side?' asked Jake.

'Just as it should be,' continued Gron. 'Much like the river people. We learnt to live together in harmony. Shunning the war outside.'

'Ignoring reality,' spat Takten.

'You can't blame them,' said Jake. 'I mean, we've only been here five minutes and we've already seen enough.'

'How did you get here?' asked Nkite.

'The craft that he stole, surely?' said Takten pointing his gun at Random, who was sitting arms folded with a concentrated look on his face.

'Well, if you must know, I was kidnapped before I stole it if that makes it any better,' he responded.

'But why? Did you not know why you were created?' asked Nkite.

'I did, yes, I'm ashamed to say. And why did I run? The obvious reason. I was scared,' Random said honestly.

'Scared of fighting?' said Takten, angered by the cowardice of the man before him.

'Sacred of sacrifice,' said Random, who got up from the boulder and started to pace about the corridor. 'I did not ask to be created. I was brought into this world for one reason and one reason only.'

'And you chose to escape,' said Nkite. 'Don't you think that's what we all want? None of us asked to be brought into this world either and like you, we didn't have a choice.'

Random sighed. 'You don't understand.'

'Then tell us!' shouted Nkite.

'Hey, hey give him a chance,' said Jake.

Anji noticed the look of sorrow in Random's eye. 'Understand what, Random?'

Random looked at his friends. 'The rebels Takten spoke of. They created me. Took elements of both their sides and made me in a laboratory. Only it went wrong. A heli-fighter crashed in the lab at the moment of my creation. It killed two people. A scientist and a rebel soldier. My parents. They extracted the best elements of their characters and installed them into one single compound. Me. After the crash, my first memory is of opening the chamber door and seeing their dead bodies just lying there on the floor. It was hell all around me. But I had their voices in my head. Somehow, they were communicating with me, talking to me, guiding me towards my sole purpose. But I was a boy, nothing but a child, unaware of the powers I had been given but fully aware of my terrible responsibility. If you were a child, given the chance to escape a terrible future wouldn't you take it?'

'I did,' replied Nkite. 'But I ran back into the fire, and I've been running back in ever since.'

'As have I,' said Random.

'It's true,' Anji said. 'The first thing Random did was save our world.'

'Yeah, then we joined him and saved one called Genocia,' chirped Jake. 'It had a terrible monster living under-'

'And so on, and so on,' said Random, talking over Jake's enthusiastic retelling. 'All the while knowing that I had to fulfil my destiny. Now I think about it, I wasn't running away from Rodas. I was running back.'

'It's a shame your epiphany didn't come sooner,' said Takten. 'The Crimson Empire's numbers have been growing stronger. There are so many in number and none of our intel knows how. Meanwhile, the Sapphire Regime is becoming an endangered race.'

'All this fighting, all this heartache, for what? I mean, what started it?' asked Anji.

'The old saying goes that the elders couldn't make the colour purple,' said Gron.

'What?!' spluttered Jake. 'That's insane!'

'It's true, apparently,' said Nkite. 'Almost too silly to make it real.'

'And yet it is,' confirmed Random.

'But you're red and blue on this planet. That's what makes purple!' said Anji, who nearly fell off her boulder she was so flabbergasted at the ridiculousness of it all.

'We know that now but we didn't know then. Rodas was a different planet in the old times,' said Gron.

'Is that why you're so special, Random? Because you are purple?' asked Jake.

'I'm the best of both worlds, even if I say so myself, now it's time to stop talking and time to prove it.' He went over to Nkite and placed his hand on her shoulder. 'Nkite, I am so sorry for all the hurt I have caused you and your people but I promise you I will make it up to you now.'

Nkite looked at him quizzically. 'What are you going to do?'

Random straightened himself up and turned to Takten. 'Takten, this war must end now and I can make it so.'

He looked at him with equal bemusement. 'How?'

'Kalor Maloso seems to have found a way to keep regenerating his army, correct? The Crimson Empire is playing dirtier to win this war than before, right?'

'Right,' replied Anji and Jake in unison.

'Then it's obvious. Maloso is fiddling with the books! He's doing something to make his Empire stronger and harder to beat which means...'

'He's bringing soldiers back from the dead?' asked Jake.

'A little far-fetched Jake, try again,' said Random.

'He's cloning his soldiers?' asked Anji, leaving Jake to shoot her an annoyed look as that was literally what he was about to say.

'Well, let's see shall we,' said Random. He marched through the corridor, past river dwellers who looked on at him in bewilderment and awe as the others followed him. He came to a stop at the pile of dead Crimson Empire soldiers and bent down to examine them. He felt along one of the corpse's helmets and found a release catch which suddenly snapped open, revealing the horrifying face of an open-eyed dead man. He pushed the catch button on another and turned the body over. Despite the ravages of war being etched across both dead faces, they looked otherwise identical. He did the same again to another corpse, leaving the on-lookers open-mouthed.

'Now either by a million to one chance I've just uncovered a family of triplets in this troop or the cloning idea is the correct one,' confirmed

Random as he got back to his feet. 'Honestly, Takten, doesn't the Sapphire Regime check the deceased?

Takten was dumbfounded and a little anxious. 'How, how is he doing that?'

'Easy. This planet has always had the technology. Think about it. If they can create someone like me in a giant test tube then why can't they clone? The Crimson Empire must have discovered this technology and hoarded it for themselves, away from prying eyes. But there's more. The security mainframe is worried that they cannot keep the war contained so there's something else going on here. I just don't know what,' said Random as he put his fingers to his lips to think and then thought against it after touching dead bodies.

'So how do we stop them?' asked Nkite.

'Not you, Nkite. Me,' replied Random.

'How?' asked Takten.

'I need to get inside the Crimson Empire's base. Find out what's really happening here.'

'That's impossible, it'll be suicide,' said Takten.

'Not if I'm the one that Maloso wants all along,' said Random.

'You're giving yourself up?!' cried Anji.

'It's the only way,' replied Random.

'Now hang on a minute!' said Jake. 'You can't do that, you'll be killed.'

'Not if I can help it,' said Random.

'And can you?' asked Anji.

'I don't know yet,' was Random's less than convincing response.

'Random you can't,' she protested.

'I can, I will and I must,' said Random stoically. 'Take a look around you, Anji. Look at these people. This is just a snapshot of centuries of torment and pain. Rodas has suffered long enough. It's time it was saved.'

'Well, you can't go in alone,' said Jake.

'Don't make me repeat myself, Jake,' warned Random.

'Look, if this Maloso bloke is half as bad as you say he is then you need help,' he replied.

'Oh always, and since I learnt long ago that there is no telling either of you to stay out of danger then I need both of you to do as exactly as I say,' said Random as he draped his arms over both his friend's shoulders. 'Now Jake, if you want to get your hands dirty, I need someone to pose as a guard. We can tell Moloso that I came willingly. Then when you are inside the base you can pass intel back to Mr Takten here.'

'Highly unlikely, I'm coming with you,' said Takten. 'You'll need more than one guard to convince the Crimson Empire that your intentions are true. If my men can escort these people back to our base then we can send the report directly to Sapphire HQ.'

'That's a great idea. You'll both have to wear a disguise. I'm sorry to ask you of this but I think you'll have to wear these men's suits to disguise yourselves,' said Random.

'Dead man's boots, lovely,' gulped Jake. 'But hang on, these won't fit me, I'm still growing after that fountain of youth business, remember?'

'Random walked up to Jake and measured himself next to him. 'You're almost back to normal, Jake. In fact, I'd say you've gained half a foot in the last hour, hadn't you noticed?'

Jake felt his body and stood up on his tiptoes. 'Oh yeah, well, there has been a lot going on I suppose.'

'You can't let him have all the fun,' said Anji. 'What about me?' Anji was smarting. So, it was fine for Jake to help Random in his dangerous mission but her? Is that what Random had in mind? Surely not? He knew her better than that. He knew what she could bring to the table.

'Of course not, I wouldn't leave you out of the fun now, would I? Okay, Anji, and Nkite, we'll report the information back to you. You need to get the river dwellers back to Sapphire HQ. Takten, can you give them a map to show them the way?' Random declared.

Anji drew a sigh of relief. That'd be a dangerous mission, for sure. Just what she was looking for!

'Yes, and Djanga knows the way, but Random, who said that you were giving the orders? I am in charge here. I'd appreciate it if you remembered that,' said Takten.

'Do you have a better plan?' replied Random.

Takten stayed silent. No, he didn't.

'Good man,' said Random.

'Is that it?' asked Anji.

'No. Whilst waiting for Jake's information, you will also need to wait for Skateboard. He'll send you a signal when he is back on Rodas.'

'Wait, what? Skateboard's gone?' gasped Anji.

'Not for long, he will be back soon. Take this device. It'll track him to you,' Random handed Anji a small little disc and placed it in the palm of her hand.

'What happens when we've got the information we require? Asked Takten.

'You get the hell out of there. Don't wait for me. Hopefully, I won't be far behind you. I'll try to disable the Crimson Empire from inside and then the Sapphire Regime can attack. You've all been in the dark for too long, it's time to emerge from the shadows,' said Random.

'Excuse me, young man, but what can I do,' asked Gron. Random put a reassuring arm around him.

'Help get your people to safety. No one else should die today. Not on our watch and not on yours, eh, peeps?'

Anji, Nkite and Gron nodded, a slight smile returning to the lips of the two Rodasian's faces. Nkite felt a warmth return in her heart. For all that she hated Random right now, he was giving her hope that she started to think was gone.

'Right, there'll be more Crimson Empire soldiers on the way so we have to act fast but we can do it. All of us. We can stop the war today and we will. So, let's get to work!' said Random as he sprung off down the corridor.

A roar came from a band of soldiers and river dwellers who had overheard everything. An optimism was growing, the tide possibly turning. The Rodasians had been beaten and broken but they could mend and they could emerge triumphant. As everyone went about their jobs, Takten instructed his men to fall in to outline the plan, a smile spread across Random's face.

He could do it. They could do it and if all went to his plan the worst part of his destiny wouldn't have to happen.

The war had raged for thousands of years. It had claimed the lives of billions upon billions of innocent people, of people coerced into a futile, race-driven war that should never have been allowed to escalate.

Random and his friends were about to draw a line in the sand.

The Battle for Rodas was about to begin...

...just as soon as Jake found a Crimson Empire uniform with boots in a size 8...

Book Two

REDEMPTION

'I have heard your pleas for help, Skateboard, but I must say that I am not convinced.'

Skateboard stood alone, back in a place he had been banished from some time ago. From the data in his memory bank, there was very little to differentiate the incredible gold splendour of the throne room on Spectronia from how it had looked when he and his friends had last been on the planet. It had been a few years back that they had crash landed upon its spectacularly colourful plains and been tricked into helping a group of sadistic archaeologists to find an incredibly powerful element. It was called the Zedron Flux and its very name caused a cache of files to corrupt in Skateboard's motherboard every time he thought of it.

The Flux itself was harmless until it was used. Torn between letting a race of gods called the Osirans from destroying Spectronia to obtain it and putting his life at risk, Random had activated the element and committed a terrible atrocity in the process. He had saved Spectronia and its inhabitants but he had wiped out a race of beings. Skateboard knew that Random's guilt over the event was something he had yet to come to terms with fully, indeed if he ever would recover from it, and the Flux's energy had almost killed him too. And after all of that, the Flux was taken into hiding again, just as the man who had it in his possession realised it was not safe to hide in this world and Random and his friends were banished from Spectronia for life by the Queen of the planet, Solenia.

It was with great surprise when they were formulating their plan that Random had requested Skateboard visit Spectronia for help first. Indeed, the great ruler who was sitting before him, resplendent in her throne and flanked by her aid and a multitude of Valkyrie guards who had escorted him from the Venus II upon landing, was thinking just the same as the AI robot.

She had listened to him plead his case for help and yet Solenia knew that it would take more than just the word of a robot to convince her to take action.

Although moments before her world had been visited once again by the Venus II and one of its occupants, she too had been wrestling with an internal dilemma. Spectronia had always been a peaceful planet and Solenia had led her people into battle against the Osirans – a battle that had it not been for Random's sacrifice – would have seen her planet obliterated. Although she had banished the outsiders, she had also taken a large number of casualties as a black mark against her own name. As she was

their ruler, she made herself an exception and made a vow to attend every funeral, and every memorial and swore that she and her people would never intervene again, so long as trouble evaded Spectronia. Indeed, it had taken some strong words, on more than one occasion, from her oldest and more trusted aid, Proctor, to finally convince her to awake from her inactivity. She hadn't expected to have to make good on her U-turn immediately, especially potentially doing so to help the only people who she'd ever had to banish from her world!

'In many ways,' she continued, 'I sympathise with your predicament. But I must give your request some careful consideration. What you ask would require me to sacrifice men and women under my rule. I have learnt from experiencing the cold loneliness of power and what it can do to my people when I make the wrong decision. I am wary not to make one so hastily that could cost the lives of so many.'

'With respect, your majesty,' said Skateboard in a calm tone. 'Every second many who know not of such a benevolent ruler are killed in the crossfire of a futile war. Men, women, children. Too many in number to tally those that have been lost. Lives have been ruined for generation upon generation and if it isn't stopped soon the war will spill out across the cosmos.

It could even reach here. Rodas is only fifteen million light years away from Spectronia. Its disease could spread if we don't act now. My friends and I can stop it but we need as many allies as possible.'

'Your Majesty,' said Proctor, 'I have heard of the problems on Rodas. Indeed, the stories of a planet torn apart by a war against races were something your father was briefed upon long ago. I believe you are also aware. It's far from a fairy tale. I humbly

---

suggest that you consider what you have been asked.'

'I am very aware, Proctor and do not need a history lesson now,' said Solenia. She turned back to Skateboard. 'The business of another planet, no matter how appalling its predicament, is not one of concern for us. Even if you say the war is on the brink of expanding across the stars there are many planets in this system with the might to withstand any trouble before it lands at our door. Why have you not asked any of them for help?'

'It is a good question, your Majesty,' replied Skateboard, 'and one I have no answer for except that we have little time to act. As we speak Random, Anji and Jake are trapped on Rodas behind a barrier that intelligence tells us is on the verge of collapse. We only have time to call upon allies. Random saved your world, no matter the aftermath. All that he asks is that you help him return the favour.'

'A favour that involves death,' said Solenia. She mused for a moment. Random had saved their world. Spectronia still hung in the sky because of the sacrifice he made. She had been surprised to hear that he was still alive. Seeing him lying in the dirt barely moving after the Flux had done its work had given her little cause to believe he would live. And now he was asking her for help, despite being banished from coming back. But if she didn't, would it make her and Spectronia seem weak? To shy behind planets in their way had been far from a noble suggestion now she thought of it.

'How would we get there?' she asked.

Skateboard felt a glimmer of hope ignite inside of him. Finally, Solenia was asking logistical questions so she must have some interest in helping, he thought. 'Do you not have any form of craft to transport you?'

'We have none. We have never left this planet,' said Proctor, who immediately felt a glare from Solenia.

'You seem eager,' she muttered. 'How much room do you have on your vessel?'

Skateboard pondered for a moment. 'Given the average height and build of your Valkyries I would say that we could make use of the engine rooms and gather a hundred inside the ship.

It wouldn't be a comfortable trip for many, but it wouldn't be a long one either.'

'And our dosas?'

'Oh,' said Skateboard. 'You'd take horses too?'

The dosas were the Spectronian's trusty steeds, much like the horses Skateboard had seen back on Earth.

'What else would my Valkyries ride into battle on?'

Skateboard was flummoxed. 'An excellent point. Well, I suppose we could fit them on but it would be a tight squeeze...' he said before starting to panic about the mess they would cause on the ship.

'And do you plan to visit any other planets to ask for help? Why was Spectronia your first port of call?' asked Solenia.

'Well, you are the planet we owe it to the most,' said Skateboard, who was lying a little about the planet being the closest to Rodas on his list.

'Proctor, I am well aware of what you think about all of this so I need not ask,' said Solenia.

'Your Majesty-'

'It's okay, Proctor. I understand the plight of Rodas. I understand that despite the robot's banishment still applying he has broken our laws, but I admire his courage and also sympathise with the cause,' she huffed, remembering a conversation she and Proctor had been having before Skateboard's arrival.

'Very well. Skateboard, your banishment is rescinded forthwith. I shall assemble my best fighters and we shall join your cause.'

Skateboard's diodes breathed a heavy sigh of relief. 'Thank you so much, your Majesty,' he bowed as much as his rigid metal framework would allow.

'Proctor, summon the Valkyries. We leave immediately. You are in charge until we get home,' Solenia strode up from her throne and down the steps to stand by Skateboard's side. She patted him gently. 'It's time Spectronia came out of the shadows and wrote its name in the stars.'

'Very good, your Majesty,' said Proctor, with a concerned look on his face. Solenia noticed this and gave him a reassuring smile.

'It's okay, Proctor. We're coming home alive. Walk with me,' she instructed Skateboard. 'We must ready ourselves with haste. Tell me of the other recruits who will help in this cause.'

'We have links with the Space Seals. They are aware of the situation. I updated our contact on the way here. She is putting a case towards the fleet to repel any potential break out from outside the security mainframe.'

'Anyone else?' asked Solenia, as the pair walked through a throne room which had suddenly became a hive of activity.

'Yes, your Majesty. We just need to make a quick trip to Genocia before we return to Rodas. We have friends there who should also be able to help.'

'So far you have a hundred of us, three people on the ground, a contact trying to convince a fleet and some friends on a world I have never heard of before who might help. My confidence wanes by the second,' said Solenia.

'Fear not, your Majesty. All will fall into place.'

'It better, because if it doesn't and if we make it out of this battle alive then I'll consider doing more than reinstating your banishment, is that clear?'

'Yes, your Majesty,' said Skateboard, who added the personal threat of execution to his ever-growing list of things that were worrying him.

'Good, now that's settled, you'd better show me where you have parked,' said Solenia as she strode off in front of Skateboard, whose concerns about Rodas, death, his friends, keeping promises and huge heaps of poo from the Valkyries horses, which he had just remembered were called dosas, had really started to put him off his stride. Meekly, he followed, hoping, praying, that all would fall into place.

The room smelt like a foul barbeque. It had been a while since Kalor Maloso's cries had been heard by his guards and so, despite the order for them not to enter under any circumstances, they were duty-bound to protect their leader.

The room was awash with thick smoke and white vapour. It was also as hot as a sauna in July. The first guard, his experience of his Lord's previous exposure to the chamber immediately made for it. Despite not seeing very clearly, he remembered its general whereabouts and the second guard followed, newer to the job and not as familiar with the gruesome place as her superior.

'My Lord?' asked the first guard.

As they approached the chamber, great tentacles of instruments, dripping in unspeakable fluids seems to be slowly snaking back into the chamber's housing. A tube high above them seemed to gurgle incessantly like a loud drain. The banging from below the floor had subsided. The room was an eerie hell hole.

As the guards peered inside the chamber interior, a terrible demonic skeleton screamed in their faces, sending them reeling to the floor and shrieking in horror. The skeleton, its blood red eyes piercing the smoky gloom like headlamps in the dark looked menacingly at them and terrified the second guard to such an extent that she emptied the contents of her bladder instantly.

'GET OUT!!!' the demon shrieked.

Both guards scrambled across the floor and left the room in such terror that upon shutting the door they both collapsed to the ground. The shrieking continued and their hearts beat so rapidly they could almost hear them as loudly as the screams coming from the room.

'W-w-was that?' stuttered the second guard.

The first guard did nothing else but nod, and faint.

Kalor Maloso started to calm down. He staggered out of the chamber and slowly and painfully made his way over to a control centre at the side of the room.

Still grunting and moaning in agony, his bony fingers reached for the controls and before long, the gurgling in the pipes above began to intensify and in return, so did the incessant banging from under the floorboards.

Slowly the cries of agony were replaced with a guttural laugh. With a final press of a button, Kalor Maloso threw himself to the floor and laughed even harder. The pipes rattled loudly; the floorboards shook.

The war on Rodas was about to get much, much worse.

III

Random shirked a little as the handcuffs clasped against his wrists and secured tightly around them.

'Do they have to be so tight?' he complained to Takten, whose expression of annoyance was noted by Random. He scanned his face and decided it might be best to get his question out in the open. 'You don't like me either do you?'

'What that girl said in the cave wasn't wrong,' said Takten, referring to Nkite's outburst minutes earlier. 'Just because I am a soldier it doesn't mean I don't feel.'

'You've lost people?' asked Random.

Takten nodded as he worked on his laser rifle and began packing his uniform away in a bag as he stood before Random wearing the commandeered suit of his sworn enemy. 'Friends. Family. Comrades. You name it.'

'Takten, I really am sorry for what I have done.'

'I don't want to hear it,' he spat, but upon looking up and seeing the remorse in Random's eyes, the battle-hardened exterior softened a little. 'What you forget Random is that being here now won't bring back anybody who has passed.'

'But it will stop more from falling. You're right I can't bring them back but I can make sure that tomorrow is a better day for Rodas.'

Takten snorted. 'Has anyone ever told you what a messiah complex you have?'

Random shook his head. 'I'm serious. What I am about to do will bring an end to this war.'

'You haven't exactly said what you're planning to do. Once we get in and get the information we need, then what?'

'For very good reason,' said Random. He looked behind him, scanning the area for any prying eyes. The river dwellers were in the process of moving out and Jake had taken himself off beyond a rock somewhere to get dressed. He couldn't see Anji anywhere but just to be on the safe side took Takten by the arm and led him aside. 'My friends. I want them to be as safe as possible. If I tell them too much then I can't guarantee that they will follow through with my instructions.'

'So?' asked Takten.

'They could put themselves in more harms way.'

'Then why bring them here in the first place?' asked Takten.

'I tried to leave them behind but in the end I know that I needed them,' whispered Random. 'Besides, if I tell them that what I am about to do might result in my death then it might end up also resulting in theirs and I couldn't live with that...especially if I was dead...anyway,' Random said, his mind running off in different directions

when it was struggling to remain focussed. 'So I want you to look after Jake and get him out of there in the slightest hint of trouble. Don't wait for me because...I might not be coming back,' he finished, with a solemn look on his face.

Takten understood. Some of his men had risen through the ranks with him. As time had gone on, he and Djanga had become inseparable. If his friend were staring down the barrel then Takten could guarantee he would throw his own body in the firing line before the trigger had been pulled.

'I understand. We might live like barbarians at times in this war Random but trust and loyalty are still commodities that make us feel like Kings. I will protect your friend.'

Random smiled. 'Good man!' His face changed to one of puzzlement. 'Now, where have Jake and Anji got to?'

*

Jake was perched awkwardly on the side of a boulder. Having snaked the Crimson Empire suit over his clothes he had tried hard to forget that it had been taken off a corpse earlier. Now he was cursing the boots.

'I'm sure Random said these were a size 8,' he muttered as he threw one of the heavy boots to the ground, the other perched hopelessly on the

end of his toes.

'Hey,' came a familiar voice.

'Anj, help us out here. This suit is all baggy and the boots might as well belong to a toy doll!'

'Can't you ask for some better ones?' she asked.

'I'm not going back into the corpse pile,' said Jake. 'Wow. There's a sentence I never thought I would say.'

Anji's face gave a wry smile and she sat down next to him.

'Look, Jake, about earlier. I... I remembered the date.'

Jake's frustrations seemed to melt away for a brief moment. 'Oh?'

'Y'see I... god why is this so awkward?' she said quietly.

'Because it's me that you are talking to and that my real name is King Awkard?' replied Jake.

'Jake, I love you-'

Jake's heart started thumping out of control. She said it. She actually said those words. He'd longed to hear them for so many years. Sure, his hormones had led him astray over the years but his real feeling for Anji had always been there, no matter how much he had tried to hide them.

'-but,' she continued.

'No, no need to continue I heard the first bit and that'll do me,' he said hastily. 'I guess it's time I said the same-'

'Jake please,' she said, putting his hand in hers. 'I love you so much, more than anyone else in my life. I've never said it so explicitly before because, well, I hoped that I wouldn't have to until now. You've been my best friend for so long and when we made that promise, back at the pond on Earth, I often wondered what we'd be like all grown up and I wanted to still have you in my life. And look, I still do,' she smiled a smile that made Jake's heart sing. 'But as time has gone by, I've changed. We've changed.'

Jake started to develop a sickening feeling in his stomach. 'What do you mean, Anj?'

'I'm sorry. I guess that the feelings I thought I would have developed leading up to prom...I just, don't love you in that way.'

'Anj, you're confusing me,' said Jake, the mask of bravado slipping. 'What are you saying? That you love me as a friend?'

Anji started to feel tears trickle down her cheeks. 'I thought that's how we both felt?'

Jake was stunned. 'Yes, so did I but...I guess,' he sniffed, wiping back his own falling tears, 'I guess there was a piece of me that was holding out for more.'

'Jake.'

'Never mind,' he looked away, unable to look his old friend in the eye.

The two old friends sat perched together on the boulder much in the same way that they had all those years ago as children. But for the first time there now felt like there was a chasm between them. Jake felt so stupid. No, he felt betrayed.

'When I was in the sand...buried alive, you only mentioned the prom to keep me-'

'I never meant to hurt you, please don't let us fall out over this, not now,' Anji pleaded. She hadn't realised it but she was squeezing his hand, which Jake quickly snapped away from her.

Nkite had watched the exchange. For a while, she had wanted to give them space but when she heard Takten's cry of instruction, she knew that she would have to step in. She walked up to the pair and she cleared her throat.

'Hello,' she said softly. 'I'm sorry to interrupt you both but Commander Takten has given the order to move out,' she said. Random and Takten also appeared.

'Right,' said Random, instantly noticing that his two friends were emotional. 'Everything okay?'

'Yeah,' sniffed Anji, wiping her face.

'Always,' lied Jake.

'Good,' said Random, who with his handcuffs firmly on beckoned them both up for a big warm hug. 'Look, we'll get through this.'

Neither Anji nor Jake smiled, with Jake looking the other way so that he didn't have to look at his old friend.

Random relinquished first, still detecting that something wasn't right with the pair but also thinking that this was neither the time nor the place to discuss it. 'Oh Jake, what's wrong with the suit?'

'Damn thing won't fit,' he said resigned.

Nkite took one look at the baggy, ill-fitting onesie and knew instantly, as did Takten, but hopped in before he had the chance to speak.

'Just press this,' she said, pushing a small button on his wrist communicator. The suit suddenly shrink-wrapped around Jake's body and also gave him extra dimensions he knew he didn't have. He looked down. He now had abs! Where had his flabby tummy gone? He also flexed his arms. He had bulging biceps!

'Wow!' he said, finally cheered up.

'It's a feature on the suits. Supposed to keep the soldiers in peak condition even if they aren't without them,' she confirmed.

'How did you know about this?' asked Takten.

Nkite flashed him a cheeky grin. 'You don't have to be a soldier to know this kind of stuff.'

'Thanks!' said Jake. 'Blimey, I'll never want to take it off now!'

Anji watched him, her eyes still sad. She had to admit to herself that he looked quite the part.

'Right, are we all set? Take care of each other,' said Random to Nkite and Anji. 'We'll see you at the rendezvous.'

Anji gave him a smile and Random walked off, followed by Takten and Jake.

'Jake,' she called after him but received no response. She sighed. This couldn't be the last time she's seeing them both. Not like this.

Nkite rubbed her arm affectionately. 'Hey,' she said.

'Sorry, right let's go,' said Anji.

'It's not the right time to be falling out with your friends,' said Nkite, not sure if she was saying the right thing or not.

Anji gave her a withering look.

They pushed their way gently through the crowd, meeting
Djanga as they reached the front. Anji looked around and just
witnessed the shadows of Random and Jake melt away into the
darkness down another path in the mountain.

'Right girls,' said Djanga, who turned to his battalion. 'Move
out!'

As Djanga barked the order his men, who were stationed at the
front and back of the crowd, started on their trip. Anji looked
down at the ground in sadness.

Nkite, who was helping Gron along the way, also held out her
hand and took Anji's in her grasp.

'We can talk about it if you like?' she offered.

'Sorry Nkite but I've just met you and I don't feel comfort-'

'Okay, just it's going to be a long walk that's all.'

The river dwellers started signing in unison behind them. Anji
was taken aback by the sheer beauty and sadness in their words. It
was an old song, from the early days of the war, one which united
both Crimson and Sapphire races in the group. Its lyrics were
about hope, about seeing the morning again at the end of a stormy
night. The river dwellers had been taught down the ages these
precious words but only vowed to sing them when times looked
like they were going to be brighter again. Now that they were
being led to safety, and after hearing Random's words, they had
so much cause for optimism.

The purple one had returned. He was going to lead Rodas to
salvation.

Even Gron had started to join in, weeping as every syllable left
his lips. Djanga and his men remained stoic. Anji bit her lip, really
trying hard not to cry again.

Nkite clicked her tongue. 'Zarks. Well, if you change your
mind...I hate singing.'

IV

'What I don't get, Benaya is why we have been asked to do this when the forces have been at it for ages.'

Delilah was moaning again. It was something her long-suffering sister had grown used to. Sadly, as Benaya herself didn't have a voice it wasn't like she could ever argue back, well, unless she deployed her well-used sign language signal for her to quit it. Ever since they had been children growing up on the planet Genocia together, she had been the one who had been unfortunate to share a room with her sister. Not like their older sibling Titu, who was lucky enough to have his own space.

She had often wondered why she had been cursed with the luck of being the youngest in her family and lumbered with the awkward middle child.

To be fair to Delilah, on this occasion at least, she did have a point. In the years that had passed since they met the mysterious Captain Random, his two human friends and his metal robot counterpart, they had continued to fight the good fight. As teenagers they had been enslaved in the mines far below the planet's surface, not that they were hardened criminals.

It was the way of the planet and as time went on, more and more people who were imprisoned with them were sent to something called "the soul destroyer" and they were never seen again.

When Random and Jake had been imprisoned with them, the sisters had helped to blow open a planet-wide conspiracy and bring down the government. After they had gone, the now free and pardoned duo were recruited by the factions that had made up the new government to carry out missions. These missions could range from arresting sympathisers to the old ways to hunting down and stunning the mutated remnants of the days of nuclear fallout in the outside wastelands of the planet.

The mutts, as they were called, had been shunned by the government as a dirty secret to the pollution that had been caused under their long reign.

Now that the planet was healing, the new regime had found a way to rehabilitate the mutts and partially restore them to how they were before they were affected by the fallout.

But the air was still dirty and the atmosphere was still dangerous and as the chemicals in the fallout changed people through their respiratory systems, Delilah and Benaya were wearing a protective piece of equipment called a rebreather, which recycled the air that they breathed instantly, meaning no need for expensive and heavy oxygen tanks.

Through the thick dangerous fog, Benaya could only just make out her sister's shaved head a few feet in front of her. She shrugged, squinting through her face mask and breathing steadily into her rebreather. The pair continued to move through the smog with nothing to guide their way but torches mounted onto their laser rifles. They were set to stun, of course. They were not killers. These mutts would be called in and taken back by a follow-up party, who as far as they were aware, were on their way.

Suddenly Delilah stopped in her tracks. Her location system began to emit a beeping sound. Then another. And another. They raised their weapons and prepared for a scrap.

'Get behind me, Benaya. This isn't going to be easy.'

Benaya sighed. It never was.

The mutts were starting to surround them. One by one they emerged like terrifying zombies through the thick fog. Delilah readied her gun. 'On my mark. Wait until they are close enough.'

The sisters stood back-to-back, ready, waiting. The mutts tore through the mist, just metres away. Delilah and Benaya opened fire, turning in a circle using their weapons with pin-point accuracy. Within moments, two dozen mutts lay unconscious on the ground.

Delilah smiled. 'Nice shooting, sis.'

She put her weapon down and reached for her communicator. 'Longboat, this is Red Fox, we have completed our mission. You are free to pick us up now.' A familiar voice fizzed back over the intercom. 'Good job as always, Delilah.' Benaya looked pleasantly surprised at her sister, who smiled back.

'Yana! You sly old thing.'

'Good to hear from you again, you two.' The voice over the communicator was that of an old ally. Yana had met the sisters through Random after she and her fellow freedom fighters, Rader and Dail had saved Anji from being sent to the mines. They had been unable to rescue Random and Jake and Yana, who had infiltrated the Grand Chamber of Genocia and acted undercover, had been discovering more and more of the corrupt and horrifying truth about how the planet was run. After the uprising, and as the dust settled on the planet, Yana had been enlisted to work for the new government as one of the new cabinet ministers. It had been a steep career change for her, one which had always seen her taking a more active role in life, but one that she had accepted on the proviso that her old friends worked with her to make the planet a better home for all of them. But Delilah and Benaya, for all of her hinting and probing, had always been hard to recruit for the jobs that she was in charge of.

'But...why couldn't you just do the job yourself?' asked Delilah.

'What good would our recruitment drive be without testing out potential employees first?'

Delilah tutted. 'Yana, we're freelancers. We don't want to work for the new Government full-time, we've spoken about this before. We are just fine where we are.'

'Trust me on this one and stand by,' Yana replied. 'We will pick you and the mutts up in a few minutes.'

'So, you've been monitoring us all along? You could have given us a lift,' said Delilah.

'Will make it up to you, I promise. A good day's work for you girls. 36 mutts collected.'

Delilah's face dropped. '36?'

Benaya stared in shock. The tracking system had been quietly beeping to itself for the last few seconds. Without warning, more mutts tore through the toxic cloud and knocked Delilah to the ground, sending her rifle clean out of her hand and the communicator far from her reach. Whatever Yana was shouting was inaudible over the screams and the shots being fired by Benaya. The bounty hunter managed to take out a few of the mutts but she too was overpowered. The duo was surrounded and held down by the terrifying hoard.

Struggle as they might, they were powerless to escape. As the mutts raised their crude instruments of death over their prisoners, a terrible roar of engines ripped over their heads, scaring them away.

The mutts left Delilah and Benaya and scattered back into the fog. Whatever had just saved them came in to land very close. Benaya picked herself up and helped her sister to her feet. It was a ship that had saved them. But who?

The sisters gingerly made their way towards it. The ship had a very distinct outline but its features were obstructed by the dust and dirt it had landed in. A ramp started to lower and a figure began to descend. As they peered through the fog, they cried out with surprise when they saw who it was.

'Skateboard!'

'Miss Delilah. Miss Benaya, I need you to come with me.'

'How did you know where to find us?'

'There isn't time now. Please, we need your help!'

Delilah's smile turned into a frown of concern. 'What's the matter? What's happened?'

Benaya signed. Where were Random and the other two?

'They are in danger. Terrible, terrible danger. And they need your help.'

'But how?'

'We really do not have time to talk now. I can explain on the way.'

Another ship roared past. 'That's Yana. She can help too. She owes us a favour.'

'I am counting on it, miss. We need all the help we can muster.'

Benaya and Delilah shot a concerned glance between themselves.

'Listen to me, the fate of our friends may well rest in our hands. We need to get back to them as soon as possible. There is no time to waste. Will you come?'

The new ship, which was bulkier and had landed with much less stealth than the Venus II settled on the hard ground very close to them. The bulkhead hissed open and the familiar face of Yana was the first to venture out into the open, her rebreather obscuring her face.

Skateboard saw her and the armed guards who were trailing her out of the ship. She looked older, as did Benaya and Delilah, but Skateboard wouldn't have said as much. It had been a number of years since he had last seen them and even in a time of great peril, he wouldn't forget his manners and mention a thing like that.

'Miss Yana,' he said.

Yana and her guard approached the gangway. 'Skateboard. It's good to see you again.'

'And you. I'm afraid I have very little time. Our friends are trapped on a planet that is at war. He has asked me to recruit our old allies to help us win. Will you all do so?'

'You want us to rescue them?' asked Delilah. She looked at Benaya unconvinced.

'Yes...I hope that if all goes to plan there will be no need to fight,' said Skateboard.

'Well, that's a shame,' said Yana. 'This desk job is so boring; I could do with a good fight. How many people do you need?'

'As many as who are willing,' said Skateboard.

Benaya walked up the gangway, having already made her mind up. She turned to Delilah and smiled.

Delilah rolled her eyes. 'Fine,' she sighed, 'but if you get me killed, you'll never hear the last of it. Yana?'

Yana looked at them. 'Okay, I might be able to rustle up some support from our armed forces. Where is this war?'

'Rodas,' replied Skateboard.

Yana's face fell. 'Ah, that's going to be tricky then.'

'How come?' asked Delilah.

'The civil war on Rodas has raged for centuries. Many planets have signed treaties not to intervene, even in a state of intergalactic emergency. Genocia signed the treaty a long time ago.'

'I see,' said Skateboard. 'It's okay, I understand.'

'Well, I didn't say that I wouldn't help. Only I can't give you an armada,' said Yana. She turned to her guards. 'Rader, Dail? Continue with our operation here and tell the Prime Minister that I'm going to be late home.'

Skateboard was surprised that he hadn't recognised them.

'But Yana, we'll come with you!' said Rader.

'I'm sorry boys but I need you to take over in my absence,' Yana replied.

'But what should we tell the PM? You'll be dismissed if they find out!' said Dail.

'Tell them I've gone off-world for a bit, and make sure they don't find out why. This is to go no further, do you both hear me?' she ordered to her old friends.

'But telling the PM that you've gone off-world will get you dismissed anyway,' said Rader.

'That's true. Oh well, I didn't enjoy the desk job anyway. Besides you both deserve a promotion,' she winked. 'I'll be fine, I'll be back before you both know it.'

She leaned in and hugged her old friends. As Rader and Dail pulled away, they waved to the three familiar faces and went off to continue their work, rather reluctantly.

As they faded from view, Yana turned towards Skateboard. 'Right, I hope you've got somewhere I can change.'

Skateboard observed her attire. She was wearing a formal business suit and high heels.

'Yes, there should be something a little more practical in the wardrobe. I'm sure that Miss Anji won't mind you borrowing a garment or two.'

'What about weapons?' asked Delilah.

'Oh,' said Yana, patting her top pocket. 'Don't worry about that. I work in politics, remember? I always carry something to cover my back.'

Benaya smiled.

'Very well,' said Skateboard. 'Let's go. We've got very little time.'

The foursome made their way up the runway.

Benaya smelt a less-than-desirable scent emitting from the Venus II the closer they got to the entrance.

'Ugh, what is that smell?' asked Delilah.

'Oh yes, well you may want to hold your noses, there's about a hundred animals on board.'

'What is this,' coughed Yana, the stench sticking in her throat. 'A rescue mission or a zoo?'

'If you would lower your tone, please, Yana, there is a Queen on board,' said Skateboard.

Delilah, Benaya and Yana all looked at each other as the gangway receded into the belly of the ship and the Venus II prepared itself for take-off. Whatever they had just signed up for, they were sure that it was going to be memorable!

V

Whilst Random had been marched out of the mountain by Jake and Commander Takten, something hideous was starting to emerge from the shadows.

Deep within the bowels of the Crimson Empire's massive headquarters lay a vast room from which Kalor Maloso's master plan was starting to converge. As technicians stood around the huge area, monitoring a catalogue of readouts that to the untrained eye would mean nothing more than utter gibberish.

Along the top gantry of what was more like a processing plant than anything else, guards strode up and down, their heavy boots clanging loudly overhead what were thousands upon thousands of steel grey vats.

Inside each of them, a hideous gurgling and churning of matter drowned out all other sounds that were struggling to be heard.

Outside each vat stood a group of lab-coated scientists, who were also monitoring the readings on the side of the vats. They wore ear protectors, not because of the deafening sounds, but because of the terrible screams of pain and agony that were groaning from within each of the tall and thick steel drums.

On each vat was a progress bar of some sort which was flowing steadily to the top of its limit line like liquid filling a cup to the brim. Steadily every single vat inside the processing plant was moving ever closer and whatever concoction that was being brewed within them would be complete.

The process was alarmingly quick. As soon as the materials had been transferred down to the plant the machines had got to work. Now, mere minutes later, they were ready.

A loud ping emitted from every single vat at the same time like a factory of microwaves all spontaneously springing to life. The screaming stopped. A scientist in front of each of these huge vats took their readouts.

High up on the gantry, a General stood eagerly awaiting the fruits of the technician's labours. He peered with huge interest and witnessed a hive of activity as the heavy industry noise – and the screams from within the vats – died down.

A hissing sound replaced them, aggravating the General's already aggressive tinnitus. From his left, he became aware of one of his soldiers marching up to him.

'Lieutenant,' he said without tearing his gaze from the action far below.

'General,' came the reply. The Lieutenant also looked over. 'How many has he requested this time?'

'250,000.'

The Lieutenant shuddered. 'It must have nearly killed him.'

The General turned to her. 'He's been dead for centuries. But now, in his final gift to our cause, we'll be triumphant. Are the heli-fighters ready?'

'Yes, General. We have recalled as many as we could, all except those currently on the front line. The aircraft carriers have all fallen back. In total, we have five hundred of them ready to do as our Lord commands.'

'Good, this first batch shall take the crafts and head for the security mainframe.'

'Is that what has been ordered, General?' said the Lieutenant, barely able to believe what she had just been told.

'It's our Lord's wish. The others shall wipe out what little pockets of the Sapphire Regime remain on this planet. As for us, we shall join our new soldiers up in the air. The security mainframe won't be able to repel our firepower this time.' The General felt so excited inside. He rarely smiled and yet he couldn't wipe his sinister grin off his face.

'We've been unable to before, the security mainframe has always repelled any attacks. Why should it work this time?'

'Two reasons,' said the General. 'One, we've never centred such a fierce attack on the containment field before and two, because we have the code to turn it off. An insider in the mainframe gave it to us. Well, he took some persuading. We were looking after his family after all. They also gave it to the purple one.'

The Lieutenant gasped. 'He's back?'

'Yes, and the trap is set. Today we win this war. There will be no other outcome.'

A loud groaning from far below interrupted their discussion. As the General and the Lieutenant looked down, every single vat appeared to be cracking open. A heavy steel door was peeling itself open allowing a cloud of smoke and gas hissing into the processing plant. The activity from the scientists and technicians became frantic as slowly red-coloured figures began to appear from within the vats.

The Lieutenant smiled. She had never seen so many soldiers being created at once before.

One by one the thousands upon thousands of newly created lives fell in like the obedient soldiers they were and marched neatly out of the processing plant. The metal doors all snapped back shut again and in the blink of an eye, the process began again.

'Good, they understand what they must do. It's amazing what those tech boys can do isn't it?' purred the General. 'You'd better return to your post Lieutenant, and inform your superiors. The new blood is on its way.'

*

'What a mess,' said Jake as he and Takten marched Random off out of the mountain.

'How far to Maloso?' asked Random.

'A fairway. We shall need to commandeer a heli-fighter,' replied Takten.

'Where are we going to find one of them?' asked Jake.

The trio dropped to the floor as not far above their heads a couple of aircraft were playing out the climax of a dogfight, culminating in the heli-fighter being chased through the sky and crashing into the side of the mountain.

'I mean in one piece?' finished Jake.

Takten shot him an annoyed look. 'We'll find on the way. Heli-fighters have to land for their engines to charge.'

As Takten finished his sentence, he spotted one such heli-fighter doing just that, landing roughly a hundred metres from the spot where they were crouching in.

'Speaking of which...' said Takten as he gestured for Jake and Random to follow him.

'Wait, we'd better stay out of view,' said Random.

'Why?' asked Jake.

'We don't know which side that heli-fighter belongs to,' replied Random.

'It's a Crimson Empire ship. They are the only ones who have heli-fighters with that livery on their doors, but you're right, we can't have any questions being asked until we are on the inside. Wait here.' Takten leapt to his feet and made for the heli-fighter.

'Won't he need some help?' asked Jake.

'I get the feeling he can handle it. Anyway, it gives us a chance to have a chat.'

Jake shuffled a bit. 'What about?'

'You and Anji. Are you both okay.'

Jake sighed. 'We're about to infiltrate the base of what sounds like the evilest people we've ever faced and you want to talk about this?'

'Jake, I don't know what is about to happen. I want to know that everything is alright between my best friends in case...'

'...in case of what?'

Random stopped himself from saying any more. 'I just want to know if I can help.'

Jake looked down at his feet. He tried his best to blot out the sound of war all around them. Then he wished he hadn't.

'It's just...before we met you Anj and I...we...made a pact. That pact has got me through some tough times. Now...I'm so stupid.'

'Jake, I know we all take a jibe at one another but I can assure you I don't think that you are stupid and I know for a fact that Anji doesn't either. She cares for you; I can promise you that. And whatever this promise was to you I'm sure that it pales in comparison to how you both feel about each other. I mean come on, your best friends. This will pass.'

'I hope so,' said Jake. 'Cheers Random.'

'Look, whatever you feel now it'll pass. Your friendship is more important than one fallout. Especially to me.' Random smiled.

Jake smiled back. 'Hey, random question, but why isn't anybody shooting at us? Two people in the middle of a war field. How come they aren't shooting at us?'

'I think they are too preoccupied. In fact, is it me or is it all getting quieter?' asked Random.

'I'm not sure, maybe we're just getting used to it?' Jake spotted a waving figure standing in the distance next to the heli-fighter. 'Hey, I think Takten has done it!'

Random got up. 'Come on.' The two friends made their way gingerly across the rocky terrain. When they reached Takten, the soldier was beckoning them quickly onto the heli-fighter, helping the shackled Random up the short ladder inside the craft.

Jake took a look around the ship.

It was cramped, with enough room for two people to carry out the piloting duties and another bank of two seats at computers that looked more like tactical positions, given the radar emitting through the dark ship.

'What did you do with the people on board?' asked Jake.

'You don't want to know,' replied Takten. 'You'd better sit with me upfront. Random, you stay in here. And belt up, I haven't flown one of these since the academy.'

'I can give it a go,' said Jake.

'Better leave it to the soldier,' said Random, who hinted at the seat belts on the seat he has chosen. 'Would you mind?'

Jake helped Random into his chair and made his way into the cockpit, immediately spotting the blood stains on the wing mirror in front of him.

'I hope that's on the outside,' he quipped uneasily as Takten chose not to reply.

'Off we go. By the way, it's more than likely that we'll be shot at as soon as we are in the air. You'll have to man the cannons.'

Jake took a look around and familiarised himself with the controls. He glanced upon a bank of buttons and a steering wheel with what looked like a crude gun and sighter on top of it. 'Gotcha.'

'Have you fired a gun before?' asked Takten as the engines began to fire up. He checked a readout on the dashboard and was relieved that the batteries were not as flat as he thought they'd be.

'A bit,' replied Jake.

'That'll do,' said Takten. 'We have enough fuel to get to the Crimson Empire's headquarters. Hold on...it's going to be a bumpy ride.'

Jake gulped as the heli-fighter shot off up into the air vertically and then sailed off into the murky, bloody fog of battle up ahead.

VI

Admiral Bagari reclined in the leather chair in her office and poured herself a glass of whisky. As she replaced the bottle back in the cabinet under her desk, she picked the glass up to her lips and took a short and sharp swig. She moved over to a bank of buttons that sat on top of her desk and pressed one, requesting the person who answered to make sure that she was not disturbed. As she released the button, she returned her gaze to the huge window and pondered out into space.

Bagari had received a call from Skateboard. In the encoded message he had notified her that he had recruited some old friends to help in the fight on Rodas and had also asked for her involvement too. It was a request that she hadn't responded to and yet it was one she had to turn down. The Space Seals Corp was almost as old as the war on Rodas and as such, was sworn centuries back not to interfere in the conflict on that planet. It was a promise that had been signed in triplicate and it was wrapped up in so much red tape that it was almost impossible to undo.

Yet whilst she was duty-bound to refuse, she didn't want to. Although she loathed calling Random and his counterparts friends, they were strong allies and had done much to help her keep the universe safe. The terrible encounter with Stratos. The wormholes opening up across the universe threatened to bring destruction, she had worked with them and in doing so she had been bumped up the ranks in the fleet. Indeed, The Stargazer was now the flagship battle freighter and she was in charge and she was bestowed that responsibility in no small part thanks to her involvement with Random.

Now here she was, in his hour of need and she was unable to do anything else other than to help him get behind enemy lines. She dreaded to think what the Admiralty would do to her if they ever found out. A demotion, a dressing down in front of peers and a loss of her command. She knew the rules and by God, she didn't want to break them.

But that didn't stop her wanting to call her peers together and try to convince them to take part but she knew they would refuse. Only if the mainframe was breached would there be a call for help for the Space Seals to step in and in a weird, very dangerous way, she kind of wanted that to happen.

She knew very well the atrocities that had taken place on that awful, shunned planet. But she wanted to see action, she wanted to help out an end to suffering.

After all, that's why she joined the Space Seals in the first place. She looked out at the stars. She knew most of them. It was part of the training when she enlisted in the academy to know them but she'd already known so many off by heart. As a little girl, she and her father would gaze nightly through the telescope in his observatory back at home and he would tell her of all the places he had been and where he still wanted to go. It used to make Bagari feel a little sad that she couldn't go with him but she would when she was older, she'd told herself. She'd enlist, just like he did, and sail the stars of the galaxy.

She tried not to think of the rest of her childhood. A locked door stopped her dead in her tracks. Instead, she thought of Rodas and thought of Random. She picked out a cluster of distant stars. It was Ursa-17 – the galaxy that contained Rodas. She could be there in a matter of hours...

Suddenly her train of thought was interrupted by a beeping sound coming from a small monitor that was rising out of her desk.

Admiral Bagari stared at the screen. It was a personal message that had bypassed her official channels. Sighing she accepted the call and a familiar face appeared.

'Commander Serridian,' she said almost with a hint of surprise.

'Admiral...it's good to see you.'

The Admiral had a smile on her lips when she saw her old friend on the screen. It had slowly started to fade when she saw the distress on Serridian's face.

'Why am I getting the feeling that this isn't going to be a happy catch-up?' Bagari said.

'I'm sorry, Vanessa. I'm so, so sorry.'

'What have you done?'

A few minutes later Bagari burst out of her office and made her way down one of the long corridors of her ship. She ignored everybody who she passed, each one of them stopping in their tracks and saluting her with the respect she had earned. Before long she had made it to the command bridge.

'Ensign. Put me through to the Admiralty now!' she barked.

'Yes, Admiral,' came the reply. Bagari's face was like thunder. Serridian. How could he do it? He should have come straight to her. They trusted each other implicitly. Their friendship had gone back to their academy days. She'd been present on the day he had got married to his wife.

Hell, she'd introduced them! She was friends with both of them.

How had he got himself tied up in such a mess? How had his family ended up getting stuck on Rodas?

It wasn't the way that she had wanted to get involved in the fight but it was just the thing that would get the Space Seals over to Rodas to help, just as she had been itching to do.

A number of people flashed up on the big screen that Bagari was standing in front of. Ignoring their unanimous calls for answers as to why they were having a sudden conference, Bagari could waste no time.

'The security mainframe surrounding the planet Rodas has been compromised. We have to go there now.'

The Admiralty fell silent. The oldest looking of the group, a thin stick-like man, spoke first.

'How have you come by this information?'

'I have been informed of a soldier working on the mainframe who has been blackmailed into giving away the shutdown code. Their deception had been notified to the mainframe high command but they are unable to change the code. There is also an attack being mounted on the mainframe, one far greater than any it has ever withstood before. We have to support the mainframe. If the war reaches the other planets in Ursa-17, or further, the consequences will be dire.'

'We will debate this news,' said another Admiral.

'There is no time,' replied Bagari. 'The Stargazer and three other battle freighters are within range. We will be there in no time at all.'

'This is too delicate a political decision for us to make on the spot,' said the old Admiral.

'Then let me take the decision for us and I'll pay the consequences if all fails,' said Bagari.

The Admiralty and the crew of the Stargazer looked at each other unnerved.

'You would lose your command,' said an octopus-like-looking Admiral.

'What's a command if you can't do anything right with it?' replied Bagari.

'You will go down for this,' said the old Admiral.

'The galaxy will go down if we don't act. I'm not debating this any further. The battle on Rodas is nearing its end. The war of an entire galaxy is on the brink. We have to go...even if no one else is coming with us.'

'What must your crew think?' asked a female Admiral.

'They can think what they like. Any disagreement with my decision will be noted in my log and I'll make sure that they will not be punished.' Bagari had barely blinked.

'We have to go now. Whether you like it or not the Space Seals must do what we were set up to do. Protect and serve.'

The Admiralty fell silent again. The older man spoke first.

'We shall discuss this. For now, the Stargazer along with the Phoenix and the Lancet will go to Rodas. Do not intervene unless provoked or it is indeed necessary. Make contact with the mainframe high command and make sure that you have all the facts before engaging. Is that understood?'

'Crystal. I hope to see you all soon. Bagari out.' The screen snapped off and returned to the impressive starscape outside the battle freighter. She immediately marched to her chair as the command bridge hummed with activity.

'Red alert. Full speed ahead to Rodas now. All hands on deck. Prepare for battle.'

VII

By an open window that overlooked the chaos of Rodas down below, Serridian was as white as a ghost. He'd let them down. He'd let them all down. There was no way that he could go on. The guilt was tearing him apart and the worst part was that it had all been for nothing.

He peered down at the electronic read-out on his tablet again. He still couldn't believe the message that it displayed.

Serridian had been conned.

He felt sick. So, they hadn't been kidnapped after all? His family were safe. When he had been informed, just earlier that day that a terrorist group, sympathising with the Crimson Empire had captured his family on his home planet, he hadn't thought to check its validity. Stupidly he had believed it.

Why had he been chosen? Was someone in the Crimson Empire looking into his file and having seen a weakness there? Whatever had happened he had caused a massive security breach and now the rest of the universe was going to pay for it.

If only his wife had picked up the phone when he called home.

He would never have sent the code on the encrypted line to the anonymous "caller" if she hadn't been out at the time but he had panicked. He'd been so foolish. He'd betrayed everyone he knew and loved and worse of all he may have condemned Rodas to a bloody end.

He returned his gaze to the view window. Out of the corner of his eye, he could see the rhymical throbbing electric charge that bolted all through the mainframe. It was like a massive metal netting containing everything that was bad and evil about Rodas inside. Serridian had been consigned to the mainframe as an Ensign when he graduated from the Space Seals and he along with 500,000 other lifeforms from around the galaxy dedicated nine months a year of their lives to stay and maintain it, making sure that it would never be compromised.

Even now he could see a distant wave of heli-fighters breaking through the clouds, the usual flashes and bangs of conflict that flashed through a hazy dust-like fog.

Then he saw more. Then more. Second, by second it looked as though the fleet was growing and heading straight for the mainframe. Serridian shivered and dropped his tablet, the screen smashing as shards of glass collided with the hard floor. He scrambled for the intercom, the loud din of the engines and blades of the heli-fighters getting louder and louder as they grew closer.

Suddenly an alarm klaxon broke the tense air in Serridian's living quarters.

All along the mainframe red lights began to flicker off and on in unison. The mainframe had withstood attempts on it before but they had never seen a number attacking such as this. Serridian saw the advancing heli-fighters. This wasn't a small battalion of crimson attackers. This was thousands.

His hands shaking, he reached for the intercom and clicked the recording button as the shadow of the heli-fighters began to blot out the bright neon sun.

'This is Commander Serridian of Rodasian security mainframe section 1401, I'm sorry...I'm just...the mainframe code has been compromised. I didn't...I was tricked. I have taken the liberty of contacting the Space Seals for help...forgive me, I know the protocol but I take full responsibility. Serridian out.'

His voice trembling with fear, he sent the message to his superior, priority urgent, hoping that they would find the time to hear it. Praying, even, that his old friend Vanessa Bagari would get there in time.

He reached for his intercom, now only too aware that his large window was completely swamped by the vision of a number of heli-fighters poised to shoot. Serridian sweated profusely, a cold fear gripping him. He scrambled to send another, final message.

'My love...we are under attack; I may not get another chance so I just wanted to say-'

Serridian's words were drowned out by the horrific sound of laser fire. With the security shield down, the sound of the klaxon suddenly fell mute in his ears as the heli-fighters opened fire.

Frozen to the spot, Serridian watched as the glass on his window shattered before long, despite being reinforced against attack it was no match without a protective layer.

His room, along with so many others exploded, a huge fireball engulfing everything within. Those manning the defence systems returned fire with equal venom but it was too late to save the likes of Serridian.

His final message would remain unsent. His final act had given the Crimson Empire a dangerous advantage.

*

It wasn't the incessant singing that was ringing in Djanga's mind. It also wasn't the fact that they were making next to no progress in getting anywhere near HQ. There wasn't the thought of the impending ambush at any moment either which was worrying him. He was pretty certain that his men could withstand it.

He knew that they were being hunted. The Crimson Empire were too omnipresent, always lurking in plain sight and in the shadows, for

them not to be hot on their scent, especially after those who had been killed by him and his men upon rescuing the river dwellers. As he and the other marched on, far too slowly for his liking, it was none of these thoughts or sounds which were making him start to worry.

It was the noise that he could hear high above them, through layer upon layer of rock, that was making him uneasy. Despite their relative safety inside the mountain, there was a hum, a soft, distant hum which he had picked up not long after they had started their trip. It was a miracle he had any hearing left, let alone hearing that was good enough for him to pick up on something he had originally thought might be shell shock. He'd carried it with him for years, ever since his days as a Private on the front line protecting the boundary of his city, Kalasias. But as their journey had continued the sound of humming had grown ever so slightly louder. Looking side-to-side with his troops, he had wondered if he was going a bit mad, a common occupational hazard in his line of work. He'd started to realise that they had picked up on it too. Cautiously, he nodded and they readied their guns.

Behind them, Anji and Nkite had been having a ball. For the last few hours, they had been nattering away, getting to know one another.

Gron, who stood arm in arm with them, smiled to himself, not uttering a word, delighted that his young friend was making acquaintance and smiling again.

'...and then he fell in it!' chuckled Anji, concluding her story.

Nkite snorted. 'Into the fountain of youth!?'

'Yes!' they both burst out in laughter.

'He's a funny one, your friend,' said Nkite.

'Yeah, you can say that again,' said Anji, her laugh dying down, her eyes lost in thought. Suddenly she was miles away.

'You speak about him a lot,' said Nkite, noticing her new friend's sudden change in mood.

'We've had a lot of adventures together. It'd be rude of me to leave him out,' said Anji.

'Well, you don't seem to speak as much about Random.'

Anji realised she hadn't. 'He's different.'

'Tell me about it. When I was a child, I remember being lost. Alone. We were being evacuated from our home. My Mother and Father, we got separated. I was so scared but then I looked up and I saw this incredible sight. A blast of colour, a colour I had never seen before. I'd seen the coming together of two explosions simultaneously and in that moment, I had hope. Guess who it was who gave me that hope.'

Anji didn't have to think twice. 'Random.'

'It was rumoured back then that something was coming to save us, to stop the war. I never thought I'd bear witness to it.'

'So, you don't hate Random then?' asked Anji.

'He inspired me. Set me on a path. I have helped save so many people thanks to what I saw that night. The things I used to do. I once lured some soldiers into a church and shot them with purple paint. You should have seen their faces. It was like I had shot them with some deadly virus!'

'Paint! Like a paint gun?'

'Kind of,' replied Nkite. 'I'd seen how that purple colour had been made. For centuries people have talked about it being the real reason why we went to war in the first place. Red and blue. In that explosion, in my paintball concoctions, I saw peace, a world in which we could both live together. You know why?'

Anji shook her head.

Nkite continued. 'It was us and them. The Crimson Empire and the Sapphire Regime come together in harmony, repelling evil. That's what your friend Random had always represented to me. To so many. And so, we waited for him to return.'

'And now that he is here, the war will end,' said Gron. 'I can feel it in my old bones.'

'For so long I had had so much hope in my heart but today...having met him, I am not so sure anymore,' said Nkite.

'They do say don't meet your heroes,' joked Anji.

'Why do they say that? And who is "they?"' asked a bemused Gron.

Anji was lost for words momentarily. She'd forgotten that her way of speaking could sometimes be lost on those who were not from her part of the galaxy. The translation programme that had installed itself in her mind the moment she had stepped onto the Venus II back in the day made it easy to forget that wherever she went she was speaking a completely alien language.

'Look. I've seen Random do the most amazing things. I've seen him fight for so many people.'

'Then why is it only now that he has chosen to come back to fight for his own?' asked Nkite.

'I don't think that I should speak on his behalf. Please do believe me when I tell you that he has struggled with his conscience ever since he left.'

Nkite looked at the ground and kicked the dirt. 'Tell that to the people he hasn't saved.'

'I wish I could. Trust me. He'll find a way. He always does.' Anji smiled.

'I'll believe it when I see it with my own eyes,' she muttered.

'You will, Nkite. I don't doubt it. You'll see the streak of hope in the sky high above Rodas once again,' Gron smiled.

'You'll have to forgive my young friend, Anji, she's had a tough time of late.'

'Haven't you all,' said Anji who then broke into a friendly smile, 'it's fine, I get it. I can't comprehend the kind of lives you've all had but I've had my tough moments too.'

'How did you get through them?' asked Nkite with an inquisitive look in her eyes.

'I had my friends,' replied Anji.

'Then wouldn't it be better to keep your friends close than to drive them away?' said Nkite.

Anji knew exactly what she was referring to. She'd been probing her about Jake for most of the journey. 'Look, it's complicated.'

Gron and Nkite fell silent for a moment, knowing to leave the subject there, so they were then shocked that Anji began blurting out to them.

'It's just I've known him for so long that any feeling I used to have might have become quite...brotherly. We've been through a lot, and when we were young, we made a promise that we'd be together for prom, and if we were home right now, we'd probably have had it, but I'm not sure we'd have gone together, probably not. I mean who knows who we'd have gone with?

He's managed to get the hots for girls all over the cosmos but I've never once been so blatant. I mean, who does he think he is? He's not the only

one who can have feelings for others, is he? I'm not saying I have feelings for anyone, well, not right now, well, I'm not sure, there's this thing that happened...sorry, I'm babbling, aren't I?'

Nkite and Gron looked stunned. 'Maybe,' said Nkite.

'Sorry. I've got a lot going on in my head,' sighed Anji. 'At the end of the day, I have such a good relationship with Jake. I don't want anything to break it.'

'Then young girl, may I suggest when he comes back to you that you tell him that. It sounds like you have such a special bond,' said Gron.

'If he does make it back,' said Nkite.

Anji started to panic a little.

'That doesn't really help,' said Gron, before Anji had the chance to say something potentially worse. She fumed. There she was, doing her best to console a stranger she'd only just met and that's what she comes back with?

'Sorry. I don't really have time to talk about boys,' said Nkite.

'It's okay, honestly you're not missing out on much!' said Anji who was starting to regain her good mood. But deep down she really was starting to worry. What if things didn't go to plan? What if she never saw Jake again? Soon she was having trouble thinking about it anymore because of a loud hum that started to interrupt her train of thought.

'Stop!' came the cry from Djanga.

The soldiers protecting the hoard of river dwellers all barked out the same order. They all readied their guns as those that they were trying to protect started to sound panicked.

'Sargeant Djanga to HQ, come in please,' said Djanga into his wrist communicator. A horrendous concoction of noise burst through the tiny speaker. Anji's heart started to beat faster.

'Djanga. This is SRHQ. We are under attack. Repeat we are under attack,' came the cry from the other end of the communicator. It kept fizzing and popping in and out like the connection was slowly breaking. 'The Crimson Empire. There are too many of them. We are trying to hold them back but we've never seen...'

'Hello? HQ come in!' yelled Djanga.

'...thousands breaking through our embankments. Protect the refugees and fall back to Hawk 159. That's an order...need every man and woman who can fig-'

The comlink died.

'That humming sound, what is it?' asked Anji. It was now so loud it was as though they were all standing on an airfield.

'Heli-fighters.'

'How can we hear them? We must be hundreds of feet away from them,' said Nkite.

Suddenly it sounded like a bomb had gone off far away. The corridor started to shake and tiny bits of rock and dust fell down upon them all.

'They are bombarding the mountain!' said Djanga.

'Captain, Hawk 159 how far away would you say that we are from there?' asked Djanga to the soldier standing next to him.

'It's almost directly above us,' he said consulting his map.

'Oh, my zark,' cursed Djanga. 'We have to get to the surface now.'

'If we do that, we'll all be killed!' cried Anji.

'If we stay here, we will be buried alive!' said Djanga.

'I don't understand, we should be well protected even by a heavy bombardment. We shouldn't be at risk,' said Nkite.

'That's the trouble. It's not just a heavy bombardment it's a number of artilleries I've never seen before.'

'How do you know?' asked Anji.

'Listen to it! It shouldn't be possible but those engines are so great in number-'

Another shock of bombs sent the group sprawling to the ground, and some of them started to scream and panic. Anji could hear babies and children begin to cry.

'Is there anywhere safe we can take them?' she asked.

'No,' said Djanga chillingly.

'Then where's the next best place!?' said Anji in an angry yell.

Djanga grabbed the map from his Captain and gave it to Anji. On it was a lime green luminous digital read-out of the mountain and its surrounding flat, ground level and underground level areas.

'Take them here,' said Djanga pointing at what Anji looked like a nearby exit from the mountain. 'It's just far enough away for now.'

'And what will you do?' asked Nkite.

Djanga cocked his gun. 'Try and hold them off. You two are in charge. Go there and don't move unless you have to. Clear?'

'Crystal,' said Anji.

'You'd better take these,' said Djanga, who reached down into two handgun holsters on both of his thighs. He handed them to Anji and Nkite. 'Now go!'

Another explosion high up above rocked the mountain. Anji fell to the floor and was helped back up by Gron, who had somehow wedged himself beside a rock for stability.

'Right men, Hawk 159, let's go! Move!' said Djanga.

He and the rest of the Sapphire Regime soldiers who were supposed to lead the river dwellers to safety tore themselves away from those they were tasked to protect.

Anji watched as the soldiers left their view. She breathed heavily. She looked at the sea of terrified people in front of her. So many men and women, children and babies both red and blue looked back at her, fear flooding from their faces.

She looked at Nkite, who looked equally as fearful. Anji looked at her trembling hand and the gun that had been forced into it. She took a deep breath and pocketed it.

'Right,' she said taking a look at the map. The exit wasn't far away, she reckoned, and she steeled herself for the task ahead. 'Let's get out of here!'

VIII

As they flew high above the devastated ground far below, the occupants of the commandeered heli-fighter were shocked by the lack of opposition they had come across. Surely the soldiers Takten had dispatched would have been discovered by now? Hadn't they raised the alarm? As time wore on and their journey continued without incident, they soon realised why it was all too easy.

As they neared Kalor Maloso's base, a shadow had begun to form over the cockpit from outside. Random, having been stowed in the cramped mid-section had noticed it too. He tried to get up from his seat but fell back.

'Jake, could you unfasten me please?'

Jake was too preoccupied gapping at what was causing the shadow.

'Jake?' Random called again.

'Random you'd better see this,' said Takten, who was also staring in disbelief at what he was seeing.

'Fine, if no one else will do it,' Random said to himself. He clenched his body until it went rigid and with his strength, broke the clasp on his seat belt and moved to join the other two in the cockpit.

When he got there, he too was astonished.

'Zarks...' he said quietly.

The three men watched as they witnessed the huge swarm of heli-fighters shooting at the security mainframe.

'How many of them are there?' asked Jake, not taking his eyes off the action unfolding above them.

'Too many to count,' replied Takten. 'This is bad.'

Random regarded the lasers which looked like they were coming from the mainframe itself. 'At least it looks like they are fighting back.'

'It's not enough,' said Takten grimly.

'But that mainframe stretches across the planet, surely it will stay intact?' asked Jake.

'Not with a force that large concentrating on one specific spot,' said Random. 'What use would a net be if there's a massive hole in it.'

'They're trying to break out of the planet,' said Takten. 'I've never seen so many enemy heli-fighters before.'

'Then where have they come from?' asked Jake.

'I don't know, but it's time I found out,' said Random.

'You mean us?' replied Takten.

'No. I'm sorry but the plan has changed,' said Random firmly.

Takten was about to protest when he intercepted an incoming transmission through the communication channel. He stared at the readout. 'Oh, my zarks.'

'What?' asked Jake who was straining to see the read-out.

'There's an imminent attack on Hawk 159.'

'Is that as bad as it sounds?' asked Random.

'It's a stronghold for the Sapphire Regime. What's worse it's the final barrier before our base, and it's close to the mountain we left the refugees in.'

Jake's stomach lurched. 'Anji,' he said to Random. 'We have to help them.'

'They might not know that they are under attack, I don't have access to my channels in here,' said Takten.

'Then that settles it, the plan changes. Takten, how far to Maloso's base?' asked Random.

'We're almost on top of it, just over the ridge, but Random-'

'It won't be as heavily guarded as we thought. You two drop me off and go back to Hawk 159.'

'But Random-' Jake said.

'Don't argue with me, Anji may need your help. Even if they haven't made it out of the mountain yet they could be ambushed by this attack. Now please, don't argue you two.

When I give the order, Takten opens the door,' Random said as he strode towards it.

'So, I'm wearing a dead man's suit for nothing?' said Jake, feeling disgusted in himself and not for the first time wanting nothing more at that moment than a really hot shower.

'Plans change,' said Random. 'I'm sorry Jake. Hopefully, this will be the last time we have to make any.'

'Shall I let you out?' said Jake brandishing the key.

'You mean he's going to jump?' said Takten in astonishment. 'We're two thousand miles above ground level.'

'Yeah, he can handle it,' said Jake brushing his concern away.

Random looked at Jake and broke his handcuffs off with ease.

'Oh, well that was pointless then,' said Jake tossing the key away.

'Ready, Random?' asked Takten.

'Ready,' confirmed Random, who was bracing himself in the doorway.

'Good luck,' said Jake.

'And to you two,' said Random. He gave his friend a smile. 'See you soon.'

'Now,' said Takten. The door burst open and Random was sucked out instantly.

The cabin alarms started to sound, warning of depressurisation, prompting Takten to close them. The howl of the inrushing air ceased almost as quickly as it had started.

'Does he usually do things like that?' asked Takten.

'It's weirder when he doesn't,' replied Jake.

Random hurtled through the air, his eyes firmly fixed below. Fixed, and watering like mad considering he was falling at a very fast velocity. He ignored the roar of the rushing air past him as he formed his body into an arrow shape, intent on penetrating the base below.

Kalor Maloso's base – the Crimson Empire's HQ – was massive. A dirty, turgid rusty red, it didn't look tall from Random's vantage point but it was monstrous in scale. The base itself had been built into the blood-red rock of a mountainside, a common thing to find on Rodas, it seemed. It looked old, battle-worn. Random noticed that some parts of it looked newer and less battle scorched by laser fire.

As he tumbled ever closer, he began to brace himself.

Then, as he counted down the seconds in his head, something he had been doing since he had chosen the more direct route to his location, he pulled on a cord at his side.

Suddenly, a parachute exploded out of a bag on his back and sent him hurtling upwards in the air, a moment that to Random felt like his organs had all shot out his body and then rearranged themselves again as the parachute sent him sailing below.

Whilst Jake and Takten had been talking, Random had noticed a parachute pack hanging up by the side of the door on the heli-fighter, so he took the opportunity to nab it while they were not looking and hopefully look as cool as could be in leaving them via the door as they were flying.

After all, he had thought to himself whilst quickly constructing the idea in his head, it might be the last time he would be able to do something so heroic in front of his friend.

As he sailed down, he surveyed the base and looked for a way in. He noticed what looked like an observation part of the complex which was jutting out of the base and deduced that this was probably the area where Maloso ran his operations.

If he was right, the war would end a lot quicker.

If he was wrong, he'd have to get his hands dirty whilst finding Maloso.

Having found a possible route in he looked up.

His parachute obscured his view of the attack on the mainframe but everywhere else around him was silent. It was like the Crimson Empire had focused itself on two main targets. Then he thought of his friends. Clearly, Anji was going to be in trouble so sending Jake back to help her would help them make up.

He'd always known how close they both were. It didn't take a genius to have seen the connection the pair had, especially after so many years with them at his side. They'd never had a fight before and although Random didn't know all of the ins and outs, as he sailed down safely onto the roof of the base and tore his parachute pack off his back, he tried his best to shake his concern for them out of his mind.

Random walked up to the mountainside and looked for an opening into the base. He found none. He put his hands cautiously against the rockface, searching for a hidden entrance or something that would trip a release mechanism to allow him entrance.

He found none. Random huffed. He heard the distant gunfire high up above and noticed that the battle was starting to be lost by the security mainframe. More and more fires blinked into existence in the sky as piece by piece more of the netting that had contained the chaos of war for so many centuries was starting to tear further and further apart.

Random grit his teeth. Had Skateboard failed to convince Bagari to fight? There didn't seem to be any sign of the Space Seals anywhere. There wasn't any way of him knowing, either, whether his robot friend had been successful in recruiting their old friends to help.

He started to clench his fists and then, the all-too-familiar voices started to talk to Random again.

'What are you waiting for?' asked the female voice.

'Back up,' replied Random, still staring helplessly at the battle.

'It's down to you, Random. It's always been down to you. This was your burden. No one else's,' said the male voice.

'Okay, just shut up a second will you? All my life I've had your voice in my head. Taunting me. Polluting my mind with the idea that I am the only one who can stop all of this. But how can I? I know I've done some incredible things but this is beyond me.'

'You doubt yourself at the moment of destiny,' said the female voice calmly.

Random felt a tear drop down his cheek. 'Will I see them again? My friends?'

The voices stayed silent almost as though they knew that this wasn't the moment to install false hope.

Random sighed heavily. 'Okay, no more interruptions now. You're right. It's time I did something on my own. No friends to help. No help is on its way in any sense. Just me, Maloso and the fate of Rodas. No pressure...' he muttered the last part to himself. He gazed at the floor. There appeared to be a trap door leading into the base.

He looked down, wiping away dirt and grime off what looked like a small handle and a window that was smeared and ancient. He tried the handle, which felt rusty and stiff, and slowly managed to open it. Unable to see through the window he had no idea what awaited him inside.

'The easy way in?' he said as he swung his legs over the opening
and dropped himself through. As soon as his boots clanged onto
the metal floor seven feet below the opening, what had been a
dark corridor suddenly turned into a red flashing, loud klaxon
shouting chaos. Under the klaxon, a dozen or so guns clicked into
life and as he straightened himself up, Random spotted the red
sighter lights on his body. He stood up and faced the gun-toting
soldiers down. He clenched his fists, ready for the fight.
    'The hard way.'

IX

'Behind you!'

Anji's warning was picked up instantly by Nkite, who twirled in the air and fired a shot that burnt straight into the chest of a Crimson Empire soldier. The blast sent him reeling back, knocking one of his comrades to the floor as Nkite reloaded her pistol. Anji bent back down under the rock and allowed herself a chance to look back at those that she was helping to save.

'Anyone else got a gun?' she cried. Some of the river dwellers, men and women who were able to fight had instantly leapt to the group's defence the moment they had been ambushed at the exit of the mountain. Nkite had been telling Anji and Gron how their path to freedom had been too easy. Upon opening the exit door, and suffering a shot to the shoulder which still flooded her mind with pain every time she shot at her enemies, she knew that she had been right.

The Crimson Empire had been waiting for them all along. This was going to be a sport for them. Nkite took out a couple more soldiers as did some of the river dwellers.

'Anji, fire!' she yelled. 'Come on!'

Anji knew she had to. It was kill or be killed.

Gron did his best to keep his head down and put a protective arm around a young child who was crying uncontrollably. Many others were sobbing tears of terror as the group were slowly being driven back into the mountain. It wasn't any good. Step-by-step more and more soldiers were starting to push their way past the small firepower that Nkite was leading.

Anji fired her pistol and managed to miss a soldier by roughly a foot.

'What are you doing?' snapped Nkite.

Anji knew exactly. She couldn't do it. She knew she had to but she couldn't bring herself to shoot and kill someone, even though they were wanting to kill her! She was trying to aim her shots in places where they would be wounded. Eventually, she felt the gun wrestled from her hand by someone.

It was Nkite and she was furious.

'Whose side are you on?' she bit as she ducked down beneath the rock to keep out of harm's way.

'I'm sorry,' said Anji. 'I can't kill them.'

'You're no leader, get out of the way then!'

Anji wanted to punch Nkite in the face but this wasn't the time nor the place. Plus, she knew deep down she was right. Anji slumped back down the rock towards the cowering river dwellers as Nkite returned a volley of fire.

Anji found Gron. He knew immediately why she had fallen back to be with him and the others but Anji felt no judging looks from the old man burning in her direction. He understood. This wasn't her fight. But Anji felt remorse still. She was so torn but she wasn't a killer. She took the map out of her pocket and inspected it hurriedly.

Upon closer inspection, there was what looked like a smaller exit quite close by.

'We can get through here!' she yelled.

'It's too close to the exit up there, we'll perish,' said Gron.

'It's worth a chance!' said Anji.

Gron nodded. They had no other option. They could keep going backwards but to what avail? If they kept falling back, they would eventually be pincered and trapped still inside the mountain. They needed help...fast.

Jake and Takten were nearly at Hawk 159 but still too far away to help. In the distance, they could see a battle taking place on the ground. The scales were imbalanced in the favour of one side by five to one, Takten estimated, and he could see his men were losing badly. To the left of them was a breakaway group of soldiers who appeared to be firing on what Jake could make out as an opening in the mountainside. He could also make out that they were slowly making their way inside.

'Anji! Hey, they are firing on Anji and the refugees!' he cried.

'Dirty red faces,' he spat.

'Woah,' replied Jake, 'that's not on.'

'Look at what they are doing! They are wiping out my battalion! We have to help them!'

Jake took a moment to compose himself. He would have to be the sensible one in the cockpit.

They were screwed, he thought.

'Commander, there are innocent people trapped in that mountainside. They are unarmed. We've got to help them first.'

'I'm the soldier, we'll do what I say!'

Jake huffed. 'Fine, one heli-fighter against thousands of soldiers who can swat us down like a fly or one heli-fighter against a few dozen soldiers attacking unarmed civilians. What's it to be, soldier?'

Takten shot Jake a look of venom. 'There're red faces in the mountain too. Who's to say that they won't turn on our kind.'

'Where's all of this coming from all of a sudden?' asked Jake, disgusted by what he was hearing.

'They do nothing but murder us and you expect me to take pity?'

Jake was getting angry. 'On people who have turned their back on fighting and who are now probably being killed unarmed yes! I know you've fought for a long time but please park your prejudices for a few minutes and help them! There's nothing you can do for your men but you can still save others. Please Takten, please?'

Jake's tone had softened as his rant had concluded. Takten took one more rueful look at his comrades. He'd been in charge of them for a few years and had got to know them all. The men and women, their stories of what had led them to fight in his battalion. They'd lost people along the way and everyone had hurt and made the glory of winning the war that more distant a goal. But deep-down Takten knew that the teenager was right.

'Take the wheel,' he grunted. Jake looked at him quizzically and jumped to attention when Takten barked the same words at him again. 'Okay,' he replied, swapping seats as the heli-fighter buffeted shortly as the pilots were changing over. He had experience flying the Venus II and some other light spacecraft in his time and familiarising himself with the controls briefly he felt confident.

'Taking us in,' he said and as he hit the throttle the little heli-fighters engines groaned as they hit maximum speed.

Takten's face was one of tortured angst as he placed himself at the controls of the guns.

He was going to make sure he wiped out every stinking Crimson Empire soldier within his sighter and every single death was going to be for every one of his soldiers who were currently being slaughtered.

'We're in range in five...four...three...two...' Jake counted down as their position got closer and closer to the mountain.

Suddenly a burst of laser fire exploded from underneath the bowels of the heli-fighter. Takten had pressed down on his trigger a second early, sending masses of rock and debris from the ground flying up into the air, creating a slight dust cloud for the heli-fighter to fly through. A number of the soldiers at the back of the hoard that were breaking their way into the mountainside turned their attention suddenly on the craft that was attacking them from above but it was too late. Takten's marksman skills were exemplary. A big number of Crimson Empire soldiers cried out in agony as they were mowed down and fell to the ground. As Jake brought the heli-fighter around for another attack, Takten continued laying down his fire, taking out more and more of his enemies in the process. Some returned fire but they were no match for the heli-fighter, even if a few lasers burrowed into the hull of the ship, it wasn't enough to bring them down.

Takten smiled at everybody that fell lifelessly into the ground.

'This is for you, team.'

Inside the mountain, Nkite was starting to lose focus. The pain was just too much. She started to wane and a couple of her shots buried themselves in the floor. One of the river dwellers noticed that she was in trouble and went to her side. As he did, Anji returned to the front line with the map to tell Nkite that they had a chance of another escape route and she was distressed when she saw that the young girl had fallen unconscious.

'We've got to fall back,' cried out the river dweller.

'Then do it!' cried our Anji.

Moments later, they noticed that the sound of the laser fire was starting to die down. Before long, it became apparent that there were not many Crimson Empire soldiers firing on them anymore.

After a time, there were only a few left after some had run away. Then there were none.

Silence fell inside the mountain.

Nkite began to stir. Her face was sweating profusely. She wiped her brow with her good arm and tried to pick herself up.

'Did we?' she muttered and Anji shook her head. Bravely, she nervously moved closer towards the opening. As she did, she could hear nearby more laser fire but there didn't appear to be any as close as it had been. As she did her best to step over the throngs of dead soldiers lying at her feet, she squinted as the daylight outside became even brighter. Somewhere close she could hear an engine, one that sounded like it was on its last legs. Tentatively she peered through the mountainside opening.

Their attackers were all dead.

'Hello Anj,' said a familiar voice.

Anji looked in the direction the voice had come from and she instantly forgot about the war, about the danger outside of the mountain and ran towards the calling voice. The figure who had called out started running towards her too. There was a second figure, gun-wielding and limping slightly as they walked away from what was now a smoking crashed heli-fighter.

Jake held his arms out to Anji and pulled her in, hugging her tighter than he had ever held her. He kissed her hard on her shoulder and pulled away, holding her head in his hands. She was crying, and so was he.

'You're okay!' he said. 'We did it. We saved you!'

'Jake, I'm so sorry,' said Anji.

Behind them, the river dwellers, led by a gingerly moving Nkite who was being supported as she walked, moved out of the mountain.

'Stay inside for now, there is a battle taking place nearby!' cried our Takten.

'What happened?' asked Nkite.

'We happened,' said Jake proudly. He looked at Takten who was in no mood to celebrate.

'I'll radio for backup,' he said as he limped past Nkite and into the mountain.

'What's up with him?' asked Anji.

'His battalion is outnumbered. I've seen it, Anj. It's awful.'

'Did you do this?' asked Nkite, who was pointing at the throng of dead Crimson Empire soldiers scattered around them.

'Well, he did, I drove...then crashed...I've never landed a heli-fighter before, still haven't technically,' said Jake.

'Let's get back inside, and tend to your wound,' said Gron, who beckoned Nkite in. She shot Jake a smile of thanks and let herself be led away.

It was just Anji and Jake now.

'Jake I-'

'Let's not fall out ever again, yeah?' Jake interrupted.

Anji smiled. 'You read my mind.'

Jake took her hand. 'Let's get undercover.'

'Where's Random?' asked Anji as they followed the others.

'He's at the Crimson Empire base.'

'We must help him!' cried Anji.

'I know. While we think of what to do, shall we talk?'

Anji nodded. 'Of course.'

The friends walked arm-in-arm, doing their best to blinker out the horror surrounding them, and just trying to be happy that through everything that was happening at least they could take some consolation that they were together.

X

As he fired another round of lasers into a wall of broken and twisted mainframe, the General beamed a smile that was so sinister it made evil look good. For years he had wanted to do this. To lead the attack, and once he was absolutely sure that they were going to win, it was going to make all of his previous achievements look like nothing. As he watched as the security officers on board the mainframe who to him were returning fire in a frenzy, he pin-pointed his sights on one person he could see through the damaged windows where they were standing. With glee, he opened fire and watched as the window shattered and exploded into tiny shards of fire. Some of the occupants of the defence post tumbled out of what was now a room ablaze and he laughed to himself as he saw someone hurl themselves out of what had been the window. As the General saw them plummet to their death, he noticed something else. There was a shard of black sky poking out beyond the mainframe. It was incredible to the General. A black abyss with scattered twinkling stars. He whooped and cheered and made for his radio.

'All units. We've almost broken through, keep going!'

He spun his heli-fighter to one side, evading enemy fire with ease. Despite the overwhelming numbers the Crimson Empire had on their side they were taking heavy casualties. In a normal attack, one of those the General had been on countless times and lost, they would have been obliterated, even if they had made some progress in their attack. After every campaign against the mainframe those that were keeping the war contained on Rodas always seemed to repair any damage quickly – and redouble their artillery also. But on this occasion, it wasn't going to be. The Crimson Empire had them. The number of ships was far too many for even the countless guns of the mainframe to handle.

The General turned to the officer who was sitting beside him in the cockpit. 'Tactical,' he asked. 'How much longer until the mainframe is fully breached?'

The officer, a young woman whose battle-scarred features were concealed by the standard issue helmet they were all required to wear, punched some instructions into her computer. 'Estimate roughly three minutes, sir.'

'Let's make it one,' he purred grabbing for the trigger again and squeezing it with all the want and abandon of a naughty child with a water pistol in summertime. 'Prepare to enter the code. I can't wait to see the entire thing shut down...'

The heli-fighter's incredible force looked like an army of flying ants in the sky and they were crawling all over the security mainframe. Inside, the people who had worked so hard for so long to maintain order and repel the attacks against them were starting to lose hope.

In a command chair, a man named Phillips sat watching the battle through gritted teeth. Like his opposite number, the General, he too was a seasoned campaigner but nothing had prepared him for anything like this. As soon as the attack had begun, he had sounded battle stations, unaware that the code had been cracked by the Crimson Empire and that they were about to fail in their lifelong mission. 'Report!' he yelled as a bank of computers near him started to spark threateningly.

In front of him, dozens of people hurried around their post, sending messages to the front line and to anyone who might be able to help. But he knew that the situation was hopeless. Down below, intel has kept them up-to-speed with the terrible surge of the Crimson Empire.

He knew that the Sapphire Regime had been driven so far back and were now in such small numbers they were practically extinct. Phillips had sat there, revolted at the detail of how Kalor Maloso's master plan had played out.

The blue side of Rodas was now on the verge of extinction and somehow, he'd swelled the number of his army to an astonishing size and they no one seemed to have any idea how he had done it.

To his immediate right, the computers that had been sparking and hissing suddenly gave out and exploded across the room, sending him and the others in the room sprawling to the floor.

Phillips picked himself up, a sharp pain shooting up through his thigh. He took a quick look down and noticed that a piece of shrapnel had embedded itself deep inside. As blood started to gush from the fresh wound, he refused the help of one of his officers and pulled himself back up into the chair.

It was forbidden to ask for help from outside. He looked at the chaos around him. The officers he knew lying wounded or worse at his feet. The mainframe he had sworn to protect went up in smoke. The impossible size of the fleet of the Crimson Empire was about to crush his previously impenetrable mainframe. As he started to black out from the pain, he had one thing firmly focused on his mind.

To hell with forbidden. They needed help.

As the hole in the mainframe was blown even bigger, he opened an outside channel.

'This is...Admiral Phillips of the Rodasian Security...Mainframe...We've-'

'We hear you loud and clear, Admiral,' came a female voice crackling over the speaker system.

Phillips looked aghast as a volley of heavy artillery pierced through the newly made hole in the mainframe and took out a dozen or so unsuspecting heli-fighters. Seconds later another bombardment took out more and again and then again.

The General looked on with rage burning under his skin as a cascade of ships that were unfamiliar to him burst into the planet's atmosphere and opened fire on his fleet. He reached for his communicator again. 'Maintain your fire on the mainframe!'

'Sir!' cried the soldier sitting at tactical. 'There's something else coming through!'

They watched on as a huge battle freighter sailed through the hole and began opening fire on the fleet. The General took note of the massive gun turrets that were firing relentlessly. 'Attack the freighter!'

Admiral Bagari stared in disbelief at what the Stargazer had flown into. 'Seal the hole in the mainframe. We have to protect it at all costs. Tactical, maintain your firepower. Give them all we can.'

'Aye, Admiral,' came the call. She watched on as her officers worked as fast as they could to repel the barrage of heli-fighters. The crew lurched as the Orbtial groaned to a halt, the vast bulk of the huge battle freighter having sealed the breach.

Bagari watched as a group of heli-fighters separated from the swarm and began to approach the Stargazer. 'Have we got the intel on the number of ships attacking the mainframe?' she asked.

'There are 21,976 of them. Falling all the time. They have minimal shields. Not enough to defend against our weapons,' said the Tactical officer.

'These are small crafts,' replied Bagari. 'But to stop just under 22,000 of them is a big ask. We need backup. How far away is the rest of the fleet?'

The comm officer pressed several buttons on her command post. '14 minutes away, Admiral.'

Bagari gritted her teeth. The Stargazer could hold her own but she knew they could be in trouble if they couldn't get there any sooner.

'Send a call out to the fleet. Tell them to step on it,' said Bagari.

'Yes, Admiral.'

The crew of the Stargazer looked on the viewscreen as a hoard of heli-fighters opened fire. The battle freighter lurched slightly.

'Divert auxiliary power to shields, everything except life support and weaponry,' said Bagari. She witnessed a crossfire of relentless red laser fire hitting the heli-fighters and picking them off one by one and seeing them sear out of the picture in a blaze of fire. Still, they attacked.

'Admiral, they are changing the code to the mainframe!' said one of the officers working on the long bank of instruments stretched out before Bagari.

'How can you tell?' asked Bagari.

'We've been granted access by the security mainframe; they want our help in resetting the code.'

'Do it!' Bagari yelled as the Stargazer was hit with more enemy fire.

'I can't. I'm locked out,' panicked the young officer. He received a message on his read-out screen. 'The mainframe is too!'

Bagari started to feel the panic hit her like a wave. In all her years in charge of the Stargazer, they had been in situations just as lethal but now the entire security of the planet was about to be compromised – and there was nothing they could do to stop it.

'Don't worry, Admiral, I believe I can help.'

A familiar old voice broke through over the intercom.

Bagari allowed herself a smile.

'You took your time,' she joked.

'We're barely any later than yourselves,' came the calm robotic voice. 'Now, might I ask you to move over a little so that we can squeeze through please?'

Bagari nodded at the helm. The battle freighter lurched again, still giving it everything it had and yet barely making a dent in the sheer volume of enemy vessels.

'Thank you, kindly,' said the voice again.

The helm and tactical officers gave each other a quizzical look. Suddenly, a battered, damaged ship, which until recently was the envy of the universe in the good-looking ship's department exploded across the viewscreen, firing upon the heli-fighters as it tore into the planet's atmosphere.

'Good to have you with us, Admiral,' said the robotic voice again.

'You too Skateboard, now any luck with the code?' replied Bagari.

'Oh, I changed it a few seconds ago. Sorry, I got slightly distracted. I managed to lock out the Crimson Empire's hacking attempts and send them a spike. You shouldn't worry about them trying to do that again.'

'Incredible,' said Bagari. 'You'd better get out of here; we'll hold the fort.'

'Agreed. The situation is looking dire on the planet's surface. We shall locate Anji and Jake and set about with our plan.'

'Best of luck to you all,' said Bagari. 'Stargazer out.'

The comm-link fell silent. Bagari watched as the Venus II suddenly became invisible. It had managed to pick off several heli-fighters and manoeuvre past any deadly attacks from enemy fighters before Skateboard had deployed its cloaking device.

'Let's just hope they are all okay,' she said to herself before turning to the matter at hand.

'Tactical, keep firing,' she anchored herself to her command chair. 'This is going to get bumpy.'

XI

Random pelted as fast as he could down one of the many identical corridors in the Crimson Empire's headquarters. Around every corner he had thought he was coming nearer and nearer to Kalor Maloso and yet the soldiers were continuing to drive him back.

But he wasn't going to let them.

As he bounced off the walls and ceiling with impeccable agility and prowess, he dismantled the soldier's guns with ease and brought everybody to their knees. The word was spreading rapidly around the base that he was there. It had left some of the most hardened amongst Kalor Maloso's troops quaking in their boots.

Some of them remembered the night that Random got away.

When the purple explosion was seen planet-wide across Rodas, it was the moment that had made the Crimson Empire shudder with fear.

It also accelerated the plans they had for total planetary domination.

Yet despite the inspiration, they knew that one-day Random would come back and the being who was created to stop them would return.

Now he was here and there was no chance of any of them putting an end to him. He was just too quick. Too strong.

It was up to Maloso now.

Random pushed aside a laser-like spear and snapped it in one swift movement. He punched the soldier who had been holding it firmly in their chest and sent them sprawling across the floor. Random was panting but didn't look tired from his exertions. He strode across what looked like a cargo hall but he had no awareness of the space of the room, only the instinct to duck and weave past the enemy shots from high above on a gantry.

He picked up what looked like a discarded piece of sheet metal and threw it high above his head.

The metal sheered through the gantry, causing it to groan and buckle. The soldiers who had been firing down upon him started to scramble to escape the gantry but before they could, the split caused it to fall inwards.

Some held on for dear life, others fell from the great height to their ends but Random didn't look behind him.

The attack on his person seemed to be dying down. As he made his way down another corridor, he grew tired of searching for Maloso and instead of incapacitating another of his attackers, he moved at the speed of light right up to the face of his latest obstacle and snapped their arm behind their back, disarming them instantly.

'Please, no!' was the pathetic cry in response to Random's brutal action.

'No more games. Take me to him.'

*

Anji sat looking out of the mountain exit into what looked like a harsh red sandstorm. Over the discontent of the people, she was trying to help, she could hear the sound of gunfire fresh as the morning sun in her ears. Rodas really was a hell hole and she was doubting their efforts to help.

It hadn't been long after reuniting with Jake that he and Takten had decided to scout the battle taking place just over the ridge. Accompanied by a few of the more keen and able river dwellers, they had taken off again in the direction of danger, leaving Anji alone in her thoughts and the people she had somehow helped to keep safe regathering themselves but she couldn't help but feel alone despite being surrounded by over a hundred other souls.

Random was in the hornet's nest, Skateboard was missing and she had almost lost Jake, her one constant in the crazy adventures they had got themselves into ever since they were kids.

She had noticed Nkite's looks of disappointment too and they hadn't been helping her mood. Sure, she couldn't fire on someone, even if they were trying to kill her.

After all that she had been through, didn't that say more about her character than Nkite ever could? Even now she could feel her disapproving gaze as Gron finished patching her up.

Gron had also clocked his young friend's annoyance. 'She didn't do anything wrong; you know?'

'She said she'd help,' replied Nkite.

'And so, she has. We're all still alive. If it wasn't for you and her, I doubt that would have been the outcome.'

Nkite groaned.

'Nkite. I know today has been a bad one but you really mustn't take it out on her.'

'Talking about me, are you?' said Anji.

Gron sighed. 'I meant no ill.'

Anji moved to join them. She smiled. 'I know. Could we have a minute please?'

Gron nodded and gave a look to Nkite. The girl snorted and looked the other way as Anji sided up next to her.

'Look. I'm not a killer. I never have been and I never will.'

'Then what use are you to us?' said Nkite.

'Nkite we're trying to save lives here not take them.' Anji gave the girl a sympathetic look. 'I know. It's hard.'

Nkite laughed. 'It's much worse than that. All we've ever known is death and killing.'

'You also know compassion. Take Gron for example. I've only known him for five minutes and he's one of the kindest people I've ever encountered. And there's you. When we were trying to escape the caves, you were telling me about why you fight, why it kept you going. At not one moment in your stories did I think that you were all about killing. Nkite, you have saved so many people. Just look at them,' she gestured to the river dwellers. Nkite watched as they went about passing around food rations. She saw mothers and fathers cradling their children. She saw every one of them putting on a brave face.

'They are doing what they can,' said Nkite.

Anji tried not to tut. 'Nkite they are alive. I can see hope in their eyes. I can still see it in yours.'

'Really? All I can feel is doubt. We are marooned. Cut off from the people who were supposed to help and why? Because they themselves are trapped.'

'Who knows? When Jake and Takten get back, they might tell us differently. Maybe the Sapphire Regime are fighting back!'

'The air feels colder now,' whispered Nkite. 'I'm sorry I was angry at you. In a way I envy you. You stood in the face of danger and said no. That was once me. Until today. Now I am not sure what that makes me.'

Anji placed a caring hand on Nkite's own. 'It makes you a hero. In a world of chaos, you are a shining light, Nkite. So are these people. Look at them. Red and blue together. There's no fighting here, even after everything that they have been through. This is what Rodas should be. As long as people like you are around it is what Rodas WILL be.'

Nkite allowed herself a little smile.

'Anyway,' said Anji, changing the subject, 'how's the shoulder?'

'It'll heal,' Nkite said wincing as she moved it a little. 'I'll take on board your words Anji if you promise to take on board mine.'

'Go on then,' smiled Anji.

'Never stoop to our level. Even in the bleakest hour, don't change who you are.'

Anji nodded. 'I promise.'

Gron had been checking up on some of his people but noticed that the two girls were getting on much better now. He allowed himself a smile and realised that today, despite all the horror they had collectively been through, he probably smiled more than he had done in a long while.

He walked into the open space outside of the mountain and looked out into the barren wilderness. He could feel the coarseness of the dirt on the ground being whipped up into the air.

'A storm is coming,' he yelled back as the wind grew louder.

'Hopefully, it'll pass,' said Anji. 'They always do.'

'Wait,' said Nkite who spotted something in the distance.

Anji and Gron met her gaze and tried to look out for what she had spotted. Slowly, a few faint outlines of what looked like people started to bleed into view. It looked like they were running. One of them was yelling something indistinctly.

'It's Jake!' cried Anji.

'What's he saying?' asked Gron.

Nkite's face hardened and she grabbed her gun from her holster. 'We don't need to hear it to know.'

It was Jake. He was pelting it back towards them at a speed that Anji had never seen before. His pace was almost fast! As they got closer, they could see that the others with him were firing shots at something behind them as the blue glow from their lasers disappeared into the gloom. A string of red lasers seemed to be following Jake and the others and they desperately zig-zagged to avoid them.

'Get back!' came the now barely audible cry from Jake.

'Oh my god...' said Anji.

Through the sandstorm, the terrifying sight of what appeared to be hundreds of Crimson Empire troops bled into view over the ridge and they were running to.

Jake, Takten and two of the river dwellers who had accompanied them finally made it into the cavemouth. Jake collapsed exhausted into Anji's arms.

'Anyone who can fight with me, the rest of you fall back!' cried out Nkite.

'The Sapphire Regime?' asked Anji.

Jake was unable to reply and was gasping for air.

'Crushed,' said Takten. 'All gone.'

'What?' asked Anji. 'What about Djanga?'

'I told you,' shouted Takten crossly, 'they are gone!'

The volume of the distressed river dwellers rang around the mountain cave.

'Please!' said Anji as she dropped Jake on the floor, winding him, 'Move back!'

'Anji, go with them,' said Nkite, who with her good arm was helping Jake back to his feet.

'I'm staying here,' replied Anji.

They took cover as shots were fired at them, sending debris all over the place.

'Return fire!' yelled Takten. The rebels did as they were instructed. Jake pulled Anji behind a rock and picked up his gun and started to fire blankly into the onrushing hoard.

Takten's face was awash with tears. His whole regiment was dead. He'd seen their lifeless bodies with his own eyes. He couldn't save them. Now they were sitting ducks. No way out. If they retreated back into the mountain, they were only delaying the inevitable. By firing back now at least they were putting up a fight.

The Sapphire Regime's HQ. Its smouldering ruin was burnt into his memory. The place he had gone to train to become a soldier, unlike so many others in his intake, willingly, was the place that had made him a soldier. No, not just a soldier. A man. It was gone. He knew not what had happened to them or just how many of the Sapphire Regime still existed but he didn't hold out much hope that many had got out alive.

As he stared unblinkingly into the onslaught, he started to notice a light up above. It tripped his concentration. Soon the other rebels also stopped fighting.

Jake trained his eyes on the intruder on the battlefield and a wide smile beamed across his face. 'Anj!!!' he exclaimed.

Anji took one look up and grabbed Jake's arm. 'Skateboard!'

The light was so much more than just a light. It was hope for all of them. A familiar sight blew through the dust and opened fire on the Crimson Empire, taking out so many soldiers in one swoop.

It was the Venus II.

The gantry lowered from the belly of the ship out of which sprung what looked like an army of fantastic multi-coloured horses. Upon their back rode an equally impressive array of people whose skin was also all the colours of the rainbow in bright gold armour and from the spears that each of them was wielding shot lightning bolts which also helped in the ambush.

'Anj, aren't they?'

'Dosas, yeah Jake,' replied Anji, who was just as stunned as her friend was. 'So that's where Skateboard has been!'

The Crimson Empire was stunned by the counterattack, almost as much as Nkite and the other river dwellers were. As the Venus II hovered close to the ground, the sound of its engine adding to the orchestra of laser fire, galloping hooves and the winds of war, a few more people bounded down the gantry and into the cave mouth.

Anji and Jake were astonished to see who they were as they jumped over the same rocks that they, along with Nkite, Takten and the fighting

river dwellers were sheltering behind.

'Hold on, you're-'

'Let's leave it until later, Jake,' said Yana, who spoke whilst simultaneously firing her weapon and landing one of her shots firmly in the helmet of a Crimson Empire soldier, which broke open like an egg.

'Delilah! Benaya!'

'Like she said Jake, later!' yelled Delilah.

'Yeah...' blinked Jake. Back to the matter at hand.

On board the Venus II, Skateboard was alone but in contact with his friends. He had fitted Solenia, Yana, Delilah and Benaya with earpieces which allowed them all to stay in contact. 'Solenia, we have to drive the troops away from the mountain. I'll lay down a spray of fire, could you mop up, so to speak?'

'On it,' came the curt reply.

'I'll reapply the cloaking device and protect the Valkyries,' he announced. After doing just that, the Venus II became invisible again. Before that some of the Crimson Empire troops had shot at the ship, leaving minimal damage but a shield system that had been weakened a little. It had been necessary to forgo the cloaking device to lower the gantry – it had been a design flaw for the Venus II that Skateboard had known about but never got around to fixing.

Also, as the Venus II had been designed on Rodas as a galaxy-class fighter ship in the first place, he had the capability to deal with pretty much any enemy hostility. It was the first time he had ever used it, and normally he was against violence, but this was Rodas, there was an entire planet, nay galaxy to save, and he would deal with his morality chip at a later date.

For now, he had to do, no, they all had to do what they were doing, and that was winning.

XII

Kalor Maloso sat in his chair, overseeing his master plan and the magnificence of it all. High above, his ships were fighting to open the security mainframe, something that they had never been able to do until now. Across the barren wilderness that had once been the proud citadel of Rodas and the brilliant architecture that until recently had once been the rotten ruins of the cities and dwellings that were now nothing but dust. He had levelled Rodas into the dirt and his forces were now using it to cull in vast numbers what remained of the Sapphire Regime. All the time the soundtrack to his chaos was screaming out over the intercom system. But it wasn't the noise from the battle outside he was purring too. He'd cut himself off from those he had full power over.

The room was cold now. He could feel a chill weaving its way through his bones. He pulled his robe up around what was left of him but he knew it wouldn't keep out the chill of what awaited him.

Like children leaving home, he'd decided to leave his forces to it. The millions of soldiers he had at his disposal knew their orders and followed them implicitly.

He'd brought about conquest for the Crimson Empire, he could see it as clear as day all around him. As he had observed, what was left of his enemies was all but gone.

All that was left now was the final confrontation, he had to be strong for that. The end was in sight.

The noise of people shouting, firing off weapons and fighting and screaming that played out over his speaker systems was what was happening within his very own base. Maloso smiled. He wouldn't have long to wait now.

He rested his eyes as he continued to wait and played out his victories in his head. Before his mind's eye, all the glorious echoes of the past came to life in front of him. The bombing of the Alixier, the end of the resistance, the time he had personally pulled the limbs from his opposite number in the Sapphire Regime and watched the horror on their face as they had bled to death before him. What glorious memories to accompany him into the darkness.

In that moment the doors to the room split open, the combination of wood and metal splintering and bending in a show of great strength. His personal triumphs folded themselves neatly back in his memories and he opened his eyes and looked at the person who had broken in and disturbed his peace.

The person in question he had been waiting to see again for so long and as he gazed down at them, his chair at a higher vantage point than the entrance to the room, he noticed the dazed, almost lifeless forms of his personal guards, dangling from the grip of the intruder like two rag dolls, and smiled a benevolent grin.

'Ah Random,' he sneered. 'What's taken you so long?'

*

On the ground, the section unit leader who had led the attack on the Sapphire Regime was lying in the mud. All around his broken frame, he could see more of his troops being brought to their knees.

These people, he thought. Who were they? They were not of red or blue colour? These were aliens who had involved themselves in a war in which he felt they had no business. As he coughed violently for the third time since an electric spear had pierced his stomach just a minute earlier, he reached for his intercom. The main battalion had to know about this.

His breakaway section, who had spotted that they were being spied on and were pulled away from the fun of the battle with their enemies, had been lured into a trap, he was certain of it.

Now, as he flipped the communication link open, it was time to turn the tide back in their favour again.

Were there more of these outsiders? What about the attack on the mainframe, was that going to plan? He had to know. As a taste of copper filled his lungs and made him choke even more, he began to call for his superior when out of nowhere, a pretty woman on a multi-coloured horse drove another spear into his flesh, this time plunging him in the chest.

The link was open, but no message made its way back to HQ. They wouldn't have heard it anyway. There was no one manning the communications link now. Not since someone had got inside the Crimson Empire base and torn it to shreds...

Solenia pulled her spear out of the soldier's chest and spun her horse around. The attacking faction was almost vanquished. She looked around her. She saw a few casualties among her own number but then after some quick mental arithmetic, relaxed in the knowledge that none of her Valkyries had been killed.

With the enemy now in full retreat, she raised her spear high above her head and cheered victoriously. The Valkyries followed in their Queen's triumph.

'I don't want to spoil your moment, your Majesty, but we have far from won. Suggest we

return to the mountainside. We can discuss there our next move and please, we must hurry before they attack again, in greater force.' Skateboard's instruction was a sound one, she thought and she led her army back across the battlefield as she heard the roar of the invisible Venus II's engines high above her.

Jake and Anji emerged from their hiding place and hugged each other before turning to their old friends and embracing them enthusiastically.

'What the hell are you guys doing here?' asked Jake.

'These are friends of yours?' asked Nkite, who along with her comrades had finished their mini-celebration.

'Old, old friends!' confirmed Anji. 'And look at you Yana, you're wearing a suit now!'

'Skateboard found us,' replied Delilah. 'He told us that you needed some help. Considering what you did for Genocia it was the least that we could do to lend a hand.'

As she spoke the roar of the Venus II's engine grew louder as Skateboard hovered the ship above the mountain opening, allowing the hundred or so dosas into the cave underneath. Upon entering the cave two Valkyries dismounted their dosas, who behaved impeccably unlike the horses Anji had seen back in her time on Earth and they helped Solenia off her steed.

'Blimey, Solenia, you too? When I see him, I'll have to tell Skateboard that if I'm ever in a hostage situation...again...I want him to do the talking!'

Benaya stood aghast at the dosas. They were the most elegant creatures she had ever seen. She turned to Delilah and signed to her that if they survived this, she wanted one for her next birthday.

'I believe that you should address me as Your Majesty before saying anything else to me, young Jake.'

Jake blushed and bowed. Anji followed suit whilst Yana, Delilah and Benaya felt that after hours of being cooped up on a small spaceship with the Queen, they were more than well acquainted to bow or curtsy again. Even if she'd requested them to do it and had refused to speak to them until she did.

'Oh yes, and, er, sorry your Majesty, about the Flux and all while we are at it,' said Jake apologetically.

'Thank you. Yes, I must concede that he is a worthy speaker, make no mistake.'

The gangway hydraulics hissed as Skateboard walked out from the Venus II. Anji and Jake threw themselves at him and hugged him so tightly that he thought they were going to buckle his metalwork.

'Skateboard, it's so good to see you! So that's where you go to? You went back to find old friends?' asked Anji, so happy to see him she could feel tears erupting in the corners of her eyes.

'Indeed, miss Anji. I'm so sorry it took us so long.'

'So, whose plan was this?' asked Jake.

'It was Captain Randoms. I fear that he is not with you?'

'He's in the Crimson Empire's base,' said a forlorn-looking Takten. He was sitting at the foot of a large rock staring into the ground. Nkite had noticed that he had been like that since the battle had been won and felt for him and all that he had lost. 'I took him there myself.'

'Then there is no time to waste. We need to implement the next part of the strategy before it's too late.'

'Woah woah woah, who put you in charge?' asked Nkite.

'We have!' replied Anji, Jake, Delilah, Yana and Solenia in unison.

'Fair enough,' replied Nkite sheepishly.

'What do you mean the next part of the strategy?' asked Jake.

'Er, shouldn't we be worried about the Crimson Empire coming back for more? They won't give up that easily,' said Anji.

'I've extended the shields from the Venus II to this entrance so we will be safe for a moment at least,' confirmed Skateboard. 'Now please, listen carefully. This planet's very future is at stake.'

'What do you mean, "at stake?" said Takten churlishly. 'It's gone. The Crimson Empire have won. I saw it myself.'

Skateboard was a little lost for words. 'He means,' said Jake softly, 'we saw the Sapphire Regime's HQ. It's been destroyed.'

'Ah,' said Skateboard. He watched as a kindly old man approached Takten with what he could only guess was liquid refreshment. 'I am so sorry for any and all losses that have occurred today. But the faster we act now the quicker we can save Rodas.'

'Save it!' Takten slapped the mug out of Gron's hand and ran right up to Skateboard. 'You're just an old service robot. What gives you the right to say that you can save it? If you and your Random friend hadn't disappeared years ago none of this would have happened!'

Nkite stood silently. She felt Takten's pain all too well.

Benaya and Delilah saddled up next to Skateboard. 'Hey, he knows what he's doing!'

'Oh yeah? And what gives you two any right to come here and get involved.'

We just saved your backside! signed Benaya.

'It's alright Benaya he's just cranky because he hasn't had his nap today,' said Delilah,

Takten's rage exploded and he hurled himself at the pair but was held back by Jake and Anji and Yana.

'Guards! Take him,' ordered Solenia as two burly Valkyries took over and restrained him.

'Jeez, Delilah, he's just lost his people,' said Anji.

Delilah suddenly looked embarrassed. 'Oh, sorry, I thought that you were just being ungrateful.'

'Please, sirs, madams, we really do have to act quickly, there is a lot to do. The mainframe is being defended-'

'By whom?' asked Jake.

'The Stargazer is up there now helping out the air defences. There are more battle freighters on the way,' continued Skateboard. 'But as far as I am aware there is little resistance on the ground.'

'I never thought that I would be relieved to see Admiral Bagari and the Space Seals again but here we are. As for resistance, well, there might not be,' said Anji. Takten was staring at her.

'Hang on, if I widen the communication signal, I can put out a call to any survivors. If these two bozos will let me go...' he hinted towards Solenia, who gave the nod of approval for Takten to be released.

'Sorry again,' said Delilah.

'So just how bad is it down here?' Asked Yana.

'Bad. The resistance has taken heavy casualties and was on the brink of extinction BEFORE today's attack. This latest wave is one that has been sent to finish us off,' said Takten.

'Are these the only people left?' asked Solenia.

'Oh no!' said Anji. These people are peaceful. We were helping to get them to safety.'

'They're with me, I'm Nkite by the way, not that I'm sure if this is the right moment to swap names.'

'It isn't, sadly, just be safe in the knowledge that everybody here is on the same side,' said Skateboard, who was growing impatient and slightly worried at how time was passing them by. 'Our main focus of attack will be the Crimson Empire's HQ. It'll pull as many of Kalor Maloso's forces back into one central position.'

'That's an idea, but there are hundreds of thousands of them out there, possibly millions,' said Takten, who was starting to repress his grief for the time being.

When the rest of the Space Seal Armada arrives it'll even the odds but for now that's our destination. It's the nerve centre for this entire operation and we have to help Random.' Skateboard started wheeling up the gantry again.

'Hold on, what shall we do with the river dwellers? They can't just stay here,' asked Anji.

'They won't. We can keep them safe here in the Venus II. Turn the cloaking device on and no one will know where they are, except us. They will be totally safe.'

'Nowhere is safe on Rodas,' said Takten mournfully.

'I didn't say that they would be on Rodas. The Venus II has the security mainframe code. I'll remote control it through the mainframe, alert the Space Seals to its whereabouts and then they can keep them safe in space,' said Skateboard.

'And we'll be marooned again!' moaned Jake.

'Only until the battle is won. The question is, who is going to look after everybody on board?' asked Skateboard.

'I will,' the elderly man stepped forward.

'Gron are you sure about this?' asked Nkite.

'Positive. Plus, I've always wanted to go into space!' a look of childish glee cheered on the old man's deep-lined face.

'Thank you, mister?' asked Skateboard.

'Gron.'

Thank you, sir. If you would care to lead your people up the gangway if you'd be most kind?'

Nkite hugged Gron with all her might. 'I'll wait for you,' he said.

'You better do,' she said with a tear falling down her cheek. He pulled away from her and smiled another broad smile and wiped the tear away.

'Ah, there it is,' he said.

'What?' asked Nkite.

'Your hope.'

Nkite smiled back.

'We'll help you all get on board, now come on everybody, follow us if you can,' said Yana as she started to help the river dwellers move onto the ship.

I'd better safeguard the cockpit,' said Skateboard to Anji and Jake. 'We wouldn't want someone to flick the wrong switch.'

'Er, Skateboard, could you lock my room too please?' Jake asked nervously.

Anji caught a whiff inside the ship. 'Pwoar! What's been going on in there?'

'Ah, yes, it's not the cleanest ship in the galaxy right now but it'll do,' said Skateboard.

Anji shot a look an accusatory look at one of the dosas, which stared her out in response.

'I'll update Admiral Bagari too and try and get a better understanding of how it's going up there,' Skateboard continued.

'How far away is the base?' asked Delilah.

'It's a fair way,' said Jake. 'Took us several minutes to fly there, oh yeah. Hang on, if we can't go on the Venus II then how are we getting there? It'll waste time to walk!'

'We'll ride. My dosas can carry us all,' said Solenia.

'Oh, great,' said Jake sarcastically. He instantly thought back to his last uncomfortable ride on the back of a dosa back on the planet Spectronia.

'Makes sense,' said Delilah who went off to help Yana. Benaya followed suit but not before she showed her excitement about getting the opportunity to ride one.

'Mind the mess,' Skateboard said as he passed the river dwellers who were starting to fill up in the midsection. He sealed the door to the cockpit and made his way back down the runway, calling Bagari on his portable intercom system as he went. 'Admiral, requesting an update.'

*

'This isn't the best time, Skateboard,' cried Bagari, her once neat hair now flopping in a sweaty mess over her forehead. 'The Stargazer is being swarmed. We're doing our best to see them off but there are just too many of them.'

'Oh dear,' replied Skateboard. 'Where is the rest of the fleet?'

'They are nearly here. One minute away in fact.'

'Good. I'm sending some refugees up through the mainframe to safety. They will be cloaked in the Venus II.'

Bagari grunted as the Stargazer lurched. The heli-fighters were covering the huge battle freighter like a big spider's web. Every one of them was firing on it.

'Shields at 4%' exclaimed tactically.

'Just a little longer,' replied Bagari. 'Skateboard are you still there?'

'Yes, Admiral. Request that you are also able to give us assistance when they arrive? We need covering fire as we embark on the Crimson Empire's HQ. I'm sending the coordinates now.'

'Sure,' said Bagari with a level of sarcasm that Jake would have been proud of. 'We'll bring the whole armada with us!'

'If you could, that'd be most satisfactory,' said Skateboard unaware of the Admiral's tone. 'We shall leave now. Estimate we will be there in ten clicks. Over and out.'

Skateboard left the ship and passed the final few people climbing on board.

'Some people wanted to stay and fight,' said Anji.

'They are brave people,' said Skateboard. 'Right then-'

The friends were all helped up onto the backs of the dosas, including a very excited Benaya and a still-hurting Takten.

Nkite waved Gron goodbye as the gantry hissed back into its closed position, who in turn waved back and whispered to her "You've got this." She smiled and then looked at Takten.

'Hey, I get it. I really do. Ready to take it out on the enemy?'

Takten powered up his gun. 'Always.'

'Do we have to hold on tight around their waists like last time?' asked Jake, referring to his previous experience hugging a Valkyrie to stop falling off.

'No, there are leather straps at the side of the saddle. Place your arms through these,' Solenia demonstrated, 'and you will be safe.'

Jake's face fell. Anji tried to stifle a laugh.

'Right, I have my bearings. I shall lead with Queen Solenia. Do your best to keep up all of you. As soon as the Venus II is out of the way then we can go. Ready?' Skateboard said as he warmed up his engines. The Venus II's engines whirred quieter and quieter as the cloaked ship disappeared from view, leaving Anji and Jake to collectively hope it wasn't too long before they saw it again.

'Okay,' said Skateboard. 'Let's ride.'

XIII

'I wouldn't come any closer if I were you, Random.'

Random dropped the two guards to the floor like they were trash and clenched his fists. His rage burnt fiercely, consuming him. He saw the frail old-looking figure of evil personified across the room and he wanted to tear him to shreds. The room in which they were was gloomy and dark, with a throbbing red light pulsing on and off which to Random was like a red flag to a bull. He yelled a guttural cry and tore off towards Maloso. Suddenly, Random was stopped in his tracks and was flung straight back into the air. As he crashed to the ground and skidded back towards the door, Maloso laughed like a tormentor bullying another child in class.

'I did try to warn you,' he said when he had finally managed to stop himself.

Random picked himself up gingerly. The whole front of his body hurt like hell. He felt a warm trickle of blood oozing from his nose. Wiping it away with his sleeve he regained his composure and straightened himself up.

'Putting a forcefield around yourself is a little cowardly, don't you think?'

'Not at all. Behind me are complex instruments that I would never want to fall into enemy hands.'

'Then come out. It's time we ended this.'

Maloso sighed. 'Oh, if only that were so my young friend. No, the end is already here.'

Random was getting angrier. 'Stop talking in riddles, Maloso. Why are you stalling? Giving your bully boys some time to get over their concussion, are you?'

'No Random I am well aware of the devastation that you bring with you. It wasn't just your demonstration of strength in getting to me. I know all about you.'

Random pulled a face of disgust. 'You know nothing!'

'I wouldn't be so sure. When you fled my clutches, all those years ago did you not think that I would do everything in my power to discover how you came to be? Why you were created? For a while, I obsessed over it and then when I discovered what I needed to know I knew then how this war would end. With you and me, standing here on the brink of the abyss with the war already won around us.'

Random shook his head. 'No, you see that's where you are wrong. The war is far from over.'

'Ha!' Maloso spluttered as he laughed, leading Random to try and peer closer through the gloom.

'You should be careful there you might choke.'

'And deprive you the pleasure of killing me yourself?'

Random shook his head. 'I am not a killer.'

'In all the time that you have been away from here, do you seriously expect me to believe that your powers haven't resulted in casualties? In deaths?'

Random didn't say anything. In the back of his mind, he thought of a few occasions when his actions had led to lives being lost. Then he tried his best to blot them out. Maloso was trying to get into his head and Random wouldn't let him.

'So go on then, you're clearly loving the fact that you know so much about me, I bet you're just bursting to tell me, aren't you?'

'The classic misdirection of a guilty conscience,' said Maloso dryly.

'At least I have one,' Random fired back.

'I do have one, Random. Don't you see? I have survived countless campaigns. I have been a scared child, a foot soldier, a prisoner, a Commander, a General and finally the ruler of the Crimson Empire. In all that time, fighting for supremacy, you grow attached to the cause. And there is nothing I wouldn't have done to see the Crimson Empire succeed. That's where you came in.'

Maloso struggled out of his chair. Random regarded him in what little detail he could see. A black, full-length cloak enveloped whatever was left of his body which seemed to have very little on it at all. In the years since their brief encounter Random had pictured a tall, gladiatorial figure.

From the stories Skateboard had told him, the only thing that had been consistent with the rumours of the demon in the dark, the ruler who hid away was the eyes. The blood-red eyes looked like they had been born in hell.

Maloso made his way over to his tubular chamber, the one that had so recently brought about the sudden influx of soldiers in the processing plant. The very same soldiers were wiping out what remained of the rest of the population on Rodas as they spoke and were trying to break out across the galaxy of Ursa-17.

'You will find this familiar; I presume?' he asked Random. As he did, Maloso flicked a switch and a white light shone down from the ceiling onto it, bringing it fully to Random's focus.

Random recognised it instantly. 'Where did you get that?'

'It was traced back to one Professor Blent's laboratory. It took us a long time to find it. So many people were...questioned...in our quest to locate the technology that had given your life and the vessel from which you came to be and here it is, the miraculous test tube that from which you were born.'

A terrible thought began to dawn on Random. As he was thinking he became aware of a terrible racket taking place underneath him under the floor. He tried not to be distracted.

'So, that's what you've done? You've created an army of Me's?'

'No. Not an army of Randoms. An army of Malosos.'

At that moment, Maloso decided to reveal his true, hideous form to Random for the first time. Random gasped in terror at the horrifying figure of his enemy as Maloso moved into the light.

Underneath the black cloak stood a man that belonged in a morgue. A truly repulsive, ghastly zombie-like figure of a man who should have been dead a long, long time ago. His face had no flesh on it whatsoever except for an ear which dangled rotting from the side of his face.

The gums in his mouth were decayed and non-existent and his torso bore the final remnants of what used to be skin and underneath his bones which jutted sharply out from his frame, Random could see his organs. Random felt a little bit sick in his mouth as he noticed his heart, blacker than the darkness of space itself, still implausibly beating.

'My god, what have you done to yourself?'

'I have given myself fully to the cause. Little by little, century-by-century, my life has been dedicated to making sure that the Crimson Empire was built in my image. In the early days, we used rudimentary cloning techniques. When I was General of the Crimson Empire, and upon the sad...murder of my predecessor, I inherited my army and piece-by-piece I allowed bits of me to go towards the making of my men.'

'You mean that you did this willingly? Centuries? You should be dead!'

'Should be, but my methods kept me alive. It was never enough though. The process was painfully slow. The Sapphire Regime – and that constrictive security barrier – kept us at bay until we discovered your creation chamber. They should have destroyed it but they had been conducting experiments – just as we had – on making organic soldiers of supreme capabilities just like you.'

'Yeah, I met one once. He wasn't too happy about what he had been subjected to. It's in-Rodasian, Maloso.'

'There are no good guys in war, Random. Only victors. Both sides took what advantage they could. It took me to make my ultimate sacrifice to tip the balance. As soon as the machine was tailored to my needs, I could input commands in the DNA that I was giving up from my own body. I could implant ideas, and commands, in the heads of my children. They would need no training, no period of growth. They would be created fully formed, in their hundreds at first, then thousands and now...millions. A drone army has organically grown from my own body. Every cell is a soldier. I have not only created life, Random. I have created a new civilisation, programmed from conception to do one thing. Conquer.

Wipe the blue stain clean from Rodas and then go out into the far reaches of space and do it again and again. It doesn't matter how many get wiped out in the process. They can always create more now that we have the blueprint. My DNA, you see? They all carry it. Purely my cellular makeup. So, my clones can keep going on and on. Now that you know why there is a forcefield.'

'My friends are on their way here. They blow this place sky-high to get through it, and your processing plants. Your plan will fail.'

'If you blow the base sky high you will risk destroying the chamber. Could you really take that risk, Random?'

Random was well and truly stumped.

'I can see your anger. I can feel your blood boiling. I find that good.'

'You're a monster, Maloso, death is the only thing that awaits you now.'

'Indeed. It is. I have given my final gift to Rodas, to the Crimson Empire. I have prolonged my agony just to see you beaten at the last, Random. I am holding back the touch of death as speak, just as I have done for so many, many years. Just to see the look on your face.'

Random felt the banging below him intensify. It was like whatever was down there was reacting to whatever was being said.

'And now...' said Maloso, lowering himself in his chair. 'The time has come.'

'This is all so pointless!' screamed Random. 'All this death, everything to do with this war is utter madness! You've overseen a genocide of your own people. It doesn't matter if you were red-skinned and they were blue, you're all on the same planet! How could you be so cruel?'

Maloso closed his eyes. 'In the old times, I used to ask the very same thing of them. You're on the wrong side Random. No one is a winner here except me. I take glory in all that I have done. I have won. You can try and break in here but you never will. I will die basking in the total glory of my victory.'

Random felt the floor move, the banging was becoming so ferocious.

'And yes, to answer your earlier question, I was luring you here. And you fell for it, well you're about to.'

In that instant, Maloso flicked a switch on a command unit on his chair and the floor below Random's feet gave way. Random was not quick enough to act and plummeted into the darkness.

A giant, red arm broke its way through the void in the floor and Maloso flicked another switch electrifying it, a deep loud moan of agony coming from the arm's owner shook the room. As it recoiled, Maloso flicked another switch.

Random fell for a good few seconds before something soft broke his fall. It was dark but he could tell he had fallen onto somebody. Random could make out the face of the person as he picked himself up on the dusty floor and he gasped in horror. The creature was almost as hideous as Maloso. Then another put his arm on Random's shoulder and Random leapt again. Random was appalled to realise that he was in a pit with a few – no – a dozen of these monsters.

'I'd like you to meet your brothers and sisters,' said Maloso, evil dripping from his words. 'Well, we all make mistakes, especially in the field of science. I won't be around to feed them anymore so I hope you'll be up to the task of doing that for me.'

Random was clambering to get out but there they were too powerful. The giant, still smarting from his electrocution, peered down and snarled unspeakable slobber in Random's face.

'Look after my abominations, would you? It's not like I did, poor things. They could do with some company.'

Random was being dragged down.

'Maloso, you can't do this!' screamed Random but it was too late.

With one final action, Maloso flicked the switch that sealed the trap door shut and Random's pleading and screams still ringing in his ears, finally gave into the dark and slipped quietly away.

XIV

Jake was struggling to fathom what was more uncomfortable. The ride or the hundreds of troops firing at them. With expert skill and grace, the Valkyries were weaving in and out of the enemy fire, which had followed them ever since they had left the mountain. Even Skateboard, who was tearing it up across the dusty, harsh terrain, was giving it both barrels from his stun gun but his long-range scanners were starting to concern him greatly.

'It appears that the Crimson Empire is trying to circle us,' he yelled to Solenia, who was herself struggling to hold off the enemy fire.

'You're flying ship would have been of great help to us now,' she cried as she continued to ride her dosa and fire at the enemy. She has witnessed a few of her people be taken out by the enemy troops, something she had felt deeply in her heart. 'If we don't get help soon, I fear that we won't reach our destination.'

Suddenly high up above, a fleet of heli-fighters began to descend upon them.

'This is it; we're done for!' shouted Anji.

'No, wait!' said Nkite pointing skywards. 'They're not Crimson Empire ships!'

'They're ours!' yelled Takten. He smiled triumphantly as these heli-fighters, which were slightly different in design except for a blue emblem on their doors, tore over their heads and opened fire on the Crimson Empire soldiers below.

'Yee-haw!' cried Jake, leading Anji to do the same.

'Commander Takten,' said a voice that fizzed over Takten's communicator. 'This is General Steyn of the 43rd Sapphire Legion. As you can see, we received your transmission, and thought you needed some help!'

'But how?' he responded. 'I saw the base at Hawk 159. You were beaten?'

'We're never beaten Takten, you know that,' said Steyn cheerily. 'We have lost a lot of our people but when we received your transmission and heard that you were heading to attack Kalor

Maloso's base we stopped fighting and thought we'd join you. The Crimson Empire thought that we had retreated and that they had won, seems we'd fooled you too?'

'I'm glad you did,' he replied.

'Commander, I just heard what your General said,' yelled Skateboard over the clip-clopping of hooves and heavy laser fire. 'We must not attack the base yet. Please can you inform your General?'

Takten looked surprised. 'Then why else are we going there?'

'To give Random time!' said Anji, as she ducked past a bolt of laser fire, to which the Valkyrie she was riding with shot back with pinpoint precision with his spear. 'We're driving them all to a focal point.'

'So that we can attack when he gives us the go-ahead, I guess,' said Delilah who was loving every minute of this. Benaya was too. Suddenly the horse that she was riding on bolted, throwing the Valkyrie to the ground. The gang looked back and looked on helplessly as the Valkyrie was surrounded by enemy troops who fires upon him at point-blank range with no mercy.

'Oh my god,' said Yana. 'Benaya, try and get it under control!'

The girl struggled to the front of the saddle as the dosa started to rear out of control. Luckily, using what little balance she had, she managed to hold on tight and pulled at the reigns and in doing so, brought it under control.

'Nice one sis!' said Delilah. 'Hee-yar!'

All the time this was happening Takten was speaking to his superior. 'I agree General but there is someone in that base who is our hope in finishing the war.'

Steyn paused for a second. 'The purple one?'

'Yes, sir.'

The General huffed. 'Well, if the war will end today let's make sure it goes out with a fight. Okay, we shall wait until further instruction to destroy the base. But if at any point we are in trouble then we must eliminate Maloso at all costs.'

'Agreed.'

'We're going to need help,' responded Steyn.

'We've got it,' said Skateboard.

'High above the fighting rebels and Sapphire Regime a flurry of battle freighters started to hone into view.

'Oh my god,' said Anji. 'Guys, it's the armada.'

'Skateboard, are you receiving me?' the voice of Admiral Bagari blared over Skateboard's audible receptors.

'Loud and clear Admiral.'

'I've transferred to the Titan. The Stargazer has taken some heavy damage. It appears that the attack on the mainframe has failed. For some reason all the ships just...left.'

'They've fallen back. They must have heard what was happening down here. The Sapphire Regime stopped defending against the attack and has joined our cause. Maybe that has led them to believe they must protect the base. Just as we wanted,' said Skateboard over the chaos.

'That as may be, there's an awful lot of them, Skateboard. What's your plan?'

'Draw the enemy to the base. Then, we try and take out as many of them as we can, buy Random time. Meanwhile Anji, Jake and the rest of us will try to infiltrate the base to lend assistance.'

'Do you know if he's okay in there?' asked Bagari.

'I don't. My long-range sensors are blinded by the thousands of Crimson Empire soldiers I'm picking up. I shall get a better reading the closer we can get.'

'We'll attack from the sky and try and lay cover for you guys on the ground. It's going to be a big fight, you guys had better take care.'

'We're almost there!' yelled Takten. As they continued to ride, they were getting closer and close to the ridge. The enemy was falling back all the time whilst still attacking and the soldiers started to disappear over the top.

'How many people do we have?' asked Anji.

'Just under one hundred Valkyries, the same number of dosas, seven of us on the ground including the Queen, four hundred and seventy-three heli-fighters and ten Space Seal battle freighters.'

'We're sending for foot soldiers,' Steyn overheard on the communicator. 'There should be roughly two thousand arriving shortly.'

'Since this is an open channel, I must interject that we also have 50,000 hornets ready to attack also,' said Bagari, referring to the light spacecraft

that the battle freighters held. 'Multiply those ten times and you've got yourself a fighting chance.'

'And how many do they have?' asked Yana.

As the rebels reached the lip of the ridge, they had their answer.

They stopped in their tracks instantly as they saw the magnitude of what they were up against.

Down below in the valley surrounding what was the Crimson Empire HQ, Kalor Maloso's base of operations was an overwhelming number of soldiers, ground vehicles which looked like tanks and heli-fighters hovering with menacing intent high above. Not to mention twenty battle freighters of their own.

Anji started to sweat.

Jake gulped hard.

Delilah and Yana were speechless.

Takten and Benaya gave each other a look of concern.

Bagari sat back in the command chair she had acquired in the Titan aghast.

'Helm. How many are we talking about here?'

The helmswoman scanned the area. Her fingers started to tremble. 'Five million, Admiral.'

Skateboard, Steyn and Takten overheard this and the number was broadcast to the rest of the group. Even the dosas were starting to move uneasily.

'Right then,' said Nkite. 'There's no turning back now, is there?'

Yana shook her head, 'No.'

Jake and Anji's dosas were close enough to allow the pair to hold hands. 'All of a sudden I'm starting to get a little bit of stage fright.'

'Why won't they attack?' asked Solenia.

'They are trying to intimidate us,' said Skateboard.

As he spoke, the Crimson Empire foot soldiers appeared to start stamping their feet in unison. The ground started to shake ever so slightly.

'General, any chance that the rest of our army might get here a little sooner?' asked Takten. In all his years of active service, he had never seen anything like this. How had they done it? How had Kalor Maloso managed to make an army of this sheer magnitude?

The heli-fighter jets and the tanks began to rev their engines. The sound of the Crimson Empire's death cry filled the air.

'We've got to do this. Even if it means that we die trying. Death or glory,' said Nkite.

'Random is in there.' said Anji. 'We have to do it for him.'

'No,' said Takten. 'We do it for Rodas.'

Those words stirred the spirit in Nkite. She held her gun up high and shouted the final two words, the only two words that mattered to her, as loud as she could.'

'FOR RODAS!!'

Her cry seemed to stoke the fire instantly in the Valkyrie, who clicked his heels into the dosas' ribs and they tore off over the ridge.

Jake and Anji steeled themselves. They all did.

Before long they were all shouting those two words, over and over and over again.

'FOR RODAS!'

The remnants of the depleted Sapphire Regime, over Steyn's open channel on his communicator, heard the battle cry and started to call out the same battle cry which implored their heli-fighters over the ridge. Even the Titan and the other Space Seals battle freighters, and the pilots of the hornets, whose engines noisily hummed into the air as they left their ships and flew out onto the awaiting battlefield, joined in.

Admiral Bagari whispered it to herself before ordering the fleet to attack.

All of a sudden, the resistance, spearheaded by Skateboard, his two human friends, his enlisted help of the Spectronian guard and the Genocian revolutionary front, joined with the oppressed Sapphire Regime and the Space Seals, was tearing over the ridge, heading towards what was about to be the battle of their lives.

Some of the Crimson Empire – including the General who had overseen the aborted attack on the security mainframe – were taken aback at the sheer determination of their enemies.

Now that Kalor Maloso had taken leave of his communication with them, it was up to him to protect the base. They'd do it with ease, he thought. Right? There are five million of them. They'd win this fight easily, surely?

Steeling his thought, he cried through the open channel to the fleet.

'CHARGE!'

The Crimson Empire's handbrake was released and they charged head-first towards the rebel alliance that was hurtling towards them.

'Jake, Anji, stay close to me please,' said Skateboard. 'You too,' he said to Delilah, Benaya and Yana. 'We have to get inside the base.'

He wasn't sure if they had heard him and that worried him. As a torrential rain of laser fire headed their way, he knew his biggest fear had come true.

There was no way he could keep his friend safe.

This was it. It was to be the end of the war on Rodas, but as the warring factions crunched together in a hail of gunfire and physical violence, the battle for Rodas was well underway...

XV

Deep underneath the bowels of the Crimson Empire, an entirely different battle was taking place. Fighting entirely in the dark against a manner of creatures he dare not wish to see, Random was throwing as many punches and kicks as he possibly could. As he felt a vice-like grip surround his midriff, it felt like he was becoming constricted. Soon he started to gasp for air and he began to choke. Although he was in a pit of total darkness, he felt a new wave of it start to fall over his eyes and he began to lose consciousness.

'Boshy, you're holding him too tight!' said one soft voice in the gloom.

'Oh,' came the reply, 'sorry.'

With that, the grip loosened and Random felt his gasping frame be carried lower until he was placed gently on the floor.

As the soles of his boots hit what felt like a sandy, dirty floor he coughed violently and fell to the ground trying to take in as much air as he could.

'But Troyus, he was hurting us,' said the same deep booming voice that had been apologising seconds earlier.

'Well, what do you expect, being chucked down a pit with us goons?' said another gravelly voice. 'Hey kid, you alright? I apologise on behalf of us all.' Random felt a hand, well, it was more like a tentacle, move down towards him.

'Speak for yourself Postanous but I think he's broken one of my noses,' said another voice in the gloom.

'And my arms!' All four of them hurt like hell,' came another.

'Wait,' croaked Random. 'Who are you guys?' he accepted the tentacle and was helped up to his feet.

'What was it he used to call us?' asked Postanous.

'I believe it was the abominations,' came a posher voice in the dark.

'Nah, I think it was worse than that,' said Boshy. 'Something really demeaning.'

'What are you all doing down here?' asked Random, who had started to recover from the tight squeeze from what appeared to now be the friendly giant.

'Well, where else would you want to hide us?' asked Troyus. 'Would you really want us all up there roaming around with our good looks?'

'Looks don't matter I mean look at him, he's purple!' said the posh voice again.

'How can you see me?' asked Random.

'When you've been down here as long as we have, your eyes begin to adjust.'

'So does your posture,' said Boshy, 'Especially when you are as tall as me.'

'Allow me to introduce myself, I am Xiros and these are my fellow abominations. I take it that you're the latest experiment that has gone wrong?'

'Far from it,' I'm the one who went right,' said Random.

'Oh yeah, we all believed that until we were captured down here,' said Postanous.

'Who put you down here?' asked Random. 'And why?'

'Kalor Maloso. We've been trying to get out since he started hiding us,' said Xiros.

Troyus picked up the story. 'We were among the first experiments on living tissues to replicate and augment super beings for the Crimson Empire. But we were shunned, failed experiments. Maloso tried to kill us all at birth, we all have pretty much identical stories. We were created from matter from the man himself, but when we were deemed unfit to fight, he tried to have us killed, only he couldn't. He tried everything. Fire, drowning, heavy artillery, starvation.'

'The poison was the worst. My taste buds have never been the same since,' said Boshy.

'So instead, he banished us down here. Sure, he'd feed us but for years we've been trying to grab his attention, to bust our way out of here when he threw food down here to keep us alive, possibly to experiment again, or maybe until the time was right to release us, I don't know.'

'But if you're superhuman then how come you couldn't use your strength to escape?' asked Random.

'He set up a force field down here. None of us could break out. Plus, the floor is electrified. As my poor friend Boshy finds out regularly,' said Xiros.

'It tickles but hurts at the same time,' agreed Boshy.

Random started to form an idea in his head. Here, he had a readymade army, powerful enough to take out the remaining soldiers inside the base and hopefully get him to the machine.

'So, you must really hate Kalor Maloso then? And your own kind. Here you are. Shunned, kept away in the dark, a dirty little secret into the failings of the Crimson Empire.'

'Don't you start,' said Postanous. 'We've heard it all from him up there all too often.'

'But you must despise your creator. The feeling of revenge must be boiling away under your skin.'

'He's got a lovely turn of phrase, Xiros, just like you!' said Troyus.

'My dear young boy, I know what you are trying to do. You're trying to stoke our flames. You want to get us angry to help you get out of here and fight against our own kind. Well, I regret to inform you that years of involuntary confinement have corrected our murderous natures.'

'If anything, it's made us much calmer,' said Postanous. 'When I bust out of here, I want to set up a fruit market.'

'But you were trying to get out, I heard you,' said Random.

'We just try and let people know that we are here in the hope that they would rescue us,' said Troyus.

'But it never works,' said Boshy sadly.

'I can help you,' said Random.

'How? You're stuck down here with us!' cried Postanous.

'What are you proposing?' asked Xiros.

'Look, if you help me, I can put an end to this war today. We can put an end to it,' he implored.

'Does it involve any violence?' asked Boshy.

'Definitely,' replied Random.

'Hmmm. It goes against my character,' said Troyus.

'Is there anything else we can do instead? Maybe we can speak to Maloso and bargain with him?' asked Xiros.

'That monster has kept you down here in this prison for years and you want to talk with him?!' said Random aghast.

'Yeah, I mean maybe he's got a nice side,' said Troyus.

Random was astounded at what he was hearing. Here was a group of super soldiers, each one of them, despite his blindness in the dark, sounded like they were bred for war and instead they want to open up fruit markets and have a chat!

'I highly doubt that and besides, he's dead,' said Random.

There was an audible sound of gasping.

'Then how are we going to get out now?'

'Well, I think I have an idea, but it'll hurt, probably a lot.'

'Oh well you can count me out then,' said Xiros.

'Not you, me!' replied Random. 'Boshy, if you would be so kind, could you please push me up to the trapdoor? I'll prize it open.'

'You'll fry! As will I!' yelped Boshy.

'You can let go as soon as I find the groove that snaps the door open. Now it's likely that I might lose consciousness after it's opened. If you could catch me and wake me up when you are all on the surface that'd be great,' said Random.

'We've tried that before. Do you think that we wouldn't have done such a thing with a giant present?' asked Xiros.

'Yes, but I've been struck by lightning before. Years ago, my body was corrupted by a powerful element, since then my nervous system doesn't feel pain as badly as it did before. I need to see if I can withstand it. Then when we are all out, there is likely to be trouble. Big trouble. Maloso might be dead but his army is far from it. I could really use your help.'

Xiros sighed. 'Okay, if you can get us out of here then I promise I will help but I'll only use my strength to fight if I am provoked. Do we have a deal, young man?'

Random smiled. 'Deal! What do the rest of you say?'

There was a grumble amongst them. 'So, you want us to fight our own people?' asked Postanous.

'Yes,' said Random.

'Kill where necessary?' said Troyus.

'Sadly, yes,' replied Random.

'And side with you and the Sapphire Regime, our sworn enemy?' asked Boshy.

'To save your entire planet and bring about peace, yes,' said Random.

There was a pause.

'Go on then' said Boshy.

'Yeah, I'm in,' said Postanous.

'This is a stupid war anyway,' said Troyus. 'It's time it ended.'

Random smiled. 'Thank you. Oh, and I'm sorry for hurting you all.'

'Ah, don't mention it!' said Troyus. 'My arms have set already.'

'Right, Boshy, if you would be so kind?' Random prepared himself for the next phase of his escape plan. As Boshy picked him up and lifted him towards the trapdoor he could hear the crackle of electricity that stood between them and freedom. He felt the heat against his face.

'I can see the crack in the door. The electricity is giving off light. Must be powerful. Right, as soon as it snaps open, Boshy, if you could let the others use you as a ladder then get them to pull you out? Is that okay with you?'

'As long as they wipe their feet then yes,' he replied.

'Okay,' said Random, preparing himself for a world of torment. 'Here it goes.'

He plunged his hands into the crack. Instantly his body was engulfed in a bright light of energy as the electricity tried to consume him. Random snarled and spat as he grimaced against the might of the trapdoor mechanism and the pain that was flooding his body. With a huge effort, he pulled the doors open and the electricity stopped.

As the doors snapped open and the electricity died away, Random lost consciousness and began to fall. Boshy caught his unconscious body in his palm.

'Hehe, he tickles!' said the giant as he calmly placed the fizzing Randon on the floor of Maloso's room outside of the trapdoor. 'Come on up, guys!'

The abominations were shocked. They had never seen anyone withstand such power before. 'Quickly!' cried out Xiros and one by one, they started climbing up Boshy's body.

'Don't pull at my hair!' he demanded and one by one they made it out.

'The ceiling looks quite high in here, chum,' said Xiros. 'You should be fine, how's the purple one?'

Troyus was checking his pulse. 'Seems a little high, but I ain't no doctor and he's still breathing so-'

Postanous was gazing out of the window at the battle taking place outside. 'Zarks...'

Xiros and two other abominations had finished picking Boshy out of the hole and then they all turned to see what Postanous was looking at. The former was having to duck a little but he didn't mind. They were free, but they had no time to celebrate.

'Would you look at that?' said Troyus. 'There must be millions out there.'

'Millions upon millions,' came a croaky voice. It was Random. The abominations weren't paying him any attention, not the fact that he was awake or that his body seemed to have steam rising from it or that some of his purple skin looked burnt. They didn't even blink at the corpse of their captor across the way.

Random limped his way over to them.

'Kalor Maloso. Ruler of the Crimson Empire. You've heard what he was doing. You know more than I did until now. Do you really think that there is any option but to fight against it?'

'Oh my god...Sergeant they are out!'

A new voice joined the room. Random and the abominations turned and saw a lone soldier standing in the crumpled doorway. Speaking into his communicator, trembling in his boots. Far away distant sounds of more of them clip-clopping their way towards the room could be heard and they getting louder and louder.

'You good kid?' asked Postanous.

Random clenched his fists. 'Never better.'

'Good...then let's do this!'

XVI

Amongst the absolute carnage that was a battle to end all battles, one that was happening on land and in the sky, a battle that had become so bad that outside help had given the underdogs a fighting chance to survive, a little AI robot was trying to have a conversation.

Upon their charge into the valley, Skateboard noticed that the base they needed to reach was a fair distance back behind endless rows of enemy soldiers. Whilst he had been keeping a watchful eye on his two human friends, who were currently letting the Valkyries they were with do all the fighting, he was thankful to see that none of them were coming to harm. But as even he kept firing his stun gun at any Crimson Empire troops that came near him, and weaved in and out of the destructive firepower that was raining down upon them, he suddenly realised that what he really needed was for everyone to just be quiet for a second.

As he was unable to be heard by his friends over the gunfire, his open channel with Admiral Bagari and General Steyn of the Sapphire Regime was at least a blessing if for nothing else but so that he could tell them what he required.

'As I was saying,' he continued, firing off more rounds at those that were trying to kill him and his friends. 'The base entrance is two hundred metres away. It is reachable, but we may need covering fire to do so.'

'And you are sure that the purple one is in there?' asked Steyn.

I am certain of it, General. And as long as he is in there, we must not fire upon it.'

'General, Skateboard,' interjected Bagari. 'I am picking up intel that there is a massive factory of some sort roughly five miles behind the mountain containing the base. Do you think we should be firing on that instead? I mean considering there are more soldiers pouring out of the doors it might be an idea?'

Steyn was dumbfounded. 'We thought that was an ammunition factory.'

'Definitely not that from our sources. I think we've found how the Crimson Empire have been restocking their forces,' said Bagari.

'How?' asked Steyn.

'I'm a bit busy to find an explanation right now, General,' said Skateboard. 'But I am certain that the answer lies in that base. Would either of you be able to lay down some covering fire, and clear a path for us to get in?'

'We're on it, Skateboard, and yes, we shall send a squadron of hornets to bomb the factory.

Considering they are still churning out soldiers – somehow – it'd probably be a good idea if we could send them a cease-and-desist notice,' said Bagari. 'I'll get straight on it. Helm?'

'On it, Admiral,' said the helm officer.

'In the meantime, we can pick you up on our sensors. We'll make a path for you now,' Bagari continued.

'I've sent you the coordinates of the entrance now,' said Skateboard. He rounded back towards his friends who thankfully were all still alive and all close by.

'Your majesty, please continue the attack,' he said to Solenia. 'The rest of you, follow me.'

Nkite and Takten broke off from their defensive fire and looked at one another. 'You go,' Nkite cried. 'This is our fight here.'

Anji looked worried. She was sure that as soon as they were inside, they would be safer than out here in the hail of laser fire. Nkite smiled at her reassuringly.

'I'll be okay, now go!'

Anji smiled back.

'Miss Anji. Sir, please come with me,' said Skateboard. Jake and Anji ducked and weaved as the hail of enemy fire was growing nearer. They approached Skateboard and stood on his body and before long, the AI robot had clamped their feet to him.

He extended his body and allowed Delilah, Benaya and Yana on and shot off full pelt as the covering fire began clearing a path.

Metre by metre, they were gaining closer and closer on the base, closer to their friend and closer, they all collectively hoped, to the end of all the madness.

XVII

In the room that had once been their prison, the abominations were fighting against their own, against those who had shunned them. But as Boshy bludgeoned a soldier with an uppercut which sent him flying up into the ceiling, Random looked upon them for what they actually were. They were liberated.

'I say,' said Xiros as he chucked a soldier into the corridor like he was a shotput in a school sports day, 'this is really rather fun!'

Still, there was a throng of Crimson Empire soldiers who were doing all they could to keep Random and the abominations back. Some had broken out electrical prongs, designed to contain and harm those on the receiving end but Random and his new friends were having none of it.

'Everyone, with me!' he yelled and together they all charged at their enemies, sending them sprawling all ways.

'Well, that felt good!' said Postanous. They all noticed that for now, things had gone quiet.

'What do we do now?' asked Boshy.

Random got up and made for the control desk. Then he remembered the forcefield.

'We have to find a way to locate my friends,' he replied. 'Boshy, Troyus, Xiros, go to the main entrance. They should find their way in there.'

'And what do we do, boss?' asked Postanous.

'We defend this room and wait for you all to return,' said Random.

'But how do we know what to look out for?' asked Troyus.

'Well, they won't be red or blue-skinned, so that should make them easier to spot. When you do see them let them in and seal this base down. Stop any Crimson Empire soldiers that you spot on the way. This had to be our stronghold, is everyone alright with that?' asked Random.

'These friends of yours, they could be wearing disguises, so that'd make it harder. And who says they won't try and shoot us dead when they spot us? We're not the nicest looking bunch, are we?' said Troyus.

'My friends, unlike those on this planet, won't judge by appearances,' said Random.

'But they might mistake us for enemies, still,' said Xiros. 'It doesn't matter if they are-'

'A young girl,' said Boshy.

'Yeah, a young girl or a' continued Troyus.

'A blonde-haired boy,' said Boshy.

'Yeah, or a blonde-haired-'

'And a flat metal robot,' said Boshy.

Random took notice of Boshy's words and went over to the giant. He craned his neck upwards to speak to him.

'How do you know what they look like?' asked Random.

'I can see them on the security monitor,' said Boshy, pointing over to the far corner of the room. His height had given him an advantage and he could see Maloso's still active surveillance desk.

Random smiled. 'That's them!'

'And it looks like they are being chased,' said Boshy with a concerned lilt to his voice.

'Quick, go now!' said Random.

'We're on it!' said Troyus and as quick as a flash he, Xiros and Boshy squeezed their way down the corridor and off to the main entrance.

'Well, since it's all a bit quiet,' said Postanous, 'Maybe you should tell me what the next part of the plan is?'

Random frowned. 'We break in through the forcefield. Then, we end this war.'

The hail of gunfire from the hornets and the heli-fighters raged up ahead. Every now and then Anji, Jake, Skateboard and the others had to jump or avoid at the last minute a piece of debris that was falling from the sky.

As they looked up ahead, they could see that the hornets were pushing their opponents back and doing much better than the alliance was faring on the ground.

For now, though, they were unscathed and as Delilah, Benaya and Yana continued to lay down fire to repel any on-coming attackers, Skateboard did his best to reach the base as quickly as he could.

'When we get there, we may have to keep fighting so I stress that we keep our wits about us, find Random and-'

'Bagari's covering fire has worked,' yelled Delilah. 'Come on Skateboard we're almost there!'

'Let's hope we can find Random quickly!' said Anji. She had tried to keep a watchful eye on Nkite but as they grew further apart she had lost her new friend in the melee.

'Anj, she'll be fine!' said Jake. All the time they had been holding onto each other for dear life. Something they had been doing ever since they had met Random. Something that would never change for either of them.

'We've made it!' said Yana.

'You should be alright now, Skateboard,' said Bagari over the AI robot's open channel. 'Will assist on the bombing of the processing plant now. Take care.'

'Thanks, Admiral,' said Skateboard. He released the clamps on his friend's feet and as they disembarked, he folded back into his normal length. There was a flight of stairs. The gang ascended it, shooting at soldiers trying to stop them as they went. Then, as they were nearly at the top, a massive explosion ripped the main entrance apart.

They threw themselves to the steps for cover and dust and dirt showered down upon them and as Jake and Anji looked they were astonished to see a massive giant of a... creature, standing where the doors used to be.

'Oh my god!' cried Anji.

'Um...Skateboard?' asked Jake.

The red, blotchy, mutated face looked down upon them. His impossibly long arms extended outwards. Benaya hid behind her sister, and Yana screamed. Jake and Anji stood terrified at the huge, hideous creature in front of them. Skateboard readied his stun gun but knew it wouldn't be powerful enough to stop such a creature of his size.

Suddenly the stern features of the giant relaxed in a cheery smile. 'Oh, hello!' he exclaimed. 'You must be Random's friends. He is expecting you. Come in quick, you'll be safer in here.' The giant reached his arm out to beckon them in.

The gang looked at each other confused. 'Are you for real?' exclaimed Jake.

Boshy felt his face and torso and nodded vigorously. 'Yep!'

Anji and Jake looked at each other. 'It's a trap, isn't it?' said Anji sideways to Skateboard.

'Come on, Boshy what's the hold-up?' came another voice. The gang shrieked when two more ugly, mutated creatures filled the door. One of them seemed to have eight limbs like a spider. The other resembled a scaley crocodile more than a humanoid.

'Hello there, we're the abominations,' said the reptile-like one in a cheery posh voice. 'Please do wipe your feet as you come in.'

The gang didn't know what to do. Each of them looked at Skateboard for guidance.

'Let's do what they say,' he said.

'Sorry, the place is a mess. Do wipe your feet as you come in,' said the posh one again. 'We'll make introductions on the way,' he looked out at the madness of the battle that was taking place. 'My, my what a terrible racket.'

Not knowing what to make of the situation, the gang did as the abominations asked but slower than they should have been doing. Behind them, the Crimson Empire soldiers had cottoned on to what was happening and were tearing up the steps behind them.

'Oh dear,' said Boshy. 'I'll deal with this.' He slammed the door as soon as they were inside and readied himself for a fight. There was none. The soldiers took one look at him and ran off, terrified.

Boshy looked confused and sniffed under his arm. Then he shrugged and turned to follow the others inside.

'What are you doing?' asked Postanous. He had been watching Random trace around the room with a stick for a good few minutes and had started to wonder if his new friend was a little mad.

'I'm trying to find a break in the force field,' said Random, who every now and then was jolting back a little. 'But so far... nope,' he said, tossing his stick to one side. 'It's hopeless.'

'What do we do now?' asked Postanous. At that moment the door to the room burst open and Random smiled broadly as a few familiar faces came through it.

'Random!' cried our Anji. She ran towards him and threw herself at him. Jake did the same and the three of them ended up on the floor laughing, barely believing that they were all okay.

'Guys! Thank zarks you made it,' said a relieved Random.

'Hey! Don't use our lords' name in vain!' warned Postanous but his comment was ignored.

Random got up and picked his two best friends up in the same motion. 'Skateboard, you did it!'

'Thank you, sir, but the mission is far from accomplished,' said Skateboard, who proceeded to scan the room.

'Yana! Delilah, Benaya! Wow! I can't believe it's really you. It's been so long!' Random hugged each of them in turn. 'Thank you so much for coming!'

'We wouldn't have missed a party like this,' said Delilah.

'Speaking of which, it's really getting hairy out there,' said Yana. 'Shouldn't we be getting on with what we need to be doing?'

'You're right,' said Random. 'Hugs and kisses later. Oh, before I do though, you've met the abominations, haven't you? They are cousins of mine; I suppose you could say.'

'Hello!' waved Xiros. Boshy re-entered the room and used a cattle prod he'd acquired from a soldier earlier to put it across the door, in turn electrifying it, meaning that no one could break in.

'So, what do we do now?' asked Jake.

'Over there is a creation chamber tube,' said Random. 'We have to get to it that entire side of the room has a forcefield running across it.'

'What about Kalor Maloso?' asked Anji.

'He's the corpse sitting next to it,' said Random. 'He's cloned the entire army. Skateboard, I think I know what we have to do.'

Skateboard finished his scans. 'I do too, sir.'

Random nodded. 'Good, then how do we get through the force field.'

'Leave that to me, sir. I'll attempt to crack the security network. If I can trip it, I can bring the forcefield down.'

'Great,' said Random. 'That's when the fun really begins.'

XVIII

As his cockpit filled up with flames and smoke, the Crimson Empire's General's hands were shaking on the wheel. Not because he was scared of the inevitable hard ground below, but because the steering wheel was going out of control. He looked all around him. Everyone else in the heli-fighter was either dead or unconscious. It was only him left.

How had this happened? Not the crashing, that had been inevitable after the Sapphire Regime had entered into battle, but first the security mainframe now this. How had the Sapphire Regime found recruitments? How were they keeping them at bay? Maloso's new clones were supposed to be indestructible. They were meant to break the mainframe and he was going to lead his new troops into space and onto further conquest whilst the foot soldiers slaughtered the remaining blue skins.

But his squadron was at a loss. When the huge battle freighters arrived, he knew that part of their plan was up. When the internal alarms had sounded for them to protect the base, they had done what, with their number, should have been unthinkable. They fell back.

Maloso had his soldiers all in a row and they hadn't heard from him since. The General tried not to think about it and as he braced for impact, trying to crash into some of the rebel alliance to take some revenge, he thought of very little. Indeed, the impact nearly killed him.

Nkite finished off her round of fire and took cover, pulling Takten down with her as the heli-fighter nearly crashed right on top of them. They held their low cover as the nearby explosion blew debris all over them. Finally, they looked up.

'You're doing well,' said Takten.

'Thanks, but I'm not sure if we are making much progress,' she replied.

'We've got to keep going. Where are those colourful horses when you need them?' he said ruing their current position. There was little cover from them and after Skateboard and the others had left them, they had lost Solenia and the Valkyries very quickly.

'We're sitting ducks,' said Nkite. 'Can you call for backup?'

Takten reached for his communicator. 'General Steyn...come in General Steyn...'

The radio was dead.

Nkite shot him a worried look.

Takten was panting hard. 'What was the name of the other one?' he asked.

'Bagari...Admiral Bagari to you,' came the reply. 'I'm afraid it looks like your General has been lost. There are a heavy number of casualties in your region, on land and in the sky.'

The Titan and its fleet of hornets were descending on the processing plant. Bagari watched on the viewscreen as the newly created soldiers continued to teem out of the factory but were immediately firing up at them.

'Tell the squadron to release their bombs on my mark. Continue to fire on anyone attacking us,' she said.

She watched on her navigation monitor as they moved into range. Lasers were exploding all around them. The tactical officer's trigger finger was getting itchy. Finally, Bagari gave the order.

'Fire.'

Instantly, the Titan released its bombs and the hornets fired their photon torpedoes. A flurry of artillery descended on the processing plant. The Titan and its hornet squadron fled instantly, careful not to be caught up in the blast.

Some of the Crimson Empire's heli-fighters tried to shoot the bombs down but it was no use, there were too many to stop them in time and it only needed a few to make a direct hit for the plan to work. Suddenly, there was a brilliant explosion.

A huge cloud of smoke and fire roared upwards into the air and within seconds the crater containing the processing plant and all that had been standing there was obliterated.

'We've done it Admiral,' said the tactical officer. 'Direct hit!'

There was a whoop and a cheer around the command posts.

Admiral Bagari remained cool. 'Great job, guys. Now let's get back to the front line. That goes for everyone on the Space Seals channel. One last push. This battle isn't won yet.'

Back in the front line, Nkite and Takten felt the ground rumble as a mushroom cloud of fire and smoke ripped into the sky far away.

'Great job Admiral!' said Takten.

'Thanks, now try and find some cover. We'll come in and pick you up. If you find Solenia tell her the same. We'll win this war from the air now,' said Bagari.

Nkite felt like hugging Takten but he didn't look the type. Takten looked at her wishing he could hug her but then thinking better of it. At that moment, just as he had remembered what feeling happy felt like, a sudden sharp pain blew up in his chest. Nkite screamed. He looked down and discovered a hole in his rib cage. He felt the worse pain he had ever felt. He looked at Nkite's face and gave her a smile as he sank to his knees.

Behind him was a very injured survivor of the heli-fighter crash. As Takten fell flat on his face,

Nkite picked up his gun and fired it at the assassin. She fired and fired again, tears streaming down her face, anger and raw agony overtaking her body as the body of the General lay motionless, his eyes open but still. She dropped the gun and ran back to Takten, who was just as lifeless as the General. She held him close and wept uncontrollably.

She thought they wouldn't lose any more friends today. Clearly, she had been wrong.

Before long she remembered where they were. She closed his eyes and placed Takten gently on the ground. Picking up her gun she moved away, running fast into the front line, taking on and beating any Crimson Empire soldier she came into contact with. Before long she found a Valkyrie, wounded on the ground. Her tears were still running down her cheeks when she picked up the injured Spectronian.

'Can you walk?' she asked them.

The man looked up at her and grimaced. 'Not well but I'll manage.'

'Good,' she said. 'We have to find your Queen. We're getting out of here.'

With that. She pulled the Valkyrie up. As she did, he swore as his bleeding leg and side were aggravated, words that Nkite didn't know but would one day use as they sounded just as colourful as this man's skin.

With great effort, she dragged him through the crowd of fighting red and blue soldiers and Valkyries, both fighting as they went.

'Come on guys,' Nkite said to herself. 'What's holding you up?'

XIX

'Hurry up Skateboard.'

Random was pensively walking up and down the little part of Kalor Maloso's war room that he could. His friend, the amazing AI robot who seemed able to do just about anything he could ask was struggling to hack into the security system and shut the forcefield down.

'I'm almost there, sir,' said Skateboard. 'Just 12,937 more combinations left to crack.'

'Yes, but how long will that take?' asked Yana.

'Roughly ninety-four seconds.'

'Wow, that doesn't seem so bad,' said Delilah.

Benaya elbowed Jake and pointed over at Random. She signed to him to ask what the matter was.

'Oh, something to do with that chamber. Apparently, it can end the war,' said Jake in response.

'It will,' said Random overhearing. 'At least it better do.'

Anji was sitting with Boshy and Postanous. 'So, you were created to fight the Sapphire Regime but you're fighting your own people?'

'Yeah, well, we haven't done much fighting to be fair. We were under this floor for years until your friend came along,' said Postanous.

'I'm kind of glad we didn't. I don't feel much like killing,' said Boshy. 'I don't think that I have it in me.'

'And that's why Maloso hid you,' said Anji. 'I'm so sorry.'

'Don't sweat it,' said Postanous. 'It gave us all time to think and to reform ourselves. Who knows, after this we might do charity work for a living?'

'If there is a Rodas after this,' said Xiros as he continued to watch the battle from outside the viewing window.

'Sir, Bagari has informed me that the processing plant has been destroyed. She's taking the Titan to pick Nkite and the Valkyries up,' said Skateboard.

'I wondered what all that banging was,' said Jake.

'Good, but please, just concentrate on this,' begged Random.

Skateboard spent another ten seconds in silence before finally, the forcefield disappeared.

'Skateboard, you legend!' said Random. He and the others raced over to the chamber.

Jake stood a little too close to the corpse of Kalor Maloso for his liking. 'Ewww. What did he do to himself?'

'This,' said Random, gesturing outside the window. 'So, Skateboard, you've scanned it. You know what it does?'

'I do, sir,' said Skateboard hesitantly. 'Maloso was right, sir. This machine is indeed the one that created you. It also created your new friends here. Except between your conception and everyone else's it has been augmented. It was retooled for mass production purposes. The DNA extracted from Kalor Maloso was transported through the tubes rising up into the ceiling and fed to the processing plant, creating millions upon millions of his troops. There's more. This machine was also keyed in with instructions. He found a way to teach his clones to think. He didn't programme them to feel.'

'How kind of him,' said Anji witheringly.

'So, what do we do? Blow it up?' asked Delilah.

'Far from it,' said Skateboard.

'We use it,' said Anji.

'I use it,' said Random.

'How?' asked Yana and Xiros simultaneously.

'This chamber, no matter how much it has been tampered with, has been coded to my DNA. Since it created me, I can use it again. By getting in and starting the process again it can create an army of Me's to fight the Crimson Empire and to stop the fighting.'

'But you'd be left looking like him!' said Jake pointing at Maloso's corpse.

'That's correct Jake,' said Random. 'And now that the processing plant has been destroyed that option is out of the window. Plus, we wouldn't have the time. However, this machine still can send out a psychic link to anyone who stems from it.'

'So, you can shut the army down?' asked Anji.

'It'll do more than that. It'll fry their brains. A signal from my mind to theirs, it'd probably blow them up. This machine is that powerful!' said Random.

'But sir,' said Skateboard, a tinge of sadness in his voice.

'I know, Skateboard, I know,' he replied.

Anji and Jake looked confused. 'Know what?' asked Anji.

Random looked up at her, his eyes starting to well up. 'I've known. Ever since I was born, I've known that what happens today will be the end of me.'

Jake's jaw dropped. 'You're sacrificing yourself?'

'That's why I ran for so long. I knew that coming back would result in my death.'

Anji shook her head, her eyes starting to well up with tears also. 'No. No, no, no there must be something else we can try, surely?'

Random spoke calmly. 'Anji, there is no other option. The only two that were open to us would have still led to this conclusion. That's one of the reasons why I asked for Skateboard to ask for

your help,' he said nodding at Delilah, Benaya and Yana. 'Old friends who I knew could help, yes, but I wanted to see everyone again. All those people I've helped save. I wanted a reminder that it was more than worth it and it was, wasn't it?'

Jake and Anji were sobbing uncontrollably.

'Is there...no chance...you could survive?' asked Jake sniffing.

'It's practically one in a billion,' confirmed Skateboard, taking no pleasure in delivering the news.

'Even if I did, I wouldn't have much of a brain left,' said Random, tears pouring silently down his cheeks.

Jake wiped his nose with his sleeve. 'It's not like you have much of one already.'

Random laughed. Trust Jake to try and joke at a time like this. He loved him for it.

'Look, this is all very distressing for your friends. If it's tailored to DNA that has passed through it already then one of us can use it, surely?' said Xiros, about to volunteer himself.

'I'll do it,' said Troyus, who had been watching in silence. 'I've got nothing in my diary for tomorrow.'

'You can't, My DNA is made up of both the red and blue factions of Rodas. My chromosomes are split 50/50 between both races of Rodasians.

Hence the purple skin. I was designed to be the one who could end this war because of that fact. I hold within me all the good and evil of the Crimson Empire and the Sapphire Regime. I've held it off for too long. With every passing second more and more innocent people die and I can't live with that guilt anymore.'

'But Skateboard, you can tailor this machine back, surely? Please someone tell me this isn't how it needs to be!' said Anji hysterically. Jake held her in close.

'I can't miss, I'm sorry,' he said. If robots could cry, he would have been inconsolable right now.

Random moved to be next to his friends. 'You three have always been the best of me. You've given me so much happiness in my life. It was a life that was never supposed to know joy. Never allowed the privilege of love but I did. I love all of you so much. Whatever happens next, wherever I go, I'll hold it in my heart forever.'

He wrapped his arms around them. Skateboard, on his hind wheels, so that he could be a part of the hug, wrapped his arms that snaked out of his body when he needed them around his friends. They all held each other tightly, knowing that this was it. There was nothing else they could do.

Just as the Oracle of Fate had told him, Random was walking hand-in-hand, finally after all these years, with his destiny.

Those watching on held each other's hands. The abominations barely knew Random but owed him their freedom and their a chance to live.

Delilah and Benaya. The sisters who had met Random in prison down in the mines of Genocia had taken part in the uprising led by the purple one so many years back and owed them their freedom.

Yana, the rebel who had also aided in the revolution on that same planet, put her arms across the shoulders of the sisters and Troyus. They were united in their thanks for Random and not just him but his three brave friends who all stood before them saying their tearful goodbyes.

Random pulled away, his face puffy and wet with emotion. 'Skateboard, look after these two and yourself. The Venus II is yours now. Do with it what you like.'

'Yes, sir,' sniffed the robot.

'Jake, never change who you are,' smiled Random.

'You bet,' sniffed Jake again, his voice faint and croaky.

'Anj...' Random held her face in his hands. 'You be whoever you want to be,' he kissed her on the forehead, making her cry even more.

He let her go and walked back a few paces.

'Look after each other and yourselves. I love you so much. No matter what corner of the universe you are in never let the light be dimmed by the dark.'

He blew them a kiss. He turned to the others. He nodded at them all and wiped his eyes.

'Right, Skateboard, you know how to program this thing?'

'I do, sir.'

Random walked over to the chamber, his hearts thumping like mad. He pressed a button on the doorway and the chamber door snapped open. 'Okay, no more to be said. It's time to end this.'

All of his friends could barely watch as Random strapped himself into the contraption. He made himself as comfortable as could be and watched as the chamber door snapped shut again.

Skateboard hated himself for having to be the one who made this all happen. He searched his databanks, desperately trying to find a reprieve but there was none. He then calculated the odds of survival again and they were just as bleak as before. As he readied the machine he looked one final time at his brave dear friends.

Random looked at him and smiled. He then looked out and saw the faces looking back at him, their faces distraught, hopeless.

Anji. Jake. Yana. Delilah. Benaya. Boshy, Troyus, Postanous, Xiros.

Then he noticed two new faces. No, not two new faces, these looked familiar.

But how? The door was fastened shut. Then he squinted.

New faces? No. These faces, although never clear before, had been with him since he had been born.

The tall, blue man and the shorter red woman. His parents. The scientist and the freedom fighter.

They had spoken in his mind over and over again, knowing what he had to do but deep down, he knew that they didn't want him to suffer or go through what his destiny had told him to.

But it was for the good of the people of Rodas.

As he gave the command for Skateboard to switch on the machine, and the sharp, protruding implements started to penetrate his purple flesh, he kept that in his mind.

Then he remembered. He remembered the good times. Meeting Skateboard, crash landing on Earth. Meeting the two schoolchildren. Posing as a pupil in a secondary school. Travelling with his two friends. The laughs. The triumphs. Nothing but the good times.

As he blotted out the pain, he allowed himself a big, broad smile. The chamber was rattling and hissing, smoke and steam pouring out of it.

It shook violently almost like a rocket about to take off. A huge build-up of energy was collecting deep within as the machine that gave Random life and Rodas hope was about to conduct its final mission.

Random, still smiling in the bliss of a life worth lived, felt the surge of energy in his body reach new limits as he prepared to do the most important thing in his life.

Save Rodas.

As the watchers moved back, the room started to flood with a glow of purple. Anji and Jake held their hands up to their faces, the brilliant light, combined with the smoke completely obscuring any final image of their best friend.

Suddenly, with a flick of a switch on the control unit of the chamber, Skateboard wheeled back.

'Get down, everyone!' he hollered over the sound of the machine as it exploded into life. The brilliant light within the room burst through the ceiling, outside of the base and formed a fantastic horizontal beam of energy that shot up right into the sky of Rodas, stopping both warring factions in their tracks.

Nkite and the Valkyrie, who had found Solenia and were about to mount her dosa stopped and watched.

The Sapphire Regime, what was left of it in the air and on the ground watched in awe.

The hoards of the Crimson Empire stopped too.

Even the Space Seals in their battle freighters and hornet fighters ceased fighting.

The security mainframe, which had also been joining in the battle by firing on those who dare come near it again, stopped and watched as the beam of energy stopped mere metres from their location.

Slowly, the beam started to spread rapidly in the sky and before long, it covered the entire planet, turning every single corner of Rodas purple. In that instance, the Crimson Empire clones dropped their arms and held their heads in agony. Those piloting battle freighters, heli-fighters and tanks lost control of their vehicles and sent them crashing. Before long, the clones began to burst into nothing but clouds of purple dust. The sight was extraordinary.

For Admiral Bagari, watching in stunned fascination from high above, it looked as though a sea of purple was washing over the battlefield. It was happening planet-wide. Within seconds, the screaming hordes of clones who had spent so many years causing so much misery, butchering millions upon millions of people were suddenly no more.

In a matter of moments, the purple clouds ascended up towards the beam's wave of energy over the planet and when all of it had been sucked up, the wave started to recede back towards the energy beam. Seconds later, the beam of light shot back down into its location below in the base and in the room where for so long Kalor Maloso had carried out his heinous acts of genocide against his own people, there was suddenly peace.

The chamber stopped shaking. The beam of light was gone.

All that remained was silence and smoke.

Those who were left behind, be it in the air, on the ground, in the mainframe, anywhere on Rodas were left stunned.

It had taken centuries for the war to end.

Now, in a hushed room at the centre of the Crimson Empire operation, it had taken seconds to bring about what the repressed people of Rodas had wanted for so long.

Peace.

XX

Silence spread over Rodas. It was as though time had stood still. Nkite dare not move in case it was all a weird side effect of being shot by an enemy soldier. Some people on the battlefield barely drew breath; forgetting to do so in the shock of it all until they began sobbing. Some cried tears of joy, others cried tears of relief. Nobody, not one Rodasian was not moved by what had happened.

Nkite let out a yell of pure elation and her fellow men, women and others who had joined the alliance followed her lead. Aboard the Titan, indeed, across all the battle freighters that the Space Seals had brought to Rodas, there were similar scenes of raw emotion and relief. Admiral Bagari sat in her command chair and allowed her guard to drop for a brief moment. She smiled. She laughed. She almost wept.

They had done it. No, Random had done it. The Crimson Empire was no more.

The war on Rodas was at an end.

Amongst the jubilation, Solenia dismounted her dosa and took a brief head count of her army. She was saddened when she realised that some of her Valkyries clearly hadn't made it. She was disturbed in her grief by an elated Nkite, who was picking her up and throwing her around, all the time repeating that they had done it.

Solenia was happy for her, but the cost of battle would be something she would have to face when they went home. Happily, however, they were going home. She hadn't thought it possible at the moment leading up to the Crimson Empire being wiped out.

Back on the Titan, messages were being relayed between the Space Seals fleet. The situation was being broadcast across the planet. War was over.

Before long Bagari, despite being beckoned by her peers to a team briefing, flipped a switch on her command chair. She had to know if they were okay.

'Skateboard,' was all she could say.

'Admiral,' was all that Skateboard could say back.

She detected a note of sadness in his voice.

'Random?' she asked.

Skateboard couldn't respond. His two friends were kneeling in the dust, sobbing and holding one another. The chamber was a mess. Inside there was too much smoke to see if Random had defied the odds but Skateboard already knew the answer.

Anji and Jake broke off for a moment when the former of the pair tore herself away from her friend and made for the chamber.

She wanted to touch it, to feel some form of connection with Random but her hand recoiled a couple of feet from the glass.

'An insurmountable energy had passed through that tube,' said Skateboard. 'We shouldn't go anywhere near it until it has cooled.'

'But Random...he could be?' asked Anji.

'Anj,' whispered Jake, his eyes streaming with tears. 'We'd know.'

Anji looked back at him and wanted to hit him. Know what? If he was alive? All she could do, however, was pull Jake back in and hug him.

The others stood motionless, not knowing what to say, knowing that there was nothing that they could say. Words were not even a crumb of comfort to the two young humans who were united in their grief for someone who had made the ultimate sacrifice, someone who most definitely was never going to make it...

...Random opened his eyes. He was surprised to find that he was still breathing. He was even more shocked to learn that he was still all in one piece. That was nothing to the astonishment he felt when he realised that he was standing in some sort of white void.

'Hello?' he called out. Nothing, not even an echo replied back.

He regarded his current position. Was he dead? Had it worked? Where on Rodas was he? Was he even still on Rodas? Finally, a voice did call to him through the void, one that he had heard very recently and was surprised to hear once more.

'See, that wasn't so bad, was it?' called the voice of a woman. The woman who had sent him back to Rodas after he had answered her call for help.

'Stung a bit,' he replied. 'Where am I? What are we doing here?'

The woman walked through the void and arrived fully formed in front of him. It was the Oracle of Fate. Random knew it was her the moment he had heard her but he was still very confused.

'I found you at a point in your time stream when you stood on the very edge of life and death.'

'So, I'm not in the afterlife?'

'What is an afterlife? It's not the same for everybody, no, you are in a point of limbo. You have yet to pass beyond the point of life and cross into the realm of the dead.'

'Okay, well, what am I doing here then? I take it the plan worked? Please tell me it worked.'

The Oracle, with dozens of pairs of eyes blinking intermittently and her tasselled dark hair matted over her shoulders, smiled at Random.

'You fulfilled the prophecy. Rodas is free once more from tyranny. The battle was won and your plan indeed worked.'

Random choked and began to well with emotion. 'Good,' he smiled. 'I'm happy that my death wasn't for nothing.'

'Death, such a finite word,' said the Oracle. 'Now that you have fulfilled your destiny my vision of Rodas' future is no longer impaired. I can see it flourishing, its people living together in harmony. Red and blue, hand-in-hand, for the rest of time. I have seen it, Random. What Rodas will one day become because of your actions. The billions upon billions of souls who shall echo throughout time who before your sacrifice would never have been given a chance of life. They shall flourish now forevermore, as will the planet. Eventually, it'll take time, but Rodas, the once shunned and ashamed planet of Ursa-17 shall take its place amongst the stars once again. It has an important part to play in the history of the universe, as you do too.'

Random scoffed. 'If what you say is true then I think you'll find that the only thing I am is history.'

The Oracle walked closer to Random and held his cheek in her palm.

'So why can't I rest now? Why can't I be at peace? Surely my work has been done? You're just here to see me off over the bridge, yes?'

'At the dawn of time, my fellow gods and I swore an oath. An oath not to interfere in the peoples of the universe's affairs but as the millennia have passed and I am now along the last of my kind, those who have survived the ravages of time with me will look upon my gift to you as a minor discrepancy.'

Random looked confused. 'You're talking in riddles, Oracle, what are you saying?'

'As you know Captain I am forbidden to interfere. But the tragedy of Rodas was so severe, indeed your part in its tale was so strong that I needed you to fulfil your destiny. If Rodas had fallen, then the universe, billions of years from now, would have been a darker place. It is for that, on our final meeting together, that I bestow to you the greatest gift I can give you as a way of saying thank you.'

Random shrugged. 'Nope, still lost me. Am I getting a medal? I mean I'm grateful but what I'll do with a medal in the afterlife I've no idea-'

The Oracle placed her palm on his chest. 'Goodbye, Captain Random and thank you.'

Suddenly, what felt like an electric bolt through his hearts sent Random reeling out of the void.

Back in Kalor Maloso's war room, a light tapping could be heard. Skateboard picked up on it first but it soon became stronger. Anji and Jake stopped crying and looked towards the chamber.

'It can't be?' said Jake.

The tap was becoming a thud.

'It is!' exclaimed Anji.

They, along with everyone else in the room circled the still-burning hot glass chamber.

'He's alive!' cried out Anji.

Skateboard instantly ran a physical scan on the chamber but it was suffering some interference.

'He can't get out!' shouted Jake.

'We'll help with that,' said Xiros. He, Postanous, Troyus and Boshy, ignoring the searing heat of the glass chamber, used all their might to tear the entrance door clean off its hinges. The glass shattered as they did and they tossed it to one side.

As the smoke cleared, the charred, injured body of Random looked back at them, smiling.

'Oh, thank god!' cried out Jake. He and Anji threw themselves at him. Random groaned loudly but reciprocated.

Skateboard was able to complete his bio-scan and he, along with the others stood disbelieving what they were seeing.

'You did it Random, you did it!' cried Anji, her tears now those of utter joy.

Random, unable to do much but hold his friends close to him looked at Skateboard. His body was still sizzling, a vapour rising from his frame like he was a meal freshly emerging from a microwave.

'Skateboard,' he said in a weak dry, husky tone that was not his usual one, 'what were the odds again?'

'About a billion-to-one, sir.'

Random smiled. 'I think I met her.'

Jake and Anji heard this and looked bemused at the comment.

'You must rest sir,' said Skateboard.

'Is he going to be okay?' asked Anji.

'It'll take time but his injuries will heal,' confirmed Skateboard.

With that, Random smiled again, allowed himself a little chuckle and sank back into the chair. 'Must rest,' he muttered.

'Admiral, we need a medical freighter here immediately,' said Skateboard to his communication channel.

Random sighed, relieved and tired, and looked up at the faces of his best friends, some old and some new and shone a smile that he had never smiled before.

'Thank you,' he sighed as he closed his eyes and drifted into a long overdue and much-needed heavy sleep.

XXI

For the next fortnight, Random spent most of his time asleep in bed. When the Titan landed on the now calm planet of Rodas it had scooped up those who had fought in the battle and took them in to tend to injuries and to generally look after those who had fought so valiantly.

The other freighters also landed on the planet and distributed aid where it was needed. There was much that Anji and Jake helped with whilst their friend recovered. Along with Nkite, they assisted in getting food and clean water to the many who had been made homeless by the constant shelling and destruction.

Skateboard, upon the return of the Venus II, had handed the river dwellers over into the care of Admiral Bagari and commenced an emergency deep clean of the ship. After seeing the terrible conditions that it had endured in transporting the dosas over from Spectronia, he was relieved to discover that it didn't take too long at all and he could set up an automatic cleaning system which worked in tandem with the self-repair nanobots.

Plus, as soon as it had been confirmed to him that Solenia and her Valkyries would be going home on one of the Space Seals battle freighters it was more than a comfort that his friends had never seen the mess that they had left behind, especially in Jake's room. It would take a while to get their home looking spick and span again but they were in no rush.

After a couple of weeks, the rehabilitation of Rodas was in full swing and Random was well enough for the debriefing with Admiral Bagari, who stood at the foot of his medical bed as Anji, Jake and Skateboard listened on. She'd already explained some of the details and Random was keen to hear every word.

'Your friends from Genocia have spent the past fortnight out on patrol across the planet with the people you found trapped in the war room,' she explained. 'They have been helping us to look for those who are homeless and in aid and spreading the word that we are here to help.'

'That's great,' said Random, his voice a little croaky still but
apart from a few grazes on his face almost back to his very best.
'I'm happy that whatever I did meant that the abominations
didn't perish, too, we've really got to call them something else,
haven't we?'

'I can explain that away, sir. Maloso's earlier cloning
experiments were given free will. When you destroyed the
psychic link, it only obliterated those who were directly under his
control,' said Skateboard.

'The Crimson Empire didn't fall?' asked Random.

'It did,' said Jake, 'but with the clones no longer around those
who were left were outnumbered.'

'And as Yana has told us those that they are finding out in the
wastelands aren't bad,' said Anji. 'They were after peace as much
as the Sapphire Regime were.'

'It's something you've always got to remind yourself in a war,'
said Bagari. 'There is good and evil on both sides. But a treaty will
be signed in due course by the highest-ranking officials from both
the Crimson Empire and the Sapphire Regime to formally
conclude the conflict. After that we hope, in time, that sides will
no longer need naming. Hopefully, as soon as the ink dries there
will be one society of Rodasians and the division will be at an
end.'

'Quite; it'll take a while for that trust to be built but they will get
there in the end,' said Random happily. 'Is there anything else?'

'The dismantling of the security mainframe has begun. They will
remain on the planet, as will some of our men, to oversee the
transition from tyranny back to democracy. But Rodas will need
help, and lots of it, to stand on its own two feet again. I spoke to
my peers earlier this week and they confirmed that we are willing
to commit to a long-term programme to restore this planet.'

'So much needs to be done,' said Random. 'The whole place will
need building up from scratch.'

'And the people of this planet will learn to trust each other
again,' said Bagari. 'We'll do what we can. I myself have been
placed in charge for the foreseeable future.'

'Ah wow, congrats Admiral!' said Anji.

'It's a tough job but someone's got to do it,' she said. 'Also, there is just one more thing. The Space Seals have decided to give you four, among the associates that you recruited, congressional medals of honour.'

'No way!' beamed Jake. 'Really? What does that mean then?'

'It means that we shall have the freedom of the universe,' said Skateboard giddily.

'I thought that we had that already,' said Anji cheekily.

'Unofficially,' replied Bagari dryly. 'Congratulations. I know it probably hasn't sunk in for you four yet but what you have done here has saved an entire planet, possibly even the universe. Great work.'

'All in a day's work for us, as you know, Admiral, but thank you, and the entire fleet for what you have done too,' said Random with a wink.

Admiral Bagari snapped to attention and saluted them all. 'I shall see you at the ceremony.'

As she left the medical bay, Random looked down at his surgical gown.

'I suppose I'd better find something better to wear for it,' he joked.

'Yet another medal of honour to add to the collection,' said Anji gleefully.

'I need to find my others. I think they might be down the back of one of my drawers,' said Jake.

'She is right you know,' said Random, 'What we did here really was incredible.'

'What you did, sir,' said Skateboard. 'We just assisted.'

'No,' said Random. 'You gave me a reason to come back. You made me face my fears and you did it by my side, no matter how much I tried to convince you to go somewhere safe. In the end, I couldn't have done it without you guys.'

'Group hug?' asked Anji.

'Why not?' said Random. All four of them embraced as Nkite walked into the room.

'Am I interrupting something?' she asked.

'Not at all, Nkite,' said Random, 'care to join?'

'I'm not really the hugging type,' she said. 'How are you feeling?'

'Much better thank you,' said Random. 'How about you?'

'The shoulder feels as good as new. I've just heard from Gron. He said that he and the rest of the river dwellers all want to go back to where they came from.'

'Back to the river, you mean?' asked Anji.

'Yes. It's a community there. Hence why I've decided that I shall be joining them. It's the only family I have now. I know you'll all understand when I tell you that it isn't something that you can't take for granted.'

'Definitely not,' said Jake beaming at his friends. 'Have you heard about the ceremony?'

'Heard? I'm getting a medal too,' she grinned. 'Admiral Bagari said that she wants to talk to me about the rebuilding of the planet too. I think she wants to keep me involved.'

'She'd be a fool not to,' said Random.

'And what about you, Random?' she asked. 'Do you know what you will do? I heard they might make you King of Rodas.'

Random's face turned serious for a moment. In truth, no he didn't. He had been thinking, in his hours lying awake, that since the voices of what he now understood to be his parents had gone and his mission was complete, he was a free entity again. There was no millstone around his neck, pulling his conscience this way and that. But did he owe it to the Rodasian people to stay with them and help rebuild the planet or to continue on his adventures with his friends?

Jake and Anji's faces fell. It hadn't occurred to them that Random may want to stay on his home planet. Random said nothing and simply smiled.

The night of the ceremony was a low-key affair. It was held in the shadow of Kalor Maloso's base and attended by hundreds of thousands of civilians. The Space Seal fleet, the surviving soldiers for both sides, well, the ones that hadn't been thrown in prison for war crimes or had shown an inkling of creating trouble, along with the rebel alliance that Skateboard had assembled all stood on the battleground where the war was finally ended.

The base, and the chamber from which Random had ended the conflict, were in the process of being demolished. Under a new act, such cloning techniques were to be outlawed on Rodas as much as it was in other parts of the galaxy as the security teams wanted to bring the planet in line with the law and order among the rest of Ursa-17. As delegates from neighbouring planets stood on the lip of the cliff that dropped into the battlefield, handing out medals to all who had fought, the ceremony was a long one. Random, Anji, Jake and Skateboard, along with Delilah, Yana, Benaya, Troyus, Boshy, Postanous and Xiros had all spruced up to look their best and were called in turn to receive their medals. Solenia and her Valkyries had elected to remain in their Spectronian armour and the Queen was awash with pride for her people when she and they were given a special recognition award for their part in the battle for peace.

Random had stood in his tuxedo, feeling slightly foolish, still pondering over what to do next. Anji, who look stunning in a flowing aqua blue ball gown alongside Jake, who had taken the effort to slick his hair back and wear a smart three-piece suit, and the two couldn't stop feeling happy for what they had helped achieve. Even Skateboard had been given a polish and was sparkling. As they received their awards the entire congregation cheered and applauded.

As the medal draped around his shoulders, Random shook hands with the Ursa-17 delegate and turned to wave at the crowd, who celebrated so loudly that Jake thought it sounded like they had all just won the Premier League! But he gave no speech and unlike his friends, Random just wanted to slip quietly away.

A little later, as the food and drink that had been provided by the Space Seals was being enjoyed and a party-like atmosphere had swept around the entire planet, Random was taking some time alone, something that was hard to do on a night like this, as everyone wanted to speak to him and hug him and thank him profusely for what he had done. Through the party goers, Nkite spotted him and made her way over.

'Hey,' she said.

Random noticed her dress. 'You look nice.'

'Thank you! Your friend Anji lent it to me.'

There was an awkward silence.

'Random I... I just wanted to say that I am sorry for the way I spoke to you back in the cave.'

Random scoffed. 'Honestly, Nkite, people have said far worse. I hurt you. It's okay I understand totally.'

Nkite bit her lip. 'So, we are good?'

'Good? We're more than that,' smiled Random. 'We saved a planet together. In my book that pretty much makes us family!'

Nkite smiled and then stared at the floor. 'We won't hold it against you, you know.'

Random looked puzzled.

'If you did decide to go?'

Random's eyes stared at the floor. 'I haven't decided yet. The thing is Nkite I'm very good at all of this revolution malarkey but I'm not one for bedding down somewhere. This might be the place of my birth but that out there,' he pointed at the stars, 'that's home to me.'

'The people will understand if you don't want to be King, I'm sure, but we all owe our lives to you Random. Just, promise me that whatever you decide that you won't forget us.'

'Forget you?' How could I ever do that? Take a look around you. The Space Seals, Spectronians, Genocians. I've never forgotten any of them. Sure, I should drop in on them more often, well, I had my reasons for not going back to one of them especially, but forget? Nkite I never will.'

Nkite smiled and took his arm. 'You know, when I saw you escape all as a child and saw the purple ripple in the sky, I thought it was the most beautiful sight I had ever seen. But this,' she guided him to look at the party. 'Red and blue Rodasians together, in peace. No, this is the most beautiful thing I've ever seen. We'll work to maintain it. Improve it even. But I don't think this as a spectacle can be bettered.'

Random smiled at her and placed his arm around her shoulders. 'You and me both, Nkite. You and me both. Then they looked down a level onto what had been a battlefield and was now a dance floor and saw two familiar figures embraced in a slow dance.

Jake's hands were a little clammy and he was thankful that they were on Anji's waist but he could tell that she was nervous too as her heart was thumping against his chest. Slowly they shared in their first dance, both a little scared of putting a foot wrong but both equally in the knowledge that the other person wouldn't care if they did.

As the Rodasian music swelled around the party, and a colourful array of fireworks exploded high ahead against a backdrop of the neon moon and the night sky, Anji let her lead

roll onto Jake's shoulder. She shut her eyes, totally content in the moment. Jake never wanted it to end.

'Well,' he said, 'this sure beats prom hands down.'

Anji laughed. 'How would we know?'

Jake spotted Random and Nkite watching them from afar and gave a knowing smile to them.

'I think,' he replied. 'we're going to find out together.'

XXII

It was the morning after. Everyone was feeling a little worse for wear. Jake and Anji had spent the whole night talking, laughing and dancing and now they were knackered. As they walked towards the Venus II, they noticed that many of their friends had lined the open gangway, wanting to see them off. There were the abominations, whose footloose dancing the previous night had caused all sorts of dance-offs to ensue. Nkite and Gron, two of the river dwellers they had helped save stood smiling at them. There were the Spectronians, who had now pardoned the crew of the Venus II and were only too happy to see them back on their planet soon. Then there was Admiral Bagari, who had sent them on so many missions since the Space Seals had helped them defeat Stratos the planet destroyer. The Genocians, who like the Spectronians had found another mode of transport home, shared in their first adventure on an alien planet.

'Blimey,' said Jake as he walked hand-in-hand with Anji with his suit jacket slung over his shoulder and his hair back to its shaggy normality. 'Feels like I'm walking through some kind of intergalactic Facebook!'

At the top of the gangway stood Skateboard, who hadn't attended the party after the ceremony and had hastily made off to make sure that the repairs would be finished in time and that the dosa poo was now completely cleaned up. If only the bio fixing that meant everyone else's excretions were transported from their bodies when they needed to go had extended to Solenia's cavalry but alas, it was all a terrible memory for Skateboard now.

'She's looking better than ever, Skateboard,' said Anji. She wasn't wrong. The Venus II's gleaming metal glistened in the Rodasian sun.

'Hey, where's Random?' asked Jake. They both looked around.

'It's probably better if you come on board,' said a sorrowful Skateboard. Anji and Jake looked concerned but bid a heartfelt goodbye to each and every one of their friends who had come along to see them off.

'Don't be strangers, please come back anytime,' said Nkite.

'Yes, drop in on us too when you're passing. I think you owe me a few rounds, Jake,' said Delilah.

'Take care out there,' said Bagari, shaking their hands.

'We will,' replied Anji. 'Seriously, though, where is Random, Skateboard?'

Skateboard said nothing but goodbye to everyone who had assembled and led his two young friends onboard. As soon as they were safely in the mid-section, he started up the engines remotely and shut them in.

'You're not telling me he isn't saying goodbye, Skateboard, he wouldn't do that!' said Jake.

'Who said anything about goodbye?' came a voice from the cockpit.

Anji and Jake's jaws dropped as Random came bounding into the mid-section, a silly grin beaming from his face.

'Ha! Gotcha!' he cried.

'Random that was mean!' said Anji playfully slapping him.

'But I thought they were going to make you King!' said Jake.

'Me? King? Crowns don't suit me, Jake,' said Random.

'You're not staying?' asked Anji, wanting confirmation that this was indeed for real.

'Nope.'

'But your people are here, and they are free, and yours Skateboard?' asked Jake.

'It almost sounds as though he wants us to stay,' said Skateboard.

'Exactly, Jake, they are free. Mission accomplished,' said Random who was making his way back into the cockpit. 'Besides,' he said plonking himself in his familiar old pilot's chair.

'Now that the security mainframe is gone, we can come and go when we like and we will. If I've learnt anything from our visit here it is that we have more friends than we care to remember sometimes.'

Jake leaned over to look out of the dashboard. There they all were, dosas and Valkyries were roaring upward in salute as their engines neared take-off velocity.

'Also,' said Random, tapping his congressional medal of honour that was hanging from the steering column. 'This gives us the freedom of the universe. It'd be a shame not to use that freedom, wouldn't it?'

'Indeed, sir,' said Skateboard. 'Where shall I set our coordinates for?'

'Guys?' asked Random.

Anji and Jake took a look at each other. 'Anywhere,' they said in unison.

'Cool, Skateboard, set a course for anywhere.'

'I'm not sure I'm aware of that one, sir, but I'll do my best.'

Anji pulled Jake in closer and leaned forward to hug Random who in turn put an arm around her as he lifted the steering column. 'Right, gang. Let's see what else is out there.'

Anji suddenly caught a whiff of something unpleasant. 'Skateboard, what's that?'

The AI robot stayed silent in shame as the Venus II took off. Its occupants waved to their friends down below as the ship was brought around and then with one final jolt, Random, who counted himself the luckiest man in the universe, stepped on the accelerator and the Venus II and its crew of heroes sailed away from Rodas, off out into the unknown.

Their adventures were mapped out in the stars, just waiting to find them.

THE END

ACKNOWLEDGEMENTS

To **Sophie** – my wife
William – my son
Anthony – the illustrator of biblical proportions
Viki - cover designer and blurb writer
extraiordinaire
Steve and Mark – podcasters supreme
David Kitchen and Jonny Dab – feedback
curators
Mum and Dad for the obvious
Mrs Bell – the teacher who encouraged me to
write
Una McCormack – who told me after writing one
Captain Random novel that I had to complete the
series, here it is!
Nicci Currie for proofing and advice
**Thomas Savill-Owen, Anna Brown and Stephen
D'Costa** – the writing gang
Eve Hopley - support

And to you for following my work and the
adventures of Captain Random.

Also Available:

Don't Panic! The Unauthorised Dad's Army Handbook

ISBN: 978-1739375201

For nearly six decades the adventures of the Walmington-on-Sea Home Guard has delighted generations of viewers. Classic quotes such as, "Don't tell him Pike!" have been copied time and again as more and more people have tuned in through repeats that continue to this day.

In this unofficial book, through an in-depth episode guide, favourite lines, memorable moments, behind-the-scenes stories from the people who made the programme and much more, Hayden Gribble discovers what really makes Dad's Army one of British television's greatest creations.

Available from all good bookshops.

Journeys in the Randomverse

ISBN: 978-1999865986

The adventures of Captain Random continue in this special collection of FIFTEEN new stories.

Join Random, Anji, Jake and Skateboard as they encounter a planet that gets inside the mind, giant bug-like creatures on a mysterious world, alternate realities, holiday planets as relaxing as being stuck in a cupboard during a fire alarm and the Oracle of Fate.

This is the FIFTH Captain Random book.

Available from all good bookshops.

Captain Random and the Stratos Conundrum

ISBN: 978-1999865979

From the darkest depths of space comes an enemy of the universe that plans to wreck havoc across the stars.

In his blood thirsty quest for revenge he will crush entire star systems and his name will make all who hear it shudder in terror.

Whilst the biggest threat the cosmos has ever known forms his master plan the only person who can possibly stop him is lying in a coma on a hospital moon that orbits a planet that is in his line of fire.

Random, Anji, Jake and Skateboard face a race against time to save the lives of all who stand in his way whilst trying to unwrap the mystery of who he is and why, in particular, he wants Random to watch the universe suffer.

His name is Stratos...and he is the destroyer of worlds...

This is the FOURTH Captain Random adventure.

Available from all good bookshops

Captain Random and the Rainbow Chasers

ISBN: 978-1999865962

The Zedron Flux is the most powerful energy source in the known cosmos. In the right hands, it has the power to end all suffering. In the wrong hands, it could bring an end to all things. After a narrow escape from an army of ancient gods, Random, Anji, Jake and Skateboard crash land on the beautiful planet of Spectronia, a paradise of colour and home to a peaceful race ruled by the elegant Solenia and her Valkyries. Upon recovering they ally themselves with a band of explorers led by Lon, who is hell bent on finding the Flux after it was taken from his grasp by a rival archaeologist. But nothing for the crew of the Venus II is ever simple. As the quest continues, danger is not far away and, as the Flux gets closer and closer, Random is left with a terrible choice that will have major consequences, not just for him and his friends, but for the entire universe…

This is the THIRD Captain Random adventure.

Available from all good bookshops

The Lurking

ISBN: 978-1999865955

Rob is a hopeless loser in the game of life. With work, his relationship with his long suffering girlfriend Claire, with everything in general. Tonight he will change for the better, make a fresh start by taking it to the next step and propose to her.

But fate has other intentions.

After an accident that leaves him stranded, Rob takes shelter in an abandoned aircraft hangar and soon discovers that he is not alone. There is something lurking in the darkness, taunting him, haunting his every movement.

Soon trapped in a living nightmare, Rob must learn the terrible truth of his tormentor and escape its clutches before it is too late...

Available from all good bookshops.

Captain Random and the Eater of Souls

ISBN: 978-1999865931

Following their explosive battle with the Sandman, and struggling to come to terms with life out in space, the crew of the Venus II decide to throw themselves into a spot of retail therapy on the friendly planet of Genocia.

But almost as soon as they arrive, they realise that this new world is not all that it seems. Outside the splendour and vast wealth of the Grand Chamber lies a neglected wasteland where terror lurks within the poisonous gloom whilst deep within the bowels of the planet lies a terrible secret.

At the very heart of it all is the ruthless leader Consula, whose designs for supremacy mean ultimate devastation to all of those who oppose her. But the greed and corruption of the government is nothing compared to what lurks in the shadows for Random and his friends. Separated and fighting for their lives, Random, Anji, Jake and Skateboard must work quickly to save the lives of the prisoners stuck in the mines deep below the surface, where death is very close by...

What is the Soul Destroyer? What part does it play in Consula's diabolical plan? Will Anji ever see her friends again? One thing is for sure. The Eater of Souls is hungry...

Available from all good bookshops.

Captain Random vs the Sandman

ISBN: 978-1999865924

Rodas. The scorned planet of Ursa-17. Ravaged by centuries of war
between two factions, the villainous Sapphire Regime and the ruthless
Crimson Empire. The reason behind the conflict of red and blue? The
people of Rodas were unable to make the colour purple.
Until one day, when two rebels, one from either side, combine to create
the ultimate warrior. A being who could put an end to the battle of ages
and bring peace to the volatile planet of Rodas once and for all.

There is one tiny drawback. The warrior is a boy.

***** Fantastic book, enjoyed every part of it!
Highly recommend it for Dr Who/Red Dwarf/Rick and Morty fans.

***** Hayden Gribble's writing is witty and clever with an essence of
Douglas Adams in there too. Would thoroughly recommend for anyone with
an adventurous spirit.

***** I really enjoyed it. I can well imagine Kids getting swept along with the
interstellar, action packed adventure and chuckling along with all the funny
scenarios and characters and wanting to know just what happens.

Available from all good bookshops.

Child Out of Time: Growing Up With Doctor Who in the Wilderness Years

ISBN: 978-1999865900

For 26 years, DOCTOR WHO was a British institution, capturing the imaginations of generations of children. But then, in 1989, it was cancelled. The Doctor and his on-screen adventures were no more. There was no longer a hero, a champion for the outcasts who struggled to fit in. It was as though he had walked into his TARDIS and set his controls for dematerialisation, never to return: a whole generation lost to the powers of Science Fiction's greatest creation. It was in this Doctor-less world that I grew up. This is the story of how one little boy would try to find the Doctor in any way, shape or form and the obstacles he faced in doing so. This is the story of growing up without Doctor Who in the Wilderness Years…and how I lived through it.

***** An engaging and enjoyable insight into a fan discovering Doctor Who during the wilderness years

***** A very passionate account of one fans discovery of the greatest science fiction of all time.

**** Perfect for fans of the Doctor in any of his or her forms.

Available from all good book shops.

The Man In The Corner

ISBN: 978-1500549862

A mysterious assassin wants out of his life as a cold and ruthless killer but must face one last assignment before he flicks the escape switch. As he closes in on the biggest criminal mind in the country, he is reminded of what he left behind and how getting closer to the light at the end of the tunnel might also reunite him with a person from his long and distant past. Who is the Big Chief? Why must he be brought down and will it be the end, not just for himself and his superior, but also to the only link to the life he has lost.

***** An exciting book! Whilst focusing on the dark story of an unnamed man, you find yourself sucked into a city of criminals. The chapters contain their own stories which really draw you in and make you want to read more. Great read! The only negative is that it was over too fast.

***** Brilliant read. Did not want to put the book down.

*** This book is a great little read about the path to redemption; not too long, in fact in some places I found myself wishing it might go on a little longer. It's got a sort of style all its own.

Available from all good bookshops.

Hayden Gribble was born in Cambridge in June 1989. He has always loved writing and released his debut novel, The Man In The Corner, as an eBook in 2013 before it went paperback the following year.

Since then, Hayden has managed to top the Amazon best seller list on three occasions, although the Booker Prize still seems some way off.

The Stratos Conundrum is Hayden's twelfth book and the second omnibus in the Captain Random saga.

Away from writing, Hayden loves reading, walking, sports, music, film and TV.

He has also been a regular member of the Diddly Dum Podcast, a show about Doctor Who, since February 2015.

He lives with his wife and son in Suffolk.

You can find out more about Hayden and Captain Random at www.haydengribbleauthor.com

---